Praise for A. A. Milne's fiction for grown-ups

'Milne has the touch of the true artist'
Telegraph

'A playful yet serious exploration of life'
New York Times

'He writes gently but thinks sharply and gives us a chronicle of quiet living'
Guardian

'The greatest fun: pure Milne throughout'
Sunday Times

'Shrewd and witty'
Country Life

'Graceful and amusing'
New York Herald Tribune

'To admirers of humour on its best behaviour there is no comedian like A. A. Milne'
Observer

'Both frivolous and thoughtful'
Saturday Review

'Peculiarly modern'
Times Literary Supplement

The

Complete
Short Stories *of*
A. A. Milne

A. A. Milne

Introduced by Gyles Brandreth

Farrago

This edition published in 2024 by Farrago,
an imprint of Duckworth Books Ltd
1 Golden Court, Richmond, TW9 1EU, United Kingdom

www.farragobooks.com

The following stories are published here for the first time: 'Happy Ever After',
'The Southey Manuscript', 'In It Together', 'My Dear Vincent', all copyright
© The Estate of the Late Lesley Milne Limited, 2024, protected by copyright
rules for posthumously published works, including the 2039 Rule.

Portions of this work appeared, sometimes in different form, in *Cornhill Magazine*
(1914), *Windsor* (1915), *Land and Water* (1918), *Living Age* (1920), *Fortnightly
Review* (1922), *Adelphi* (1923), *Ladies' Home Journal* (1925, 1926), *The Saturday
Book* (1943, 1946), *Good Housekeeping* (1948, 1949, 1950), *Collier's* (1948), *Birthday
Party and Other Stories* (1948), *A Table Near the Band* (1950), *Cosmopolitan*
(1949, 1950), *Evening Standard* (1950) and *Ellery Queen* (1950, 1951).

A catalogue record for this book is available from the British Library.

Paperback ISBN: 978-1-7884-2449-3
eISBN: 978-1-7884-2450-9

Cover design and illustration by Emanuel Santos

Contents

Introduction

The publication of this complete collection of his short stories would have given A. A. Milne so much pleasure.

Alan Alexander Milne (18 January 1882–31 January 1956) was one of Britain's most brilliant, prolific and successful authors. As a journalist, playwright, screenwriter, poet, polemicist, novelist and crime writer, he was proud of his versatility. As a man, he was disappointed, frustrated, and even at times despairing, that for half his working life he was known chiefly – and by some only – as the man who invented Winnie-the-Pooh.

Milne's four slim children's books – *When We Were Very Young, Now We Are Six, Winnie-the-Pooh* and *The House at Pooh Corner* – published between 1924 and 1928, made him wealthy and world famous. They came to define him and, thanks to the skilful exploitation by The Walt Disney Company, they generate millions of dollars to this day.

As Milne pointed out in almost every interview he gave in the last 25 years of his life, his four children's books amounted in all to no more than 70,000 words – the length of a single novel. Before them, and after them, he was writing so much else, including the wonderfully varied stories in this collection, eighteen plays that enjoyed considerable success in London's West End and on Broadway, and a whodunnit

(*The Red House Mystery*) in the best tradition of the Golden Age of Detective Fiction. He called his autobiography *It's Too Late Now*, in part because he knew he had to accept that with Pooh centre-stage and in the spotlight, the rest of his considerable literary output was destined to be consigned to the semi-darkness of the wings.

Happily, thanks to the book you are holding in your hands now, it's not too late to enjoy the best of the rest that the great A. A. Milne had to offer. As the children's author, certainly, he created a unique and magical world peopled by a handful of characters destined for immortality. But as a story teller for adults, as you are about to discover, he wrote with his own special brand of humour, elegance and ease, and was a shrewd observer of the human condition – especially of the relationship between men and women (his own marriage was not always an easy one) and within families.

Born in the London suburb of Kilburn, where his parents ran a small independent school, Milne was educated at Westminster School and Trinity College, Cambridge, where he studied mathematics and began writing humorous pieces for the university magazine, *Granta*. His father hoped he might one day take on the family school, but Milne was determined to be a writer. For a decade and more he wrote weekly pieces for the magazine *Punch* (where he became the assistant editor) until the First World War, when he enlisted in the army – the experience that led him to write his anti-war tract many years later. Then, in the teens and twenties of the twentieth century, he became one of Britain's most popular playwrights and a pioneer screen-writer in the fledgling years of British cinema. The stories in this complete collection were written between 1914 and 1953, and, excitingly, include four pieces not seen in print before. From satire to fairy tale, from crime to romance, this is a collection that truly reflects the imagination and world of A. A. Milne.

'I suppose,' he reflected once, 'that every one of us hopes secretly for immortality; to leave, I mean, a name behind him that will live forever in this world, whatever he may be doing himself in the next.'

Well, I can picture Milne in the next world right now, sitting on a heavenly cloud with two of his good friends, and personal heroes: Arthur Conan Doyle and J. M. Barrie. (They played cricket together in a celebrated Authors' XI.) 'Well, gentlemen,' Milne is saying, sucking on his pipe with some satisfaction, and raising his glass towards his companions, 'you two each did a great deal more than invent Sherlock Holmes and Peter Pan and I did rather more than create Winnie-the-Pooh and here is this handsome new edition of *The Complete Short Stories of A. A. Milne* to prove it. Shall we drink to that?'

Gyles Brandreth

The Woman

(1914)

I

It was April, and in his little bedroom in the Muswell Hill boarding-house, where Mrs Morrison (assisted, as you found out later, by Miss Gertie Morrison) took in a few select paying guests, George Crosby was packing. Spring came in softly through his open window; it whispered to him tales of green hedges and misty woods and close-cropped rolling grass. 'Collars,' said George, trying to shut his ears to it, 'handkerchiefs, ties—I knew I'd forgotten something; ties.' He pulled open a drawer. 'Ties, shirts—where's my list?—shirts, ties.' He wandered to the window and looked out. Muswell Hill was below him, but he hardly saw it. 'Three weeks,' he murmured. 'Heaven for three weeks, and it hasn't even begun yet.' There was the splendour of it. It hadn't begun; it didn't begin till to-morrow. He went back in a dream to his packing. 'Collars,' he said, 'shirts, ties—ties—'

Miss Gertie Morrison had not offered to help him this year. She had not forgotten that she had put herself forward the year before, when George had stammered and blushed (he found blushing very easy in the Muswell Hill boarding-house), and Algy Traill, the humorist of the establishment, had winked and said, 'George, old boy, you're in luck; Gertie never packs for *me*.' Algy had continued the joke by smacking his left hand with his right, and saying in an

5

undertone, 'Naughty boy, how dare you call her Gertie?' and then in a falsetto voice: 'Oh, Mr Crosby, I'm sure I never meant to put myself forward!' Then Mrs Morrison from her end of the table called out—

But I can see that I shall have to explain the Muswell Hill ménage to you. I can do it quite easily while George is finishing his packing. He is looking for his stockings now, and that always takes him a long time, because he hasn't worn them since last April, and they are probably under the bed.

Well, Mrs Morrison sits at one end of the table and carves. Suppose it is Tuesday evening. 'Cold beef or hash, Mr Traill?' she asks, and Algy probably says, 'Yes, please,' which makes two of the boarders laugh. These are two pale brothers called Fossett, younger than you who read this have ever been, and enthusiastic admirers of Algy Traill. Their great ambition is to paint the town red one Saturday night. They have often announced their intention of doing this, but so far they do not seem to have left their mark on London to any extent. Very different is it with their hero and mentor. On Boat-race night four years ago Algy Traill was actually locked up—and dismissed next morning with a caution. Since then he has often talked as if he were a Cambridge man; the presence of an Emmanuel lacrosse blue in the adjoining cell having decided him in the choice of a university.

Meanwhile his hash is getting cold. Let us follow it quickly. It is carried by the servant to Miss Gertie Morrison at the other end of the table, who slaps in a helping of potatoes and cabbage. 'What, asparagus *again*?' says Algy, seeing the cabbage. 'We *are* in luck.' Mrs Morrison throws up her eyes at Mr Ransom on her right, as much as to say, 'Was there ever such a boy?' and Miss Gertie threatens him with the potato spoon, and tells him not to be silly. Mr Ransom looks approvingly across the table at Traill. He has a feeling that the Navy, the Empire, and the Old Country are in some way linked up with men of the world such as Algy, or that (to put it in another way) a Radical Nonconformist would strongly disapprove of him. It comes to the same thing; you can't help liking the fellow. Mr Ransom is wearing an M.C.C. tie; partly because the bright colours make him look younger, partly because unless he changes *something* for dinner he never feels quite clean, you know. In his own house he would dress every night. He is fifty; tall, dark, red-faced, black-moustached, growing stout; an insurance agent. It is his great sorrow that the country is going to the dogs, and he dislikes the setting of class against class. The proper thing to do is to shoot them down.

Opposite him, and looking always as if he had slept in his clothes, is Mr Owen-Jones—called Mr Joen-Owns by Algy. He argues politics fiercely across Mrs Morrison. 'My dear fellow,' he cries to Ransom, 'you're nothing but a reactionary!'—to which Ransom, who is a little doubtful what a reactionary is, replies, 'All I want is to live at peace with my neighbours. I don't interfere with them; why should they interfere with me?' Whereupon Mrs Morrison says peaceably, 'Live and let live. After all, there are two sides to *every* question—a little more hash, Mr Owen-Jones?'

George has just remembered that his stockings are under the bed, so I must hurry on. As it happens, the rest of the boarders do not interest me much. There are two German clerks and one French clerk, whose broken English is always amusing, and somebody with a bald, dome-shaped head who takes in *Answers* every week. Three years ago he had sung 'Annie Laurie' after dinner one evening, and Mrs Morrison still remembers sometimes to say, 'Won't you sing something, Mr —— ?' whatever his name was, but he always refuses. He says that he has the new number of *Answers* to read.

There you are; now you know everybody. Let us go upstairs again to George Crosby.

Is there anything in the world jollier than packing up for a holiday? If there is, I do not know it. It was the hour (or two hours or three hours) of George's life. It was more than that; for days beforehand he had been packing to himself; sorting out his clothes, while he bent over the figures at his desk, making and drawing up lists of things that he really mustn't forget. In the luncheon hour he would look in at hosiers' windows and nearly buy a blue shirt because it went so well with his brown knickerbocker suit. You or I would have bought it; it was only five and sixpence. Every evening he would escape from the drawing-room—that terrible room—and hurry upstairs to his little bedroom, and there sit with his big brown kit-bag open before him ... dreaming. Every evening he had meant to pack a few things just to begin with; his tweed suit and stockings and nailed shoes, for instance; but he was always away in the country, following the white path over the hills, as soon as ever his bag was between his knees. How he ached to take his body there too ... it was only three weeks to wait, two weeks, a week, three days—to-morrow! To-morrow—he was almost frightened to think of it lest he should wake up.

Perhaps you wonder that George Crosby hated the Muswell Hill boarding-house; perhaps you don't. For my part I agree with Mrs Morrison that it takes all sorts to make a world, and that as Mr —— (I forget his name; the dome-shaped gentleman) once surprised us by saying, 'There is good in everybody if only you can find it out.' At any rate there is humour. I think if George had tried to see the humorous side of Mrs Morrison's select guests he might have found life tolerable. And yet the best joke languishes after five years.

I had hoped to have gone straight ahead with this story, but I shall have to take you back five years; it won't be for long. Believe me, no writer likes this diving back into the past. He is longing to get to the great moment when Rosamund puts her head on George's shoulder and says—but we shall come to that. What I must tell you now, before my pen runs away with me, is that five years ago George was at Oxford with plenty of money in his pocket, and a vague idea in his head that he would earn a living somehow when he went down. Then his only near relation, his father, died ... and George came down with no money in his pocket, and the knowledge that he would have to earn his living at once. He knew little of London east of the Savoy, where he had once lunched with his father; I doubt if he even knew the Gaiety by sight. When his father's solicitor recommended a certain Islington boarding-house as an establishment where a man of means could be housed and fed for as little as thirty shillings a week, and a certain firm in Fenchurch Street as another establishment where a man of gifts could earn as much as forty shillings a week, George found out where Islington and Fenchurch Street were, and fell mechanically into the routine suggested for him. That he might have been happier alone, looking after himself, cooking his own meals or sampling alone the cheaper restaurants, hardly occurred to him. Life was become suddenly a horrible dream, and the boarding-house was just a part of it.

However, three years of Islington was enough for him. He pulled himself together ... and moved to Muswell Hill.

There, we have him back at Muswell Hill now, and I have not been long, have I? He has been two years with Mrs Morrison. I should like to say that he is happy with Mrs Morrison, but he is not. The terrible thing is that he cannot get hardened to it. He hates Muswell Hill; he hates Traill and the Fossetts and Ransom; he hates Miss Gertie Morrison. The whole vulgar, familiar, shabby, sociable atmosphere of the place he hates. Some day, perhaps, he will pull himself together and move again. There is a boarding-house at Finsbury Park he has heard of ...

II

If you had three weeks' holiday in the year, three whole weeks in which to amuse yourself as you liked, how would you spend it? Algy Traill went to Brighton in August; you should have seen him on the pier. The Fossett Brothers adorned Weymouth, the Naples of England. They did good, if slightly obvious, work on the esplanade in fairly white flannels. This during the day; eight-thirty in the evening found them in the Alexandra Gardens—dressed. It is doubtful if the Weymouth boarding-house would have stood it at dinner, so they went up directly afterwards and changed. Mr Ransom spent August at Folkestone, where he was understood to have a doubtful wife. She was really his widowed mother. You would never have suspected him of a mother, but there she was in Folkestone, thinking of him always, and only living for the next August. It was she who knitted him the M.C.C. tie; he had noticed the colours in a Piccadilly window.

Miss Gertie went to Cliftonville—not Margate.

And where did George go? The conversation at dinner that evening would have given us a clue; or perhaps it wouldn't.

'So you're off to-morrow,' Mrs Morrison had said. 'Well, I'm sure I hope you'll have a nice time. A little sea air will do you good.'

'Where are you going, Crosby?' asked Ransom, with the air of a man who means to know.

George looked uncomfortable.

'I'm not quite sure,' he said awkwardly. 'I'm doing a sort of walking-tour, you know; stopping at inns and things. I expect it—er—will depend a bit, you know.'

'Well, if you *should* happen to stop at Sandringham,' said Algy, 'give them all my love, old man, won't you?'

'Then you won't have your letters sent on?' asked Mrs Morrison.

'Oh no, thanks. I don't suppose I shall have any, anyhow.'

'If you're going on a walking-tour,' said Owen-Jones, 'why don't you try the Welsh mountains?'

'I always wonder you don't run across to Paris,' said the dome-shaped gentleman suddenly. 'It only takes—' He knew all the facts, and was prepared to give them, but Algy interrupted him with a knowing whistle.

'Paris, George, aha! Place me among the demoiselles, what ho! I don't think. Naughty boy!'

Crosby's first impulse (he had had it before) was to throw his glass of beer at Algy's face. The impulse died down, and his resolve hardened to write about the Finsbury Park boarding-house at once. He had made that resolution before, too. Then his heart jumped as he remembered that he was going away on the morrow. He forgot Traill and Finsbury Park, and went off into his dreams. The other boarders discussed walking-tours and holiday resorts with animation.

Gertie Morrison was silent. She was often silent when Crosby was there, and always when Crosby's affairs were being discussed. She knew he hated her, and she hated him for it. I don't think she knew why he hated her. It was because she lowered his opinion of women.

He had known very few women in his life, and he dreamed dreams about them. They were wonderful creatures, a little higher than the angels, and beauty and mystery and holiness hung over them. Some day he would meet the long-desired one, and (miracle) she would love him, and they would live happy ever afterwards at—He wondered sometimes whether an angel *would* live happy ever afterwards at Bedford Park. Bedford Park seemed to strip the mystery and the holiness and the wonder from his dream. And yet he had seen just the silly little house at Bedford Park that would suit them; and even angels, if they come to earth, must live somewhere. She would walk to the gate every morning, and wave him good-bye from under the flowering laburnum—for I need not say that it was always spring in his dream. That was why he had his holiday in April, for it must be spring when he found her, and he would only find her in the country … Another reason was that in August Miss Morrison went to Cliftonville (not Margate), and so he had a fortnight in Muswell Hill without Miss Morrison.

For it was difficult to believe in the dreams when Gertie Morrison was daily before his eyes. There was a sort of hard prettiness there, which might have been beauty, but where were the mystery and the wonder and the holiness? None of that about the Gertie who was treated so familiarly by the Fossetts and the Traills and their kind, and answered them back so smartly. 'You can't get any change out of Gertie,' Traill often said on these occasions. Almost Crosby wished you could. He would have had her awkward, bewildered, indignant, overcome with shame; it distressed him that she was so lamentably well-equipped for the battle. At first he pitied her, then he hated her.

She was betraying her sex. What he really meant was that she was trying to topple over the beautiful image he had built.

I know what you are going to say. What about the girl at the A B C shop who spilt his coffee over his poached egg every day at 1.35 precisely? Hadn't she given his image a little push too? I think not. He hardly saw her as a woman at all. She was a worker, like himself; sexless. In the evenings perhaps she became a woman ... wonderful, mysterious, holy ... I don't know; at any rate he didn't see her then. But Miss Morrison he saw at home; she was pretty and graceful and feminine; she might have been, not *the* woman—that would have been presumption on his part—but a woman ... and then she went and called Algy Traill 'a silly boy', and smacked him playfully with a teaspoon! Traill, the cad-about-town, the ogler of women! No wonder the image rocked.

Well, he would be away from the Traills and the Morrisons and the Fossetts for three weeks. It was April, the best month of the year. He was right in saying that he was not quite sure where he was going, but he could have told Mrs Morrison the direction. He would start down the line with his knapsack and his well-filled kit-bag. By-and-by he would get out—the name of the station might attract him, or the primroses on the banks—leave his bag, and, knapsack on shoulder, follow the road. Sooner or later he would come to a village; he would find an inn that could put him up; on the morrow the landlord could drive in for his bag ... And then three weeks in which to search for the woman.

III

A south wind was blowing little baby clouds along a blue sky; lower down, the rooks were talking busily to each other in the tall elms which lined the church; and, lower down still, the foxhound puppy sat himself outside the blacksmith's and waited for company. If nothing happened in the next twenty seconds he would have to go and look for somebody.

But somebody was coming. From the door of The Dog and Duck opposite, a tall, lean gentleman stepped briskly, in his hand a pair of shoes. The foxhound puppy got up and came across the road sideways to him. 'Welcome, welcome,' he said effusively, and went round the tall, lean gentleman several times.

'Hallo, Duster,' said the gentleman; 'coming with me to-day?'

'Come along,' said the foxhound puppy excitedly. 'Going with you? I should just think I am! Which way shall we go?'

'Wait a moment. I want to leave these shoes here.'

Duster followed him into the blacksmith's shop. The blacksmith thought he could put some nails in; gentlemen's shoes and horses' shoes, he explained, weren't quite the same thing. The gentleman admitted the difference, but felt sure that the blacksmith could make a job of anything he tried his hand at. He mentioned, which the blacksmith knew, that he was staying at The Dog and Duck opposite, and gave his name as Carfax.

'Come along,' said Duster impatiently.

'Good morning,' said the gentleman to the blacksmith. 'Lovely day, isn't it? … Come along, old boy.'

He strode out into the blue fresh morning, Duster all round him. But when they got to the church—fifty yards, no more—the foxhound puppy changed his mind. He had had an inspiration, the same inspiration which came to him every day at this spot. He stopped.

'Let's go back,' he said.

'Not coming to-day?' laughed the gentleman. 'Well, good-bye.'

'You see, I think I'd better wait here, after all,' said the foxhound puppy apologetically. 'Something might happen. Are you really going on? Well—you'll excuse me, won't you?'

He ambled back to his place outside the blacksmith's shop. The tall, lean gentleman, who called himself Carfax, walked on briskly with spring in his heart. Above him the rooks talked and talked; the hedges were green; and there were little baby clouds in the blue sky.

Shall I try to deceive you for a page or two longer, or shall we have the truth out at once? Better have the truth. Well, then—the gentleman who called himself Carfax was really George Crosby. You guessed? Of course you did. But if you scent a mystery you are wrong.

It was five years ago that Crosby took his first holiday. He came to this very inn, The Dog and Duck, and when they asked him his name he replied 'Geoffrey Carfax'. It had been an inspiration in the train. To be Geoffrey Carfax for three weeks seemed to cut him off more definitely from the Fenchurch Street office and the Islington board-ing-house. George Crosby was in prison, working a life sentence; Geoffrey Carfax was a free man in search of the woman. Romance might come to Geoffrey, but it could never come to George. They were two different persons; then let them be two different persons. Besides, glamour hung over the mere act of giving a false name. George had delightful thrills when he remembered his deceit; and there was one heavenly moment of panic, on the last day of his first holiday, when (to avoid detection) he shaved off his moustache. He was not certain what the punishment was for calling yourself Geoffrey Carfax when your real name was George Crosby, but he felt that with a clean-shaven face he could laugh at Scotland Yard. The down-ward path, however, is notoriously an easy one. In subsequent years he let himself go still farther. Even the one false name wouldn't satisfy him now; and if he only looked in at a neighbouring inn for a glass of beer, he would manage to let it fall into his conversation that he was Guy Colehurst or Gervase Crane or—he had a noble range of names to choose from, only limited by the fact that 'G. C.' was on his cigarette-case and his kit-bag. (His linen was studiously unmarked, save with the hier-oglyphic of his washerwoman—a foolish observation in red cotton which might mean anything.)

The tall, lean gentleman, then, taking the morning was George Crosby. Between ourselves we may continue to call him George. It is not a name I like; he hated it too; but George he was undoubt-edly. Yet already he was a different George from the one you met at Muswell Hill. He had had two weeks of life, and they had made him brown and clear-eyed and confident. I think I said he blushed readily in Mrs Morrison's boarding-house; the fact was he felt always uneasy in London, awkward, uncomfortable. In the open air he was at home, ready for he knew not what dashing adventure.

It was a day of spring to stir the heart with longings and memories. Memories, half-forgotten, of all the Aprils of the past touched him for a moment, and then, as he tried to grasp them, fluttered out of reach, so that he wondered whether he was recalling real adventures which had happened, or whether he was but dreaming over again the dreams which were always with him. One memory remained. It was on such a day as this, five years ago, and almost in this very place, that he had met the woman.

Yes, I shall have to go back again to tell you of her. Five years ago he had been staying at this same inn; it was his first holiday after his sentence to prison. He was not so resigned to his lot five years ago; he thought of it as a bitter injustice; and the wonderful woman for whom he came into the country to search was to be his deliverer. So that, I am afraid, she would have to have been, not only wonderful, mysterious and holy, but also rich. For it was to the contented ease of his early days that he was looking for release; the little haven in Bedford Park had not come into his dreams. Indeed, I don't suppose he had even heard of Bedford Park at that time. It was Islington or The Manor House; anything in between was Islington. But, of course, he never confessed to himself that she would need to be rich.

And he found her. He came over the hills on a gentle April morning and saw her beneath him. She was caught, it seemed, in a hedge. How gallantly George bore down to the rescue!

'Can I be of any assistance?' he said in his best manner, and that, I think, is always the pleasantest way to begin. Between 'Can I be of any assistance?' and 'With all my worldly goods I thee endow' one has not far to travel.

'I'm caught,' she said. 'If you could—' Observe George spiking himself fearlessly.

'I say, you really *are*! Wait a moment.'

'It's very kind of you.'

There, he has done it.

'Thank you so much,' she said, with a pretty smile. 'Oh, you've hurt yourself!'

The sweet look of pain on her face!

'It's nothing,' said George nobly. And it really was nothing. One can get a delightful amount of blood and sympathy from the most insignificant scratch.

They hesitated a moment. She looked on the ground; he looked at her. Then his eyes wandered round the beautiful day, and came back to her just as she looked up.

'It is a wonderful day, isn't it?' he said suddenly.

'Yes,' she breathed.

It seemed absurd to separate on such a day when they were both wandering, and Heaven had brought them together.

'I say, dash it,' said George suddenly. 'What are you going to do? Are you going anywhere particular?'

'Not very particular.'

'Neither am I. Can't we go there together?'

'I was just going to have lunch.'

'So was I. Well, there you are. It would be silly if you sat here and ate—what *are* yours, by the way?'

'Only mutton, I'm afraid.'

'Ah, mine are beef. Well, if you sat here and ate mutton sandwiches and I sat a hundred yards farther on and ate beef ones, we *should* look ridiculous, shouldn't we?'

'It *would* be rather silly,' she smiled.

So they sat down and had their sandwiches together.

'My name is Carfax,' he said, 'Geoffrey Carfax.' Oh, George! And to a woman! However, she wouldn't tell him hers.

They spent an hour over lunch. They wandered together for another hour. Need I tell you all the things they said? But they didn't talk of London.

'Oh, I must be going,' she said suddenly. 'I didn't know it was so late. No, I know my way. Don't come with me. Good-bye.'

'It can't be good-bye,' said George in dismay. 'I've only just found you. Where do you live? Who are you?'

'Don't let's spoil it,' she smiled. 'It's been a wonderful day—a wonderful little piece of a day. We'll always remember it. I don't think it's meant to go on; it stops just here.'

'I *must* see you again,' said George firmly. 'Will you be there to-morrow, at the same time—at the place where we met?'

'I might.' She sighed. 'And I mightn't.'

But George knew she would.

'Then good-bye,' he said, holding out his hand.

'My name is Rosamund,' she whispered, and fled.

He watched her out of sight, marvelling how bravely she walked. Then he started for home, his head full of strange fancies …

He found a road an hour later, the road went on and on, it turned and branched and doubled; he scarcely noticed it. The church clock was striking seven as he came into the village.

It was a wonderful lunch he took with him next day. Chicken and tongue and cake and chocolate and hard-boiled eggs. He ate it alone (by the corner of a wood, five miles from the hedge which captured her) at half-past three. That day was a nightmare. He never found the place again, though he tried all through the week remaining to him. He had no hopes after that day of seeing her, but only to have found the hedge would have been some satisfaction. At least he could sit there and sigh—and curse himself for a fool.

He went back to Islington knowing that he had had his chance and missed it. By next April he had forgotten her. He was convinced that she was not the woman. *The* woman had still to be found. He went to another part of the country and looked for her.

And now he was back at The Dog and Duck again. Surely he would find her to-day. It was the time; it must be almost the place. Would the loved one be there? He was not sure whether he wanted her to be the woman of five years ago or not. Whoever she was, she would be the one he sought. He had walked some miles; funny if he stumbled upon the very place suddenly.

Memories of five years ago were flooding his mind. Had he really been here, or had he only dreamed of it? Surely that was the hill down which he had come; surely that clump of trees on the right had been there before. And—could that be the very hedge?

It was.

And there was a woman caught in it.

IV

George strode down the hill, his heart thumping heavily at his ribs ... She had her back towards him.

'Can I be of any assistance?' he said in his best manner. But she didn't need to be rich now; there was that little house at Bedford Park.

She turned round.

It was Gertie Morrison!

Silly of him; of course, it wasn't Miss Morrison; but it was extraordinarily like her. Prettier, though.

'Why, Mr Crosby!' she said.

It *was* Gertie Morrison.

'You!' he said angrily.

He was furious that such a trick should have been played upon him at this moment; furious to be reminded suddenly that he was George Crosby of Muswell Hill. Muswell Hill, the boarding-house—Good Lord! Gertie Morrison! Algy Traill's Gertie.

'Yes, it's me,' she said, shrinking from him. She saw he was angry with her; she vaguely understood why.

Then George laughed. After all, she hadn't deliberately put herself in his way. She could hardly be expected to avoid the whole of England (outside Muswell Hill) until she knew exactly where George Crosby proposed to take his walk. What a child he was to be angry with her.

When he laughed, she laughed too—a little nervously.

'Let me help,' he said. He scratched his fingers fearlessly on her behalf. What should he do afterwards? he wondered. His day was spoilt anyhow. He could hardly leave her.

'Oh, you've hurt yourself!' she said. She said it very sweetly, in a voice that only faintly reminded him of the Gertie of Muswell Hill.

'It's nothing,' he answered, as he had answered five years ago.

They stood looking at each other. George was puzzled.

'You are Miss Morrison, aren't you?' he said. 'Somehow you seem different.'

'You're different from the Mr Crosby I know.'

'Am I? How?'

'It's dreadful to see you at the boarding-house.' She looked at him timidly. 'You don't mind my mentioning the boarding-house, do you?'

'Mind? Why should I?' (After all, he still had another week.)

'Well, you want to forget about it when you're on your holiday.' Fancy her knowing that.

'And are you on your holiday too?'

She gave a long deep sigh of content.

'Yes,' she said.

He looked at her with more interest. There was colour in her face; her eyes were bright; in her tweed skirt she looked more of a country girl than he would have expected.

'Let's sit down,' he said. 'I thought you always went to Mar—to Cliftonville for your holiday?'

'I always go to my aunt's there in the summer. It isn't really a holiday; it's more to help her; she has a boarding-house too. And it really

19

is Cliftonville—only, of course, it's silly of Mother to mind having it called Margate. Cliftonville's much worse than Margate really. I hate it.'

(This can't be Gertie Morrison, thought George. It's a dream.)

'When did you come here?'

'I've been here about ten days. A girl friend of mine lives near here. She asked me suddenly just after you'd gone—I mean about a fortnight ago. Mother thought I wasn't looking well and ought to go. I've been before once or twice. I love it.'

'And do you have to wander about the country by yourself? I mean, doesn't your friend—I say, I'm asking you an awful lot of questions. I'm sorry.'

'That's all right. But, of course, I love to go about alone, particularly at this time of year. *You* understand that.'

Of course he understood it. That was not the amazing thing. The amazing thing was that she understood it.

He took his sandwiches from his pocket.

'Let's have lunch,' he said. 'I'm afraid mine are only beef.'

'Mine are worse,' she smiled. 'They're only mutton.'

A sudden longing to tell her of his great adventure of five years ago came to George. (If you had suggested it to him in March!)

'It's rather funny,' he said, as he untied his sandwiches—'I was down here five years ago—'

'I know,' she said quietly.

George sat up suddenly and stared at her.

'It was you!' he cried.

'Yes.'

'You. Good Lord! … But your name—you said your name was … wait a moment … that's it! Rosamund!'

'It is. Gertrude Rosamund. I call myself Rosamund in the country. I like to pretend I'm not the'—she twisted a piece of grass in her hands, and looked away from him over the hill—'the horrible girl of the boarding-house.'

George got on to his knees and leant excitedly over her.

'Tell me, do you hate and loathe and detest Traill and the Fossetts and Ransom as much as I do?'

She hesitated.

'Mr Ransom has a mother in Folkestone he's very good to. He's not really bad, you know.'

'Sorry, wash out Ransom. Traill and the Fossetts?'

'Yes. Oh yes. Oh yes, yes, yes.' Her cheeks flamed as she cried it, and she clenched her hands.

George was on his knees already, and he had no hat to take off, but he was very humble.

'Will you forgive me?' he said. 'I think I've misjudged you. I mean,' he stammered, 'I mean, I don't mean—of course, it's none of my business to judge you—I'm speaking like a prig, I … oh, you know what I mean. I've been a brute to you. Will you forgive me?'

She held out her hand, and he shook it. This had struck him, when he had seen it on the stage, as an absurdly dramatic way of making friends, but it seemed quite natural now.

'Let's have lunch,' she said.

They began to eat in great content.

'Same old sandwiches,' smiled George. 'I say, I suppose I needn't explain why I called myself Geoffrey Carfax.' He blushed a little as he said the name. 'I mean, you seem to understand.'

She nodded. 'You wanted to get away from George Crosby; *I* know.'

And then he had a sudden horrible recollection.

'I say, you must have thought me a beast. I brought a terrific lunch out with me the next day, and then I went and lost the place. Did you wait for me?'

Gertie would have pretended she hadn't turned up herself, but Rosamund said, 'Yes, I waited for you. I thought perhaps you had lost the place.'

'I say,' said George, 'what lots I've got to say to you. When did you recognize me again? Fancy my not knowing you.'

'It was three years, and you'd shaved your moustache.'

'So I had. But I could recognize people just as easily without it.'

She laughed happily. It was the first joke she had heard him make since that day five years ago.

'Besides, we're both different in the country. I knew you as soon as I heard your voice just now. Never at all at Muswell Hill.'

'By Jove!' said George. 'Just fancy.' He grinned at her happily.

After lunch they wandered. It was a golden afternoon, the very afternoon they had had five years ago. Once when she was crossing a little stream in front of him, and her foot slipped on a stone, he called out, 'Take care, Rosamund,' and thrilled at the words. She let them pass unnoticed; but later on when they crossed the stream again lower down, he took her hand and she said, 'Thank you, Geoffrey.'

They came to an inn for tea. How pretty she looked pouring out the tea for him—not for him, for them; the two of them. She and he! His thoughts became absurd …

Towards the end of the meal something happened. She didn't know what it was, but it was this. He wanted more jam; she said he'd had enough. Well, then, he wasn't to have much, and she would help him herself.

He was delighted with her.

She helped him … and something in that action brought back swiftly and horridly the Gertie Morrison of Muswell Hill, the Gertie who sat next to Algy and helped him to cabbage. He finished his meal in silence.

She was miserable, not knowing what had happened.

He paid the bill and they went outside. In the open air she was Rosamund again, but Rosamund with a difference. He couldn't bear things like this. As soon as they were well away from the inn he stopped. They leant against a gate and looked down into the valley at the golden sun.

'Tell me,' he said, 'I want to know everything. Why are you—what you are, in London?'

And she told him. Her mother had not always kept a boarding-house. While her father was alive they were fairly well off; she lived a happy life in the country as a young girl. Then they came to London. She hated it, but it was necessary for her father's business. Then her father died, and left nothing.

'So did my father,' said George under his breath.

She touched his hand in sympathy.

'I was afraid that was it ... Well, Mother tried keeping a boarding-house. She couldn't do it by herself. I had to help. That was just before I met you here ... Oh, if you could know how I hated it. The horrible people. It started with two boarders. Then there was one—because I smacked the other one's face. Mother said that wouldn't do. Well, of course, it wouldn't. I tried taking no notice of them. Well, that wouldn't do either. I had to put up with it; that was my life ... I used to pretend I was on the stage and playing the part of a landlady's vulgar daughter. You know what I mean; you often see it on the stage. That made it easier—it was really rather fun sometimes. I suppose I overplayed the part—made it more common than it need have been—it's easy to do that. By-and-by it began to come natural; perhaps I am like that really. We weren't anybody particular even when Father was alive. Then you came—I saw you were different from the rest. I knew you despised me—quite right too. But you really seemed to hate me, I never quite knew why. I hadn't done you any harm. It made me hate you too ... It made me want to be specially vulgar and common when you were there, just to show you I didn't mind what you thought about me ... You were so superior.

'I got away in the country sometimes. I just loved that. I think I was really living for it all the time ... I always called myself Rosamund in the country ... I hate men—why are they such beasts to us always?'

'They *are* beasts,' said George, giving his sex away cheerfully. But he was not thinking of Traill and the Fossetts; he was thinking of himself. 'It's very strange,' he went on; 'all the time I thought that the others were just what they seemed to be, and that I alone had a private life of my own which I hid from everybody. And all the time *you* ... Perhaps Traill is really somebody else sometimes. Even Ransom has his secret—his mother ... What a horrible prig I've been.'

'No, no! Oh, but you were!'

'And a coward. I never even tried ... I might have made things much easier for you.'

'You're not a coward.'

'Yes, I am. I've just funked life. It's too much for me, I've said, and I've crept into my shell and let it pass over my head ... And I'm still a coward. I can't face it by myself. Rosamund, will you marry me and help me to be braver?'

'No, no, no,' she cried, and pushed him away and laid her head on her arms and wept.

Saved, George, saved! Now's your chance. You've been rash and impetuous, but she has refused you, and you can withdraw like a gentleman. Just say 'I beg your pardon,' and move to Finsbury Park next month ... and go on dreaming about the woman. Not a land-lady's vulgar little daughter, but—

George, George, what are you doing?

He has taken the girl in his arms! He is kissing her eyes and her mouth and her wet cheeks! He is telling her ...

I wash my hands of him.

V

John Lobey, landlord of The Dog and Duck, is on the track of a mystery. Something to do with they anarchists and such-like. The chief clue lies in the extraordinary fact that on three Sundays in succession Parson has called 'George Crosby, bachelor, of this parish', when everybody knows that there isn't a Crosby in the parish, and that the gentleman from London, who stayed at his inn for three weeks and comes down Saturdays—for which purpose he leaves his bag and keeps on his room—this gentleman from

London, I tell you, is Mr Geoffrey Carfax. Leastways it was the name he gave.

John Lobey need not puzzle his head over it. Geoffrey Carfax is George Crosby, and he is to be married next Saturday at a neighbouring village church, in which 'Gertrude Rosamund Morrison, spinster, of this parish', has also been called three times. Mr and Mrs Crosby will then go up to London and break the news to Mrs Morrison.

'Not until you are my wife,' said George firmly, 'do you go into that boarding-house again.' He was afraid to see her there.

'You dear,' said Rosamund; and she wrote to her mother that the weather was so beautiful, and she was getting so much stronger, and her friend so much wanted her to stay, that—and so on. It is easy to think of things like that when you are in love.

On the Sunday before the wedding George told her that he had practically arranged about the little house in Bedford Park.

'And I'm getting on at the office rippingly. It's really quite interesting after all. I shall get another rise in no time.'

'You dear,' said Rosamund again. She pressed his hand tight and …

But really, you know, I think we might leave them now. They have both much to learn; they have many quarrels to go through, many bitter misunderstandings to break down; but they are alive at last. And so we may say good-bye.

Rosemary for Remembrance

(1915)

I

When I have shaken hands with my hostess and apologized for being so late, I never know what to do next. Some men make a beeline for the son of the house and ask him what's for dinner, but I have been better brought up. Generally I find myself standing first on one leg and then on the other, fingering my tie, and wondering if there is anyone present who would like me to point out that the day has been a beautiful one.

I was carrying on in this way when my host came up to me.

'You're taking in Miss Daintry,' he said. 'I don't think you know her.' He brought me up to a lonely girl and explained: 'This is Mr William Denny.' I bowed and said to myself: 'Her nose is too short.' It is not, of course, a remark which one makes aloud. I then prepared to say something pleasant to her.

But what?

'Are you *the* William Denny?' she said brightly, just as I was thinking of something.

As soon as the ice is broken, I am all right. Anyway, I am always fluent—and, I think, well informed—on the subject of myself.

'I seem to be to-night,' I said. I wondered who the other—the famous William Denny—was, or if she could possibly have read my little brochure—or book, as ordinary people say—called *The Road to Happiness*. My theory of happiness is roughly that—But you will understand it better if you buy the book. It costs two shillings and sixpence, and the publishers give me a penny or so for myself every six months, according to whether one or two copies have been sold.

'I always ask everybody that,' smiled Miss Daintry. 'It's much the best way of beginning.'

I looked at her in surprise.

'Do you mean you've never heard of any sort of a William Denny at all?'

'Not any sort. Are there lots of you?'

'Yes. No. I don't—Hallo, they're all going in!' I gave her my arm. 'Now,' I said, on the stairs, 'please explain.'

'Well, it's like this,' said Miss Daintry. 'Suppose Mr John Brown is introduced to me. Well, of course, I might say: "What a lovely day it's been! Have you done anything exciting?"'

'You might,' I agreed, and I shuddered to think how nearly I had said it myself.

'And it isn't a bad opening, either. Because if he says, "Golf," then I ask him what his handicap is, and how many bunkers he's been into, and so on all through dinner. And if he says, "Only work," then I say pleasantly, "Is that exciting?" and, of course, he tells me all about it, which may take weeks. One way or another there's bound to be conversation.'

'Mostly by him.'

'Oh, well, I do my share.' We found our seats, and she went on: 'Well, this year I thought I'd try and get a little more fun out of it. So, as soon as we're introduced, I say in an interested voice: "Oh, are you *the* John Brown?"'

'You mean the one whose soul goes marching along?'

Miss Daintry smiled and accepted some soup.

'Well, let's call him John Smith,' she said. 'I say: "Are you *the* John Smith?" Then he can do one of two things. He can be funny.' She stopped and helped herself to toast.

'I don't quite see how he can be funny,' I said thoughtfully. 'At least, it doesn't come to me at the moment.'

'Well, he might be jocular.'

I tried to think of something jocular for him, but failed. Still, that doesn't say that some other John Smith mightn't have had a dash. 'All right,' I agreed, 'he might be jocular. Next.'

'Next he might be pleasantly—er—pleasantly courteous.' She gave me half a smile and added, 'Like you. I mean,' she explained, 'he might be rather nice, and ready and—'

'I know,' I said. 'Like me.'

'But in nine cases out of ten he just tells me all about himself. He says with a modest smile: "So you've read my book?"'

I blushed into my soup. I could see the rich tomato reflection.

'What a conceited thing to say!' I exclaimed loudly, and began to eat a lot of bread.

'Oh, men are perfectly lovely when they talk about themselves!' said Miss Daintry happily.

I looked at her again, and decided that her nose wasn't too short—it was just short enough.

'I wonder,' I said, 'how it would work if the man talked first. Let's just try, shall we?'

'All right,' said Miss Daintry, with a smile waiting at the corners of her eyes.

'We'll suppose we've just been introduced. H'm! Are you *the* Miss Daintry?'

'So you've read my book?' she said modestly.

'I'm afraid not. I have very little time for reading. What is it called?'

'*Dinner Table Topics*,' she laughed.

'Ah! And the author's name?'

28

'Rosemary Daintry.'

'Rosemary!' I murmured to myself.

She waited for the next question.

'No,' I said. 'That's all—that's all I wanted to know.'

Rosemary! I liked the name. And, since her nose wasn't too short, I liked the face. I decided that one day I would tell her all about myself.

II

'Mr William Denny,' said a superior gentleman with brass buttons all over him. So I walked into the drawing-room.

Miss Daintry looked up in surprise.

'*The* William Denny,' I explained nervously.

'How do you do?' she said, holding out her hand with a smile. But she still looked surprised.

'My hat and stick,' I said, when I had shaken her hand and returned it to her, 'are in a strategic position in the hall. I can get to them immediately. Say the word, and I am downstairs and out of the front door in a flash.' I waited anxiously.

Miss Daintry continued to regard me with an air of wonder.

'This is a formal call,' I said hopefully. 'I mean I've come to ask for a subscription for the waits. Or, to put it another way, I know your uncle very well. I'm afraid I've come to the wrong house. I—Oh, can't you see how nervous I am? Do let me sit down and tell you all about it.'

Rosemary laughed out loud. Then she indicated a chair, and I sat down gratefully.

'I am so sorry,' she said. 'But I was wondering whether I oughtn't to pretend I didn't recognize you. Supposing I had said, "Let me see, didn't we meet at the Warringtons?" Would you have gone?'

'I should have departed,' I said.

'Yes. The bother is, I remember you perfectly well. To make it worse, I was reading your book when you came in. To make it still worse—'

'One moment,' I said, whipping out a pencil. 'Did you buy it or did you get it from the library?'

'I bought it.'

I made a note on my cuff.

'To keep a check on the publishers,' I explained.

'And to make it still worse,' Rosemary went on gravely, 'I was thinking of writing to the author of the book and saying how much I liked it. Isn't it awful?'

'Awful! I don't know what your great-grandmother would have said.'

'So, you see, I couldn't very well turn you out, could I?' She smiled encouragingly at me. 'But, all the same, I shall like to hear what you're going to say. You must have *some* reason for coming.'

The superior gentleman entered at this moment with an accomplice, and proceeded to arrange the tea. There was an interval while I explained how much sugar I liked, asked for it a little weaker, ate a couple of sandwiches, gave away another, and balanced a fourth on my saucer. Then I ventured into my explanation.

'This,' I said, 'is my after-dinner call.'

'Let's see,' said Rosemary, with her head on one side, 'when did you dine with us?'

'Never—at least, not yet. One still hopes. But I dined with the Carews last week. Now, an after-dinner call is, I take it, a way of expressing thanks. "In return for your delightful caviare last Thursday," one says to one's hostess, "I have come to show you my new spats." Isn't that so?'

'Well, something like that.'

'Yes. But supposing the thing which struck one most about the dinner was not the caviare, but the conversation of one's partner, then one might say to oneself, "I dined last Thursday, not with Mrs Carew, but with Miss Daintry," and it would be to Miss Daintry that one's after-dinner call would be due.'

'Yes,' said Rosemary, 'but it wouldn't prevent one saying, "Where on earth does the creature live?"'

'Oh, that was child's play. I looked you up in the telephone book.'

'But we aren't the only Daintrys.'

'My dear lady—don't you hate being called "my dear lady"? It's what bishops always say. I ought to pat your hand, really—my dear lady, I once met Conan Doyle. I know all about inductive reasoning.'

'Oh, do tell me how it's done!' pleaded Rosemary.

'It's quite easy,' I said. 'There are nine Daintrys in the book. *A priori*, as Sherlock used to puzzle Watson by saying, you might be any one of those nine. But the first five were A. H. Daintry and Co., plumbers, so that washed five out.'

'I don't see why my father shouldn't sell plums,' complained Miss Daintry.

'Even if he did,' I pointed out, 'I shouldn't call at the orchard and expect to meet his daughter. You were bound to be one of the other four. The first was John Daintry, artist; the second was Henry Daintry, artist. An artistic family the Daintrys. But was Miss Rosemary Daintry the daughter of either of them?'

'Yes,' pleaded Rosemary, 'let me be an artist's daughter.'

'I looked them up in *Who's Who*. John was there. He painted that remarkable picture *Slice of Lemon on Plate*, purchased by the Middlesborough Art Gallery; his recreations are polo and stamp-collecting; his age is fifty-seven, and he has two sons. Two sons,' I said sternly, 'and no daughter.'

'Bother!' said Rosemary. 'Still, what about Henry?'

'Henry was not in *Who's Who* at all. No one I spoke to had ever heard of Henry; no one had ever seen his pictures. It was impossible that so unsuccessful an artist as Henry should support a grown-up daughter.'

'She might have sat for him,' said Rosemary, 'and earned her keep that way.'

'Then he would have sold his pictures,' I said, looking at her thoughtfully, 'and Henry didn't. No, you were either the daughter of C. E. Daintry, of Queen Anne's Gate, or of Reginald Daintry, of

Norfolk Street. Yesterday afternoon I had a sudden intuition that you lived in Norfolk Street.'

'How funny!' said Rosemary. 'How did the intuition come?'

'It came yesterday afternoon,' I said, 'as I was being urged out of the drawing-room of Queen Anne's Gate.'

III

I was passing the British Museum when the thunderstorm broke. My umbrella was new—a young one, out for the first time—and I did not want to get it damp. Besides, what is one umbrella against the majesty of Heaven? So I pushed my way through the pigeons and went inside. An attendant took my umbrella from me.

'Be careful with it,' I said. 'This is the first time it has left its father. Don't let it have the India-rubber ring; it's so unhealthy for it.'

I left him and wandered upstairs. There are, of course, other things than mummies in the British Museum, but it is to the Egyptian Rooms that I always make my way when it rains. For once I was rewarded. Standing opposite the case of one of the most notorious of our mummies was—

'Allow me to introduce you,' I said, stepping up briskly. 'Miss Rosemary Daintry—my aunt, the Princess Ra.'

Rosemary turned round quickly.

'Why, it's Mr Denny!' she said. 'How do you do?'

'How do you do? Everybody is at the British Museum to-day.'

'Yes, but what are they all doing? *I'm* here on business, only I'm doing it very badly. Perhaps you can help me.'

I began to look as capable as possible.

'It's like this. There's a book called *The Beginnings of Assyrian Ethnology*. Do you know it?'

'By heart. I sleep with it under my pillow every night.'

'It's in twenty volumes,' went on Rosemary gravely.

I sighed.

'Who should know it better than I?' I said sadly. 'Doctors are baffled by my insomnia, but I dare not tell them the truth. I have got to love the book so much that I cannot be parted from it. In the daytime I carry it—I mean it follows me in a lorry—everywhere.'

'Oh, well, that's splendid, because now you can tell me the real name. I came to look up something in it for Father, and I know it was something about ethnology, but I've got the name of the book wrong.' She waited expectantly.

I thought for a moment with my head on one side.

'No,' I said, 'no, I've never heard of the book. I misunderstood you. I thought you were referring to the poems of Ella Wheeler Wilcox.'

Rosemary laughed.

'I knew you couldn't help me,' she said.

'I wasn't sure that I could myself, but I was determined to try. "Always be helpful"—that's the motto of the Dennys. When we came over with William the Conqueror—I should say, when William the Conqueror came over with us—it was Guillaume de Saint-Denys who pointed to the shore and said to William: "This is England, sire." He recognized it from the maps.'

'Yes,' said Rosemary, 'but that still doesn't explain what you're doing here now.'

'No, it doesn't, does it? It ought to, but it doesn't. The truth is—and I say this without prejudice to anything I may think of later on—the truth is, I came here to meet Miss Daintry.'

'We must have had an assignation,' said Rosemary remorsefully, 'and I had forgotten it.'

'It wasn't an assignation; it was just a sort of feeling that Thursday was your day for the British Museum. Monday, I told myself, the Zoo; Tuesday, the Tower of London; Wednesday, a little needlework at home; but Thursday—well, here we are.'

'I believe you only came in because it was raining.'

'Let us rather say that it only rained because Miss Daintry was in the British Museum and Mr Denny happened to be passing.'

'Said he gallantly,' smiled Rosemary. 'A quotation from your next magazine story.'

'From *The Beginnings of Assyrian Ethnology*, Book VII, Chap. 16,' I corrected her. 'That was the reference Mr Daintry wanted, I expect. Do you think, now that we've found it, we might—' I hesitated, not quite knowing how to put it. 'Do you ever have tea?' I said.

'You saw me having it only the other day. Don't say you've forgotten.'

'There you are, then. I owe you seven sandwiches, two cups of tea, and a piece of cake. There's a refreshment room here somewhere, but probably they only give you marble tops to the tables—and water-cress. If we went outside, I could pay my debt properly, and I could also show you my new umbrella. I lent it to an attendant when I came in, but he's promised to give it me back when I go out.'

'Tea *would* be rather jolly,' said Rosemary thoughtfully, but with a bit of a smile lurking somewhere. 'Do you know that it's only ten days ago that I first met you at dinner?'

'We always seem to be having meals together, don't we?' I said cheerfully. 'One can talk so much better when one is eating—I mean, of course, in the intervals. But to speak seriously, to quote again from the immortal work, Book VIII, Chap. 16, "I should be very much honoured, Miss Daintry, if you would take a dish of tea with me," said he, with a low bow. This,' I added, 'is the "low bow".' And, look-ing round to see that the policeman wasn't watching, I took off my hat and bowed low to her. 'Do come.'

Rosemary nodded her head slowly at me.

'Miss Daintry,' she said, 'has much pleasure in accepting Mr Denny's kind piece of cake.'

IV

For a week I had not seen Rosemary. A whole week had passed—had, indeed, elapsed—without a single invitation from her. Dinner-parties, wedding receptions, dances, christening ceremonies, funerals—at none of these had the pleasure of Mr William Denny's company been looked for by Mr and Miss Daintry. One wondered what the younger generation was coming to.

However, two days later, things began to move. At four o'clock of a fine afternoon Miss Daintry might have been seen tripping lightly down Regent Street, and five yards behind her, padding sleuth-like in her track, came a tall man of handsome exterior. Could it have been W. Denny? It was.

Rosemary stopped and looked critically at a hat in the window. W. Denny slipped past and looked critically at a shop-walker in the next window. Rosemary moved on. Mr Denny turned round and hurried back in the direction from which he had been coming. He had forgotten his umbrella, perhaps.

'Hallo!' said Rosemary, her face lighting up.

'Well,' I said, 'this *is* a surprise!'

'I'm buying a birthday present,' she volunteered. 'Something for a father. But I can't *think* what he wants. If you aren't going in entirely the other direction, you might walk along and make brilliant suggestions.'

We walked along.

'Fathers are very difficult to give things to,' I agreed. 'They always have everything. It's disgusting the way they indulge themselves.'

'I generally give him a book. He just lives in his library.'

'What about a bull-terrier this year, for a change?' I suggested hopefully. 'We must get him out of his groove.'

Rosemary laughed.

'Try again,' she said.

I tried again.

'A sword-stick?' I said, after profound thought.

Rosemary looked doubtful.

'The advantage of a sword-stick,' I pointed out, 'is that if you are attacked suddenly by a madman, you—Well, probably the spring doesn't work. There *is* that, of course. But you get a good notice in the papers. "Mr Daintry, who would have defended himself vigorously, if the safety-catch hadn't got stuck, leaves a daughter and a bull-terrier to mourn him." Oh, I was forgetting he refused the bull-terrier.'

'And the sword-stick, I am afraid,' smiled Rosemary.

I sighed sadly.

'Wouldn't you call him rather a particular man?' I asked. 'One can't please him. Of course, you really ought to have been knitting him something ever since last birthday, and hiding it under the sofa cushions when he came in. It almost looks as though it would have to be books again, doesn't it?'

'It does, I'm afraid. The question is, what book?'

I looked up at the sky. It's very awkward when anybody says 'What book?' to the man who has written *The Road to Happiness*, price two shillings and sixpence at all booksellers, or direct from the publishers, Messrs. ——

'Yes,' said Rosemary, 'but I've given him that one already.'

Wonderful intuition women have! I hadn't said a word.

'Why not give him another copy?' I suggested. 'In case the first copy wears out.'

'Much as he admires the author, whom he particularly wants to meet——'

'He shall,' I said firmly.

'He thought you might come down to our country cottage for a week-end,' Rosemary explained parenthetically.

'I should love to.'

'Hooray! Well, much as—I've lost that sentence. Where was I up to?'

'You were saying how your father admired me. Dwell on that for a little. I shan't mind.'

Rosemary laughed.

'What I really want to dwell on is some tea,' she said. 'It's your turn to have tea with me. If you're one of those manly men who can't bear the idea of a woman ever paying for anything, then you'd better say so now, to avoid a scene inside.'

'I should love you to pay for me,' I said; 'and I'd better warn you—it's my day for cream buns.'

We had a very jolly tea—one more meal with Rosemary. Towards the end of it she took a newspaper cutting from her purse. I leant forward with interest.

'Read that,' she said. 'I cut it out of the paper this morning.'

'It's a penal offence, defacing papers in the public libraries,' I protested. 'But perhaps you take it in privately?'

'We do,' said Rosemary severely. 'We did even when it was three-pence,' she added, with a grand air.

'Then I'm glad you're paying for tea. Now, then, what's this about?'

It was a cutting from the Agony Column.

'If Henry S. Boldero will be at the Oxford Circus Tube at 3.45 p.m. this afternoon, with—you know what—the man in the false whiskers standing by the bookstall will be ready to receive it.'

'Well?' I said.

'You remember I told you the other day how I always read the Agony Column, and what fun it would be to keep one of the assignations, and see what happened? Well, I kept this one.'

'What happened?' I asked eagerly.

'I don't know. There was a huge crowd—I suppose they'd all read that paper—and, after a bit, I came away. That was just before I met you.'

'Ah,' I said profoundly, 'I expect it was a secret code, and meant something quite different.'

'Do you really think so?' said Rosemary.

'I really do.'

And I did. In fact, I knew. It meant: 'I love you, and I *must* see you again soon. You read the Agony Column—you told me so. Then read this, and come to see what it means, just for fun. I shall be there, too.'

'Yes,' I said, 'I expect it's a bit of a secret.'

V

I don't know if you have ever been in love. If you have, you will understand how wonderful it is to wake up in the morning and realize suddenly that she, the beloved one, is for the first time under the same roof as yourself. No hopeless prayers that there shall be a letter from her to-day; no lingering forlorn in the Park, on the chance that she will pass. You have only to dress and go down to breakfast, and there she is bound to be. Very likely she will ask you to pass the marmalade. Could anything be more delightful?

'What would you like to do?' asked Mr Daintry, after breakfast.

'Well—' I said doubtfully.

'You must just do whatever you like,' he said, and retired to the library.

'What Father really means,' explained Rosemary, 'is, do you want to go to church or not? He *doesn't* mean, would you rather go up in an aeroplane, or play polo, or swim the Channel. So, if there's anything like that which you want to do, you must be polite and try to forget about it. I told you there was nothing to do here, didn't I?'

'Yes, but I like doing nothing. Is there a church anywhere about?'

'There's one about three miles away.'

'Well, I should love not going to that.'

'It's Early Norman,' said Rosemary reproachfully.

'Then we should certainly be too late for it. Let's go for a walk, and you can show me all the sights. We can take the church cautiously, from the outside, on our way back.'

Rosemary nodded.

'In half an hour, then. I must put on a shorter skirt, or I shall be one of the sights myself.'

And so, half an hour later, we started.

'I ought to warn you,' I said, 'I know very little about the country. I don't know if a cuckoo-wort is a bird or a—a wort.'

'What *is* a cuckoo-wort?' said Rosemary.

'That's just it—I don't know. But I feel it must be something. And probably to-day's just the day when it will be in flower—I mean in song. So if I don't say anything about it, you mustn't think that I don't admire it. May I borrow a stick of Mr Daintry's, in case we're attacked by anything?'

'Here you are. Now, which way shall we go?'

'Anywhere. Round and round the stables. I don't mind a bit on a day like this.'

'I thought we might try Pulman's Gap.'

'Do let's. And then, if it turns out that there isn't such a place, we can come home again.'

We set off hopefully. Gap or no Gap, it was good to be out with Rosemary.

'Don't you really know much about the country?' she asked suddenly.

'I know more about London.'

She looked at me with a smile.

'Really, I know very little about you, don't I?'

'Name of Denny,' I explained.

'Yes, that's almost all I'm sure of.'

'Christian name, William; commonly called Billy. This leads to a huge joke. When people say to you, "Do you know Billy Denny?" you answer, "Yes, isn't that the stuff people put into their eyes?" thus causing great merriment.'

'Go on.'

'What else is there? Publications: *The Road to*—No, I feel sure I've mentioned that before. It's a funny thing how the conversation always comes round to my book. I try desperately hard to avoid it. I start talking about the most unlikely things, such as cuckoo-worts, but, somehow or other, I always end up with the name of my publishers. And yet I am not a conceited man. I—'

'Have you written any other books?'

'I am writing one. Mr William Denny is at present engaged upon a full-length novel. It's rather exciting. You just go on until you're stuck, and then you begin a new chapter with "Meanwhile—" Life is rather jolly, don't you think?'

'It's heavenly,' said Rosemary. 'What made you suddenly say so?'

'Oh, just the weather and the country, and talking to you, and talking about myself. I don't see what else one wants.'

Rosemary was silent.

'I wish you'd tell me something,' I said, after a pause.

'Perhaps I will. What is it?'

'When they christened you Rosemary, how did they know you were going to look like Rosemary when you grew up?'

Rosemary stared at me, utterly astonished, and yet it was a simple enough question.

'When they christened you Rosemary—' I began again.

She gave a little laugh and turned away.

'That's Pulman's Gap over there,' she said.

I took my hat off to it.

'I suppose,' I went on, 'they gave you a name like Madge as well, to fall back upon, and then they thought you'd be safe, either way.'

She continued to look over the fields at Pulman's Gap.

'I just wanted to know,' I said humbly.

Rosemary turned round to me with a pleasant smile.

'I'm sorry,' she said, 'but you took me by surprise. I didn't know we were talking about me; I thought you were telling me about yourself.'

(Oh, Rosemary, Rosemary, I am telling you about myself now, and you know it!)

'Myself,' I said. 'Well, I give you my nurse's verdict. "Master William may not be handsome, nor clever, to speak of, but he *have* got a cheek."'

Rosemary laughed.

'I agree with some of that,' she said.

VI

'This is our dance,' I said to Rosemary. 'Come along.'

'I don't think so,' she smiled. 'I'm dancing this with'—she consulted her programme—'Mr Twigg.'

'Twigg? Oh, I know Twigg—at least, I know his family tree. You can't dance with *him*!'

'But I promised.'

'Yes, but where is he? Where are the twigs of yester-year? Gone with the leaves of Vallombrosa. His last words were: "Denny, old man, lend me half-a-crown for a taxi. My aunt's ill." That's his aunt on the other branch ... I wish you wouldn't dance with people called Twigg. It's so easy to make up things about them.'

Rosemary looked round the room hopefully. 'He's a stout man with an eye-glass. I don't see him.'

'What's the good of his having an eye-glass if you can't see him?'

'He must have forgotten me. It seems rather a pity to waste this dance, doesn't it?'

'It does,' I said firmly. 'Come on.'

We came on.

It was my first dance with Rosemary. Oh, the nearness and the dearness of her!

'You're twenty something, and I'm twenty something, and we've never danced together before,' I said at the end of it. 'I don't know what's coming to the world.'

'It's coming all right now,' said Rosemary.

We found a shady corner. I had known, when I was dressing that evening, that it would have to be done now.

'Rosemary,' I said—believe me, a little queerly, as though it was somebody else speaking, and I was listening to him.

'Yes?'

'I—I love you!' the absurd voice went on, and said it again and again, making an anthem of it.

Rosemary said nothing.

The ridiculous fellow went on. I tried to push him away and assert myself, but he stuck to it. It was stupid of him, because I had planned some delightful things to say to Rosemary—the sort of things that Lewis Waller says. But then he knows what the lady is going to answer—it's in the prompt book—and that makes it easier for him. A hint of independence, and he sends for the understudy.

'I love you!' said the muffled voice again.

'Oh,' said Rosemary, 'don't! I don't know. It's absurd!'

At the word 'absurd' the usurper collapsed altogether, and I stepped back into myself and took command.

'We hardly know each other at all,' Rosemary went on.

'We never shall until we get married,' I said. 'We could meet a hundred times, and we'd know just as much of each other as we do now. Perhaps at the fifty-eighth time it might come out that I sang a bit, and at the seventy-fourth time that you had an uncle in the Diplomatic Service. We needn't wait for that. I'll sing now, if you like. You see, you don't get engaged because you know a person, but because you want to know them.'

'I don't know. I am afraid,' said Rosemary wistfully. 'I think I'm a little afraid of men.'

'I promise you it will be all right; I won't let you down, really. Besides, both our names begin with a "D", so that you needn't have new initials put on your luggage. And if you've got "D—Y" on any of your handkerchiefs, then that will be all right, too. We can even allow you an "n" in the middle. You can't do that when you marry Twiggs. Oh, Rosemary, just try saying "Billy!"'

Rosemary sighed.

'I've never even thought of you as anything but Mr Denny,' she said.

'Then begin with William. Say "William—William—William—William—William!" like that to yourself, and after a bit "Billy" will come quite easily to you.'

'Oh, I must talk to somebody about it! Father likes you, I know.'

'And I like him. When we are married, we will often meet him at the British Museum. And I'll go and talk to him to-morrow. It isn't only the three and fourpence from my publishers; I've got other money, too. We shall have about five and ninepence altogether. I'm sure Mr Daintry will be satisfied. What shall I call him when we're married? What a pity he isn't a major, and then I could say "Colonel". They like that. I suppose I shall have to call him "Hi!"'

'Oh, Billy, Billy,' said Rosemary, 'you do talk! I love to listen to you now. Shall I love to listen to you always?'

'There's an awful lot of listening in marriage,' I said.

She was silent for a little, and then said suddenly—

'Oh, why did you do this at a dance? You don't really mean it—proposals at dances mean nothing.'

That did make me laugh.

'I love listening to *you*,' I said, 'when you talk such heavenly rubbish! Meet me in the Park to-morrow morning at eight o'clock. It's sure to be wet, and then you shall have a proposal before breakfast in the rain. "Carried away by hunger and the gentle trickle down his neck, Mr Denny flung himself at her feet." Oh, Rosemary, silly girl, it isn't the glamour of the dance—it's the glamour of *you*!'

'Is it?' said Rosemary, turning to me eagerly. 'Say that again.'

But I didn't. Before I could say anything, that other silly person rushed up and took Rosemary into his arms and told her his old story again. And somehow she didn't seem afraid.

Mullins

(1918)

There are always bores in a Regimental Mess who want to talk about their adventures when you want to talk about yours. Mullins was as bad as any of them, but with this difference. The adventures of the others were adventures in search of the material; a petticoat, a golf ball, a gun emplacement. Mullins had only spiritual adventures. If, during those early days of training, he had fallen off the cliffs into the sea, he would have told you of his emotions on the way down, and said not a word of the splash at the bottom. Recovering in hospital, he would not have wondered whether he would always carry on his body the scars of the accident; he would have contemplated only the new scars on his soul. 'Do I look different?' he would have asked his nurse quite seriously, his face swathed in bandages, and would have been surprised at her polite prevarication. What he would have meant would have been, 'Don't you understand that, as a result of this extraordinary experience, I am a finer Mullins altogether?'

This is not to say that he was indifferent to his personal appearance. He was very tall and thin, talked in a high voice, and walked with his head well back in the endeavour to balance a pair of glasses on a nose apparently not meant for glasses. Had he been indifferent to his appearance, he would have worn spectacles. Spectacles may or may not be ugly, but they would have hidden from you the essential

Mullins. The essential Mullins, in a material world where people fight each other, and the short-sighted must suffer no handicap in the battle, could be expressed more clearly by *pince-nez*. So Mullins strode past you on the parade-ground with his head in the air, and if you did not realize at a glance all the astonishing things that he meant to himself, you did at least admit that he was an interesting-looking person. Which would have pleased him enormously to hear.

He went to France. He had often spoken of the changes in his mental and spiritual attitude which were likely to be caused by the battlefields of France, but he had never wondered, as many so much less introspective have wondered, whether he would be afraid. He knew he would not be afraid, simply because whatever might come to him only offered him yet another of those spiritual adventures for which he hungered. Death least of all he feared. For to a man like Mullins, whose every adventure is an adventure of the soul, the next world was simply an escape from the trammels of the body; a communion of spirits unfettered by spectacles and such-like matters, in which (I suspect) Mullins would do most of the communing.

But he had another reason for looking upon Death with a kindly eye. He was already in communication with many of those who had begun the adventure of the next world. In his actions in this world he was influenced by what they of the next world told him—(indeed, that is my story, as will be seen)—and now he was eager to join them, and himself to get to that great work of helping and guiding the earth-bound mortals whom he had left behind, but of whom he had never quite been one.

All this sounds strange, and perhaps a little uncanny, but it was Mullins. If I say simply that he was a Spiritualist, you will think of table-rappings and other stupidities, and do him an injustice. If I say that he was just a Christian who really believed all that other Christians profess, I may be nearer the truth; save that I do not know at all what his religion was. All I know is that he believed the barrier between this world and the next to be a slight one, and was himself quite ready to pass it.

And, of course, still more ready to talk about it.

To be absolutely without fear is not the only virtue required by a Company Commander in action. Mullins was given his company, and then taken away from it. He disregarded the material too openly. He saw beyond the crown on his sergeant-major's arm into the blankness in his sergeant-major's soul—and preferred to consult his batman, whose arm was devoid of anything but wound-stripes, but whose soul shone with crossed swords and stars. He was wrong about the sergeant-major, and wrong about the batman; and of course still more wrong about the proper duty of an officer. So he was taken from his company and made Intelligence Officer instead.

He did not mind. As Intelligence Officer he had much more scope. No soul is so clogged by the material as a company commander's, whose twin cares must ever be the stomachs and the feet of others. True, a company commander is the lord of his Company Mess, and nobody can stop him doing all the talking, whereas the Intelligence Officer at H.Q. Mess must let the Colonel say something on occasion. But it must be remembered that the Intelligence Officer's duties will take him to every part of the line, and consequently into all four Company Messes, and that if one Mess is temporarily alert, another may be in that peaceful state when the uninterrupted soliloquy of a soul contemplating itself is inexpressibly soothing.

But it was not all soliloquy, of course. He had his arguments with the unbelievers. The unbelievers were of two kinds; the materialists who held that there was no life beyond the grave, and the religious who held that there was such a life and that we should know all about it one day, but certainly not to-day. All alike scouted his pretence that the spirits of the dead could and did communicate with the living. Mullins argued earnestly with them, but did not resent their attitude. They were just blind; they were waiting until he could open their eyes with the proof; possibly in this world, but more probably from that next world, when, as a spirit of the dead, he would have something to say to them.

It was after Mullins had been out a year, had won the Military Cross, and had shown himself as good an Intelligence Officer as he was a bad Company Commander, that he came into possession of the famous stick. A great friend of his had been killed, and Mullins, home on leave, had called on that friend's people. He had been asked to choose a memento of the dead man, and had chosen his stick, a short heavy one with plenty of weight in the head. During that night the dead man talked with Mullins, and told him how glad he was that Mullins had his stick. 'That stick will do great things for you,' he said. 'It will save the lives of many of your battalion.'

Mullins still had four days of leave; four days in which to tell everybody in London of this wonderful communication with the dead. Some, perhaps, believed; some smiled. Mullins himself was happy and excited. To the friends who saw him off his last remark was: 'Look out for news of the old stick,' and he waved it gleefully at them. Two days later everybody in the battalion had heard that Mullins' new stick was going to save their lives, and had indicated that he was a silly ass … They also told him that he was just in time for the new push.

The battalion was held up, and resented it. The leading company on the left licked its wounds in a disused trench—God knows what trench or whose, for this bit of country had been fought over, backwards and forwards, for two years—and wondered what to do about it. A hundred and fifty yards away a German machine-gun was engaged in keeping their heads down for them. The Company Commander squinted up at it, and squinted again at his watch, and cursed all machine-guns. Suppose they charged it—but a hundred and fifty yards was the devil of a way, and that damned machine-gun had killed enough of them already. Suppose he sent a couple of men out to stalk it? Slow work, but—he looked at his watch again. Why the devil had this happened, when everything had been going so well before? And here they were—stuck—and seemed to have lost the swing of it. Momentum—that was the word—momentum all gone. Well, something would have to be done.

He looked along the trench, considering …

And from the extreme right of it a tall, thin figure emerged from the ruck and hoisted itself leisurely over the top. Mullins. He carried no revolver. His tin-hat was on the back of his head, his coat-collar, for some reason, turned up. Both his hands were in his pockets, and in the crook of his left arm lay the famous stick.

With an air of pleasant briskness he walked towards the machine-gunner. He did not hurry, for this was not so much an operation against the enemy, as a demonstration to unbelievers on the home-front. Neither did he dawdle. He just went to the machine-gun as in peace days he would have gone to the post on a fresh spring morning.

He had a hundred and fifty yards to go. From time to time his right hand came out of his pocket, fixed his glasses more firmly on his nose, and returned to his pocket again. So, at Oxford, he must have walked along the High to a lecture many, many times, hands in pockets, hunched shoulders, coat-collar up, and gown or books tucked under the left arm. So he walked now … and still he was not hit.

I have tried to explain Mullins to you; I shall not try to explain that machine-gunner. He may have thought Mullins was coming to surrender. The astonishing spectacle of Mullins may have disturbed his aim. The numerous heads popping up to gape at the back-view of Mullins may have kept him too busy to attend to Mullins. Or—there may have been other reasons.

So Mullins walked up to the machine-gunner. A yard away from him he took his right hand from his pocket, withdrew the stick from the crook of his left arm and in a friendly way hit the machine-gunner over the head with it. The man collapsed. Mullins picked him up by the collar, shook him to see if he was shamming, dropped him, replaced the stick in the crook of his left arm, fixed his glasses on his nose, took the man by the collar again and started to drag him back to the British trench. Once or twice he got a little entangled between the stick, the prisoner and the attention necessary for his glasses, hesitating between dropping the stick and fixing the glasses with his left hand, and dropping the prisoner and fixing them with his right. But in the end he arrived safely at the trench with all three possessions. Once there, he handed the prisoner over, and then stood beaming down at the Company Commander.

'Well,' he said, pushing his glasses firmly on to his nose, 'and what about the jolly old stick *now*?'

If this were not a true story, I should say that Mullins got the Victoria Cross. Actually they gave him a bar to his Military Cross. The real 'Mullins', if he reads this, will recognize the incident, though he will protest that I have quite misunderstood his personality and have failed altogether to appreciate his spiritual attitude. Perhaps I have. A writer must be allowed his own way in these matters. We start with a fact or two, the impression of a face, and in a little while we do not know how much is reality and how much is our day-dream.

Bad Lord Blight

(1920)

(A Moral Story for the Middle-aged)

I

Seated in the well-appointed library of Blight Hall, John Blighter, Seventeenth Earl of Blight, bowed his head in his hands and gave himself up to despair. The day of reckoning had come.

Were appearances not so deceptive, one would have said that Lord Blight ('Blight', as he was known familiarly to his friends) was a man to be envied. In a revolving bookcase in the middle of the spacious library were countless treasured volumes, including a complete edition of Thackeray; outside in the well-kept grounds of the estate was a new lawn-mower; a bottle of sherry, freshly uncorked, stood upon the sideboard in the dining-room. But worldly possessions are not everything. An untroubled mind, as Shakespeare knew (even if he didn't actually say it), is more to be valued than riches. The seventeenth Earl of Blight's mind was not untroubled. His conscience was gnawing him.

Some people would say, no doubt, that his conscience was too sensitive. True, there were episodes in his past life of which in later years he could not wholly approve; but is not this the case with every one of us? Far better, as must often have occurred to Milton, to strive for the future than to regret the past. Ten years ago Lord Blight had been plain John Blighter, with no prospects in front of him. Realizing that he could expect little help from others, he decided to push for himself. He began by pushing three cousins over the cliffs at Scarborough, thus becoming second heir to the earldom. A week later he pushed an elder brother over the same cliff, and was openly referred to in the Press as the next bearer of the title. Barely a fortnight had elapsed before a final push diverted the last member of the family (a valued uncle) into the ever-changing sea, the venue in this case being Whitby, presumably in order to avoid suspicion.

But all this had happened ten years ago. The past is the past, as Wordsworth probably said to Coleridge more than once. It was time for Lord Blight to forget these incidents of his eager and impetuous youth. Yet somehow he could not. Within the last few days his conscience had begun to gnaw him, and in his despair he told himself that at last the day of reckoning had come. Poor Blight! It is difficult to withhold our sympathy from him.

The door opened, and his wife, the Countess of Blight, came into the library.

'Blight!' she whispered. 'My poor Blight! What has happened?'

He looked up haggardly.

'Gertie,' he said, for that was her name, 'it is all over. My sins have found me out.'

'Not sins,' she said gently. 'Mistakes.'

'Mistakes, yes—you are right.' He stretched out a hand, took a letter from the desk in front of him and gave it to her. 'Read that.' With a groan he buried his head in his hands again. She took it and read, slowly and wonderingly, these words:

'To lawn-mower as delivered, £5 17s. 6d.'

Lord Blight looked up with an impatient ejaculation. 'Give it to me,' he said in some annoyance, snatching it away from her and throwing it into the waste-paper basket. 'Here, this is the one. Read it; read it quickly; for we must decide what to do.'

She read it with starting eyes.

'DEAR SIR, I am prepared to lend you anything from £10 to £10,000 on your note-of-hand alone. Should you wish—'

'D—n!' said the seventeenth Earl of Blight. 'Here, where is the blessed thing?' He felt in his pockets. 'I must have—I only had it a—Ah, here it is. Perhaps I had better read it to you this time.' He put on his spectacles—a present from an aunt—and read as follows:

'MY LORD, We regret to inform you that a claimant to the title has arisen. It seems that, soon after the death of his first wife, the sixteenth Earl of Blight contracted a second and secret marriage to Ellen Podby, by whom he had eleven sons, the eldest of whom is now asserting his right to the earldom and estates. Trusting to be favoured with your instructions in the matter, We are, my lord,

'Yours faithfully,

'BILLINGS, BILLINGS & BILLINGS.'

Gertie (Countess of Blight) looked at her husband in horror.

'Eleven!' she cried.

'Eleven,' said the Earl gloomily.

Then a look of grim determination came into his eyes. With the air of one who might have been quoting Keats, but possibly wasn't, he said firmly:

'What man has done, man can do.'

That evening the Countess of Blight gave orders for eleven spare bedrooms to be got ready.

II

On the morning after the arrival of the eleven Podbys (as they had been taught to call themselves) John, seventeenth Earl of Blight, spoke quite frankly to Algernon, the eldest.

'After all, my dear Algernon,' he said, 'we are cousins. There is no need for harsh words between us. All I ask is that you should forbear to make your claim until I have delivered my speech in the House of

Lords on the Coast Erosion Bill, upon which I feel deeply. Once the Bill is through, I shall be prepared to retire in your favour. Meanwhile let us all enjoy together the simple pleasures of Blight Hall.'

Algernon, a fair young man with a meaningless expression, replied suitably.

So for some days the eleven Podbys gave themselves up to pleasure. Percy, the youngest, though hardly of an age to appreciate the mechanism of it, was allowed to push the lawn-mower. Lancelot and Herbert, who had inherited the Podby intellect, were encouraged to browse around the revolving bookcase, from which they frequently extracted one of the works of Thackeray, replacing it again after a glance at the title page; while on one notable occasion the Earl of Blight took Algernon into the dining-room at about 11.31 in the morning and helped him to a glass of sherry and a slice of sultana cake. In this way the days passed happily, and confidence between the eleven Podbys and their cousin was established.

It was on a fair spring morning, just a week after their arrival, that the Countess of Blight came into the music-room (where Algernon was humming a tune) and said, 'Ah, Algernon, my husband was looking for you. I think he has some little excursion to propose. What a charming day, is it not? You will find him in the library.'

As Algernon entered the library, Lord Blight looked up from the map he was studying and nodded.

'I thought,' he said, coming to the point at once, 'that it might amuse you to drive over with me to Flamborough Head. The view from the top of the cliff is considered well worth a visit. I don't know if your tastes lie in that direction at all?'

Algernon was delighted at the idea, and replied that nothing would give him greater pleasure than to accompany Lord Blight.

'Excellent. Perhaps we had better take some sandwiches and make a day of it.'

Greatly elated at the thought of a day by the sea, Lord Blight went out and gave instructions to the Countess for sandwiches to be cut.

'In two packets, my love,' he added, 'in case Algernon and I get separated.'

Half an hour later they started off together in high spirits.

It was dark before the seventeenth Earl of Blight returned to the house and joined the others at the dinner-table. His face wore a slightly worried expression.

'The fact is, my dear,' he said, in answer to a question from the Countess, 'I am a little upset about Algernon. I fear we have lost him.'

'Algernon?' said the Countess in surprise.

'Yes. We were standing at the top of Flamborough Head, looking down into the sea, when—' He paused and tapped his glass. 'Sherry, Jenkins,' he said, catching the butler's eye.

'I beg your pardon, my lord.'

'When poor Algernon stumbled and—Do any of you boys know if your brother can swim?'

Everard, the ninth, said that Algernon had floated once in the Paddington Baths, but couldn't swim.

'Ah! I was hoping—But in any case, coming into the water from that height—Well, well, we must face our troubles bravely. Another glass of sherry, Jenkins.'

As they passed through the hall on their way to the drawing-room, Lord Blight stopped a moment at the aneroid barometer and gave it an encouraging tap.

'It looks like another fine day to-morrow,' he said to Cuthbert, the second Podby. 'The panorama from the Scalby cliffs is unrivalled. We might drive over and have a look at it.'

III

Fortunately the weather held up. A week later the Podby family had been thinned down to five, and the seventeenth Earl of Blight was beginning to regain his usual equanimity. His health too was benefiting by the constant sea air and change; for, in order that no melancholy associations should cast a gloom over their little outings, he took care to visit a different health-resort each time, feeling that no expense or trouble should be spared in a matter of this kind. It was wonderful with what vigour and alertness of mind he sat down in the evenings to the preparation of his speech on the Coast Erosion Bill.

One night after dinner, when all the Podby family (Basil and Percy) had retired to bed, Gertie (Countess of Blight) came into her husband's library and, twirling the revolving bookcase with restless fingers, asked if she could interrupt him for a moment.

'Yes?' he said, looking up at her.

'I am anxious, Blight,' she answered. 'Anxious about Percy.'

'So am I, my love,' he responded gravely. 'I fear that to-morrow'— he consulted a leather pocket-book—'no, the day after to-morrow, something may happen to him. I have an uneasy feeling. It may be that I am superstitious. Yet something tells me that in the Book of Fate the names of Percy and Bridlington'—he consulted his diary again—'yes, Bridlington; the names, as I was saying, of—'

She interrupted him with an impatient gesture.

'You misunderstand me,' she said. 'That is not why I am anxious. I am anxious because of something I have just learnt about Percy. I am afraid he is going to be—'

'Troublesome?' suggested Lord Blight.

She nodded.

'I have learnt to-day,' she explained, 'that he has a horror of high places.'

'You mean that on the cliffs of, as it might be, Bridlington some sudden unbridled terror may cause him to hurl himself—'

'You will never get him to the cliffs of Bridlington. He can't even look out of a first-floor window. He won't walk up the gentlest slope. That is why he is always playing with the lawn-mower.'

The Earl frowned and tapped on his desk with a penholder.

'This is very grave news, Gertie,' he said. 'How is it that the boy comes to have this unmanly weakness?'

'It seems he has always had it.'

'He should have been taken in hand. Even now perhaps it is not too late. It is our duty to wean him from these womanish apprehensions.'

'Too late. Unless you carried him up there in a sack—?'

'No, no,' protested the Earl vigorously. 'My dear, the seventeenth Earl of Blight carrying a sack! Impossible!'

For a little while there was silence while they brooded over the tragic news.

'Perhaps,' said the Countess at last, 'there are other ways. It may be that Percy is fond of fishing.'

Lord Blight shifted uncomfortably in his seat. When he spoke it was with a curiously apologetic air.

'I am afraid, my dear,' he said, 'that you will think me foolish. No doubt I am. You must put it down to the artistic temperament. But I tell you quite candidly that it is as impossible for me to lose Percy in a boating accident as it would be for—shall I say?—Sargent to appear as "Hamlet" or a violinist to wish to exhibit at the Royal Academy. One has one's art, one's medium of expression. It is at the top of the high cliff with an open view of the sea that I express myself best. Also,' he added with some heat, 'I feel strongly that what was good enough for Percy's father, ten brothers, three half-brothers, not to mention his cousin, should be good enough for Percy.'

The Countess of Blight moved sadly from the room.

'Well,' she said as she stopped for a moment at the door, 'we must hope for the best. Perhaps Percy will overcome this aversion in time. You might talk seriously to him to-morrow about it.'

'To-morrow,' said the Earl, referring once more to his diary, 'Basil and I are visiting the romantic scarps of Filey.'

IV

On the day following the unfortunate accident at Filey the Earl and Countess of Blight reclined together upon the cliffs of Bridlington.

'If we only had had Percy here!' sighed the Earl.

'It was something to have got him as far as the beach,' said the Countess hopefully. 'Perhaps in time—a little higher every day—'

The Earl sighed again.

'The need for self-expression comes strongly upon the artist at a time like this,' he said. 'It is not for me to say that I have genius—'

'It is for me to say it, dear,' said his wife.

'Well, well, perhaps in my own line. And at the full height of one's powers to be baulked by the morbidity, for I can call it nothing else, of a Percy Podby! Gertie,' he went on dreamily, 'I wish I could make you understand something of the fascination which an artist finds in his medium. To be lying here, at the top of the world, with the lazy sea crawling beneath us so many feet below—'

'Look,' said the Countess suddenly. She pointed to the beach.

The Earl rose, stretched his head over the edge and gazed down.

'Percy,' he said.

'Yes. Almost exactly beneath us.'

'If anything fell upon him from here,' said the Earl thoughtfully, 'it is quite possible that—'

Suddenly the fascination whereof he had spoken to her came irresistibly home to the Countess.

'Yes,' she said, as if in a trance, 'if anything fell upon him from here'—and she gave her husband a thoughtful push—'it—is—quite possible—that—'

At the word 'that' the Earl reached Percy, and simultaneously the title expired.

Poor Blight!—or perhaps, since the title was never really his, we should say 'Poor Blighter!' It is difficult to withhold our sympathy from him.

The Return

(1922)

I

The office of Mr Stephen Cosway, literary agent, may elude the stranger at a first visit. It is in one of those difficult streets near Long Acre, and although it distinctly announces itself as '8' on its note paper, we wander vaguely from '7' to '9' several times before we decide that the unimportant and unnumbered door between the two is worth a trial. Once inside, the impression returns to us that we have mistaken the street, and we retire hurriedly to contemplate '7' and '9' again. But, being at heart as brave as a lion, we go back whistling, and mount the stairs to the first floor, where a door marked 'Private' asks us what the deuce we think we are doing. Realizing that they cannot eat us, we knock. 'Mr Cosway?' we ask without much hope. 'What name, please?' says the girl. And we are so surprised to find ourselves there that we answer instinctively, 'Columbus.'

I am writing of 1910, when Michael had been with Mr Cosway for two years. Cosway, a hearty little bachelor with the complexion of a baby and the baldness of a grandfather, had surprised his friends in his middle-age by discovering a sudden passion for the country. The flat in Knightsbridge was replaced by a cottage in Kent, a cottage which called loudly to Mr Cosway on golden afternoons. Week-ends gradually acquired a habit of beginning on Fridays. Even on a Wednesday morning the waste-paper basket of No. 8 might be called upon suddenly to receive the plan of a projected herbaceous border. But a business will not look after itself because a man loves his garden. So young Michael Wentworth, light of heart, but grave of face, joined the very efficient Miss Perkins in representing an absent Mr Cosway on Saturdays, and restoring an urbane outlook on other days to a Mr Cosway who might be only nominally present.

After two years at No. 8 Michael married. If a man is afraid to make an adventure of marriage, he does not deserve any other adventures which come his way. Michael was earning £180 a year. It is not a large salary, but Audrey had a whole £50 a year of her own. Add £50 to £180 and you get the incredible sum of £230 per annum, an income for Emperors. So at least Michael and Audrey thought. They married on it and were prepared to be happy.

From the first Audrey was convinced of her husband's importance in the world of letters. Great men wandered in and out of Mr Cosway's office, and Michael said 'Good morning' to them. Herbert Bannerman himself, with a circulation of 100,000, had told Michael that the evenings were drawing in. Michael could inform his wife's visitors that Cyril Floyd, 'England's only poet', was quite a good fellow, and that Benham, the Cabinet Minister, whose *Recollections of My Boyhood* had bored everybody so much, was not a bit like the cartoons. It was in this magic circle that Michael moved, and Audrey, in spirit at least, moved with him.

But not only in spirit. On the Saturdays when Mr Cosway was in the country Michael was left in charge. That was Audrey's great day. Soon after twelve o'clock she would appear at No. 8 and make her way to Michael's room. Miss Perkins had gone; Michael was alone in his glory, with the litter of a week's work to clear up. Audrey became his secretary. She wrote to 'Dear Mr Bannerman' with her own hand; she made an appointment with Dear Mr Benham. She sat on Michael's table and said, 'Oh, I say, Mike, what's this?' And Michael, very busy, said, 'Wait a minute, darling.'

At one o'clock she brought out the sandwiches, and they perched on the table together, swinging their legs, and Audrey said between mouthfuls and kisses, 'I *do* help you, coming up like this, *don't* I?' And Michael said, '*Of course* you do, my sweetheart.' And she did. When they worked together, it hardly seemed like work. There was no little house in Bedford Park calling to him to be done; no reason now for hurry. Michael could say truly that Mr Cosway was never served more faithfully than on those happy Saturday afternoons.

By 1914 Michael's salary had risen to £240. Audrey's little dowry had given them £60 in the last year, so that their joint income was now £300. It seems almost too much. But there were even better things to come. Audrey was sure that her husband was now indispensable to Mr Cosway, and an eventual partnership was (she told Michael) almost a certainty. Michael was more doubtful, although her design for a notepaper headed 'Cosway and Wentworth, Ltd.', appeared to carry conviction. A more inspired design, which announced 'Mr Michael Wentworth, Literary Agent', the senior partner having succumbed to an imaginary heart attack, was kept in reserve for the moment, as were the numerous dinner-parties, overloaded with Benhams and Bannermans, which Audrey had already planned. But no limit could be set to her private dreams.

However, in August of that year dreams for the moment were shattered. The Saturdays were no longer the Saturdays they used to be; the little dinners at home were eaten now in silence. There was a constraint between them, a weight upon both their hearts which was felt almost as a physical pain. For Michael knew that he must tell Audrey of his decision to enlist, and Audrey knew what Michael was wanting to say, and by all her silences, by her every look, had told him that she couldn't let him go.

Yet he went. The scene which they had dreaded came at last, as it was bound to come.

'I suppose I'm not p-patriotic,' sobbed Audrey, 'but I do love you so much, and I can't bear it, Michael, I can't bear it.'

'You don't suppose I *want* to go,' growled Michael, biting hard on his pipe; 'I hate the idea. But I know I shall never be happy until I do go.'

'L-look at Mr Spencer; he's younger than you, and not even m-married.'

'Look at Howard,' said Michael; 'he's forty-three and has two children.'

Audrey clung to him weeping.

'Oh, why do I love you so much?' she cried. 'Why couldn't I be like other wives, and just be fond of you? We've been married four years—why couldn't we have got used to each other by now? I should have missed you horribly; I should have been horribly anxious about you; but it wouldn't have been like this ... You're tearing yourself out of my heart. It hurts so much, Michael, so much.'

'Oh, *damn*,' said poor Michael, and he jumped up hastily, muttering that his pipe was out.

She was calmer in the morning. They talked of leave, of the healthy life of training, of her pride in him when he was in khaki; above all, of the great joy of coming back to the old life when the war was over.

'You see,' said Michael, 'it isn't as though we were enjoying ourselves now. We aren't. We can't. But when it's over, and I come back, fairly bursting with medals, just *think* how happy we shall be! Much, much happier than if I had stayed at home.'

'You *will* come back?' said Audrey, looking at him earnestly.

'I promise.'

'And you won't let the war go on too long?'

'A year at the most.'

'I think I can bear it for a year,' said Audrey gravely, never taking her eyes off him. 'Yes, if you come back at the end of a year I can bear it.'

'And *then*—think of our Saturdays at the office! All those lovely times together again.'

'I'm thinking of them,' said Audrey, her big eyes fixed upon him. 'That's all I'm thinking of.'

Arrived at the office, Michael broke the news to Mr Cosway. Mr Cosway had seen it coming.

'I mustn't say anything to stop you,' he said affectionately, 'much as I should like to for my own sake. You're doing the right thing, and I'm proud of you. I only wish I were your age, my boy, and could shoulder a rifle with you.'

'You can get somebody in my place, sir?'

'I shall have to try. Some old gentleman or consumptive youth, I suppose. But he'll never take your place, Wentworth. As soon as ever the war is over, I shall expect you back.'

'Thank you, sir.'

Mr Cosway picked up a paper-knife and played with it.

'There's another thing, Wentworth. Money. You're giving up everything to go into the Army: wife, home, safety, all that. You know what I mean? I think the least that we can do, those of us who are staying at home, is to take care that you have no financial worries. Let me see, what are you getting now?'

'Two forty, sir.'

Mr Cosway looked surprised. 'Well, well,' he said at last, 'we can talk about that when you come back to us. Only two forty? Perhaps we can make some other arrangement. Meanwhile, as long as you are in the Army I shall give you £150 a year. Call it the back pay that you ought to have had, or a retaining fee to bring you home to us. Call it what you like. You understand? I want you not to bother about money. You will have plenty of other things to worry about, and—no, don't thank me,' he added hastily as Michael began. 'Damn it, boy, you're going to fight, and I'm going to stay comfortably at home! Bless my soul, it's the very least I can do.' He blew his nose vigorously, called for Miss Perkins, and waved Michael out of the room. Lunching at his club later on, he felt very patriotic and well disposed towards everybody. He mused over a glass of port ...

'A good fellow, Wentworth ... We must all pull together nowadays ... Least I can do is to see that that nice little wife is well provided

for while Wentworth is away … Only wish I were Wentworth's age …
Damn these Germans!'

He finished his port and lit a cigar.

But Michael and Audrey also had their thoughts. That reference
to 'some other arrangement' in the future surely meant a partnership.
But would he give Michael a partnership if Michael had no capital to
put into the business? They must begin saving at once.

'I'll get something to do,' said Audrey. 'I shall always be all right
because of the hundred and fifty, and then I can save all that I earn.
And if you *can* save anything out of your pay—oh, but you mustn't!'

'I will,' said Michael with determination.

This was a much happier evening than the last. Discussion of
the future took their minds off the present. They grew quite eager
together over the great days that were coming—after the war.

'And when you're a partner,' said Audrey, 'will you still like me
coming on Saturdays and helping you with your work?'

'I shall love it more than ever.'

'I do love helping you so,' said Audrey, looking at him with a kind
of wonder that she should be allowed by heaven to help him.

Michael took her in his arms suddenly.

II

Captain and Adjutant Wentworth was enjoying the October sun in
the little open-air shelter outside the H.Q. Mess. It was a quiet part
of the line, for the battalion was recuperating after its three weeks on
the Somme—the Somme of 1916. In the comparative peace of his
present position Michael felt supremely content with the world. For
the moment all that he wanted to make him happy was a letter from
Audrey. The post corporal was late.

A bench ran round the three sides of the shelter, and there was
a table in the middle. Here, when the weather was fine, and Fritz
sufficiently inactive, the H.Q. Mess had its tea; a change from the

stuffiness of the official dug-out. Tea was over, the Major and the doctor had gone about their business, and in the other corner of the shelter, opposite to Michael, the Colonel was addressing a letter to his wife.

He looked up at Michael with a smile.

'Finished yours?'

'Before tea, sir. The post is late to-day.'

'It's always late. And it never gives me all the letters I want … Michael, what are you going to do after the war?'

'Go back to my job, sir.'

'Any good?'

'Literary agent. We have an idea that I shall be a partner one day, but I expect we're rather sanguine.'

He smiled suddenly. 'Anyway,' he went on, 'we're saving in case.'

The Colonel was silent while he filled his pipe.

'Oh, well, anyhow,' he said at last, 'the war won't be over for a long time yet.' He laughed and added, 'Having just told my wife that it will be over by Christmas. But we must buck them up somehow.'

'Every year I say Christmas,' smiled Michael.

'Quite right. It *will* end some day, and I shall go back to my business. So if ever you do want a job …' He stopped and lit his pipe.

'It's awfully decent of you, sir,' said Michael, 'and you know how much I like working with you, but …' He blushed and went on rather shyly, 'You see, all our married life is wrapped up in this work that I was doing. Going back to it means going back to happiness, the happiness we had before the war. We talk about it in every letter, and—oh, *damn* the war!'

'I concur. Anyhow, we shall both be in London—if we're lucky … If we're lucky,' he murmured wistfully to himself. There were so many of them who had been left behind on the Somme, good fellows who had not been lucky.

Michael took out his last letter from Audrey. He knew it by heart, but he wanted to read again in her own writing the bit which began,

'Do you remember our Saturday afternoons together?'—When—when—*when* would those Saturday afternoons come back?

He had written occasionally to Mr Cosway in these last two years without getting back much in the way of an answer. On two of his leaves he had paid a visit to the office.

He had called, of course, with Audrey; leave was too precious to allow a moment away from her. Mr Cosway had insisted on taking them both out to lunch.

'My dear young friends,' he said gaily, 'you must, you simply must. We will leave the office to Miss Perkins—and Snider. You haven't seen Snider yet, Wentworth. Your substitute. All lungs and knuckles. You know what I mean, Mrs Wentworth? Tries hard, but *breathes* everywhere. Oh, I daresay he'll be all right when he's learnt his way about. He's willing enough. But I often wish you were back, Wentworth. "Your nice-looking clerk", was what my clients used to call him, Mrs Wentworth, but we mustn't tell the Field-Marshal, or he'll blush.'

And Michael blushed very happily.

He made a second appearance at No. 8 nearly a year afterwards, and saw the unhappy Snider for the first time. Snider was still knuckly and unhealthy-looking, but he had evidently 'learnt his way about'. He apologized at some length to Michael for the lungs which prevented him from enlisting, and (with many more apologies for the trouble) asked for Michael's expert advice as a soldier on the subject of Tuolite.

'What on earth's Tuolite?' asked Michael.

'Some new sort of explosive, isn't it, Lieutenant Wentworth?'

'Never heard of it,' said Michael, and went into Mr Cosway's room.

'Rum chap, that Snider of yours,' he said after they had shaken hands.

'Oh, haven't you seen him before?'

'No. You were quite right about him, sir.'

'What did I say, Wentworth? If it was anything about his capacity for work, I probably under-rated it. He's got ideas too.'

'Oh?'

'Yes. He …' Mr Cosway stopped abruptly and turned over some papers with his hand. 'Well, Wentworth, glad to have seen you,' he said, and gave the appearance of rather a busy man who has been interrupted. 'I suppose you'll be going out directly?'

'Any moment now, sir.'

'Well, good luck to you.' He held out his hand. 'The sooner you get this war over, the better for us all.'

Michael said good-bye and went out. He had not seen Mr Cosway since.

But when—when—*when* were Audrey and he going to sit on the office table, and swing their legs, and eat their sandwiches together? Not this Christmas, anyhow.

'Letters, sir,' said the mess waiter, and handed the Colonel his packet.

'Thanks.' He glanced at the envelopes, and looked across at Michael. 'Any luck?'

'Just one, sir.'

'I've beaten you to-day; I've got two. That's five since Sunday.'

'I had two yesterday,' smiled Michael. Unknown to themselves, Audrey and the Colonel's wife were engaged in a competition to decide which was the more regular letter-writer. As they both wrote every day, the result depended from week to week on the vagaries of the Army Post Office, but this did not make it the less exciting. Of course, if it came to quality Audrey won easily. At least, Michael thought so.

'… And oh, Michael, what do you think? I was passing the office this morning and thought I'd look in. Because you were so *bad* when you were on leave, and wouldn't go there, and we *must* keep Mr Cosway interested in us. I looked rather a duck in the hat I told you about yesterday. But when I saw the table where we used to sit, and thought of all the *times* we had together, I could hardly bear it, Michael. Oh, my darling, you *must* come back safe to me; you *have* promised, *haven't* you? Well, Mr Cosway was ever so nice and interested in you, sweetheart, and I told him what a great man you were nowadays. Fancy, he didn't even know you were a Captain! I do think he likes us, you know. He was so interested about the Government work I'm doing. (Audrey swanking!) Of course, I didn't tell him that it was mostly envelope-addressing. I like him to think you've got a clever wife, darling. "Say I'm clever, *quick*! Oh, quicker than *that*, Michael." Do you remember all the lovely little silly jokes and private sayings we used to have? Oh, I want you back so badly, beloved …'

Michael finished his letter and fell into a pleasant daydream. Cosway and Wentworth, the well-known literary agents. The senior partner would retire deeper and deeper into the country, leaving the junior partner to manage the business. Gradually he would get into the habit of bringing famous writers home with him to Bedford Park. No, not Bedford Park; they would have one of those jolly old houses in Kensington. In Michael's library would be all the newest books, and signed photographs of the authors. Mrs Michael Wentworth's parties would be famous in literary London … Mrs Michael Wentworth's week-end parties. Little Audrey as hostess, the duck, trying to be dignified. What fun they'd have. 'I *do* help you, don't I?' He would bring her down manuscripts to read, and take her advice about editors and publishers; she would soon get into the way of it. Oh, *damn* the war!

The mess waiter appeared round the corner of the trench.

'A letter, sir—got among the Major's some 'ow.'

'Oh, thanks.'

No luck, not from Audrey. From Cosway, though. Funny he should have been thinking of him.

DEAR WENTWORTH,

I hope you are keeping fit. I had the pleasure of a visit from Mrs Wentworth this morning, and she gave me news of you. I am glad that you are doing so well as to be Adjutant of your battalion—a position, I understand, of some responsibility.

This brings me to a matter upon which I have been meaning to write to you for some time. When you joined the Army I promised you, as you remember, an allowance of £150 a year. We both of us thought that the war would be over in a few months; you were enlisting as a private on a private's pay, and I naturally wished to do something to make your circumstances easier for the short time that you would be away from me. I think you will agree with me that the case is now rather different. You are earning a Captain's pay, with, I presume, something additional as Adjutant, and your wife also is, she tells me, occupying a remunerative position in a Government office. Under these circumstances I imagine that the need for an allowance from me hardly arises.

So much for that. Your place, of course, is waiting for you when you return. You will find that we have made some changes while you have been away. Snider, who seems to know most people in the theatrical world, has persuaded me to extend the business of the office so as to include dramatic agency also. This naturally comes under his care more particularly, and I have no doubt that he will develop it with his usual energy and acumen. He was called up last week under this new Conscription Act, but fortunately was able to convince the doctors that his lungs would not permit of active service in the trenches. For myself I should have thought that his proved business ability was of much more value to the country in his present position than it could possibly be in the Army, but unfortunately many people do not realize that those of us at home are in our own way doing as much to win the war as the soldiers and sailors. Life really is hardly worth living in London just now, and I shall be thankful when the war is over. No doubt you feel much the same about it.

I am, yours very truly,
STEPHEN COSWAY

Michael read the letter with an ever-growing feeling of anger. 'Damn the man, *damn* him!' he cried to himself. 'Oh, to have had him on the

Somme for five minutes! And he says life isn't worth living in London! *London!* My God! *Damn* him!'

He lit his pipe and read the letter again.

'You look as if you're going to kill somebody, Michael,' said the Colonel. 'Don't.'

'Here's a man, sir, who says that life isn't worth living in London just now.'

'Oh! Why not?'

'Because of this very inconvenient war,' said Michael bitterly.

The Colonel smiled.

'I seem to remember about eighteen months ago a very young subaltern who thought that life wasn't worth living in Essex.'

'Yes, you've got me there,' laughed Michael. 'I look back now on those days of training and think what a paradise it was.'

'Exactly. And no doubt there are prisoners in Germany who wonder why they ever groused in the trenches. I don't think you really need kill your man in London.'

Having read the letter a third time, Michael was inclined to agree.

At any rate Cosway was quite right in what he said about the allowance. Michael was spending about five francs a day on his mess bill, and that was really all. He and Audrey were saving much more than they could have saved in London. Perhaps it wasn't quite fair to drag in the fact that Audrey was earning money too. Audrey was working for a special purpose—to put by something for the partnership. Of course, Mr Cosway didn't know that. And, of course, there *had* been some talk in 1914 about the allowance making up for Michael's pay in the past. It really depended how you regarded it; whether as backpay, or retaining fee for the future, or charity for present needs. Mr Cosway evidently looked on it as charity, now unnecessary. Well, one couldn't blame him.

But for many hours afterwards Michael's brain was busy in 'not blaming' Mr Cosway. All his reason told him that Mr Cosway was being perfectly fair and sensible about it. Yet he knew that in his heart he felt a bitterness against Mr Cosway.

'It's absurd,' he told himself for the twentieth time.

'I've got no grievance whatever.'

Yet he dreaded telling Audrey. Audrey was not so reasonable as he. Audrey would certainly feel that they had a grievance.

III

Michael and his Colonel were wounded by the same shell. They went down to the same base hospital, crossed to England together, and found themselves in the same hospital in London. This was after the autumn fighting of 1917. By April, 1918, the Colonel was again a civilian.

'Michael won't be long in following you,' smiled Audrey to him as they said good-bye.

'Wish you *could* persuade him to follow me,' said the Colonel. 'I don't want to lose him, Mrs Michael.'

Audrey shook her head and looked at Michael.

'We've got our work to go back to,' she said, and there was so much pride in her voice and look, mixed up with so much tenderness for her crippled Michael, and yet so much happiness because he was now hers again for ever, that the Colonel had some difficulty in getting out of the room without (as he told his wife afterwards) making a damn fool of himself.

So there came a day later on when Michael also was a civilian again, with a permanently crippled arm, but (heaven be thanked) his own work waiting for him, and Audrey always near to help and encourage.

Behold him, then, leaving the little house at Bedford Park (in a tweed suit of 1914) on his way to No. 8.

'Good-bye, darling one,' says Audrey at the gate. 'Mind you tell me everything that he says. When do you think you'll start? Monday? Then I shall come and help you on the Saturday. Shall I, Michael?' (Michael nods.) 'Oh, hooray for it all! I wonder what salary he'll give you. Much more, I should think, because of prices going up, and you're four years older.' (Michael smiles.) 'You must tell me *everything* when you come back.'

So Michael goes. But she stops him at the last moment.

'Michael?'

'Yes?'

'Thank you, my dear, for having come back safe to me.'

There were two girls in the outer office of Stephen Cosway's, strangers to Michael. He told one of them his name, and she asked him to wait a moment. Michael looked round the familiar room, and then looked down at himself to make sure that he really was in civilian tweeds. It was an extraordinary thing; he was in tweeds, not khaki. Somehow he had got through those four years and had come back.

Mr Cosway would see him.

'Ah, Wentworth,' the familiar voice was saying, 'how *are* you? I saw you were wounded. Going on all right?'

'As right as I ever shall be, I expect,' smiled Wentworth. 'But no more use as a soldier. I'm invalided out.'

'Really? Ah, yes, now I see. Having a bit of a holiday?'

'I've had my holiday,' said Michael. He hesitated a moment, and then said with a sudden smile, 'I've come back, sir.'

Mr Cosway looked up at him in astonishment.

'Come back?'

'Yes. To work. That is to say, if you want me still.'

Mr Cosway continued to gaze at him blankly.

'Of course I want you, Wentworth,' he stuttered at last. 'That is to say ... well, you ... you take me by surprise, rather. You ... sit down, won't you?' He fumbled on his desk. 'Have a cigarette?'

'Thank you.'

'You see, Wentworth, I had no idea. One must have time to consider things. You have finished with the war, I understand? Precisely. And you want to come back? Quite so. A match? ... Yes. Well, one has to consider. This is all very sudden. I think, perhaps, a letter informing me of your situation ...'

'I'm sorry, sir,' said Michael. 'Audrey … my wife … I mean we did think of it, only … only somehow I didn't.'

'Yes.' With the paper-knife in both hands he was feeling more at home with the situation. 'Well, let us talk it over calmly.'

'Yes, sir,' said Michael, with a sudden weight at his heart.

'You see, Wentworth, there have naturally been changes here while you have been away. And I am wondering—I ask myself—whether it would be wise for you, from your own point of view, to come back now to the position you held before the war. I feel strongly that you can do very much better for yourself elsewhere. After all, what were you when you went away? To put it frankly, Wentworth, a clerk. Do you want to be a clerk again? Your place, of course, is waiting for you; there is no question about that. Nobody shall say that I go back upon my word, or that I am capable of treating a returned soldier with injustice. Come back by all means, my dear Wentworth, if you wish it. You will find things different, of course, but no doubt you will soon get into our new ways. I am afraid I cannot let you have your old room—that is Snider's now. Perhaps I may tell you in confidence that I am taking Snider into partnership. He deserves it, if only for the new business he has brought in, but he has also been able to provide the necessary capital. Some fortunate investment, I understand, in connection with war material. And such a worker. Here till eight o'clock, even on Saturdays … However, we are talking of your position, Wentworth. You see what I mean? It is for you to decide.'

'I see,' said Michael aloud. To himself he was saying: 'And I've got to tell Audrey, I've got to tell Audrey, I've got to tell you, Audrey.'

'A clerk at—what was it—£200 a year?'

'Two forty.'

'Well, two forty.'

'That is all it would be if I came back?'

'Well, what am I to do? I want to be just to you, but I must also be just to my partner. Will you be worth more to me—at first? By the way, you get a pension for your disablement?'

'Yes.'

'And the ordinary war gratuity. That will all help, of course. I shouldn't like to feel that you were uncomfortable. And suppose we make it £250? But I strongly advise you to reconsider your position before you decide to come back to me. You see, it leads nowhere, Wentworth, it leads nowhere.'

'Cosway and Wentworth, Literary Agents,' said Michael to himself. 'And I've got to tell Audrey.'

He stood up.

'Well, I'd better write to you to-night about it,' he said mechanically, holding out his hand.

Mr Cosway shook it warmly.

'Yes, do, Wentworth. You must have made many friends in the Army who would be glad to give you employment. Work which gives you real scope for your talents. I'm sure you will have no difficulty about that. Well, then I shall expect to hear from you, and I shall wish you all luck in whatever you take up.' Holding Michael affectionately by the arm, he guided him through the outer office. He could not have been more tender with the great Herbert Bannerman himself. The girl clerks wondered who the nice-looking new author was. 'Then good-bye, Wentworth, good-bye. Let me see you now and then.' The door closed behind him, and Michael walked down the stairs of No. 8 ...

So that was the end of all the dreams. Kicked out! Kicked out to make room for a profiteering skrimshander. Damn Snider! Damn Cosway! What did you do in the Great War, Daddy? Made money out of Tuolite, my boy, and bought a soldier's job. What did *you* do in the Great War, Daddy? Kicked out the man who had been fighting, my son. Cosway and Snider, the men who won the war!

He must walk home. Walking would help him to think. What was that headline in the paper the other day? '*Justice for our Fighting Men.*' Justice! ...

No, no, one must be reasonable. One must try to look at it from the other side. Look at it from Cosway's side …

Snider's got money. (Damned profiteer!) He's good at his job. Probably better, much better, than Michael. Michael has been away for four years. Some sort of excursion on the Continent. Snider had a bit of a headache and didn't feel up to travelling. Well? Well, then, Snider stays at home and does Michael's job—very cleverly, much more cleverly than Michael—and, naturally, Cosway wants to keep him. That's all right …

One *must* be reasonable …

Confound it, the whole thing was perfectly reasonable. One must look at it from Cosway's side … Audrey wouldn't. She would be furious. That would be silly of her. Michael would have to explain. Hang it all, Audrey, what *has* Cosway done that isn't perfectly correct and just and straightforward? There's my job waiting for me. It won't be the same, of course; it can't be the same. We couldn't have our Saturdays together, for instance. Well, says Cosway, if I were you I should try and find a better job. The fact is, Wentworth, you're too good for this. You can do better, my boy. Is *that* being unjust?

And yet …

Well, what did he want? Did he want to live on Cosway's charity for the rest of his life? No!

Did he want to stay in a job which offered him no hope for the future? No!

Well, then!

After all, Cosway didn't know of all their hopes of a partnership. One couldn't blame Cosway because they had had these ridiculous dreams. Cosway probably regarded him just as an ordinary clerk, a clerk to whom he had behaved with perfect correctness. It was absurd to say that Cosway had been unjust …

And yet—

JUSTICE FOR OUR FIGHTING MEN …

And as he came to the gate of the little house in Bedford Park, Michael suddenly seemed to find a glimmer of the light towards which he had been groping his way.

'Perhaps it isn't justice that we want,' he said to himself.

The door opened before he could get his key to it.

'Well?' said Audrey excitedly.

The End of the Peer of Wotherspoon

(1923)

You remember Morton Vaile. No? Dear, dear; so soon forgotten. Well, I must tell you of him.

Morton Vaile. I suppose the truth is that we, too, have tried to forget him. 'There, but for the grace of God …' No, no, do not let us say that. We shall never fall as he fell. Yet his fall was such that we do not care to think of it, to speak of it, even now; even now that you, the public (the wart-hogs, as Vaile used to call you) have forgotten that terrible year when he blazed into publicity, and fell back dead in its ashes. But in the cause of literature one must put aside one's personal feelings. Vaile flourished in '22 and early '23; a new generation of critics has sprung up which knows not his end; let it be told to them for a warning.

In 1922 there was (though he is forgotten now) no writer better known among his intimate friends and fellow-critics than Morton Vaile. It would be difficult to say whether he was more admired as poet than as critic, as essayist than as poet. He belonged to the Vaile school of poetry. When he was least like himself, then he was most like himself—as Kaynes, the critic, finely said. Kaynes, in reviewing his *Songs of Desolation*, gave it as his considered opinion that Morton

Vaile was 'one of the two poets who count in England to-day'. This, from H. R. Kaynes, was high praise, for Kaynes was, in Vaile's words, 'one of the two critics England has produced since Wotherspoon died'. But Vaile was too severe. What of himself, who, as critic, was hailed by Jabez Cuff as 'peer of Wotherspoon'? And if himself was meant as the other of the two, what, then, of Cuff? What of A. Z. Tinkler? What of Reginald Quigley? Let us be more generous. Let us say that (since Wotherspoon *was* dead) there were five critics, five poets, five essayists alive in England in 1922, of whom Morton Vaile was not the least.

Every critic has, or had in those days, his favourite author. Jabez Cuff, as we have seen, admired Vaile, but 'The Art of Quigley' in *The Literary Mirror* remains his monumental work. Quigley's well-known essay in the same paper (though in the following issue) 'The Art of Cuff' expressed an admiration sincerely felt; yet H. R. Kaynes was his hero. From above Tinkler's beard escaped often the name of Vaile, but to Cuff was his homage given. And though to Vaile Morton Vaile seemed most wonderful of all, he wrote not of Vaile. He wrote always of Henry Harrison.

It was as far back as '21 that Vaile first discovered Harrison. He discovered him in the 1/- box; '2 for 1/6'. *Sauterne*, A novel by Henry Harrison, and on the inside page 'First published in 1921'. Already in the shilling box! Vaile dropped it, and picked up the next one. Surely the colour of its back was familiar! It was. *Rhinoceros, and other Moments*, by Morton Vaile, said its front. He laughed cynically. The dear old wart-hogs! And there were Blank and Dash, those impostors, going into edition after edition, piling up bank balances, lecturing to admiring school-girls, taking the chair at Literary Dinners ('Literary', ye gods!) and all the wart-hogs stood around and slobbered on them! Thank Heaven he was not as they.

He felt in his pocket for a shilling, but encountered a florin. While waiting for change, he picked up Sauterne again, and glanced at the opening pages. This man did not write for wart-hogs either. He had style. '2 for 1/6'. *Sauterne* balanced *Rhinoceros* in another pocket;

a lower pocket received the sixpence change; and they all went home together.

After dinner he strolled round to Tinkler's rooms. Quigley was there and Kaynes; but not Cuff, for Cuff was still at school. This was in 1921, remember.

'Ever heard of Henry Harrison?' he said, dropping into a chair.

'Has one?' said Tinkler to Kaynes.

'Let me see,' said Quigley, 'didn't he write—what's the name of the book?'

'*Sauterne?*'

'That's it,' agreed Quigley gratefully.

'Oh, that man?' said Kaynes. 'He's written something else, hasn't he?'

'*Corybantic.*'

'*Corybantic,* that's it,' agreed Kaynes, thus hearing of it for the first time. 'Have you read it?'

'Not yet. I only discovered *Sauterne* this morning. He's good.'

'Oh, rather. You'll like *Corybantic* too.'

'What's it about?' asked Tinkler maliciously.

Kaynes had no difficulty in answering.

'My dear Tinkler,' he said with a faint smile, 'if Harrison, who, as Vaile will confirm, is a considerable artist, cannot tell you what it is about in less than so many thousand words, you can hardly expect me to tell you in ten.'

Vaile broke in quickly. This always-showing hostility between Tinkler and Kaynes was tiresome. Why, they even carried it into their reviews of each other's books; Kaynes going so far as to say that Tinkler had still something to learn from Shelley, and Tinkler hinting that some of Kaynes' essays were not so brilliant as others.

'He's good, A. Z., he really is. You must read *Sauterne.* I'll lend it to you.'

'Thanks. It'll be a change. I've been reading Wells.'

'Good God, why?'

'Not for pleasure, obviously. I'm doing him this week in my "Exploded Georgians" series. Poor old Wells! And I used to think he could write.'

'He could once,' said Quigley.

'He could once. That's the tragedy of it,' said Vaile. 'And now what's happened? The wart-hogs eat him; simply eat him. He's popular—and dead.'

'It's all very strange,' said Kaynes. 'I have a father who reads Meredith. It's all very strange and interesting. He said Meredith is a little obscure sometimes. Obscure. They use such curious words.'

Well, it was thus that Vaile discovered Henry Harrison. Thereafter he kept him always at hand. For instance, if it were his painful duty to castigate a novel of Mr Arnold Bennett's, he would say, 'How much better Henry Harrison would have managed this scene!'—and Mr Bennett would be left searching for Harrison in his card index; or again, contemptuously, 'Probably Mr Wells has never heard of *Sauterne*,' and Mr Wells would order a bottle at once. Perhaps he was at his most trenchant in an estimate of Mr Galsworthy. 'Of a public,' he wrote, 'which accepts the *Forsyte Saga* and rejects *Corybantic*, nothing need be said but what, in those words, has been said.' This was in 1922; and it was as a result of this article that Cuff, who had now left school, and was writing for the *Weekly Review,* called him 'the peer of Wotherspoon'. They met shortly afterwards by arrangement; for Vaile had formed the opinion that Cuff, though three years his junior, had already a well-formed literary taste.

Henry Harrison, it was discovered, lived in Switzerland. 'My health,' he wrote, 'is none too good.' Vaile had addressed a letter to his publishers, in which he praised *Sauterne* and *Corybantic*, and took the opportunity of enclosing a little book of his own, *Rhinoceros and Other Moments*, a copy of which he happened to have by him. Naturally he had erased first the pencilled second-hand price. Harrison acknowledged it gratefully. 'It is very good of you,' he wrote; 'and good of you to say the things you do about my books. I suppose they sold about a hundred copies each, and, together, brought me five pounds in cash. I have another coming along slowly, which I hope will do better.' And lower down: 'I suppose every artist flourishes on praise, for vain though he may seem in public, in private he descends to depths of humility such as no other can sound. He must be reassured by others, for he cannot reassure himself. Your praise encourages me, and I am grateful.' And then again: 'One feels so helpless out here. I tell myself that if I were in London I could say, "You *shall* read me!" but here I can do nothing. Yet if I were in London, what could I do? Well, even to find someone to whom I could say "Damn!" would be something; yourself, for instance.'

Vaile was better placed. He could say 'damn' to Kaynes, and said it.

'It's a damned shame.'

'My dear, what did you expect?' said Kaynes.

'Well, there's one thing I can do. I can say to the public: "You *shall* read his next book."'

'You can say it, but they won't.'

'Wart-hogs!'

'Yes, but very amusing wart-hogs.'

In the autumn of 1922, Henry Harrison's third novel made its unheralded appearance. '*To-day and To-day*, by Henry Harrison'.

This was, he opined, the novel for which England had been waiting. *Sauterne* had been well enough; *Corybantic* had been well enough; but with *To-day and To-day* Henry Harrison entered into the Kingdom which was his by undisputed right. There was a ripeness, a rotundity … a rhythm … Subjective rather than objective … In this respect the Russians and Harrison … Harrison and de Goncourt … a Proust or a Harrison … Dostoevsky, for all that he would have acknowledged Harrison as his master … Only Wotherspoon among the moderns … And SO forth.

He ended up thus:

'To say, as we must say, that this is incomparably the greatest novel of our generation, is no doubt to condemn it to the obscurity of the shilling box in the book-shops of the Charing Cross Road. The British public is only at ease with mediocrity. Yet, Mr Harrison, we feel, would prefer it so. In the fine words of Reginald Quigley:

'For them the coloured beads of *Brummagem*; for us, the rubies.'

Quigley, meeting Vaile the day after this appeared, was quite frank about it.

'I liked your notice.'

'I said what I felt, that's all. You agreed with me?'

'Not altogether,' said Quigley, who hadn't read the book. 'In some ways I felt that *Corybantic* … of course what you say about the rhythm of *To-day and To-day* … Still …'

'I see what you mean,' frowned Vaile. 'But you can't deny that the …' he made curves in the air with a cigarette-clutching hand … 'taking it as a whole …'

'Oh, as a whole, yes.'

'It's big. That's what I feel.'

'Big, undoubtedly.' And then after a pause, 'What you said about Harrison and de Goncourt was absolutely right.'

'It needed saying.'

'Yes … I'm doing a little article for the *Weekly Review* …' And the conversation took another turn.

But Reginald Quigley was not the only person who had read Vaile's review. The attention of Mr Albert Pump, the publisher of *To-day and To-day*, had also been called to it. In his next advertisement in the *Literary Supplement* he handed the good news on.

TO-DAY AND TO-DAY
by HENRY HARRISON

Mr Morton Vaile writes in the *Literary Mirror*: 'Incomparably the greatest novel of our generation.'

It would be ridiculous to say that Vaile was proud when he came thus across his name; he had a horror of the publicity which is accorded so carelessly to writers; to other writers; but certainly there seemed to be an added warmth in the air that day. More than once he found himself wondering to what he owed this feeling, and he decided that it could only be pleasure at the thought of Harrison's incomparable novel. And they were actually advertising it! How splendid if he could help to sell a copy here and there!

Mr Pump would deny that he helped to sell a copy. Mr Pump has a theory that no book sells except by recommendation from mouth to mouth. We must suppose, therefore, that the first few people, who at the beginning bought *To-day and To-day* by accident, found something in it to their liking, of which they could speak frankly to their friends, and that so, copy by copy, the book was sold. However it was, Mr Pump was able to write another advertisement:

TO-DAY AND TO-DAY
(Second Edition)
by HENRY HARRISON

Mr Morton Vaile writes in the *Literary Mirror*: 'Incomparably the greatest novel of our generation.'

The Peer of Wotherspoon was at Margate when the second edition was announced, having been sent for by his father (who still had the privilege of giving him an allowance) to help amuse the children in a late seaside holiday. But the phenomenon was discussed in Tinkler's rooms.

'I see Harrison's in a second edition,' said Kaynes.

There was an awkward silence. Then Cuff, the youngest of them, spoke.

'We all make mistakes,' he said.

'In what way?'

'Vaile. *To-day and To-day* is good, damned good, but *Corybantic* was incomparably better.'

'So I told him,' put in Quigley.

Tinkler grunted in his beard.

'Don't you think so yourself, A. Z.?'

'H'm.'

'My dear, doesn't it always happen?' said Kaynes. 'A writer's first books, his best books, are ignored. Later on, when he is beginning to fail—'

'That's just what I felt about it,' said Quigley. 'What I told Vaile. The feeling one gets that Harrison is beginning to write down to the public. As Kaynes says, it always happens.'

'H'm. When's he coming back?'

'Vaile? Next week, isn't it? Or the week after.'

'He'll be pleased. Just that one notice of his, and—'

'Oh, he's a great man, Vaile. Still I do feel that in this case, perhaps, he went a little too far.'

'Oh, rather,' said Quigley.

But Vaile, coming back a fortnight later, was not sure that he was pleased. *To-day and To-day* was now in its fourth edition. So much was announced to him by his paper that morning, bought at the Margate book-stall. But London had another surprise waiting. It was broken to him by a motor-omnibus in the King's Road. The omnibus said very loudly and clearly:

EVERYBODY IS READING
TO-DAY AND TO-DAY

'Incomparably the greatest novel of our generation.' MORTON VAILE in the *Literary Mirror*.

And everybody *was* reading it. Everybody.

He went round to Quigley's that evening, feeling a little uncomfortable.

'Hallo,' they said. 'Had a good time?'

'I was staying with my people,' explained Vaile by way of answer.

'Oh, I see.'

Dead silence.

'You've seen about Harrison?' said Kaynes at last.

'Yes.' He laughed easily; or tried so to laugh. 'Funny, isn't it?'

'Oh, I don't know,' said Quigley. 'I always felt it might catch on, didn't you? I mean, it's just the sort of book—'

'In what way?' said Vaile coldly.

'Oh, my dear fellow, it's no good pretending that it's as good as *Sauterne* or *Corybantic.* Now, is it, Kaynes?'

'I never liked *Corybantic,* my dear.'

'Oh, you're wrong there, Kaynes,' said Cuff. *Corybantic* and *Sauterne* were the genuine thing. But I do agree with Quigley—'

'Of course,' said Quigley, 'there are fine things in *To-day and To-day.* That I admit. But, taken as a whole, I've always felt that it was just the sort of book that the public would wallow in. You know what I mean?'

'I don't agree with you,' said Vaile curtly.

'My dear Vaile,' put in Kaynes gently, 'we all know why you wrote as you did. Harrison, poor fellow, neglected, ill, perhaps dying in some beastly Swiss *pension*, away from all his friends—here, you said, is a writer of distinct ability, who badly needs a helping hand. You gave him that hand. It was magnificent, but it wasn't criticism. All the more do we admire you for it.'

'I was damned sorry for him,' mumbled Vaile.

'We know, we know.'

'One gets carried away,' said Cuff. 'Inevitably.'

'Inevitably,' said Quigley.

'That's right,' said Tinkler.

'Yes, I suppose one does,' admitted the Peer of Wotherspoon reluctantly, but with a certain relief.

'My dear, of course one does,' smiled Kaynes, and patted him on the shoulder.

They all breathed freely again. The flag was still flying.

But the position was not yet saved. Indeed it began now to seem that it would never be safe. For *To-day and To-day* was more than a success, it was a triumphant riot. This was the sort of advertisement with which Mr Pump at the beginning of 1923 was plastering the Underground stations of London:

500,000—COPIES SOLD!
TO-DAY AND TO-DAY
THE NOVEL EVERYBODY IS READING
The Archdeacon of Westborough says:
'An inspiring tale.'
Morton Vaile (the critic) says:
'Incomparably the greatest novel of our generation.'

Nor did Mr Pump's malignity (as it seemed to Vaile) stop there. A member of the Royal Family, in opening a hospital, made what must have been the first royal reference to a printed book in our later history, and the book was *To-day and To-day*.

Mr Pump announced:
750,000 COPIES SOLD!
Royalty is speaking of
TO-DAY AND TO-DAY!
The Church is preaching on
TO-DAY AND TO-DAY!
The Critics are praising
TO-DAY AND TO-DAY!
Everybody is reading it!
What does Royalty say?
'That wonderful story.'
What does the Archdeacon of Westborough say?
'An inspiring tale.'
What does Morton Vaile (the critic) say?
'Incomparably the greatest novel of our generation.'
READ IT

And Reginald Quigley, H. R. Kaynes, A. Z. Tinkler and Jabez Cuff read and trembled. For the flag was not yet saved. It could never be saved now for Morton Vaile, but surely it might yet be for them. More desperately than did ever Henry Harrison they needed now re-assurance. For a terrible thing had just happened to one of their number; Reginald Quigley, no less.

He had met Penn Wilkins that afternoon; Wilkins, destined to be perhaps the greatest literary personality of late '23 and undoubtedly even then (this was April) one of the coming poets, novelists, essayists and critics. Wilkins, on his way back to Oxford, had lunched with Quigley.

Said Wilkins with a good-humoured laugh, in the manner of one quoting, 'Have you read *To-day and To-day*?'

'Good lord, no,' said Quigley.

'I have. I thought I would. And the other two. Ninth Edition *Corybantic* and Twelfth Edition *Sauterne*. My God!'

'Terrible, aren't they?' agreed Quigley. 'At least, I mean, *Corybantic*, I haven't read the other. Is that as bad?'

'My dear man, there's no choosing.'

'Of course he's an absolute impostor, Harrison,' said Quigley.

'Oh, why blame Harrison? If he wants the money why shouldn't he write like that? I don't suppose he pretends that it's anything but extreme tripe. But this fellow—what's his name?'

'Who?' said Quigley nervously.

'The innocent babe—what does he call himself? Morton Vaile, that's it—who tells us it's the greatest novel—incomparably the greatest novel—Again, oh, my God!'

Quigley laughed awkwardly. 'Absurd, isn't it?' he said.

'Who *is* the fellow?'

'Morton Vaile? Morton Vaile, I suppose.'

'Anybody ever heard of him?'

'He wrote a book called—'

'I had an idea he was some old maiden lady with shares in the paper. But not, you think? By the way, did you read my article ...'

And so on. Most of which Quigley had reported to the others. No wonder that they trembled.

For what were they to tell themselves? That great work could be popular? Never! The implications were too disturbing. That Vaile was wrong, then, hopelessly wrong, in his estimate of Harrison? Undoubtedly. Then they were wrong, hopelessly wrong, in their estimate of Vaile. The peer of Wotherspoon!

But this alternative was no better. For if they were wrong in their estimate of Vaile, why not in their estimates of each other? Even—and now the ground shivered beneath their feet—in their estimates of themselves? No, no, not that. But it was disturbing. On the citadel of their self-esteem the flag might still be kept flying, but …

They looked at each other and shook their heads.

'I don't see how we can,' said Cuff.

'The fact is, he hasn't been well for a long time,' said Quigley. 'I've noticed it.'

'Breaking up,' growled Tinkler.

'If he's wise, my dears,' said Kaynes, 'he'll take a holiday. It's the only thing that can save him.'

And the Peer of Wotherspoon thought so too. Fortunately his father had some influence with a shipping firm in Liverpool, and to Liverpool a few days later Vaile made his way. Lingering by the book-stall at Euston for a moment, he had his attention called by the clerk to the great new novel which everybody was reading, *To-morrow and To-morrow*.

'Incomparably,' the clerk assured him, 'the greatest novel of our generation.'

But the new shipping-expert did not seem to be interested.

The Green Door

(1925)

One day when Prince Perivale was a little boy, he was walking with his father the King in the gardens of the palace. There was a high stone wall round the garden so that no venturer from outside could get in; nor was there any way by which those inside the garden could get out, supposing, as was less likely, that they wished to do so. But as the young Prince was walking with his father, now leaving his hand and running this way and that, now coming back to it again, he espied suddenly, hidden in a tangle of trees, a little green door in the wall. And he gave a cry and ran back eagerly to his father.

'There's a door there, Father. I saw a door, a little green door. Shall we go through that door, Father? Where does that door go to?'

His father the King frowned and said nothing.

'Did you know that there was a door there, Father?' went on the Prince. 'I didn't. Shall we see where it goes?'

The King tugged at his beard and frowned again. 'No, my son,' he said at last, 'we will not go through it.'

'Oh!' said Perivale, and the corners of his mouth began to turn down. 'I did want to go through that dear little door.'

'If you had gone through that door,' said the King solemnly, 'you would never have come back again.'

'Is it a magic door?' asked the little Prince in an awed whisper.

The King pushed his way through the tangle of trees and stood looking at the door. It was locked, and there was no key in the lock. It looked as though it had not been opened for years, nor could ever be opened again. With a little sigh of relief the King turned round for Perivale's hand and drew him away to another part of the garden.

'What was it, Father?' whispered Perivale, now a little frightened.

'It was through that door that King Stephen, your great-grandfather, passed on a summer evening, and was seen no more.'

'What happened to him?'

'Nobody ever knew. Some said he was killed by robbers, some that he was eaten by wild beasts. There is a legend that through that door a man steps into an enchanted forest in which he wanders for ever. The King, my father, was of the opinion that, as the door is opened, a bottomless pit forms itself on the other side into which one falls headlong. However it be, this is certain—that no one of our ancestors who has ventured through that door has been seen again.'

'Perhaps there's a dragon waiting on the other side,' said the little Prince excitedly.

'Perhaps there is. But we shall do well not to talk of it. We could not unlock the door now if we would, and we would not if we could. The trees will grow over it again, and we shall forget it.'

But the little Prince did not forget it. Often he thought of it, and told himself strange stories of the wonders to which the green door led. Sometimes it came into his dreams, and then the way was full of terrors, but when he awoke to the sunlight, then the way led by ripple of brooks and twittering of birds to a happiness beyond his understanding.

And as he grew up he heard much idle talk of it by those who had never seen the door: and he noticed that each one who talked of it told a different story, yet each one pledged his word that his story was the only true story of it; but on this they all agreed, that whoever had passed through the door had passed out of mortal sight for ever.

* * *

In due time Perivale grew up and succeeded his father as King of Wistaria. At the time of his coronation there was great account in the country of the new king. It was said by those who should have been in a position to know that King Perivale was the handsomest, the wisest, the most manly and the most gallant young king that had ever sat upon the throne. It was reputed that there was no science within the knowledge of the most learned magicians of the country at which he could not better them, no form of manly exercise at which he did not surpass the most talented of his subjects. With his bow he could split a wand at two hundred paces, with his sword he could engage at the same time any three swordsmen in his army. He knew more of the art of fighting than any of his generals, of the art of hunting than any of his huntsmen, and, had only Wistaria been in possession of a seacoast, he would undoubtedly have been fully qualified to take his country's fleet into a victorious action. All this, and more, was commonly reported of him.

A little later there were other stories told of him. For by this time it had been announced that the beautiful Princess Lilia was coming to Wistaria to wed with the King. And it was told how the King and the Princess had happened across each other in the forest, neither knowing who the other was, and how they had met secretly on many a day afterward and had fallen in love with each other, but had feared that they could not marry, because Lilia—as Perivale thought—was not a princess, and Perivale—as Lilia thought—was not a king. How delighted then were they when they discovered that a marriage which would bring everlasting happiness to themselves would also bring pleasure to the people of their countries! This and other stories were told of the King and his bride; and when the Princess sent a picture of herself, done by her own court painter, as a gift to King Perivale, all who saw the picture said that indeed she was the loveliest lady in the world, and that His Majesty was blessed above all men in taking her to wife. But Perivale was not reconciled to his happiness. For, in truth, he had not yet seen the Princess Lilia; and though it was the custom of his family to marry in this way, yet he would have preferred to choose for himself the lady who he would wed.

It had been his father's wish, and the wish of his people, that Wistaria and the country of Princess Lilia should be united by his marriage, and Perivale was ready enough to do what it seemed to be his duty; but, as he wandered through the palace on the day before the royal wedding, he was a little melancholy, feeling that the happy life which he had known until now was over. And, wandering thus, his thoughts in the past, carelessly opening a chest here or a cupboard there, he came suddenly upon a silver key.

Not for a moment did he doubt. It was the key to the little green door. And as he held it between his fingers all his childish memories of the green door came back to him—the fears, the wonders and the fancies; and suddenly he knew that if ever he was to go through that door it must be now, before his fate was linked with that of the Princess Lilia. As yet she had not seen him. If she never was to see him now, how could she grieve for him?

He hurried through the palace and into the garden. None saw him go save a waiting maid, who watched him idly. The trees had hung new branches over the little door, and he had to force his way through, but in the end he came to it; and with a thrill of anticipation, half fearful, half eager, he turned the lock, and so passed through the green door into the unknown world beyond.

And there was nothing there—no dragons, no robbers, no bottomless pits! Alas, not even an enchanted forest! The door shut with a click behind him, and he was on the outside of the palace wall, with the royal deer park in front of him. He moved a dozen paces away, looked about him and saw that he was still in the world he knew. A little amused, a little angry, he came back again. Better to have gone on imagining than to have found the reality so commonplace.

Yet, perhaps, not entirely commonplace. For now that he looked for the door he could not find it. That was curious. Yet the explanation might be simple enough. The door, no doubt, had been made of stone on this side, the same colour as the wall, so that it should not be seen by the passer-by. For a little while Perivale amused himself by searching for it, and then, remembering that in any case he had left the key on the other side of the door, he laughed and set out leisurely on his walk round the palace walls, until he should reach the main gate of the castle.

The waiting maid, watching idly, had seen His Majesty push through the trees which fringed the wall; watching eagerly, had seen him come to a little green door and put a key to its lock; watching fearfully, had seen him open the door and pass beyond her sight. Breathlessly she ran to tell the others.

As Perivale came to the main gate, he remembered that it was on this afternoon that the Princess was to set foot in the palace for the first time, and for the first time to see him. Looking down at his clothes, torn and dirtied by the trees through which he had pushed his way, he smiled to think how she would regard him if she met him thus, and he made the more haste to reach the privacy of his room.

But he was never to reach it. A soldier at the gate barred the way. 'Well,' he asked gruffly, 'what do you want?'

'Nothing, my man, but to get to my own chamber,' said Perivale mildly.

'Then right about turn and get to it,' said the soldier, lowering his pike.

'I perceive that you are new to your duties,' said Perivale pleasantly. 'I am the King.'

Other soldiers lounged up from the courtyard. 'What's this?' said one, who seemed to be in some authority.

'The silly fellow says he's the King. What shall we do with him?'

'Fool, I am the King!' thundered Perivale.

At this declaration there was a roar of laughter.

One of the soldiers came and looked at him more closely 'Aye, you're not unlike,' he said, 'save that a king is a king, and a common man is a common man. Take my advice, friend, and get along home before trouble comes to you.'

At this moment one of the women came running into the courtyard.

'The King!' she cried. 'The King! He went through the green door! The green door! He will never come back!'

Many of the soldiers ran to her, eager to hear more, but he who was in authority came and looked again at Perivale.

'Aye, he will never come back,' he murmured to himself, 'but one who is like the King comes in his place, saying that he is the King. My friend,' and he put a hand on Perivale's shoulder, 'this is very curious. Your tale came pat to the moment. Doubtless you will be able to tell us that you knew the King was not in the palace to give you the lie.'

He gave an order, and Perivale was seized and marched into the palace. 'After all,' he said to himself, 'that little green door seems not to have been as commonplace as I thought.'

And so it proved. An hour later the chancellor was summing up the matter to the satisfaction of all but the prisoner.

'It is clear,' he said, 'what has occurred. His late lamented Majesty, in spite of all warnings, ventured through the green door. On the other side of that door lurked a fiend, a monster, capable of assuming the shape, and in some measure the appearance, of his victim. To rend His Majesty in pieces, to garb himself in His Majesty's clothes, is the work of a moment; and, so garbed, with designs upon the throne itself, this monster presents himself at the palace gates. But though he can assume, to some slight extent, His Majesty's appearance, he cannot assume His Majesty's great qualities. Can he engage three swordsmen at once? He refuses even to try. Can he surpass in excellence of learning our wisest philosophers? He laughs at the idea of it. How then can he be that most endowed of all monarchs, our noble King Perivale?'

'True,' said Perivale grimly to himself. 'How can I be?'

But there came an interruption in the cheers which greeted this pronouncement. Amid whispers which rose to shouts of 'The Princess! The Princess is here!' Her Royal Highness made her way into the hall. And men murmured: 'Now indeed we shall know if he be the King, for true love, such as the Princess Lilia has for His Majesty, cannot be deceived.'

'What is this they tell me, that His Majesty has been basely murdered?' she cried out. The chancellor explained.

'Then why do none of you follow him through the green door?' she asked scornfully.

The chancellor explained, not only how useless, but also how dangerous it was.

'Cowards!' she cried. 'Afraid of a little green door!'

'It is rather a mysterious little door,' put in Perivale apologetically.

She wheeled round at his voice. 'Who is this?' she demanded.

And now each man nudged his neighbour and muttered: 'You see? She does not know him. It is not the King.'

The chancellor explained that Perivale was certainly an impostor, and that probably he was the wicked monster who had made away with His lamented Majesty.

'And yet he is not ill-looking,' murmured Lilia.

'Indeed no,' agreed Perivale. 'There was a time when I was spoken of as the handsomest man in Wistaria.'

'Silence, fellow!' called those nearest to him, and hustled him out of her sight.

'Well,' said Lilia when all were silent again, 'who is going through that door to find the King?'

Each man waited for his neighbour to answer.

'No wonder your king left you,' she said scornfully. 'Show me the door, and I will go.'

So they went with her to the garden; and they watched her as she passed through the little green door. Then they came back to their prisoner.

'Perchance,' said one, 'since we have caught the fiend who lurked behind the green door, she will come safely back.'

Suddenly, while they were questioning their prisoner, a commotion arose at the other end of the hall, and people cried, 'The Princess! The Princess! She has come back to us!' And in a moment all were crowded round.

'What did your Royal Highness see?' they cried.

'There was nothing there,' she said, and looked long at Perivale; and she nodded at him as if now she understood; and Perivale smiled, and she smiled back at him.

'Did your Royal Highness find the body of His lamented Majesty?' asked the chancellor.

'I found the King,' said Lilia, smiling.

'Where? Where?' they cried.

'Here,' she said, and pointed to Perivale.

Then there arose a great uproar of talking, and one said, 'Yet why did she not recognize him at first?' and another, 'He has admitted that he is not the King,' and a third, 'But we know that the King is dead.' Then, as they talked thus, a whisper ran through them, like wind over corn, and none ever knew who started it.

And the whisper said:

'Is it the Princess?'

When the whisper came to Perivale he threw up his head, and laughed loud and long.

'What is it?' said Lilia anxiously to him.

'My dear, they say now that you are not the Princess, but an impostor like myself. This is indeed a magic door.'

And now the certainty grew that this also was a fiend, passing itself off as the greatly-to-be-lamented Princess Lilia. Then the chancellor was inspired; and to put the matter beyond all doubts, he ordered that Lilia should be taken beneath the portrait of the Princess which had been sent to His Majesty as a wedding gift. And as soon as she stood beneath it there came a shout of derision, for all saw that, whereas the portrait was of a surpassingly beautiful lady, with regular features, the girl beneath was of no more than a certain wayward prettiness.

'Bind them together,' ordered the chancellor, 'while we consider what to do with them.'

'I had not intended to give you a wedding ring so rough,' smiled Perivale, 'but we are indeed joined together now.' He looked down into her eyes. 'The painter did not do you justice,' he murmured. 'You are something better than the Princess Lilia.'

But now the chancellor had made his decision as to their fate. Burnings, drownings, stonings, all these happy suggestions of the people had been considered, and rejected as beneath the merits of the case.

'I have,' said the chancellor softly, 'a prettier plan. These two inhuman monsters have failed in their audacious plot. Think you how that failure will be punished by their brother fiends now waiting for them outside the green door! Let us drive them, then, through the door, and listen, safely on this side of it, to the vengeance which is wreaked on them!'

There was a shout of approval. Perivale and Lilia looked at each other, and a little sob of relief broke from her. Then, bound wrist to wrist, they were driven to the little green door.

'Last time,' murmured Lilia, 'we went through the door as King and Queen, and came out as man and woman. This time we go through as man and woman, and come out—how?'

'Perhaps as lovers,' said Perivale gently. 'For that is again to be King and Queen.'

She dropped her eyes, and the colour came suddenly into her cheeks. 'I wonder,' she whispered.

So for the last time they passed through the little green door together, and out into the world beyond.

The Secret

(1926)

Once upon a time there was a princess who was so beautiful that she could not do anything for herself. If she wished to get up in the morning, somebody had to dress her, and if she wished to go to bed in the evening, somebody had to undress her. She could not go into a room until somebody had opened the door for her, she could not sit down until somebody had arranged a chair for her, she could not admire a piece of embroidery until somebody had found a piece of embroidery for her to admire, and had shown her the place where she had left off admiring it the day before. She was very proud, she was very beautiful; and because she was so beautiful, everybody said what a sweet nature she had.

One day she was riding through the forest with her attendants when she came upon a young man who was seated on a fallen tree, whittling at a lump of wood with his knife. She drew in her horse so that he might have the opportunity of rising and bowing to her, but he just looked up and nodded in a friendly way and went on whittling. She sat there, looking down at him, and frowning to herself, waiting for him to speak. But he was not thinking of her.

'Well?' she said coldly, when she had waited as long as she was able.

'It is well,' said he.

'Do you know who I am?'

'No,' said he.

'I am the Princess Elvira.'

'Oh!' said he. And then, fearing that he was discourteous, he added, 'I am called Simon.'

'You did not hear me,' she said more coldly still. 'I am the Princess.'

He looked up at her then, and his eyes went from her face to the faces of her companions, and back to hers again.

'That explains it,' he nodded, and went on with his work.

The attendants of the Princess hastened to tell Her Royal Highness that the man was some poor crazy fellow, yet harmless, and that if it was Her Royal Highness' kindly wish that an end should be made to his sufferings, she had but to ride on, and there would be those left behind who would see to it.

'You hear?' she said to Simon.

'No,' said Simon, looking up in surprise, 'I wasn't listening. What was it?'

'They were asking me if they should kill you.'

'What did you say?'

'I have not answered yet. I am wondering.'

'Doubtless I shall know when you have decided,' he said, and fell to whittling again.

'Kill him!' said the Princess in sudden anger, and two of them got down from their horses and drew their swords. But the young man took no notice of them.

'Wait!' called the Princess. She turned to the young man and asked petulantly, 'Do you wish to be killed?'

He smiled and said, 'Do you wish to kill me?'

For a long time the Princess made no answer. Then all at once, as if against her will, she cried out 'No!' and called harshly to her attendants, and in a sudden scurry of hooves and jingle of harness they were gone.

'What a strange young woman,' said the man called Simon to himself, as he went on with his work.

Now the Princess was eighteen years old, and it was considered well by her father the King that she should marry. This or that Prince was sent for, and came gladly to the Court because of the great beauty of the Princess and the great wealth of her father; and this or that one, seeing her, vowed that he lived only to please her, and that, when the light of her eyes was turned away, the world held no more joy for him; whereat she turned her eyes away from him, and the young man went back to his feasting, and thought of some new thing to say to her on the morrow. But the Princess took no pleasure in them, neither in their words nor in their faces. So a morning came when she could bear with them no longer, and she left them and rode again into the forest, taking but one servant to attend her; and in a little while, whether by accident or intent, they came again to the man called Simon.

He was there, as before, carving his wood.

'Well?' said the Princess, looking down at him scornfully.

Simon looked up.

'Oh, it's you,' he said, and looked down again.

'You remember me?'

'There are not many who come into the forest.'

'You remember my name?'

Simon rubbed his head in a puzzled sort of way.

'How should I? I have other things to think of. Viola, was it? Let it be Viola.' He went on with his carving. Then, fearing that he was discourteous, he added, 'I am called Simon.'

The attendant broke in roughly: 'Fool, this is Her Royal Highness, the Princess Elvira.'

'Elvira, of course,' he nodded.

'You remember,' asked the Princess, 'what happened last time?'

'I remember. I was carving a heron in flight. You interrupted me. I finished it later. It was a good heron.'

'I spared your life,' said the Princess with great dignity.

'Alas, I did not know that it was yours.'

'Am I not the Princess?'

'Am I not Simon?'

'What of that?'

'There are many Princesses, but I know of no other Simon.'

'That would not stay me, if I wished to have you killed.'

Simon looked up at her, wrinkling his brow.

'You talk always of killing,' he said plaintively. 'Does it interest you so much?'

The Princess Elvira opened her lovely mouth to say something, but could think of nothing to say. There was silence for a little …

Simon held his work at arm's length and pondered it, his head on one side. It was the figure of a crouching leopard. He turned it this way and that.

'A crouching leopard!' he murmured to himself. 'Oh, my poor Simon! It is a tame cat at milk-time. I hear it purr. No, no!' And he fell upon it urgently.

'Oh, I hate you, I hate you!' cried the Princess in fury, and wrenched her horse's head round, and spurred it to a wild gallop, her silver whip rising and falling until she was out of the forest. So, without drawing rein she fled to the safety of the castle and the comfort of her Princes and courtiers, to whom she said, 'Am I not beautiful?' and they to her, 'More lovely than words can tell,' which brought her ease again.

And the days went on, and still she would not pledge herself to marry. One day she said to her Father:

'Are there no other Princes, for I am weary of these?'

'There is the great Prince Simon,' said the King.

'Send for him.'

'If he will come,' said the King.

'He will come,' said the Princess, looking at herself in a mirror.

So the King sent messengers to him. Then the Princess told herself that she would ride into the forest for the last time, and would come back and marry the great and powerful Prince Simon, and live with him ever afterwards. So she rode into the forest …

He looked up as he heard her come to him, and nodded.

'Have you come to kill me?' he smiled.

'No,' she said meekly. Then after a little silence, 'May I look?'

He stood up and gave her the figure he was carving.

'She is very beautiful,' said the Princess.

'She is beautiful,' said Simon.

'I seem to know her face.'

'You have never seen her.'

'Is it someone you love?' she asked, a little scornfully.

'I would not love her,' he said quickly. 'She has a temper. She is cruel.'

The Princess looked at the figure again.

'You have shown it,' she said.

'Yes.'

'What is her name?'

'Her name,' he said thoughtfully. 'Her name. Wait … It is on the tip of my tongue. Yes, I have it. Elvira.'

'I?' she cried in amazement.

'You,' he nodded. 'Did you not recognize it?'

Indignation flamed in her face.

'How dare you!'

'What have I dared?'

'You dare to talk of being in love with *me*?'

He shook his head.

'I talked of not being in love with you,' he said pleasantly.

'That is worse!'

'Would you have me in love with you? To what end? You would not marry me.'

'I marry *you*!' She laughed scornfully.

'Well! Why should you want me to be unhappy?' He looked at her wonderingly. 'You are a strange girl,' he went on. 'First you want to kill me, and then you want me to break my heart for you. You never seem contented unless somebody else is suffering. What a creature!'

'It is not true,' she cried indignantly.

'What is not true?'

'That I am what you say I am.' Then, almost in tears, like a little child, she said, 'I—I don't mean any harm.'

For a while neither of them spoke. Then he held out his hand, and said gently, 'May I have it back?'

She unclenched her hand, and he took from her the little figure of Elvira.

'It is not right,' he said, shaking his head over it. 'I saw what was not there. When you come again, I will show you.' And he continued to look intently at the face he had carved.

'I shall not come again,' she said coldly.

'Then good-bye,' he said, without looking up.

She seemed about to speak, but no words came. She turned her horse and rode slowly out of the forest. The great Prince Simon was waiting for her ...

He was not waiting. Messengers had come to say that he was on a journey in distant lands. They brought with them a hundred tales of the market-place, but this only was certain. He was not coming.

The Princess Elvira dismissed her attendants and sat alone. There were thoughts and hopes and wonders in her heart which she could show to no other, and feared even to show to herself. This man Simon whom she so nearly loved—was this love?—this man Simon whom she had hated, who despised her, this man whom she loved—ah, how she loved him, but could never marry him—this man Simon who might be brought to love her—could he? Oh, if he could, not that she might indeed marry him—this man Simon was—Who was he?

What had he said? 'I know of no other Simon.' It was true. There was only one Simon. The great and powerful Prince Simon. Who but a Prince could be so sure of himself? Who but a Prince would treat her as an equal? And where was Prince Simon? It was rumoured this and rumoured that, but who could say with certainty? Surely only she! He was in the forest waiting for her! Then, if he were in the forest, he had come there for her sake! He had wanted her love. But he would have her love him for himself, not for what he was. Ah, but she had indeed loved him for himself, before she had guessed his secret. It would still be a secret until he chose to declare it. He was Simon, she Elvira, and they loved each other. How wise, how beautiful of him to have it so! Even from the beginning he would not call her 'Princess'. She was to be just Elvira, he just Simon. Now she would go to Simon.

In the morning she went.

'I have come,' she said.

He held up to her the little figure of Elvira.

'I think it is better now,' he told her.

She looked at it.

'There is no cruelty here, no scorn,' she said wonderingly.

He nodded.

'It is better so,' he answered; 'it is more like her.'

'Is it, Simon?' she asked wistfully.

'That is how I think of her now.'

'Always think of her like that, Simon, even if it be not true.'

'If I have put it there, it is true.'

'Oh, it shall be true,' she cried passionately. 'I will make it true.'

'Then you will be happy,' he said. 'I am glad.'

'And you?'

'I have my work.'

'Is that enough?'

He looked at her suddenly ... and looked away again. 'Enough,' he said.

She nodded, but did not move. Then, with a sigh, 'Farewell, Simon,' she said.

'Farewell, Princess.'

He moved away from her as if to busy himself with this work of his, and fingered this and that, but still she did not move ... She was there, behind him ...

'Why have you not gone?' he cried, turning round on her violently.

'The Princess *is* gone, Simon,' she said meekly.

He stared at her, but could not speak.

'But Elvira,' she went on, 'is—oh, Simon, have you nothing to say to her?'

But still he could only look … and suddenly she smiled adorably on him.

'You mean to say the *Princess* is gone?'

'Yes, I think that is what I mean, Simon,' she nodded.

He held out his arms to her, and she slipped into them. But the secret remained a secret. Many times in the days that followed Elvira would look at Simon, and smile to herself, and say to herself, 'Why does he not tell me?'—and say to herself, 'He wants to try me further; he wants to be sure that he can trust my love.' When they talked, they talked of Simon's work, and how much he could earn by it, and how she could help him by going into the town and selling it for him.

'Wait,' said Simon. 'In a few days we will go from here. The people here are foolish. They do not love good work. One here, one there; that is all. We will wander from this place to that; always we shall find one or two who will understand. That will be enough for us, enough for our simple wants.'

And Elvira smiled to herself. She saw what was coming. They would wander here, they would wander there, until at last they came to his own country. Then, having proved her, he would reveal himself to her, and they would take their places again as Prince and Princess. Happy days those would be, but meanwhile these were happy days too. It was fun being married to Simon. The bargaining was fun; the little hardships were fun; marrying was fun; watching him work was fun. She loved him.

The secret was fun too.

'What did you mean, Simon,' she asked him mischievously one day, 'when you said that there was only one Simon?'

'There is only one Simon,' he smiled back.

'And who is he?' she went on innocently.

He tapped his chest.

'I, Simon the Carver. There is none who carves as I. Kings come and go, and lie forgotten, but the artist endures for ever. A thousand years from now men will say "Simon carved that," and none will ask, "Which Simon?" There is no other Simon.'

'Little bits of wood,' she scoffed.

'Not always wood,' he said seriously. 'Bone and ivory one day, perhaps. Why not? Perhaps even stone or metal—who knows?'

'And will you always—just carve?' She had to turn away then to hide the sudden smile.

'What else is there to do?' he asked, grave-faced like a child.

'Oh, I love you, Simon,' she cried impetuously, and took his head in her hands, and kissed it. 'Whatever you do, whenever you do it, I shall be content.'

He said nothing, but went on with his work.

So they wandered from place to place, living their gypsy life on the outskirts of this town and that; he following his fancies; she planning, managing, buying, selling, cooking, tending; she always watching over him.

It was fun. Was it fun? There were hard days, weary days, bad days; days when she longed to cry out, 'Simon, Simon, have I not proved my love? Simon, I cannot go on. Let us go back to your own country, and take our places in the world. How can you doubt any longer that I love you? See what I have given up for you!' But she did not. She could be as obstinate as he. Let him speak first, if that was how he wished it.

She loved him. Did she love him? If it was love, that which she had first felt for him, then this was not love.

That was something outside her which came gloriously upon her; this was something growing up from the very roots of her, until it was part of her body, of her soul, of herself, to be separated from which was death. Was this love? Then the other was but a little thing. How strange that by so little a thing she should come upon life.

Yes, she loved him. But was life fun? Was she happy? She did not know.

It was two years later. In the forest which was their home Elvira sat and watched her baby; her two babies. She was content. The secret was still a secret, but it was a golden secret; a magic key to unlock the prison doors whenever her prison was too hard for her. She had but to say, 'Simon, I am tired of being Elvira, I wish to be a Princess again,' and she would be a Princess. She had but to say, 'Simon, we must think of our child,' and they would go back to their kingdom. She had but to say, 'Simon, we have pretended long enough,' and the secret would be out.

But she did not want to say it. Not now. She was happy. It was enough that she could say it when she needed to say it. Perhaps now she would never use that key. So long as she had it, she was not in a prison, she was free. What happiness to be so free! With her two babies. Big Simon and Little Simon.

Outside the hut Simon the Carver was still carving. In ivory now. He, too, was happy; happy in his work, happy in his wife, happy in his child. Perhaps one day his son would be a great carver too. Another Simon! Simon the Elder and Simon the Younger. Two of them ...

There was a third Simon somewhere. Prince Simon. But of him Simon the Carver had never heard. The son of a charcoal-burner has not much acquaintance with Courts, however great an artist he turns out to be.

In Vino Veritas

(1943)

I am in a terrible predicament, as you will see directly. I don't know what to do …

'One of the maxims which I have found most helpful in my career,' the Superintendent was saying, 'apart, of course, from employing a good press agent, has been the simple one that appearances are not always deceptive. A crime may be committed exactly as it seems to have been committed, and exactly as it was intended to be committed.' He helped himself and passed the bottle.

'I don't think I follow you,' I said, hoping thus to lead him on.

I am a writer of detective stories. If you have never heard of me, it can only be because you don't read detective stories. I wrote *Murder on the Back Stairs* and *The Mystery of the Twisted Eglantine*, to mention only two of my successes. It was this fact, I think, which first interested Superintendent Frederick Mortimer in me, and, of course, me in him. He is a big fellow with the face of a Roman Emperor; I am rather the small neat type. We gradually became friends, and so got into the habit of dining together once a month, each in turn being host in his own flat. He liked talking about his cases, and naturally I liked listening. I may say now that *Blood on the Eiderdown* was suggested to me by an experience of his at Crouch End. He also liked putting me right when I made mistakes, as so many of us do, over such technical matters as finger-prints and Scotland Yard procedure. I had always supposed, for instance, that you could get good finger-prints from butter. This, apparently, is not the case. From buttery fingers on other objects, yes, but not from the pat of butter itself, or, anyhow, not in hot weather. This, of course, was a foolish mistake of mine, as in any case Lady Sybil would not have handled the butter directly in this way, as my detective should have seen. My detective, by the way, is called Sherman Flagg, and is pretty well known by now. Not that this is germane to my present story.

'I don't think I follow you,' I said.

'I mean that the simple way of committing a murder is often the best way. This doesn't mean that the murderer is a man of simple mind. On the contrary. He is subtle enough to know that the simple solution is too simple to be credible.'

This sounded anything but simple, so I said, 'Give me an example.'

'Well, take the case of the magnum of Tokay which was sent to the Marquis of Hedingham on his lordship's birthday. Have I never told you about it?'

'Never,' I said, and I, too, helped myself and passed the bottle.

He filled his glass and considered. 'Give me a moment to get it clear,' he said. 'It was a long time ago.' While he closed his eyes, and let the past drift before him, I fetched another bottle of the same: a Château Latour '78, of which, I understand, there is very little left in the country.

'Yes,' said Mortimer, opening his eyes, 'I've got it now.'

I leant forward, listening eagerly. This is the story he told me.

The first we heard of it at the Yard (said Mortimer) was a brief announcement over the telephone that the Marquis of Hedingham's butler had died suddenly at his lordship's town house in Brook Street, and that poison was suspected. This was at seven o'clock. We went round at once. Inspector Totman had been put in charge of the case; I was a young Detective Sergeant at the time, and I generally worked under Totman. He was a brisk, military sort of fellow, with a little prickly ginger moustache, good at his job, in a showy, orthodox way, but he had no imagination, and he was thinking all the time of what Inspector Totman would get out of it. Quite frankly I didn't like him. Outwardly we kept friendly, for it doesn't do to quarrel with one's superiors; indeed, he was vain enough to think that I had a great admiration for him; but I knew that he was just using me for his own advantage, and I had a shrewd suspicion that I should have been promoted before this, if he hadn't wanted to keep me under him so that he could profit by my brains.

We found the butler in his pantry, stretched out on the floor. An open bottle of Tokay, a broken wine-glass with the dregs of the liquid still in it, the medical evidence of poisoning, all helped to build up the story for us. The wine had arrived about an hour before, with the card of Sir William Kelso attached to it. On the card was a type-written message, saying, 'Bless you, Tommy, and here's something to celebrate it with.' Apparently it was his lordship's birthday, and he was having a small family party for the occasion, of about six people. Sir William Kelso, I should explain, was his oldest friend and a rela-tion by marriage, Lord Hedingham having married his sister; in fact, he was to have been one of the party present that evening. He was a bachelor, about fifty, and a devoted uncle to his nephew and nieces.

Well, the butler had brought up the bottle and the card to his lordship—this was about six o'clock; and Lord Hedingham, as he told us, had taken the card, said something like, 'Good old Bill, we'll have that to-night, Perkins,' and Perkins had said, 'Very good, my lord,' and gone out again with the bottle, and the card had been left lying on the table. Afterwards, there could be little doubt what had happened. Perkins had opened the bottle with the intention of decanting it, but had been unable to resist the temptation to sam-ple it first. I suspect that in his time he had sampled most of his lordship's wine, but had never before come across a Tokay of such richness. So he had poured himself out a full glass, drunk it, and died almost immediately.

'Good Heavens!' I interrupted. 'But how extremely providential—I mean, of course, for Lord Hedingham and the others.'

'Exactly,' said the Superintendent.

The contents of the bottle were analysed (he went on) and found to contain a more than fatal dose of prussic acid. Prussic acid isn't a difficult thing to get hold of, so that didn't help much. Of course we did all the routine things, and I and young Roberts, a nice young fellow who often worked with us, went round all the chemists' shops in the neighbourhood, and Totman examined everybody from Sir William and Lord Hedingham downwards, and Roberts and I took the bottle round to all the well-known wine-merchants, and at the end of a week all we could say was this:

1. The murderer had a motive for murdering Lord Hedingham; or, possibly, somebody at his party; or, possibly, the whole party. In accordance, we learnt, with the usual custom, his lordship would be the first to taste the wine. A sip would not be fatal, and in a wine of such richness the taste might not be noticeable; so that the whole party would then presumably drink his lordship's health. He would raise his glass to them, and in this way they would all take the poison, and be affected according to how deeply they drank. On the other hand, his lordship might take a good deal more than a sip in the first place, and so be the only one to suffer. My deduction from this was that the motive was revenge rather than gain. The criminal would revenge himself on Lord Hedingham, if his lordship or *any* of his family were seriously poisoned; he could only profit if *definite* people were definitely *killed*. It took a little time to get Totman to see this, but he did eventually agree.

2. The murderer had been able to obtain one of Sir William Kelso's cards, and knew that John Richard Mervyn Plantaganet Carlow, Tenth Marquis of Hedingham, was

called 'Tommy' by his intimates. Totman deduced from this that he was therefore one of the Hedingham-Kelso circle of relations and friends. I disputed this. I pointed out: *(a)* that it was rather to strangers than to intimate friends that cards were presented; except in the case of formal calls, when they were left in a bowl or tray in the hall, and anybody could steal one; *(b)* that the fact that Lord Hedingham was called Tommy must have appeared in Society papers and be known to many people; and, most convincing of all, *(c)* that the murderer did *not* know that Sir William Kelso was to be in the party that night. For obviously some reference would have been made to the gift, either on his arrival or when the wine was served; whereupon he would have disclaimed any knowledge of it, and the bottle would immediately have been suspected. As it was, of course, Perkins had drunk from it before Sir William's arrival. Now both Sir William and Lord Hedingham assured us that they *always* dined together on each other's birthday, and they were convinced that any personal friend of theirs would have been aware of the fact. I made Totman question them about this, and he then came round to my opinion.

3. There was nothing to prove that the wine in the bottle corresponded to the label; and wine experts were naturally reluctant to taste it for us. All they could say from the smell was that it was a Tokay of sorts. This, of course, made it more difficult for us. In fact, I may say that neither from the purchase of the wine nor the nature of the poison did we get any clue.

We had, then, the following picture of the murderer. He had a cause for grievance, legitimate or fancied, against Lord Hedingham, and did not scruple to take the most terrible revenge. He knew that Sir William Kelso was a friend of his lordship's and called him

Tommy, and that he might reasonably give him a bottle of wine on his birthday. He did *not* know that Sir William would be dining there that night; that is to say, even as late as six o'clock that evening, he did not know. He was not likely, therefore, to be anyone at present employed or living in Lord Hedingham's house. Finally, he had had an opportunity, for what this was worth, to get hold of a card of Sir William's.

As it happened, there was somebody who fitted completely into this picture. It was a fellow called—wait a bit, Merrivale, Medley— oh well, it doesn't matter. Merton, that was it. Merton. He had been his lordship's valet for six months, had been suspected of stealing, and dismissed without a character. Just the man we wanted. So for a fortnight we searched for Merton. And then, when at last we got on to him, we discovered that he had the most complete alibi imaginable. (*The Superintendent held up his hand, and it came into my mind that he must have stopped the traffic as a young man with just that gesture.*) Yes, I know what you're going to say, what you detective-story writers always say—the better an alibi, the worse it is. Well, sometimes, I admit; but not in this case. For Merton was in gaol, under another name, and he had been inside for the last two months. And what do you think he was suspected of, and now waiting trial for? Oh well, of course you guess, I've as good as told you. He was on a charge of murder—and murder, mark you, by poison.

('Good Heavens,' I interjected. I seized the opportunity to refill my friend's glass. He said, 'Exactly,' and took a long drink. I thought fancifully that he was drinking to drown that terrible disappointment of so many years ago.)

You can imagine (he went on) what a shock this was to us. You see, a certain sort of murder had been committed; we had deduced that it was done by a certain man without knowing whether he was in the least capable of such a crime; and now, having proved to the hilt that he was capable of it, we had simultaneously proved that he didn't do it. We had proved ourselves right—and our case mud.

I said to Totman, 'Let's take a couple of days off, and each of us think it out, and then pool our ideas and start afresh.'

Totman frisked up his little moustache, and laughed in his conceited way.

'You don't think I'm going to admit myself wrong, do you, when I've just proved I'm right?' Totman saying 'I', when he had got everything from me! 'Merton's my man. He'd got the bottle ready and somebody else delivered it for him. That's all. He had to wait for the birthday, you see, and when he found himself in prison, his wife or somebody—'

'—took round the bottle, all nicely labelled "Poison; not to be delivered till Christmas Day".' I had to say it, I was so annoyed with him.

'Don't be more of a damned fool than you can help,' he shouted, 'and don't be insolent, or you'll get into trouble.'

I apologized humbly, and told him how much I liked working with him. He forgave me—and we were friends again. He patted me on the shoulder.

'You take a day off,' he said kindly, 'you've been working too hard. Take a bus into the country and make up a good story for me; the story of that bottle, and how it came from Merton's lodging to Brook Street, and who took it and why. I admit I don't see it at present, but that's the bottle, you can bet your life. I'm going down to Leatherhead. Report here on Friday morning, and we'll see what we've got. My birthday as it happens, and I feel I'm going to be lucky.' Leatherhead was where this old woman had been poisoned. That was the third time in a week he'd told me when his entirely misconceived birthday was. He was like that.

I took a bus to Hampstead Heath. I walked round the Leg of Mutton Pond twenty times. And each time that I went round, Totman's theory seemed sillier than the last time. And each time I felt more and more strongly that we were *being forced* into an entirely artificial interpretation of things. It sounds fantastic, I know, but I could almost feel the murderer behind us, pushing us along the way he wanted us to go.

I sat down on a seat, and I filled a pipe and I said, 'Right! The murderer's a man who wanted me to believe all that I have believed. When I've told myself that the murderer intended to do so-and-so, he intended me to believe that, and therefore he didn't do so-and-so. When I've told myself that the murderer wanted to mislead me, he wanted me to think he wanted to mislead me, which meant that the truth was exactly as it seemed to be. Now then, Fred, you'll begin all over again, and you'll take things as they are, and won't be too clever about them. Because the murderer expects you to be clever, and wants you to be clever, and from now on you aren't going to take your orders from *him*.'

And, of course, the first thing which leaped to my mind was that the murderer *meant* to murder the butler!

It seemed incredible now that we could ever have missed it. Didn't every butler sample his master's wines? Why, it was an absolute certainty that Perkins would be the first victim of a poisoned bottle of a very special vintage. What butler could resist pouring himself out a glass as he decanted it?

Wait, though. Mustn't be in a hurry. Two objections. One: Perkins might be the one butler in a thousand who wasn't a wine-sampler. Two: even if he were like any other butler, he might be out of sorts on that particular evening, and have put by a glass to drink later. Wouldn't it be much too risky for a murderer who only wanted to destroy Perkins, and had no grudge against Lord Hedingham's family, to depend so absolutely on the butler drinking first?

For a little while this held me up, but not for long. Suddenly I saw the complete solution.

It would *not* be risky if *(a)* the murderer had certain knowledge of the butler's habits; and *(b)* could, if necessary, at the last moment, prevent the family from drinking. In other words, if he were an intimate of the family, were himself present at the party, and without bringing suspicion on himself, could bring the wine under suspicion.

In other words, and only, and finally, and definitely—if he were Sir William Kelso. For Sir William was the only man in the world who could say, 'Don't drink this wine. I'm supposed to have sent it to you, and I didn't, so that proves it's a fake.' The *only* man.

Why hadn't we suspected him from the beginning? One reason, of course, was that we had supposed the intended victim to be one of the Hedingham family, and of Sir William's devotion to his sister, brother-in-law, nephew and nieces, there was never any doubt. But the chief reason was our assumption that the last thing a murderer would do would be to give himself away by sending his own card round with the poisoned bottle. 'The *last* thing a murderer would do'—and therefore the *first* thing a really clever murderer would do. For it couldn't be explained as 'the one mistake which every murderer makes'; he couldn't send his own card accidentally. 'Impossible,' we said, that a murderer should do it deliberately! But the correct answer was, impossible that we should not be deceived if it were done deliberately—and therefore brilliantly clever.

To make my case complete to myself, for I had little hope as yet of converting Totman, I had to establish motive. Why should Sir William want to murder Perkins? I gave myself the pleasure of having tea that afternoon with Lord Hedingham's cook-housekeeper. We had caught each other's eye on other occasions when I had been at the house, and—well, I suppose I can say it now—I had a way with the women in those days. When I left, I knew two things. Perkins had been generally unpopular, not only downstairs, but upstairs; 'it was a wonder how they put up with him'. And her ladyship had been 'a different woman lately'.

'How different?' I asked.

'So much younger, if you know what I mean, Sergeant Mortimer. Almost like a girl again, bless her heart.'

I did know. And that was that. Blackmail.

What was I to do? What did my evidence amount to? Nothing. It was all corroborative evidence. If Kelso had done one suspicious thing, or left one real clue, then the story I had made up would have convinced any jury. As it was, in the eyes of a jury he had done one completely unsuspicious thing, and left one real clue to his innocence—his visiting-card. Totman would just laugh at me.

I disliked the thought of being laughed at by Totman. I wondered how I could get the laugh of him. I took a bus to Baker Street, and walked into Regent's Park, not minding where I was going, but just thinking. And then, as I got opposite Hanover Terrace, who should I see but young Roberts.

'Hallo, young fellow, what have *you* been up to?'

'Hallo, Sarge,' he grinned. 'Been calling on my old school-chum, Sir Woppity Wotsit—or rather, his valet. Tottie thought he might have known Merton. Speaking as one valet to another, so to speak.'

'Is Inspector Totman back?' I asked.

Roberts stood to attention, and said, 'No, Sergeant Mortimer, Inspector Totman is not expected to return from Leatherhead, Surrey, until a late hour to-night.'

You couldn't be angry with the boy. At least I couldn't. He had no respect for anybody, but he was a good lad. And he had an eye like a hawk. Saw everything and forgot none of it.

'I suppose by Sir Woppity Wotsit you mean Sir William Kelso?' I said. 'I didn't know he lived up this way.'

Roberts pointed across the road. 'Observe the august mansion. Five minutes ago you'd have found me in the basement, talking to a cock-eyed churchwarden who thought Merton was in Surrey. As it is, of course.'

I had a sudden crazy idea.

'Well, now you're going back there,' I said. 'I'm going to call on Sir William, and I want you handy. Would they let you in at the basement again, or are they sick of you?'

'Sarge, they just love me. When I went, they said, "Must you go?"'

We say at the Yard, 'Once a murderer, always a murderer.' Perhaps that was why I had an absurd feeling that I should like young Roberts within call. Because I was going to tell Sir William Kelso what I'd been thinking about by the Leg of Mutton Pond. I'd only seen him once, but he gave me the idea of being the sort of man who wouldn't mind killing, but didn't like lying. I thought he would give himself away ... and then—well, there might be a rough house, and young Roberts would be useful.

As we walked in at the gate together, I looked in my pocket-book for a card. Luckily I had one left, though it wasn't very clean. Roberts, who never missed anything, said, 'Personally I always use blotting-paper,' and went on whistling. If I hadn't known him, I shouldn't have known what he was talking about. I said, 'Oh, do you?' and rang the bell. I gave the maid my card, and asked if Sir William could see me, and at the same time Roberts gave her a wink, and indicated the back door. She nodded to him, and asked me to come in. Roberts went down and waited for her at the basement. I felt safer.

Sir William was a big man, as big as I was. But of course a lot older. He said, 'Well, Sergeant, what can I do for you?' twiddling my card in his fingers. He seemed quite friendly about it. 'Sit down, won't you?'

I said, 'I think I'll stand, Sir William. I wanted just to ask you one question if I might.' Yes, I know I was crazy, but somehow I felt kind of inspired.

'By all means,' he said, obviously not much interested.

'When did you first discover that Perkins was blackmailing Lady Hedingham?'

He was standing in front of his big desk, and I was opposite to him. He stopped fiddling with my card, and became absolutely still; and there was a silence so complete that I could feel it in every nerve of my body. I kept my eyes on his, you may be sure. We stood there, I don't know how long.

'Is that the only question?' he asked. The thing that frightened me was that his voice was just the same as before. Ordinary.

'Well, just one more. Have you a Corona typewriter in your house?' You see, we knew that a Corona had been used, but there was nothing distinctive about it, and it might have been any one in a thousand. Just corroborative evidence again, that's all. But it told him that I knew.

He gave a long sigh, tossed the card into the waste-paper basket, and walked to the window. He stood there with his back to me, looking out but seeing nothing. Thinking. He must have stood there for a couple of minutes. Then he turned round, and to my amazement he had a friendly smile on his face. 'I think we'd both better sit down,' he said. We did.

'There is a Corona in the house which I sometimes use,' he began. 'I dare say you use one too.'

'I do.'

'And so do thousands of other people—including, it may be, the murderer you are looking for.'

'Thousands of people including the murderer,' I agreed.

He noticed the difference, and smiled. 'People' I had said, not 'other people'. And I didn't say I was looking for him. Because I had found him.

'So much for that. There is nothing in the actual wording of the typed message to which you would call my attention?'

'No. Except that it was exactly right.'

'Oh, my dear fellow, anyone could have got it right. A simple birthday greeting.'

'Anyone in your own class, Sir William, who knew you both. But that's all. It's Inspector Totman's birthday to-morrow—' ('As he keeps telling us, damn him,' I added to myself.) 'If I sent him a bottle of whisky, young Roberts—that's the constable who's in on this case, you may have seen him about, he's waiting for me now down below'—I thought this was rather a neat way of getting that in— 'Roberts could make a guess at what I'd say, and so could anybody at the Yard who knows us both, and they wouldn't be far wrong. But *you* couldn't, Sir William.'

He looked at me. He couldn't take his eyes off me. I wondered what he was thinking. At last he said:

'A long life and all the best, with the admiring good wishes of—How's that?'

It was devilish. First that he had really been thinking it out, when he had so much else to think about, and then that he'd got it so right. That 'admiring'; which meant that he'd studied Totman just as he was studying me, and knew how I'd play up to him.

'You see,' he smiled, 'it isn't really difficult. And the fact that my card was used is in itself convincing evidence of my innocence, don't you think?'

'To a jury perhaps,' I said, 'but not to me.'

'I wish I could convince *you*,' he murmured to himself. 'Well, what are you doing about it?'

'I shall, of course, put my reconstruction of the case in front of Inspector Totman to-morrow.'

'Ah! A nice birthday surprise for him. And, knowing your Totman, what do you think he will do?'

He had me there, and he knew it.

'I think *you* know him too, sir,' I said.

'I do,' he smiled.

'And me, I dare say, and anybody else you meet. Quick as lightning. But even ordinary men like me have a sort of sudden understanding of people sometimes. As I've got of you, sir. And I've a sort of feeling that, if ever we get you into a witness-box, and you've taken the oath, you won't find perjury so much to your liking as murder. Or what the Law calls murder.'

'But *you* don't?' he said quickly.

'I think,' I said, 'that there are a lot of people who ought to be killed. But I'm a policeman, and what I think isn't evidence. You killed Perkins, didn't you?'

He nodded; and said, almost with a grin at me, 'A nervous affection of the head, if you put it in evidence. I could get a specialist to swear to it.' My God, he was a good sort of man. I was really sorry when they found him next day on the Underground. Or what was left of him. And yet what else could he do?

I was furious with Fred Mortimer. That was no way to end a story. Suddenly, like that, as if he were tired of it. I told him so.

'My dear little Cyril,' he said, 'it isn't the end. We're just coming to the exciting part. This will make your hair curl.'

'Oh!' I said sarcastically. 'Then I suppose all that you've told me so far is just introduction?'

'That's right. Now listen. On the Friday morning, before we heard of Sir William's death, I went in to report to Inspector Totman. He wasn't there. Nobody knew where he was. They rang up his block of flats. Now hold tight to the leg of the table or something. When the porter got into his flat, he found Totman's body. Poisoned.'

'Good Heavens!' I ejaculated.

'You may say so. There he was, and on the table was a newly opened bottle of whisky, and by the side of it was a visiting-card. And whose card do you think it was? *Mine!* And what do you think it said? A long life and all the best with the admiring good wishes of—*me*! Lucky for me I had had young Roberts with me. Lucky for me he had this genius for noticing and remembering. Lucky for me he could swear to the exact shape of the smudge of ink on that card. And I might add, lucky for me that they believed me when I told them word for word what had been said at my interview with Sir William, as I have just told you. I was reprimanded, of course, for exceeding my duty, as I most certainly had, but that was only official. Unofficially they were very pleased with me. We couldn't prove anything, naturally, and Sir William's death had looked as accidental as anything could, so we just had to leave it. But a month later I was promoted to Inspector.'

He filled his glass and drank, while I revolved his extraordinary story in my mind.

'The theory,' I said, polishing my pince-nez thoughtfully, 'was, I suppose, this. Sir William sent the poisoned whisky, not so much to get rid of Totman, from whom he had little to fear, as to discredit you by bringing you under suspicion, and entirely to discredit your own theory of the other murder?'

'Exactly.'

'And then, at the last moment, he realized that he couldn't go on with it, or the weight of his crimes became suddenly too much for him, or—'

'Something of the sort. Nobody ever knew, of course.'

I looked across the table with sudden excitement; almost with awe.

'Do you remember what he said to you?' I asked, giving the words their full meaning as I slowly quoted them. '"The fact that my card was used is convincing evidence of my innocence." And you said, "Not to me." And he said, "I wish I could convince you." *And that was how he did it!* The fact that your card was used *was* convincing evidence of your innocence!'

'With the other things. The proof that he was in possession of the particular card of mine which was used, and the certainty that he had committed the other murder. Once a poisoner, always a poisoner.'

'True ... yes ... Well, thanks very much for the story, Fred. All the same, you know,' I said, shaking my head at him, 'it doesn't altogether prove what you set out to prove.'

'What was that?'

'That the simple explanation is generally the true one. In the case of Perkins, yes. But not in the case of Totman.'

'Sorry, I don't follow.'

'My dear fellow,' I said, putting up a finger to emphasize my point, for he seemed a little hazy with the wine suddenly; 'the *simple* explanation of Totman's death—surely?—would have been that *you* had sent him the poisoned whisky.'

Superintendent Mortimer looked a little surprised.

'But I did,' he said.

So now you see my terrible predicament. I could hardly listen as he went on dreamily: 'I never liked Totman, and he stood in my way; but I hadn't seriously thought of getting rid of him, until I got that card into my hands again. As I told you, he dropped it into the basket, and turned to the window, and I thought, "Damn it, *you* can afford to chuck about visiting-cards, but I can't, and it's the only one I've got left, and if you don't want it, I do." So I bent down very naturally to do up my boot-lace, and felt in the basket behind me, because of course it was rather an undignified thing to do, and I didn't want to be seen; and it was just as I was putting it into my pocket that I saw that ink-smudge again, and I remembered that Roberts had seen it. And in a flash the whole plan came to me; simple; fool-proof. And from that moment everything I said to him was in preparation of it. Course we were quite alone, but you never know who might be listening, and besides'—he twiddled the stem of his empty wine-glass—'p'r'aps I'm like Sir William, rather tell the truth than not, and it *was* true, all of it, as I told the Super, how Sir William came to know about Totman's birthday, and knew that those were the very words I should have used. Made it very convincing, me just repeating to the Super what had really been said. Don't think I wanted to put anything on to Sir William that wasn't his. I liked him. But he as good as told me he wasn't going to wait for what was coming to him, and he'd done one murder anyway. That was why I slipped down with the bottle that evening, and left it outside Totman's flat. Didn't dare wait till the morning, in case Sir William closed his account that night.' He stood up and stretched himself. 'Ah, well, it was a long time ago. Good-bye, old man, I must be off. Thanks for a grand dinner. Don't forget, you're dining with *me* next month. I've got a new cocktail for you. You'll like it.' He swaggered out, leaving me to my thoughts.

* * *

'Once a murderer, always a murderer ...' And to-morrow he will wake up and remember what he has told me! And I shall be the only person in the world who knows his secret! ...

Perhaps he won't remember. Perhaps he was drunk ...

In vino veritas. Wasn't it the younger Pliny who said that? A profound observation. Truth in the bottle ...

'Once a poisoner, always a poisoner ...'

'I've got a new cocktail for you. You'll like it.'

Yes, but—shall I?

The Lost Diary of Shakespeare

(1946)

Extracted from the secret diary of a horse-holder, and deciphered for modern reading.

Thursday. April 23, an. dom. 1594. With this my Birth Day I begin a new volume. Well, I am 30. How many more years have I in which to discharge the rich cargo of my mind? Never have I been so laden with notions, and with words, words, words in which to set them free. If I could stop thinking for a little, then I could write as I wish to write: if I could stop writing for a little, then I could think. But thoughts and words tumble in my head so restlessly, day and night, that no sooner does a thought present itself than pat! there comes a line of verse for it. This is not the way to write, this is not the way to think. And I am 30, and have little time left.

May 1. Dick Burbage grows more difficult every day. There are no half-shades in his character, as there are (far too many) in mine. To him a thing is Yes or No. Either a play is a tragedy, in which case all the leading characters must be strangled, poisoned or stabbed (himself last of all): or it is not a tragedy, in which case they must all marry each other willy-nilly, the villains, if any, repenting at the church door. Also he has this fixed idea that no actor can leave the stage without saying a rhymed couplet first. Nothing in nature corresponds with this; one can leave the stage at any time. Also his notion of humour is hard to bear. The scenes between rustic clowns which he inserts into my plays to tickle the ears of the groundlings are so lacking in true comedy that I can no longer listen to them at rehearsal. When I am not to be found, they say that I am 'holding a horse for somebody' outside the theatre. This is because, the first time I got up and left the rehearsal, I made the excuse that I had promised to hold a man's horse for him. If only I had my own theatre, and could produce and write my plays as I wish to!

On reading this through I see that I might have begun, 'Will Shakespeare grows more difficult every day.'

May 3. I suddenly found myself writing an Essay this morning. Of Innovations. It is good discipline for me to write prose. Short sentences packed with meaning. No getting carried away by my own music. I must do more of this. I have an idea for one on Youth and Age.

May 10. Dick is a good fellow, and I have been unjust to him. He tells me now that these, as they are called, comic scenes with which he peppers my plays are not written by him but by an obscure lawyer called Bacon; who is persuaded that Nature meant him for a playwriter. I asked Dick why an obscure lawyer called Bacon should have a right of entry into my plays, and he said that Bacon was a very clever young man of good family who would probably be Lord Chancellor one day; in which case one would wish not to have offended him. Dear Dick! To lick absurd pomp, and crook the pregnant hinges of the knee—well, as he must do it, he must. But if I had my own theatre ... Wrote an Essay on Fortune.

May 14. Last night I went through my plays and read again what are called the comic scenes. The strange thing is that this man Bacon is reputed a wit in his conversation. No, that is not strange. The pen and mouth are separate instruments. The strange thing is that a man of high birth should neglect the life which he knows, and insist on writing of common people of whom he is ignorant.

On reading this it came to me that I, a country man of middle-class birth, write mostly of Kings and Courts.

May 15. Have begun a play of rustic life, to be called, I think, 'A Village Revel', and to contain many true comedy scenes for lowly characters.

June 25. I have been much occupied with my play, Dick wanting me to set the scene in Athens, as we have the dresses from *Titus Andronicus*. I know not what my rustics will be doing in Athens, and have therefore called it *A Midsummer Night's Dream*, which excuses all. I have nearly enough Essays for a book.

July 1. My book is ready. Dick is opposed to my putting it out over my own name. He says that I am known as a play-writer and a poet, and that it is not good for his theatre that I should play tricks with my reputation. I fear he is right. So I must think of a name for myself ... 'Essays by John Falstaff'.

There is an air about that.

July 2. Curious. All day I have been seeing him as a tall, stout, roystering fellow. Then I do not see how he could have written these Essays.

July 9. For the last week I have been working at a play on the Life of Henry IV. It is written round a jolly, fat fellow called Sir John Falstaff, I think my best character so far. He came into my head complete, so soon as I had written down the name. I must think of another author for my book.

July 15. I have met this man Bacon. He came to the theatre when I was with Dick. He is a shifty-eyed creature, with a lean and hungry look. He has three ambitions, as I read him. To be Lord Chancellor—which he may be, since he is apt at intrigue; to be known as a writer—which he will never be, as he cannot write; and to make money—which he is well qualified to do, having no scruples. Let no such man be trusted.

July 20. 'Essays by William Page'. 'Essays by John Oldcastle'. 'Essays by—'

July 22. I do not like this idea of putting out these Essays under a made-up name. I would rather that Dick Burbage lent his name to them, for then at least he could recommend the book to his acquaintance. John Oldcastle can do nothing to sell so much as one copy. I did but write them as a curb to my style, and for my own instruction, and if now they be of profit to others, and make a little money for myself, I care not who fathers them.

July 23. Met Bacon again. I have no doubt but that I judged his character aright.

July 25. I think Bacon is the man.

July 31. Bacon comes to my lodging to-morrow.

August 1. It is done! My book is to come out as 'Essays, by Francis Bacon'. He has read them, and is proud to think that he wrote them—as, in truth, he does almost persuade himself. It is a deception after his own heart, for it gives him all that he most wants. I offered him one half of the money; but in the end he has given me his Note (so worded that he dare not repudiate it) for One Hundred Pounds within six months of its putting out. This, without doubt, will be at the moment which he considers most favourable to his advancement; for there is a tide in the affairs of all men, which, taken at the flood, leads most quickly to fortune. But I care not for that, for now it is off my mind, and I can give myself to my Great Project.

August 2. Began *The Advancement of Learning.*

The Birthday Party

(1948)

I

David Alistair Shawn Baker came into the world at half-past three on an April morning; and at four o'clock William Henry Baker was kneeling at his wife's bed, her hand, wet with his tears, held against his cheek.

'Oh, Will,' she sighed.

'Oh, Maggie!' he sobbed, and felt for his handkerchief with his left hand.

'Have you seen him?' she asked faintly.

'Yes, no, it's only you, Maggie, that's all that matters.'

'Well, that's a nice thing to say of your son and heir,' put in Mrs Shawn from the basket wherein David Alistair Shawn lay. Maggie, she considered, had had a very easy time, much easier than her own had been when Maggie was born. All her emotion was for her first grandchild.

'You must see him, darling.'

He kissed her hand; he wanted to go on kissing it for ever, but knew that he couldn't. He got up clumsily, and went over to the basket, wiping his eyes. He looked at his son, and felt, as other husbands have felt looking at their firstborn, 'All that for this; so small, so ugly; and yet what a burden to have borne.'

'Hallo!' he said, and had an absurd impulse to chuck it under the chin, but restrained himself, no obvious chin being there. He looked from his son to his wife, wondering at the miracle of their union.

'Now you must be off,' said Mrs Shawn. 'Try to get some sleep, and you may come and say good-bye just before you catch your train.'

He bent down and kissed his wife's forehead, whispering, 'Thank you, Maggie dear.' She gave him a loving smile, so tired, so remote, that the tears came back into his eyes, and he felt again for his handkerchief. He went back to the camp-bed in what was going to be the nursery. 'Bars on the windows,' he said to himself. 'I mustn't forget that. Oh well, there's no hurry.'

He had a few minutes with her alone before he caught his train. She had come back into the world, she was herself again; proud and happy.

'You promise to have a really good dinner, darling? I don't mean a midday dinner. Proper dinner, and drink David's health.'

He had had it made clear to him by Mrs Shawn that there was enough to do in the house without looking after a grown-up man who could look after himself. He was to have his meal in town, and come back by a late train. Orders.

'I will, Maggie. I shall be thinking of you both all day.'

'You'll tell them at the office? They knew he was coming, didn't they?'

He said 'Yes' to both questions, and asked again, 'You did want a boy, didn't you, dear?' as if he would have changed it even now if it had not been satisfactory.

'Of course! Didn't you?'

He nodded proudly.

William Henry Baker was nearly forty when David was born, and he had been married for ten years. Because his son had been so long in coming, he had been more than usually frightened. He would have been frightened in any case, for he was a timid little man, and his love for Maggie was almost the whole of his life. He had longed for a son: a son, a Shawn Baker, who would not be timid, would not be ineffectual, as he knew himself to be; would not be a clerk in an office who was treated with a tolerant, only just not contemptuous, familiarity by his fellow-clerks. Shawn Baker would be one of those big, strong, masterful men: an explorer, perhaps; a statesman, a great general. That was why Mr Baker had insisted—well, not insisted, he could never do that—had wanted the Shawn in his boy's name. There must be a hundred David Bakers about, but Shawn Baker was unique. He sounded like somebody. Perhaps, when he became Lord Mayor of London, David would hyphenate the name: Sir David Shawn-Baker.

Yes, he had told his fellow-clerks that the baby was coming; far too often, most of them would have said. Never had a baby been so generously shared. The brighter spirits had suggested a sweepstake on the day and hour of its arrival; anything to make a commonplace event more interesting. There had been opportunities for humour which the humorous had not missed. At times Mr Baker wished that he had been more reticent; at other times he was glad to think that Shawn Baker was being talked about already. He pictured them in after years: young Henderson, an elderly man now, managing director of the firm, perhaps, saying to an important client, 'Yes, I remember the very day he was born, his father coming into the office as pleased as Punch—oh, yes, Shawn Baker's father was with us then—just an ordinary sort of fellow, you'd never have thought he'd have had such a brilliant son.' And Miss Clissold, retired and living in the country, saying proudly to the Vicar: 'Oh, yes, I knew Sir David's dear father *very* well. Quite a little excitement, I remember, when Sir David was born. We all drank his health—oh, only in tea, of course.'

But there was another reason why he was sometimes glad and sometimes sorry that he had confided in them. The elder married men were comforting. 'Pooh, old man, it's nothing. Danger? Nonsense! In the old days, perhaps, but not to-day. Well, I suppose you and I wouldn't like it much, but I always say women don't feel pain in the way men do. Not so sensitive. Besides, they give 'em anaesthetics now. Easy. No, it's the damned expense of it that's the real trouble. You're not having anything to do with these blasted nursing-homes? Quite right. It's a racket.' But the younger ones told agonizing stories of what they had suffered (and, by inference, their wives) through the long hours of labour. They went into clinical details which both terrified and outraged him; as if, in some way, by talking of these intimate things, the speaker was admitting himself to intimacy with Maggie. Then he wished with all his heart that he had kept his secret to himself.

And the jokes. Horrible.

So now, as he hurried to the station, it came over him suddenly that he did not want to tell them, not to-day. His happiness, his pride, his relief, were too great to share with strangers who could feel none of these things. Just for to-day it would be his secret. Miss Clissold would raise enquiring eyebrows, and he would shrug his shoulders. Henderson would say: 'Well, old boy, any news of the twins?' and he wouldn't answer. He would just be smiling quietly to himself.

He smiled now as he thought of the private happiness which would be his; of the secret which he would carry with him throughout the day.

II

At 6.45 that evening Mr Baker was walking up and down outside the entrance to the Savoy Grill, looking at his watch from time to time, and giving the impression of a man of the world, a well-known clubman, who preferred to meet the Lady Patricia (late as usual) as her Rolls-Royce drew up, and personally to conduct her inside. The Lady Patricia might be a little bewildered, left to herself, having always dined at the Ritz before; might be uncertain of the way into the restaurant—as, indeed, Mr Baker was. He was also not quite sure whether evening dress was necessary. He proposed, therefore, to follow the first arrivals obviously not in evening dress through the swing door with the air of being in their party, leaving his hat and coat where they left theirs, and accompanying them into the restaurant. Up till now he had somehow failed to do this. Each time that the opportunity had come he had told himself that it was still a little before his usual hour for dinner and that there was just time for one more saunter to the Strand and back. In this way, if he were lucky, he would miss the next opportunity also.

The terrifying decision to dine at the Savoy had been taken at lunch that morning. The cup of coffee slopped into the saucer, the baked beans overrunning the side of the plate, the stained marble-topped table which had satisfied William Henry Baker for so long, suddenly disgusted the father of Shawn Baker. Not in these surroundings, not even in the homely comfort of a City chop-house, should Sir David's health be drunk. To go West into the bright world of fashion, and be one with the heroes and heroines of so many serialized meals was indeed an alarming adventure to him; but to Shawn Baker it would be routine, and the friendly 'Good evening, Sir David,' of head-waiters a familiar sound in his ears. Perhaps Mr Baker's ideas of heredity were a little muddled. Perhaps he was wrong in thinking that a sudden, uncharacteristic display of moral courage by the father can influence the character of a son already born. Perhaps he was right in thinking that a post-natal virtue, if some sign of it could be achieved, would at least be evidence of a latent virtue such as a son might have inherited and would bring to maturity. Right or wrong, fearfully he had pledged himself to dine in style that evening; right or wrong, he had told himself that on the keeping of his pledge the whole future of David Alistair Shawn Baker depended.

The Savoy was the obvious tourney-ground. It was nearest to the familiar City, which was in itself a sort of comfort; it was the most advertised in novels. Moreover, young Dugdale, son of old Dugdale and now taken into partnership, who had begun his career in the clerks' room (in order to 'start at the bottom and work my way sideways', as he put it cheerfully) had spoken so often of the girls he had taken to the Savoy that he had given it a solidity which made the adventure a little more plausible. Mr Baker was one of the firm, dining, as was the firm's custom, at the Savoy. What was there frightening in that? Nothing. He had the money in his pocket, he was ready for anything, afraid of nobody.

A taxi drew up at the door, and a man and a girl got out. With a weak feeling at the knees and a sick feeling in the stomach, Mr Baker followed them in.

III

The man was Mr Basil St John Wender, and the girl was Miss Charmian Flyte. Unlike David Alistair Shawn Baker, they had chosen (and who better?) their own names. Mr Wender was good-looking in a business-like way; a solid man of fifty with what he thought of (and hoped you would think of) as a Roman nose commanding a strongly coloured face, the red of a sanguine temperament fighting it out with the blue-black of a jaw which, for all his care, never seemed freshly shaved. To make up for this there was always an air of eau-de-Cologne about him. His hands were beautifully manicured; as indeed they should have been, seeing that Miss Charmian Flyte herself attended to them every week. She was what he would have called a pretty little thing; with more character of her own and less admiration for his than he supposed. This was the first time he had taken her out to dinner. Being a man of generous impulses where his own tastes were concerned, he had ordered champagne, and, as a result, they amused each other a good deal.

They also found easy amusement in others. In Mr William Henry Baker, for instance.

He was at a little table in the gangway, alone. With their backs to the glass screen separating them from the lounge they had him under their eyes; had so had him all through his dinner. It would not be true to say that Mr Baker was particularly conscious of them, for he felt that the eyes of all the early diners were upon him, that all the waiters were whispering about him; that, in short, what he was undergoing was not a romantic adventure, but an unpleasant ordeal. The prices of the strangely named foods were far beyond what he had expected, prices more suited to a purchase of the whole animal (whatever it was) from which the dish came. Conveying as best he could the suggestion that he was under doctor's orders, he chose the most moderately priced dish he could identify, to be followed by the most translatable sweet; and, since wine was essential for the drinking of David's health, he added a half-bottle of the cheapest Burgundy, telling himself, as he did so, that he was throwing money away, had been a fool to come, and that David's chance of inheriting anything worth while from his father was now remote. Perhaps he would be like his mother, sons often were, and Maggie was perfect. What would she say when he confessed how wickedly extravagant he had been? He would have to tell her; he had never had any secrets from Maggie.

Some, but not all, of his emotions were visible to Mr Wender and Miss Flyte. As Miss Flyte so well put it, the poor little man seemed like a fish out of water; and though neither of them had seen a fish out of water except on a fishmonger's slab, when it bore little resemblance to Mr Baker, they agreed laughingly that this was exactly what he did look like.

'Thought it was an A.B.C.,' suggested Mr Wender, 'and then found too late that it wasn't. Having a little difficulty with his French, isn't he?' This was when Mr Baker was deeply involved in the menu. 'Wonder what he'll make of the wine-list?'

'That's easy, darling. He just says "25", and there you are.'

'*I* may be, but he isn't. "25" is champagne. He won't be having champagne,' said Mr Wender, with the simple ostentation of one who was. 'Well, girlie, enjoying yourself?'

She nodded. 'I always say there's nothing like the dear old Savoy. It's sort of different, if you know what I mean.'

'Another glass of Pommery?'

'Just what Mother ordered,' laughed Miss Flyte, as he picked up the bottle.

All through his dinner Mr Wender's eyes invited the attention of his neighbours. The pretty girl he was entertaining, the lavishness of his entertainment, the forceful personality of the entertainer, were shared with them; even the people drinking cocktails in the lounge behind him could look enviously, admiringly, through the glass screen. Picking up the second bottle, he flicked an eye in that direction so as to include them, said 'Good God!' suddenly, and put the bottle down.

'What's the matter?' asked Miss Flyte.

His hand to his cheek, his head averted, he told her.

IV

It might have been Sir David Shawn Baker himself who lay back in his chair twirling his empty glass. He was at ease with the world. He saw himself taking Maggie to the Savoy on her next birthday. He imagined somebody asking him—not that anybody would—what he thought of the Ritz, and heard himself answering, 'Well, personally, I prefer the Savoy,' and perhaps something about 'my usual table'. He wondered why he had ever been frightened. The whole thing was so easy. You just decided where you would dine that night, went there, chose your dinner (and, of course, your bottle of wine) and dined. There was one trifling impediment which escaped him for the moment. Something which, in certain circumstances, might prevent full enjoyment of the evening. No, not Maggie's absence; she and David had been with him all the time; at first encouraging him, then, as the half-bottle did its work, sharing his pride and satisfaction. But there had been a moment, a little while back, just before he had begun that second glass of Burgundy, when the roseate cloud in his mind had suddenly darkened. It couldn't have been very important, because now everything was rosy again. Still, it was silly not to remember …

The folded bill on his plate caught his eyes. Ah, that was it. He couldn't pay the bill. All these potatoes and things added up surprisingly, and the waiter seemed to have made a mistake about the number of the Burgundy. 'My son, Sir David, will pay it next time he comes in.' Doubtless something could be arranged. He would give his mind to it directly. Just now it was resting with its feet up in a cosy warmth of contentment.

A big important-looking man was coming to his table. Probably—what was that fellow's name in that book?—Prince Florizel of Bohemia. Mr Baker was glad to see him.

'How *are* you?' said Mr Wender genially, holding out a large white hand.

Mr Baker, shaking it, said that he was very well. Never better, in fact.

'That's good. I noticed that you were dining alone. My friend,' he indicated her over his shoulder, and added confidentially, 'one of the most famous actresses from the Comédie Française, is most anxious to meet you. I wonder if you would give us the great pleasure of finishing your meal at our table?'

Mr Baker said that in fact he had finished it, three, or possibly four, minutes ago.

'Still,' smiled Mr Wender, in the persuasive voice which had launched a thousand companies, 'you will let us give you a glass of champagne, a cigar, and a cup of coffee.' He stopped a passing waiter and said, 'Sir Joseph is dining with me. Just put that,' he indicated the bill carelessly, 'on to mine.' He bowed to Mr Baker. 'If you will give me that great pleasure?'

Mr Baker made it clear that he was glad—in a sense, relieved—to give it to him.

'And now,' said Mr Wender, helping his guest up, 'we will join Mademoiselle de—but no. For reasons which you will understand she wishes to remain incognito while in London. By the way, she talks English perfectly—unless, of course, you insist on conversing with her in her own language.' He waited a moment in case Mr Baker insisted, and went on, 'Should it be necessary to refer to her by name I am permitted to call her Lady Witterman. You won't mind my introducing you as Sir Joseph?'

(Undoubtedly Prince Florizel of Bohemia.)

'Well, actually, my name is—'

Mr Wender waggled a genial hand.

'No names, no pack-drill, as we used to say in the Guards.'

(Or the Duke of Westminster?)

They came, arm-in-arm, to the table by the glass screen.

'This, darling,' said Mr Wender, 'is Sir Joseph.'

Miss Flyte nodded sulkily.

'A glass of Pommery, Sir Joseph?'

Mr Baker wondered if champagne went well with Burgundy, and didn't see why it shouldn't try.

'Your very good health. My dear, we must drink Sir Joseph's health.'

Miss Flyte, her mouth still sullen, raised her glass to Mr Baker. Then, seeing something in his insignificant face, something which she didn't see in the faces of the men who made love to her, she gave him a sudden warming smile, and said, 'All the best.'

'The same to you,' said Mr Baker, 'both of you,' he explained, remembering that the Duke was paying his bill. But, as he drank, he was drinking to Maggie and David. He was drinking their healths in champagne. Real champagne. Pommery. What an evening!

The Pommery seemed to like the Burgundy. It reminded the Burgundy of a very funny thing which their lessor knew about and nobody else did. That was what made it so funny. That was what made Mr Baker laugh so surprisingly.

'Yes?' said Mr Wender encouragingly. His eyes went round again to the doorway.

'What,' Mr Baker invited them to tell him, 'do they know of England who only England know?'

'What?' wondered Miss Flyte, assuming that it was a riddle.

'That wasn't what I said,' he explained with a happy smile. 'What I said was nobody knows what happened this morning. Now why does nobody know what happened this morning? Because it's a profound secret.'

'What did happen?' asked Miss Flyte.

'When I say nobody, I mean nobody-but-three. No,' said Mr Baker, working it out, 'four. Probably five. Or six or seven. Things get about. Have you ever,' he asked on a different note, 'come across Sir David Shawn Baker in Paris or elsewhere?'

'I seem to have heard of him,' said Miss Flyte, feeling that it was expected of her. 'I've never actually met him.'

'I have. Just for a moment.'

'What's he like?'

Mr Baker reflected for a little.

'On the short side,' he said, summing it up.

Mr Wender rose to his feet. One felt that he had been waiting for this moment. Three people in evening dress were coming in. The big woman who led the way, magnificently under-gowned and over-jewelled, glanced at Mr Wender, stood for a moment in surprise, committed Miss Flyte and Mr Baker to memory, and inclined her head to Mr Wender's bow. The party moved on. Mr Wender sat down and poured himself out the rest of the champagne. 'I think that's all right,' he murmured, gulping it down.

The waiter brought the bill. Mr Wender put a £10 note on the plate.

'Look, girlie,' he said, 'I think I'll just go and say a word to those people, while you powder your nose. I'll meet you both outside.'

They all got up. Mr Baker, surprised to find that he could walk, not only effectively but with a certain dignity, followed Miss Flyte out. She turned to him as soon as they were through the doorway.

'Hat and coat!' she snapped. 'Quick!' She indicated the cloak-room. Then, as soon as he was ready, 'Come on!'

'But what about Mr—er—'

'Come on!' She led the way. 'Ask for a taxi. Tell him Victoria.'

Completely bewildered, Mr Baker, as so often before in his life, obeyed instructions. As he took his place in the taxi beside her he was still saying, 'What about Mr—er—'

'To hell with him!' said Miss Flyte bitterly. 'Thinking he was going to get away with *that*!'

V

The fresh air through the open window was doing Mr Baker good. He still wondered why he was there, but now he felt benevolently and intelligently interested in his position.

'Married men!' said Miss Flyte. 'They make me sick.' Mr Baker waited for further details.

'He asks me to have dinner with him. Well, why shouldn't I have dinner with him? What else did he think he was going to get? Not bloody likely. (That's a quotation, ducky, you needn't look shocked.) And then suddenly there's his darling wife in the lounge, plastered with Koh-i-noors and looking like the Queen of Sheba's Aunt Rachel. He's told her, see, that he's dining with Sir Joseph Wotsit so's to discuss a—what's that thing men like that discuss, financiers I mean?'

'Well, they might discuss so many things. Would it be a merger?'

'Something like that. So now when she comes in and sees him— well, am I going to look like I'm discussing a merger with darling hubby? So I've got to be explained somehow, see? Well, he's a quick thinker, I will say that for him. Well, you see, we'd noticed you at your table—"I wonder who that nice-looking man is," I said, "seems sort of lonely"—I'd just passed the remark, not thinking any more of it, so now he gets his idea. Because once you're at our table, he's all right. There he is, dining with Sir Joseph, and if Sir Joseph brings his wife along, well he can't help it, can he? So he gets up and bows to her—don't suppose you noticed, you were telling me about that secret of yours—and then goes up to her table and says, all smiles and handwash, I can just hear him saying it, "Sir Joseph brought the wife along, used to be his secretary, knows all the ins and outs of the business; well, I must be getting along, got to get back to his flat, he's left some papers behind; how are you, John, how are you, Mary, nice of you to look after the wife while I'm so busy." Gah! It makes me sick. I'm as good as she is, aren't I?'

'But not as married to him as she is,' said Mr Baker mildly.

'Who said I was, and who wants to be? He asked me to come out with him, didn't he? I didn't ask *him*. What's it matter to *me* what his wife thinks? If he couldn't stand up to her, he oughtn't to of asked me. How did I know he had a wife at all? What would he of thought if I'd said, "Don't look now but there's my husband over there, you'd better pretend to be the Archbishop of Canterbury"? What sort of a way is that of having a nice little dinner together?'

Mr Baker didn't feel competent to answer any of these questions, nor did he suppose that an answer was expected. All that mattered was that he had dined at the Savoy and had drunk David's health in Burgundy and champagne. Now he was sitting in a taxi with an extremely pretty girl. All this on David's birthday. Miss Flyte seemed to remember suddenly that he was there, and that she had certain obligations towards him.

'Victoria all right for you?' she asked.

'Yes. Oh, yes.' He looked at his watch. 'Catch my train, nicely.'

'I'm on the District. Ealing. D'you know that part?'

'No.'

'Retired Indians mostly. You know what I mean. Nice part, near the Common where we are. Married, I suppose?'

'Yes.' She knew by the way he said it that he was in love with his wife.

'What I said about married men making me sick, of course I didn't mean you.'

'I'm sure you wouldn't have said so to me, even if I had.'

'I just say anything that comes into my head when I'm angry, and if there's one thing that makes me angry, it's bad manners. What's your real name when you aren't Sir Joseph?'

He laughed and said, 'Baker.'

'Mr Baker,' she said, looking at him, pondering the name and its owner. 'Fancy! If it hadn't been for that wife of his we should never have met. Seems funny, doesn't it? What was that secret you were telling me?'

He coughed apologetically.

'I'm afraid I was a little—I must have been—it's the first time I've ever drunk champagne. And I'd already had half a bottle of Burgundy.'

'I say, you *were* going it! What will Mrs Baker say when you tell her?'

'She wanted me to have a good dinner, because, you see,, she—we—we had a son early this morning.'

'First?'

'Yes.'

'Was that the secret?'

'Yes. I didn't tell them at the office, because I thought—well, it was something rather—I know this sounds silly—'

'I shan't laugh.'

'Well, sort of sacred between Maggie and me. Just for to-day. I didn't want jokes about it.'

'And now you've told me?'

'Yes, but that's different somehow.'

She looked at him wonderingly.

'How long have you been married?'

'Ten years.'

'What are you calling him?'

'David Alistair Shawn,' said Mr Baker shyly. 'Shawn was his mother's name.'

The taximan opened the window behind him, and said, 'Which line?'

'Main line,' said Miss Flyte, and to her companion, 'I'll pay.'

'No, no,' he protested. 'You forget, I didn't pay for my dinner.'

'D'you mean *he* paid?' Miss Flyte laughed happily. 'Well, that's a good one. That's cheered me up a lot. All the same, I'm going to pay the taxi, and you can put half a crown in David's money-box specially for me. See?'

'Oh, that *is* kind—'

She leant across to him suddenly and kissed him on the cheek. 'And that's for yourself. Because you're different from all the others. See?'

The taxi drew up at the station, and they got out.

VI

Mr Baker was happy. He'd done it. He had dined where he had said he would, he had toasted David in champagne, and it hadn't cost him a penny. His son, he felt modestly, could be proud of him. The Bakers were not to be despised. When put to it, they could hold their own with the best in the land.

What a story to tell Maggie!

Except for that last moment. That, he felt instinctively, must remain untold. The fragrant memory of that touching, unexpected kiss was for himself alone. The thought of keeping anything from Maggie made him a little uneasy, but he assured himself that men and women must always have secrets from each other. When, for instance, Sir David Shawn Baker was Ambassador in Paris, there would be many matters which he would not confide to his wife.

The Dear, Dead Past

(1948)

I

Mr Cedric Watherston (Watherston and Reeves, Solicitors), a stout, old-young man of forty, sat at his office table, knitting. He was not a good knitter, but he was proud of the fact that he could knit at all. He had learnt when a prisoner-of-war in 1917, having walked straight into a German trench on his first journey up the line; and with the passage of years the circumstance of his capture had also become, in some odd way, a matter for pride. He liked sentences which began 'I remember when I was a prisoner in Holzminden', and would go a long way to encourage them. When a client was announced he put the ball of wool, the needles, and the unfinished sock in the top left-hand drawer, drew a bunch of keys on the end of a chain from his right-hand pocket, locked the drawer, returned the keys, smoothed his hair with both hands, and waited for the visitor to be shown in.

'Sir Vernon Filmer.'

Mr Watherston rose to shake hands with one of his most distinguished clients. He would shake hands again with him when the interview was over. He seemed to like shaking hands.

'Glad to see you, Sir Vernon. You don't often give us the pleasure. On no unpleasant business, I trust?'

Sir Vernon did not look as if he were glad to see Mr Watherston. He was a tall, fair, cold man, with pale blue eyes, a prominent nose, and a small prim mouth. He was one of those natural politicians who are always conveniently there when Ministerial posts are being given out. If there were to be ten Knighthoods on New Year's Day for what could only be described as 'public services', and nine had been decided upon, his name would come irresistibly to the mind for the tenth place. It might be difficult to think of a reason why Vernon Filmer should have a Knighthood or a seat in the Cabinet, but it was almost impossible to think of a reason why he shouldn't; and that goes a long way in politics.

'Cigarette?'

Sir Vernon waved it away. Mr Watherston lit one for himself, leant back in his chair, remembered to put his finger-tips together, and said, 'Well?'

'I am being blackmailed.'

'Dear, dear, we must do something about that,' said Mr Watherston with an exaggerated calm which hid most of the emotions. Surprise was the least of them, for he had a dislike of politicians.

'That is naturally what I am expecting.'

Mr Watherston tried over a few sentences in his mind until he got the right opening.

'Blackmail,' he said delicately, 'implies the previous commission, or alleged commission, of some offence. Offences can be classified as offences against the Law, offences against morality, and offences against the social code. Perhaps, in this case, one should add political offences. Which class or classes of offence, Sir Vernon, does the threatened exposure allege?'

'Legal,' said Sir Vernon; adding primly, 'I have nothing whatever on my conscience.'

Yes, yes, thought Mr Watherston, but your conscience must be in pretty good training by now, and it is precisely the legal offence which is most serious to a lawyer.

'To put it frankly, then, Sir Vernon, the blackmailer is threatening to reveal some action of yours which is punishable by law; an indictable offence?'

'Yes. To put it with greater accuracy, if the truth had come out at the time, I might have been charged, but need not necessarily have been convicted. I should think that to-day there was no possibility of conviction.'

'When did this happen?'

'Nearly thirty years ago. 1909, to be exact.'

'Ah! So it is the social and political consequences which really matter to-day?'

'Obviously. As they did, to an overwhelming extent, at the time. Do you not think it would be illuminating if I told you about it?'

Mr Watherston held up a hasty hand. He had had no experience of blackmail, and he disliked the idea of being accessory after the fact to an apparently undiscovered crime. His mind wandered vaguely back to 1909, trying to think of the sort of contemporary illegalities in which Sir Vernon, a young man of twenty-two, might have been mixed up. Having himself been a boy of twelve at the time, he came to no conclusion.

'Sir Vernon,' he said. 'It will be distressing for you to confide this story to anyone. To have to make a needless confession of it would be intolerable. Let us consider the matter on general lines for the moment. There are three ways of dealing with a blackmailer. The first is to submit to his demands.'

Sir Vernon indicated what he thought of that.

'The second is to prosecute him. As you know, this can be done anonymously.'

Sir Vernon gave another short, unpleasant and obviously sarcastic laugh.

'Under the disarming soubriquet of Mr X,' the solicitor went on, unperturbed. 'There is a pleasant legal fiction that nobody ever gets to know who Mr X is. In the case of a public personality like yourself, this legal fiction is even more amusing than most legal fictions. Prosecution means complete publicity.'

'Of course.'

'The only remaining method is to deal with the blackmailer out of court. I could pay his demands for you; I could instruct the prosecution for you; but frankly, Sir Vernon, I am not competent to get the better of a scoundrel whether by negotiation, threat or personal violence.' He let this sink in for a moment, and then added, 'Fortunately I know the man who is.'

'Private detective, or shady solicitor? I have no use for either.'

'Solicitor. A shady solicitor in the sense that he usually acts for the submerged classes, but entirely loyal to his clients, whether prostitutes or Prime Ministers. And a very able man.'

'You know him personally?'

'Oh, yes. A most pleasant fellow. The fortunes of war threw us together at Holzminden, where we happened to be prisoners.'

'H'm,' said Sir Vernon doubtfully.

'I understand your dislike of confiding in a stranger. Perhaps I should have added that he has very strong feelings about the detestable crime of blackmail. It is the one charge which he has always refused to defend in Court—which is more than can be said for the whole of the Bar. To get the better of a blackmailer he would go to the extreme length of his purse, his time, and—the Law.'

There was a short silence.

'Your firm,' said Sir Vernon pompously, 'has been my legal adviser for many years, Mr Watherston. I come to it now for advice, and that is its considered advice?'

'Yes.'

'Very well. I agree to accept its advice. I had better see this fellow in my own house at, say, nine o'clock this evening. Will you arrange that?'

Mr Watherston made a note, saying, 'His name is Scroope.' He meditated a small but well-tried joke about 'unscrupulous', looked up into Sir Vernon's face, and decided that it would not be helpful. He got up and held out his hand.

'Perhaps you will let me know how the matter goes on. And if there is anything else I can do, Sir Vernon—'

They shook hands and went to the door together.

'Cold fish,' thought Mr Watherston, as he returned to his table. 'One can't help disliking him. I wonder what he did.'

He picked up the telephone. Afterwards, there being nothing else to do, he went back to his knitting.

II

Being asked by an interviewer to what he attributed his success in life, Mr Scroope replied, 'My eyebrows.' These had a natural quirk which seemed to express a good-tempered amusement with the world, and to admit his companion of the moment to an equal share in that amusement. 'You and I,' they seemed to say, '*we* know.' Whether the eyebrows had conformed to the man, or the man, subconsciously or deliberately, to the eyebrows, need not be considered. They were now all one piece. It is doubtful if anybody had ever had a private joke with Sir Vernon, nor was he the man to wish to be on confidential terms with anyone less important than himself, least of all a shady solicitor; but even he recognized the eyebrows as evidence of a knowledge of the world. Mr Scroope obviously knew his way about.

'A cigar, thanks,' said Mr Scroope. 'Nothing to drink. Now then, Sir Vernon, Watherston tells me that you are being blackmailed. Who told *you*?'

'I don't understand,' said Sir Vernon coldly.

'Dammit, one doesn't wake up in the morning and say, "I've a sort of feeling that there are blackmailers about." Something must have given you the idea.'

'Naturally I had a letter.'

'Why naturally? You might have had a telephone message. Or,' went on Mr Scroope, enjoying himself, 'a dark but exotic lady in whose toils you were entangled might have—Is that the letter?'

Sir Vernon released it, saying, 'It came this morning through the post.'

'H'm. Typed. Signed "Well Wisher". Humorous. D'you know who wrote it?'

'Not with any certainty.'

'Five hundred pounds in pound notes on Saturday as a guarantee of good faith, followed by five hundred every quarter-day. Sounds as if he wanted to get married. Well, that gives us six weeks before the second payment. Six weeks in which to think of something.'

'You suggest that I should pay the first five hundred?'

'Oh, certainly. At least, *you* won't, I will. We'll keep you out of it.'

'Read the rest of the letter.'

'I have. You are given till Saturday to get the money; you are to communicate with nobody; you are to have your car waiting outside your door on Saturday morning, ready to drive yourself to a *rendezvous* which will be given you by letter just before you start. A cautious gentleman.'

'Perhaps you are not aware that I am lunching at Chequers on Saturday?'

'Nobody tells me anything,' said Mr Scroope sadly. 'But why shouldn't you? The food's quite good, I hear. And who could give you a better alibi than the Prime Minister?'

'You propose to keep the *rendezvous* yourself?'

'As Sir Vernon Filmer? Do I look like it? But I dare say I can find somebody who will pass for you at a distance. All you'll be asked to do, I fancy, is to leave the money in a certain spot, where he will pick it up afterwards. He's giving nothing away. Now then, he says, "I have a letter written on board the *Ladybird* in September, 1909. Don't tell me you've forgotten it."' He looked up. 'Have you forgotten it?'

'No.'

'Right. Then you'd better tell me.'

There were three of them on the *Ladybird* on that summer afternoon: Robert Hayforth the owner, Filmer, and a local hand called Towers. They had been fishing close inshore. Hayforth, a powerful and devoted swimmer, had suggested a bathe. The wind was freshening, the sea uninviting now, and Filmer stayed on board. Hayforth, whose idea of a swim was half a mile out and half a mile back, had been gone about ten minutes, when suddenly—

'He came sidling up to me, his right hand behind his back. I'd never liked him, nobody in the place did, but he was a useful man in a boat, and Hayforth often took him on. He had a bottle in his hand, and he was holding it like a club. He—he accused me of'— Sir Vernon's face could still show disgust at the idea—'"messing about with his wife".'

'Were you?'

Sir Vernon looked at him contemptuously, and went on, 'I asked him what the devil he was talking about. I thought he was drunk. He said that when he had finished with me I'd have the sort of face that nobody's girl would want to mess about with. It was horrible. Such a foul weapon, and he was much more powerful than I. Hayforth was out of sight and hailing distance. I was at the man's mercy. It was his life or mine. I saw red.'

He poured himself out a brandy and swallowed it quickly. In another moment, thought Scroope, all his past life will flash before his eyes. Why must politicians always talk in clichés?

'And you killed him. How?'

'I don't know to this day how I did it. I seemed to be endowed with superhuman strength. Fear, I suppose, and furious indignation at that loathsome weapon.'

'You killed him, and you went on killing him. Is that right?'

'Yes.'

'And when you had finished, it didn't look like self-defence, it looked like deliberate, premeditated, brutal murder. Is that right?'

'Yes, but it wasn't.'

'It's what things look like which matter to the Law. Well, and then Hayforth yelled "Ship ahoy!" from under the starboard counter or whatever you call it, and you helped him on board, and he saw the body and said, "Lawks a mussy, what's all this?" And you told him. And he agreed to help you. Is that right?'

'Agreed on conditions.'

'Ah, yes, now I'm seeing it. That letter was to him. Exonerating him and admitting sole responsibility. Why a letter? Couldn't he trust you?'

'If anything had happened to me, and the body had been washed up later—'

'It would have been damned awkward for him. Because, stop me if I'm wrong, *he* was the man who had been messing about.'

'Yes. I had had no idea of it, but I suppose there were other people who had guessed.'

'So, when he had got the letter safely in his pocket, you put out to sea—the wind was freshening, you said—and it sounded sufficiently plausible to say that Towers had been washed overboard. No attempt to save him?'

'It blew up into a gale, we didn't pick up our moorings until three o'clock next morning; we put the accident at just after midnight. In the dark, in that weather, only two of us to work the boat, what could we have done? We nearly followed him as it was. I never expected to see land again.'

'Convincing. And no suspicions by anybody?'

'None that I heard of. He was a thorough-paced rascal. Nobody missed him.'

'Not even his wife?'

'She least of all.' Sir Vernon cleared his throat and added, 'I should explain that my whole career was in the balance at this time, and that I had no other course open to me. I had just left Oxford with unusually brilliant prospects—'

'Yes, well, that's for the Archangel Gabriel or somebody. All that matters now is that politicians stand to be shot at, and here's some good ammunition.' He picked up the letter. 'D'you think this is Hayforth?'

'It might be, of course. Equally, I suppose, he might be dead, and somebody might have found my letter among his papers. I lost sight of him in the war, and haven't heard of him since.'

'That sort of man?'

'Obviously not in those days, or he wouldn't have been my friend. But he was always a reckless fellow, and might have been knocked about by the war, have fallen on hard times, and slowly sunk to— this. The war,' said Sir Vernon, who had fortunately missed it, 'did not improve people's characters.'

'That also can be discussed with Gabriel. Is there anything in this letter which indicates knowledge not contained in your letter to Hayforth?'

'I don't think so.'

'For instance, why should it be taken for granted that you can drive your own car? Lots of people can't.'

For the first time that evening Sir Vernon looked at Scroope with respect.

'That's true,' he said thoughtfully.

'Were you driving a car at this time?'

'My wife gave me a Rolls as a wedding-present a few months later.'

'I congratulate you. Driven Hayforth in it?'

'Probably. I saw something of him up to the war.'

Scroope got up and threw the end of his cigar into the fire.

'Obviously we must find the man first. I shall sleep here on Friday night, so as to be with you when your instructions come.' He took a note-book and pencil from his pocket. 'Turn your head to one side, I want the profile.' He began to draw. 'About five feet eleven inches, aren't you? I think I've got just the man. Muffled and goggled, of course, which is what anyone would be who was keeping a date with a blackmailer. My man—Dean is his name—will come in the back way at eight o'clock on Saturday morning. With false moustache. This is going to be fun. There, that's not bad.' He held the drawing up and admired it. 'Thank God, it's money that he's after.'

'What else are blackmailers ever after?' asked Sir Vernon contemptuously.

'Seats in the Cabinet,' said Mr Scroope. 'The way I'm going to work, that would have made it more difficult.'

III

At eight-thirty on Saturday morning Sir Vernon Filmer came out of his front door and walked across to his garage. It was a chilly February morning, and even for that short distance he thought it well to wear a thick, fawn travelling coat and a check cap. He brought his car round to the front door and left it there. Mr Scroope and breakfast were waiting for him in the morning-room. The former had already introduced himself to the latter.

'Now then,' he said, his mouth full of omelette, 'let's get down to it. You are to be at the fifth milestone between Wellborough and Chiselton at twelve-thirty. You say you know the road. How?'

'It was near Chiselton that Hayforth kept his boat.'

'Good. How long would it take you to get there?'

'Three hours.'

'Then Dean must take three hours. We'll have him in directly, and you can show him the place on the map. What's the country like?'

'Absolutely flat. No houses, no trees, no possibility of concealment, as I remember. A long, almost straight road of ten or twelve miles.'

'You hide the money behind the milestone—nothing elaborate, just enough not to catch the eye of a passer-by. Then you drive on, turning off at Chiselton and coming back to London another way. Obviously he'll be a little way behind you up to the milestone. He may be outside the house now—he was in London last night to post the letter—in which case he'll follow you down. Well, it doesn't matter, but we're taking no risks. Dean in your coat and cap will be good enough for him. So that's that.'

Sir Vernon had picked up the letter again, and was studying it.

'You talk of "him" all the time,' he said. 'Does it not occur to you that it is more likely to be the work of a gang?'

'With a master-mind at the centre of the spider's web?' said Mr Scroope hopefully.

'You notice he says that one of his men will be watching me at this end, one will be at Chiselton to see that I turn off there, one will collect the money for him, and he himself—'

'That's four; and with Moriarty and the Ace of Spades and Red Anna we have seven. I must build up my strength. I must have another piece of toast.'

'I gather,' said Sir Vernon coldly, 'that you think otherwise.'

Scroope pushed the toast away, and spoke seriously.

'I'll tell you what I think,' he said, 'and then I'll tell you my plans. You're paying for this treat, and you're entitled to know. I think that if two young men go out in a boat for a summer afternoon's off-shore fishing and bathing, they will not be wearing oilskins. I think that if one of them has just had a desperate fight for his life, any letter which he writes immediately after, with a shaking hand and under the stress of great emotion, will be uncharacteristic and only just legible. I think that if a small boat, manned by two people in flannels, is fighting a gale for eight hours, the occupants will not merely be wet, but soaked literally to the skin. And I think that after it's all over, and now that the unexpected storm has removed all possibility of suspicion, Mr Robert Hayforth will find a piece of sodden paper in his pocket with not a single decipherable word on it, will wonder what the devil it is, and then throw it away with a laugh at the ridiculous caution which inspired it. What that piece of paper would have looked like thirty years later baffles the imagination. In short, Sir Vernon, you may be quite certain that the blackmailer is Hayforth himself, and that it is only his word against yours.'

Sir Vernon permitted himself a little enthusiasm.

'But that is most satisfactory, Mr Scroope. You relieve my mind considerably.'

'Yes, but even so he can be extremely mischievous. So, since black-mailers are better out of action, I propose, with your financial assistance, to put him out of action.'

'Now that we know who he is—'

'We don't. We only know who he was; a face and a name of thirty years ago. That doesn't help. But this letter shows that he is sticking to familiar ground. It is probable that he is living in the district, and almost certain that he has a car. Ever studied History?'

'I got a First in History in my Final Schools at Oxford,' said Sir Vernon, obviously surprised that this was not generally known.

'Pooh, I don't mean that sort of dead-alive History. Real History. Criminal History. There is no variation of crime which a criminal has not already employed, no method of detection which has not previously found him out. If you know History, you know everything. Ever studied the Lindbergh case?'

There was no need to wait for an answer, Sir Vernon's delicate shrug had given it.

'What it came to in the end was that they knew all about the man except who he was. However, he had the ransom notes—numbers taken, of course—and one day he would use them. That was their only hope of getting him. But how? By the time a tradesman has identified the note he has forgotten who gave it to him, and anyway the man has gone. So what? Every gasolene station in the neighbourhood was given a list of the notes, and told to write down secretly on the back of any ten-dollar bill paid in exchange for gas, the number of the car which was filled. Then the list of ransom notes could be consulted at leisure in the evening. Simple. And so, after weeks of waiting, they got him.'

'Most ingenious. And you have taken the numbers of the notes?'

'Of course. And I shall go down to Wellborough this afternoon and make arrangements. Not being official it will cost money. But by the time we've made the second payment to Hayforth, I shall know what he's calling himself and where he lives. I'll tell you something else. He says that he will give you the second *rendezvous* on March 25th, and that it will be in an entirely different part of the country. It won't. If his plan works successfully to-day, as I mean it to do, he will repeat it exactly. It leaves you just as uncertain until the last moment, and saves him the trouble of looking for an equally convenient place. He's clever—but so am I.'

'And when you've found him, what then?'

'Then,' said Mr Scroope with a happy, anticipatory smile, 'the real fun begins.'

IV

When Mr Reginald Hastings was arrested for possessing and uttering forged notes he did what all intelligent prisoners do, he sent for Mr Scroope. Luckily Mr Scroope was able to attend him.

'Well,' said Mr Scroope, twinkling at him, 'what's the story, Mr Hastings?' He looked at the man with interest, summed him up as a gentleman gone to the bad, than which nothing was worse, and offered him a cigarette.

'Thanks. I've been arrested, God knows why, for—'

'Yes, I know the police story, now I want to know yours.'

'I swear to you that I am—'

'—absolutely innocent. Naturally. But we still need a story to explain why a quantity of forged notes was found in your safe, and why several others which had been passed in the neighbourhood were traced to you. What is that story?'

'Just that. I know nothing about them. They were planted on me.'

'By whom?'

'God knows. Some enemy, I suppose.'

'Got a lot of enemies like that?'

'Anyone who knocks about the world makes enemies.'

'No particular one in your mind?'

'No.'

'I see. What about the notes in circulation which have been through your hands?'

'They must have gone through many hands. Why pick on me?'

'Obviously because you had such a large store in your safe from which to draw. It isn't good enough, Mr Hastings, is it? An enemy might plant forged notes in your safe, but he couldn't force you to circulate them. The ordinary chances of circulation might pass a few forged notes through your hands, but it wouldn't fill your safe with them. We want a better story than that.'

'I can't tell you anything better than the truth.'

'The truth being that you have no idea how these particular notes got into your safe?'

'None. It's a complete mystery to me.'

'Then,' said Mr Scroope politely, 'I will wish you good morning.' He got up. 'Just one word of advice, if I may. The story which you will be telling to some other solicitor need not be true; but it must sound sufficiently like the truth to allow him a temporary hallucination that it was possible.' He held out his hand with a smile. 'Good luck to your invention.'

Mr Reginald Hastings waved the hand away.

'Wait,' he said, and gnawed his forefinger.

'Thinking?' asked Scroope.

'You may as well have it. I found the damned things.'

'That's better. That's much better. Where?'

'Oh, hidden under a stone somewhere.'

'You know, I don't think that that will quite carry conviction— using the word "conviction" in its less technical sense, of course. It must have been rather a moment in your life when you found such a large packet of notes. You would be expected to remember the historic spot.'

'Oh, well, if you want the exact place, it was behind the fifth milestone on the Wellborough–Chiselton road.'

'You counted—and remembered?'

The man who called himself Reginald Hastings looked up angrily.

'What the devil do you mean? It said "Wellborough, 5 miles", didn't it? Naturally I noticed.'

'You were looking behind milestones for something?'

'I happened to sit down there. Convenient to lean against for a few minutes. I noticed that the ground was disturbed, and, idly, as anyone would, investigated, and—'

'And said, "Hallo, what's this?"—'

'Exactly.'

'And what was it?'

'A parcel of pound notes. Damned odd, I thought.'

'Well, anyway, you counted those. How many?'

'Five hundred, in packets of a hundred.'

'And nine hundred and fifty were found in your safe six weeks later. Nobody would think anything of it if they had been rabbits; but Treasury notes—'

'I must have counted wrong. Perhaps it was a thousand.'

'And so, five hundred or a thousand, and not minding which, you decided to steal them?'

'What's that?'

'You wish to plead guilty to an alternative charge of stealing by finding. Is that right?'

Mr Reginald Hastings gnawed his forefinger again.

'Right!' he said suddenly. 'I stole them. Like that. Finding. That's not very serious, is it? Well, now you've got the truth.'

'At least we're getting on. So, having found them accidentally, you decided to say nothing about them, stuffed them in your pocket, and drove off with them?'

'That's right.'

'Fill up with petrol anywhere on the way home, paying with one of the notes?'

'No,' said the man, surprised. 'I'd filled up before I started. Why?'

'I just wondered why a man, driving along the Wellborough-Chiselton road on a cold and frosty morning, should stop at precisely the fifth milestone, lean against it rather than against the cushions of his car, fiddle about behind it, and—'

The man calling himself Reginald Hastings jumped to his feet, and said angrily, 'What's all this? You trying to trap me?'

'I'm trying to do,' said Scroope mildly, 'what Counsel for the Prosecution will do much more thoroughly. Because it is necessary for you to know what you will be up against.'

'Sorry. I see the point; but naturally'—he gave an awkward little laugh—'I'm a bit upset about the whole thing. But I do absolutely swear, and it's Gospel truth, that I didn't know that the notes were forged, and that I found them precisely where I said I did.'

'Knowing that they would be there?'

'I've told you my story, and I'm sticking to it. I *happened* to find them. Let them make what they bloody well like of that. It's all they're going to get.'

'Oh, come, we must give them a little more. They know now that you happened to find them, they know where you happened to find them, what about telling them when you happened to find them?'

'When?'

'Take your time—When?'

'I can't remember the exact date. Does it matter?'

'Well, it depends which date you can't remember.'

Mr Reginald Hastings wiped his forehead with the back of his hand, and said, 'I haven't the vaguest idea what you're talking about.'

'I want the date which you can't exactly remember, when you got out of your car, leant against the fifth milestone, and accidentally found a packet of notes. Just a rough guess.'

'Roughly about the first week in February. Satisfied?'

'Quite. The first forged note which came to hand was paid to the Lion Garage at Chiselton on February 18th. So that fits nicely. Now what about the second date? When you again got out of your car, leant against the fifth milestone, and accidentally found a second packet of notes.'

Mr Reginald Hastings licked his lips and said, 'What makes you think I did that?'

'Two parcels were found in your safe. One, opened, contained about four hundred and fifty forged notes. The other, unopened—or, possibly, opened, examined, and tied up again—contained five hundred.'

'Wait a moment.'

'No hurry.'

'I can explain that. It's all coming back to me. The parcel which I found—'

'In the first week in February?'

'Yes. It was really two parcels, done up together. I counted the top one and it was £500, which was what made me say five hundred just now. I was forgetting for the moment about the other parcel, which I didn't open. Obviously there was another five hundred in that. Making the thousand as you were saying.' He drew the back of his hand across his forehead again and added, 'Silly of me.'

'Not at all. Very natural. Then all that we have left to explain,' said Mr Scroope cheerfully, 'is why the inner wrapper of the second parcel was a double sheet of the *Western Morning News* dated March 24th.'

'I—I—'

'You are about to tell me that on March 25th you suddenly decided to repack the second parcel in the previous day's paper; explaining that, as you live on the East Coast, you preserve your mental balance by taking in the *Western Morning News*. Tell me, by all means, Mr Hastings, I have a romantic nature; but don't tell twelve hard-headed British jurymen.'

Robert Hayforth banged the table with his hand, and cried, 'God damn and blast him, he's framed me!'

'Who?'

'The snivelling devil!'

'Who is sniveller? Who is he?' murmured Mr Scroope to himself.

'The Right Honourable Sir Vernon Filmer.' He dragged the words out sneeringly. 'All right, you've got it. It was hush money. He killed a man, murdered him; that's your—Right Honourable. You want me to tell the truth in Court. Right, I'll tell it—and we'll go down together.'

Mr Scroope got up.

'You must arrange that as you please, Mr Hastings, with whatever solicitor you engage. I must tell you now that I have made it an inexorable rule never to defend blackmail cases. On the other hand, of course, everything which you have told me is in the strictest confidence, and I now fade out of the case entirely. But I will just warn you in parting that the penalty for blackmail is, next to that for murder, the severest known to the Law. Any written evidence which you may have had against Sir Vernon Filmer will be in possession of the police, and you will not be permitted to use it. An unsupported accusation of murder made in defence against the present charge would only make your case worse and your punishment more severe. If you take my unprofessional advice, you will plead "Not Guilty" to the present charge, give no evidence, and leave it to your Counsel to suggest that in some undefined way you are the innocent victim of a conspiracy.'

He picked up his hat and went to the door.

'Oh, by the way,' he added, 'if it gets about, though I don't see why it should, that I declined this case, you will not be prejudiced.' The eyebrows went up in that humorous quirk of his. 'It may even do you good. There is an absurd legend in legal circles that I only defend the guilty.'

V

Mr Watherston returned his keys to his pocket, picked up the telephone, and said, 'Watherston here.'

'Busy?'

'Just turning the heel.'

There was a laugh, and the voice said, 'Anyone listening in?'

'My dear fellow!'

'Right. Then I thought you would like to know that your friend is relieved of all anxiety for five years.'

'Five years! Or would it be four?'

'Well, it might be four.'

'Fancy! I do congratulate you. I was reading an interesting case this morning, forging and uttering and all that sort of thing, and oddly enough—but, of course, it's only a coincidence.'

'I expect so. A respectable family lawyer shouldn't read criminal cases.'

'It just caught the eye. Tell me, where did you get the—er—ground-bait from, if I am not overrating your ingenuity?'

'Legacy from an old case.'

'Did you get him off?'

'Of course. But he's a reformed character now.'

'Says he and says you.'

'I never defend the same man twice.'

'Ah, then he would have to be. Going back a little, what do you think will happen at the end of the five, or possibly four years?'

'That's going forward a little, isn't it? Leave the future to take care of itself. But if you want my personal opinion—'

'I should value it highly.'

'I think that you will lose a distinguished client, and the country a distinguished servant. Quite suddenly.'

'Ah! I was fearing the same thing myself.' Mr Watherston chuckled. 'You know, you're a very naughty man. Here was a perfectly ordinary case of blackmail, such as must be almost normal procedure in the Cabinet, and there is hardly a crime in the calendar which you have not committed, in order to bring the blackmailer to Justice. If,' he added, 'you know what I mean by justice.'

'Well, you see,' the voice said apologetically, 'I don't *like* black-mailers.'

'Neither do I.'

'Come to that, I don't like Sir Vernon Filmer.'

'How right you are,' said Mr Watherston cheerfully.

A.V. and R.V.

(1948)

I

'Mummy!' said Pamela on the last Sunday afternoon of the holidays.

'Yes, dear?'

'It *is* true that everything in the Bible's true, isn't it?'

Mrs Haverstock, a little surprised, looked up from her knitting.

'Darling! What a question to ask!'

'Yes, but *is* it?'

'Well, of course, darling! It was just that it was such a funny question to ask. The Bible is God's Word.' Uncertain whether to be shocked or amused, she added, 'You didn't think that God would tell *lies*?'

'You mean He wrote it Himself?'

'Pamela, dear, you aren't a little girl now, you're growing up. You oughtn't to ask these silly questions.'

'Why is it silly what I asked?'

'Darling, you were taught all these things in the nursery by Nanny and me, you had everything explained to you by Mr Donkin at the Children's Afternoon Services, you go to church every Sunday, you were actually top of your scripture class this term—Daddy was very pleased about that—and Miss Waters was talking to me only the other day about your taking Confirmation next Easter. And now you ask me if God wrote His own Book!'

'Did He, Mummy?'

'Yes, dear, of course,' said Mrs Haverstock sharply. She went on with her knitting in silence for a little, and then, feeling that some modification of this was needed, said, 'When Daddy writes letters at his office, he dictates them to his secretary; he tells his secretary what to say; it doesn't mean that he writes the letters with his own hand.'

'You mean God dictated the Bible?'

'Yes. That's to say, certain very good and very wise men, prophets and so on, wrote it under His inspiration. Everything which they wrote was put into their hearts by God. He *inspired* them. So that's how we *know* that it is true.'

'Miss Kellaway said that Shakespeare—'

'Kellaway? Oh, that's your new English mistress.' Glad to change the subject, she asked, 'Do you like her, darling?'

'No. She squiggles.'

'How ever do you do that?'

'*You* know. All spectacles and wriggles. We're doing Shakespeare's *As You Like It*.'

'Yes, I was talking to Miss Waters about that. I did wonder a little—but she assured me that it would be all right.'

'Wondered about what?'

'Never mind, darling.'

'Squiggles said that Shakespeare was inspired.'

Mrs Haverstock saw that she had still a little way to go.

'Oh! Well—yes,' she said. 'But that's rather different. Of course, all poets are inspired in a way, but—well, it's different. God may put it into one man's head to write a little play to amuse people, and into another man's heart to write the beautiful Psalms. But it isn't quite the same thing. It is the difference between Fiction and Truth. All Shakespeare's plays—you do understand that, dear?—are Fiction.'

'And all the Bible is Truth. That's what I wanted to know, Mummy. Thank you.'

Mrs Haverstock endured a rather ominous silence for as long as she could, and then said:

'Pamela, dear, there is something on your mind. I wish you would tell me. It isn't'—her voice became more anxious—'it isn't Adam and Eve?'

'Of course not!' said Pamela scornfully.

Mrs Haverstock put down her knitting, and gave her whole mind to her daughter.

'I think, darling, I may have misled you just now. There are certain stories in the Bible which are just—stories. They are put there in order to teach us lessons. It doesn't really matter whether they are true or not, as long as we learn from them what God is trying to teach us. When we are told that Jonah was three days in the—er—stomach of the whale, it is just a picturesque Eastern way of saying that he was in—in spiritual darkness for three days, shut off from God. And the Flood and the Tower of Babel, I'm sure that Mr Donkin has explained to you the *moral* of these stories. So you see, darling, it doesn't matter whether they are *actually* true or not, they are true in spirit, that is the great thing.' A little uncertain of the spiritual truth of Methuselah's recorded age and other matters which occurred to her, she went on firmly, 'What you must *not* think, Pamela, is that, because you can't believe this or that story which doesn't matter, you needn't believe the things which *are* true and which do matter. Do you see what I mean, darling?'

'I don't mind about Noah and the silly old whale,' Pamela burst out, 'but if it's something about God Himself, then I've *got* to believe it, and I *don't* believe it, and that's why I asked you if the Bible was true.'

Mrs Haverstock was shocked. For a moment she wished that her husband were there to help her; and then she remembered that he was playing golf, as he always did on Sunday, and she saw how much more helpful it would be if Mr Donkin were there.

'I think you had better tell me about it, dear,' she said quietly.

Pamela told her very loudly and quickly.

'It's in Samuel, we did Samuel last term, and I've been thinking about it ever since, because David numbered the people, and I asked Rosemary, she's in the Sixth, if numbering people was wrong, and she said do you mean in drill, and I said no, numbering people in a country to see how many there were, and she said of course not, silly, we do it every ten years, it's called Ascensus. I don't know how you spell it but *we* do it every ten years, and when David did it God was very angry with him and sent a pestilence which killed seventy thousand people, little babies who'd never done any wrong to anybody, because babies always die first in pestilences, and even if David *was* wrong, though I don't see why if *we* do it every ten years, I think that to kill innocent little babies just to punish *him*—oh, Mummy, how can people get up in church and pretend that God loves little children if *that's* what He does, *I* think He's cruel, and I *don't* love Him, I *don't*, I *don't*!' She found a rather dirty handkerchief somewhere in her clothes and sobbed noisily into it.

Mrs Haverstock got up and shook her until she stopped.

'Pamela, dear, please! Here!' She took out her own handkerchief. 'Wipe your eyes, and blow your nose properly. No, I'm not angry, dear, I quite understand; but if we lose control of ourselves, we can't think it out together quietly, which is what we are going to do.' Seeing her daughter's woebegone face, she went on, 'If it is any comfort to you, darling, I was just as unhappy about it all, when I was your age, as you are now. And then Granny explained it all to me so clearly that I never had any doubts again. I wish I could remember all that she said. It was so comforting.'

'About David?' asked Pamela hopefully.

'I forget just what it was that I couldn't understand. It was something about that time, I mean David, or it may have been Abraham, but I just felt I *couldn't* believe it; and then, knowing how many unhappy people there were in the world, and sick people—Granny's sister was paralysed all her life!—I just didn't see how there *could* be a loving God who looked after us, as He looked after the Israelites when He took them through those terrible deserts. Daddy was there in the War, you know, with General Allenby, and he says they are simply terrible.'

Mrs Haverstock had hoped that if she went on talking, she would suddenly remember what her own mother had said which was so comforting; but it still hadn't quite come back to her.

'Well, now, darling, we've got to remember first that God can see into people's hearts. We can't. All we can see is what people *do*; we can't see *why* they do it. One can do quite innocent-looking things with a bad motive, and one can do what seem like wrong things with a good motive. You do understand that, don't you?'

'You mean like drowning Fluff's kittens last week?'

'Well—yes. Of course we were all very sorry for poor Fluff, but it *was* the best thing to do. Daddy did explain. And in the same way every wicked man does things which are perfectly innocent in themselves, but they are done for his own wicked purposes.'

'You mean like sharpening a carving-knife, which Daddy's so good at, in order to plunge it into somebody's heart?'

'Well—yes. Though that's rather a gruesome example, darling. So you see, we don't know what was in David's heart when he numbered the people, but God knew; and we can easily see that David *may* have had some unworthy reason for it, like pride or vainglory or—or something, which *we* don't have when *we* do it.'

'Killing seventy thousand babies because somebody else was proud—'

'Pamela, Pamela, one thing at a time. We can now be sure, can't we, although it isn't explained very clearly to us in the Bible, that David sinned in *some* way. He must have done, or God wouldn't have been angry with him. That's logic, isn't it?'

'Y-yes. But—'

'Well then, that's something. Now about the pestilence. This does seem at first rather hard to understand. Yes, I remember now this *was* one of my difficulties when I was your age. But Granny pointed out to me, and I think it's so true, that God's ways are not our ways. He can see into our hearts, but we cannot see into His. We are not told anything about these people who were killed, but we can be sure of two things. Those of them who were wicked were rightly punished for their wickedness, and those of them who were innocent were mercifully released from the troubles of this world, and have been ever since in the company of God's angels, in that other more beautiful world which God has prepared for us. Yes, I think it was something like that which Granny pointed out to me, and it made it so clear, it made all the suffering in the world so beautifully clear, because it's just a *preparation* for the next world. Now, darling, don't think about it any more; all these little difficulties will be made clear to us one day, not in our time but in His; just ask God in your prayers to-night to strengthen your faith in Him, and you will find that He always answers. *Faith*—that is what we want. Whatever happens, and whatever happened in the past, whether in Jerusalem or anywhere else, we know that it is God's will, and for the best. Now run along, and wash your face properly before tea, there's a darling; Mrs Parry is coming, but I think you'll do as you are, and you can escape to the nursery as soon as you like afterwards.'

'Oo, thank you, darling,' said Pamela, relieved that attendance on Mrs Parry was not to be compulsory; and she kissed her mother and ran along. And as she got into the House basket-ball team next term, and was working very hard for the School Certificate, she didn't think of these disturbing things any more. Indeed, when, many years later, her own little girl had similar misgivings about those seventy thousand poor, disfigured bodies, she was able to give her an explanation of it all, just as beautifully clear as the one which her own mother had once given her, on that distant Sunday afternoon ...

There is, for those who are interested, another explanation, another version of what happened, which makes it, perhaps, even clearer.

II

Abiezer the Physician came to David and said, 'Have I the King's leave to speak?' And David said, 'Speak on.'

'Well,' said Abiezer, 'it's what I was saying.'

'Not that again?' said David, frowning. 'I understood that we had finished with the subject.'

'The trouble is that it hasn't finished with us.'

'Nevertheless,' said David, adroitly ignoring this, 'I am glad that you dropped in this morning, because I want you to have a look at the Queen. She has been a little feverish lately.'

'Which Queen?' asked Abiezer tactlessly.

'Bathsheba, of course.'

'And she is feverish?'

'In a feverish mood. Nothing to speak of, but since you *are* here—'

'As I was saying, and have been saying for the last six months,' observed Abiezer, returning to his theme with equal adroitness, 'unless the drainage system of Jerusalem is entirely re-planned— assuming that what we have can be called a drainage system—in a short time many thousands of your people will have begun by feeling a little feverish, and will have ended—' David sat up alertly.

'You are not suggesting that the Queen—'

'As far as she is concerned, you need have no immediate alarm. But there are a million other of your people—'

'Oh, many more than that. That reminds me, I must have them numbered again. The Queen is always on at me about it. But it was a good many more than a million some years ago. I could send for the figures, if you were interested.'

'One million, or five million, or fifty million, when once the plague gets among them, there will not be many left.'

'Oh, nonsense! Why do you come here to talk such nonsense?'

'I have the honour,' said Abiezer stiffly, 'to be the King's Physician.'

'At the moment, yes. It isn't a life appointment.'

'So long as I hold it, I shall try to do my duty; and my duty is to warn you that Jerusalem must be given a proper drainage system at once. If that is impossible, then some form of sanitary drill must be enforced.'

'Drainage system! Drill! You don't seem to realize that these things cost money.'

'I prepared an estimate for you the last time we spoke on the subject.'

'I should say you did! How many million shekels was it? Where do you think the money is coming from? What do you think my Army costs, as it is?'

'One might reply, David, that your third question answers your second.'

King David pulled at his beard, giving himself a little time in which to think this out. Then he said coldly:

'You know, Abiezer, I am almost certain that that amounts to treason. Indeed, I am not at all sure that it isn't blasphemy. When you remember how Yahweh feels about war, and that our whole history under His beneficent guidance has been one long battle, then—well, I must consult the authorities, and see how you stand. Treason *and* blasphemy, I am inclined to think, and I don't know which is worse.'

Abiezer bowed.

'Then you will not wish me to look in on Queen Bathsheba?'

'Now don't be hasty,' said David. 'I am only warning you. Of course you must go and see her. A little run down, that's all. I just want—I mean, she just wants you to tell her not to be so interf—so active. Tell her to take things quietly for a spell; perhaps a change of air for a few days might do her good. And about this other matter; I am sure that you are drawing too gloomy a picture. Did I ever tell you in this connexion of a rather odd experience I had once in the Cave of Adullam?'

One of the penalties of being the King's Physician is that one has to listen to rather odd experiences in caves, however often one has heard them before. Abiezer listened …

Abiezer came to David a year later, rubbing his hands, and said, 'Have I the King's leave to speak?' And David said, 'Speak on.'

'Well,' said Abiezer cheerfully, 'I bring good news. I think we have got it under.'

'Look, Abiezer, I am getting an old man now. How old would you say I was?'

'Sixty-eight.'

'Nine hundred and sixty-eight, that's right. It's a considerable age. If I am no longer able to pick up what was evidently left over from a conversation of some previous month and have it immediately under control, you must forgive me. You say that we have got it under. What have we got under? What are we talking about?'

'The plague,' said Abiezer grimly.

'The plague. Ah, yes, I remember now. And you say that we have got it under?'

'I think I may say that the worst is over. I think I can promise that we have turned the corner now. But during those terrible first three days it looked as if the whole of Jerusalem would be wiped out. If we had gone on like that—'

'In the circumstances you were quite right not to alarm me unnecessarily. Have you any idea of the death-toll? I am afraid, from what you have been telling me, that it must run into several hundreds!'

'It is impossible to give actual figures. We have been burning and burying the bodies in heaps as soon as we could, without much thought of anything else. But at a rough estimate I should put it at between sixty and eighty thousand. Say seventy.'

'Seventy thousand? Dear, dear! That's bad. That's worse than I thought.' He considered for a little, and asked anxiously, 'You haven't been able to classify them at all?'

'As one would expect, mostly women and young children. Particularly children. I should say that the Army, if that is what is worrying you, David, is pretty nearly intact.'

'Things don't *worry* me,' said David, annoyed. 'One cannot rule over a great nation for nearly forty years, and allow oneself to be perpetually *worried* by things. "Worry" is a superlatively ill-chosen word. Looking at my reception of your news with scientific detachment, I should say that my emotional response had been, in part, kingly calm; in part, overwhelming grief at the calamity which has overtaken my people; and, in part, profound gratitude that so many of us have been spared. Indeed, I may tell you that the first phrases of a suitable psalm of thanksgiving are already in my mind. As for the Army, you overlook the religious aspect of the matter. We are Yahweh's chosen people, destined by Him to conquer the world. Naturally, then, my first thoughts must always be for my Army. That is why I numbered the people the other day; that is why I rejoice now that of the recorded million and a half fighting men—a million and a half, Abiezer, think of that!—only a few have been taken from us. *Worry*, indeed!'

When he had made an end of speaking, Abiezer said:

'Nevertheless, David, your Army is—worrying. If I do not use a stronger word, it is that I may not—alarm you unnecessarily.'

'What have *they* got to worry about? Of all my people the most favoured!'

'Pestilence distributes her favours more doubtfully. The Army objects to seeing its wives and children die in agony before its eyes.'

David started up.

'What are they saying?'

'They know what *I* have been saying these twelve months past. They paid little heed to me; and now that the calamity has come upon them, they do not blame themselves for their heedlessness. As is the way of men, they tell themselves that somebody else should have done something. They say that their King should have given them their orders. Are they not soldiers? How could they act if they had not been given orders?'

'They blame *me*?'

'They think that if Adonijah the son of Haggith had been King, this would not have happened.'

'Rebellion!' cried David.

'No, not rebellion yet. But they murmur it among themselves and soon they will say it more loudly. Then it will be rebellion.'

David muttered in his beard, and looked this way and that. He felt very old suddenly.

'Have I the King's leave to speak?' said Abiezer.

'Speak on.'

'When you took Bathsheba from Uriah—'

A wistful look came into David's eyes.

'She was very beautiful,' he said simply. 'I have never seen anything so beautiful as she was that day.' He sighed. 'What a difference a few years make to a woman!'

'It is many years now, David. But, even so, you remember that, when her son was born, you gave orders that it should not live, fearing that it might be Uriah's son.'

'How was anyone to know whose son it was?'

'But when your orders had been obeyed, you were afraid of what you had done, and you lamented openly, and declared that Yahweh had punished you for your sin in the matter of Bathsheba by taking away your beloved child. And the people believed you and pitied you.'

'You use such strange words, Abiezer. Kings are not pitied!'

'But they may sometimes be believed?'

'You seem to have an idea in your mind. What is it?'

'There is a young woman named Aiah—'

'I don't know *what* you're talking about,' said David hastily.

'Wife of Alihud—'

'The whole story is completely untrue.'

'Soldiers do not blame a man for such things. Rather they admire him and envy him. As I understand, she is an unusually beautiful young woman—'

'She is one of the most—I have never even seen her.'

'If you were to give it out that Yahweh had sent this pestilence as a punishment for your sin in the matter of Aiah—'

'Now I see your point. You think that they would be more reconciled to what has happened?'

'Men can rebel against the acts of a King. They cannot rebel against the acts of a God.'

David was silent for a long time. Then he said:

'In this matter of Maraiah, if I heard the name correctly, I mean this young woman whom you were telling me about, you say that soldiers do not blame a man for such things. Has it occurred to you that Bathsheba bears a marked dissimilarity to soldiers in this respect?'

Abiezer's face fell. It had not occurred to him.

'We must therefore,' said David firmly, 'think of something else …

'Something, however,' said David, 'on the same lines, but not involving a beautiful young woman …

'Something, rather, if this were possible, involving Bathsheba …

'Something I had done,' said David, working it out, 'which was generally known to have been approved by the Queen …

'Or, better still, instigated …

'In short,' said David triumphantly, 'as I always maintained, this pestilence has nothing to do with the extremely efficient sanitary system of the city. It was sent by Yahweh as a punishment on Bathsheba for the wicked and vain-glorious pride which insisted that I should number the people. But, of course,' he added magnanimously, 'I accept all responsibility. I shall take the blame on my own shoulders.'

Abiezer regarded him with reluctant admiration. It must be wonderful, he thought, to be like that.

'Well?' said David jauntily.

Abiezer nodded slowly.

'It will do,' he said. 'It seems a little—what shall I say?—out of proportion. But if the people will swallow it—'

'People, I find,' said David, 'will swallow almost anything. If it concerns their God,' he added, 'then they will swallow anything.'

Anne-Marie

(1948)

We had had a good year, and by way of celebration I was giving a little dinner in my Hampstead flat to heads of departments. We had seen quite enough of each other in the last twelve months, but a dinner is a dinner, and something of the sort seemed to be expected of me. I reckoned that if I gave them enough to drink we should get through the meal somehow, but that the hour or so afterwards, before I could decently kick them out, might be a little sticky. Then I had the brilliant idea of engaging a conjurer. Everybody likes a conjurer.

He introduced himself as the Great Rinaldo. He wore his evening clothes as if they had been fancy dress; young, apparently, but with a face like old ivory, and thick black hair which he kept shaking back from his forehead. He had the most beautiful hands I have ever seen. I told him that card-tricks would be the most suitable form of entertainment, and he said in a low, melancholy voice that he only did card-tricks now. So card-tricks it was.

They were brilliant. I suppose they could all be explained, but some of them seemed sheer magic. For instance, he held up the four aces between the fingers of his right hand; they were there, they were not there, they were there again. 'Spade to the Gardener,' he murmured, 'Club to the Clubman, Heart to the Lover, Diamond to— well, you must find your own way, I cannot help you. Off with you!'

He snapped his fingers. 'And now, gentlemen, if you would feel in your breast-pockets—' Well, he could have looked me up in *Who's Who* and seen that I belonged to half a dozen clubs; but how did he know that Rogers never stopped talking about his tomatoes, and that Nason was still indecently in love with his wife after twenty years of matrimony? The diamond went to Jewell, the head of our Education department.

One of the most attractive things about him was that he gave us none of that dreary, facetious patter which you get from most con-jurers. He talked, of course: conjurers, I understand, have to do this in order to distract the attention; but his talk was more like a musical incantation to the cards, very soothing and restful in his melancholy voice. Altogether he was a great success, and when it was over, I had another bottle of champagne up, filled a glass for him, and we all gathered round his end of the table.

'You say you only do card-tricks?' I said, to start him off.

'Only!' said Nason, and everybody laughed.

'Only card-tricks now,' said the Great Rinaldo. He drank and sighed. I filled his glass again. We all waited …

It was three years ago (said Rinaldo), on a Saturday night at Blackpool, that Carlotta left me. Between the shows we had had our last quar-rel. Once more she had accused me of loving Anne-Marie more than I loved her, and now at last it was true. One cannot go on saying this to a man without it becoming true in the end. Did I, then, want her to leave me? Not consciously, for I needed both of them. Both of them were indispensable to my art. But down in the subconscious, I suppose, I was saying 'To hell with Carlotta'.

Carlotta was my partner. She stood by my table looking gay and pretty, and she gave me the accessories of my art as I needed them. From her wide but lovely mouth I drew the flags of all nations; as the Vanishing Lady from the hermetically sealed cabinet she brought our turn to its triumphant conclusion.

I am an artist, and I take my art seriously. When I found Carlotta, she was with a juggler who called himself Hal I. Butt; that, gentlemen, gives you an idea of the life she was leading before she met me. I rescued her from this, but unfortunately I was unable to blot out the past altogether. Our first few months together were happy, and then she began to relapse. She played for laughs. At the close of one of my most brilliant feats, as the audience was about to thunder its applause, Carlotta would look at me with a comically exaggerated awe, and say, '*Coo!*'—and the applause would turn to shouts of laughter. A serious artist does not want laughter. When I asked any gentleman in the audience to lend me his watch, she would frown and shake her head warningly at them, implying by this that I was a confidence trickster. I, the Great Rinaldo! Once, when a gentleman in the front row of the stalls was fumbling for his watch in one pocket after another, she leant over to him and said helpfully, 'Or a sundial'; which was foolish, and would have made the trick impossible. Always now, when the show was ended, we would have a scene, and always the scene would end with Carlotta in tears, crying that I did not love her any more. Gentlemen, how can one love a woman who says 'Or a sundial' when I ask any gentleman in the audience to lend me his watch?

'You love Anne-Marie more than you love me,' she would cry for the hundredth time, and now it was true. Anne-Marie was sweet and gentle. She never made a mockery of my art, never tried to be funny at the climax of my professional skill. She had been with me for two years before I found Carlotta, and knew all my ways. We loved each other dearly …

Anne-Marie was my rabbit …

That last performance at Blackpool. Always, previously, we had made it up before we did our turn again, but now, for the first time, Carlotta and I went on to the stage at enmity with each other. I was afraid. I told myself that she was planning a great humiliation for me to-night, a louder laugh than she had ever got before. To my surprise she played her part perfectly; not a smile from the audience, nothing but that wave of wonder and applause which is so necessary for the serious artist. So we came to the Grand Finale, the Vanishing Lady. I knew then that she had been saving herself up for this. Once she had said to me in her frivolous way, 'It would be rather funny if I didn't vanish one night, and when you threw open the doors of the cabinet, I was still there.'

'*Funny?*' I exclaimed.

'Yes, and I said reproachfully, "Darling, you forgot to leave the corkscrew." Get a good laugh that would.'

A good laugh! To-night, I told myself, she was playing for the greatest laugh of all.

We came to the finale. She is in the cabinet. Six of the audience, including two sailors, have examined it, have assured themselves that there is no way out. The band plays. I stand there exercising all my will-power, for I feel that it is a struggle of wills between us, and I stand there compelling her to play her part, to do what is needful and to vanish. The band stops. The whole house is hushed. I make a pass over the cabinet, the one that my grandfather has taught me. I cry '*Voilà!*' as I fling the doors wide. What shall I see?

All is well. She is not there.

The audience applauds. I bow. I hold the applause until Carlotta comes tripping down the centre aisle. She joins me on the stage, and together we make our final bow …

But what is this? She does not come! I signal for the curtain to descend. I rush to the wings. 'Where is she? Where is she?' The men shake their heads. Nobody has seen her. They ring the curtain up again. I am there bowing. Still no Carlotta tripping down the aisle; still, however, the torrents of applause. And then, suddenly, the applause turns to laughter! Never, gentlemen, have you heard such laughter. It thunders in my ears, and I cannot understand it. Furiously I tell myself that Carlotta has not left the stage, that she is here behind me, making funny faces at the audience. I take a quick look round. She is not there. But at my side—what do I see?

Ah! I know then that, as I had often suspected, the true magic of my grandfather has descended upon me! Carlotta has vanished for ever … and down by my feet is Anne-Marie, sitting up on her back paws, and blowing funny kisses at the audience!

The Great Rinaldo tossed the hair back from his eyes, and gulped down what was left of his champagne. I filled his glass again, and said in a matter-of-fact voice, 'Where was Carlotta?' He shrugged his shoulders, and made a vague gesture towards the ceiling. We all looked up there, God knows why.

'Gentlemen,' said Rinaldo mournfully, 'have you ever thought what it is for a serious artist like myself to have a funny rabbit who plays for laughs?'

Speaking for all of us Jewell said that he hadn't.

'There is a trick, very popular at private parties, in which one cooks a plum pudding in a gentleman's hat. Is it nice, when I say "Hey Presto!" and remove the handkerchief, not to know whether it is plum pudding or stewed rabbit? When I make the magic cactus grow beneath my fingers, what is this which slowly pushes its way through the sand? The first shoots of the cactus—or Anne-Marie's ears? She could no longer say "Coo!" at my most baffling trick, but she would fall on her back in a mock swoon, with her paws crossed on her breast—and the house would rock with laughter.'

'Surely,' said Jewell, 'you could have shut her up after you had done your first trick with her?'

'How many times had Carlotta escaped from the cabinet? She knew all about escaping.'

'Carlotta?' said Rogers stupidly.

'Or Anne-Marie. Call her what you like.'

'I should have said that there was a fortune in a rabbit like that,' suggested Nason.

The Great Rinaldo looked at him. Just once. Nason hurriedly swallowed another glass of my port.

'So what?' I said. 'You gave it up?'

'I wanted no more partners, I wanted no more rabbits. We came up here to your Heath at dead of night, Carlotta and I, and I pushed her down a burrow, and ran. That was a year ago. Now I do only card-tricks. Nobody can interfere with my card-tricks.'

Lying back in his chair, he put a hand in his pocket and drew out a pack of cards. He shuffled them with one hand, threw them to the ceiling and caught them again. He snapped his fingers and they were gone. Mechanically he leant forward to bow … and there on the table beside him, believe it or not, was a rabbit, sitting up and blowing kisses to us.

'My God!' he cried. 'You!'

He seized it by the ears and rushed from the room.

What an artist! What an actor! His fee was twice the usual for this sort of thing, but I couldn't complain.

Breitenstein

(1948)

I

I was dining with the Hammersleys at Richmond that night. The old man—well, he would seem pretty young to me now, but he was twice my age then—old Hammersley was having his usual birthday party. There were just the three of them, and a few friends. No relations, because, as he said, he saw enough of his relations anyhow, and they would feel that they had to bring presents. Presents were not encouraged. As a matter of fact, I did bring one, a book on decorative iron work which everybody was talking about—I mean everybody who talked about decorative iron work anyway; and I knew he wanted it, because he had said something about not being able to get the damned thing; so I just turned up with it casually, and said I'd happened to see it in a bookshop that day. He took it very nicely, and seemed really grateful—until Sheila told me that she and her mother had both given it to him as a surprise, and he'd bought his own copy as well. Which shows you why I thought him a nice old man, and worthy of being Sheila's father. He was very keen on iron gates for some reason.

I don't know why I am telling you about him, because he doesn't come into the story. This is the story of the only real adventure I have ever had, and I have never told it to anybody. It came back to me suddenly this morning when I found myself driving along one of those little plane-shaded roads in St John's Wood, and I caught the name Lauriston Gardens just as we turned out of it. And then I thought that perhaps I had better get the story down for you to read, because it ought to be on record somewhere, even though it happened so long ago. Of course, I had the usual experiences, some of them exciting, most of them dull, in the First World War, and of course I talked about them; but what I call an adventure is something which only happens to oneself, and happens out of a clear sky; and when it's over, you wonder if you dreamt it all. Well, I know I didn't, because a lot of it got into the papers …

Sheila was the girl I was in love with that year. She was fair and slim, and had good features without being exactly pretty, and a mouth which was always breaking into a smile. She also had the most lovely colouring, and this was in the days when all that sort of thing was left to Nature. Nature had been very good to Sheila. Thinking of her as she was then, I feel that what I ought to have said was that she had such an appearance of prettiness that you didn't notice what good features she had. We played golf together at Sudbrook Park once or twice, and if she had ever hit the ball more than fifty yards, we might have played more often, and she might have learnt to love me, and I might never have learnt, until it was too late, that I didn't love her. She married an Anglo-Indian. I saw her once when she came home with the children; sallow and hard-mouthed, and full of little prides and grievances on various points of Anglo-Indian precedence which I couldn't follow. I was glad that I had married your mother.

But you must understand, because it is the reason for bringing Sheila into the story, that I was (or thought I was, which is the same thing) completely in love with her that evening; and when we said good night at the gate, I held her hand and looked unutterable things at her, and she, I thought, at me. Good Heavens, no, I didn't kiss her; one didn't in those days, not unless one was actually engaged, not a daughter of Mrs Hammersley's; I just said, 'I love you, I love you, my darling,' but quite inaudibly, while taking off my hat. I should have mentioned before that, being in what lady novelists of that time called faultless evening dress, I was wearing a silk hat, a thin black overcoat with silk facings, and a white scarf. Does it matter, you wonder, raising tolerant eyebrows. I have often wondered too. I think perhaps it did matter; yes, I think that in the end it mattered a good deal.

II

I had rooms in Westminster Broadway at that time, and a District train from Richmond to St James's Park took me almost to the door. I sat alone in a first-class carriage. It is a long time since I travelled on the District Railway, and it may be that class distinctions therein, like so many good and inevitable things, have now been abolished. Did you ever, as a child, have an India-rubber ball with a dent in it? You worked the dent out very carefully and cleverly until the rubber came up with a little pop—and then you found that you had made an entirely new dent in another place. That's what happens when you try to abolish class distinctions. I'm sorry; that's as irrelevant as old Hammersley; what I meant to say was that first-class compartments were long corridors just like the others, except that the seats were of red plush.

At Bedford Park, I think it was, two people joined me, waving good-bye to two others on the platform as the train moved off. They sat down in the far corner; and, in the way which foreigners seem to have of always being in the middle of a conversation, continued an unceasing and simultaneous stream of French. The man was big and handsome. He had a finely cut upturned moustache, which, with his bold good looks, qualified him to be the villain in a melodrama. The woman was younger; not more than my own age, I thought, which was twenty-five; and definitely not attractive. I mean not attractive to me, not, as they say, my style; not, I should have said in those days, any Englishman's style; very much made up, and with nothing which goes in England for beauty or prettiness, but, I dared say, plenty of what they liked in France. At twenty-five the fact that a girl was *chic* (if she was *chic*) meant nothing to me. Sheila wasn't *chic*, thank Heaven; nor was she 'a very nice girl', nor 'an awfully good sort', nor any of the things with which one excuses the absence of beauty. I loved her.

I didn't take much notice of these two people at first, because I was deep in my own happy thoughts. It is not a discovery of my own that anticipation and recollection are the highlights of happiness; but I may be peculiar in this, that, even when I am enjoying my happiness in company, I am looking forward to, and, in a way longing for, the moment when it will be over, so that I can be alone to enjoy it in retrospect. I had Sheila's happy face and comradely laugh on which to look back. In front of me were three weeks of the perfect holiday— golf and bathing in Cornwall. Further on still, at the end of the three weeks, was this new job which I had just got at Lancasters, the marine engineers—well, as you know, I am head of it now, though only nominally this last year or two. So, you see, I was happy and everything in the garden was lovely, and in thirty-six hours or less I should be standing on the first tee, with the blue sea twinkling 400 yards away in the gap in the cliffs where the green lay. I would start with a five, one mustn't expect too much on the first morning …

I came out of my thoughts to hear the girl say in a high, emphatic voice, '*Non, non, non!*' a translation of which was about as far as my public-school French took me. I looked across at them, wondering what it was all about. It was clear from the tones of their voices and their gestures that she was urging something on him which he rejected firmly, and that he was offering some other solution of their problem which she didn't like. They being foreigners, and I being in an idly romantic mood, I made up the story for them. She was asking him to take her away from it all, and he was saying that Georges was his best friend, he couldn't betray him, and things would look differently to-morrow, and she was saying, No, no, *no*, she would never, never go back to Georges, he must take her away … And then I thought that as they were foreigners, I might make it a little more exciting; and now he was telling her that there was only one way out, she must poison Georges, and he would send her the arsenic to-morrow, and she was saying, No, no, *no*, why should *she* do all the work, he must come home with her tonight and stab Georges, it was quicker … And then the man turned round and looked at me, and I looked guiltily away and as if out of the window, and found that I could see them reflected there. And the odd thing was that the man still kept looking round at me, as if considering, as if wondering how he could work me into the story. You can leave me out of it, I thought sleepily. I don't like your girlfriend anyway, and I'm going to Cornwall to-morrow. Write and tell me all about it.

III

The train stopped. I realized that it was Sloane Square as we moved on again, and thought pleasantly of bed, now only two stations away: Victoria, St James's Park. The man got up and came towards me. He raised his hat.

'I make all my apologies, sir,' he said, 'but the situation is a little difficult. I have to catch a train at Victoria, while my friend goes on to Charing Cross. She is unused to travelling alone, and does not know your railways. Would you be so very kind as to see that she gets out at Charing Cross, where her brother will meet her? She is very nervous of being alone, but you see how I am placed.'

'Well, as a matter of fact,' I said—why does one always say 'as a matter of fact'?—'I am getting out a little before Charing Cross myself, but I will explain it all to her very carefully before I go. It will only be two stations more, and I will see that she understands.'

'I am very much obliged to you, sir.'

'Not at all,' I said kindly.

He raised his hat again, and went back to his friend, reassuring her, as it seemed. So that was all it was. No elopement, no murder.

Simply that she wanted him to come on to Charing Cross with her, and he, naturally, wanted to catch his train at Victoria. And they had been arguing about it simultaneously since Bedford Park. Very French, I told myself complacently.

As we came into Victoria, he bent over her hand and kissed it, raised his hat to me, and left us quickly. Nobody else got in. As soon as the train was moving, I went over to her. I talked to her as one would talk to a deaf child, wondering how much English she knew. I explained very slowly that I got out at the next station; that the station after was Westminster, where she did *not* get out, and that the station after that was Charing Cross, where she did get out. Simple? You'd have thought so.

She knew English all right. Lots of it. She told me over and over again how 'nairvous' she was, how she admired our brave English girls who went everywhere alone, how frightened she was of our railways, how in her country girls never travelled by themselves, but yes, her brother was meeting her, but suppose he were late, what then, suppose he were not there, and she alone on the platform, so nairvous, I was so kind, it was so kind of me to help her, never before had she been alone in a train, not like your brave English girls.

Well, what would you have done? I didn't find her any more attractive close up, and I wanted to get to bed. Don't think that she was in any way repulsive or even ill-looking, she was just damned plain, or so I thought, with painted lips and a patch of rouge on sallow cheeks, such as, if she were English, only a prostitute would have shown in those desirable days. The very opposite of clean, fair-haired, sunny Sheila. But what could I do? She was French. I couldn't help telling myself that the English hadn't got a very good reputation abroad for manners, for chivalry; that I should be at Charing Cross and back again in ten minutes; and that surely I could give ten minutes to a frightened girl, without demanding first that she should be pretty. For wouldn't I have gone on with her if she had been pretty? Of course I would. That settled it for me.

'All right,' I said resignedly, 'I'll come on to Charing Cross with you, and then you'll have nothing to be nervous about. Is that right?' I gave her a smile, she gave me a little nervous one back (which made me think that perhaps, after all, she wasn't much more than twenty), and told me how brave the English girls were. This seemed to be on her mind rather.

We didn't say much, I was too sleepy. I didn't take her hand and pat it comfortingly. I didn't touch her the whole time but just the once, as you will hear; and if you are as clever as a son of mine should be, you will know why I touched her then. We came to Charing Cross.

IV

And there was no 'brother'.

You are not surprised? Nor was I. Even as the train began to slow up, I was putting that brother into inverted commas. All the time we stood on the platform, waiting for it to clear, I was telling myself, with the cynicism which is the self-protection of the young, that of course there had never been a brother; that the whole story, to use that horrible word which we have imported from America, was 'phoney'. People got out of the train, people got in; it moved away, we were alone on the platform, and there was no brother.

The girl cried, as if making a terrible discovery, 'My brother! He is not here!'

I said, as politely as I could manage, 'He may be waiting for you upstairs,' knowing that he wasn't.

We went up and looked. Another train came in. We went down to the platform again. It filled and emptied, and of course there was still no brother.

What was the idea, I wondered. I was hardly worth robbing. I had two pounds on me—golden sovereigns in those happy days—two pounds in a silver sovereign purse, a metal watch, valueless studs and links, and a silver cigarette-case. Not worth all the planning. Or was it just an ordinary pick-up? But why so elaborate, when there were a hundred more likely men in Regent Street? Well, the sooner I crossed the line and went back to bed, the better.

She went on crying for her brother, wondering where he was. Well, a real brother might forget whatever arrangement was made, start late for it, fail to find a taxi, go to the wrong station, anything; but I wasn't going to waste time talking about a brother I didn't believe in. I said coldly:

'I'd better get you a taxi. Where do you live?'

'Yes, but my brother will not be there!' She said it with an exclamation mark, like that.

I wanted to say of course he won't, but I said, 'Does it matter, as long as you've got home safely? If he does turn up after you've gone, and I'm still here, I'll tell him.' And smiling to myself at the thought of this imaginary brother, I added, 'What's he like?'

She said, looking at me gravely, 'He is very like you, you remind me of him very much,' and then, as if it were a separate means of identification, 'He is very handsome.'

No. I didn't fall for it, it was too obvious, but I couldn't help warming to her a little. Before I could do anything but blush stupidly, she said:

'But since he is not there, how can I get into the house?'

I said, 'Doesn't anybody else live there?'

She shook her head.

'Well, but you have a latch-key?'

She hadn't. In her country the young girl—I didn't want all that again. I said, 'If you and your brother live alone, I suppose you do the housekeeping. Well, how can you do that, if you can't shut the door behind you when you go out to shop?' I thought, complacently, that that had blown up the whole story, until she explained that a woman came in every day. Even so—but it was much too late for this sort of discussion.

'Are you on the telephone?' I asked firmly.

She was, luckily.

'Then give me your brother's address and telephone number, and I'll ring up. If anybody is in, I'll put you in a taxi. If not, we'll wait a little longer.'

She didn't seem to think much of that, but I felt that it was something to do. She told me an address: Paul Verray, The Sycamores, Lauriston Gardens, and the telephone number. I wrote them down on the letter I had had from Sheila, asking me to the party. Just as I was going, she stopped me and gave me the purse from her bag, saying, 'For the telephone.' I took it, rather surprised, rather ashamed, thinking, 'Well, I've got the first purse anyway.'

Of course, as soon as I had worked it out, which I did as I climbed the stairs to the telephone, I saw why she had done it. If I had her purse, then I had to come back to her. Otherwise—

I gave the number. I put in my 'two pennies please', the girl's two pennies. I said, 'Is that The Sycamores?' Fancy calling a house The Sycamores!

To my great relief a voice with a slight foreign accent said, 'Paul Verray speaking. Who is there, please?'

Well, why should I give him my name; and how go into a long explanation; or say, 'I've got your sister here'; or—Well, what? It was enough that he existed, and was there to open the door. I did begin, 'Your sister—' and he said quickly, 'Marguerite, yes?' and I said, 'Yes, it's like this,' and saw that it was hopeless and rang off; but I thought I heard him say, a little anxiously, 'Is that you, Breitenstein?' And I wondered if Breitenstein was the man in the train.

So I went down to the girl, and gave her the purse, less twopence, and said cheerfully, 'It's all right, he's there. Come on, we'll find a taxi in the Strand,' and I added, rather fatuously, 'So you're Marguerite?'

She nodded, saying, 'Paul? Was he all right?'

'Of course.' I didn't know what she meant.

'Why had he not started?'

'We didn't go into that,' I said. 'Come along.'

All the way up Villiers Street to the Strand she was telling me again how kind I was, and how clever to understand that other girls were different from English girls, so brave, she admired them so much; and once more I wondered if she really did. All the way up Villiers Street she seemed to be hinting that terrible things happened to a girl, a French girl, alone in a taxi. Well, if she had lived until to-day she would have known that worse things happened to a girl when she wasn't alone in a taxi; but this was forty years ago, and, as she had told me many times, she was nairvous. So—yes, you have guessed it—I put her into the taxi, gave the address to the driver, and ... got in after her.

You see, I was feeling a little disgusted with myself. I had been sure that there wasn't a brother, and there was a brother; and because this part of her story was true, I felt that it was all true, and that I had been a churl about it; had been absurdly suspicious; had not recognized, as I did now, seeing her suddenly by the lights of a jeweller's shop, that she was just a frightened child under her silly make-up. But I still didn't understand why she should have been so frightened ... I don't really know now.

V

We didn't talk much. I asked her a few polite questions: did she like London, what part of France did she come from (as if I knew it all), where did she learn English, and so on; but she didn't seem to want to go into all that, and I certainly didn't care. So we left it. But she did say one thing which surprised me.

'You think I am French, yes?'

'Well, but—'

'Because I talk French in the train?'

'Well, yes.'

'And now I talk English in the taxi. So I am English, yes? And if I talk German in the steam-boat—'

That was clever of her, and I laughed appreciatively. She looked across at me and said, 'It is nice to hear you laugh.'

'Don't you and your brother have jokes together?'

She shook her head, and looked away from me out of the window.

I felt my gloves, thin evening ones, in my pocket, and put them on. I don't quite know why. Something to do, perhaps; or a sub-conscious assertion of physical immunity from her ... or just one of those things.

As we came into St John's Wood, she said:

'You will meet my brother? When I tell him how kind you have been, he will want to thank you.'

I would have preferred him to want to give me a drink; but all my suspicions were now gone, and I was anxious to see this man who was so handsome—and so like me. Well, anybody would. It isn't vanity, it's—well, perhaps it is vanity.

'If you like,' I said.

We passed a red telephone-box, and she tapped on the window, and waved a turning to the left. Almost immediately after we had turned she tapped again, and the taxi stopped. She was out and pay-ing the man before I could do anything about it. Even while I was protesting to her, he had let his clutch in again, and was off.

'You shouldn't have done that,' I said.

'But why should you pay for me?'

I was beginning to explain that I didn't mind her paying for herself, but I did mind having now to find another taxi for myself at—I looked at my watch—ten minutes to twelve. However, it seemed polite to say nothing. I followed her through the gate and up a little flagged walk to the house. We were within a few yards of it when she stopped. It is difficult to describe the complete suddenness and stillness of her change from motion to immobility.

She whispered, 'The door is open.'

Fear is infectious. My reassuring laugh got me nowhere; but I did manage to say in quite an ordinary voice, 'Why not? He went to the post, and left the door open in case you came back while he was out. Should we have passed him if he had?'

'No,' she said thoughtfully. 'No.'

'Well, there you are.'

'Yes.' She looked back at me, and I could not read her face in the darkness. She said, 'You have been very comforting.' I hope I had been, for those were the last words she said to me.

VI

The door was only just open. She pushed it back with her left hand, and put her right hand out to the switch. There was a click, and nothing happened.

'Hallo,' I said, coming in behind her. 'Fuse gone? Wait a moment, I'll give you a light.'

Usually I can't do anything with gloves on, but by some accident I got a match alight at once. I held it up as high as I could reach. She saw him first.

'Paul!' she said in astonishment.

He stood up against the coat-rack with his hands outstretched. It looked as if he were just going to get out of his coat … and then, as the match burned brighter, as if he *had* just been going to get out of his coat at the moment when—and, even as we looked, he began to topple sideways, and I saw the red mark under his left shoulder-blade, and he crumpled on to his back, but soundlessly as it seemed to me, and the flame reached my gloved fingers and burnt itself out.

The girl had not moved, only stared, and now it was dark, and I was fumbling for another match.

'Telephone!' I whispered. 'Quick! Police—doctor—'

There was a rustle as now she moved. I was still struggling in my gloves to get a match alight. Then I heard a little 'O-oh!' and a long drawn-out sigh which went on and on as if it were the last breath of the world; and the match flared and went out, and I had seen her on her face with that red mark under her left shoulder-blade; and there was a patter of quick footsteps somewhere at the back of the house, running, running, running; out of a window, out into the garden, I saw them still running, all the way back to Charing Cross, the way we had come, and still on, over hills and valleys, to a great beach with the sun setting red at the end of it, very small they looked now, pattering on to the red sunset, but the noise of them like thunder in my ears … and then the sun went out, and it was night, and somehow I was sitting on a chair, clinging desperately to consciousness, and telling myself that I would not, would not, *would not* faint …

If I did, it was just for that moment. I got hold of myself again. I struck another match and looked at my watch. It still seemed to be ten to twelve. Then I thought that perhaps I had only imagined those running feet, and the murderer was still in the house, and I blew the match out quickly, and put the stub in my pocket. I felt the back of the chair, and it was wood, not wicker, and right up against the wall, and I knew that, whatever happened, I couldn't be stabbed as the others had been, under the left shoulder-blade. So I could sit there for a little and think.

It was only when I was in the Cornish Riviera Express next morning that I really thought it out—I mean what it all meant and why I mustn't be found there. I knew that there were good reasons; but just at the moment I had only this angry determination, not to be involved any further in a business which was none of mine, and into which I had been dragged so reluctantly. Read through what I have written, and you will see that from the very beginning I could have said 'I told you so' to the fool who sat in that chair. Well, I would be a fool no longer. Equally I would not be a knave; and it would be a knavish trick just to leave them there, dying or dead. 'Telephone—police—doctor,' I had said to Marguerite, and I could not refuse to say it, just as urgently, to myself.

Well, why not? Telephone and then disappear. Yes, and have the whole police force of London looking for me, and the girl's photograph in the papers, and the taximan coming forward with his evidence, and perhaps people who had noticed the girl (and me) at Charing Cross, and those two at Bedford Park, and Breitenstein, identifying the train, and the Hammersleys knowing that it was the train which I must have caught. Better, much better, to throw my hand in at once ...

I felt steadier now. I lit another match, and got up from my chair. The girl was lying on her face, her right arm over Paul's outflung left arm. Yes, Paul *was* a little like the man whom I saw every morning as I shaved; same build, same colouring, same type of face, only more lined, more mature. Not a double by any means, but like. I looked up at the rack where a silk hat was hanging. Silk hat; thin black coat with silk facings, white scarf. And I said what's to stop me? Nothing. For suddenly I knew what to do.

Standing there, looking, thinking, had taken more than one match. I picked up all the match-ends which I had dropped, and added them to those in my pocket. I thought for a little, and then let one fall by the door, and two by the girl. I bent over Paul and felt in his overcoat, wriggled out a box of safety-matches from one of the pockets and put my own box of 'Swan vestas' in its place. Then, by the light of the last match I was using, I put my hand on the girl's wrist, and moved her arm gently off Paul's arm, and raised his arm, and dropped it on Marguerite.

Yes, I told you that you would understand why I touched her—just that once.

VII

Don't go in for crime, my dear boy. There is always some little thing which it is too easy to forget. It was only as I was stepping into the telephone-box that I remembered, and went back to the corner. I had remembered to count the houses to the corner, but I had forgotten to look at the name of the road as I turned into it. Manton Road. I ran back to the telephone-box ...

'I am Paul Verray,' I said breathlessly, in what I hoped was a foreign accent. 'You must come quick, there has been murder!'

'And just where do we come, sir?' said a deep, lazy voice, with all the stolid comfort in it of all English policemen.

'My sister, she has been stabbed! We drive up in a taxi, there is no one in the house, she go into the house in front of me, she turns the light and there is no light, and then I hear a cry, and she lies there dead!'

'Quite so, sir, but you still haven't said where.'

'The Sycamores, Lauriston Gardens, perhaps she is not dead, you will bring a doctor? *Please*, a doctor!'

'Lauriston Gardens.' The voice became firm and businesslike. 'Is that where you're speaking from?'

'No, no, you see, there are no lights, and the murderer perhaps he is still there.'

'I see.' There was just that touch of contempt for the foreigner who ran away. 'Then where are you now?'

'I speak from the telephone-box in Manton Road. Now I go back to be with my sister. But you must come quick!'

'That's all right, sir.' His voice became more friendly suddenly. 'But I shouldn't go inside. Wait for us at the gate.'

'Yes, yes, but—'

'And the name again?'

'Paul Verray. It is the fifth house on the left. You won't forget the doctor?'

But he had rung off.

Had I been too foreign? But I had just seen my sister murdered, I was excited, out of breath—and who now could demonstrate just how pronounced, or mispronounced, Paul's accent had been?

I hurried back as if to the house. Manton Road was well-lit and somebody might be looking out of a window, to see a figure leaving the telephone-box, to notice which way it went. Lauriston Gardens was darker, and I walked past the house, trying to walk firmly and naturally, but desperately wanting to run, until I got to a turning. Then quickly again by little side-roads to a main street; and then, since there was life here, back to the unhurried but purposeful stride of the home-returning diner-out, who had stayed a little too long. My only fear had been lest I should meet the police-car. They would not be looking out for the man who telephoned, but anybody they passed might be the murderer.

I walked back to my rooms. It was a long way, a deadly long way at that time of night, but I walked back. Do you know why? 'Oh, well,' you say carelessly, 'I suppose in a sort of way it was safer. Never mind about that, tell me who these people were, and what the police did, and … I'm sorry, dear boy. You may not find this a very satisfactory story, because there is a great deal of it which I can't tell you, which I never knew; but I have said no word of it for forty years, and now at last that I am telling somebody my side of it, I am going to enjoy telling it. I am the hero of this story, make no mistake. For forty years I have wanted to tell somebody how clever this hero was, how he thought of everything; I mean, of course, how clever he suddenly became, after the incredible event. So now you will have a paragraph from my *Manual for Criminals*, as composed by me in those few age-long minutes which I could spare for the work.

Nowhere is one such a target for eyes as in a bus, and particularly in a bus at night when there is nothing to draw the eyes outside. Notice for yourself next time you are in one. Automatically your eyes will fasten on somebody and suck the meaning out of him. I don't count myself a very observant person, I have had so many things to think about in my life, but I have never left a bus or a tube without having one face, one personality, completely registered in my mind. That night I didn't want to be registered in anybody's mind. The same with a taxi? Oh, no. A taxi-driver would only have the vaguest impression of his fare. I was already counting on that confidently, as you have seen. I was completely certain that our taxi-driver would identify the dead bodies of Paul and Marguerite Verray with a 'That's right, that's the couple I picked up in the Strand.' But just suppose that he had picked me up again at the Marble Arch! A thousand-to-one chance, you say. My dear boy, criminals are caught because the thousand-to-one chance comes off against them. If you must take a two-to-one chance, take it boldly. If you need not take a million-to-one chance, don't take it. That was what I taught myself, coming away from Lauriston Gardens.

I got home. I had the only flat in the building; the rest of it was offices, and a housekeeper lived somewhere underground. Nobody ever knew when I came in. I threw the match-stubs into the waste-paper basket and burnt Sheila's letter. It was one o'clock as I wound my watch up. It seemed only a few minutes later that I woke to broad daylight and a knocking on the door. My golfing holiday had begun.

VIII

In a corner-seat (first stop Plymouth) I thought it all out. First, had I been a cad; or, to put it with more dignity, had I betrayed my own ethical standards? One can defy, unhorse, and place a triumphant foot on, any adversary but Conscience. Conscience is always back in the saddle and at you again. Secondly, whether or not running away was justified, had I in fact escaped? Thirdly—the question to which you want the answer—what was it all about? I thought it out in this order, for it was in this order that the answers seemed important.

My self-justification, then, first. Looking back, I see that I told you of old Hammersley's interest in iron gates, and admitted that it had nothing to do with the story. It would have been more helpful to have said something of Mrs Hammersley. She was a shortish, well-kept-in woman of imposing frontage, whose life-work was the finding of a suitable husband for Sheila. Every unmarried man who came into the house was looked at, and accepted or rejected, as a possible candidate. He could not get on to the short list until his financial position and prospects had come under favourable consideration; but a 'mere boy', like myself, with his way to make, could be entered on the books if he were 'nice'; partly as company for Sheila while waiting, partly as a spur to the more solid candidate of the moment. But there must be no 'nonsense'; no social impropriety by the Victorian standards of her own girlhood; nothing which could give rise to a suspicion in the genuine suitor's mind that Sheila was not a 'thoroughly nice' girl. I told you that I played golf twice with Sheila. On the first occasion Mrs Hammersley walked round with us; and asked her daughter on every tee why she didn't hit the ball as far as I did, adding, 'I'm sure you could if you really tried, dear.' On the second occasion some other duty kept her at home, and we were only allowed to play on my solemn promise to take two caddies round with us. Well, that was Mrs Hammersley.

I loved Sheila, and I didn't mean to lose her. If I had stayed for the police to come, I should have lost her. Nice men who are allowed into the houses of thoroughly nice girls do not get mixed up with murder. They do not pick up painted young women of foreign extraction in trains, and offer to see them home. They do not—Mrs Hammersley's massive bosom was too well corseted to shake, but it would have struggled to indicate her horror—they do not, my dear Sheila, *deliberately go into their houses*! 'Of course Mr—er—' she would pretend not to remember my name, it was so completely to be put out of Sheila's mind—'of course he is not a *murderer*; at *least* I can say that no *murderer* has ever come into this house; but I have been *grossly* deceived as to his character.'

So I am to lose Sheila, for—I think I may say—no fault of my own. I am also, and don't smile at the anti-climax, to endanger my golfing holiday. For though it was (I thought) extremely unlikely that I should be arrested for murder, my story might well sound thin to the police; they might want to keep me under observation for some time; and they would certainly want me for the inquest. So I should not be going down to Cornwall next day; should not be thinking happy thoughts as we glided through Newbury, Westbury, all the old landmarks; should not look out of the window at Exeter Cathedral as I finished my lunch; should not be filling my pipe as we slid down the estuary, smoking it as we turned westward and came out of little red sandstone tunnels to glimpse for a moment the sparkling sea. All the old landmarks, all the renewals of anticipation to which I had looked forward for twelve long months, all these little preludes to the delight of a crazy golfer in a three weeks' golfing holiday, gone; gone for a Paul and Marguerite Verray, who were nothing to me.

Well, that's my side. Now let's consider theirs. They were dead when I left them. I was absolutely sure of this. I don't mean that I *am* absolutely sure, just because they said so at the inquest. I mean that I was sure at the time. Even if they hadn't been, I had only lost a minute or two, and that could hardly have made the difference. It was merely callous, then, to be thinking first of myself, not of them, poor souls? No, no; one can be sentimental about many things, but not about the sudden, instantaneous death of strangers. One could only be sorry for those who loved them, and were left behind. Who were these? Even if I had known of their existence, and I never did, I could have been as sorry for them (I told Conscience) in Cornwall as in a Coroner's Court.

No, if I had left a debt unpaid, it was to the community, not to individuals.

Are you interested in the community? Most young artists aren't. I was not an artist, and I was rather community-minded in those days: Lloyd George (1906) vintage. I did feel that, if a policeman blew his whistle, one ought to join in, however dangerous or inconvenient it might be. I believed in Law and Order and the Pursuit of Murderers. Had I handicapped the police by running away? Well, what did I know which they didn't know? That Paul had died a minute before, not a few minutes after, Marguerite. I didn't see that that mattered. What else? Only this: that Paul knew a man called Breitenstein, and that Marguerite knew two people at Bedford Park and a tall man whose description I could give, and who might be Breitenstein. But the Bedford Park people (I thought) were bound to come forward, and they could tell of the man in the train. I should have to wait for the inquest before I knew whether he were Breitenstein or not; whether I still had that one tiny piece of information to give the police.

Fancy worrying about that, I can hear you say; if your Conscience was so prim, I wonder she didn't point out that whatever happened, you seemed to be telling a good many lies. I don't think Conscience ever got on to that. Nothing about lying ever passed between us at that time. I admit that, when the story came back to me a few days ago, and I began to write this, she made an absurd attempt to jog me. But I put her in her place. 'My good woman,' I said, 'if circumstances tell wicked lies against me, I am entitled to defend myself with the weapons which they have chosen.' And to that I hold. So let us get on to Breitenstein, who was the final answer to my first two problems, and, I have always thought, the key to the third.

IX

Yes, Breitenstein was the man in the train, though I didn't know it at the time. So I shall call him by that unlovely name, while I am considering, a little way past Reading, my second problem: had I escaped? For it all depended on him.

If you were called to the telephone and a voice said, 'This is James Alcott of the Spencer Galleries,' and if everything which he said made professional sense to you, and you looked him up when he had finished speaking, and found that he was what he said, well, what more would you want? Of course James Alcott rang you up. And of course Paul Verray rang the police up. And then he went back to the house (as he said he would) and went inside (as a loving brother would, though warned not to) and found the murderer still there (as the police had feared was possible), and was himself murdered … and fell across the body of his sister. There's the hat he was wearing when they came in together. Lit a match for his sister when the switch didn't work—to see her way into the sitting-room probably—there's the stub—what did she go for? Torch perhaps—hangs up his hat and the match goes out. The other man's hiding in the sitting-room; stabs her; she screams, runs into the passage and falls. He lights a match and bends over her, gets into a panic and runs out. Then remembers the telephone-box and runs to it. Comes back, strikes another match as he looks at his sister again ... Ordinary Swan matches—better just look in his pocket ... that's all right—and then, as he stands up, the murderer comes out again, flashes a torch and stabs him ...

'Yes, sir, them's the two I picked up in the Strand. Didn't see the gent's face very clearly, not when he give me the address, bit 'ard of 'earing and I bends me 'ead down, and it was the lady wot paid at the other end. But that's the couple, I'd swear to that, couldn't mistake the lady, and I sees enough of the gent to know there couldn't be no mistook about 'im neither. Yes, sir, that's wot 'e was wearing, top 'at and scarf and all. Time? Well, as it 'appened, I did look, wanting to get 'ome, and expecting a bit more when it's as late as that. Ten minutes short o' twelve it is when I drops 'em, and I remember thinking, well I'll be home by twelve, and that's the first time this week ...'

Almost too easy.

But then there was Breitenstein. If he came forward, as I felt sure that he would, what was he going to say?

Well, it depended on whether he were as innocent as I, or, as I was inclined to think, the murderer.

Why on earth should he be the murderer? you ask. No reason at all, except that he was the only man I knew who could be, and that I had idly cast him for the part of villain when I first saw him.

First, then, if he were innocent—and truthful. I said 'as innocent as I', but I don't mean as little truthful as I. Let us suppose him completely truthful.

'... Yes, sir, it was understood that Miss Verray was to be met at Charing Cross by her brother. Unfortunately I have to catch a train at Victoria. She has not been in England long, and is not used to travelling alone—yes, she speaks English well. I ask a young gentleman in the carriage if he will tell her when to get out. He is not going to Charing Cross himself, but says he will see that she gets out there. For myself I do not even know how many more stations are to come, I use the Underground very little. So I say good-bye to Miss Verray at Victoria, and that is the last I see of her.'

'Thank you, Mr Breitenstein. There is, of course, no doubt that she did get out at Charing Cross, and was duly met by her brother. What I should like you to tell us now, if you can, is whether she showed any particular apprehension in the course of that evening. Mr and Mrs—er—Pargo tell us that she seemed in her usual *not* very high spirits. Was that how it struck you?'

'You must understand, sir, that I did not know Miss Verray at all well—even less well than I knew her brother. But from the little I had seen of her she seemed a girl who took life very seriously.'

'As if she always had something on her mind?'

'You might say that—yes. She always seemed—nervous.'

'Ah! But you talked, no doubt, in the train. How was she then?'

'Well—like that. I supposed, of course, that she was nervous of being left alone in the train. She kept begging me to come on with her to Charing Cross, even to see her home. Almost as if she were afraid that her brother mightn't be at the station.'

'Ah! That is very significant. She feared that already something might have happened to her brother. As we know, he met her, and it was not until later—Thank you, Mr Breitenstein, your evidence has been most helpful.'

I could imagine the scene in the Coroner's Court—just like that. What I could not imagine was that anybody would take the slightest interest in the anonymous young gentleman who was not going to Charing Cross himself. What evidence could he give?

But if Breitenstein were the murderer, then what? I had to put myself in his place, and consider his part in the business, before I could decide how I should be affected. So let us make up a story for him, I said, as we glided through Newbury, and on to Westbury.

Breitenstein had decided to murder Paul. Don't ask me why. I can think of a hundred reasons why one man should want to murder another; this was one of the reasons. Tonight is to be the night. He has called for Marguerite, and taken her down to the Pargos. Paul cannot come. He has important business (he always has important business) and must be in all evening. Breitenstein will bring the girl back. A little while before they leave to catch their train, he pretends to remember something which will make it extremely inconvenient for him to take her home. But it is all right; he will see her to Charing Cross, and will now ring up Paul and arrange that he shall meet her there. He withdraws to the telephone, smokes a cigarette, and comes back to say that it is all very lucky. Paul is just starting off to keep a sudden appointment in the West End, and will go on to Charing Cross at eleven-thirty to collect her.

'Was he all right?' she asks anxiously.

'Y-yes,' he says hesitatingly. And then quickly, 'Yes, of course. Why not?'

'Who is he meeting?' she asks, almost frightened now.

'He didn't say.'

Chapter II of my *Manual for Criminals* says, 'Simplicity pays. Be as simple as you can.' Here was the very simple plot, the very simple alibi. He gets out at Victoria, slips into a carriage at the back, and is out at Charing Cross and into the North London tube before we begin to move. He gets out at the nearest station to Lauriston Gardens, kills Paul and is away. Marguerite is not met, waits an indefinite time for her brother, gets home somehow … and finds him dead. Breitenstein's alibi is confirmed by her later. Simple.

But it didn't happen quite so simply, because he dragged in me.

Why did he drag me in? Perhaps because she insisted. She had supposed he was coming on to Charing Cross with her, and she refused to be left alone. Perhaps because he thought she would be more willing to wait patiently on the platform if she had a young man with her. Perhaps because—a man of the world summing up the innocent young boy at the other end of the carriage—he knew that in the end I would take the girl home, and so provide another suspect for the police and another witness to his alibi. Yes, there were good reasons why he should drag me into it. What was unknown to him was that the girl didn't attract me, and that I wanted to get back to bed as quickly as I could. What was unexpected was that Paul had slipped out to the post, and that, by the time he returned, we were on the top of him. So, when Marguerite came into the sitting-room, he had to kill her too. He didn't want to. He was rather sorry for her.

But why not kill me also, while he was about it? Well, why should he? I hadn't seen him there, and was no danger to him. On the contrary, I was now the only witness to his alibi, I alone could swear that he had left the train at Victoria. Obviously, then, he would emphasize my share in the party—which meant that the police would be looking for me ... So, you see, I *haven't* escaped. I'm for it! ...

I was for it until we got to Westbury.

But at Westbury—wait!

When he reads the papers, he will know that I have left the party. The police have not seen me, know nothing about me. I am evidently lying low. Suppose I don't appear? Suppose I do ... and say that I saw him slipping back into the train at Victoria ... or merely deny that he ever spoke to me. He is a murderer and knows it. I am innocent, and he knows it. Whose word will he expect to be believed? Mine. He will not dare to say anything which I might contradict: he will hardly dare to say anything about me which I might not be there to confirm. So he will wait to hear what I say. And if I am not there to say anything; if no one is bothering about the harmless young gentleman at the other end of the carriage (not so harmless now, he realizes, but fighting to keep out of it); then he will not bother either. He will be as casual about me as if he had nothing to hide.

'I ask a young gentleman if he will tell her when to get out. He is not going to Charing Cross himself ... So I say good-bye to Miss Verray at Victoria ...'

'Thank you, Mr Breitenstein. There is, of course, no doubt that she did get out at Charing Cross and was duly met by her brother …'

It looked as if I were all right anyway. The only danger—an infinitesimally small one, I thought—was that Breitenstein and the Verrays and the Pargos might all be in an international spy story together, and that none of them would get in touch with the police. Then I should have to speak.

The attendant came along, and I booked a seat for lunch. As I began on the fish, I remembered that I should also have to speak if the man's name were not Breitenstein.

X

I was lodging with a farmer called Lambrick, whose sheep were occasionally to be seen on the course, and on that first evening, just as she had done in previous years, Mrs Lambrick brought in the duck and green peas, and asked me what papers I would like ordered.

'Mrs Lambrick,' I said firmly, but with a smile, 'I'm not going to *look* at the papers for the next three weeks. I'm going to think of nothing but golf, and get my handicap down to six.'

She smiled back, and said well of course if ever I did want to see anything particular I had only to ask, and she would bring in theirs for me of an evening.

'You can't tempt me,' I said. 'I don't care what Lloyd George or the Kaiser do, or who murders whom, I'm here to enjoy myself. And thanks to you, Mrs Lambrick, I'm quite sure I'm going to.' And I got to work on the duck.

Well, that was the first precaution I took. The other was this.

I looked very young in those days, younger even than the incredibly youthful age, as it seems to me now, of twenty-five. When I went for my interview with Lancasters, the Managing Director commented on it, and advised me humorously to grow a beard if I didn't want to be mistaken for one of the apprentices.

I replied (equally humorously—one needs to keep in step with one's Managing Director) that I had an old pair of whiskers at home which I would bring out and dust. So next morning I began on a moustache; and I told myself that with three weeks of perpetual golf and sea-bathing, and a three weeks' old moustache, I should look very different from the pale, clean-shaven Paul Verray who had followed his sister into a taxi at the top of Villiers Street.

For of course you understand that, if in the end I went to the police, it would not be with bowed head, saying, 'Oh, sir, forgive me, it was I who impersonated Paul Verray and told those wicked lies.' No, I saw the scene going quite differently.

'Well, sir, what can I do for you?'

'Well—er—the fact is, Inspector, I've been away on a holiday and haven't been seeing the papers. So I've only just heard about this Verray case.'

'And you think there's something you can tell us about it?'

'Well, I don't know, but—I say, look here, is it true that the two of them were at the Charing Cross District station late that night, and got a taxi in the Strand?'

'And if they were, sir?'

'Well, because I came from Richmond to St James's Park that night, and at Bedford Park two foreigners got in, and the girl was being met at Charing Cross, and I just wondered—'

'Ah!' He becomes interested.

I describe Marguerite. The girl without a doubt. I describe the man. He makes a note of it. Not Paul evidently.

'And he got out at Victoria, you say, sir? You didn't happen to hear the girl mention his name?'

I tell my story truthfully—up to Victoria. But I say that, in the short conversation we had before I got out at St James's Park, she mentioned somebody or something called Breitenstein.

'I was very sleepy, Inspector, and not paying much attention. I thought she was referring to the man who had just left her, but she may have been telling me where she was born. She jabbered a lot—you know the way they do.'

'Breitenstein,' says the Inspector thoughtfully. I seem to have got the name across. He looks up, as if surprised to see me there. 'Thank you, sir. Quite right to come forward. That might be helpful.'

I retire, respected of all men. The good citizen.

Well, I had to wait for the inquest to know what Breitenstein would do. But, as you see, I wasn't taking any risks. I remember on my third day playing in a foursome with three people from the hotel, I forget their names, and one of the women asked me what I thought of Asquith's speech, or whatever it was. We were standing on the fifth tee. I said, 'S'sh. No politics. I haven't looked at the papers since I've been here and I'm not going to.' She seemed to think that I was an Under Secretary or something. But I felt that my immunity from current affairs was really getting established.

Of course I did see the papers. I went into the kitchen every night after the Lambricks had gone to bed, and kept in touch with Our Crime Correspondent. And then one day there was an account of the inquest …

And Breitenstein—yes, that was his name—gave his evidence. And he said nothing about me!

Did that prove him guilty? At first I thought that it did. If he were innocent, why should he conceal anything? Then I remembered that I was innocent—and was concealing a good deal. But it was funny, wasn't it? If he were guilty, he must have wondered what I knew, must have thought it safer to keep me out of it, must have been a little frightened of me. Well, I was also a little frightened of him. I hoped that we shouldn't meet again. In fact, we never did.

I'm sorry, dear boy, but that's really all. The Verrays were a mysterious couple, and nobody seemed to know much about them. Nobody was ever arrested. To come to more important matters: my moustache was a great success with the Managing Director, and we had a lot of laughs about it. I don't know whether it would have been a success with Sheila. You see, I had a letter from Mrs Hammersley a few weeks after my return to say that the dear girl had become engaged to a *most* delightful man in the tea business. I didn't mind so much as I had expected, because on my last day I had found a much dearer girl in the bunker by the twelfth green. I apologized for driving into her, and she took it so sweetly that—

Well that, my dear John, was how I met your mother …

No, I didn't tell her anything about it. Husbands, you will find, are born complete on the day when they first meet their wives. Adventures in a pre-natal existence, particularly when involving two other young women, are as profitless to recount as last night's dream.

C.O.D.

(1948)

'Did I ever tell you,' said Mr Reginald Sprocket, that charming but little-known essayist, moistening the stamp and placing it on his letter, 'of my war-service in the Ministry of Transport?'

The girl behind the counter at the village post-office, drapery and sweet-shop gave him 3½*d.* change, and said that he hadn't. It was, in fact, the first time she had seen him.

Mr Sprocket pushed the office scales a little further along the counter and sat negligently down. 'This will interest you professionally,' he said. 'Stop me if you have heard it.'

Owing to a difference of opinion with the Director as to the relative importance of news (said Mr Sprocket), I had just retired from my post of announcer at the B.B.C.; to the regret of many millions of listeners, some of whom, we may surmise, had already cast on the first stitches of the Christmas bed-socks which they proposed to knit for me. I had held my post for a comparatively short time, and had been unable, therefore, to effect the revolution in the Corporation's policy for which I had hoped. I mention this because I do not wish you to hold me responsible for the many shortcomings which you find in the service; such as, to take a case, the habitual levity of the Scandinavian Folk Songs in the Third Programme. The blame lies elsewhere. But perhaps I had better tell you first the full story of my connexion with that autocratic body.

For some months I had been Deputy Assistant Director of the Dramatic Sounds Department, being personally responsible for all those noises which give so much more reality to a radio play than mere dialogue: storms at night, mounted men crossing a cobbled bridge, seagulls taking leave of a liner, and rats gnawing their way through woodwork—to give the examples which will occur most readily to your mind. But it had long been my wish to exchange the yellow pullover of the Sounds Department for the full evening dress of the Announcer Corps, and it was with this purpose that I sought an interview with the Chief of Staff.

'What can I do for you?' he asked courteously.

I explained that I wished to better myself.

'What are you now?'

I said that for the greater part of the previous week I had been an Austin 7 going into first on mounting a hill, but that for the last two nights I had been a flock of sheep in a mist on the mountains.

'And what would you like to be?' he asked kindly.

'I should like to be an announcer,' I said.

He looked surprised.

'You are accustomed to wearing full evening dress?' he asked.

'From a child,' I said.

'And what other experience have you had?'

I told him that once when Red Hot Roper had had a severe cold, I was the American who said, 'This is Red Hot Roper and his Razzle Dazzle Swing Boys bidding you all good night, good night, everyone, good night and carry on.'

He seemed impressed.

'How did it go?' he asked. 'Was reception good?'

I said that it might have been a coincidence, but Red Hot had had two proposals of marriage and a box of candied fruit next day.

'That sounds very promising,' he said. 'In the circumstances I think you might announce the six o'clock news this evening.'

I thanked him and went home to dress.

When I was handed the script from which to announce, I found that it was full of such clichés as are the despair of a writer like myself. Black smoke habitually poured from tails; patches of oil continually rose to the surface. It was my intention to give new life to all these outworn phrases.

('And did you?' asked the girl, moving along the counter to the sweet department, at which a younger patron was holding out an urgent penny.

'Unfortunately, no,' said Mr Sprocket.)

I began (he said) in the orthodox way. 'This is the B.B.C. Home Service. Here is the six o'clock news, and this is Reginald Sprocket reading it, better known to most of you, I dare say, as the author of many charming essays, of which the latest volume, *Daffodil Days*, to be published shortly by Crump and Webster at the moderate price of seven shillings and sixpence—' It was at this point that there occurred, without warning, what is technically known as a technical hitch; and before it could be put right I was asked to take my pocket-comb with me and leave the building. From the public's point of view it was a calamity, since I had much to say to them, but from my own it was merely an inspiration to new and greater fields of endeavour. Forgive me for interrupting myself a moment, but what were those charmingly coloured balls which appealed so strongly to our visitor?

('Assorted fruit-drops, penny an ounce.'

'I will have an assortment weighing four ounces,' said Mr Sprocket …)

My first step (continued Mr Sprocket) on being relieved of my arduous duties at the B.B.C, took me to the Ministry of Soap and Whitewash. The Minister, who had recently been promoted or degraded (it was never clear which) from the Ministry of Food, was an old friend of the family. A cousin of mine of the same name had recently written a small monograph on Pressed Flowers, and by some confusion of sound between 'flour' and 'flower', or miss-association of the subject with the separate industry of Pressed Beef, the book was fortunate enough to catch the attention of the Minister of Food. Meeting me at a Memorial Service, and accidentally hearing my name when I was introduced to him, he said kindly, 'Ah, Mr Socket, I'm delighted to make your acquaintance. I have been reading with great interest your book on old English porcelain.' This, I felt, gave me a certain claim on his attention, and I was not surprised when I heard that he would receive me.

'Well, Mr Spigot,' he said, 'I am delighted to meet you again. I have not forgotten the pleasure your book on Chinese coins gave me. Now what can I do for you?'

I explained that I wished to put myself at the service of my country.

'Yes, well, we are full up here at the moment, but there might be something for you somewhere else. You had better go and see Hammersmith this afternoon. Good morning to you, and let me know how you get on. You must write another book one day.'

I withdrew, and, after a light lunch, boarded a bus to Hammersmith. The Minister had not mentioned what his object was in wishing me to become acquainted with this particular quarter of London, and I may say at once that I spent a profitless afternoon there; but the news which greeted me on my return, that Lord Hammersmith would like me to ring him up, threw a new light on the matter, and almost reconciled me to my fruitless journey.

It never became clear who Lord Hammersmith was, but he appeared to be a capable young man, who found no difficulty in securing me a well-paid post in the Ministry of Transport. I forget who was Minister at the time. They came and went with a certain regularity. One got into the way of calling any new face which had an air of authority 'Chief', and assuming that it had come into one's room in order to raise one's salary; instead of which (as we writers say) it would reveal itself, as often as not, as a humble addition to the staff, desiring to know its way to the lavatory. When, however, I did at last meet the Minister, I had no difficulty in identifying him as the tall, thin man whose pint of beer I had accidentally drunk at the canteen two days before, leaving him, on some vague impulse of compensation, to pay for both of us. Naturally I did not presume on our previous acquaintance, but said, 'You sent for me, sir?' respectfully, and waited to hear why he had summoned me to his presence.

(Mr Sprocket opened his bag of assorted fruit-drops, and chose a green one; but, realizing as it approached his lips that it might impede his natural flow of words, checked, and replaced it in the bag.)

Transport in war-time (said Mr Sprocket) is always a difficulty, whether it is Hannibal trying to get his elephants over the Alps or King John conveying the royal baggage across the Wash—though perhaps, to make my meaning quite clear, and avoid unnecessary scandal, I should have used the word impedimenta rather than baggage. In modern war the problem assumes a different shape, and may, perhaps, best be exemplified by the fact that a parcel of unbound essays, travelling from, as it might be, Frome towards the office, to take a case, of Messrs Crump and Webster in London, would think nothing of spending three months on the journey, and being last heard of in Market Bosworth as a box of dried prunes.

(The girl nodded. 'Shocking it was,' she said. 'They used to blame *me* for it, just as if *I* had anything to do with it.')

I had ventured to call the Minister's attention to this and other matters which were delaying the moment of victory, and now it seemed that he had sent for me to discuss the matter. For if things are put on trains and never get anywhere, where, as the Minister well said, do they get to?

'Where indeed, sir?' said I.

'Suppose, for instance,' said the Minister, 'the line is damaged, and the train is unable to proceed? Well? Is it just left there? For ever? That's bad, Sprocket. We must improve on that. Trains mustn't be left just lying about.'

I reminded him that passenger trains were similarly inconvenienced, but that there was no record of a passenger being lost entirely.

'Exactly my point,' he said. 'If the line is damaged at Chipping Podbury, the passenger alights and re-embarks at Chipping Salterton. But what does the *train* do? These are the things we ought to know, Sprocket.'

I suggested that the train backed into a siding until the line was repaired, and then proceeded on its way.

'With goods on train if goods-train?' said the Minister tersely.

'Presumably so, sir.'

'Then why don't the goods arrive in course of time, with the train, so to speak, in support?'

'Perhaps,' I tried again, 'they are unloaded at Chipping Podbury before backing, and then when the train resumes its journey, it forgets that it is empty, and accidentally—'

'But would not somebody—as it might be, a porter at Chipping Podbury—be aware of all this?'

'He should be, sir.'

'But apparently he is not. Here are these poor dumb crates dotted about the railway systems of Great Britain, unable to call for help, unable to indicate their latitude and longitude, and nobody can do anything about it. It's up to *us*, Sprocket. The Ministry of Transport. Note that word "transport". *Not* the Ministry of Immobility in Sidings.'

And then I had my brilliant idea; an idea which, little though I anticipated it, was to lead me into the charming company in which I now find myself.

'Chief,' I said, 'how would it be if *I* travelled as a crate of goods from Frome to Paddington? I, at least, should not be inarticulate.'

'You mean,' he said, 'that you would put your head through the straw and call for help from time to time?'

'No, no, sir, you misunderstand me. I should remain silent, but I should be taking notes all the time. Whatever happens to packages on a goods train, or for that matter a passenger train, will happen to me, for I shall be one of them. The only difference will be that when we all arrive at Paddington I shall be in a position to make a full report, as the other packages will not, of the sequence of events which brought us there.'

The Minister was thoughtful.

'It's an idea, Sprocket,' he said at last. 'Quite an idea. The only objection which occurs to me at the moment is that, when your report is presented on your arrival at Paddington, it may be dismissed by the Cabinet as the senile reminiscences of a garrulous old man.'

I need hardly tell *you*, dear lady, that I had foreseen this objection. For it was my idea to present a series of interim reports from week to week, as circumstances allowed; emerging from the crate by means of a sliding panel at (as it might be) Chipping Slowcombe-on-the-Whiffer, and dispatching a letter to the Ministry from the local post-office, drapery and sweet-shop.

I explained this to the Minister. His chief apprehension removed, he shook me warmly by the hand.

'Sprocket,' he said, 'you are a gallant fellow, and the Government will not forget it. You will take every precaution? The Ministry cannot afford to lose you.'

I assured him that I should be well prepared.

'You must keep in mind,' he said kindly, 'not only the months which lie ahead of us, but the ensuing seasons as they will recur. Thus, Sprocket, it is a question not only of winter woollies, to which, no doubt, you have given your attention, but of summer light-weight zephyrs, mesh or otherwise. But I can safely leave all this to you. Good luck, to you, my dear fellow.'

I thanked him and withdrew.

Next morning I went down to Frome by car. Naturally our Ministry had its agents everywhere, and at Frome I got into contact with one of our most knowledgeable men. We discussed the venture from every angle. As an example of the minute attention we paid to detail I may instance the consideration we gave to the question whether I should be labelled *'China and Glass, Fragile'* or, as I was inclined to prefer,

'*Dynamite, Handle with Care*'. Obviously I did not want to be thrown about. I had boasted to the Minister that I should be in a position to make a continuous report, and it was necessary to remain in that position. On the other hand the whole point of this experiment was that one should not receive special treatment. Any such *cri du cœur* as '*Urgent*' would be entirely misconceived. In the end we decided that I should travel quite simply as '*Books*', with the one small concession to human frailty, '*This Side Up*'.

My home for the next few months (as I supposed) was comfortably padded, and had a sliding panel which could be worked from the inside. Besides clothes for the varying climatic conditions, and a certain amount of tinned food, I had provided myself with refreshment for the mind; notably *Paradise Lost*, a work with which I was insufficiently acquainted, and an early volume of essays *Mornings at Seven* (Crump and Webster, 5s.) by the well-known author of *Daffodil Days*. My idea was that at the many sidings to which I was clearly destined, I would get out, stretch my legs, and eventually fetch up at some house of refreshment, returning to my fellow-travellers in ample time to resume the journey. Emergency rations, therefore, were all that I needed.

I shall not weary you (said Mr Sprocket kindly) with the full tale of my adventures. My companions, as I discerned through one of the many peep-holes with which I had provided myself, were a likely looking lot of young packages, though inclined to be over-familiar. However, a certain irregularity of shape in the roof of my house, which I had thoughtfully insisted on, gave me the freedom of the upper air, and the unrestricted use of my panel. Throughout the whole of my wanderings I was only superimposed upon by one bicycle; a bicycle, however, which seemed, particularly at night, to be composed exclusively of pedals.

At the beginning the procedure was much as would have been expected. We left Frome at seven o'clock one Monday night, and, travelling uneventfully backwards for some 28 miles, reached Long

Sutton and Pitney at eight-thirty on Wednesday morning. Here we rested for three days before returning to Frome, and by the following Tuesday were safely back at Long Sutton and Pitney again. I sent a brief report to the Minister giving 'Poste Restante, Long Sutton and Pitney' as an accommodation address, and resumed my comfortable quarters and the delightful company of *Mornings at Seven* …

The full tale of my travels will no doubt be published shortly in a White Paper. The life would have been monotonous but for the occasional glimpses we had of the sea. I have always had a passion for this element, and the first sight of the waves breaking on the beach at Bognor Regis gave me new courage for my task. By now I had re-read that charming work *Mornings at Seven* sixteen times, and if I had not completely mastered *Paradise Lost*, I had at least got some idea of the plot and general scope of the work. It was not, however, until we were wintering at Merthyr Tydfil that I first encountered the hero, by name Adam; and it was in the Manchester Ship Canal, I remember, that he was joined by his dear wife—Eve, if I recollect the name aright …

'And that, roughly speaking,' said Mr Sprocket ten minutes later, 'is how we brought the guns up from Aix to Ashby de la Zouch. Of my arrival at Basra labelled *Small Arms Ammunition*; of my life as a vaulting-horse in the gymnasium at Haifa; and of my eventual return labelled *Not Wanted on Voyage* to Long Sutton and Pitney, this is not the place to speak. Suffice it to say that I am now making what must surely prove to be a temporary stay at your own charming marshalling-yards. For here in this letter'—he held it up—'I have sent in my resignation to the Minister. The war, I understand, is over, and my publishers, Messrs Crump and Webster, tell me that *Daffodil Days* has at last made the grade, and will be published next month. I feel once more at liberty to resume my profession of writing. Disappointing though the news will be to admirers of the essay as an art-form, I think of trying my hand in my next volume at some form of fictitious narrative. Sadly inexperienced as I am,' said Mr Sprocket regretfully, 'I hope in time to develop some slight talent for it.'

He put an assorted fruit-drop in his mouth, swung himself from the counter, and wished the girl a very good afternoon.

'Crackers,' said the girl, as the door closed behind him. She went on stamping letters.

Dear Old George

(1948)

Two, shapeless, middle-aged women were discussing the latest scandal in their little country town. Ethel Baradell-Smith was the stouter and more dowdy of the two. Nobody could say where her figure ended. Her hair was a grey turmoil. She had a rasping voice, suited to conversation in a tunnel; she seemed always to be talking something or somebody down—the clank of wheels, operatic music, or an equally talkative companion. But now it was time for her to go back to her own house. George would be home, and she had all this to tell him. All this about Tim Ferrars, who had left his wife.

'Well, there's one good thing,' she said with a satisfied smile, 'I don't have to worry about dear old George. Dear old George isn't like that. Somehow I can't quite see *him* running away.'

'You never know, dear,' said the other woman maliciously.

'Believe me, I do, darling. Now I shouldn't wonder at all if Jane wasn't getting a little anxious about the Major. I think, if I was Jane, I should be getting just a little anxious. He always strikes me as that sort of man. But George is quite, quite different. He's a different *type*, if you see what I mean. I haven't been married twenty-five years to dear old George without knowing what his faults are, and believe me, Polly, he's not that *type*. I mean that either you are or you aren't. And George—well'—she gave her unmusical laugh—'look at him!'

She touched cheeks with her friend and left, calling out something as she went.

She was quite right. George himself could have told her that he would never leave her now.

I

The four children had grown up together: George and Roger Baradell-Smith, Mary Somers and Ethel Pritchard. Roger was a cousin of George's and spent his holidays with them; his parents lived in India. Mary was the over-worked doctor's daughter, and was at the square house at the end of the village. Ethel was the much-petted, orphaned granddaughter of the old Vicar. George's father was an engineer, and always going away. In the holidays the four children went in and out of each other's houses, and did pretty much what they liked.

Mary was George's first love. She was quieter than Ethel and not so pretty, but then George was rather a stolid child, and the chattering, laughing, jumping-up-and-down Ethel bothered him. Ethel was better suited to the more dashing Roger. At the awkward age Ethel's self-consciousness sobered her down. She was now not quite so ready of tongue, fearing to be attacked herself. George found himself liking her better, and for the first time her prettiness attracted him. When they were all grown up, or what they thought was grown up, he was at first as happy with the two of them together as with either alone. They were both of them delightful girls. There was something restful about Mary, and this last year or two had given her a bloom, so that she was almost as pretty as the other. Yet being slow of speech himself, he admired Ethel's readiness, her flow of high spirits. She was good company when one felt in that mood.

He seemed to take it for granted in his unromantic way that he would marry one of them. He wasn't in love with either, but he was in love with the idea of getting engaged, getting married and settling down. He was still a little uncertain which one he preferred, when

Roger decided it for him. Roger and Mary announced their engagement. So naturally George married Ethel. Ethel had already promised herself George; Roger was the more dashing, but the more unreliable; George was the safe one. Also, and this was important, he was the better listener.

Roger and Mary went off to South Africa. There was a little correspondence at first between the two girls; but correspondence at that distance was too one-sided to keep them together, and Mary passed out of George's life. He settled down with Ethel.

Ethel was pretty in those days, attractive of face and body; and George was a born husband. They had one child whom they adored, Penelope. For five years George was happy. Then, when they were all off for a holiday together, Penelope fell out of a train and was killed. Perhaps he thought it was Ethel's fault—the child was on her side of the carriage; probably she thought he thought so; in fact, it was nobody's fault. Ethel abandoned herself to grief and an exaggerated remorse. She had killed her child. Never, never, never would she have another. Both George and the local Vicar had tried to console her. The Vicar drew a picture of Penelope in Heaven, released from the cares of this world, and, with more assurance, spoke of Time the Great Healer. He was right. Time went on, and they forgot Penelope. But long before this Ethel had let her figure go, for what did anything matter now; and George had ceased to be a husband, and was dear old George.

II

George was a year or two short of fifty when Mary came back into his life. He still had thick black hair without a sign of grey in it, a little close-clipped black moustache, and a trim, well-carried figure; with these to help him there was no reason why he should ever show his age. In the train which the more important people in offices caught every evening he was not noticeable. He wore, like so many of them, a short black coat and striped trousers; he carried, sometimes, a dispatch-case.

A fellow-traveller, remote from the business world and contemptuous of their conventional, unimaginative pattern, might perhaps have picked out George from the others as somehow a little more human. He looked likeable, which some of the others didn't; he might have had, which none of the others had, a quiet sense of humour. He didn't talk much. One would be safe in putting him up for one's club. But obviously on the Stock Exchange or somewhere—poor devil.

Mary recognized him at once.

'Hallo, George,' she said, as if they had parted last week.

He turned round, taking off his hat automatically, looked at her for a moment, wrinkling up his eyes in that way she knew, and said, 'Why, it's Mary, isn't it? Well!'

They told each other a little of their immediate news, standing on the pavement. He had a business call to make just round the corner in Arlington Street; couldn't they have tea somewhere afterwards? Roger had died three years ago; she was over in England for a visit, she wasn't sure if she would stay. Yes, she smiled, she was quite alone in the world; she had a little flat in Chelsea. Couldn't he come and have tea with her there? He'd love to, he had to catch the 5.30, but he would be with her at four, and that would give them time for a real good talk. How nice. And Ethel? Ethel was quite well, down in the country. I *am* glad to see you again, Mary. So am I, George; you don't look a day older. Nor do you, Mary. She laughed and shook her head at him. She knew how far from the truth it was.

But much further from the truth, thought George, as they sat happily over tea together, was the absurd suggestion that she and Ethel were the same age. Mary was twenty years younger than Ethel, with a figure well under control, a beautifully made-up face, and her own fair hair as shining, as wavy, as ever. Not a day over forty, and a modern forty at that. Whereas Ethel—he looked at her dispassionately when he got home that night. Sixty? Well, it didn't really matter. It was just the difference between a woman whom you would like to introduce to strangers as your wife, and—and Ethel.

'Oh, who do you think I ran into to-day? Mary!'

'Mary Somers?'

'Yes. She's a widow now. Roger died three years ago. She's over in England for a bit.'

'Well, she might at least have told us. Who do you think *I* met to-day? The new Mrs Viner!'

'Who on earth is she?'

'My dear old George, don't pretend to be so stupid. You knew that John had married again, and naturally we all wondered what she was going to be like. I said—and I generally know these things, it's a sort of instinct, I suppose—that he would choose somebody as much like dear Amy as possible. You see, I always feel that there are two *types* of husband. There's the type which—'

He listened as he always listened now; saying 'Yes' and 'I think you're right' and 'Really?', while his mind was elsewhere. How restful Mary was. How nice to be with somebody who liked to hear you talk, who listened, who was interested.

The new Mrs Viner disposed of, Ethel remembered Mary.

'Fancy Mary again! Would you like to ask her down here, darling?'

'No. I don't think so.'

She smiled affectionately at him. 'How right you are, George. It never does, trying to renew old friendships. It isn't as if we hadn't got plenty of nice friends here. Too many, I sometimes say.' She gave the laugh of an almost too popular woman. George felt glad that now he would keep Mary to himself.

He had tea again with her next week. Soon it became a habit. Tea with Mary on Wednesday at four; leave at five; catch the 5.30. On special occasions—her birthday, for example, or his, or some still remembered red-lettered day from their childhood—they had lunch together, and shopped, or sat in the Park; but still were back for tea at four, and always he left at five, and caught the 5.30. It was his rest hour, an hour of peaceful happiness with a dear woman; the woman whom he ought to have married. The week now was reckoned from Wednesday. One was never more than three days away from it. However harshly, however persistently, Ethel talked, only three days ago Mary's gentle voice ... in three days from now Mary's placid understanding ... At the end of a year Mary was as much part of his life as the more frequent 5.30.

When she told him one Wednesday that she might be giving up the flat and going back to South Africa, he knew at once that he couldn't let her go. At first he supposed that he was just asking her not to leave him; begging her not to spoil his Wednesdays, not to take away the one day in the week which made his life consciously happy again. Then he realized that he was saying more than that; he was telling her that if she went, he must go with her. He was reminding her that as children they had sworn to get married. He was on the verge of telling her that he had always loved her.

Mary listened, surprised and deeply touched. She knew that she would miss their Wednesdays as much as he. She could imagine, and would have welcomed, a week of Wednesdays, for she was tired of being alone. Her life with the dashing Roger had reached the heights and the depths. She would never be in love like that again, nor did she want to be. Life with George, she thought, would be very restful, very comfortable. Dear old George! So good, so kind, so right. One could trust him always. One would never see that look in his eyes, that awareness of the other sex, which she had seen so often in Roger's; so miserably, jealously, often in Roger's.

They talked it over sensibly. They were two sensible, middle-aged people. George was a good business man, and as soon as he saw that she was wavering, he began to be business-like. At the back of his mind he was still feeling astonished that it was he, George Baradell-Smith, who was actually 'running away' from his wife! Getting divorced!

'Of course,' he pointed out, 'you being Mrs Baradell-Smith already—'

'Wait a moment, George.' She held up a plump but pretty little hand.

'What, dear?'

'You mustn't rush me.'

'Mary dear, you do *want*—I mean—'

'And I mustn't rush you.'

'You did that when you said you were going away. You didn't think I'd stand for that?'

'Darling George,' she smiled. 'But what I mean, and I mean it seriously, is that we must both think it over.'

They argued about that; George protesting, of course, that he didn't need to, she saying that neither of them had considered Ethel yet, he saying that—well—er—*Ethel*—but he was quite sure ...

'It's no good, dear. There are things which we shall both have to think of. Now this is my plan. If neither of us has written to the other in the meantime, we will meet again next Wednesday and decide just how we're going to go about it. But in this next week we must think it over alone. If you decide, for any reason whatever—I can't advise you whether or not to talk it over with Ethel—you know best about that; but you must think of her, and of everything else, and if you decide that it would be a mistake to go on with it, just write me a little line, saying that you won't be here next Wednesday. I shan't feel injured or resentful in any way. I shall understand perfectly. And if I decide, then I will do the same. But if neither of us hears from the other, then, dear George'— she stood up, holding out her hands to him with a smile, half-mocking, half-loving—'I am yours. And now you must catch your train.'

He looked at the clock on her mantelpiece. 'Good Lord,' he said, 'I've missed it! Oh well, I can catch the 6.25.'

III

One could get a carriage to oneself on the 6.25; it was only the Third-Class passengers, the clerks and the office-girls, who had to keep their elbows out of each other's papers. Mary was quite right, one had to think these things out. Dispassionately. Neither in the cosy quiet of

Mary's room, in the restfulness of her company, nor within sound and sight of Ethel. Here in the train, alone. Money, for instance. If Ethel divorced him, she could claim a third of his income. No, he would be generous, he would give her more than that. He would settle a lump sum on her as well …

The train began to move. There were shouts from the platform as the door was swung open. He saw a girl on the running-board, dangerously off-balance. Suddenly and horribly Penelope came into his mind. He jumped up and pulled her in. By the time he had managed to get the door closed, she had fallen, a little breathless, into the seat opposite.

'Thank you,' she said. 'I oughtn't to have bothered you.'

He had been prepared to curse her, he had been so shaken by that memory, but now he mumbled that it was all right. 'You gave me rather a fright for a moment, that's all.'

'I know. And that always makes one angry. I was expecting you to say "What the hell?" It was nice of you not to.' She gave him a grateful smile, took out her compact and considered herself.

This is what Penelope might have been, he thought; a young Diana, with all the spring of life in her. Why did one always think of goddesses as over-size? Juno, Venus, even Diana—compare a woman to one of them, and one immediately pictured a great strapping creature—ridiculous!

She was now looking at her watch a little doubtfully.

'This *is* the 6.25 I've caught, isn't it?' she asked.

'6.25, that's right.'

'Then why does my watch say 6.10?'

'Does it generally say 6.10?' asked George, rather amused.

'Well, not generally. Only at ten minutes past six.'

'It must have stopped.'

'Then it chose a very inconvenient place to do it in.' She held the watch to her left ear. Then she held it to her right ear, explaining, 'It's possible to be stone deaf in one ear without ever finding it out, I mean until you do something like this.'

'I hope you're not finding it out now,' said George politely.

'Well, I can't hear anything in either, so I suppose that's a good sign.' She shook it and listened again. 'Do you know anything about watches?'

'I've learnt one or two things lately,' he said rather bitterly.

'Oh, do tell me.'

'They're not very helpful, I'm afraid. One is that, if you send a watch to be mended nowadays, it will take six months, and you will be charged the extortionate price of twenty-five shillings.'

'Well, but they're giving you all that time in which to save up. I think that's rather nice of them.'

'The other is that if your watch was being very fast or very slow before, you'll have nothing of that sort to complain of in the future. It now won't go at all.'

'I see. And if it didn't go at all when you sent it, I suppose it would now start going backwards?'

He laughed, and said, 'Probably. It's a hell of a world just now. Or don't you find it so?'

'Well, I seem to be in it, and I can't see my way to any other. So I do the best I can.'

He looked at her for a little, and said, almost to himself, 'Yes, it would be all right for you. You're young and beautiful.'

'That seems to want a compliment in exchange.'

'Good Heavens, no, I wasn't dreaming of such a thing.'

'All right, then you won't get it. So, speaking for myself alone, I'll say that one can't spend one's whole life looking in the glass and saying "God, how beautiful I am!"; and that, if the world is Hell, the younger you are, the more you're going to have of it. So, if you really think that it's all right for me, please stop saying it's a hell of a world.'

'I'm sorry,' said George. 'You must forgive me. It's the sort of silly thing one gets into the habit of saying without meaning anything.' He smiled to himself and added, 'As it happens, I discovered this afternoon that it wasn't at all a hell of a world. On the contrary, it has great possibilities.'

'That would cheer it up if it knew,' she said. 'Somehow I thought you were enjoying it, in a quiet sort of way.'

With the graceful half-bow of the courtier paying his lady a compliment, George said, 'Well—er—naturally—I mean—er—you—'

'Take a little time,' she nodded, 'and do us both justice.'

He gave her a very boyish smile suddenly, and shook his head. 'You've ruined it.'

'Oh!' She said it like a child who has had its visit to the circus postponed. 'Never mind. Something else will come to you without thinking, and you'll blurt it out, and I shall pass it over quickly, and then dwell on it happily after you've gone.'

'Is that what you do?'

'Always. Don't you?'

He considered it, trying to recall any compliments which had been paid to him—not, of course, by Ethel.

'Yes, I think I do,' he said seriously, 'only of course I don't get so much opportunity.'

'Oh well,' she smiled, 'I'll try to give you an opportunity just before you go.'

'That's very kind of you. But why are you so certain that I am going first? You don't know what my station is.'

'I know what mine is.'

'Of course. Stupid of me. You're going on to the end.'

'Yes. You ought to have done that more quickly, oughtn't you?'

'I'm not very quick, I'm afraid,' he said humbly.

'Oh, I don't know, you're not doing badly. Do you go up and down every day?'

'Yes. It's only an hour each way by my usual train.'

'Isn't this your usual?'

'Oh, no! The 5.30. And the 8.45 in the morning. Full of business men, all going up and down like me.'

'And what do you all do to pass the time?'

'Read the papers, and curse the Government, and somebody says "Did you hear about old So-and-so"—getting a divorce or going into liquidation or something, and we all say "Good Lord!" and "Well, I always did think—" and go back to our papers.' And that has been my life, he thought, and I never knew it.

'Two hours every day,' she murmured to herself.

'You must add a quarter of an hour each end to and from the station.'

'Three hours a day. Six days a week?'

'Well, lately, five. You see, I'm head partner now.'

'Fifteen hours a week. How many weeks a year?'

'On an average, say, forty-four.'

'That's—wait a moment—'

'Six-sixty.'

'Why did you say you weren't very quick? Well now, would you like to get that into days first, or shall we multiply by the number of years and then do it?'

'It's twelve years—where I am now.' He didn't say 'Where we are now.' Instinctively he kept Ethel out of it; not knowing whether it was because he had now left her for Mary, or because a married man might be less interesting to a girl like this.

'Well, come on. Six-sixty hours multiplied by twelve—'

'Three-thirty days.'

She nodded to herself, saying, 'Evidently there's a way of doing these things which I haven't been told about. Well, that's nearly a year.'

'Two years altogether, I should say. I used to live nearer to my work, but then it was six days a week and much less holiday.'

'Two years of your life! Wasted?'

'Absolutely. Except for this evening.'

She clapped her hands delightedly.

'That was just right! I knew you'd do it.'

'It wasn't a compliment,' he said seriously. 'Just an obvious fact.'

'Better and better! I must be looking rather special.' She felt in her bag.

'I was going to ask you,' said George, with the sudden bravado of the quiet man; 'do you always look as nice as this, or —'

'I'll tell you.' She took out her mirror again.

'I wondered if there was to be a civic reception on the platform, and you'd dressed up for it.'

'It's the hat,' she announced firmly. 'That's what's doing it.'

'I have got a theory about hats.'

'So have I. What's yours?'

George felt very wise, very much a man of the world, laying down the law about women's hats.

'It's simply this. If a woman's hat doesn't make her face more attractive, then it isn't doing its job. The hat isn't anything in itself. It's a beautifier—or nothing.'

'The exact opposite of a mink coat, in fact.'

'Precisely. It's the picture-frame, that's all.'

'And the mink coat is the red label saying "Sold",' she murmured. 'And if you guess from that remark that nobody, alas! has ever given me a mink coat, you would be right.'

He felt a sudden wild desire to give her a mink coat; and a more compelling urge not to be a damned fool.

'What was your idea—I mean about hats?'

'Oh, much more personal. Simply that this is my sort of hat, and I always knew it was, and, thank Heaven, I can't afford another for a long, long time. But I think you're quite right. Tell me some more of your ideas.'

They discussed everything they could think of; she lightly, he a little heavily at times, with an occasional break into lightness which was the more attractive for being long out of use. He had never realized before how few girls had come into his life. All his wife's friends, now he considered them, were as middle-aged as she; if not as dowdy as

Ethel, then, more regretfully, made up beyond all nature to look less dowdy than Ethel. The few girls who lived there—well, he had hardly noticed them, which meant, he supposed, that they were hardly worth noticing. The Travers girl, for example. Or Freda Williams. Nice healthy girls, and who cared?

Her voice fascinated him; and, when it came, her laugh. He wished that he were more amusing. No, he didn't. It wasn't her laugh when she was amused which he wanted, but her laugh when she was happy; when she was happily interested in what they were saying to each other. And what was it? Nothing very much. Just two friends eagerly talking. He laughed himself suddenly.

'Yes?' she said expectantly.

'I was just thinking how funny it was that I feel I know you so well, and yet I don't even know your name.'

'Miranda,' she said.

Quite naturally. Just like that. Well, perhaps better like that. 'Mine's George,' he said, absurdly conscious of it as his own intimate property.

'Oh, no!' She shook her head. 'That's not a bit like you. Not really. Do you mind if we change it?'

'Into what?'

She looked at him consideringly. 'I shall call you Peter. It isn't quite your name yet, but you'll find yourself gradually getting to feel like it. You've been George too long.'

He was going to be George again very soon. Only one more station. 'The next is mine,' he said, and hated it.

'Oh dear! And there are such a lot of things we haven't discussed.'

'That's just it. When are you coming to London again?'

'I'm coming up to-morrow. After that—I don't know.'

'To-morrow.' He nodded, and made up his mind. 'Miranda?'

'Yes, Peter?'

'Will you lunch with me to-morrow?'

She looked at him frankly.

'Sure you want me to?'

'Very much.'

'All right, Peter.'

'Thank you.' He tried to remember a fashionable restaurant. 'The Millamant? 1.15? I mean 1.15 for you; I shall be there long before, trying to believe that you are really coming.'

'I shall come.'

'Well'—he got up—'good-bye, Miranda, till to-morrow.'

'Good-bye, Peter.'

'I'm so glad I missed my train.'

'I'm so glad I caught mine,' she laughed.

'Millamant, 1.15.' The train stopped. He gave her a little bow, and went out.

IV

He sat in the lounge of the Millamant, near the swing door. Every time a taxi stopped, every time the door revolved, he anticipated the hat. It would be the same hat. For the first time he realized how many people there were in the world who were not Miranda; how many girls there were, well-dressed girls, pretty girls, who might have been Miranda but weren't. All followed by men; or waving fingers, as they came in smiling, to men who waited for them—as he was waiting for Miranda's up-held hand and warming smile. For Miranda's hat stooping out of the taxi. It was 1.15. She would be a little late; it was a woman's right; but at any moment now she would come.

Sometimes they didn't come. A page-boy went through the lounge calling for Mr Peters, and disappeared into the restaurant. He, or another, had come in again, calling for Mr Ransom, and this time Mr Ransom at a near table had beckoned him, and gone off, presumably to the telephone. George had watched him idly, had seen him later, hat in hand, making for the door. Mr Ransom's girl couldn't come; she was making some other arrangement. Tea perhaps. George had felt condescendingly sorry for Mr Ransom, because at any moment Miranda would be here …

'Millamant, 1.15.' There could be no mistake, no mistake about the promise to come. Millamant, 1.15, and already it was 1.30.

He ordered himself a drink. She would understand. She would explain why she was late, and say of *course* he was having a drink, poor man, and of course he must have another, and then she could have one too. At 1.45 he was having that other one, but she need not know that it was his second. Yes, she was a little late, but he had liked waiting for her, knowing that she would come, and he'd just ordered himself a drink, and what would she have? And then they would raise glasses to each other, and he would be looking at her again, and hearing her voice again, and hearing her laugh …

It was two o'clock when he left, it was so obvious now that she was not coming. He thought of all the places where she might be, the restaurants where she might have gone by mistake. What about the Mirabelle—was that its name? something like that—but it was too late now, she wouldn't be waiting there now, not all this time. He felt that he ought to have done something earlier, but he didn't know what. A younger man would have known. He was both too old and too inexperienced for this kind of thing. He didn't know what to do when these things happened.

Then, with a sudden lightening of the heart, he told himself that she would be going back by the 6.25. Of course! Then so would he. Why not? He was his own master, and he could go by whatever train he liked. He would see her on the 6.25 again!

He had a hasty lunch at his club, and went back to his office, almost happy. But all through the afternoon's work she made fleeting visits to his mind, asking him each time if he were sure she would be on the 6.25. Fool, he thought suddenly. Of course I'm not. It is she who has broken our engagement, who for no fault of her own was forced to break our engagement, and it is she who will try to make up for it. She knows that the 5.30 is my usual train, and she will look for me there.

Or won't she? Isn't that too much to expect of her? Won't she look to me to come by her train?

Oh well, which? Obviously both. He must be there for the 5.30, and, if she didn't come, wait for the 6.25. He would be at the barrier. His friends would say, 'Hallo, coming along?' and he would explain that he was waiting for somebody.

He waited. She did not come. He waited until the 6.25 was moving out of the station. She had not come …

He had a carriage to himself again. Yesterday she was sitting there opposite to him. To-day, only her ghost. He still had that feeling that he had been stupid, that he had missed something … The train was coming to his station, he was standing, hat in hand again, saying, 'Good-bye, Miranda, till to-morrow,' when suddenly he remembered; when he heard again her voice saying, 'I shall call you Peter. You have been George too long,' and heard again a boy's shrill voice calling, 'Mr Peters! Mr Peters!'

'Oh God!' he cried aloud. 'I deserve it!'

Ethel was very much Ethel that evening. She had all this to tell him about Tim Ferrars. As soon as possible after dinner he escaped to what she called his den, saying that he had letters to write. He only wrote one letter. It was to Mary.

The General Takes off his Helmet

(1948)

Gisco walked behind the General, his thoughts, as usual, rioting round himself. They were inspecting the 27th Division, a mixed crowd of Libyans and Moors under Carthaginian officers. The Division stood to attention and looked unwinking to the front, so that at every step you came under fire from a new pair of eyes; and every pair of those eyes was acknowledging that you were the finest-looking young fellow of them all (as you obviously were), and at the same time pretending to despise you, but really envying you, because you lived so safely and so comfortably—as in a way you did. Well, safely anyhow. You didn't lead forlorn assaults, and have hot lead poured on you from the walls by shrieking women. No, you were spared that. Comfort, too, up to a point, though not quite what they thought. Good food and good quarters, yes; but it was anything but a comfortable life being A.D.C. to the General when he was in one of his moods. A fellow simply didn't know where he was.

Hannibal was in one of his moods to-day.

The siege of Saguntum had gone on too long. Gisco was not quite sure why it had started. He had understood that they were just marching on Rome, wherever that was; and he had promised the girl he had left behind him in Carthage—the three girls he had left behind him in Carthage—to bring back the head of one of those Senators who were making all the trouble, and a jewelled comb such as the Roman ladies wore. But passing Saguntum on their way, they had stopped to take it ... and that was eight months ago, and here they still were. Most of the troops had thought, and had gone on thinking, that they were besieging Rome, and that the war was nearly over; but Gisco, being so close to the General, had only thought so for a very short time. Now he knew that the war was just beginning.

The plains between the city and the sea had become an immense parade-ground, and the siege seemed but one of the many activities of barrack life: troops drilling, troops at sword play, troops going through physical exercises, troops under inspection, and troops advancing on Saguntum and drawing off again, leaving their dead behind them. Here and there under the hard blue sky tattered men hung on crosses. To Gisco they meant as much or as little as all the other features of military life by which he was now becoming bored: a life lived under discipline. But to the Commanders of Divisions about to be inspected they offered a problem; for one could never be sure whether the General would be more struck with the vigour of their discipline or with the previous indiscipline which it implied. Discipline, he had told them, must be maintained; maintained at all costs; but the cost must always be reckoned, and to crucify a discontented man was to save the enemy the trouble of killing him. This, he suggested mildly, was a pity—or didn't they think so? They hastened to think so. In private they told themselves that the General was queer, you never knew where you were with him; and they decided that, since bodies hanging about the place made it look untidy, for the special occasion of a General's Inspection they had better be taken down. So, in the 27th Divisional quarters this morning there were no dead or dying men looking down on Gisco and envying him his more comfortable lot.

He was taller than Hannibal, but the General's golden helmet with its flashing plumes overtopped his own, and he had to admit that for an oldish man of thirty Hannibal made a fine figure from the back. And when the General turned round, as he sometimes did, if that were his humour, to test his A.D.C. on some point of equipment, well, you also had to admit that there was something about his face: not beautiful, of course, not like Gisco's; but with something in it, something behind it, which nobody, not even a foolish young man of twenty, could ever feel quite sure about.

This foolish young man was incapable of putting his feeling for Hannibal into definite words. Had he tried to do so, he might have discovered to his surprise that he felt a sort of affectionate pity, almost contempt, for the Great Man; as for a dreamer who was missing all the good things of life (women, and—well, women) in pursuit of some inescapable end to which, the story went, he had been pledged as a child. You might say that he was something of a child still—sometimes—and though you had to admit that he was a good General and all that, nobody who talked as he did, when he was in that sort of mood, could be called really intelligent. Not like Gisco. But when you had promised your sister (who, after all, had got you the job) to look after the man, you had to look after him. You had to humour him. And somehow—but Gisco never quite knew how—you couldn't help liking the fellow. You would have liked him, even if he hadn't written to your sister: 'I can never thank you enough. Your Gisco is a constant delight and inspiration to me.'

The inspection was over. The General acknowledged his last salute, this time from the Nubian sentries outside his headquarters, and strode to the inner tent, followed by his faithful A.D.C. As soon as they were alone, his hands went to his head. Wincing slightly he raised the massive golden helmet with its waving plumes until it was clear of his forehead, lowered it in front of him, looked at it malignantly, and then flung it on the ground.

'Ye gods,' he cried, 'how I *hate* these helmets!'

Gisco picked it up, cosseting the feathers into shape again as he said soothingly, 'It's a hot day for helmets anyhow, sir.'

'*You've* nothing to complain of. Look at the size of yours compared with mine. Here, take this.' He unbuckled his sword-belt and hung it over the helmet in Gisco's hands, ruffling the plumes again.

'True, O Hannibal,' said Gisco, 'but then look at the size of your brain compared with mine.' He said it kindly, with an encouraging smile. This was what an A.D.C. was for. This was what a Gisco did so well.

'If that's meant for flattery,' snapped Hannibal, 'I don't want it, and if it's meant for irony, I won't have it.'

'It was meant for the truth, sir,' said Gisco untruthfully.

'In that case it was a gross understatement. My helmet is only twice the size of yours.'

'Quite so, sir,' said Gisco firmly. Hannibal was in one of his moods, and it was better to close the conversation. Even as it was, he had an idea that he had been insulted. He put the helmet and the sword-belt away; and, as soon as Hannibal had settled himself on his divan, saw that a drink was ready to his hand. Hannibal drank.

'Those fellows in the little leather caps,' he said, wiping his mouth and leaning back with a sigh, 'I envied *them*, Gisco, I envied *them*!'

'The sanitary squads, sir?' said Gisco, surprised.

'Oh, were those the sanitary squads?'

'Yes, sir.'

'H'm.' He frowned to himself. Looking up and seeing Gisco there, he waved at the drinks, murmuring, 'Oh, my dear boy, please,' and went back to his thoughts. Gisco helped himself with a 'Thank you, sir,' and sat cross-legged on the ground; waiting. The General was coming to an important decision; you could see it in his face. Perhaps he would decide to call the whole campaign off. Perhaps they would be back in Carthage by the autumn. Perhaps Thalyctra and he—if he decided on Thalyctra—

'Those sanitary squads,' said Hannibal.

Gisco came back from Carthage with a start, and said automatically, 'Yes, sir.'

'How would it be if in future they all wore helmets like mine, and the Commander-in-Chief wore a little leather cap like theirs?'

Gisco gaped and stammered, 'W-with what object, sir?'

'Damn it,' said Hannibal reasonably, 'with the object that they'd get headaches and I shouldn't.'

'Quite so, sir. Is it an order?' The poor fellow was crazy, but one must humour him. Take it all quite seriously.

'I don't know. I'll tell you later.'

'Yes, sir.'

'We must consider both sides. I suppose all these feathers and things are more dignified?'

Gisco had a good one for that. One wasn't an A.D.C. for nothing. One knew instinctively what to say.

'If you wore the leather cap, sir,' he said, little knowing how near the truth he was, 'then very soon the leather cap would be more dignified.'

'Obviously one would hope that such would be the case, but in actual fact it wouldn't.'

'No, sir.'

'On the other hand, it *would* be cooler.'

'Yes, sir.'

Gisco took up his drink again sulkily. There was no doing anything with the man when he was in this mood. He returned to Carthage and Thalyctra, but with no hope now of seeing her in the autumn.

'Gisco,' said Hannibal—

(There! He was off again. What now?)

'—tell me, just for interest, I've often wanted to know. If I do make it an order, what exactly happens?'

'Naturally, sir, it is carried out.' That was an easy one.

Hannibal considered him thoughtfully.

'You know,' he said, 'sometimes you give the impression of being quite intelligent, and sometimes you give the impression of being completely the reverse. Is there a reason, or is it just chance?'

Gisco began to say as politely as he could (only there were times when it was difficult) that he didn't know what the poor fellow was talking about; but Hannibal wasn't listening.

'There are fortunate men who rose from the ranks to be commanders,' he went on. 'Alas, I didn't. I was born to it. That puts me at a disadvantage. There are things which I don't know.' He sipped his drink and explained, 'What I want to know now is this: what happens to this order as soon as I have given it to *you*?'

'Oh, I see, sir,' said Gisco, quite cheerful again. Now he was in his element; explaining things to his General, explaining what he knew so well—military routine. 'It's like this, sir. I write it out, and when you have signed it, I hand it to your Chief of Staff.'

'Never mind the signature. *I* tell *you*; *you* tell the Chief of Staff. Whom does *he* tell?'

'The Divisional Commanders.'

'And they?'

'The Captains commanding Companies.'

'And they?'

'The officers commanding the Companies' sanitary squads.'

'Ah! And they?'

'They would make out a requisition for the number of helmets they wanted—and, I suppose, the sizes—and that would go back to the Captains commanding Companies; and they—'

Hannibal held up a hand.

'Don't tell me. They would pass it back to the Generals commanding Divisions—'

'Exactly, sir. And *they* would pass it back to the Chief of Staff.'

As if he had been through all the motions himself, Gisco helped himself to the second drink which he had so fully earned, and wondered what else he could do for the General.

'Excellent,' said Hannibal. 'You will be glad to hear that so far I have followed you with ease. You will also observe that so far nobody has done anything at all, except tell somebody else to do it. But there must be a terrifying moment when somebody actually has to set to and *make* a helmet, simply because there is nobody else he can get to do it for him.' He drank, and said dreamily, 'Who is that unlucky man?'

Gisco had seen the question coming, and where lesser men might have fallen down, he was ready to stand up to it.

'Well, sir,' he said, improvising a little doubtfully, 'I suppose the requisition would eventually come to the Master-Armourer—'

'Ah!' said Hannibal. 'Thank you.'

'And *he* would tell the armourer-sergeants—'

'I was hasty,' said Hannibal, making a motion of apology. 'I beg your pardon.'

'Who would tell the armourers to—er—make the helmets.'

'And they would make them?'

'Yes, sir.'

There was a short silence, which just gave Gisco time in which to congratulate himself again, and to tell himself that now the General knew all about that; and then Hannibal spoke.

He said, 'How?'

'I beg your pardon, sir?'

'I said—how?'

'Er—do you mean how would they make them?'

'What else could I mean?'

'Well—er—'

'Imagine yourself to be an armourer. The armourer-sergeant has just told you to make a hundred and forty-nine helmets. Damn it, Gisco, you can't *do* it!'

'I am not an armourer,' said Gisco stiffly. I am nursemaid, he told himself, to an infuriating child.

'You start with a wedge of gold,' said Hannibal, following out his thoughts, 'and you beat it into a thin plate. Then you—sort of'—he made arcuate motions with his hands—'bend it—or don't you?'

Gisco had only heard one word of all this, but it was enough.

'Sir!' he said, shocked out of his usual complaisance. 'Really!'

'What's the matter?'

'You wouldn't have *gold* helmets for the *sanitary* squads?' Hannibal looked at him solemnly.

'If even my elephants have ivory tusks,' he said, 'are my sanitary squads to be grudged gold helmets?'

'Quite so, sir,' said Gisco hastily.

'What I want you to observe is how very much easier it is to be a Commander-in-Chief than it is to be an armourer. All *I* do is to say "Let the sanitary squads wear gold helmets," and in a week from now—'

'Better say a fortnight from now, to be on the safe side,' said the man of affairs kindly. One could at least keep him right in matters like that.

'In three days from now—' Hannibal corrected himself.

'Three days, sir, yes, sir.'

'In three days the sanitary squads are wearing gold helmets. Marvellous! Incredible! I go down to History. And yet what have I done? Nothing that demands the exercise of the intelligence or the operation of manual skill.' He sighed. 'Any fool can give orders, Gisco, but it takes a clever man to execute them.'

Gisco had the brightest moment of his day. 'It takes a genius to give the right orders,' he said.

Loud applause? No applause. For some reason it was the one thing which was wanted to bring the whole simmering morning to the boil. Hannibal jumped to his feet.

'And who the Hades,' he shouted furiously, 'is to know whether they *are* right? Do *you* set yourself up as a judge?'

'The gods forbid, sir,' said Gisco, up and backing away.

'Then who?'

'Nobody in the army would dare to, sir.'

'Exactly. I give the order to besiege Saguntum'—his voice rose almost to a scream—'and for two hundred and thirty-seven days we've been besieging the blasted town'—his voice dropped almost to a whisper—'and who is to tell me whether I am right or wrong?'

He fell back again on his divan. Gisco refilled his cup and passed it to him, while searching in his mind for something helpful, something soothing, something inspiring.

'I always understood, sir,' he said, in case the General had forgotten, 'that it was meant to be a declaration of war against Rome, Saguntum being under Roman protection.'

Hannibal gave him a gentle smile.

'What other commander has ever taken two hundred and thirty-seven days to declare war? Why not march straight on Rome?'

'Well, sir,' Gisco tried again, 'you can't leave a fortified town in your rear to cut off your line of retreat.'

'My line of *what*?' said Hannibal coldly.

Naturally, thought Gisco, he'd be touchy about a thing like that. Silly of me.

'I mean, sir, that you can't have a fortified town like Saguntum harassing your rear as you advance—'

'My dear Gisco, use words in some relation to their meaning. How can a fortified town harass the rear of a rapidly departing army? It can't run after us.'

'No, sir.'

There was another pregnant silence. If you hadn't known that the General was delighted with you, if you hadn't known for a fact that you inspired him, there were times when you might have felt a little doubtful about yourself, wondering if you were to take him seriously when he seemed to be differing from you. As it was, one knew that it was just the General's way. Once again Gisco had given him something to think about; but naturally a Commander-in-Chief doesn't want to acknowledge too openly that—

'Or take elephants,' said Hannibal.

Gisco sat up with a jerk, spilling his wine on the floor of the tent. 'Take what, sir?'

'Elephants.'

'Yes, sir.' All right, all right, take elephants. They were off again.

'Am I right to burden myself with all these elephants? Who knows?'

'Surely, sir, they will strike terror into the hearts of the Romans.' At least, they would if Romans were at all like Gisco.

'Possibly—if they ever get within trumpeting distance of one. At present it looks as if some of the young ones may just see the siege of Saguntum out.' He considered this for a moment, and added: 'How long do elephants live?'

'About eighty years, sir, isn't it?'

'Some of the very young ones,' amended Hannibal, closing his eyes.

'Yes, sir,' said Gisco dutifully.

'Suppose I sent them back to Carthage—'

'Yes, sir?'

'Somebody takes them?'

'Yes, sir.'

'I shouldn't know how to take thirty-seven elephants back to Carthage—would *you*?'

For one wild moment Gisco thought of saying Yes: of saying that as a boy he had been brought up with elephants—(only Hannibal knew his sister too well to believe that the family was in the elephant business); of saying that he would like to try (only there was nothing he would hate more); of saying anything to get back to Carthage and Thalyctra (and, of course, Daphnis and Melitta) and away from the camp and the questions … And the knowledge that there was nothing he could say, and that here he was for another how many years and they hadn't even begun the real war yet, and that he would never see Melitta again *(or* Thalyctra *or* Daphnis), all this turned him suddenly from a charmingly tactful A.D.C. into a very hot, very annoyed young man.

He said contemptuously: 'I don't happen to be an authority on elephants,' and turned his back on his General, and drank to show his indifference.

Still with his eyes shut, Hannibal said:

'You aren't an authority on elephants, and you can't make a helmet. What,' he asked with interest, '*can* you do?'

Gisco's temper began to go.

'If it comes to that, Hannibal,' he snapped, 'what can *you* do?'

Hannibal sighed.

'This is one of your bad days. For the last twenty minutes I have been confessing my complete inability to do anything; and now you ask me insolently, and with the air of making a point, what I can do.'

'Oh, I was insolent, was I?' sneered Gisco.

'You were. You still are.' He considered this for a moment, and added, 'It's a hot day, of course.'

'I'm insolent, am I?' shouted Gisco, his temper quite gone. 'All right, then, crucify me.'

As soon as he had said this, he wished that he hadn't. Supposing Hannibal took him at his word? It was an unpleasant form of death, and he didn't want to die anyhow. Of course his sister might do something at the last moment—Perhaps, even now, if he apologized to the old man—

He waited to see what Hannibal would do …

Hannibal did nothing, said nothing. He still lay there with his eyes closed; thinking (Gisco told himself) that this was only a young fool who didn't know what he was saying. Well, he'd show him. He wasn't going to stand that sort of thing.

'Go on!' he shouted. '"Discipline must be maintained"—you've said it often enough. Go on! Crucify me!'

Hannibal opened his eyes, and turned to Gisco, shaking his head at him.

'There you go again,' he sighed. 'You're making a ridiculously unwarranted demand on my powers. I simply don't know how to begin crucifying anybody.' He lay back, and looked up at the roof of the tent, thinking it out.

'One starts by making a cross, I suppose. Well, but where do I get the wood from? And then it has to be shaped—and nailed—no, that wouldn't do—fitted together in some way, with a—tenon, do you call it?—and braced—is that it?—braced at the back with—You know, the more I think about it, the more complicated it seems.' He sighed again.

'You've only got to look outside,' said Gisco viciously. 'There are plenty of old crosses ready for you. "Discipline must be maintained."'

Hannibal pulled himself into a sitting position, and looked at Gisco with a new interest.

'That's funny,' he said. 'That's twice you've said that, and in the same unnatural voice. Is it supposed to be an imitation of me?'

'It is.'

'Is my voice really like that?'

'Yes. And I'm sick of the sound of it.'

Hannibal leant forward anxiously.

'Just let's try, if you don't mind. I want to get this established. I'll go first.' In the voice in which he might address a conference of his commanders, he said firmly, 'Discipline must be maintained!' and added, 'Now *you* say it.' He turned his head slightly, his ear raised to Gisco, and waited, chin on hand.

'Discipline must be maintained,' Gisco said sulkily.

Hannibal shook his head.

'It's not very good, is it? Apparently you add to your inability to make helmets and conduct elephants across country, an inability to give recognizable imitations.'

'Inabilities,' said Gisco with a low bow, 'which I have the honour of sharing with my lord Hannibal.'

'True. And in addition *I* can't wear a helmet without getting a headache, *I* can't take Saguntum, and *I* can't even keep the respect of a very ordinary young man with red ears.'

For perhaps the first time in his life Gisco spoke without hearing himself speak. For perhaps the first time in his life he recognized himself as a very ordinary young man, possibly with red ears. 'Sir!' he cried remorsefully. 'Forgive me! I am ashamed, I am not worthy to live!' He put his hand to his sword-hilt, and at the feel of it became himself again. 'Say the word,' he cried dramatically, 'and I will fall on it!'

Hannibal shook his head.

'You'd probably miss it,' he said.

Gisco was beginning to wonder about that too. It was easy enough to say, but how exactly did one do it? He took the short sword in both hands and pressed the point to his chest. That, anyhow, was easy.

'Say the word,' he cried again, 'and I will plunge it into my heart!'

He wished Thalyctra could see him now. He also wished Daphnis could, and Melitta. But they would hear about it. His sister would get a letter from Hannibal, and in a little while the news would be all over Carthage …

Hannibal had told Gisco's sister that her brother was a constant inspiration to him. Perhaps he hadn't meant it quite in the way that they supposed. But at least Gisco had inspired him now. He leapt to his feet.

'Ah!' he cried. 'There's something we both could do! We've found it at last. No orders to give to others. No wondering afterwards if we were right, or wrong. A decision, private in application, personal in execution, which we can never regret. My sword, Gisco!'

'Hannibal!' said Gisco, aghast.

'At least my orders are obeyed.'

'I would rather obey any other than that.'

It was true. If Hannibal killed himself, then Gisco must needs kill himself too, and there would be nobody to write to his sister, and tell her how bravely her brother had died. And Thalyctra—and of course Melitta and Daphnis—would never know. Yes, he would obey any order sooner than that one.

'Curious!' said Hannibal in a gentle voice. 'It is the most humane order I have ever given. My sword, Gisco.'

Gisco came forward with the sword-belt and the helmet. Hannibal smiled.

'The helmet, too,' he said. 'We are going to a place where there will be no headaches, we hope. Well, let me try to look like a real General for the last time.'

Gisco stopped suddenly.

'What's that?' he whispered. 'Listen, sir!' He held up his hand.

Distant shouts could be heard, voices in argument close at hand, scufflings; and then rapid footsteps, as an officer burst in on them.

'Well, sir?' said Hannibal in that cold terrifying voice which all knew.

'My lord!' the officer cried. 'Surrender, my lord! An embassy of surrender from the town! Surrender!'

A little sigh came from Hannibal, so gentle that Gisco could hardly hear it.

'Ah!'

He turned to his A.D.C. and said, 'You have my sword there?' He took the belt and fastened it on. 'They are being conducted here?'

'Yes, my lord. It is in here that you will receive them?'

'Yes. My helmet, Gisco.'

The officer went out. Two of the Nubian bodyguard came in, and stood one on each side of the entrance to the inner tent. Hannibal took the great helmet, and lowered it on to his head. As it touched his forehead, he flinched slightly. The envoys could be heard shuffling through the outer tent.

Hannibal gave the helmet back to Gisco. He took off his sword-belt. With great dignity, and in a loud voice he said:

'No! They are brave men and have fought bravely. In respect for their valour I shall receive them as equals.'

He took up a commanding position, his hand on his hip, his A.D.C. a little behind him on the left. Helmet or no helmet, sword or no sword, every inch a General. The Nubians stood to attention. The envoys from Saguntum, walking dispiritedly between their guards, came through the opening.

'My lords!' said Hannibal. 'I have the honour to receive you as you come, unarmed and—bare-headed.'

As he said the last word, his chin made an infinitesimal movement towards Gisco. His left eye caught Gisco's eye. He winked …

Well, you couldn't help liking the man.

Luck Nothing

(1948)

Aurora Delaine was holding a reception at the Savoy in preparation for the first showing of *Souls Asunder*. She had been smuggled into England with the advance privacy which her prestige required; a privacy calling for an escort of all the unemployed policemen of the country to carry her through the hysterical crowds who fought and fainted in the approaches to the docks at Southampton, the platform at Waterloo, and the swing doors of the Savoy. Now, after an interval for repairs and the slipping on of a thousand dollars'-worth of something simple, she was telling pressmen how glad she was to be back in dear old England; that England which she would always regard as her native country. This announcement was thought to be very good of her, and was received with applause.

Somebody asked her, possibly in other words, to what she attributed her present monolatric position in the sidereal system. She turned swimming eyes beneath long, curling lashes upon him, and said modestly, 'My! *That's* a question to ask a girl! Just luck, I reckon.' There was a murmur of 'No, no,' which seemed to give her confidence. In the voice of one who finds herself suddenly in front of a loud-speaker, the world waiting, she said, 'Well, boys, I'll be frank with you. Here's my say. Hard work; hell's own ambition; and luck'—she waved it away with a flip of her hand—'nothing! But, of course—well, say,

I don't like giving you this—' ('Go on, Miss Delaine.') 'Well, then, you've got to *have* something first. I don't say for beauty'—she gave them a ravishing smile which said all that was needed for beauty—'but *talent*. Mean to say, you gotta be an artist!' One young pressman, flushed with South African sherry, cried, 'A genius!' She gave him a private smile, neither confirming, nor denying, just thanking. He began to work his way a little nearer to her.

When, later, in response to a request from her manager, they streamed out, some of them may have been thinking of the little differences which made the difference between World-Wide Fame and Complete Obscurity; between Aurora Delaine, say, and—well, any little girl one sees, a name only to her friends, running beneath one's window to catch a bus.

For instance, I used to know a little girl called Mary ...

I

She was born in a small way, Mary Briggs; and for as long as she could remember, which was between the ages of two and twenty, she had lived alone with her Aunt Hester at Sydenham; 'near the dear old Crystal Palace', as Aunt Hester would explain, remembering that wonderful day, thirty-five years ago, which had seemed to be the beginning of Romance, and had, in fact, been the end of it. Mary had another aunt, Aunt Julia, who lived at Sandbeach; but Aunt Julia had two daughters of her own, and a little house near the sea almost as small as the house at Sydenham, and as little capable of entertaining visitors—visitors, that is, beyond the age of sharing bedrooms, or even beds, with chattering young cousins. So, for the last few years the families had been—if I may sully these pages with the horrible phrase—'pen pals' only. Hester corresponding with Julia, and Mary receiving the confidences of Ada, in letters full lately of a certain dispenser in the local hospital at Shrimpington, a less refined resort three miles to the east. The younger daughter, Hilda, was in love with Clark Gable, who needed no introduction to Sydenham.

Mary was neither pretty nor plain. She had a pleasant little face, freckled in the summer, a shy but friendly smile for everybody, and a figure of which she was alternately proud and apprehensive. 'No true lady,' Aunt Hester had told her, 'calls attention to herself in these matters'; and there was an absence of stress, a polite evasion of the point, if we may so put it, in the upper half of her wardrobe, which all true ladies would have approved. Only in the Sydenham Baths could Mary's figure be compared, and generally to her advantage, with the figures of the unladylike. But though, in her unpretentious way, she never came within the purview of the Casanovas of Sydenham, she had an extraordinary attraction for all stray animals. Lost dogs looked at her with pathetic, lustrous eyes, and followed her home. Cats, appearing from nowhere, did figures of eight between her ankles. As Aunt Hester said, 'Animals always *know*.'

If you are one of those girls who 'Tell Aunt Hester Your Troubles', as advised to every Thursday, you will have felt all the time that the name was familiar. Yes, it is the same one. She was 'Aunt Hester' of *Girl, Wife, and Mother.* Another expert, Nurse Sunshine, answered the more embarrassing questions of Wife and Mother; Aunt Hester dealt with the problems of the Growing Girl. Of late she had begun to feel that the line of demarcation between the two experts was not so firm as it should be. Indeed, it was almost her weekly custom now, on her visit to the office, to place a few of her letters on Nurse Sunshine's (Mrs Hopwinkle's) desk, with the words, 'I think, dear, you had perhaps—er—yes, I am afraid so, very distressing.' But in less hygienic matters, on all questions of pure etiquette (and both Aunt Hester and I emphasize the word pure) she remained authoritative. *Should a girl accept chocolates from a married man in her office?—Does one bow or shake hands on being introduced?—Would it be all right to go to the pictures with the young man who has been going out with one's best friend?*—You don't know, I don't know; but Aunt Hester knew.

Our ignorance can be excused; but it will be seen that Mary, any-how, should have known all the answers. It does not follow, of course, that she would always give them. She was twenty; and often thought that it would be nicer to be Dorothy Lamour.

II

For some months now Tom Perry had stopped talking about prescriptions to Ada, interested though she seemed to be in them, and had made one or two tentative excursions into compliment; the most promising being an assertion that any day on which Miss Ada came over to Shrimpington was, whatever the barometer said, a fine day. But it was not until the day after the Fête that she could write incoherently to Mary, to give the news that she was 'really and truly engaged!!!' The Fête took place in Shelley Park, so named after the Mayor who had presented it to the town, and whose statue, sometimes confused by illiterate visitors with the other Shelley, stood opposite the Bandstand. In one part of the grounds the hospital, always in debt, had made itself responsible for a Fun Fair, a shilling to go in, and sixpence for almost anything when you got there; all profits to the Building Fund. Tom Perry was, though not of course officially, the chief organizer of the Fair, with Ada as his enthusiastic assistant. The harmony of their combined efforts brought £18 8s. 6*d.* to the Building Fund, and Tom to Ada—or, as it would be more chivalrous to say, Ada to Tom. Whoever was chiefly responsible, they were now engaged.

It was the engagement, I think, the sudden need for Aunt Julia and Ada to come to London for pre-nuptial shopping, which led to the suggestion that the two sisters should exchange houses for the last fortnight of August. So, Hilda being with a school-friend in Suffolk, Aunt Julia and Ada came to Sydenham. And Aunt Hester and Mary, pleasantly excited at the thought of the sea, came to Sandbeach.

They made the great change on the same day. Their trains crossed, as for a week past their letters had crossed; and this had made it necessary for each side to leave in a prominent place an elaboration of notes: on such matters, for example, as the best and quickest laundry in an emergency, the relative altitude of the Vicar's liturgy, and what to do if, as sometimes happened, a flush of water was delayed. What interested Mary most was the presence of a key labelled 'Hut 26', and the information that, though undressing behind the boulders in the West Bay was now allowed to visitors, the residents naturally preferred to use the huts in the East Bay, and dear Mary would, of course, wish to do the same. But it was most important that the hut should always be kept locked. When the girls bathed, they buried the key in a hole in the sand while actually in the water. It was safer, as there were always *prowlers* about, and there were cases of clothes being actually *stolen*.

Mary loved swimming. She had, as a real swimmer should have, a blue one-piece which gave her the freedom of the water. Aunt Hester had tolerated, if she had not altogether approved, her niece's appearance in this in the Sydenham Baths (Ladies' Days); but for mixed bathing, in the very mixed society of a seaside resort, she considered it a little, just a little, unladylike. Faced by a slightly rebellious Mary with the pattern in *Girl, Wife, and Mother* of an attractive two-piece, in which each piece attended to its own business and made no attempt to meet the other half-way, she admitted sadly that she was old-fashioned, and Mary must do as she pleased. Mary kissed her, and said that she was an old darling. However, old darlings do not surrender so easily. When Mary, towel over shoulders, left Hut 26, Aunt Hester followed, camp-stool in hand, key in bag. Mary slipped off the towel and plunged into the sea. When she came, wet and shining, like Venus from the waves, and almost as revealed, Aunt Hester was at the water's edge to throw the towel of invisibility over her, and hurry her back to sanctuary.

They made many nice friends on the beach. There was old Mrs Gosling, who had had children and operations in abundance, and who gave them much interesting information about both. Some of the grandchildren were almost ready to have their tonsils out; which may have explained her expressed hope that they would meet again in London in the winter. There were also the Amersham girls, who had a great fund of anecdote about the upper reaches of Society, which they were not unwilling to pass on. Mrs Manders, who came to Sandbeach every summer, could tell them of the changes in the amenities and tone of Sandbeach in the last forty years. There were many nice people about … and sometimes Mary wondered what Dorothy Lamour would have thought of them.

III

On Saturday they were going back to London. Packing—which always took Aunt Hester a long time, being planned in detail, as a general plans a campaign—would occupy most of Friday. To-day was the last free day, Mary's last opportunity for a lovely swim in the lovely, lovely sea.

'I am very sorry, dear,' said Aunt Hester after breakfast, 'but I shall not be able to come with you this morning. I have my girls to look after.' She held up a bunch of letters, which had been sent on, a little unexpectedly, from the office. She had already opened one of them: from BLUE EYES (16), whose boy was taking some other girl to the next dance, and who naturally wanted to know if Life had anything else to offer. Aunt Hester was very sound on this, and would explain in the firmest but kindest way that suicide was altogether out of the question.

'Oh, well, darling, I can go by myself.'

'Of course, dear, but not, I think, to bathe. Just sit with old Mrs Gosling for a little; or take a look round the shops, or you could listen to the band with those nice Amersham girls.'

'Very well, Aunt Hester,' said Mary meekly.

But up in her room she stamped her foot and said that she *would* bathe, yes, she would. Only, of course, she mustn't be seen leaving the house with a towel and bathing-dress …

She undressed. She put on the blue one-piece. She put a skirt and a hand-knitted jumper over it. Aunt Hester, like the American Board of Censors, didn't approve of jumpers, but this one had been a present from Aunt Julia, and evidently intended in the first place for Ada, a bigger proposition altogether. It was a catholic jumper, which made no distinction between left and right, back and front; an outrage in orange which even Ada had rejected violently. To Mary this morning it was just a covering to get her down to Hut 26, and out into the sea. She would dry in the sun, slip on the skirt and jumper, and hurry back.

So off she went; and at the gate the golden Labrador, who had been hanging about wistfully for days, joined her.

Nobody ever knew whose dog he was; nobody but the Labrador, who knew he was Mary's. Previously, when he had proposed to accompany them to the beach, and carry Mary's towel for her, save her life if drowning, or render any other little service for his beloved which she asked of him, Aunt Hester had shooed him away. He had promptly sat down in the middle of the road and given them one look, of such unfathomable reproach that Mary could hardly bear it. '*Couldn't* we take him, Aunt Hester?' she would ask, and Aunt Hester would say, 'We don't know whose dog he is, dear. He hasn't even a collar,' as if this put him definitely among the submerged classes.

But the Labrador knew. To-day there was no one to shoo him away. Only the beloved was there ... and the two of them went down together to the beach.

Of Mary's swim, almost to France and back, we will say nothing. The Labrador went in a little way with her, assured himself that she was a real swimmer, and came back to the water's edge to wait for her. They returned together to Hut 26.

'Oh, dear!' said Mary. 'I forgot to bury the key!' She opened the door, and went in. The Labrador, knowing his place, sat on guard outside.

And the skirt and jumper were not there!

It was no good looking for them; telling oneself that they had fallen off their hooks. Even in a well-furnished bedroom the orange jumper would have let its presence be known, however carelessly flung aside. Here concealment was impossible. One of those prowlers, while Mary was off Ushant, had prowled by, seen the key in the door, entered and taken what she could find. Luckily, to-day, only that hideous jumper and a very old skirt.

Well, that didn't matter so much. What did matter was that she had to get back to Cragsyde, ten minutes' walk up the hill. She couldn't, she simply *couldn't*, walk all that way in a wet bathing-dress! She didn't need Aunt Hester here to tell her that no nice girl could. There was only one thing to do. Round two sides of the hut, as a sort of frieze (and very decorative, Aunt Hester had said when they first saw it) was pinned a broad gaily painted streamer, relic of that history-making Fête. Designed, presumably, by Tom Perry, and executed, undoubtedly, by Ada, it said in red letters on a yellow background: 'DON'T MISS SHRIMPINGTON HOSPITAL'S FUN FAIR', a pleasing way, when strung over the entrance into the Park, of calling attention to the Fête's chief attraction. Here, anyhow, was something to drape round the upper half of the body, something to give her a little more the feeling of being dressed; however casually, in however holiday a spirit.

She draped it diagonally across her chest, over the right shoulder and under the left, and brought it round to the right shoulder again and pinned it; and she shifted it about until it was doing all that Aunt Hester would have liked it to do; and then she went out into the sun. In the bright sun, under the thoroughly approving eye of the Labrador, her self-consciousness left her. She felt a little Spanish, and really a little like Dorothy Lamour—say, a little like Dorothy Lamour at a bull-fight. Almost as if fully dressed, she walked along a singularly deserted beach, followed by the Labrador. Everybody, it seemed, had moved, or was moving, towards a platform by the bandstand. Wondering why, she began to follow them. As she got closer to them, a policeman noticed her, and at once realized the situation. He pushed his way out of the crowd, and came to her.

'You're only just in time, Miss,' he said. 'I'll get you in round at the back.' He took her arm, and, using his authority, made a passage for her. She supposed that the thief had been found, and that she was now to identify her property. She was helped on to the platform; yes, there were other girls there in bathing-dresses who had had their clothes stolen; yes, that's what it was. Well, thank goodness, now Aunt Hester would never know.

'Stand here, Miss, at the end,' said the policeman.

So they stood there—from L to R. 'Miss Torquay', 'Miss Weston-super-Mare', 'Miss Brighton', 'Miss Bridlinghampton', 'Miss Slowcombe-on-Sea', 'Miss Bognor Regis', and 'Miss Shrimpington', with their titles on their chests, the finalists in the Bathing Beauties competition for the proud super-title of 'Miss Southern Resort'.

Next to Miss Shrimpington sat the Labrador, the most beautiful of them all. Among the judges was Mr Lionel Springe of C.Q.N— certainly the most unattractive.

IV

C.Q.N., the world-famous Film Company, once Hollywood had heard of it, was the inspiration of Mr Finkelstein. Having had a classical education (until his father discovered that that was what he was having, and removed him to another school), he decided that it would be a pleasant conceit to call his child the Ciné-qua-non Film Company. As such it began its career; as the Cinequanon it disclosed itself as impossible of a standardized pronunciation. It also sounded un-British, an idea which Mr Finkelstein's name should have dispelled. Reluctantly he surrendered his joke, but kept it in being as C.Q.N. The fact that nobody outside a few pioneers in the firm could tell you what the initials stood for was not to the Company's disadvantage. The 'Q', one felt, was both intriguing and masterful; and, as it turned out, symbolic.

Mr Lionel Springe was talent-spotter for C.Q.N. He took his powerful field-glasses to a convenient recess in the cliffs and spotted talent. He had been spotting it all yesterday among the boulders in the West Bay. When the Mayor of Sandbeach was unable to fulfil his duties as one of the judges, owing to a scene with the Mayoress at breakfast which was better described as urgent municipal business, hasty search was made for a substitute. It was known that Mr Lionel Springe of C.Q.N. was staying in the town; it was usually known that he was staying in a town, either through Mr Springe himself or the police; and he was immediately approached. Both for business and personal reasons he was delighted to accept.

Mary still didn't quite know what was going on. Unpleasant people came and peered at her, and once or twice the Labrador growled warningly. After a little she was removed from the platform; partly because there was a complaint from 'Miss Torquay's' end that the dog at the other end was getting too much attention; partly because somebody in authority had discovered that she ought not to be there at all. 'Miss Shrimpington', he remembered, had been eliminated in the semi-finals, and in any case there should only have been six competitors. But though she and the Labrador left the stage, they had already been spotted. As she turned to go, Mr Springe said softly, 'Wait until this is over. I *must* speak to you.'

No, it was not her pleasant little face which appealed to Mr Springe; not even the full charm of her figure, momentarily revealed when the pins came out, and the streamer dropped to the ground—to be picked up hastily and placed, as it should have been at first, over her shoulders, the lettering inwards. The others—Miss Bridlinghampton particularly—had twice what Mary had, everywhere, and a technique which made it look like three times. No; it was the Labrador.

Dogs, horses, fawns, elephants had all woken lately to find themselves famous film-stars: there seemed to be a sudden craze for them.

C.Q.N., always in the van of progress, though nearly always on the tail-board, decided that a film about a faithful animal would be original and moving. At a recent conference the executive had been advised to 'think up some ideas quick'. Mr Springe now had a quick idea. The Company had recently paid £10,000 for the film rights of a novel on the Black Prince, and half a dozen of the best authors in England were turning it into a scenario of the life of Bonnie Prince Charlie. If Bonnie Prince Charlie were followed everywhere in glorious technicolour by a golden Labrador, what a picture it would make! A moment's doubt in Mr Springe's mind as to whether Labradors would follow people up oak-trees was accompanied by another moment's doubt as to whether it was Bonnie Prince Charlie he was thinking of, and the two of them dismissed. The six authors could work that out for themselves.

As soon as the judges had come to their decision—and it is only fair to record that it went to Miss Bridlinghampton—Mr Springe made for Mary.

'Now, Miss,' he said, in his well-known imitation of a business man, 'about that dog of yours—what d'you call it, by the way?'

'It's a golden Labrador.'

'Yes, yes, I know that. I mean what's its name?'

'Well—er—' began Mary uncomfortably.

'Weller, eh? That's good. The faithful servant, eh?'

Mary looked vague.

'You're a well-read girl, ain't you? Know all about that fellow what's-'is-name, who wrote the book of that film *Pickwick Papers*, eh? Well, now, I want you to come and see me this afternoon. Here's my card. I'm at the Royal. And bring the dog. See? Three-thirty sharp.'

Mary looked doubtful. Should a girl accept an invitation from a gentleman who had never been introduced? Aunt Hester would know.

'Quite all right, Miss—er—'

'Briggs.'

'Quite all right, Miss Briggs. I'm a married man.'

This reassured Mary. Perhaps if she had known how very much married he was, she would not have been so reassured. If she had known that he had a date for that evening with Miss Bridlinghampton—well, that would have worked both ways. Most reassuring of all, perhaps, would have been the knowledge that as a man he felt no attraction to her, and as a talent-spotter no interest in her. She never knew this. She never knew that it was Weller whom he had so unerringly spotted.

'All right,' said Mary breathlessly. 'I'll come.'

V

Mary was still a little breathless when she found herself at the C.Q.N. Studios a few weeks later. It was Weller who had seen her through the whole business. Aunt Hester's first reaction to the idea of taking somebody else's valuable dog to London was not favourable. 'Practically tantamount to stealing, dear Mary. Whose dog *is* it? All we can say with certainty is that it is not ours.' Weller answered that one. He followed them to the station; he followed them into a third-class carriage; he retired under the seat. Nothing would get him out. 'Very well,' said Aunt Hester. 'You will write to your Aunt Julia, saying that we have the dog, and that if anyone advertises for it—'

No one ever advertised for him, no one claimed him. Nobody ever knew where he came from. The suggestion was made, but did not meet with general acceptance, that he was Mr Gladstone, returned to earth in order to reorganize the Liberal Party. I think that this is unlikely. Anyhow, there he was; and it was he who convinced Aunt Hester that Mary was safe under his chaperonage, even in the wanton atmosphere of a film studio. Secretly she was not sorry to get a little inside knowledge of the Film World, a world in which her girls spent so much of their lives.

The difficulty, for Mary, of getting to the studios was surmounted; the difficulty, for C.Q.N., of keeping her out of the picture was insoluble. Weller was prepared to bound over the heather with Bonnie Prince

Charlie and Mary; pace, with Lord Nelson and Mary, the quarter-deck of the *Victory*; swim the Hellespont with both Byron and Leander, if Mary came too; but without Mary he would do nothing. Expert cutters and cameramen told the Director to leave it to them; Weller probably told Mary to leave it to him; in the end Weller always won. However cleverly they cut, there was a bit of Mary left over, or a bit of Weller missing. The six authors were told to think up some more ideas.

The idea finally accepted was a good one. Lightly tracing and retracing history, the Black Prince had ended up as Richard Cœur-de-Lion. You remember how Richard was imprisoned in a castle in France, and how somebody who Mr Springe always thought was Blondin sang beneath the walls of all the castles until he came to the right one? One of the executives in a dark-blue singlet, who normally pulled on a rope, suggested that Weller (and Mary) should take the place of Blondin, and that Weller should howl mournfully until he got an answering howl, or cry of recognition, from Richard. The suggestion was promptly elaborated. What about making Mary Margaret of Ongjew, come to save the man she had always loved; photographing her entirely from the back, or when she bent down to confide in Weller; and in the preliminary and subsequent love-scenes (and in constant interpolated close-ups, to remind one of what Margaret was looking like if one could only see her) letting the beautiful and popular Lorna Dooney stand in for Mary? But that is now ancient history. Everybody remembers *Wella, the Lion Heart,* and the notices which Weller, and in a lesser degree Lorna Dooney, received from the critics …

Everybody also remembers (with the exception, of course, of the Russians) that in 1939 Britain declared war on Hitler. This seemed a favourable moment to Mr Finkelstein and most of the executive to explore new openings for British markets in America. Mr Finkelstein had started to do this in a small way in September, 1938, but had decided, almost as soon as he landed in New York, that the moment was not quite ripe, and had returned as from the necessary reconnaissance. Now he had no doubts. All that was best of C.Q.N. hastened to

Hollywood to amalgamate on what terms they could with P.K.Z., the terms naturally including C.Q.N.'s trump-card (as he now was) Weller.

It was in Hollywood that Mary first began to make a frontal attack on the emotions of her audiences. I use the word 'audiences' deliberately, for it was there also that she first found her way on to the sound-track. Mr Finkelstein had explained the Mary technique; but Mr Zerfi, with a sentimental weakness for the English at a time when they had their own troubles, and a conviction that he knew their language, said kindly, 'Hell and Thomas, old eggs, we give the little filly her socks.' Mr Finkelstein looked as if he were going to explain again, but decided not to. So Mary Bridge, as she now called herself, played the small part of Lynette in the great Arthurian romance *Atlantis*; and she and Gelert (you remember) saved the life of King Arthur in the famous Mutiny of the Round Table.

But alas! Hollywood did not agree with Weller. He pined for something; a glimpse, perhaps, of an English postman again. He drooped, he took to his bed, and, all too soon, passed to that bourn where beautiful golden Labradors, who are not Mr Gladstone, must all go. Hollywood gave him what almost amounted to a state funeral. Mr Zerfi returned from it, wiping his eyes, to look up Mary's contract. The enormous salary which he was pledged to pay her for the services of Weller (and, since the two were indivisible, herself) should have had a release clause in the event of Weller's death. Someone, as Lord Tennyson observed to Lord Palmerston in the super-colossal picture *Victoria and Albert*, had blundered. There was no release clause. He had Mary on his hands, and, more regrettably, on his salary list, for three more years.

What were they to do with her? It was a question which Hollywood had never found it difficult to answer. They made her into a star. They gave her a new face, they gave her new hair, they gave her a new stream-line, they did something to her tonsils to give her a new, husky voice, and they gave her a new name.

They called her Aurora Delaine.

Night at the Aldwinckles

(1948)

It seems that I have lost Gabrielle. I don't admit that it is my fault, because I don't know what else I could have done. Looking at it in another way, you can say that Gabrielle has lost me. Well, she has only herself to blame. If she had listened to my explanation, she might have been happily married to me by now. 'Happily' is, perhaps, putting it too strongly. I don't see how a marriage can be happy when one party to it does not trust the other party; when one party refuses to accept from the other party, as occasion demands, simple, straightforward explanations of what (admittedly) may seem unusual circumstances.

'When a guest, on his first visit to one's house,' said Gabrielle coldly, 'is discovered by the butler at eight o'clock in the morning, stretched out on the drawing-room floor in crumpled evening clothes and a drunken sleep, surrounded by a litter of smashed glass and china—'

'It was the housemaid who broke in on my sleep,' I corrected her, 'and I should put it at nearer seven-thirty than eight. But since you have made it clear that you do not wish to know the truth, what do these details matter?'

'What indeed? After a drunken debauch like that—'

'I understand that, thanks to the kindly forethought of Mrs Aldwinckle, my bags have already been packed, and that the car will be at the door in half an hour. In the circumstances, I prefer to walk to the station and pick up my luggage there. Good-bye, Miss Aldwinckle.'

'Good-bye, Mr Wibberley.'

As you see, I left with dignity. I did not write to Mrs Aldwinckle thanking her for a very pleasant visit, because there are, I hold, limits to the conventional insincerities of Society; nor did I make any further attempt to justify my behaviour on the night of January 25/26 by a reassertion of the facts. None the less, having thought the matter over in the weeks which followed, I have now decided that the truth shall be known; if not to Mrs and Miss G. Aldwinckle, then to those of our mutual friends who have been hearing a garbled version of the incident. Here, then, is the plain, unvarnished truth.

Perhaps I have misled you into thinking that I was actually engaged to Gabrielle. Such was not the case. I desire my readers to feel confident of the good faith of the present historian, and I shall therefore confess that at the time of my projected visit to The Towers I was still hesitating between Gabrielle and Mrs Aldwinckle. It was only the discovery on my arrival that Mr Aldwinckle was still alive which made me realize that Gabrielle, beyond a doubt, was my predestined mate. She was (or so I thought then) a charming girl: frank, merry, good-natured, and at times quite pretty. Mrs Aldwinckle (Bella, as I had been calling her in my mind) was physically even more attractive, and, during her lifetime, the bulk of the money would presumably be hers. Of course, the discovery that Mr Aldwinckle was still alive altered the financial position considerably; but I would emphasize that money never played a major role in my emotional reactions to the two ladies. Mrs Aldwinckle, charmingly youthful though she might be, was a year or two older than I, and this, I always think, is a mistake. Gabrielle was seven years younger, which seemed to me the correct interval between husband and wife.

You will have guessed by now that Gabrielle was Mrs Aldwinckle's stepdaughter. Old Mr Aldwinckle had married three times. When he was in the sixties, his first wife died, and he then married a girl forty years younger than himself, Gabrielle's mother. When Gabrielle was fifteen, he divorced this second wife; and being now eighty, and unable to profit by experience, married a still younger third wife, Bella. Even after what has passed between us, I have no wish to say anything against the present Mrs Aldwinckle, however temporary she may turn out to be; but if she did not marry him for his money, it is difficult to surmise what she did marry him for. He was an extremely disagreeable old man.

I had met Mrs and Miss Aldwinckle in London on several occasions, and, as I say, had found myself attracted by both of them. When I was asked to The Towers for some late January dances in the neighbourhood, I had no expectation of meeting a Mr Aldwinckle. I arrived at about five o'clock, and was shown by a devious route into the drawing-room. The topography of the house, which is important to my story, will be explained later. The two ladies rose to welcome me, and led me up to an old gentleman glooming by the fire. Naturally expecting Mrs Aldwinckle to say 'This is my grandfather', I was startled to hear that he was her husband; but I pulled myself together, bowed to him, and murmured politely that he was not to get up. This was an unfortunate beginning. He immediately put his hand to his ear and shouted, 'What's that? Speak up! I can't hear'; after which it was obvious that the need for begging him to remain seated would have passed by the time I had made myself audible. I therefore substituted a word of friendly greeting, which Mrs Aldwinckle broadcast for me, and we left it at that.

'My husband likes his tea punctually at 4.15,' she said to me, 'so we are having ours in the billiard-room. Take him along, Gabrielle. I'll join you in a minute.' As we went out of the room I heard Mr Aldwinckle say, 'And who the devil might that be?' referring evidently to myself, and then the door closed behind us.

When I say that the door closed behind us, I mean just that. All the doors in the lower regions of the house closed themselves automatically. Moreover, when one room led into another—as now, when we passed from the drawing-room into the library—there were double doors: that is, each room had its own door, and there was a sort of Priest's Hole between the two. This, as I guessed from my brief sight of Mr Aldwinckle, was a protection against draughts and noise, such as would be demanded by an ill-tempered old man of seventy with a child of five in the house. Protection against noise was no longer needed, but careless young women might still leave doors open. In Mr Aldwinckle's house they couldn't.

There was a big log-fire in the billiard-room and a cheerful-looking tea laid out. With its comfortable armchairs it was a welcome change from the drawing-room. I had only had a glimpse of this, of course, but it was enough for me to be sure that it had been furnished by the first Mrs Aldwinckle under the personal influence of Queen Victoria. It was full of occasional tables and uneasy chairs; and *objets d'art*, as they used to call them, and silver photograph frames were crowded on to every piece of furniture which could hold them. Even with its full-size table the billiard-room seemed open country in comparison with it.

A Mr and Mrs Stephens, I was told, were coming to dinner; after which we were driving to a small private dance some miles away. When I say 'we', I do not include Mr Aldwinckle. However, he was a great nuisance at dinner, though one recognized that his presence there could not be helped. All I need to say about the dance is that Gabrielle was my partner for the greater part of the evening, and that Mrs Aldwinckle, almost literally, went straight into the arms of a Major Fosdyke and remained there until we left. Loth as I am to saying anything against Mrs Aldwinckle, it is, I think, my duty to record that, even though several hours were to elapse before she ordered my bags to be packed (and this despite a perfectly simple explanation of my position on the drawing-room floor), yet even now I realized how fortunate it was that Mr Aldwinckle was physically incapable of listening to rumour.

We drove back, dropping Mr and Mrs Stephens on the way. I suppose it was about two o'clock when we got home, and found whisky and soft drinks laid out in the billiard-room. The fire was still flickering, the room still warm. I poured orange squash for the ladies, and mixed myself a whisky-and-soda. I had this in my hand as they got up to go to bed.

'And what about you, Mr Wibberley?' said my hostess. 'You haven't finished your drink. Don't hurry, so long as you remember to turn the lights out.'

'That's very kind of you,' I said. 'I did rather want to look at the evening paper before I went to bed. I suppose there will be one somewhere?'

Gabrielle laughed. Mrs Aldwinckle said, 'Oh, yes, you'll find it in the drawing-room. This naughty girl laughed because her father takes it there after dinner and reads it from the first word of the leading article to the last word of the advertisements. We never get a sight of it. But he doesn't take it to bed with him. So if you know your way to the drawing-room—'

'Oh, yes,' I said, 'I think so.'

'Through the aquarium and the library, and on the left,' said Gabrielle.

Mrs Aldwinckle laughed and said, 'Naughty girl' again. We all went out into the hall.

'You switch on the upstairs lights from here,' she explained, 'and you'll find a switch outside your bedroom which turns it off. I suppose you remember which your bedroom is?' she added, with a smile which I should have thought provocative, had I not remembered Major Fosdyke—and, of course, Mr Aldwinckle.

'I remember,' I smiled back. I did think of saying something a little daring in reply (but lightly, of course), and doubtless should have done so if only one of them had been there. With the two of them it was difficult.

'Then good night and pleasant dreams.'

'Good night, Mr Wibberley,' said Gabrielle, from a little way up the stairs, waggling her fingers at me; 'I enjoyed our dances.'

'So did I,' I said. 'Enormously. Good night—and thank you.' I said this to both of them, gave them a little bow, and went back to the billiard-room, making a mental note to get engaged to Gabrielle before I left. She was delightful.

My particular reason for wishing to see the evening paper (a local one, I supposed) was to acquaint myself with the progress of our cricket team in Australia. Though I have never played games myself with any proficiency, I consider that it is an Englishman's duty to take a patriotic interest in his national side, particularly when it is engaged in the most national of all pastimes, cricket. Moreover, I had wagered £5 against an old college friend of mine, a Trinity man, that England would not win a single one of the Test Matches, as they are called, and I was anxious to see what my prospects were. I suppose it would be true to say that, if I had not had this patriotic enthusiasm for the game, I should never have lost Gabrielle. Well, I am not ashamed of it. It is an enthusiasm which I share with many distinguished men. The other contributory cause to my downfall, as far as I can see, was a dogged determination not to be beaten by events. Of this also I am not ashamed. It is a boast of the Wibberleys that when they set their hand to the plough, they do not turn back.

Having finished my drink, I put down my glass and went into the hall. I walked across this into what Gabrielle called the aquarium. If you can imagine the Palm Court of a seaside hotel in the off-season, slightly reduced in size and only in touch with the outside world through its glass roof, you will get some idea of this curious inter-position within the architecture of The Towers. I am too young to have seen The Towers as first designed in 1860 or thereabouts; I was denied the opportunity of seeing it from outside in its yet more splen-did rejuvenescence. Doubtless its name was well-derived; doubtless it had also an observatory which offered for a moment of indecision an alternative name. As I say, I never saw it from the outside; and I am glad that I didn't.

The shortness of my visit also prevented me from discovering whether the aquarium actually held fish. All I can say is that it looked as if it ought to. It was lit by a faint green light in the lofty roof, apparently always kept burning. There may be fish for whom this is a pathological necessity; or it may have been designed to give an under-water feeling to the night visitor. It was all a little eerie, and I was glad to get across the place and into the library.

I was now in Mr Aldwinckle's territory, and the outer library door closed behind me as I opened the inner one. I put my left hand up for the switch, but could not find it. Almost certainly it should have been there; and undoubtedly I should have investigated the matter in daylight to discover why I had missed it. The biased attitude of Mrs Aldwinckle in ordering bags to be packed immediately after breakfast explains why I am still (as I was then) in the dark. I can only hazard the opinion that the switch was hidden within one of the bookshelves which lined the room. However this may be, my natural reaction was to take out my match-box, and so to make the unfortunate discovery that it was empty.

Possibly a less resolute character would have gone back at this point to seek illumination from the billiard-room. This was a weakness which I would not allow myself. It was easy to feel my way along the books until I reached the far left-hand corner of the room, where the door led into the drawing-room. I did this; I passed through the first door into the Priest's Hole; and I stood there for a moment, the second door held open with my right hand, my left hand feeling for the switch …

I will ask my readers to pause with me in this moment, and to search their hearts to see if they can find anything as yet with which to reproach me. Let me recapitulate. I have good and patriotic rea-sons for wishing to see the evening paper. I have the permission, even encouragement, of my hostess to fetch it from the drawing-room.

I am arrived there in face of a set-back which might have deterred a less resolute man. Is there aught for blame in all this? Nothing, you say. Then I shall assume that you are with me in spirit, your hand, metaphorically, also on the switch, waiting, as I, for more light to be thrown on the matter.

Again there was no switch. But this time the explanation, or so I thought, was simpler. My hand touched, not the wall, but a screen; pulled up close to the door as a further reinforcement against an imaginary draught. I suppose that, at the age of about forty, Mr Aldwinckle had woken up one morning with a crick in the neck, and had decided to spend the rest of his life guarding against another. Very gently I pulled my end of the screen a little towards me, so as to get my hand behind it, and immediately wished that I hadn't. It was one of those folding screens, stretched out, evidently, to its limit, and the least movement made it wonder nervously if its limit hadn't been reached. When it had settled down again, I reconsidered the position. A weak character would have groped his way back to the billiard-room, had another drink, and gone to bed. An ordinary man would have carried out the first two parts of the programme, but returned, suitably equipped, to fulfil his original intention. The Wibberleys come from a different mould. I have a cousin who shoots lions, rhinoceroses, and other local inhabitants of Central Africa. I shall refer to him again later, but I mention him now to say that we are of the same blood.

Since the screen could not be moved, I must walk round it; guiding myself gently by the finger-tips until I reached the end, and returning by similar means on its other side to the switch in the wall. I reached the end safely, and turned. My left knee struck a small table; there was a gentle tinkling sound, not unmusical in itself, which seemed to indicate that some *objet d'art* had fallen into disuse. I moved hastily away, and struck another table with the other knee. This table was more lightly balanced. It see-sawed from side to side, sliding things off its slippery top with each movement: photograph frames, I judged, from the more metallic noise of their fall, a surmise which the occasional crack of broken glass seemed to confirm. I realized that any further attempt to reach the switch would be ill-judged.

Reculer pour mieux sauter, I am not ashamed to confess, has often been the practice of the Wibberleys. I remember my cousin Bernard telling me how he had once surprised a lioness (or more accurately, I suppose, had been surprised by one) when strolling a little way from his tent; and how he had withdrawn backwards, keeping his eye firmly but reassuringly on the animal, until he was within reach of his gun. The skin now hangs in the smoking-room. In the same spirit I was prepared to withdraw to the billiard-room until I reached a box of matches, keeping my eye firmly, so to speak, on my object, the evening paper. I turned therefore to the door, bumping my hip painfully against something more solid than usual; made a short detour to avoid this; turned again, like Whittington, but, unlike him, striking some sort of *jardinière* with the other hip; felt ghostly fingers playing over my face and heard the dull crack of breaking pottery; stretched my hands out to guard against any more of these enforced contacts, sweeping something, I know not what, to the floor ... and in a sudden panic, such as I have never before experienced, realized that I was lost.

My cousin Bernard was lost once in the Njaio Forest. He has described the scene to me. The tall impenetrable trees which the fiercest rays of the sun could not pierce; the matted undergrowth; the cold realization that it was as impossible to go forward as to go back, since one did not know which was which; the awful knowledge that nothing human was within sight or sound; the sharp cry of some animal; the sudden deathly silence. Then the panic.

So it was with me.

In these circumstances, my cousin Bernard told me, the only thing to do is to sit down quietly and reason the thing out. I sat down, therefore, but not so quietly as I had hoped. It is immaterial to the authenticity of my story whether it was a photograph frame or a piece of pottery on which I sat, but I had let out a sharp cry before silence again descended upon the forest. I was lost; of that there could be no sort of doubt. The door might now have been in any direction. At three o'clock in the morning in an English January the sun's rays are not fierce; but even if they had been of tropical intensity no faintest gleam could have penetrated the thickness of the draught-proof curtains. All round me—and, as I had just discovered, underneath me—dangers lurked. Here I was; and here I must stay, until a rescue-party found me.

It was not an inviting prospect, but once one has made up one's mind to anything, one can bear it. Like an old campaigner I set about making myself as comfortable as possible. Thanks to Mr Aldwinckle's early experience at the age of forty, the floor was draughtless, the room fairly warm. Squatting down and extending my arms cautiously, as if swimming, I cleared a space on the floor for my torso. My head was under one occasional table, my feet under another. For pillow I had my pocket-book wrapped in two handkerchiefs. As I settled down on my right cheek and side, my customary position in bed, my outflung left hand felt something. Disgusted, possibly, with the closing advertisements, Mr Aldwinckle had hurled his evening paper to the floor. Now I had it in my hands. I withdrew my head cautiously from its table, and wrapped *The Northampton Evening Courier* round my ankles. It was this, you remember, which I had come into the drawing-room to get. I had got it.

There is no need to go into the morning's proceedings at any length. I slept the sleep of a good man with nothing on his conscience but the knowledge that he had done what he had set out to do. The housemaid's immediate reaction on drawing the curtains and turning to face the room again did not wholly wake me. Her piercing scream, her shrieks of 'Help! Murder! Thieves!' as she rushed to the domestic quarters, left me with the vague feeling that it was time to rouse myself and drink my morning tea. The fact that I greeted the arrival of the butler (poker in hand) with a loud oath and a crash of yet more broken china was due to the fact that I had (naturally) sat up in bed for this purpose, thus hitting my head violently on the underside of the occasional table. I was already feeling in my pocket-book, in reply to his 'Well, well, *well*, Mr Wibberley!', hoping that we could come to some arrangement by which the debris was swept up, and the remaining *objets d'art* reshuffled on the occasional tables so as to avoid any noticeable vacuum, when the attendance of the rest of the staff, with further shrieks of horror, made any business-like ending to the affair impossible. Within minutes the parlourmaid was taking up tea to her mistress, and Mrs Aldwinckle was giving orders that my bags should be packed.

That is the true story. Looking back on it, I still fail to see in what respect my conduct fell short of good manners, good sense, and a high standard of endeavour. Mrs Aldwinckle and Miss G. Aldwinckle made it quite clear that they did detect a shortage. So be it. Yesterday, by a curious coincidence, I met Mr Aldwinckle's second wife. She is still quite young, a widow, and apparently well provided for. I told her the whole story, and she was greatly amused. I am going to tea with her to-morrow.

Spring Song

(1948)

I

In the spring (said a more popular poet than either of them, but popularity isn't everything) a young man's fancy (and they were both young) lightly turns to thoughts of love. So it was with Claud Byles and Cecil Urbage. It was unfortunate that in this particular spring their fancies turned in the same direction.

She also was young, and to a lover beautiful. Possibly her nose was a shade too long, her mouth a trifle too small, her chin—but we need not anatomize her. Beauty lies in the eye of the beholder, and at this frenzied moment of the year they both thought her beautiful. By day she was 'Miss Smith, forward' in the Glove Department of the Riverstead Bon Marché; by night she was Jessie to her father and mother at Rose Villa.

Claud could be described (and, in fact, was by Cecil) as a whipper-snapper, just as Cecil might strike one (and did so strike Claud) as a jelly-bag; which is saying little more than that one was small and neat, and the other large and unconfined. Claud described himself diffidently as a poet; he was hoping that his genius or his size or some-thing would prevent him from being pushed down a coal mine before he had written his masterpiece. At this time he was trifling with what used to be called *vers de société*. Cecil described himself truculently as a poet. He also was relying on his genius or his size, but particularly his genius, to keep him above ground until he had made his name. At this time he was experimenting with what is now called poetry.

All this being so, it was fortunate that each of them had an independent income of £500 a year, and still more fortunate that this came from Government stock 'not taxed at source'. When, a year ago, Claud had received his first income-tax form, followed by a series of demands that the matter should engage his immediate attention, he returned his professional earnings truthfully and, in a broadminded way, halved his unearned income on the rational grounds that the price of everything had doubled. Cecil had received half a guinea six months before for an appreciation of T. S. Eliot, but pride forbade him to exhibit this as a year's earnings. He added, therefore, half his patrimony to it, and then, very naturally, forgot about the other half. His official income was thus established at £250 10s. 6d., or 10s. 6d. more than Claud's.

It was an invitation to a wedding which first brought Claud and Jessie together. He had remembered as the hour approached that he had left his only pair of gloves in a waiting-room at Waterloo three weeks ago, and as it was his pride to be the best-dressed man in any company (which may have been what Cecil meant by a whipper-snapper), and since it was too late now to go back to Waterloo to look for them, he had dropped in at the Bon Marché.

'Gloves? Certainly, sir. Miss Smith, forward,' said an obviously over-dressed gentleman with a wave of the hand, and, Jessie thus introduced, strolled magnificently away. Except for the other customers and an assistant or two, the lovers were alone together.

Claud took a deep draught of oblivion. All the girls of all the previous springs were forgotten.

'Gloves,' he whispered, with as much emotion as the word would bear.

'Size?' she asked, with as little emotion as the question warranted.

This was their first exchange of thought.

He held out his hand, hoping that she would now fondle it with a tape-measure, forgetting that hands were an open book to her. She gave it a brief glance and said, 'Seven. Colour?'

Claud realized that any prolonged conversation with the loved one would have to receive its impetus from his end.

'Lavender, grey, slate, elephant,' he said nervously; 'stop me when I strike a chord. Or possibly you have other suggestions. What we want is something appropriate for a wedding between a heedless young cousin and the profound mistake she is making.'

'Black?' offered Miss Smith.

'No, no, you misunderstand me. Not now, not now. Far from it, my dear Miss Smith. I will be frank with you,' he went on, though she had not asked him to be, 'there *was* a time—'

She handed him a pair, and stated the price. His love-life seemed of less importance to her than the needs of other customers. One of them was a tall, stout young man on whose ears the words 'Scarves? Certainly, sir. Miss Smith, forward' had just fallen. She wrote out a bill with one hand, held out the other for his Clothing Book, gave a seemingly casual glance at the name, snipped out the coupons, returned it with the bill, said, 'Pay at the desk,' and offered herself to the next customer, wondering what 'Claude Byles' did for a living. Claud gave the side of her face a look which said all, and went over to the cashier. 'A marvellous day,' he said enthusiastically. 'How are you feeling?' She gave him his change without telling him. The Riverstead Bon Marché was doing little this morning to promote that Host-and-Guest relationship of which it boasted in its advertisements.

Cecil Urbage was not a well-dressed man. Like many stout people he was careful of his health, and one cannot be well-dressed and wear three pullovers at the same time. There was a pleasant freshness in the spring air this morning, and such mornings were dangerous. I need not enter into the reasons why he could not get so close to his side of the counter as Claud; nor could he look into her eyes from the same level; but even a distant, foreshortened view of Miss Smith was enough. He quivered with emotion. Possibly this is what Claud meant by a jelly-bag.

'I want a warm scarf,' he said.

'Lady or gentleman?'

'Gentle—Well, I mean it's for me.'

'Any particular colour?'

'So long as it affords protection for the throat, the colour is immaterial.'

She brought him a box.

'Have you anything thicker?' he asked.

She brought him another box.

'I suppose these are guaranteed to wear well?' he wondered.

'Should do. You never know nowadays.'

'I'll have this,' he said, picking out a dirty yellow one. 'No, don't wrap it up.' He wound it round his throat several times. 'Rather a sharp morning.'

Miss Smith seemed indifferent to the sharpness of the morning. She said, 'You pay at the desk. I'll take the coupons.'

'Ah, coupons. I was forgetting,' said Cecil. He unwound himself to get at them. 'I seem to have two books,' he discovered. 'Would that be right?' He put them both on the counter.

Miss Smith showed the first real flicker of interest in her morning's work. Mr Claud Byles had had only twelve coupons left. Mr Cecil Urbage, as he seemed to be, had fifty-four. A young man, however stout, who has fifty-four clothing coupons left is worth any girl's attention. It was this which gave Cecil his start over Claud. She smiled at him, as she had not smiled at his rival. Cecil gave her a return smile, which for a moment put him back where he began, but the fifty-four coupons had the greater staying power. She decided to see more of Mr Urbage. When she had attended to the wants of the next seventeen customers, all women, she thought that it would also be nice to see Mr Byles again.

II

Well, there we have the Eternal Triangle once more, with Cecil in the more advantageous corner. The next phase was confusing and difficult for both of them. In order to see the beloved they had to make purchases at her counter; in order to make purchases they had to have clothing coupons.

Claud's problem soon became simple. He had seven pairs of gloves and no coupons.

Cecil's problem was more complex. He had all the coupons which a lover needs; but every one which he exchanged for the delight of the loved one's presence made him that much less attractive to her. He had misunderstood that first smile, supposing it to be of admiration at the approach of so big and handsome a gentleman, or of shyness in the presence of genius. Unknown to him, she was calling for the invitation which never came: the invitation to tea in the Queen Alexandra Café on early closing afternoon, when she could have told him about that new spring costume, and lamented that a mere lack of coupons separated her from it. 'I suppose,' she would have said innocently, 'you don't know of anyone who has a few to spare?' and Mr Urbage (it was hoped) would unwind himself and feel for his pocketbook.

She knew something of both of them by now, and they knew something of each other. On the day when he bought his last pair of gloves she had said carelessly to Claud, 'Did you ever meet a Mr Urbage?'

'Urbage?' said Claud. 'Do you mean—he made a swimming motion with his hands, indicating a semicircle about four feet in diameter—'that man?'

'Taller than you by a good bit,' she said coldly. 'Matter of fact, he's a well-known poet.'

'Well known for what?' asked Claud.

'Poetry,' said Jessie, after a little thought.

'Oh, I thought you meant—'

'Fancy! He's got fifty-four clothing coupons left! At least, he had,' she amended. 'He's only got forty-eight now.'

Later, when she was serving him, she asked Cecil if he had ever come across a boy called Claud Byles.

'Claud Byles?' said Cecil. 'Do you mean'—he held a hand, palm downwards, about three feet from the ground—'that man?'

'A slim boy with a very good figure,' said Jessie coldly. 'He writes—like you.' She picked up her scissors.

'Not in the least like me,' said Cecil with dignity. 'An artist is a unique personality. I don't write like Milton. Milton,' he added, to avoid any misapprehension, 'doesn't write like me.'

'Then who does he write like?' she snapped—and clipped.

'Like Milton,' said Cecil.

'Well, anyway, you've only got forty-seven coupons left. What do you *want* with all these scarves?'

She wondered a little sadly next day if Claud had now left her life, but he was there as usual.

'I want,' he said, 'a pair of gardening gloves. My spies tell me that they come under the heading of "Industrial", and are thus coupon-free. How are you this morning, Miss Smith? You're looking as charming as ever.'

'Anything like that would be in Garden Implements on the second floor, Mr Byles.'

'Believe me, there is nothing like that on the second floor. Charm in the Riverstead Bon Marché is confined entirely to the Glove Department.'

'Don't be silly, Mr Byles,' said Jessie, trying to be business-like, but handicapped by a slight feeling of pinkness. 'And I can't spend my time talking to customers if I'm not selling them anything.'

'Not if I promise to buy several garden implements immediately afterwards? The Directors wouldn't want you to miss a good stroke of business like that.'

'There's Mr Urbage coming in. I expect he's wanting to buy a scarf. Excuse me.'

'Very well. But I shall be back to-morrow to make another small purchase.'

The rivals met; one going, the other coming. They stood and looked at each other. Cecil drew his chin in, as one peering down at something on the floor. Claud moved his head slowly from side to side; what one wanted, he seemed to be saying, was a wide-angle lens ...

Claud was there next morning as he had promised.

'I want,' he said, 'a small bicycle-lamp. Leaving that for the moment, how are you this morning, Miss Smith? Isn't it a lovely day? I have just heard a small boy imitating a cuckoo.'

'This is the Glove Department,' said Miss Smith, with all the dignity she could manage.

'Then why do you sell scarves to a captive balloon?'

'Well, anyway, we don't sell bicycle-lamps to—'

Claud held up a hand.

'Don't say anything which you will regret afterwards. And I didn't ask you to sell me a bicycle-lamp, Miss Smith. I merely mentioned, by way of making conversation, that I was in need of a small one; just as you, it may be, long for a diamond tiara and a little cooking-fat. Surely we can give voice to our simple aspirations without introducing a sordid financial element. Have you seen Mr Urbage, some of Mr Urbage, again?'

'He bought another scarf half an hour ago,' said Miss Smith with a sort of gloomy pride.

'Have you ever thought of strangling him in one?'

'He's a poet, did I tell you? He's got a piece of poetry coming out in the *Messenger* next week. That's more than some people could do.'

'Has he, indeed? Very well. I accept the challenge and fling back the gauntlet. Do you sell gauntlets, by the way? I want the heavy iron sort, coupon-free, for flinging. Put it down on your order list. For, mark my words, Miss Smith, if poetry wrings your heart, I, too, will have a poem in the *Messenger* next week. What is more, it will be addressed, not to a drain-pipe, as Mr Urbage's best poems are, but to the most beautiful girl in Riverstead; and the original manuscript will be presented to her in the course of a short ceremony in the Glove Department, on, let us say, next Tuesday. Meanwhile, I shall be making another small purchase to-morrow. Until then, farewell.'

He raised his hat and left her.

III

So began the third phase: the local Eisteddfod, so to speak, in the *Riverstead Messenger*.

Miss Smith was truly informed when she said that Mr Urbage had a piece of poetry coming out in that paper. Moved by the ferment in his blood at this season of the year, Cecil had been delivered of a poem called *Spring in Alicante*. It went roughly like this: I say roughly, partly because there is a rugged grandeur about it which is characteristic of all Urbage's work, and partly because I quote from memory and may have left out some of the words. There will be those who think that this can't have mattered much, but they will understand that an author might be sensitive on the point. Here, as I was saying, is the poem.

Spring in Alicante

> Steam-hammers like white thoughts clanking
> as once (once)
> 'as once' in Nanking
> once in months the visceral bull
> target-centred enters
> papal palpable
> China-town China-town China-town
> crockery and mockery
> thighs dew-ridden in the pastoral yoke
> egg-white rag-red
> steam-hammers
> pulsing and repulsing equal and opposite Ice.

It is not my business to annotate the work of an Urbage, and I should hesitate to do so now, were it not for that one word 'Ice', which I remember so vividly: a word singularly out of place, as it seemed, in a poem on spring. Up to that last electric line we feel that we have followed the poet's train of thought through its numerous changes, shuntings, backings, and overrunning of points. Then, suddenly, just as we reach the terminus with a sigh of satisfaction, we are jerked into a confusion of doubt by that startling ice. I cannot leave it like that. I dare not entrust an Urbage *opus* to the speculations of posterity, the *varia lectio* of some as yet unborn critic, when a glance at the MS (at one time in the possession of Mrs Jessie Waterfield, and under the short leg of the kitchen table, but I think not now extant) has made the whole matter clear to me.

Like all poets Urbage was an experimentalist. He had tried leaving out capital letters at the beginning of his lines, and he had tried putting them into the middle of his words, in the hope of so achieving what has been called the Great Thrill of poetry. Italics and Roman type were equally at his command. In this poem he had tentatively essayed a more daring experiment. It will have been noticed that the word 'once' comes four times into the first four lines. It is, in fact, the keynote of the poem, as it should be of any poem if poetry is to preserve its reputation as 'emotion recollected in tranquillity'. Now, it is always effective to strike the keynote again at the end of an improvisation, and this is exactly what Urbage had planned to do. But on this occasion he had given a new touch to it.

He had written it 'Ice'.

Claud Byles was wedded to a more old-fashioned Muse who thought that poetry should rhyme, and the oftener the better, and if it didn't scan why was it called poetry? I'm afraid that she took it all rather lightly anyhow. Claud and his Muse got together on Sunday morning, and prepared to write an ode to Miss Smith.

They began by considering rhymes to Smith. All that his Rhyming Dictionary could give them on the subject was 'pith' and 'frith', neither of which seemed to express what he wanted to say, even if he had known what a 'frith' was. 'Monolith', which came to him in a flash of inspiration, received only a shake of the head from his Muse. If Miss Smith were Mrs Byles, the situation would be easier, but in that case he wouldn't want to write a poem to her. 'Irony,' he said to his Muse, and she agreed with him.

He wondered what her Christian name was. If Mabel, then able, stable and cable; full of promise. If Ruth, then youth and truth; still better. If Jacynth—no, that was worse than Smith. Damn it, he said suddenly, why don't I choose an imaginary name, as all the Elizabethan poets did? Chloe, Amanda, Lucasta, Julia? None of these. Who was the most beautiful girl in the world? Miss Smith of Riverstead. Who was the most beautiful woman in history? Helen of Troy. *To Helen*. Why, the lines almost wrote themselves.

To Helen

When I fell in
Love with Helen—
O, the sweet entrancing creature!
(One supposes
That her nose is
Probably her fairest feature)—

Did I dare to
Hope, and swear to
Love and cherish, have and hold her,
Fears arrested
As she nested
With her head upon my shoulder?

> Was she guessing
> (I confessing)
> What the throbbing of my heart meant? …
> 'Tis a dream, I
> Only see my
> Helen in the Glove Department.

No editor, he felt, could refuse such a poem, no true woman refuse the hand of its author. On his way to the *Messenger* office next morning, he looked in at the Bon Marché to ask Miss Smith if she had any silk-lined boxing-gloves with the town arms worked on the back. Hearing, with a start of surprise, that she hadn't, and was not expecting any in for the next few days, he said that he would just come round early to-morrow in case, and that he was now going to enter into financial negotiations with the Editor of the *Riverstead Messenger* for the publication of an important work.

'Oh, Mr Byles,' said Jessie, excited, as what girl would not be, 'does that mean—'

'It means,' said Claud, 'that we shall be going down to posterity together; one of the advantages of posterity being that no coupons are required there. *Au revoir.*'

When the Proprietor and Editor of the *Riverstead Messenger* received *Spring in Alicante*, he read it, blotted out the title with his blue pencil, and passed it to the Assistant Editor, as his son and office-boy called himself when the Editor wasn't there.

'What would *you* call that, Tom?'

The Assistant Editor read it and told him.

'I meant title. Would you call it *Spring in Alicante*?'

'No,' said the Assistant Editor, 'I told you what I'd call it.'

'I think we'd better just call it *Spring*,' mused the Editor.

'Or what I said,' repeated the Assistant Editor doggedly.

The Editor wrote 'Mag. Page Fill-Up' in the corner and sent it down to the printer. The Thursday 'Magazine Page', which started going to press in a leisurely way ten days beforehand, was still not quite filled up when Claud reached the office. This was because the latest instalment of 'Behind the Scenes in the Secret Service', by Raymond Strong, which was making such a sensation in Riverstead, had had to do without its usual illustration this week, the artist having been directed into the cotton industry. Claud was even more welcome than he had expected.

'I have brought you a little poem,' he said to the Editor's back.

Without looking round, the Editor held out a hand for it, glanced at it for length, said, 'Fine,' wrote 1 on it, and passed it to the Assistant Editor.

'That other bit's "2". General title "Poetry" and let readers sort it out for themselves.'

'Bit dogmatic, isn't it?' said the Assistant Editor. 'Just "Poetry" like that. "Poetry Corner" would sort of ease it in better.'

'Have it your own way.' He looked round and seemed surprised that Claud was still there. 'Thank you, Mr—er—good morning.'

'There's just the little question of the fee,' said Claud with an ingratiating smile. 'You haven't said anything about that.'

'That's all right, Mr—er—' said the Editor kindly. 'On the assumption that you will be buying at least a dozen copies to give to your friends, we don't charge any fee. Good morning.'

'Good morning,' said Claud, a little dazed. The financial negotiations seemed to be over.

When the Magazine Page came up it was still a couple of lines short.

'We'll give Poetry Corner a sub-title,' said the Editor. 'Think of something.'

The Assistant Editor thought of what he had thought of before, but it was again passed over.

'Give that first one its old title "To Helen". That'll do it.'

But it didn't come under the 'T' as it should have done, and both poems were thus addressed to Helen.

IV

For the last phase we go over to Rose Villa.

'Well, which of them do you like best, dear?' said Mrs Smith.

'I thought you were engaged to young Waterfield,' said Mr Smith, scowling at his daughter. He was a morose man who suffered from indigestion and too many women in the house.

'Well, yes and no,' said Mrs Smith. 'A girl must do the best she can for herself these days. Joe isn't all that.'

'He's making £600 a year, *and* his mother's dead,' said Mr Smith, looking up at the ceiling; not as a last salute to the departed, but because Mrs Smith's mother was still there.

'Well, what's Mr Urbage making, Dad? You ought to know.'

'Of course your father ought to know, and he'll make it his business to know. How many scarves do you say he's bought?'

'Twelve.'

'That sounds like money. And Mr Byles sounds like money too. But which do you *like* best, dear? It's always something to fall back on, if you like them.'

'Do they *mean* anything,' said Mr Smith, 'or are they just trifling with the affections of another man's fiancée? That's the point.'

'I thought it was a very nice bit of poetry Mr Byles wrote,' said Mrs Smith, 'but I don't quite know why he called you Helen. I thought Helen was the girl at the ribbon counter.'

'So she is. I said thank you for nothing until he told me who she was, the most beautiful woman who ever lived, he said. They fought a great battle over her, she was so beautiful.'

'When was that?' asked Mr Smith.

'Four thousand years ago. Fancy!'

'Dead now?'

'Of course, Dad.'

'That's something,' said Mr Smith, looking up at the ceiling again. 'Though it's a long time to wait,' he added gloomily.

'Writers make a lot of money,' said Mrs Smith. 'Look at what that Raymond Strong must be making, with all those stories he writes.'

'I don't think poetry is so well paid, from what Claud said.'

'Well, we'll go into all that on Sunday,' said Mr Smith. He helped himself to bicarbonate of soda, put on his hat, and went round to his club.

'Mr Urbage doesn't use his clothes coupons,' said Jessie to her mother. 'I mean not in the ordinary way. One's got to think of everything.'

'I didn't think his poem was very nice,' said Mrs Smith. 'I don't say I understood it, but there was something about "thighs" which I thought was better left unsaid. It isn't a word one likes to see used in a public print about one's own daughter.'

'It was the bull, Mum, not me.'

'All the same, people get ideas,' said her mother darkly. 'One can't be too careful.'

So Mr Byles and Mr Urbage came to tea on Sunday, and as Claud was nervous and talkative the meal went gaily enough, except that Mrs Smith's mother tapped twice on the ceiling to ask (presumably) how she could be expected to get her afternoon's nap with all that noise going on. 'Poltergeist,' explained Mr Smith briefly, 'we have a lot of trouble with it,' and asked Jessie if she had seen young Waterfield lately.

As soon as tea was over, he took the two young men into his office and came to business.

'Now then, gentlemen,' he said, 'I understand that you both want to marry Jessie, been writing poetry to her and all that, so naturally, as her father, I'd like to know something about you. For instance, supposing my little girl's fancy should turn towards one of you, and I don't say it will, mark you, I should want to be sure that he could support her properly.' He took out his pocket-book and fingered the pencil absently.

'What would you call properly?' asked Claud.

'Suppose we say £700 a year.'

Cecil quivered slightly, recovered himself, and said, 'Chicken-feed.' Mr Smith made a note, and looked towards Claud.

'I don't keep chickens,' said Claud, 'but I can only say that, if I did, I should be ashamed to starve them like that.'

'Well, that's very satisfactory. And earned, I hope? I shouldn't care to have an idle son-in-law. Mr Urbage?'

'All except a trifling £500 a year,' said Cecil. 'I suppose you wouldn't object to that?'

Mr Smith made another note, and turned to Claud.

'Well,' said Claud, 'there *is* a little something which comes in every six months. I forget exactly how many hundreds it is. My chief income, of course—' He looked at the fingers of his right hand and waggled them, as if all this writing was beginning to give trouble.

'That's good. Now, Mr Urbage, you won't mind my asking just *how* you earn your money.'

'I am a poet,' said Cecil proudly.

'As a spare-time occupation I have nothing against it, but—'

'I write other things as well. Naturally.'

'Such as—'

Cecil swallowed and said, 'I don't want this generally known, Mr Smith, but I am—I am—I am Raymond Strong.'

'Good Heavens,' said Claud, 'are you the man behind the scenes in the Secret Service?'

'I am.'

'They must be very big scenes,' said Claud thoughtfully.

'I was under the impression,' said Mr Smith sarcastically, 'that your name was Cecil Urbage.'

'He writes under an omnibus,' explained Claud. 'Lots of us do,' he added, seeing that his turn was coming next.

'Let's have this clear. Your real name is Urbage, but when you write under an omnibus'—he frowned at Claud, and corrected himself—'when you write anonymously—or, rather, under a pseudonym—you call yourself Raymond Strong?'

'That's right.'

'You must make a great deal of money, Mr Urbage. Raymond Strong is a very popular author, according to all accounts.'

Cecil shrugged modestly.

'In fact, we might put your income at'—he poised his pencil over the note-book—'what shall we say? About £5,000?'

'About that.'

'That's very satisfactory,' said Mr Smith, making another note. 'And now, what about you, Mr Byles? Apart from this hobby of poetry indulged in under your own name, do you also write under an om—' He stopped himself just in time. '—anonymously, or under a pseudonym?'

'Of course. One has to nowadays.'

'And what have *you* been writing—under what name?'

'*Forever Amber*,' said Claud simply. 'I,' he went on dramatically, without really stopping to think, 'am Charlotte Brontë.'

There was an awed silence … Anyway, there was a silence.

'Same initials, you see,' said Claud, noting the coincidence with surprise, and feeling that it ought to mean something. 'Because of underclothes,' he explained. 'Or rather,' he corrected himself, 'dressing-cases. Underclothes would be different anyway. Silly of me.'

Mr Smith, who was no strip-tease artist, but a serious-minded business man, said, 'Never mind underclothes, let's come down to figures. What do you make? Can we say £5,000 a year like Mr Urbage?'

'Six,' said Claud, determined not to be like Mr Urbage.

'Six thousand,' said Mr Smith. Having made a final note, he permitted himself to rub his hands lightly together; and what he thought of as a smile flickered out of one side of his moustache and crept back again.

'Thank you for being so frank, gentlemen. It is up to me to be equally so.' He put his note-book back in his pocket. 'You have told me who you are in your professional capacities, and it is only fair that I should tell you who I am.'

'Don't say you're not Jessie's father,' pleaded Claud. 'You can't be sure.'

'I,' said Jessie's father grimly, 'am F. X. Smith.'

The two young lovers left together; they left almost at once; they had the same appointment with the same man about the same dog; they would have gone arm-in-arm if they had been more nearly the same height.

After a long silence Claud said:

'I always hated that name.'

'So did I,' said Cecil. 'Indecent.'

There was another silence.

'I rather think of going to live in London,' said Claud. 'More scope there for a writer.'

'Much. God knows why we've stayed here so long.'

After another interval for thought Claud summed the matter up.

'Jessie,' he said, 'is a very nice girl, but one got carried away.'

'Spring fever,' agreed Cecil.

'Looking at it in the more mellow light of approaching summer, one sees that one simply cannot marry the daughter of one's Income-Tax Collector.'

'Practically incest.'

'By the way, that reminds me—you're not really Raymond Strong, of course?'

'No.'

Claud decided to be frank.

'I—' he said, 'am not Charlotte Brontë.'

Tristram

(1948)

I

On a certain morning towards the end of September, 1943, Colonel Philibert Kaye came into the revolving summer-house at the end of his garden with three unopened air-letters in his hand. The rest of his mail had been read at breakfast, but these three letters were from his boy; and it was his sentimental custom to read all such letters in the garden-house which he had built for Lydia. Here, in the last year of her life, she had followed the sun across the sky; here, on the last day, she had said good-bye to it for ever, her hand in his. That was eight years ago, when Tristram was thirteen. It would be difficult to say which of them she had loved more. The Colonel never knew that almost her last words to Tristram had been, 'You will be looking after him for me, won't you? Please, darling.' She had no need to ask her husband to look after Tristram. Tristram was all of herself which she had left to him.

Twenty years ago a board had stood where the Colonel now sat, offering 'this valuable freehold building site of 70 acres' for sale; and all the old inhabitants, who lived in beautiful time-worn houses which seemed to have grown up with the country, shuddered, and told themselves bitterly that in a year or two they would be having the trams. It was not so bad as that. Only twelve houses were put up, each with its five or six acres, and the houses were as much in keeping with local conditions as a modern architect could make them. The first concern of all the new-comers was to screen themselves from their neighbours, and so to give themselves the privacy which a true Englishman demands, they set about planting hedges. The patient ones were more successful than the others. The impatient ones began with lordly thoughts of yew, changed to lonicera, experimented with beech, privet and hawthorn, and returned years later to lonicera, thus falling behind in the race. But Nature is very persistent; and, in spite of what he now admitted to have been mistakes, Colonel Kaye had made his castle fairly safe from enemy observation. Only in one corner, close to where he now sat, could a spy from Wychelm look over the hedge. Fortunately, when Lydia had lived in the garden-house, Wychelm had been empty.

At breakfast that morning Colonel Kaye had achieved his most supremely happy moment since Lydia's death. Tristram was an eager and regular correspondent. He had taken his father all round the Cape and into the Middle East; had talked to him from messes and bivvys, deserts and battlefields; had never left him alone for more than a few days at a time ... and suddenly had vanished. The Colonel waited. Something was 'on'. When he heard of the landing at Salerno, he felt sure that this was it. When the Germans announced that the whole landing-force had been annihilated, his heart hammered out, 'Yes, but not my boy. All—but not my boy.' He knew that he would have to be patient; there could be nothing from Tristram yet; but whenever he heard the postman's knock he was torn between hope for a letter and fear for a telegram. At a sudden ringing of the bell, 'Well, this is it,' he would say, his thoughts a scrap-book of well-weathered phrases: 'Stiff upper lip ... bite on the bullet ... *pro patria mori* ... I wouldn't have had it otherwise.' And if it were just a woman at the door selling tickets for a dance in the Village Hall, he would gladly have bought them all in gratitude for the respite.

Now, after nearly three weeks of waiting, he came down to breakfast, a well-set-up little man, trim greying moustache, trim greying hair, whistling casually to himself to show that he didn't expect a letter of any consequence, but one might as well look ... and there it was: One—Two—Three! Three letters! He studied the postmarks anxiously. As far as he could make out, Sep. 17th, 22nd, and 23rd; all written after that first terrifying week; the last ones written when we were well on the move again. His boy was safe! All through breakfast his eyes went back to the addresses in Tristram's delicate handwriting, and his heart swelled with happiness at the happiness in store for him. In Lydia's house, alone with her and Tristram.

So, on this morning, he opened the first of his letters and read, 'Very dear old man and respected Sir'—Tristram always had some new way of beginning—and smiled to himself, and looked up gratefully to Heaven for his happiness ... and there, only a few yards away, on the other side of the waist-high hedge, was a stranger.

'Damn!' said the Colonel, and put his letters back in his pocket. Monstrous thing to do, to come spying on him like this.

'Could I speak to you, Colonel Kaye?' a soft, pleasant voice called to him.

He had seen her in the distance once or twice. She was the nurse who looked after Miss Alladyce. Miss Alladyce, it was understood, had been bombed out of her house in London, and had been herself badly injured. When she had come to Wychelm six months ago, she had let it be known that she couldn't receive visitors. She was bedridden and invisible. Nobody knew anything about her.

'Of course, Nurse, of course,' he said, getting up and coming to the hedge. Why hadn't she gone to the front door in the proper way?

'Miss Alladyce wondered if you would be so very kind as to help her. Well, it was really me who suggested it, but she was so pleased at the idea, I wouldn't have felt right if I hadn't come to you, I mean after brightening her up like that.'

'Well, of course, quite right, only too glad. Tell me all about it.'

'You see, Miss Alladyce has a nephew she's very fond of—out there'—she waved a hand vaguely—'and he writes to her regularly every week, and he hasn't written for more than three weeks, and she's getting so anxious, and it's upsetting her, and I don't like that. It's not good for her.'

'I should think not indeed. She mustn't be upset, poor lady. Well now, will you tell her from me that I've been in just the same case. I hadn't heard from my boy for more than three weeks, and then suddenly, this morning, look!' He whisked the letters out of his pocket, and held them up to her. 'One, two, three!' As he took them down, an idea came to him. 'Of course!' he said. 'He's probably in the same Division.'

'I've got all about him written down,' said Nurse, feeling in the pocket of her apron. 'Here we are. Fifty-six. Would that be it?'

'I thought so. Same Division as my boy's. They were in this Salerno landing.'

'Miss Alladyce thought it might be Salerno, that's what's been worrying her, he wouldn't tell her, of course—'

'No, no, they're not allowed to tell. But they can't stop us guessing, can they?' He gave her a friendly laugh, and she laughed in return.

'Fancy their being together!'

'London Division. Best Division in the Army,' said Colonel Kaye proudly, meaning best now that my boy is in it. 'Yes, well now, you tell Miss Alladyce from me that that's why she hasn't heard. And tell her this from me. No news is good news. The War Office will tell us soon enough if anything happens; she would have had a telegram by now—at least, the boy's next of kin would—anyway, she would be hearing soon enough—'

'But that's just it, Colonel Kaye. That's really why I came to you.'

'I don't quite understand, Nurse.'

'You see, the next of kin is young Mr Roger Dixon's father, and Miss Alladyce and he, well, she doesn't even know where he is now.'

'But surely his son—'

'No, you see, they have nothing to do with each other.'

The Colonel was horrified. Father and son having nothing to do with each other! His hand went into his breast-pocket and fingered his letters.

'Miss Alladyce doesn't like to talk much about it, but Mr Dixon was separated from his wife, that's her sister, and the boy had been living with his mother, and then she died—I think Mr Dixon had been very unkind to her, and he didn't see the boy again. This was at the beginning of the war, and Mr Roger went straight into the Army after his mother died, and of course the father was the next of kin. It doesn't seem right somehow.'

'Dear, dear,' said Colonel Kaye thoughtfully. 'A very awkward situation. And she wants me to see if I can find out about the young man—'

'If you possibly could. It *would* be kind of you.'

'Well, give me that bit of paper, and I'll see what I can do. But you must come here and tell me at once if she hears from him. I'm generally here for an hour or so after breakfast.'

'Oh, thank you, Colonel Kaye. This will do her so much good.'

As she turned away, he called after her, 'And tell her not to worry. It will be quite all right.'

When she was out of sight, he went back to his letters. A little of the glory of the morning was gone. He felt uneasily that it was selfish to be so happy. Something of the weight of all the unhappiness which Salerno had brought to other men and women was on him as he began to read. Then Tristram made him laugh. He forgot all the others and read on, thinking only of Tristram, seeing him there, hearing him laugh too.

Later in the day he wrote to his son, telling him about Miss Alladyce and asking him to find out what he could. He also wrote to a friend of his in Records at Liverpool. So in a little while Miss Alladyce knew that on Sep. 10th T./Capt. R. Dixon of the Queen's Royal Regt. had been killed in action.

II

It had been the custom of Nurse to come up to the hedge by the garden-house once or twice a week in order to report to, and receive news from, the Colonel; and she was so talking to him one morning at the end of October, giving him, he was distressed to hear, a very poor account of her patient.

'You see, Colonel Kaye, it was the one thing which kept her going. If she wasn't knitting him something, she was thinking up a parcel for him, and then I had to buy the things, and we'd have them all out on the bed, and she would wrap each one up so lovingly, and pack them all so carefully in the box, so that they all fitted in, and paint the address beautifully with a brush and very black ink—better than Hitler could do, she said once—I mean it just made it a day to look forward to, it was just—Well, I mean, now she's *got nothing*.'

'Poor lady, I understand. But couldn't she make things for one of these Societies? I'm sure there's one in the village—'

'Well, of course, I did suggest it, but she didn't seem to take to it somehow. I mean it isn't personal, is it, it isn't like anything you're doing for somebody you love. I mean you can't *see* the person opening the parcel, and wearing what you've made, and—You do see what I mean, don't you, Colonel Kaye?'

He nodded absently. He was thinking. He put his hand into his breast-pocket and brought out a letter-case. From the letter-case he took a photograph, looked at it for a moment, and passed it across the hedge to her.

'My boy Tristram,' he said awkwardly.

She took it, and held it close to her rather short-sighted eyes.

'Oh, what a sweet face!' she said impulsively.

'Isn't it?' agreed the Colonel, proudly but shyly. 'The image of his mother. Give him one of those tight-fitting hats, and paint in some curls, and you couldn't tell the difference.'

'I can imagine her. She must have been sweet.'

'She was lovely,' said the Colonel, looking back at the dead Lydia, almost with awe. 'Oh, but you mustn't think that Tristram is a namby-pamby,' he added quickly. 'Bless you, no. He was in his school Fifteen, *and* in the Eleven. A thorough boy.'

'You must be very proud of him,' she said, passing the photograph back to him across the hedge.

He didn't take it. He puffed at his pipe and said, 'Nurse. Do you think that if you showed that photograph to Miss Alladyce, and told her that in his last letter Tristram had said that the sock situation was rapidly getting out of control—do you think that she might be persuaded to do something about it? It would be very kind of her, and the boy would appreciate it enormously. You see, I'm not very good at socks.'

To her surprise Nurse felt a foolish tear coming into one eye.

'Oh, Colonel Kaye!' she said. 'It's just what—I'll take it to her at once. Oh, I do think you're—oh, *thank* you!'

As she turned to go, he called after her, 'Tell her I don't want the photograph back, I've got another copy.' And then more loudly, 'Size seven! He's got a very small foot!'

Left alone, the Colonel went back to his chair, shaking his head at himself. It was one of those still, sad, autumn days, bringing nothing for encouragement, offering nothing to fight. A day of regret for the lost opportunity which was never there; of remorse for the wrong which one does not remember to have done. But Colonel Kaye knew what he had done. He had shared his boy with a stranger. He had given her some part of Tristram. No longer would he be Tristram's only confidant, Tristram's only outlet for self-expression. Tristram would write to Miss Alladyce, thanking her; she would write long letters back, much better letters, he thought, than I ever write, though, of course, I give him all the news of the Home Guard, and the people in the village; and perhaps when I am thinking that there should be a letter from him this morning, it will be going to her.

'Oh, well,' he thought. 'Poor dear. One couldn't do less.'

He put his hand to his pocket, and drew it out again. 'I must look for that other copy,' he thought. 'I know I've got one somewhere.'

But Miss Alladyce could match his sensitive kindness with her own. When the first pair of socks went out, a letter went with it. Tristram was *not* to write to her; she knew how busy he was. He could send her a message through his dear father to say he had received them, and to let her know what else he particularly wanted. And she would be sending him a parcel directly, and if there was anything in the parcel which he didn't much care about, or anything else which he would rather have had, he must tell his father. 'Now is that quite understood, dear boy? Because I really do mean it. God bless you and keep you safe. Your unknown friend, Christine Alladyce.'

So, in his office, where he filled up innumerable forms for his company of Home Guard, the Colonel typed out the relevant passages in Tristram's letters; at first no more than an expression of gratitude, with perhaps some extravagant reference to the envy which the socks had excited in the Company Mess, and the subsequent suicide of the O.C. But, as the weeks went on, he found himself going from there into a description of Italian scenery, or a humorous account of a conversation with the Mayor, telling himself that this would interest Miss Alladyce, but also telling himself that he would like her to appreciate his boy's charm as a letter-writer, his boy's qualities. In the end he was typing almost the whole letter, only leaving out the love and the little private jokes; and once, as if by accident, letting the love slip in, so that she should know how near and dear his boy was to him. Every morning now Nurse would be at the hedge to give and receive the messages which passed between him and Miss Alladyce.

'Oh, thank you, Colonel Kaye,' she would say, taking the envelope from him, 'we didn't expect him to write again so soon. And Miss Alladyce wants to know, does he like Turkish Delight?'

'Well, tell her that I've never actually seen him eating it, but I feel quite sure he does.'

'Oh, that's good, because we've got some. Colonel Kaye, I can't tell you what all this has meant to her.'

'And to Tristram,' he laughed. 'We mustn't forget that. Nurse—' he went on hesitatingly, and then stopped.

'Yes, Colonel Kaye?'

'I suppose it would be quite impossible for me to see Miss Alladyce? Talk to her?'

She shook her head sadly.

'She was so dreadfully burnt. She can't bear for anyone to see her poor face now. Except me, of course. And the doctor.'

'Yes. I understand. Poor lady.'

'And so brave.'

'She must be. Is there no hope? They do such clever things nowadays.'

'We pretend sometimes. She says, "When I'm the Belle of Saffron Walden again," in her joking way. But she has a weak heart; and to go through all *that*—I don't think she has very long now, you know.'

'I see. Yes, I understand.'

'It's so wonderful of you to have made the end so happy for her.'

The Colonel put his hand to his eyes, thinking of Lydia, thinking of Tristram disfigured, thinking of that poor woman. Then with a shake of his shoulders—'stiff upper lip' and all that—he turned away, throwing a 'Thank you, Nurse,' at her as he went.

III

It was on an early spring morning in March that Nurse came to the hedge and waited for the Colonel to come out of the garden-house; but he did not come. For some reason she wouldn't call to him, but moved along the hedge until she could see into the room. And he sat there, with his arms spread out on the table, and his head on his arms.

On the floor by his side was a crumpled piece of paper. Before she knew what she was doing, she had cried out.

He started up. She turned away, she could not bear to look at him. Even Miss Alladyce's injuries could be looked at more easily. She put her hand up, as if warding him off, and began to hurry out of his sight. She had gone some twenty yards before he called to her, loudly, firmly.

'Nurse! Come here!' It was an order.

She turned. He waited for her. She could look at him now. He was the man she had known: trim, upright, composed, but an older man than she had thought.

'You are not to say a word of this to Miss Alladyce. You understand?'

'Yes, Colonel Kaye.'

'Let her go on just as before. You understand?'

'Yes, but—'

'We must plan it out.'

'There are the parcels—she was just making one up now. To-morrow's our day for it.'

'She must send it as usual.'

'Yes, Colonel Kaye.'

'Does she put letters in the parcels?'

'Sometimes.'

'Tell her it's safer to send them separately. The letters will come back to me. I'll arrange with his Company Commander to open the parcels. They won't be wasted.'

'Oh!' cried Nurse, excited now. 'Yes! We *could* do that!'

'Of course we can't keep it secret from anybody else. You realize that?'

'Nobody sees her but me and the doctor.'

'Dr Matthews? I'll warn him.'

'But what about the letters? His letters, I mean? The bits you send on to her?'

Colonel Kaye fiddled with his pipe and blew down it.

'She shall have them,' he mumbled.

'Oh, Colonel Kaye!' Poor man, she thought. That lovely boy. It's worse for him than ever it was for her.

'Well, Nurse, do you think we can manage it?'

'Oh, I'm sure we can!'

'Got to think of everything, you know. One slip and we crash. Ah! There we are, you see. The parcels. Who addresses them, and who posts them?'

'She addresses them, like I told you, and I take them on my bicycle to the village.'

'Yes, well, that won't do. The village will know, and wonder what's up. Parcels going off every week.'

They both thought this out.

'I could alter the name before I posted it,' she said doubtfully. 'To the one you were saying, the Company Commander. But it seems sort of—well, not quite—I mean, sort of unkind, after all the trouble she has taken, painting the address on. Oh well, that's just silly, of course.'

'Not silly at all, Nurse,' said the Colonel sternly. 'Only silly to a silly person. I agree with you entirely. What you must do is to bring the parcels to me, and I'll post them in the town.' Battalion H.Q. was in the local town ten miles away, and the Colonel's car made weekly journeys to it.

'Yes, that would be better.'

'And when you bring me the parcels, you must bring me a list of what's inside. You understand? You understand why?'

She understood. She shook the tears out of her eyes as she nodded to him. Poor man! Typing out those imaginary letters, saying Thank you for this and that which his dead boy had never seen.

'Right. Then I think we've got it set. You must exercise your own judgment about the staff.'

'It's just the cook and the gardener. They never see her.'

'Well, I leave that to you.' He looked at her, giving her for the first time his full attention. 'Do you think we can keep it up?'

'Yes, I think so. It won't be for long, Colonel Kaye. Just midsummer perhaps.'

Without thinking, she stretched out her hand to him across the hedge. He took it, pressed it, and let it go. 'Fellow conspirators,' he said, and achieved a smile. She went quickly away.

IV

Colonel Kaye was in his office, writing a letter from his son. At first he had found this difficult, for he was not, as Tristram had been, a ready writer. But he had kept in touch with his son's battalion; he knew within limits where it was; and he had Tristram's old letters to help him. The Division had gone to Palestine to refit; a year ago it had passed through Palestine on its way to Tunisia; in any case (he reassured himself) one desert was very much like another. Moreover, Tristram's great friend, Jimmy Ludlow, wrote to him now and then; which made it possible to superimpose on a rather prosaic description of Jerusalem Tristram's more lively embellishment of an afternoon in Bombay. In the same spirit he had transferred the flora and fauna of Cyrenaica (in which Tristram had taken so much interest) a thousand miles or so to the north-east.

He was glad when the Division had left Italy. Italy had been difficult, because Miss Alladyce knew most of the Italian letters. So, for the first few weeks, Nurse had had to explain that Tristram was very busy, and that what they were doing now was all most secret. Even so, a page or two could be filled; partly with expressions of gratitude, partly with undated and unplaced adventures from the earliest letters. Indeed, there was material from O.C.T.U. days, if carefully edited.

As before, Nurse came to the hedge in the mornings: every day still, for they were always afraid that something might threaten which would have to be guarded against. But nothing threatened. It was just as it had been when Tristram was alive.

'When Tristram was alive'—but Tristram was living again in these days. The realization of his death was subdued to this need for keeping him alive in Miss Alladyce's mind. In the lonely hours of wakefulness, as he lay in his narrow bed, memory did not torture him with pictures of Tristram on his last leave, Tristram in the car with him, Tristram playing golf with him, laughing, singing gaily to himself in his bath; it probed his mind for something to say in his next letter, something amusing from an earlier irrelevant letter which might be worked up.

'Now those people he met in Cape Town. There was a delightful description of the elder daughter. Oh no, that wouldn't do; no women. Oh well, I don't know. W. A. A.F.'s and A.T.'s and all. Might do. And that Major on the boat who always had the correct nautical term for everything—damned if I remember what the joke was, but he could meet him again in Palestine, and say, "Did I ever tell you about that Major on the boat?" I must remember to look that up to-morrow. It was his first letter after he had sailed. Easy to find. Yes, to-morrow. Sapper Major, wasn't he? … Look it up to-morrow … to-morrow.' And he drifted into sleep.

He had explained about the parcels to Tristram's Company Commander, and, since he knew what was inside them, it was easy to say, 'Tell Miss Alladyce—no, Aunt Christine, I'm adopting her—that the soap is absolutely wizard.' And then, as Tristram had written once in his non-commissioned days, 'People come from miles around just to sniff at me.' It was because he had 'never been much of a writer', as he put it to himself, that he took it all so seriously, gave to it so much of his mind; and so, almost unconsciously, made a protective tent for his broken heart.

So the weeks went on.

It was on July 6th, the eve of Tristram's birthday, that Nurse brought him the news.

'Quite peacefully, dear lamb. In her sleep.'

'Ah!' he said, looking at her blankly.

'A merciful release, Colonel Kaye, I think that's the way we must look at it.'

'Yes ... Indeed, yes ... Poor, dear lady ... Yes ... A merciful release.'

He turned away from her as if she were not there, and she watched him, a little surprised, as he made his hurried way across the lawn. Suddenly and overwhelmingly he had realized that he was alone in the world, and that there was no to-morrow.

A Table Near the Band

(1949)

I was giving Marcia lunch at the Turandot.

She is a delightful girl to give lunch to; very pretty, very decorative; drawing the eyes, admiring or envious, of all the other lunchers, but not (and this, I think, is her most charming characteristic)—not showing any consciousness of it; devoting herself with all her heart (if any), her soul (probably none) and her eyes (forget-me-not blue) to her companion. With it all, she is amusing, in the sense that after a couple of cocktails she makes you feel that either you or she or somebody is being extremely funny, smiles and easy laughter being the pleasant condiments of the meal. In short, a delightful person to take out to lunch.

It is one of the advantages of lunch that it rarely leads to an unpremeditated proposal of marriage. I have a suspicion, which has never been confirmed, that I did propose to Marcia once, after dinner. If so, she must have refused me, because I am still a bachelor. There is no doubt that up to that evening (a year ago now) I had regarded myself as in love with her, and had assumed that, as a consequence, the moment would arrive when I should suddenly hear myself asking her to marry me. I woke up next morning with the conviction that I had so heard myself. I spent the next six hours trying to imagine our married life together, from dawn to dawn and December to

December; and I concluded that the immediate and, indeed, obvious pleasures of such contiguity, enjoyable as they could not fail to be, would have much to contend against. A little nervously I rang her up at tea-time. I am not at my best in a telephone conversation with Marcia, because, even more than most men, I detest telephone conversations, and, even more than most women, she revels in them. She is never handicapped, as I am, by the fear, or even the knowledge, that other people are within hearing. On this occasion I was handicapped further by the uncertainty whether or not I was talking to my betrothed. I gathered fairly soon that I was not, and, a little later, that neither was I a rejected suitor. Our table had been near the band, and I suppose she hadn't heard.

Marcia lives in a highly polished flat in Sloane Street. The economics of this flat are something of a mystery; I mean to me, not, of course, to her. Indeed, the economics of Marcia's whole life are a little mysterious. She has, or has had, a father and a mother. Casual references to one or other of them keep me in touch with their continued existence, but I have never seen them, nor do I know where they live. However, I gather that the father is, or was, in some unnamed profession or business, which permits of his making a quarterly allowance to his daughter; while Marcia herself earns part of her living in some confidential relationship to a firm in Richmond. I know this, because on one or two occasions when she has had to cancel a date with me it has been some sudden need of this firm in Richmond which has so untimely compelled her. 'You seem to forget, David darling, that I am a working woman,' she has said reproachfully; and, looking at her, one has, of course, been inclined to forget it. In addition to this, one must remember that the flat is not actually her own, but has merely been lent to her by a friend, referred to sometimes as Elsa and sometimes as Jane. Doubtless this friend has two Christian names, like most of us. Elsa (or Jane) is either on her honeymoon or exhibiting new dress designs in South America; or, possibly, both. I understand that she is likely to be away for some time. One of my delightful discoveries about Marcia is that she has almost as many women friends as men friends; and they are all eager to lend things to her.

It will be seen, then, that with all these resources Marcia is well able to afford the Sloane Street flat. I am not sure now why I suggested that there was anything mysterious about it. For all I know she may be a rich woman in her own right, with money inherited from an ancestral brewery or a doting godfather. She has not mentioned yet that this is so, but it may well be. In any case it is no business of mine. All that matters to me is that she is a delightful person to give lunch to; and that this is what I was doing at the Turandot one day last week.

At the moment we weren't lunching, we were sitting in the lounge drinking cocktails. They were doubles, of course, because in these days one is apt to mislay a single at the bottom of the glass, and one can't afford to do that. We raised our glasses to each other, and murmured compliments. One of the things which I like about Marcia is that she doesn't expect all the compliments for herself. She is the only woman who has told me that I remind her of Robert Montgomery. She will say 'You look divine in that suit, darling, you ought always to wear brown'—or whatever it is. This is a very endearing habit of hers, and one which none of my female relations has fallen into as yet.

She took the mirror out of her bag; I suppose to see if she was looking as lovely as I had just said she did. She has beautiful hands, and, possibly for that reason, made a good deal of play with this bag, so that I felt impelled to say, 'Hallo, I haven't seen that before, have I?' This is a fairly safe line to take with anything of Marcia's, and often gets me credit for that habit of 'noticing' which all women expect from their men.

'This?' she said, holding the bag up at me. 'I shouldn't think so.'

Some comment was called for. Unfortunately bags do very little for me. I never know what to say to a new one; just as, I suppose, a woman wouldn't know what to say to a new cricket-bat. Obviously the thing has got to be the right shape and, in the case of a bag, the appropriate colour, but one can't praise a thing for its obvious qualities. 'It's charming' was the best I could do.

'David!' she said reproachfully. 'This old thing? Oh, but I oughtn't to say that. Let's talk of something else. Wait a moment.' She opened the bag again, seemed to be looking for something, and then, realizing that she wouldn't find it, snapped the catch and murmured, 'Of course! I was forgetting.'

I took the bag off her lap. I considered both sides of it, and put it back. I saw now that it wasn't new.

'Mother lent it to me,' she explained. This, as it were, gave her mother another six months of life. She was last heard of in the spring.

'But why?' I asked. I felt that she was using up her mother unnecessarily. A bag is as essential to a woman as braces to a man; one doesn't have to explain how one comes to be wearing them.

'Just motherly love, darling,' she smiled.

'Yes, but—'

'Oh, David, don't go on about it, or I shall cry. If I've got a handkerchief,' she added, opening the bag again.

'Marcia, what *is* all this?'

She looked at me pathetically, and her eyes glistened as though she were crying already.

'I didn't want to tell you, and spoil our lovely lunch together, but the most tragic thing has happened.' She emptied her glass, as if to give herself courage to look back on it, and said, 'I lost my bag yesterday. With everything in it. Oh, but *everything*!'

'Clothing coupons?' I asked in horror. It was the first thing I thought of.

'Of *course*! The whole ration book. How do you think I live?'

Well, I didn't know. But thinking it over, I did see that she might want a ration book for breakfast.

'Everything,' she went on quietly. 'Identity card, ration book, driving licence, car insurance, money, latchkey, flap-jack, of course, and lip-stick, everything.' And in a whisper she added, 'Including my cigarette-case.'

I knew that cigarette-case. It was in gold and platinum with an 'M' in little diamonds. Desmond had given it to her, just before he went out to Burma, where he was killed. She was to have married him as soon as the war was over. He wouldn't marry her before: he said it wouldn't be fair to her if he were missing.

While I was wondering what to say which didn't sound either callous or sentimental—(after all, he died three years ago)—she added in a smiling voice, 'I felt absolutely naked when I discovered what had happened.'

This took us off the emotional plane, and I asked the obvious question, 'When did you discover?'

'Getting out of the taxi last night. I'd been down to Letty's for the week-end. Morrison paid the man and let me in with his pass-key, and I rang up Victoria at once, of course, but it was one of those trains which goes backwards and forwards all day—darling, what a life!—and it was now on its little way to Brighton again. With my lovely bag in it. Of course, somebody has just taken it.'

'No news of it at Brighton?'

'No. I rang up again this morning.'

'But Marcia, darling—wait a moment, we want some more drinks for this.' I caught a waiter's eye and ordered two more doubles. Marcia gave me her loving, grateful smile—'What I was going to say was, however does a woman leave her bag in the train? It's part of her. I should have thought you'd have felt absolutely naked as soon as you got on to the platform.'

'That was the idiotic part. I'd been reading a magazine in the train, and I'd put my bag down, and then I put the magazine under my arm—oh, David, I know I'm a fool, but it's no good saying it.'

'I wasn't going to, darling. I'm terribly sorry, and I wish I could help.'

'I know. You're sweet.'

'How about all the things you've got to renew? Ration book and licences and all that? Can't I help there?'

'It's lovely of you, David, but it's all what they call "in train".' She laughed and added, 'Like the bag, unfortunately. I've been rushing about like a mad thing all morning.'

'Was there much money in it?'

She shrugged and said, 'About ten pounds, and quarter-day a long way off. I shall have to go carefully for a bit. But, of course, that's the least of it. It's—everything else.' I felt uncomfortably that she was thinking of Desmond again. She must have realized this—she is very quick, bless her—because she said at once, 'I mean the bag itself, it's so hateful to think of my lovely, lovely bag being worn by some horrible woman in Brighton, or wherever she is.'

'Do I remember it?'

'Well, darling, you ought to, seeing that it's the only one I've got. Only I haven't got it.'

I always thought that women had lots of bags, but I suppose it's like men with pipes. We have half a dozen, but the others are always the ones we can't smoke at the moment.

'I seem to remember a black one,' I said tentatively.

'Of course, darling. I always wear a black bag—when I have it. But never mind my silly troubles, tell me about yourself. You wrote that you were spending the week-end with your married sister. How was she?'

Marcia has a very sweet way of taking an interest in people she has never met. I told her that Sylvia was well. We then went in to lunch. It was, for these days, a very good lunch, and we chattered and laughed and said no more of the bag.

Marcia didn't want me after lunch. I took her to where her car was parked, and she went off to Richmond or somewhere; on business for the firm, I suppose, as otherwise she wouldn't have had the petrol. I wasn't sorry to be alone, because I had something I wanted to do.

I had thought of it almost at once, and now I thought of it again; and the more I thought of it, the more I felt that it was up to me to replace that bag. No doubt it was the cigarette-case for which Marcia was really grieving, but Desmond had given it to her, and I couldn't do anything about that. Nor could I have afforded to do anything about it: the economics of my life don't include platinum and gold cigarette-cases. But I thought that they did include a bag on an occasion like this for a very attractive and much-to-be-pitied young woman. After a few enquiries I wasn't so sure. However, I was committed to it now, at whatever cost, and in the end I felt fairly satisfied with the result. Bags, as I think I have said, all look much the same to me; but this one was certainly black and certainly expensive, and presumably, there-fore, just what Marcia wanted. The girl in the shop was sure it was. She said Moddom would rave about it.

And, in fact, Moddom did.

I spent the week-end at Waylands. I am thirty-six, and what is called a commercial artist. No doubt you have seen me among the adver-tisements: represented as often as not by an athletic young man and a superb young woman in very little on the beach. This can call your attention to anything, from your favourite laxative to your favourite cigarette or soft drink; from National Savings (the holiday you can look forward to, if you save now) to pocket cameras (the holiday you can look back upon afterwards). Altogether I don't do too badly; and the only reason why I am mentioning this is because a bachelor of thirty-six, who is understood not to be doing too badly, gets invited to houses a little out of his social and financial class. It was in this way, and again at this week-end, that I met Maddox.

Maddox, I suppose, is about fifty, and something pretty big in the City. He has known Marcia longer than I have, and he talks to me about her whenever we happen to meet; as if I were waiting anxiously for him to talk to me, and this was the only subject of conversation which could possibly interest us both; as, indeed, it is. Then, having put me at my ease, he leaves me as soon as possible for somebody richer or more noble. He has this natural flair for putting people at their ease. If he had met Shakespeare in his prime (Shakespeare's prime) he would have asked him if he were doing any writing just now—thus showing that he was in touch with the literary fashion of the moment—and drifted away without waiting for the answer.

He is not in the least jealous of my friendship with Marcia. The fact that I am a bachelor assures him in some way that there can be no rivalry between us. He himself is married; and the only thing which has prevented him from marrying Marcia (so Marcia tells me) is this wife of his. Either she is a Catholic and won't divorce him, or she is in a Home for Incurables and he can't divorce her. I forget which, but I know that it is all very hard on him—and, of course, on his wife, if she is in a Home for Incurables.

On this occasion we saw more of each other than usual, because we travelled down together. I stepped into his carriage when it was too late to step out again, and he went through the usual drill of seeming surprised to find me in such good company.

'Hallo, young fellow! You?'

I admitted it.

He nodded, as if to confirm my admission, and gave himself a moment in which to place me. Then he asked if I had seen the little girl lately.

'Marcia?' I asked coldly.

'Who else?'

I said that I had seen her fairly lately.

'You didn't hear what the little idiot had done? No, you couldn't have.'

'What's that?'

'Left her bag in the train, with £20 in it.'

'Good lord!'

'*And*, of course, everything else. What's really worrying the poor girl is the cigarette-case.'

'Cigarette-case?'

'A beauty. Platinum and gold. But the tragic thing is that it's the one Hugh gave her.'

I wanted to say 'Who's Hugh?' because I had never heard of him, but it didn't sound right somehow. It was no matter, because he went on: 'The feller she was engaged to. You wouldn't have met him, you've only known her for the last year.'

'Two years,' I corrected.

'Poor kid, it was a tragedy for her. Hugh was in the Air Force, and they were going to get married as soon as he got a ground job. And then, just at the end of his last tour, on his very last operation, he was shot down over the North Sea. That cigarette-case was all she had had of him. He'd meant to make a will, he had quite a bit to leave, but like a damned young fool he put it off. Tough luck on Marcia.'

'Very tough,' I said. 'I know the cigarette-case, of course, but she's never told me about Hugh. I suppose she wouldn't like to talk about him.'

'That's right. Naturally she told *me*, because—well, that's different.'

'Naturally. No hope of getting the bag back?'

'Well, hardly—with all that in it. Of course, one would gladly give her a cigarette-case to take the place of Hugh's, but'—he gave a little shrug of his shoulders—'one can't, can one?'

I saw that he wanted to be admired for the delicacy of his feelings, so I shook my head and said, 'Too expensive nowadays, with the purchase tax.'

He almost decided to leave me then. He said coldly, 'It's hardly a question of money. I shall certainly give her a cigarette-case at Christmas, but that's different.'

'I see what you mean,' I said quickly. 'You're quite right, of course. Absolutely.'

That soothed him, and he felt that he could take me into his confidence again. For a man who admires himself so much he is curiously eager to be admired by others.

'All the same one had to do something at once. I mean, the poor girl was in tears, and I don't wonder. So I've given her a new bag. Apparently she only had the one, poor kid. She'd actually had to borrow one from her mother! And then losing £20 like that, and quarter-day a long way off, I felt it was the least I could do.'

'It was extremely generous of you,' I said warmly. 'And just what she'd want. I suppose you know all about these things. I mean you would know the sort and the colour and all that. I'm afraid I'm no good at bags.'

'That's right. Well, I had to ask about the colour, of course. She'd naturally want it to be the same colour.' He gave a little chuckle of self-appreciation. 'But I did it very tactfully, so that she couldn't guess anything.'

'I am sure she wouldn't guess. It will be a tremendous surprise. What colour was it? I should have said black, but I'm afraid I never notice bags very much.'

He shook his head with a condescending smile.

'No, no, not black. I knew it wasn't black. Green. As soon as she told me, I remembered. She always carries a green bag.'

A day or two later (which is how these things happen) I was sitting in the smoking-room of my club when young Hargreaves came in. With a shy smile and an apology he leant over me to ring the bell.

'I've just rung it,' I said. 'Have one with me instead.'

He said, 'Oh, I say!' and then, 'I say, that's very decent of you, I'll have a sherry, but look here these are mine,' and as the waitress came in, 'What'll you have?'

I waved him down, and said firmly to the girl, 'Two large sherries, and put them on my luncheon bill.' As she went, I said to Hargreaves, 'I spoke first, you can't get away from that.'

'Oh well, thanks a lot.'

Hargreaves is very young; at least he seems so to me. He has only just joined the club, and as I am ten years older and have been a member twelve years longer, I feel a world-weary veteran when I talk to him. Like so many young men these days he passed straight into the Army from school. On demobilization he went up to Cambridge, cramming what should have been three leisurely years of graduation in life into a hectic twelvemonth struggle for a book-learning degree. Then he was free to earn a living. Luckier than most, he had a family business to go into, with money to come (I get my gossip from the secretary); so we need not feel too sorry for him. But like all these young people he is a curious mixture of experience and innocence. He has seen half the world, met people of all countries in every class of life, had adventures of which, at his age, we knew nothing. Yet in many of his contacts with civilian life he still has the *naïveté* of a schoolboy.

We sipped our sherries and talked about the weather. The conversation came to its natural end. He pulled out his cigarette-case and offered me one. I called his attention to the pipe I was smoking. He said, 'Oh, sorry,' and lit one for himself. With this to give him confidence, he began:

'I say, I wish you'd tell me something.'

'If I can.'

'I don't know London very well, I mean I don't know the best places to go to, and all that. What would be the best place to get a bag?'

'What sort of bag? Dressing case?'

'No, no, *you* know, the sort women carry about.'

'Oh, that sort? What Americans call a purse.'

'Extraordinary thing to call it,' he said, opening his blue eyes wide. 'Still,' he added generously, 'if they call braces suspenders, I suppose it isn't so extraordinary. Well, anyway, that sort.'

I gave him the name of the shop at which I had got Marcia's bag, and mentioned one or two other possible places.

'That's grand,' he said, and made a note of them. 'Thanks very much.'

'They're expensive, you know, at that sort of shop. I'm assuming that you want a really good one.'

'Oh, I do.' He hesitated and said, 'Er—about how much?'

'Ten to fifteen pounds.'

'Oh!' He was more than surprised, he was taken aback. His round pink face became even pinker.

'Of course,' I said quickly, 'you can get them much cheaper at some of the big places—well, obviously it depends on the bag.'

'No, it must be a good one, but—' He gave an awkward little laugh. 'I mean fifteen pounds is all right by me, but would the girl—I mean, I've only just met her, and it isn't her birthday or anything, so would she feel—I mean it's quite a present, not like flowers or chocolates or taking her out to lunch. What do you think?'

'I should think she would be delighted,' I said with some confidence. 'I shouldn't worry about that.'

'Oh, good. Then that's all right. And anyway it *is* rather special. I mean there's a special reason for it.'

It was clear that he wanted me to ask what it was, so I asked him. Besides, I was getting interested suddenly.

'Well, you see, she left her bag in the train, with everything in it, and there's no news of it, and it's been a frightful shock for her. Apart from everything else, she'd just cashed a cheque for fifty pounds—'

'I shouldn't do anything about that,' I put in quickly.

'Well, I could hardly offer her money,' he said with a delightful man-of-the-world air. 'Actually there was something even worse—a gold and platinum cigarette-case with her initials in diamonds—God knows what that cost, but of course it's the sentimental value which made it so precious to her.'

'Of course,' I said. I wasn't surprised.

'You see, she was engaged to a man who was killed just after D-Day. He was in the Commandos, and he was dropped behind the lines with the Maquis, *you* know—'

'I know,' I said. 'So was I.'

'I say, were you really? I was in the Burma show.'

'So I heard. Sooner you than me.'

'Oh, it wasn't so bad. I should say your job was a much stickier one.'

'I'd lived in Paris for a good many years. I talked French. That was all there was to it. What was this man's name? I may have come across him.' But I didn't think it was very likely.

'She just called him John. I didn't like to ask his other name.'

'Quite right,' I said firmly.

'This was his engagement present to her. They were to be married on his first leave, and then—Pretty bloody.

'And now she has lost all she had left of him.' He was silent for a little, contemplating life, and then threw his cigarette end into the fire, and said, 'Well, of course I couldn't do anything about that, but I thought I could at least replace the bag.'

'A very nice thought, if I may say so; and one which I'm sure she will appreciate. What colour did you think of getting? They'll help you in the shop with all the rest of it, but you must be able to tell them the colour. Most women have their own special colour.' Or, of course, colours.

'I know. So, to be quite safe, I'm getting one exactly like the one she lost. Luckily she happened to describe it, it just came out accidentally, but I was on to it like a shot. I mean in my own mind, of course. It was yellow.'

'And a very pretty colour too,' I said.

This should have been the end of it, for other people dropped in, and the conversation became general. But he came up to me again, hat in hand, as I sat alone in the lounge after lunch drinking my coffee.

'Thanks very much for that address,' he said; and I thought it was nice of him to seek me out as he was leaving the club, to thank me for so little. But apparently he had something else to ask. Very casually, as if he knew the answer and wanted to see if I did, he said:

'I say, I suppose there's nothing much to choose nowadays between the Berkeley and the Ritz? I mean for dinner.'

'Nothing,' I said. 'You'll be perfectly safe at either.'

'That's what I thought.' He turned to go.

And then I wondered, a little anxiously, if he would be perfectly safe. He is a thoroughly nice boy, and he is going to meet a thoroughly nice girl one day.

'Just a word of advice, if I may,' I called after him.

'Of course!' He came back to me eagerly.

'Get a table near the band if you can.'

He looked surprised, as well as he might be.

'Why?' he asked, very naturally.

'It's safer,' I said.

All the same, I still think that she is a delightful girl to take out to lunch.

The Three Dreams of Mr Findlater

(1949)

I

Mr Ernest Findlater, bank manager, forty-eight, married, had two day-dreams of which he was very fond.

The first was of himself and a beautiful local girl lying side by side on the white sands of a Pacific island. He is wearing a hat of palm-leaves which she has woven for him, she a coral necklace which he has strung for her. Otherwise they are in all their naked beauty, Mr Findlater's heightened by a lightly sketched-in six months of tree-climbing, hut-building and so forth before the dream begins. Soon they will plunge into the lagoon ('without hat', he remembers just in time) and swim lazily side by side through the blue translucent waters. Mr Findlater is now a good swimmer. At first he had thought of saving her from a shark somewhere about here, but he soon saw the folly of this. Not only would sharks be a nuisance in the lagoon, but, since she had given herself to him already, there was really no need for one. Back, still lazily, to the beach, and a deep draught of—kvass? kava?—he must look that up, one wants to get the details right—and luscious guavas, tamarinds and pomegranates. And then—love. Or would it be better the other way round: love first and refreshment afterwards? Well, that would be for Lalage to say. He thought of her as Lalage; Hula-hula, his first choice, presenting itself to him later as either a bird or a dance.

The second dream was that he came home from the Exminster Conservative Club one afternoon to find a car outside the gate. As he opens the front door, Bridget comes rushing from the kitchen, tears streaming down her cheeks. 'Oh, sir!' she wails. 'The mistress! The poor mistress!' Firm steps are heard overhead, and Dr Manley's legs are seen coming down the staircase. Arrived in the little hall, Dr Manley puts a kindly hand on Mr Findlater's shoulder. 'You must be brave, Findlater,' he says. 'Death, the Great Reaper. He cometh to one and all. A sudden stroke. I could do nothing.'

It might be thought that one of these dreams was a natural sequel to the other, but this was not so. The two dreams were distinct in Mr Findlater's mind. In the first one Minnie had neither present nor past. Obviously she would have been out of place in person on his island, but he refused to have even the memory of her with him. Just as the dream presupposed six months of rejuvenation to fit his body to lie beside Lalage's, so it may be said to have derived from that glorious day twenty years ago when he decided *not* to ask Minnie to marry him; or, asking, was rejected. He and Lalage were alone in the world; they always had been, they always would be.

Nor must it be thought that Mr Findlater was just a man who hungered for amatory adventures in his real life, and, denied them by a jealous wife, pursued them in dreams. Lalage was no mistress. She stood for all which he had wanted from Minnie, and had never had; sympathy, companionship, appreciation, peace of mind and body, love, happiness, rest. Since Lalage had to be everything which Minnie wasn't, her body must be beautiful, and she must not be ashamed of it; nor scornful of his. So they lay side by side, happy in each other on their island beach, talking as old friends talk. Lalage's English was the prettiest thing imaginable (her father, Mr Findlater sometimes thought, had been a shipwrecked Irishman), and just to lie there and listen to her was to listen to celestial music. There were times in his waking life when Lalage's voice seemed to Mr Findlater her most precious gift of all.

The second dream was also complete and self-contained. Its realization, if such were to happen, would not lead Mr Findlater straight to the South Seas, in the hope of meeting an actual Lalage. Its realization would be happiness enough in itself. To be able to have breakfast in bed on Sunday just because he wanted to have breakfast in bed on Sunday; to do his crossword or his Patience of an evening without having it referred to as his 'everlasting Patience again' or his everlasting crossword; to read what he wanted to read without comment on his childish taste for stories of adventure; to sit and dream without a harsh accompaniment of contemporary scandal; to talk to a charming woman at a party without hearing her disparaged all the way home, without being reminded of his own approaching baldness, greyness, deafness and stiffness in the joints, such as would prevent any charming woman from being interested in him except from pity: Mr Findlater could have gone on for ever like this, recounting the benefits which would follow Dr Manley's delightful announcement that he could do nothing. No need to go to a desert island to look for them. To be free, to be his own master again, was enough.

Now most people would have said that the realization of Mr Findlater's first dream would have needed a miracle, and that his second dream merely assumed a natural, however unlikely, happening. To him it was otherwise. He could believe more easily in the first dream than in the second. Perhaps this was because the first was fantasy, which creates a living world for itself, while the other was so close to reality that only its realization could bring it into being. All the facts of life, all his experience of the world, told him that the second dream must remain a dream. Whoever else died, Minnie was imperishable …

And then a third dream began to form itself in Mr Findlater's mind. It was conceived, though he did not know it at the time, in the lavatory of the Exminster Conservative Club; and it was born on that hot, silent afternoon when he came down the hill into the sunken lane, and saw the empty Buick.

II

Mr Findlater was accustomed to lunch at the Club. He was the highly respected manager of the Exminster branch of his Bank; an undistinguished figure of middle height, his lean face clean-shaven and melancholy. He wore, and from his first entry into the Bank had always worn, horn-rimmed spectacles, to enhance his dignity rather than his vision, and he dressed in a short black coat, grey flannel trousers and a bowler hat, thus putting both town and country clients at their ease. He meditated the writing of a history of Exminster, but in spite of the encouragement of his friends and the discouragement of Minnie he had not yet begun it. He found it easier to meditate.

On this particular day Mr Findlater had been called to the lavatory suddenly after lunch, and, as is customary, had bolted the door on himself. Some defect in the bolt made it difficult to release himself later; indeed, for a little while it seemed that he must subdue his dignity to the needs of the Bank, and shout for help. Wondering if it were possible to escape by the window, he opened the lower half of it and looked out. He discovered to his surprise that there was a drop of nearly thirty feet to the ground; and that the angle of the wall in which the window was set cut him off, not only from the basement windows of the Club, but from all outside observation. If he had happened to have with him a rope thirty feet long, he could have escaped to the Bank without anyone being the wiser. As it was, he renewed his attack on the bolt, deciding this time to take it by surprise. A quick but nonchalant pull, and—'There you are!' said Mr Findlater triumphantly. As he hurried out of the Club, he noticed that Rogers, the hall porter, looked up, identified him and crossed his name off the list of members still within. 'Probably the last,' thought Mr Findlater. 'There'll be nobody now till tea-time. What does Rogers do with himself for the next hour or so?'

A few weeks later Mr Findlater found himself again in an unpleasant position. He had gone out by train to discuss some matter of business with an important but temporarily immobile client; had been met in the Rolls, entertained frugally to lunch, and, business done, had been offered the car, a little reluctantly, for the return journey to the station. But it was a fine, summer day, this was a new part of the county to him, and he had protested his eagerness to walk to the station. His host, disregarding the implications of Mr Findlater's bowler hat, gave him a cross-country direction which soon deserted him; within half an hour Mr Findlater knew himself to be completely lost in what seemed to be as deserted a spot as Lalage's island. Trudging on in what he vaguely hoped was the right direction, he came suddenly out of the wild upon a sunken lane. He pushed his way through the hedge and down the bank; and saw, to his great relief, a saloon car twenty yards to his right. It was just in time, for he was beginning to panic. He walked up to it eagerly to ask for further directions, hoping, indeed, that he might even be offered a lift. For he was now tired of this part of the county.

The car was empty. The windows were open, and it was plain that it was not locked; which suggested that the occupants were strolling somewhere not far off. Mr Findlater, therefore, hovered around, listening for sounds or voices. None came. It was one of those still, hot days when the whole countryside seems, in the shimmering light, to be a little unreal. There might be nobody else in the world; the car might be a magic car, it might move off suddenly of its own will, leaving him to wonder if it had ever been there. For the moment, however, it existed. The thought came to him that there should be a map in the flap-pocket of the driver's seat which would give him some idea of his position. A little nervously, after a last look round in the stillness to make sure that he was alone, he opened the door and put his hand in the pocket. There was no map. Instead, he found himself fingering what his detective stories called a gun ...

He took it out and looked at it. Like all small bowler-hatted men with a literary taste for adventure, Mr Findlater had always wanted to own a gun. But now there was a new, compelling reason why he should have one. For the moment he couldn't quite remember what it was; he just knew that he had to have one, and that this was his first, and probably his last, chance to get one. Even if the owner of the car came back, as presumably he would, it was unlikely that he would discover his loss until some time later. In any case it was probable that he had no licence for it, and would be unable to report matters to the police. This would be the first time that Mr Findlater had ever stolen anything, but somehow he didn't think of it as stealing. It was obedience to an Inner Voice which said 'Don't argue. Take it and Go,' and he took it and went. His sense of direction told him that the car was pointing the way he should have gone, but, fearing to be overtaken, he went the other way for safety. Not surprisingly, it led him to the station.

III

And now Mr Findlater's third dream began; neither fantasy nor mock-reality, but a dream which, at the right moment, would incorporate itself in the real world. He did not tell himself at first that he was going to murder his wife; he just thought that it would be a nice thing to do, and that he might have to do it if nobody would do it for him. Meanwhile it was pleasant to think about it. How, he asked himself, *would* one do it?

Means, motive, opportunity: every murderer had followed those three sign-posts to death—the death of his victim, and, more often than not, the death of himself. One could commit a murder safely, then, if one could conceal those sign-posts. Ah, but that was just what he could do! Consider them for a moment.

The Undiscovered Means: The gun. He had a gun locked up in his safe, which was completely untraceable to him.

The Undiscovered Opportunity: The lavatory window. He hadn't thought it out yet, but he knew, he had always known, that somehow through that window an alibi could be found; so that Rogers would swear that he was in the Club when he was not in the Club.

The Undiscovered Motive: This was easy. All the detective stories made it clear that the police recognized only two motives for the murder of a wife: Money and Another Woman. There had never been any other woman but Lalage; no husband's life could have been more blameless. As for money, there was little enough in any case, and that little could easily be renounced. There was plenty of time.

Time, Mr Findlater saw, was what every murderer lacked, for he never thought of murder save as the last immediate resort. Buy the false beard on Monday and the strychnine on Tuesday; wear the one and dispense the other on Wednesday, and what hope had you of avoiding suspicion? But wait a year after making your purchases before putting them to use, and who is going to trace them to you? Given time, one could do anything. Let us take it easily, allowing ourselves a year from now; a year of preparation, a year in this delightful new dream.

He began that evening.

'You'll excuse my asking, Minnie,' he said, Patience cards spread out in front of him, 'it's entirely your own business, of course, but have you ever made a will?'

'What on earth put that into your head suddenly?'

'Oh, just that I was witnessing a will this afternoon for a lady—we are often asked to at the Bank, you know—and I wondered. So few ladies ever think it necessary.'

'Well, I suppose she had money to leave. I haven't.'

'There are your personal possessions. And I seem to remember your buying some Savings Certificates during the War.'

Minnie made a noise of reluctant agreement; and then added, 'What's the good of a married woman making a will? It all goes to her husband anyhow.'

'Only if she doesn't make a will. You can leave your personal possessions and your money to anybody you like. We have will-forms at the Bank. Morgan would explain it to you.'

'You seem to have arranged it all for me very kindly. Have you any suggestion as to who I leave all my diamond tiaras and mink coats to?'

Mr Findlater smiled to himself at his cleverness, put the black seven on the red eight, and said, 'Me.'

'I shall do nothing of the sort! What would *you* want with my things I should be glad to know?'

'Oh, I could always sell them. That brooch your Uncle Herbert gave you—one could get quite a nice little sum for that.'

'Well, of all—'

'The question hardly arises, however, because you are leaving it to your sister Carrie's eldest girl. Or so I have always understood.'

'You have understood correctly.'

'Then doubtless you will say so in your will. Otherwise the brooch will come to me, and I might give it to—ah! the ace at last. Now we can get on.' He got on in silence for a little, and then said casually, 'I had a letter from Robert this morning. Grace goes to school in September. Did I tell you?'

So Minnie made a will a few days later, leaving everything to her sister, except the brooch which went to Mona. If she had had a rattle-snake, she would have left it to Grace. Grace was Mr Findlater's niece.

Motive, like Means, being thus untraceable, there only remained Opportunity. To the leisurely preparation of an alibi Mr Findlater now gave his attention. But still, of course, in an academic spirit.

IV

At first Mr Findlater thought of writing down the Pros and Cons of his alibi after the manner of Robinson Crusoe, and then he saw that he must put as little as possible down in writing. What he wanted was an imaginary confederate, an *advocatus diaboli* almost, who would pounce upon the weak points, and so help him to strengthen them. He decided at once that the ideal person for this was Lalage. It was much pleasanter to lie on the beach with Lalage, and talk it over in a lazy, light-hearted way as it came into his head, than put the case seriously before some hard-faced ex-Superintendent of Police. One of the nice things about Lalage was that you didn't have to call the lavatory window the bathroom window, as you would have to do if (supposing such a thing possible) you discussed the matter with Minnie.

MR FINDLATER: Well, that's the rough idea, darling. Now let me have your comments. I mean on the general plan—we'll discuss how to get out of the lavatory window afterwards.

LALAGE: It is the girl's afternoon out, you say?

MR FINDLATER: That's right. It must be, of course. Wednesday.

LALAGE: Then it would be a good idea if you were always in the Club on Wednesday afternoon, not just on the one day.

MR FINDLATER: That's good, darling, that's very good. I'll make a note of that. *(Note* 1). I must think up some reason. Next?

LALAGE: There must be a back way out of the Club through the kitchens. You want to be sure that nobody could go out that way without being seen.

MR FINDLATER: I never thought of that. Oh, dear!

LALAGE: When is the time you leave?

MR FINDLATER: Three-thirty. Back by three-fifty, I should say. Of course we shall have a rehearsal and time it exactly.

LALAGE: There would be people in the kitchens at three-thirty, surely?

MR FINDLATER: Yes, but I must make certain. *(Note* 2). And also that Rogers doesn't leave his post. *(Note* 3). This is splendid. Anything else?

LALAGE (*lazily*): Not at the moment, darling. Except that I love you.

There was a short interval here, while Mr Findlater forgot his third dream, and went back to his first.

MR FINDLATER (*coming back to business*): Now then, let's see how we stand. I am known to be always at the Club on Wednesday afternoons. On this particular one Rogers sees me come in for lunch—

LALAGE (*sleepily*): Late for lunch.

MR FINDLATER: What's that?

LALAGE: Always be late for lunch on Wednesdays so that you don't come past Rogers with all the others, and people say how can you notice them all, Rogers, when so many come in together.

MR FINDLATER: Good. *(Note* 4). Well, Rogers sees me come in, and doesn't see me go out. Oh, but then again, I might have slipped out with the others—that's awkward.

LALAGE: Get Rogers to ring up on the telephone for you at three. Not every Wednesday, but just now and then, so that it doesn't look as if you were doing it on purpose on this one day.

MR FINDLATER: Darling you're wonderful. *(Note* 5). Very well, then. I'm in the Club at three, and Rogers swears that I haven't left by the front, and the people in the kitchen—did I make a note of that? Yes, I did—swear that I didn't leave by the back, and there's no other way out. And it's all quite natural, because I'm there every Wednesday afternoon after the lunchers have gone. Excellent. And now, darling, what about a swim to the reef and back?

So it was that Mr Findlater began at last his *Short History of Exminster.* The Bank closed early on Wednesdays. He had been accustomed to come home for tea, helping Minnie to prepare it in the absence of Bridget; and anything which he had been accustomed to do with Minnie's approval was not easily to be renounced. However, he brought it off. He pleaded the reference library at the Club as his reason for working there; he suggested humbly that Mrs Bryce, who came into Exminster every Wednesday and dropped in to tea, would much prefer to find Minnie alone. This, of course, was obvious. Indeed, it had often been suggested to him, as soon as he had swallowed his first cup, that if he wanted to get on with mowing the lawn, Mrs Bryce (Minnie was sure) would excuse him. Mrs Bryce had a routine for Wednesday which included a hair-set in the morning, followed by lunch with her sister-in-law and a visit to her dead husband's grave. This brought her to Balmoral at precisely 3.45, and put her on the 5.20 omnibus home again. Mr Findlater was getting rather tired of Mrs Bryce, and it was pleasant to think that it was she who would discover the body.

MR FINDLATER: Well, that's all settled. I've attended to all your points, darling, and everything is satisfactory.

LALAGE: You are taking a bag with you every Wednesday to the Club?

MR FINDLATER: I wasn't. Why? So far I have only been making notes for the book.

LALAGE: Darling! What would you do without me! *There was another short interlude here.*

MR FINDLATER: You were saying something about a bag?

LALAGE: But think on the day of what you will want to carry there. So many things.

MR FINDLATER: Yes, let's think. It's difficult to think of everything at once. Of course, I shall want the rope and—this is a good idea, Lalage—some towels to prevent the rope marking the cistern-pipe and the windowsill. What else?

LALAGE: Your disguise, of course, darling!

Disguise! Just as Mr Findlater had always wanted to have a gun, so he had always wanted to disguise himself. Of course he must disguise himself! But he would do it cleverly, careful not to overdo it. What was the minimum? As regards clothes, a sports coat and a soft hat, to take the place of the black coat and bowler, with perhaps rather a highly coloured tie; no more. Face? A false moustache, no spectacles, and pads in the cheeks; this would also disguise the voice if anyone spoke to him. Walk? False heels, which would also add to his height. It was, he remembered from his detective stories, the presence of horn-rimmed spectacles on the mysterious stranger which always suggested disguise to the police. But Mr Findlater would be disguised by the absence of them, which would suggest nothing. His disguise, he told himself, would be simple but impenetrable.

He had to go to London from time to time on business. He bought a large, yellow cavalry moustache (for *Patience*, he explained, humming the Colonel's song), clipped it short and dyed it. At another costumier's he bought heel and cheek pads (*Ruddigore*). He bought a ready-made sports coat and a soft easily folded hat. When he talked it over with Lalage, they agreed that everything was going splendidly. Until suddenly one night—

LALAGE: Darling!

MR FINDLATER: Yes?

LALAGE: Can you climb a rope?

MR FINDLATER: I imagine that anyone moderately active can go down a rope.

LALAGE: But you have to go up it again.

MR FINDLATER: Oh!

Fortunately, as he had always told himself, there was no hurry. He had bought the rope—'a swing for my little boy, but strong enough to bear his mother too if necessary. Oh, about my weight, I suppose, the two of them together'—and now he had to learn to climb it. He began by training his muscles in the garden: an eagerness to do all the heavy work which surprised Minnie, and left her uncertain whether to approve or disapprove. There was always plenty of heavy work to be done which she was glad to point out to him, but she hated to think of him keeping fit and strong when she was getting flabby. It was part of her creed for him that he was too old now for any other woman to take an interest in him. However, he went on: morning exercises in the bathroom, digging or cutting down trees in the garden and the little plantation beyond, more exercises at night. Then at a wet week-end, when Minnie had gone to her sister's for a few days, he took off his coat and waistcoat, wrapped himself in his rope, covered it with a macintosh, and went off to Lakeham Woods. He found a suitable tree, climbed it, fastened his rope—(at Lalage's suggestion he had made a study of knots)—and experimented. It was difficult at first; but when he came away he had been down and up, untied and pulled in his rope in two minutes twenty seconds. But it had taken him six months to get there …

And still the planning, the daily and nightly talks with Lalage, went on. This was to be the perfect crime.

V

The perfect crime, like the perfectly produced play, needs a dress rehearsal. On a Wednesday afternoon in June, a week before The Day, a strange man might have been seen in Potters Lane. He was on the tallish side, and walked with a curious forward-thrusting gait, rather like a pre-war débutante. He came to the gate of Balmoral, hesitated a moment, fingered his moustache nervously, and then, with a sudden squaring of the shoulders, walked in. 'Oh, well,' he murmured to himself, but without much conviction, 'I can always say it was a joke.' He rang the bell. 'Coming!' called Minnie, and, a minute later, opened the door.

'You're early, dear, aren't you?' she was saying, and then, 'Oh, I beg your pardon!'

Mr Findlater began to smile apologetically, and then thought that he had better not. He began to take off his hat, and thought that he had better not do that either.

'Er—does Mr Sanders live here?' he asked in a muffled voice.

'Who?'

'Mr Sanders.'

'This is Mr Findlater's house.'

'Oh, I beg your pardon. I must have been misdirected.' He put his hand to his hat again, and turned away.

'There's no—Sanders, did you say?—in Potters Lane. You must have taken the wrong turning.'

'Oh, thank you.'

He went out of the gate and back the way he had come with his curious shuffling walk. As he came out of Potters Lane, he met Mrs Bryce coming in. They passed, ignoring each other. It was pleasant to cut Mrs Bryce. Five minutes later he was back in the lavatory.

In another five minutes Mr Findlater might have been seen in the Club library, hard at work on *A Short History of Exminster*.

So that was that. It had been done, it could be done. The only variation necessary was the shooting, and the departure through the plantation at the back, this being not only a quicker but a safer way of return in case anybody heard the shot. Perhaps it would be better to make his approach also from the back, and avoid using his latch-key.

But however successful a dress rehearsal may be, an actor still dreads the first night. Indeed, it is a superstition of the stage that the more smoothly a play goes at the dress rehearsal, the worse the actual performance will be. In the week which followed Mr Findlater had many a talk with Lalage, and always on the same monotonous lines. Indeed, had she not been the angel she was, she must have got very tired of it.

'You see, darling, up to the very last moment I can pretend—I mean I haven't *done* anything yet. It's only just preparation … Well, of course, darling, I'm going to, but what I mean is it needn't be next Wednesday. It could be the Wednesday after. No, no, of course, it *will* be next Wednesday, I'm only just saying …'

And then, pleadingly:

'It's just a story we've made up, isn't it, Lalage? You and I. Just one of our stories. Say it is, darling. I mean, one doesn't *seriously* murder one's *wife*!'

And then:

'Yes, of course I'm going to. She's detestable. She's ruined my life. My God, I've had twenty years of it, twenty years of hell. Yes, it *is* hell. I daresay it doesn't sound much, just little things day after day, week after week, year after year. But all added together—I doubt if any other man could have stood it as long as I have. Nobody knows what I've been through. Even if I were caught and hanged, it would be worth it. But I shan't be, shall I? We've been too clever for them.'

And so on.

On the Tuesday he came back from the Bank at his usual time. He had made up his mind. He would give Minnie one more chance. If she were the same to-night as she had always been, then to-morrow— But if she—His mind thus made up, he put his key to the door and went in.

Bridget came rushing from the kitchen, tears drying on her cheeks.

'Oh, sir,' she wailed, 'the mistress!'

Firm steps were heard overhead, and a pair of legs was seen coming down the staircase. Arrived in the little hall, Dr Manley put a kindly hand on Mr Findlater's shoulder.

'You must be brave, Findlater,' he said; 'you must brace yourself for a great shock. Your dear wife—a sudden stroke. It was all over before I could get here. My poor, dear fellow.'

The Prettiest Girl in
the Room

(1949)

The door of her bedroom opened a little way, the tap of knuckles on it
a polite afterthought rather than a request for admission.

'Nearly ready, old girl?'

'Just on, dear.'

'I'll go and get the car.'

'Right.'

The door closed. She had another five minutes. The walk to the
garage, trying the self-starter, feeling in the dark for the starting-
handle, getting out of the car, winding, getting back into the car,
starting, backing, coming to the house, turning, stalling, starting
again, warming up the engine for the hill, and then a loud whistle like
a siren; she knew it all. Going up the hill he would say, 'I hope to God
the Traills aren't there,' and she would say, 'Oh, they won't seem so
bad after you've had a drink or two,' and he would grunt and be silent
until they were turning into the Hewitsons' lane, and then he would
say, 'Well, we needn't stay long. Three-quarters of an hour should
about see it. Leave at seven-fifteen. All right by you, old girl?' And she
would say, 'Of course, darling.' And at eight o'clock she would say,
'Charles! You really *must* come away.' All just as usual.

Sometimes she wished that he didn't call her 'old girl'. She tried to remember if he had always called her so, or only since she had become—well, older. After all, a grandmother, but only just a grandmother, couldn't complain. She wasn't complaining. She had nothing to complain about. She had two delightful grown-up sons, both with jobs, and a married daughter with the sweetest baby. And Charles—everybody liked Charles. It was just that the winter seemed so long in the country, and life so short; and now that Charles had retired, they always seemed to be saying and doing the same things together, and had nothing new to tell each other. Inevitable, of course; but every now and then one got the feeling that life oughtn't to be so inevitable. Not even when you were a grandmother.

He whistled; she whistled back on her fingers, as he had taught her more than thirty years ago. The war-cry of the Allisons, he had called it. Well, you couldn't say that a marriage was a failure when two people had gone on whistling to each other in the same way for thirty years. Could you? She took a last look at herself in the glass—oh, well!—and went down.

'I hope to God the Traills aren't coming,' said Charles, as they went up the hill. 'Can't stand 'em.'

'Never mind, darling, perhaps Betty will be there.'

Charles cocked an eye at her, and they both laughed. Betty was Mrs Hewitson, and it was supposed that Charles was in love with her. Well, you couldn't still be having jokes like that with your husband if your marriage was a failure. Could you?

'Mustn't stay too long.'

'No, darling. Seven-fifteen.'

Considering that it wasn't a party, but just a ring-up and a 'Why don't you come in on Sunday and have a drink?' there seemed to be quite a collection of people. Charles kissed Betty, and winked at his wife, and Mary offered her cheek to Tom; and then they walked into the crowd, and said the usual things to the usual faces. Presently Mary found herself on a sofa with a drink in her hand, listening once again to the General. When he told her that he had got a three at the seventh that morning, she said, 'Oh, but that's marvellous! It's hard enough to get a four there'; because with a husband and two growing sons you couldn't help knowing all about the seventh. When he told her about the political Brains Trust which they were holding in the village next week, she said, 'How interesting! Oh, I must certainly come to that'; having promised to do so after Charles' exhaustive account of it the day before. She talked to other people, and other people talked to her, and it was all just as it always was; and now she looked at her watch and it was 7.15 and there was Charles with a full glass in his hand, chattering away to Willy and Wally Clintock, those inseparable brothers who had resisted the designs of all the local match-makers for twenty years or more. Of course he liked going into other people's houses and getting away from her for a little, only he always made such a fuss about starting. She couldn't see Mr Traill, but there was Mrs Traill in the wrong clothes again, looking as lonely as usual. She got up, meaning to go across to her, but was stopped by Betty.

'No, don't get up, dear,' said Betty, taking her hand and inclining her back to the sofa, 'sit down and talk to Sir John Danvers-Smith. I've been telling him all about you, and he says he's sure he has met you before. I'll get you a drink.'

Mary acknowledged Sir John with a smile, wondering where they had met, and they sat down together. He was a tall, heavily built man with a close-cut, black moustache going grey, and a head of greying hair going bald; and though his complexion spoke of easy living, his features were still good—a little like a Roman emperor side-face, she thought. She had noticed as he came up behind Betty that he walked firmly with a complete assurance of solid worth. She thought that he was probably older than Charles, but then he would always look older, whatever their ages. He had that 'set' look which Charles had never got. It was difficult to imagine him young and carefree, just as it was difficult to imagine Charles old and important.

'You know,' she smiled, 'I'm afraid I don't remember you, and I think I should if we had met before. Was it a long time ago?'

'Thirty-eight years,' he said, evidently priding himself on remembering anyone so long. 'You were just eighteen.'

It flashed through her mind that he oughtn't to have disclosed so exact a knowledge of her age, and another flash revealed him to her as the sort of man who got on without consideration of what was in the minds of other people. Anyhow she had never bothered to conceal her age.

'What a memory you have! For there must be very little of that girl left to remember.'

'True. But just something. Whatever else you are, Mrs Allison, you are not—ordinary.' (Good gracious, she thought, whatever else is he suggesting I might be?) 'At first I wondered if perhaps I had seen your daughter somewhere—'

'That seems very possible. Or even,' she added, wondering how he would take it, 'my granddaughter.'

He went on as if she had not interrupted him: 'And so I asked our hostess if she knew what your maiden name was. It was what I had expected.' He waited for a moment, and then said, almost in reproof, 'I see that you still have no recollection.'

'I think I must be allowed one or two more questions first, Sir John. We have already decided that it was in this century, and fact not fiction, so I shall now ask, England or abroad?' She said it with a smile, but it was wasted on him.

'At the Prince's Gallery in Piccadilly. A subscription dance in aid of the School Mission. Your family had connections with my old school, I gathered. Am I correct?'

She looked at him. Through thirty-eight years of war and peace, happiness and unhappiness, adversity and prosperity, thrusting its way through a hundred more familiar faces, a face struggled into life. Now she remembered it all: a girl, an evening, a young man; and then she was looking at Sir John Danvers-Smith again, and he was saying,

'Our hostess seems to have forgotten that drink she promised. Let me get it for you.' He moved away from her. She was alone … on a chair up against the wall in the Prince's Gallery.

It was her second grown-up dance.

The first one had been on her eighteenth birthday in the Lancaster Gate house. Her hair was up for the first time—oh, the excitement of it! She was surrounded by her friends and her mother's friends in her own home. Everybody wanted to dance with her. She was the toast of the evening, the belle of the ball. 'Mary!' All glasses raised at supper, and 'God bless you, darling' from a suddenly emotional mother. Her first real ring from her godmother; an amethyst necklet from her father. All her own favourite waltzes on the printed programme, and the little orchestra playing encores whenever *she* rushed up and asked them. Oh, all such fun! And everybody said that it was an even better party than the one two years before, when Kathleen came out. And Kathleen had been engaged for three months, so perhaps in eighteen months from now … what was it like being engaged?

It was six years before she knew.

Derek's old school was giving a dance to raise money for its mission in Bermondsey. Derek wasn't noticeably interested in missions, but it was a dance, and an opportunity to display Kathleen to all the fabulous Cheesers and Bills and Tuppys of whom she had heard so much. Derek's mother got up a party. Wouldn't it be nice, darling, now that Kathleen's sister was out, to ask her too? So Mary, longing for another triumphal dance, her hair up, wearing all her jewellery, and in her pretty, white coming-out dress with the blue sash, squeezed—oh, so excited—into one of those new taxis with Kathleen and Derek (holding hands, of course) and was driven to Prince's. There she was introduced to Derek's mother, who promptly forgot about her; and in a little while she was sitting on one of the chairs which lined the walls of the gallery, waiting for her first partner.

Of course Kathleen and Derek ought to have looked after her—Cheeser would have been delighted to dance with such a pretty girl—but they went straight off into a trance in each other's arms, and nobody else existed for them. So Mary sat there, an empty seat on each side of her, almost the only young girl among the chaperons, waiting to be chosen ...

She couldn't believe it at first. Surely somebody did something. People were introduced to you, or young men, even if they didn't know you, asked you if they could have the pleasure of the next dance, and wrote their names in your programme. Surely among all these young men there should have been somebody who wanted her. She had said to Derek in the taxi, 'Are you going to dance with me, Derek?' almost as a joke, almost as if it would be a favour on her part to dance with a sort of relation who was in love with somebody else. And he had said, 'All right, infant, put me down for the third.' And so when the second dance was beginning, and she was still waiting, she wrote down 'Derek' on her programme, the only name there, and thought, 'Well, anyhow, that's something'; and he and Kathleen had disappeared after the second dance, and she hadn't seen them again until the middle of the third dance, and there they were, right across the room, dancing together ...

She didn't know which was worse, sitting there alone when everybody else was dancing, or sitting there alone when everybody else was chattering round her. What should she be trying to do, what sort of face be bravely trying to wear? Look as if she were waiting for a partner who had gone to get her an ice; or as if she were not feeling very well, and thought that she would sit out this one quietly by herself; or as if she didn't dance, being unfortunately lame from birth, but loved watching other people dance? How did one look like any of those things? How did one look anything but what she felt, utterly humiliated? And—oh God, help me!—there was the supper dance to come; and she would have to look as if the doctor had said, 'Now mind, no supper, a glass of hot milk when you get home, but no supper.' Oh God, how does one look like that? How can I sit here for an hour, while everybody else is having supper? …

She got up and went into the ladies' room; it was something to do. She passed young men in other rooms: some alone, smoking a cigarette, perhaps longing for a partner too, some in groups, talking, she supposed, about the dear old school. She passed happy couples sitting out. She came back; well, that was another five minutes gone, five minutes when nobody felt sorry for her. She sat down again and studied her programme, with Derek's name, and only Derek's name, on it. This was the eighth dance, and the next was her favourite, the one she had made them play so often at her own dance—and she had thought then that she liked dancing! Never, never would she go to a dance again, never again go through this awful humiliation …

Suddenly she knew what she would do. She would sit through the next one, because it was her favourite tune, and perhaps she could go off into a dream while it was being played, and if she didn't get a partner for the one after that, the tenth, then she would find Kathleen and Derek and tell them that she felt terribly ill, and make them take her home—probably they would like being in a taxi together coming back—and then she wouldn't have to face that awful supper dance. And if everybody was in bed, she would find something in the kitchen, and take it up into her bedroom—oh, the utter joy of being alone in your own dear little room with nobody to look at you and pity you. Yes, that's what she would do. Oh, thank God, that's what she would do! Why hadn't she thought of it before?

With this sudden, though so comparative, happiness in front of her, she lost her self-consciousness. She smiled to herself with the confidence of one who was no longer defenceless. She smiled, and then told herself that she mustn't be smiling if she were to counterfeit a splitting headache or appendicitis pains, and smiled again at that. She was ridiculously pretty when she smiled, and an assured young man, standing for a moment in the doorway, told himself that it was absurd that the prettiest girl in the room should be wasting herself on the empty chairs each side of her, and that the whisky-and-soda could wait. He came up to her, and bowed.

'I wonder if I might have the pleasure of the next dance?'

She heard the words from a long way off, telling herself that that was what they said to you when they thought that you were pretty, and wanted to know you. That was what they said to the lucky ones. Vaguely she looked up and saw a tall young man bending over her.

'Oh! I beg your pardon! Did you—were you—'

'I was venturing to ask you if we could have the next dance together.'

He was saying it to *her*! In a confusion of wonder and happiness and gratitude she stammered, 'Oh yes, thank you—oh, please, yes!' And then some instinct made her say coldly, 'Well, I hadn't been meaning to, because I feel rather tired, but—'

'Of course we could sit it out, if you were tired.'

'Oh no, no!' she cried eagerly. 'It's my favourite waltz. I should love to dance it.'

'That's good. Then let's sit the rest of this one out, if you allow it—'

'Oh yes, please let's!'

'And then we can introduce ourselves properly.' He sat down beside her.

She wouldn't let him see her programme with only Derek's name on it. She couldn't. She put it into the hand furthest away from him, and held it underneath her dress. If he asked for it, she could let it fall, and say, 'Oh dear, I seem to have lost it!'

'My name is—oh, but first you must promise not to laugh.'

She looked at him in surprise.

'Why, is it such a funny name?'

'Well, the police always seem to think so. They always laugh when I tell them. On Boat Race night,' he explained, in case she didn't understand.

'Oh, I see.' She smiled at him confidently. 'All right, I promise not to laugh.'

'And you promise to believe me? Some people don't.'

'Yes!' She nodded eagerly.

'Well, my name is John Smith.'

She laughed; a spontaneous, irresistible, increasing gurgle of laughter, showing the prettiest little teeth; and then, with a remorseful 'Oh!' and her fingers over her mouth, she cut it short.

'You promised not to,' he said reproachfully.

'I know, I'm sorry. But it *is* so funny.'

'I told you it was.'

'Because, you see,' she began to laugh again, 'my name is Brown.'

He looked at her with awe.

'Don't say—no, it's too good to be true—*don't* say it's Mary Brown?'

She nodded delightedly.

'Well! To think that we've never met before. All over the world John Smiths are meeting Mary Browns, and somehow we've missed it. You haven't got an "e" at the end of your name, by any chance or mismanagement?'

'Oh, no!'

'That's good. We are the people, we Smiths and Browns. All these toffs round here'—he waved his hand at the pictures on the walls— 'they think no end of their pedigrees, but there's a John the smith or a brown Mary somewhere in every one of them. By the way, you don't know any Robinsons, do you?'

'Well one, sort of. But I don't like him very much.'

'Quite right. An inferior brood.'

Mary laughed. She could have laughed at anything he said.

They danced. The band played her favourite waltz, 'Caressante'. Her eyes were closed in happiness. He danced beautifully, and, like a good dancer, was silent. Life had never been so wonderful. Perhaps, she thought, it is like this when you're engaged.

When the band stopped, he murmured, as if to himself, 'The prettiest girl in the room, *and* the best dancer,' and then he looked down at the vivid little face and said, 'Thank you, Mary Brown.' And very shyly, and wondering if she ought to, she said, 'Thank you, John Smith.' Then they both laughed.

'What about an ice?' he asked, as he led her off the floor. 'Or shall we wait till supper?'

Had he really said 'we'? Did he mean—but of course he didn't mean 'we' together, but just 'we' wherever each of them happened to be. So perhaps if she didn't have an ice now, she would never get one at all.

'Well, I think perhaps—'

'You *are* giving me the supper dance, aren't you?'

(Oh, it was true, it was true!)

'It's no good saying you are engaged,' he went on, 'because the man you were going to have it with—I meant to have told you this before—was arrested half an hour ago, poor chap, I saw a couple of policemen taking him away, they would have it that he was Soapy Robinson, the safe-cracker. Was he?'

She shook her head, swallowed a little nervously, and said in a stage whisper, 'Jones, the Confidence King,' hoping that it would please him. It did. He smiled at her, rather as her History mistress used to smile at her when she got one right.

'Then that settles it, we have the supper dance.'

The supper dance was number twelve. She had two dances to wait, but waiting meant nothing to her now. She went to the ladies' room again, because she simply had to look at herself in the glass to see why he called her the prettiest girl in the room, and then, of course, she had to make herself a little prettier so as to be ready for him when he claimed her again. Then she went back, happy to sit there, and watch the dancers, and dream.

He was dancing with a tall girl in red. Mary hadn't noticed the girl in red before, so perhaps she had only just come. One couldn't not have noticed her if she were here, because she was so—so different. She made Mary, she made all the others, even Kathleen, seem like schoolgirls. She looked so exciting, like one of those beautiful adventuresses one read about. Not *really* wicked, of course, but very, very grown-up, and knowing everything; and they had to steal papers because they were being blackmailed, and their fathers would be exposed if they didn't. She was talking to him all the time, so probably she didn't dance very well.

As soon as the dance was over he left her, and came over to Mary.

'Miss Brown,' he said, 'I make you all my apologies, but I have just had a message sent round from my rooms, and it means that I have to leave. I was leaving after supper anyway, but now it seems that I must go at once. I am so very sorry to be deprived of the pleasure of having supper with you. Please forgive me.'

With a sick feeling inside Mary said, 'It's all right. I quite understand.'

'It isn't all right, at least not for me. I had been looking forward so much—Now, will you do me a favour, just to show that you forgive me? Will you let me find you a partner for supper, to take my place? I am quite sure that I can.'

She wanted to say, 'Well, as a matter of fact it's really very lucky, because I've just remembered'—but she wasn't quite sure what she remembered, and it would be such a relief to be having somebody for supper after all, anybody was better than nobody, and any girl might be left without a partner if her partner was suddenly called away.

'I expect they're all engaged now,' she smiled bravely.

'Well, if you don't mind waiting here just for a few minutes, we'll see.'

He came back with—was it Cheeser or Tuppy? She never got the name, so put him down as Robinson. He was a shortish young man with a round beaming face and spectacles. They were very shy with each other at first, but by the time they were at the supper table he was in what seemed to be his usual cheerful mood. They sat with a gang of other Cheesers and Tuppy and their girls, all equally cheerful, and they laughed a great deal, and Mary was as brilliant as any of them. And all the other Cheesers and Tuppy wanted to dance with her, it was great fun trying to fit them all in. They didn't dance very well, but they were nice.

The girl in red seemed to have gone …

In the cab going home Mary said:

'Derek, was there anybody called Smith at school with you?'

'Lots, baby, I expect. I can remember two anyway. No, three. Not in my house, though. Why?'

'Oh, a man I danced with. John Smith. Tall. I just wondered.'

'There was a J. D. Smith—are you all right, darling?' This was to Kathleen who said, 'A bit squashed. That's better,' as she rearranged herself. 'He was a toff when I was a squeaker, captain of Cory's and in the Fifteen, that sort of bloke. Would that be the man?'

'I expect so,' said Mary.

'Sure you're all right, darling?' asked Derek, and Kathleen assured him that she was.

J. D. Smith. Mary wondered what 'D' stood for.

She wondered about him a good deal in the months which followed. She wondered why he had been called away so suddenly. Sometimes she thought that he was a war-correspondent; they were always being sent off to the ends of the earth at a moment's notice. Probably he had had his pith helmet and revolver already packed before he came to the dance, and was just waiting for the summons. In that case she wouldn't see him for a long time, but she could look for his name in the paper and cut out what he had written. Of course it might be a paper which they didn't take in. It would be better if he were a King's Messenger, taking one of the Crown Jewels (strapped to his waist) to a Foreign Monarch for a present, because you couldn't send that sort of thing by post. In that case he would be coming back with a priceless snuff-box, because monarchs always exchanged gifts in order to keep relations friendly. So she would see him again quite soon. Or, of course, the Prime Minister might have wanted to consult him suddenly about something, or offer him a seat in the Cabinet. Pitt was in the Cabinet when he was twenty-two, and Mr Smith was older than that.

When, and how, would they meet again? They would run into each other suddenly at Harrods. Or she would be in the stalls and see him looking down at her from a box, and she would say, 'Look, there's Mr Smith!' to her mother or whoever she was with, and they would go up to his box in the interval, or would that be rather forward? Better wait in the *foyer* as they came out, and let him see her sort of accidentally. Or perhaps it would be nice if they met at Studland Bay in the summer, swimming in the sea perhaps, or wouldn't he recognize her in a bathing cap, and she would bring him back to lunch. But really, of course, it would be nicest of all if her father said to her mother at breakfast one day, 'Oh, by the way, my love, I'm bringing a young fellow back to dinner to-night, a Mr John D. Smith, very clever young fellow, I think of making him a partner.' Wouldn't he be surprised when he saw her? Of course, if he were a partner, they would get married quite soon. And once they were married she would devote her whole life to him. She didn't know *what* she would have done if he hadn't rescued her, she would have died of shame. Never, never would she stop being grateful; never, never would she leave him out of her prayers ...

She left him out a year later. Kathleen was married now, and was telling her how she and Derek had gone to a dance the night before, and there wasn't a proper sit-down supper, so they had slipped out and had supper at the Carlton, such fun. Suddenly Mary knew that that was what Mr Smith and the girl in red had done. Suddenly she Saw it All. A wave of old-age and disillusionment swept over her, leaving her with the life-long conviction that all men were beasts, and you couldn't believe anything they said, and she would never fall in love or marry anybody, or at least not for a long time. It was, in fact, not until she was twenty-four that she married Charles, who had been in love with her for many years, and had almost given up hope ...

'Mary dear, Sir John wanted me to make his apologies to you. He had to hurry off. I've brought you a drink.'

Betty sat down beside her, and began a long story about the latest treasure from the village who had come to help, but, as it proved, had only helped herself. Mary hardly needed to listen, she had heard it so often.

So once again he had deserted her! What a blesséd, blesséd comfort it was to know that it mattered no longer. How cosy to feel that there was one man who would never desert you; never grow old and insensitive. Though you would never again be the prettiest girl in the room, though your dancing days were over, how restful it was to know that you were truly poised at last, and that all the turbulent uneasiness and pathetic silliness of youth was behind you. There was much to be said for autumn—with an occasional sweet reminder of spring, a sudden memory which brought the scent of its flowers into the present, yet left you undisturbed.

It was eight o'clock again. 'Charles, dear, we simply must be going.' The usual goodbyes, the usual trouble to get the car started, the usual, 'Sure I can't help, old man?' from their host at the door, the usual, 'Don't stand out in the cold, *please*!' from Mary. Then they were off, hands waving, the lights from the house caught between the trees as the drive swung round. All as usual—but not quite as usual.

As they came into the road, he said:

'Well, old girl, you did it again.'

'Did what again?'

'Knocked 'em all. The prettiest girl in the room, *and* the best dressed.'

'Charles! Darling!' She could hardly believe that he was saying it. To *her*!

He dropped his left hand for a moment on to her thigh and squeezed. 'Proud of you.'

'Darling!' In a bewilderment of crazy happiness she put her fingers to her mouth and gave the war-cry of the Allisons.

'Good God, what's that for?' said a startled Charles. 'Still, if you feel that way—' He gave the answering call, louder, more piercing.

'The whole village will hear us,' said Mary, laughing weakly. 'They'll think we're mad.'

Presently she found that she was not laughing, she was crying.

Before the Flood

(1949)

We are told that Lamech was 182 years old when he begat Noah, and that he lived 595 years afterwards. So we are not surprised when we read that 'all the days of Lamech were seven hundred, seventy and seven years: and he died'. It is just what we should have expected. But the next verse gives us material for more sustained thought. It says 'And Noah was 500 years old: and Noah begat Shem, Ham and Japheth.' Now it is improbable that this verse is meant to convey two independent items of news, for then the chronicler is merely telling us in the first one that at some time in his career Noah was 500; which we could have worked out for ourselves, remembering that he was 595 when his father died. But if, as therefore seems likely, the two statements are related, then he is giving us the really interesting information that at the age of 500 Noah begat triplets. As he says a few verses later, 'There were giants in those days.'

The present chronicler, however, finding it difficult to distinguish in his mind between a hearty, middle-aged man of 500 and an elderly gentleman of 840, and suspecting that it is arithmetic rather than nature which has changed so remarkably since those days, has thought it better to divide patriarchal ages by ten, in the hope of so arriving at some picture of the truth. He proposes, therefore, to regard Noah as a man of sixty when he entered the Ark, and the ages of his sons as twenty-eight,

350

twenty-four and twenty. And since the old chronicler has said little of the women, the present one, wishing to say more of them, would remind his readers that the name of Noah's wife was Hannah, of Shem's Kerin, of Ham's Ayesha, and of Japheth's Meribal. Now we can begin.

Noah was accustomed to dream at night, and to recount his dreams to the family over the breakfast table. These dreams were either straightforward prophecies of ill-fortune, or were so oblique that they would only be interpreted accurately after the event. For example, if a plague of locusts destroyed his crops, he would remind the family complacently of his dream a month earlier that he was emptying a bottomless well with a sieve; acknowledging that he had misinterpreted this at the time as meaning that his second son would come to no good. Noah never did like Ham much. Ham would argue.

One night Noah had a peculiarly vivid dream. He dreamed that the Tigris and the Euphrates had joined together and rushed at him, and that he and Ham were sitting on a log in the middle of the waters, and Ham was saying 'Why didn't you dream about this, and then we could have built a boat and saved my mother and my brothers, and my brothers' wives?' And, as an afterthought, he had added, 'And Ayesha.' And then Ham had turned into a crocodile, and the crocodile said 'What about *my* wife?' And suddenly all the animals were saying, 'And what about *our* wives?' But he wasn't sitting on a log, he was sitting on the top branch of a cypress tree, sawing it off so as to build a boat, and suddenly he found to his horror that he was sitting on the wrong side of the branch. And he gave a great cry as he fell, and his wife awoke and said, 'Who is it?' and lo! it was a dream. So he said, 'Just a dream, dear. I'll tell you in the morning.' And he lay awake for three hours pondering it, at the end of which time he had forgotten that it was a dream. He fell asleep again as the day was breaking, and this time Yahweh Himself spoke to him; and now all was clear in his mind.

'Shem, my boy,' he said at breakfast, 'what did you think of doing this morning?'

Shem was his favourite son. He was strong and willing; he could do anything with his hands, and had very little brains to do anything else with; so he could be trusted to do what he was told without arguing. Ham was cynical and unsatisfactory. He didn't seem to believe any of the things which were commonly believed: among them that a father was the embodiment of wisdom, and should be honoured even when he differed from you. Japheth had just got married to Meribal, and Meribal had just got married to Japheth. They sat together and thought together and walked together; and neither of them had said 'I' for six months, but always 'we'. They were regarded as a temporary but total loss to the establishment.

Before Shem could collect in his mind the facts with which to answer his father, Noah went on: 'Well, I want you to put all that on one side and help me to build a boat. Ham, no doubt, will now wish to ask me why a boat, seeing that the only water we have here is a well. Ham, my boy?'

'My dear father,' said Ham, raising his eyebrows in that way he had, 'it never occurred to me to ask you why a boat. On the contrary, I have always thought that the one thing this farm lacked was a boat. Really we ought to have one boat each. Seven boats,' he explained, looking at Japheth-and-Meribal. 'You never know when a nice boat mightn't be useful.'

'You have spoken a true word there, Ham. You never know when a boat mightn't be useful.'

Hannah, scenting trouble between them again, said:

'Oh, you were going to tell us about your dream, dear. Was it about boats this time? I don't think you have ever dreamed about boats before.'

'I have had no occasion to, Hannah. But on the eve of the most terrible catastrophe in History, when a Great Flood is about to cover the face of the Earth and destroy all the people thereon, I have been mercifully forewarned, and instructed what to do.'

The family took it calmly, as if all that was to be expected from this dream was that a sheep would fall into the well. As a matter of academic interest Ham wanted to know where the water was coming from.

'Where everything comes from, my son,' said Noah sternly. 'From Heaven.'

'Amen,' said Hannah, feeling vaguely that it was called for.

'Oh, you mean it's going to rain?'

'For forty days and forty nights, until the waters cover even the crest of Ararat.'

'And we shall all be in our boat?'

'Not only we, but representatives of all the animals in the world, two of each, male and female.'

Japheth-and-Meribal had a secret smile for this.

'What's the idea?' asked Ham.

'As I understand it, Yahweh is weary of the wickedness of the world, and intends to destroy every living creature in it, with the exception of this household, and these—er—specimen animals I was telling you about. We, or perhaps I should say, I, have been fortunate enough to find favour in His sight.'

'And what happens afterwards, or do we live in our boat for ever?'

'When the waters subside, we shall all start again, and found a new generation.'

'Us eight and all the animals?'

'Yes.'

Ham looked at Ayesha and said, 'Fancy that!' Ayesha looked away from him and said nothing.

'It seems rather a roundabout way of doing things,' said Hannah. 'You don't mean that I've got to start again, too?'

Noah ignored the question, and said sternly:

'Woman, do you dare to tell the Lord Yahweh how to do things?'

'Mercy, no, I just said it seemed rather a roundabout way of doing them.'

Japheth and Meribal had been whispering and laughing together, and now Meribal said: 'Daddy Noah, we want to ask you, are you going to save two scorpions?'

'Certainly, my child. Yahweh makes no exceptions.'

'We think,' said Japheth, 'that you ought to give scorpions a miss. We think that if Meribal's father and mother are going to be drowned, it is rather unflattering to save the lives of two scorpions. Couldn't you leave them out? Say you couldn't catch them, or got two males by mistake, or something?'

'What's the difference between a male scorpion and a female scorpion?' asked Ham. 'Docs anybody know?'

'I thought,' said Noah coldly, 'that I had explained the facts of life to you on the night before your marriage.'

'Oh, was *that* what you were doing?' said Ham, a little surprised. 'I thought—well, anyhow, we never touched on scorpions.' He glanced at his wife, and added, 'It didn't seem necessary then.' Ayesha flashed hate at him, and dropped her eyes.

'Isn't one bigger than the other?' asked Hannah. 'Or is it smaller?'

'It might be younger, Mother,' Shem pointed out.

'Well,' said Hannah, 'I can't see that Yahweh would mind very much if we all started again without scorpions.'

'He *would* mind. Very much,' said Noah.

'So would the scorpions,' said Ham. 'Don't forget that.'

'So will Father and Mother,' said Meribal brightly, making, she felt, a good point.

'Aren't you glad you married into our family?' Japheth asked her, kissing her nose. Meribal took a quick look round the room and bit his ear.

'All these matters,' said the Patriarch importantly, 'sink into insignificance beside the problem of building the boat. Obviously it will have to be a big one to contain all these animals. My instructions are that it shall be 450 feet long, 75 feet broad, and 45 feet high.'

Shem gasped. Hannah said, 'Gracious!' Japheth whistled.

Ham said negligently: 'Oh, would you call that a big boat, Father?'

* * *

Though the patriarchs had seen to it that the lowly position of Woman in the Home was established by Divine Law, it is doubtful if her authority differed very much from that which her glorious emancipation has since given her. Hannah, it may be said, frequently confused Noah with Yahweh, and, regarding them both as children, felt it her duty to do what she could for them.

'Just a moment, dear, before you go off to your tree-cutting,' she said after breakfast.

'What is it, Hannah? All right, Shem, meet me at the Well Gate.'

'Yes, Father.' Shem shouldered his axe and strode off.

'Now, dear.'

'All this about the boat—'

'I think we'll call it the Ark. Yes, I remember now that that is what Yahweh called it. The Ark.'

'You really do believe it? You know, dear, sometimes your dreams— there was that prophecy of yours that Ham was going to be struck by lightning—'

'If you remember, my love,' said Noah patiently, 'Ayesha had a miscarriage shortly afterwards, which is exactly what the grief and shock would have caused, if Ham *had* been struck by lightning. There was nothing wrong with the prophecy, I just didn't follow the implications far enough.' Even now Noah could surprise his wife. She looked at him pityingly. How anybody over the age of five could suppose that Ayesha—couldn't he see how it was between them?

'You do believe in this Flood, then?'

'I was never more certain.'

'Naturally there will be preparations to make if we are all to live in this Ark for—how many days did you say?'

'The actual rains will last for forty days. But then, of course, the water has to go down again. I don't know how long that will take. It might well be a year before normal conditions were restored.'

'A year's provisioning for eight people and all those animals. Have you any idea of how many sorts of animals there are, and what they all eat?'

'N-no,' said Noah cautiously. 'I shall—er'—he brightened up and ended—'I shall leave that to Ham. We must all do our share.'

'They won't bring their own food with them?'

'I—er—no. Don't think, my dear,' he added hastily, 'that I don't appreciate the enormous responsibility which this command of Yahweh's has placed upon you.'

'As long as you appreciate it, that's all I ask of you. It's just that, if some of the rarer animals, of whose habits we know so little, do happen to find themselves running short at the end of the tenth month, I don't want you to say "How like Hannah".'

'My dear, I shouldn't dream of saying it.'

'You dream of so many strange things, Noah, that that might well be one of them. Very well, dear, now run along and get your axe. Shem will be waiting for you.'

When he had gone, she went in to Kerin and said, 'It's serious this time.'

And now even the neighbours were beginning to take it seriously.

'You seem to be building something,' said Nathaneel one day. He was an observant man.

'Yes,' said Noah, wiping away the sweat which was running into his eyes.

'You won't have much wood left if you go on like this.'

'No.'

'What's the idea?'

Nathaneel was the thirty-second person who had said, 'What's the idea?' and Noah was now a little tired of it. He said 'Oh, just an idea,' and went on sawing.

'If I blink my eyes rapidly, and then look away, I get a curious sensation of a house of some sort. Would that be right?'

'Yes.'

'Bit big for a house, isn't it? But perhaps you are expecting an addition to the family?'

'Yes.'

'Ah, that's good. I like to see young people—' he was about to say 'enjoying themselves', but substituted 'realizing their civic responsibilities'.

'Yes,' said Noah.

Nathaneel felt that he was doing most of the work. However, he had now arrived at the point for which he had been making.

'As I was saying, you will be running out of wood at this rate. I could let you have a couple of acres of cypress, if it interested you.'

'The North wood?' asked Noah, straightening up and showing interest.

'Yes. Matter of fact it's a little over the two acres.'

'What do you want for it?'

'You've got some good-looking sheep,' said Nathaneel cautiously.

'I dare say we could do something on those lines,' said Noah. The fact that all his sheep but two were doomed anyway offered, he thought, a good basis for bargaining. The fact that Nathaneel was equally doomed might also be worked in somehow: post-dating delivery or something.

'Come along to my place to-night,' said Nathaneel, 'and we'll talk it over.'

Noah nodded a little condescendingly. It was hard not to be condescending when the Lord has told you that you are the only man in the world worth saving. The only man, that is, with a beard.

'How are you getting on?' Ham asked his brother at dinner some weeks later.

'Oh, all right,' said Shem.

'If you worked as diligently as your brother,' said Noah, 'your elder brother,' he explained, glancing at Japheth-and-Meribal who were still one, 'then you would be getting on all right too. You are responsible for the animals, and so far you seem to have done nothing.'

'On the contrary,' said Ham, scratching his elbow, 'I have collected a flea. Whether male or female, and with or without companion, I cannot say. But it's a start.'

'Tchah!' said Noah through his beard.

'Well, there's one thing,' said Hannah. 'With all these animals I needn't provide food for the fleas.'

'That's just what I wanted to ask you, Father. Don't imagine that I have been idle. I have been thinking. And, believe me, this needs a great deal more thought than anybody had yet given it.'

It was so obvious that 'anybody' included Yahweh that Hannah was a little frightened. You never knew with Yahweh. He was so easily offended, and *so* impulsive. She hastened to substitute herself, saying that she had had to think about it a great deal, with all that food to provide.

'Exactly the point, Mother. Father insists that there must be two of everything. One male, one female. No more, no less.'

'Yahweh insists,' corrected Noah.

'Quite so. But some of these animals eat each other. If we are to satisfy a couple of lions for a year, we want more than two gazelles. Otherwise you will end up with no gazelles and no lions. Lions, I have estimated, want about a gazelle a day each. So, merely looking at it from the lion's point of view, we shall have to start with 730 gazelles.'

'Yahweh distinctly said two only,' repeated Noah obstinately.

'Take it or leave it,' shrugged Ham. 'Why should I mind either way?'

Noah scratched at his beard. ('This is the other one,' Japheth whispered to Meribal, and they both giggled.) 'The solution is obvious,' he said, as soon as he had thought of it. 'There is always a way if you look for it. Dead meat. Yahweh said nothing against dead meat.' He looked round at them triumphantly. There was a heavy silence.

'I am only a woman,' said Hannah very clearly, 'and my one desire is to obey the Lord's and my husband's commands. But if I *should* be offered the choice of drowning comfortably with my friends, or living for a year in a box with 730 dead gazelles—'

'Oh, why don't we *all* drown, and have done with it!' cried Ayesha passionately. Amazingly she burst into tears and rushed from the room. Ayesha! Ham felt a sudden lightening at the heart. If she were unhappy too—! He started up to follow her. But what was the good? She would only say, 'Oh, leave me *alone*!' He sat down again, but still with that strange excited feeling. Ayesha!

Noah said bitterly: 'I have walked with the Lord all the days of my life. I have obeyed His testimonies. If the commands of the Lord are now to be as naught with my own people, then it were indeed better that we should all drown.'

'Yes, dear,' said his wife soothingly, patting his head, 'but we shan't. Not when you've built that nice boat.'

'Ark.'

'Yes, dear, ark. That boat you're building so cleverly.'

Ham said, choosing his words carefully, 'Nobody would be so foolish as to set up his wisdom against that of the Creator of All Things. But if He seems to have given us an order which no man can possibly carry out, do we not follow the path of wisdom by telling ourselves that the order cannot have been fully heard, fully understood, fully interpreted?'

Noah combed his beard with his fingers, saying nothing.

'May we speak, Father?' asked Japheth, holding up his hand.

'Yes, my son, let us all speak.'

'Well, we've been talking it over, and what we think is this. Fleas. You can't have an ark full of all sorts of furry animals, and only have two fleas. Then think of flies. *Flies!* Can you see Ham examining all the million flies in the ark until he's got one boy-fly and one girl-fly—' (Meribal giggled)—'and then trying to catch and kill all the others? Think of birds. You can let two of each in by the front door, but what of the hundreds which settle on the roof? Cats! How many kittens are you letting yourself in for? And how can Ham be sure of finding all the animals anyway? There may be a particular sort of rare beetle, which lives in a hole at the top of a mountain a hundred miles from here—what does he do about that one?'

'I shall be up there anyway,' said Ham, 'getting that second eagle.'

Noah was silent. There was nothing to say. He looked up and saw that Shem seemed to be in trouble with an idea.

'Well, my boy?'

'I was just thinking—if we didn't have to have all those animals it would mean a much smaller ark, and we could do with the wood we've got.'

Noah nodded.

'Kerin? Have you any contribution to make?'

'May we just say one more thing, Father?' Japheth interrupted.

'Well?'

'We just want to know. When the flood is at its height, and Meribal's father and mother drift past us on a barrel, what do we do? Wave?'

'Kerin? You were going to say—?'

Japheth, realizing that he had been snubbed, restored confidence in himself by pointing out to Meribal what an unanswerable point he had made. She agreed, and kissed his nose.

Kerin was fair, and her hair came down in two plaits over her shoulders. She was very beautiful. Not dangerously, frighteningly beautiful, like the dark and passionate Ayesha, but tranquilly beautiful, as if she knew what she was and where she wanted to go.

'In the end,' she said slowly, 'we have to trust to our own minds and hearts and consciences. If it be Yahweh's will to destroy the whole world, then we can neither help Him nor hinder Him. But if He gives us, and us alone, the opportunity of saving ourselves, then we must use all our efforts to save ourselves, efforts not only of body, but of mind and judgment. Our judgment may be wrong, but we shall have done our best, and nothing which we do or leave undone can alter His plans for the world.'

They were all against him. All!

'I think, dear, if I may speak again—'

'Yes, Hannah?'

'Wouldn't it be better to wait until you have had *another* dream, one in which things are made *much* clearer?'

Even Hannah!

'I cannot have dreams to order, Hannah! I cannot summon Yahweh to speak to me!'

'No, dear, but I have noticed that that sort of thing so often happens after you have been eating Lebanon honey. Kerin, dear, you will find the jar on the top shelf of the larder. Would you mind? Just put a little out on a plate.'

In the end Noah did what mankind always ends by doing. He compromised. He had Divine Authority for this; that is to say, he put the difficulty before Yahweh when he went to bed, talked it over with Hannah until they both went to sleep, and in the morning came to a decision. No man could have done more.

'About the animals,' he said at breakfast.

'And Meribal's father and mother,' murmured Japheth.

'I have now received clearer guidance.' (Hannah looked across at Kerin and nodded.) 'The wisdom of the Lord is too deep for the mortal mind to comprehend it at the first instruction, and in substituting his own imperfect wisdom for so much of the Divine wisdom as he does not understand, Man may fall into grievous error.'

He paused a moment, as if for comment, but since it was not quite clear whether reverent assent or polite dissent was called for, nobody said anything.

'As should have been plain to you all from the first, my reference to animals was to domestic animals only. If it be Yahweh's will to destroy all evil men, must it not be equally His will to destroy all evil beasts and creeping things? Ham, you should have seen this. Is it not also manifest that among beneficent cattle and sheep no distinction of goodness can be made, and that the numerological reference, the mention of "two", applied therefore to the sex, not to the individual? Japheth, my boy, I am surprised that this did not strike you. Moreover Hannah, my dear, it was always obvious, or so I should have supposed, that we could not sustain ourselves unless we had a surplus of living animals from which to replenish our stocks of fresh meat. This of itself would have made the idea of two sheep only'— he waited to get it under full control, and then gave an amused chuckle—'quite ridiculous!'

'Of course now that you put it so logically, dear, I do see,' said Hannah. 'Men,' she went on to Kerin, 'are so much more logical than women. Such a help. Meribal, darling, when I see you eating Japheth's ear, I always feel that it is a reflection on my housekeeping. You should keep that in reserve, in case the Flood lasts longer than we expect.'

'I have the Divine Authority,' announced Noah a little pompously, 'for saying that, after all, we may be back on dry land in as little as eight weeks from the beginning of the rains. Eight weeks, Hannah. Nevertheless,' he added, 'you should cater for the whole year, so as to be on the safe side.'

'Of course, dear,' said Hannah. 'As you will find later on, Kerin, when you set up house for yourself, it is these little authoritative hints which make housekeeping so much easier.'

'Now as to the human element,' Noah went on, 'and this of course includes Meribal's father and mother. Whether owing to my intercession or of His own bounteous mercy (and it is not for me to say), Yahweh has relented towards them. Our friends and neighbours are to be warned of the Flood, and so to be given a chance of saving themselves.'

'Very handsome of Him,' said Ham.

'Oh, thank you, Daddy Noah,' said Meribal, after being nudged by Japheth, 'that *is* kind of you both.'

'Do you mean, dear, that they are to be given a chance of saving themselves in *our* boat—'

'Ark.'

'—ark, or a chance of building and stocking one for themselves?'

'Well—' said Noah, and left it at that, not being quite sure.

'You do see the difference, dear?' Hannah asked anxiously.

'I think, Hannah, that we might leave that point for the moment. The immediate duty is to warn them.'

'Surely by this time,' said Ham, 'everybody knows why we are building an ark. Don't they, Shem?'

'They come and ask me, and I tell them, and then they scoff.'

'Isn't that good enough, Father?'

'In a general way, yes, my boy, but I feel that in certain cases the situation should be explained in a little more detail.'

'To Nathaneel, for instance.'

'I wasn't thinking so much of Nathaneel, as of Meribal's father and mother.'

'I agree,' said Hannah firmly. 'I shall call upon your mother this afternoon, Meribal, and make it all *quite* clear to her.'

So Hannah called on Meribal's mother, and no two people (you would have said) could have been more delighted to see each other. When they had got over their delight, Hannah began:

'What lovely weather we are having, but of course we could do with a little rain.'

'I understood,' said Meribal's mother archly, 'that we were going to have some.'

'Oh, you've heard our news?' Hannah laughed. 'Forty days and forty nights? Fancy!'

'Is it—official?' asked Meribal's mother, glancing up at the ceiling.

'I'm afraid so. But then everything is which Noah thinks of. It makes things *so* difficult.'

'Shobal used to be like that, but I got him out of it.'

'You're so clever, Tirzah,' sighed Hannah. 'If only I had taken it earlier! But it's too late now, I'm afraid. I shall have to go on saying "Yes, dear", for the rest of my life.'

'You don't believe it, of course,' asked Tirzah, with the uneasy laugh of one who didn't want to.

'About the Flood?' Hannah's laugh sounded much more genuine. 'Darling, how can you ask? Raining all that time!'

'I said to Shobal, "Whoever's heard of rain for forty days?"'

'Who indeed? Oh, but you haven't heard the best of it. With all this rain, there's going to be a flood which will cover the top of Mount Ararat, and everybody in the whole world is going to be drowned! Isn't it amusing? The things Noah thinks of!'

'Oh, is *that* why you're building this extraordinary box? What did Shobal call it? It made me laugh so. "Noah's Ark", that was it.' She tittered, and said again, 'Noah's Ark! I think that's a wonderful name for it. "Have you heard about Noah's Ark?" he asked me. I didn't know what he meant.'

'My dear,' said Hannah grimly, 'it may be a joke to you and Shobal, but it's no joke to me. I've got to provision that box for a whole year!'

'I thought you said forty days—'

'Yes, but the water has to subside—I think that's the word—and apparently that takes another year.'

'Hannah! It's crazy!'

'Of course it is, but what can I do?'

'I said to Shobal when I first heard of it, "Well, our daughter has married into a crazy family."'

'I'm afraid she has, poor girl. And such a sweet nature. But, Tirzah, can you imagine us all shut up in that box for a year or more, with as many animals as we can squeeze in, shut up in a box for a whole year?'

'Horrible,' said Tirzah with a shudder. 'But, of course, if it *doesn't* rain—'

'Oh, but we shall have to go into our box just the same. Noah is determined on that. Just sit there boxed up, and wait for the rain to begin. And then wait for it to stop. And then wait for another year.

And then—Oh, Tirzah, how I envy you and Shobal, such a nice sensible man, Shobal, with none of these strange ideas.'

'I'm thinking of Meribal. It's very hard on her.'

'It is. Luckily she can't see an inch beyond Japheth's nose at the moment, so she's quite happy. But as for the rest of us—*and* all those smelly animals—oh well, dear, I mustn't bother you with our little troubles. It has been lovely to see you.'

She got up, laid her cheek against Tirzah's, and moved towards the door. But suddenly she remembered.

'How silly of me, darling!' she laughed. 'I had a special message for you from my husband, and I had forgotten all about it. Well, the fact is, I'm ashamed to give it. You'll think I'm making fun of you.'

'Oh, go on, Hannah, you know I'm not one to mind.'

'Well, do forgive me, dear.' She paused, and then went on quickly, 'Tirzah, it's really too absurd, but Noah says that if you and Shobal like to join us all in our box—for the whole year, of course, and I'm *afraid* you'd have to bring your own provisions, men never think of that, but *you* understand, darling—well, you know how delighted we should all be to have you.' She took a deep breath and ended, 'There! I've done it!'

'Oh, dear!' said Tirzah. 'Of course, it's sweet of you, Hannah, but—well, I know Shobal is rather busy this next week or two—and, as a matter of fact, I'm supposed to be out in the open air as much as possible just now, no, nothing serious, but you do see, dear—'

'Of *course*, darling! Don't think any more of it. But my husband insisted that I should ask you, so naturally I had to do it. Good-bye, darling. My love to Shobal, please. Good-bye!'

So at dinner that night Hannah said:

'I'm afraid it's no good, Meribal darling. Your father and mother just *won't* believe about the Flood. So foolish of them.' She caught Kerin's eye, and added, 'I did my best.'

'I'm sure you did,' smiled Kerin.

The words 'father' and 'mother' came to Meribal from a long way off. She was smoothing out Japheth's eyebrows for him.

The Ark was nearly finished. The neighbours had stared, and made their jokes, and lost interest. Shem was resting for a moment when Kerin came down from the house with a jug of milk in her hands.

'You will be thirsty,' she said, 'and tired. Sit for a little and talk to me.'

'I'm all right,' he said. He took the jug from her and they sat down together.

'How much longer will it be?'

'Just the roof to finish off,' said Shem. He drank and said, 'That was good. Well, say three more days.'

'And then—?'

'How do you mean?'

'Then we all go into the Ark together, and there we all are. Together.'

He nodded and said, 'The same as we have always been.'

'Don't I know? But even so, you and I have managed to be away by ourselves sometimes. Now, for a whole year—'

'Oh, I expect we shall be all right. Bit crowded at first perhaps.'

'If it is to be for a whole year,' began Kerin, 'I don't think I—' and then suddenly, 'Shem!'

'Yes?'

'Will you promise me something?'

'Anything I can. Of course.'

'When it is all over, will you come away with me?'

'Where?'

'Anywhere, so long as it is a long way, and we are alone.'

He looked at her in astonishment.

'Why, what's the matter, Kerin? Aren't you happy with us?'

'I think that Husband and Wife should be alone together.'

'Yes, dear, but with their children. Like Father and Mother.'

'No, no,' she said urgently, 'not with their children, not when the children are grown up.'

'It is the custom,' said Shem, a little bewildered.

'Is it? Then why isn't Meribal with her father and mother? Would you like me to be with mine, if they were alive?'

'Oh, daughters, no.'

'Oh, daughters, no,' repeated Kerin. 'So you see, children don't have to be with their parents for ever. There is no Divine Law about it.'

Shem scratched his head, took another draught of milk, and tried again.

'What's wrong with being all together? I don't understand. Everybody loves you. Who is it who makes you unhappy? I know Mother loves you.'

'I like your mother very much. I admire her, and she amuses me a great deal.'

'Amuses?' said Shem, shocked by the word. One oughtn't to think of mothers as amusing.

'And of course everybody respects your father. He's a dear old man. Sometimes he amuses me too,' she added, with a reminiscent smile.

That word again! 'Kerin!' he cried. 'I don't know what you're saying!'

'Yes, I like them both very much; I have been very lucky. But you see, dear, I don't *love* anybody but you.'

Shem groped his way after her as well as he might, but he was still in the darkness. All he found to say was, 'I thought we were all so happy together'; but he didn't sound happy as he said it.

'All!' she said scornfully. 'Ham and Ayesha never speak to each other! Japheth and Meribal are only happy because they can still behave as if the rest of us weren't there. For all they mean to anybody else they might be gone already.'

'You don't want us to behave like Japheth and Meribal?'

'Do you ever wish that I did?' she said softly.

Shem turned to her in surprise. He found himself looking into the depths of her deep blue eyes, and was lost. Suddenly he took her in his arms, crushed her until she could scarcely breathe, and kissed her ...

'All right, I promise,' he said. 'Now I must get on with the roof.' Kerin went singing back to the house, swinging the empty jug.

'I have it on High Authority,' said Noah that evening, 'that the Ark will come to rest on the summit of Mount Ararat. This may not be until the seventeenth day of the seventh month. From that moment the waters will gradually subside.'

'And what do *we* do?' asked Japheth.

'We gradually get out, darling,' giggled Meribal.

'And there we all are on the top of Ararat,' said Ham. 'Mother, how good are you at climbing down a 17,000-foot mountain?'

'Not very good, dear. I haven't been practising lately. But I expect to be a little better than some of the cows.'

Noah pulled at his beard.

'I may have got that bit about Ararat wrong,' he said reluctantly.

'I hope so, dear,' said Hannah.

Ham came into his wife's room. She looked round and said coldly: 'What do you want?'

'Not to disturb you,' he said. 'And not to annoy you; at least, not before I have begun.'

'Begun what?'

'Saying what I want to say.'

'Oh, are we talking again?' said Ayesha. 'How nice! It will be the first time for months.'

'And it may be the last time for ever. But perhaps it was a bad moment to choose. You're packing.' He had come to rest at her dressing-table, and now, sitting down in front of it, he picked up a carved wooden hair-brush. 'I made this for you. Do you remember? It's rather good.' He looked at it appreciatively.

She took it away from him, saying, 'Don't muddle things up, please. And wouldn't it be better if you got on with your own packing? We move in to-night.'

'You do, perhaps. I don't.'

She was startled. She said, 'What do you mean?' putting the brush down, and backing away from him. He got up from his seat and said, 'Sit down here and brush your hair. It will give you something to do, if you don't want to listen to me. Here!' He gave her the brush again, and she sat down. 'I used to like watching you brush your hair—your serious, so remote, face, and the ripple of your arms. But I won't watch you now. You're alone, and I'm alone, and—What were you asking me? Oh, about the packing. Well, I shall have very little to pack. You see, I'm not going into the Ark.'

'You mean you don't believe there's going to be a Flood? You wouldn't, of course.'

'Sometimes I do and sometimes I don't. What I don't believe is that I'm a particularly good person to save. I can't help thinking "Why Ham?" I can see why Father and Mother, and why Shem and Kerin; they're good. I am not so sure about Japheth and Meribal, because, when you are as happy as that, it seems to me rather a good time to die; but they are nice children and have never done anybody any harm. And I can see why Ayesha, because beauty, sheer beauty, is the one thing which mustn't be destroyed. But when I think of Ham, then I begin to doubt. Then I begin to feel that it's absurd and wrong to choose a little group of eight people out of the whole world, and to set them above all the rest. There are wicked men on the earth, and I daresay I'm one of them, but not children, not babies. I can't quite believe in a God like that.'

'So you're taking a chance?'

'Yes ... Ayesha, I want you to take it with me.'

'Now?'

'Yes.'

'Why?'

369

He said, as if to himself, 'I should never have dared to ask you. But when you cried, "Oh, why don't we all drown, and have done with it?" then I knew that you were no happier than I, and that there was still a chance for us. I want you to come with me and take it. To put it in another way,' he went on more firmly, 'I'm damned if I'm going to live with you in that damned Ark for a whole damned year, watching Japheth and Meribal, and knowing that I love you a hundred times more than he will ever love her, and that without some help from you I shall never have the courage to do anything about it.'

The brush had ceased its regular motion. There was silence. Then slowly her hand moved again, and, still looking in her mirror, she said, 'Stand where I can see you.'

He came and stood behind her, a little to one side. They looked at each other in the mirror.

'Is that where you used to stand when you liked watching me brush my hair?'

'Yes.'

'I don't think you ever told me.'

'I thought you knew.'

'Never think that of me. Never think that I know.'

'You know now.'

'Yes. All the same, I think that we will go into the Ark together. Just to be safe. Will you mind?'

'Not now.'

'Perhaps,' she smiled, 'Japheth and Meribal will be able to give us a few hints on how to be happy.'

'I don't think so. I have a very good memory.'

'So have I. Oh, so have I!'

'Ayesha!'

'When it is all over, then I promise that we will go off by ourselves—oh, a long, long way—and start that family.'

'Thank you, my very lovely one.'

'Is your courage coming slowly back?'

'Slowly,' he nodded.

She turned round to him and said:

'Show me.'

Under a cloudless sky that evening, they all went into the Ark. After they had seen to the animals, they assembled in their own living-room; and when they were together, Noah said:

'Let us now call on the Lord God to bless our enterprise. Let us pray that the light of His countenance may be a shining beacon, our faith in Him a sure shield, through all the perils which confront us.'

Young or old, thoughtful or frivolous, believing or unbelieving, they fell upon their knees, each of them in their separate way moved by a sense of their own littleness, the knowledge of their own ignorance. And, as Noah prayed, it seemed to them that the beating of their hearts kept time to his words, at first gently, then more loudly, until the words were lost in the monotony of its rhythm … and they knew that what they heard was just the beating of the rain upon the roof.

A Man Greatly Beloved

(1950)

I

I am fifteen, and extremely advanced for my years. This is not self-recommendation which, as the youngest of us has been told much too often, is no praise, but a *précis* of last term's report by Julia Prendergast, Headmistress, on Antonia Fell, Modern VIb. I am Antonia Fell, and most people call me Tony. I do not care for either of these names, and would rather have been christened Amaryllis and called Meriel for short, which is what I should have been if immersed when of riper years. In the novel which I am writing the heroine is so named and is the admiration of all. I have a father and a mother, as so often happens to young people, and a little brother of thirteen, which is not so inevitable. He was christened Charles Robert. Father calls him Robert and Mother calls him Paddy and I call him Bill, which is somewhat confusing for elderly visitors who have just dropped in. However, life goes on just as if they weren't confused.

What I am going to tell you about is the Strange Case of John Anderson. This is not the my Jo John whose bonny brow was brent, but the one who came to live at Essington, which is our village.

I am not quite sure whether I ought to describe the village or Father first. This is the sort of thing which the experienced writer knows by instinct, and I don't; being inexperienced. Probably whichever I do I shall feel when I read it through afterwards that it ought to have been the other one. This will be a pity, because it is too late when you only have one small exercise-book, and the big one is being kept for the novel. So I shall take a chance and start with Father.

Father is the Vicar of Essington. Most of his opinions are out of date, as is natural to a Vicar who has to believe what people believed before they knew that the earth was round and had taken millions of years getting that way; and so we don't agree on quite a lot of things. He doesn't know this, because I am careful not to argue with him. There is no object in arguing unless you want to convince the other person that you are right. I argued with Prendy about getting off net-ball now I was in the Sixth, even if VIb. We remained of our own opinions still, but I did try to convince her that she was wrong, although without visible success. But if I convinced Father that he was wrong, then he would have to resign his living and we should starve, which would be lamentable for all. Of course, when my novel is published and makes a lot of money, then it won't matter so much. So I am really waiting for that. Meanwhile I go to church twice every Sunday, when I would much sooner be writing my novel.

Father looks like an actor; and though it is a sad thing to say of one's father, a very bad actor at that. Perhaps if he were really an actor, I should say that he looked like a Vicar and a very good Vicar. He has a deep voice, and deep soul-compelling eyes; and his thick black hair, just beginning to go grey at the sides, is full of curls which he ought to have given to me, but hasn't, having wasted them on Bill. Altogether he is the sort of father you feel rather proud of and nervous about simultaneously, wondering whether the new visitor can take it. I mean some people say 'What a handsome man for a Vicar, my dear'; and others raise their eyebrows, as if he had gone too far. It depends on what you're used to. He is very eloquent in the pulpit, if you don't think about what he is saying but only how he says it, and in the home he makes everything sound just as religious and deep meaning, even if he is asking Mother where she left the Slug Death.

Mother is lovely in every way, and I am devoted to her. Bill is a nice little boy, but of course only a child. Mother calls him Paddy, because he was the next best thing, Father having ordered another daughter. There used to be a book called 'Paddy-the-next-best-thing', and the reason why Father didn't want him was because he feared that Vicars' sons always went to the bad. Bill hasn't gone to the bad yet, being a bit young for it and getting a prize for Divinity last term. Next term he will be at Harrow, which is where you generally begin going to the bad if you have any leaning that way. We shall have to wait and see.

Essington is a pleasant little, old-world village, but the only building in it of antiquarian interest to the visitor is Ballards, a charming black-and-white cottage dating from the thirteenth century—photograph on p. 81. That comes from *Rural Rambles Round England*, which I got for half a three-legged race at the sports; and my friends at school were greatly surprised when I showed them the photograph and told them that I had often been inside it. It is not often that one goes inside a photograph in a book. Father was more hurt than surprised, because the author said nothing about his church being of antiquarian interest, and it quite spoilt his breakfast. He kept on asking for the book again, in case a bit about it had got into some other chapter by mistake, and muttering to himself when it didn't. I was hoping that he would decide to take me away from school and send me somewhere where they didn't have sports, but his dislike of *Rural Rambles Round England* didn't seem to go as deep as that, and I went back at the end of September as usual. Of course what I am really hoping is that one day, in a later edition, the author will add: 'My literary readers will doubtless wish to make an excursion to the famous Vicarage where Antonia Fell, our great woman novelist, was born.'

But it looks as though I shall have to wait a little for that.

II

It is now time that our great woman novelist introduced you to the hero of her story. But as I wasn't there all the time, being at school,

I must explain first how it is that I can tell you about it. Authors don't do this as a rule, being unable. I read a book once about a woman dying alone on a prairie, and it went on for pages describing her last dying thoughts; and I did wonder, being very young at the time, how the author got to know them so well when he wasn't there and couldn't have been told by anybody. Of course I am aware now that this is the Art of the Novelist. But when he is telling you a true story, and is one of the characters in it, then the Art of the Novelist hasn't got so much scope, and he can't describe people's dying thoughts unless he says 'Probably' or 'It may well be'. Of course his Art encourages him to touch up conversations a little, particularly anything which he said himself, and I shall probably do this, but you will have to guess for yourselves what my characters are thinking. Except when I tell you of my own ruminations.

Well, Father is the Vicar, and has to take a spiritual interest in everybody in the village, which is quite different from being nosey, but has the same result. And Father always tells Mother everything, mostly twice. So when Mother goes into the kitchen to see Rose (who is our cook and has been with us since I was born, which shows what a sweet thing Mother is) naturally they talk about everything including what Father said. In the holidays I spend a good deal of time in the kitchen, because I shall be living in a little flat in Chelsea one day doing my own cooking, and Rose and I are very great friends in consequence. So I really know everything, including when Father gives Mother a melodious cough meaning 'Not before the child'.

I was only ten when old Mrs Hetherington died, but of course I remember her well, and I remember my excitement when I heard that Ballards had been sold, and wondering who the new owner would be, and whether he would have any great influence on my young life; because Ballards is the sweetest cottage, and I was always in and out of it when Mrs Hetherington was alive, and she left me a moonstone necklace which I used to wear in bed, because I was too young to wear it in the daytime, and Father wanted to lock it up until I was older, but Mother said, 'Who would look in a child's bedroom for jewels?' and as the answer was Nobody, I was allowed to keep it under my handkerchiefs when I had any, which is why I wore it in bed when nobody but myself could see; but I don't now, that sort of excitement wearing off very quickly.

(I fear that my memories have run away with me, and I shall try to make my sentences shorter in future.)

Ah me!

How young one was!

'A Mr John Anderson,' said Father at breakfast on that well-remembered morning. He made it sound like the Archbishop of Canterbury.

'Coo! I bet he stinks,' said Bill.

Bill had just inherited this unlovely word from one of the choir-boys, and couldn't be separated from it. Father told him to leave the room and not come back until he had learnt to talk like a gentleman. He went out, and should be there still, but being in the middle of his porridge, he began to cry, and Mother brought him back. He was only eight. The conversation was then resumed.

'Married?' asked Mother.

'I presume so,' said Father, as if this state were natural. Little did he know that his only daughter would never marry, an author's books being her progeny.

'When do they move in?'

'Any moment, I understand. The house is in perfect condition, of course.'

'Shall I still be allowed to go there, Mummy?' I asked.

'When I have called, darling, and if Mrs Anderson invites you,' said Mother.

'When will that be?' I piped. I am afraid I was very young then, asking all these silly questions, but I want my readers to feel that I am hiding nothing from them.

'Next holidays, perhaps,' said Mother.

That's the worst of school, it interrupts the holidays so remorse-lessly. I said, 'Oh dear,' and changed the subject, not caring to think of the coming term.

But I couldn't wait all that time. So in the afternoon I got on my bicycle and rode over to Ballards, which is only three minutes away on a bicycle, and there was Mr John Anderson and a large furniture van, and the one was superintending the unloading of the other. There were furniture men too, but they had aprons, so one knew at once which was Mr Anderson. He was the very big, elderly one.

'Good morning,' I said to him.

'Good morning,' he replied.

'Are you Mr John Anderson?' I asked.

'I am,' he said.

'I am Miss Antonia Fell,' I announced.

He gave me a funny little dip of the head, not having a hat on. He had a sad sort of face, not unhappy-sad, but wistful-sad, like a spaniel's when you have to explain that you can't take him for a walk. I think it is possible that Alfred, Lord Tennyson's cocker spaniel wanted to be taken for a walk just when his master was beginning 'Tears, Idle Tears', and it was this which gave it that yearning sadness.

'My father is the Vicar of this parish,' I said rather grandly. People generally say 'Oh' when I impart this information, but there are many ways of saying it. I should describe his as really wondering more if the wardrobe could possibly make its way into the house, and what he would do if it couldn't.

'Are you married?' I asked.

'No.' He was silent for a long time, as if thinking of something else, and then said, 'Are you?'

'No,' I replied. I didn't say that I was bound to celibacy, not having decided on this at that time, but I did explain that I was only ten, and that in England one couldn't be married until one was fourteen, though in hot climates like India it was different. He didn't seem to know this. Of course I see now that he may have been still wondering about his wardrobe.

I stood, leaning over my bicycle and shifting about from one foot to another (I was very young and *gauche* in those days), and whenever he looked in my direction I smiled at him, and then I rang my bell once or twice to see if it was working, and at last he said, 'Well, thank you very much for calling' and went into the house. So I got on to my bicycle and rode home. Do I need to tell my readers that I am bitterly aware of my lack of poise throughout this encounter, and that though it was not until last Easter that Miss Prendergast informed my parents that I was much more poised this term, I had been uncomfortable about it long before that?

But five years ago I was a carefree child, and you can imagine with what pride I told them all about it at tea. But when I told them that he wasn't married, Father said that I was a very rude little girl to have asked such a personal question; a remark which I attributed at the time to jealousy, because Father asks people if they are saved, which is much more personal.

Well, that was how I met Mr John Anderson, and I didn't see him again until the Christmas holidays, as I had to go back to school. Although I was only ten, I was already going to boarding-school, because I am so advanced for my years.

Of course by Christmas Father and Mother had got to know him, and he was what is called *persona grata* in Essington society. So now I will tell you what I knew about him, both from the inhabitants of the Vicarage and my friends in the village.

He was fifty-five, and had retired from business; but as he hadn't told anybody what business he had retired from, it was thought to be something that one wouldn't want to linger on in conversation. Like suspenders. Because when at a dinner-party one of the guests says, 'I remember when I was Governor of the Bermudas,' it is rather a falling-off and embarrassing for all concerned, if you say at the end of his story, 'That reminds me of when I was making suspenders.' Far better to remark, 'Of course in the business world we often get examples of what you were saying. I remember in 1923,' leaving it possible that you were Lord Mayor of London in 1924.

This was the first time he had lived in the country, he had always wanted to, but if you're in business in the City you cannot unless you go up to London every day, which isn't living in the country, and isn't really country if it is as near to London as that. Of course he might have gone to Nottingham and made lace like the Beaver, but somehow we were sure that London had been his commercial home. And he had brought a man and his wife from London to look after him, a Mr and Mrs Watkins. He had only engaged them a few weeks before coming to Essington, so all their confidences revolved round His Lordship. Mr Watkins had been with His Lordship for years and years, and had only left him because he wanted to be with Mrs Watkins; but when you asked him what Lordship, he suddenly remembered that he hadn't polished the silver, and you had to run along.

Well, that was all we had found out by Christmas, and now I suppose I ought to describe his looks, because if you can't get a picture of him in your mind, this story might as well not have been written. It is very difficult to describe looks. The easiest way would be to say that he looked a little like an overgrown, slightly moth-eaten Uncle James, only then I should have to describe my Uncle James, which would be difficult again. Of course if he looked like the King or Mr Churchill, then that would tell you all you want to know, but people are rarely so obliging.

He was big and slow-moving, and he walked with the fingers of his hands open. I don't know if that matters but he did. He had a big, clean-shaven face, rather like what Long John Silver's must have been. His hair was grey and sort of fuzzy-looking, as if it had been singed, and if you rubbed it, it would all rub off. He had those lost-dog eyes I told you about, but only when he wasn't really talking to you. When he was interested in what you were saying, his eyes were quiet and kind, and suddenly he would be quite boyish, and he would laugh very softly to himself, as if he didn't want to wake his memories. I told myself later on, when I understood life better, that he had lost some-body very near and dear, and was always remembering; and some-times, if you were lucky, you could make him forget. So I never knew whether he was really a little deaf, as they said, or just remembering.

He was the kindest man I ever knew.

But of course I didn't really know him at all in those holidays, so I shall now pass lightly over two years and come to when I was twelve.

III

Father once preached for twenty minutes on the difference between 'requisite' and 'necessary', the chief one, which he didn't think fit to mention, being that they are spelt differently. My own feeling about this sermon was that it was neither. Of course one can't go on about goodness and Moses Sunday after Sunday, but I did think that he was getting a little out of his depth that morning through not knowing anything about the ways of writers. The author of 'Dearly beloved brethren' used both words, either because (a) he liked the sound of them together; or (b) meant to cross out one of them when he had made up his mind which, but forgot; or (c) was afraid he was on the short side anyway, and didn't want to waste anything. In the same way we need not ask ourselves why I have already written fifteen pages in my exercise-book, and am only just beginning. Every real author knows that the first anxiety of literary composition is how one can possibly drag the story out so that it gets up to the sixth page of one's exercise-book, and that the next is what one will do for another exercise-book when the thirty-two pages are finished. Because one is suddenly filled with the sustaining knowledge that one could go on for ever. So in future I shall try not to be so discursive, but confine myself to a straightforward narration of events. It will be difficult, because I fear that I am of the same school as Mr Henry Fielding and the Rev. Laurence Sterne, who evidently had all the exercise-books they wanted.

We get most of our news of the great world from *The Spectator* and Miss Viney's Fred, Miss Viney's Fred being the more in touch with events of interest. Miss Viney lives at Rosemount, and I always go to see her on the first day of the summer holidays, which is partly politeness and partly raspberries. She is a very nice lame person, and gets along quickly with a stick in a sort of wriggle from side to side, which makes her seem more bustling than she really is. Fred is her nephew. He works in a Bank in London; and owing to being said Good-morning to by all sorts of influential people, gets to know things like how many husbands Myrna Loy has had and if we have a secret naval base in the Black Sea.

So Miss Viney asked if he knew anything about a Mr John Anderson of London who had lately come to live among us, because of course we were all wanting to know if it really *was* suspenders. I suppose she must have described him very carefully, so it was not surprising that once again Miss Viney's Fred came to our help. Miss Viney showed me his letter, I mean the part she was letting me read.

It said:

'There was a Superintendent John Anderson who retired last year, one of the Big Four at Scotland Yard, would that be the man? Don't you remember the Luton case, the one that first put him on the map? And then the Cave Murders and The Girl in the Cistern, in fact most of the really gory ones. He was badly knocked about by a gang just before he retired, and I should think, if he's your man, and he sounds just like it, that Essington must seem a haven of peace to him after all he's been through.'

So *that* was who he was! Well, of course, as soon as I had settled with the raspberries I went straight back and asked Rose about the Luton case and the Cave Murders and the Girl in the Cistern, because she reads it all in the Sunday papers and says it gets you out of your groove. I thought Luton was a place, I know it used to be when I was in IVA, but it was the man's name, and he strangled his wife and buried her under the floor of the summerhouse, which is a very good place which nobody thinks of, and was pursued to Morocco; and I was too young to hear about the Cave Murders which were just murders in a cave, and Rose says that the girl whose body was found in the cistern wasn't murdered by the man who was hanged, but by somebody else. I suppose this often happens.

Well, you can imagine how interesting this was, and I just couldn't wait to find out if it was really our Mr Anderson. So I got on my bicycle and went to Ballards. Of course I shouldn't have done this at my present age, but I was only a child.

Mr Anderson and I were great friends by this time, and as soon as he saw me he led the way to the sort of little terrace behind Ballards, and Mr Watkins brought out drinks. I had some orange-squash with ice in it, and he had a glass of sherry. He asked me all about the last term, and I told him, because I never mind this in the first week of the holidays, and only stupid people ask you about it in the last week. Mr Anderson never did. And then, heartened by the orange-squash but a little swallowy, I put my question to him. I must remind my readers that this was a long time ago, and I was only twelve.

'Mr Anderson,' I began, and swallowed.

'Yes, dear?'

'Are you the Superintendent Anderson who solved the Luton case?'

I only asked him about this one, because I didn't want him to think that I knew about the one I was too young for, and even in those distant days I could feel how tactless it would be to ask him about the one when he hanged the wrong man.

He was just going to drink, and he stopped and put his glass of sherry very slowly down on the little table in front of us. Then he picked it up and drank it off.

'Who told you that, Tony?' he said in a sort of muffled voice.

'*Are* you?' I asked obstinately and very rudely.

He shrugged his big shoulders, and said, as if it had nothing to do with him, 'I don't think it can ever be claimed that one man solved a case. It wouldn't be fair to all the others who helped.'

'But you can say that but for one man it *wouldn't* have been solved,' I said rather cleverly.

'Well, yes, sometimes perhaps.'

'And were you that man?'

'If you must have an answer—I suppose I was. Perhaps everybody wouldn't think so. There was a Sergeant Blythe who—' He broke off suddenly and said, 'Are you greatly interested in crime?'

'No!' I said indignantly.

'Neither am I.'

'I think it's silly.'

'Most of it is,' he agreed. Of course, he wasn't really agreeing with me, because I meant it was silly to read detective stories like Bill, and he meant it was silly to be a criminal.

The silence got rather oppressive after that, so I said meekly, 'I'm sorry I asked you, but I just wanted to know if that was who you were.'

He nodded, and murmured, 'Miss Viney's Fred,' and I blushed, being liable to this in those days.

'I want you to understand,' he said at last. 'Look!' And he pointed.

'You mean Ballards?'

'Yes.'

'It's just too lovely,' I said, 'because it is the loveliest house I have ever seen.'

'Can you understand that there are horrible things in the world which one mustn't talk about in its presence?'

'Yes,' I whispered.

'And then—look!'

He brought his hand round in a sort of semi-circle, and there was the garden a glory of snapdragons and marigolds and mallows and hollyhocks, and beyond it the quiet meadow going down to the stream, with the brown cows gently swishing their tails, and the hum of bees in the peaceful blueness of the morning. I felt rather choky, it was all so beautiful suddenly.

'Do you understand,' he said, 'that, sitting here, one just can't think of men and women, people like ourselves, shut away, seeing nothing but a little patch of sky through a barred window?'

'But if they were wicked,' I said, 'weren't you right to put them there?'

'Who is to say how wicked each one of us is?' he said gently. 'Who knows but God?'

Somehow when he talked about God like that it seemed real to me, as it never does in Father's voice.

'Yes,' I said.

He poured himself a little more sherry, and drank it. Then he wiped his mouth and said:

'So that is why I am just Mr Anderson here.'

'Yes, Mr Anderson,' I said humbly.

'Or, of course, Uncle John to my little Tony, if she likes,' he added, looking down at me with his funny smile.

'Oh!' I cried, and put my arms round him, and kissed him. It was the first time I had kissed him. I am not one of those girls who treat kisses lightly.

'Let's go and look at the raspberries,' he said, getting up and blowing his nose.

Full though I was of raspberries, I went.

IV

The news that our Mr Anderson had been one of the Big Four soon became what Mademoiselle Stouffet (more widely known as Stuffy) would call *un secret de polichinelle dans le village*. At least, I think she would. For the benefit of those of my readers who never reached Modern VIʙ I will translate this as meaning that everybody now knew it but nobody talked about it. In case anybody thinks that it was I who betrayed Mr Anderson's secret, I will merely remark that all Essington knows anything which Miss Viney's Fred has told her, and that it was because of me telling everybody that Mr Anderson didn't want to talk about it that nobody did. For we were all too fond of him to disregard his wishes.

Nevertheless it made a difference in our feeling for him. He had always been everybody's friend, but now he had a sort of halo of authority which made us look up to him. He took a great interest in cricket, though too old to play, and was ever ready to umpire in our matches, which is an unrewarding task, leading to acrimony and disillusion. Yet now he had only to lift a finger up, and all argument was stayed. This is unusual in village cricket. If Mr Prossett of The Three Fishermen was having a little trouble round about closing time, which I understand is when you most often have a little trouble, a hasty message down the road to Mr Anderson, and all was harmonious again. When he was unanimously elected People's Churchwarden, it was at the back of everybody's mind that *he* wouldn't help himself from the plate. I don't wish to imply that Churchwardens generally do this, but it is a thing which it is easy to suspect other people of doing when you haven't the chance of doing it yourself. And I blush for my sex (this is not a real blush, of course) to have to admit that it is mostly the women who suspect other women's husbands of behaving in this nefarious manner.

And to give one last example of our hero's position in the village I will add that when one of the inmates escaped from the County Asylum seven miles away, and was understood to be making in our direction, mothers just said calmly, 'I suppose Mr Anderson has been told,' and went on with their washing. How different from the escape six years earlier when even I was not allowed to leave the Vicarage unattended by Father and a sheep-dog.

Of course Uncle John had been elected Vice President of the Cricket Club, the Football Club, the Horticultural Society, the Archaeological Society and the Girl Guides Association as soon as he arrived in the village, but these are honorary posts entitling the holder to subscribe not less than a guinea a year to the funds of the Society. Now he was promoted to President of most of these organizations and Treasurer of all of them. In fact, he became not only the most loved but the most influential person in Essington. Some would add politely, 'After the Vicar, of course.' But I think that he had more influence than Father. When Father said anything, people thought, 'Well, of course, he had to say that, because he's a parson.' But when Mr Anderson said it, he was just a man like themselves, and this made it more believable. His goodness was part of himself. To be with him was to feel it.

V

That was a short chapter, because now I have to tell you that he died. He died quite suddenly a few weeks ago of a stroke. I don't know enough to explain what this is, but it is something which comes suddenly to people of a certain age. It happened on the last day of term, and the first news which greeted me when I got home was that my dear Uncle John was dead. I was very unhappy, even though it was the beginning of the holidays.

Father had a telegram from a solicitor in London asking him to make arrangements for the funeral, and saying that he would come down as soon as he could, but it mightn't be for a few days. So we decided to give him a public funeral; by which I mean that we, and by 'we' I mean the village of Essington, were going to pay for it and not take the money back from the solicitor. So one of the first questions to decide was what we were to put on the tombstone.

'I know!' I said suddenly at supper that night.

'What, darling?' asked Mother.

'"He was a good man and did good things,"' I said rather proudly.

Father cleared his throat musically and feared that he did not recognize the text. I was not surprised, because his reading has been different from mine, so I explained that it came from *The Woodlanders* by Thomas Hardy, and was what Marty said of Giles Winterbourne. Father raised his noticeable eyebrows.

'Thomas Hardy?' he said, in the voice of one who had been expecting Isaiah. 'An unsuitable choice for a churchyard, Antonia.' Mother shook her head gently at me, meaning, 'Don't go on now. I'll explain afterwards.' She often does this.

Mother said rather diffidently, 'Couldn't you just put those few words from Daniel, dear? "A man greatly beloved"?'

'Daniel X. 11,' said Father at once. 'As it happens, I had already chosen that as my text on Sunday.'

The funeral was on Saturday, and I could see him feeling a little hurt at Mother's suggestion; because it was such a perfect text for a valedictory sermon, and if it were already ordered for the gravestone, everybody would know about it, and its announcement on Sunday would be less dramatic. Father has to think of these things.

Mother, who always knows what Father is thinking, said, 'There's no real hurry, of course, we can't give orders for the stone until we have seen the solicitor.'

'He has given me a free hand, my love, and it is the village's responsibility.'

'But not to choose the date of his birth, dear.'

'True,' said Father, and he gave her a little smile, partly because he loves her (and who could help it?) and partly because he saw that now his sermon wouldn't be spoilt. So that was what we decided.

A funeral is a terrible thing, even if you don't care much about the person. The grave is so deep, and so concluding. He was my first dead friend, and I could not stop my tears. This is not a thing I like doing in public, but the whole village was there, and everybody was crying, so I did not mind. And on Sunday Father's sermon sounded so beautiful that the tears came again; as they are coming now while I write this. But then they would come anyhow, I expect, even if I were writing about an imaginary person who died in my novel.

On Monday the solicitor arrived. He went into Father's study, and was there for a long time. When they came out, Father looked utterly shattered.

I think I shall put some dots here …

Because Mr Anderson's real name was John Luton. And he strangled his wife …

I thought at first that he had told me lies about himself on that
morning three years ago, and I couldn't have borne it. But if you read
what I have written, you will see that he didn't. He was in prison
for fifteen years, and when he came out he changed his name to
Anderson, but I don't think he meant it to be the name of the man
who had arrested him. Or perhaps he did. I don't know very much
about him. Except that, when I knew him, he was a good man and
did good things.

It still says on his tombstone 'A man greatly beloved'. But Father
added a text from the 31st Psalm; and though I have often differed
from Father, I felt that he had chosen the last perfect words for the
story of my dear Uncle John.

*'Into thy hands I commend my spirit: for thou hast redeemed me,
O Lord, thou God of truth.'*

The Rise and Fall of Mortimer Scrivens

(1950)

Extract from 'Readers' Queries' in *The Literary Weekly*:

Q.   What is it which determines First Edition values? Is it entirely a question of the author's literary reputation?

A.   Not entirely, but obviously to a great extent. An additional factor is the original size of the first edition, which generally means that an established author's earliest books are more valuable than his later ones. Some authors, moreover, are more fashionable than others with bibliophiles, for reasons not always easy to detect; nor does there seem to be any explanation why an author, whose reputation as a writer has never varied, should be highly sought after by collectors at one time, and then suddenly become completely out of fashion. So perhaps all that we can say with confidence is that prices of First Editions, like those of everything else, are determined by the Laws of Supply and Demand.

Mr Henry Winters to Mr Brian Haverhill
DEAR MR HAVERHILL,

It may be within your memory that on the occasion of an afternoon visit which you and Mrs Haverhill were good enough to pay us two years ago I was privileged to lend her Chapman's well-known manual on the Viola, which, somewhat surprisingly, she had never come across; I say surprisingly, for undoubtedly he is our greatest authority on the subject. If by any chance she has now read it, I should be very much obliged by its return at your convenience. I would not trouble you in this matter but for the fact that the book is temporarily out of print, and I have been unable therefore to purchase another copy for myself.

Miss Winters is away for a few days, or she would join me in sending compliments to you and Mrs Haverhill.

Yours very truly,
HENRY WINTERS

Mr Brian Haverhill to Mr Henry Winters
DEAR WINTERS,

I was much distressed to get your letter this morning and to discover that Sally and I had been behaving so badly. It is probably as much my fault as hers, but she is away with her people in Somerset just now, and I think must have taken your book with her; so for the moment I can do nothing about it but apologize humbly for both of us. I have of course written to her, and asked her to send it back to you at once, or, if it is here in the house, to let me know where she has hidden it.

Again all my apologies,
Yours sincerely,
BRIAN HAVERHILL

Brian Haverhill to Sally Haverhill
DARLING,

Read the enclosed and tell me how disgraced you feel—and how annoyed you think Winters is. I don't care for that bit about purchasing another copy for himself. He meant it nasty-like, if you ask me. Still, two years is a long time to take over a book, and you ought to have spelt it out to yourself more quickly. I could have helped you with the longer words.

The funny thing is I don't seem to remember anything about this viola book, nor whether it is the sort you play or the sort you grow, but I do seem to remember some other book which he forced on us— essays of some sort, at a guess. Can you help? Because if there were two, we ought to send both back together. I have staved him off for a bit by saying that you were so devoted to Chapman that you had taken the damned book with you. It doesn't sound likely to me, but it may to him. And why haven't we seen Winters and his saintly sister for two years? Not that I mind—on the contrary—but I just wondered. Are we cutting them or are they cutting us? One would like to know the drill in case of an accidental meeting in the village.

My love to everybody, and lots of a very different sort to your darling self. Bless you.

Your

BRIAN

Sally Haverhill to Brian Haverhill

Darlingest, I did mean to ring you up last night but our line has broken down or the rent hasn't been paid or something, and I couldn't do it in the village, not properly.

How awful about Mr Winters! It was flowers of course, silly, not musical instruments, because I was talking about violas to him when you were talking about the Litany to Honoria, I remember it perfectly, I was wearing my blue-and-yellow cotton, and one of her stockings was coming down. But you're quite right about the other one, it was called *Country Filth* and very disappointing. It must be somewhere. Do send them both back at once, darling—you'll find Chapman among the garden books—and say how sorry I am. And then I'll write myself. Yes, I think he's really angry, he's not a very nice man.

No, I don't think we've quarrelled. I did ask them both to our cocktail party a few weeks later, but being strict T.T's which I only found out afterwards, Honoria was rather stiff about it. Don't you remember? And then I asked them to tea, and they were away, and then I sort of felt that it was their turn to write. I'll try again if you like when I come home …

Brian Haverhill to Sally Haverhill
DARLING SAL,
1. Don't try again.
2. I have found Chapman nestling among the detective stories. I deduced that it would be there as soon as you said garden books.
3. Books aren't called *Country Filth*, not in Honoria's house anyway, and if they were, what would you be hoping that they were like? Tell your mother that I'm surprised at you.
4. There are a thousand books in the library, not to mention hundreds all over the place, and I can't possibly look through them all for one whose title, size, colour and contents are completely unknown to me. So pull yourself together, there's a dear, and send me a telegram with all that you remember about it.
5. I adore you. BRIAN.

Sally Haverhill to Brian Haverhill
Something about country by somebody like Morgan or Rivers sort of ordinary size and either biscuit colour or blue all my love Sal.

Country Tilth: The Prose Ramblings of a Rhymester by Mortimer Scrivens (Street & Co.)
Ramble the First: *A World Washed Clean*.
Long ere His Majesty the Sun had risen in His fiery splendour, and while yet the first faint flush of dawn, rosy herald of His coming, still lingered in the east, I was climbing (but how blithely!) the ribbon

of road, pale-hued, which spanned the swelling mother-breasts of the downland. At melodic intervals, with a melancholy which little matched my mood, the lone cry of the whimbrel …

Brian Haverhill to Sally Haverhill

O Lord, Sally, we're sunk! I've found the damned book—*Country Tilth* by Mortimer Scrivens. It's ghastly enough inside, but outside—darling, there's a large beer-ring such as could never have been there originally, and looking more like the ring made by a large beer-mug than any beer-ring ever did. You can almost smell the beer. I swear I didn't do it, I don't treat books like that, not even ghastly books, it was probably Bill when he was last here. Whoever it was, we can't possibly send it back like this.

What shall I do?

1. Send back Chapman and hope that he has forgotten about this one; which seems likely as he didn't mention it in his letter.
2. Send both back, and hope that he's a secret beer-drinker and made the mark himself.
3. Apologize for the mark, and say I think it must be milk.
4. Get another copy and pass it off as the one he lent us. I suppose Warbecks would have it.

What do you advise? I must do something about the viola book soon, I feel. I wish you were here …

Sally Haverhill to Brian Haverhill
One and four, darling. Sal.

Mr Brian Haverhill to Messrs Warbecks Ltd.
Dear Sirs,
I shall be glad if you can find me a first edition of *Country Tilth* by Mortimer Scrivens. It was published by Street in 1923.

If it is a second-hand copy, it is important that it should be fairly clean, particularly the cover. I should doubt if it ever went into a second edition.

Yours faithfully,

BRIAN HAVERHILL

Mr Brian Haverhill to Mr Henry Winters

DEAR WINTERS,

I now return your book with our most profound apologies for keeping it so long. I can only hope that you were not greatly inconvenienced by its absence. It is, as you say, undoubtedly the most authoritative work on the subject, and our own violas have profited greatly by your kindness in introducing us to it.

Please give my kindest regards to Miss Winters if she is now with you. I hope you are both enjoying this beautiful weather.

Yours sincerely,

BRIAN HAVERHILL

Mrs Brian Haverhill to Mr Henry Winters

DEAR MR WINTERS,

Can you ever forgive me for my unpardonable carelessness in keeping that delightful book so long? I need hardly say that I absorbed every word of it, and then put it carefully away, meaning to return it next morning, but somehow it slipped my memory in the way things do—well, it's no good trying to explain, I must just hope that you will forgive me, and when I come home—I am staying with my people for three weeks—perhaps you will let us show you and Miss Winters how well our violas are doing now—thanks entirely to you!

A very nice message to Miss Winters, please, and try to forgive,

Yours most sincerely,

SARAH HAVERHILL

Sally Haverhill to Brian Haverhill

DARLING,

I hope you have sent the book back because I simply grovelled to the man yesterday, and I had to say I hoped they'd come and see our violas when I got back, but of course it doesn't mean anything. What I meant by my telegram was send the book back, which I expect you've done, and try and get a copy of the other just in *case* he remembers later on. If it's such a very bad book it can't cost much. Bill is here for a few days and says that he never makes beer-rings on books, and it must be one of *your* family, probably Tom, and Mother says that there is a way of removing beer-rings from books if only she could remember what it was, which looks as though she must have got the experience from my family not yours, but it doesn't help much. Anyhow I'm sure he's forgotten all about the book, and it was clever of you to find it, darling, and I do hope my telegram helped …

Messrs Warbecks Ltd. to Mr Brian Haverhill

DEAR SIR,

We have received your instructions re *Country Tilth*, and shall do our best to obtain a copy of the first edition for you. If it is not in stock, we propose to advertise for it. We note that it must be a fairly clean copy.

Assuring you of our best attention at all times,

Yours faithfully,

H. & E. Warbecks Ltd.

(p.p. J. W. F.)

Mr Henry Winters to Mr Brian Haverhill

DEAR MR HAVERHILL,

I am glad to acknowledge receipt of *The Care of the Viola* by Reynolds Chapman which arrived this morning. My impression was that the copy which I had the pleasure of lending Mrs Haverhill two years ago was a somewhat newer and cleaner edition, but doubtless the passage of so long a period of time would account for the difference. I am not surprised to hear from Mrs Haverhill that the book has been of continued value to her. It has been so to me, whenever in my possession, for a good many years.

Yours very truly,
HENRY WINTERS

Brian Haverhill to Sally Haverhill
DARLING SALLY,

Just to get your values right before you come back to me: it is the Haverhills who are cutting the Winterses, and make no mistake about it. I enclose his foul letter. From now on no grovelling. Just a delicate raising of the eyebrows when you meet him, expressing surprise that the authorities have done nothing and he is still about.

Warbecks are trying to get another copy of *Country Tilth*, but I doubt if they will, because I can't see anybody keeping such a damn silly book. Well, I don't mind if they don't. Obviously Winters has forgotten all about it, and after his ill-mannered letter I see no reason for reminding him …

Sally Haverhill to Brian Haverhill
SWEETIE PIE,

What a *brute* the man is, he never even acknowledged my letter, and I *couldn't* have been nicer. I think you should definitely tell Warbecks that you don't want the book now, and if he *does* ask for it ever, you either say that he never lent it to you, or else send back the copy we've got, and say that the beer-mark was always there because you remember wondering at the time, him being *supposed* not to have beer in the house, which was why you hadn't sent it back before, just seeing it from the outside and not thinking it could possibly be *his* copy. Of *course* I shall never speak to him again, horrible man. Mother says there used to be a Dr Winters in Exeter when she was a girl, and he had to leave the country suddenly, but of course it may not be any relation ...

Brian Haverhill to Sally Haverhill

Sally darling, you're ingenious and sweet and I love you dearly, but you must learn to distinguish between the gentlemanly lies you *can* tell and the other sort. Don't ask your mother to explain this to you, ask your father or Bill. Not that it matters as far as Winters is concerned. We've finished with him, thank God ...

Mr Henry Winters to Messrs Warbecks Ltd.

DEAR SIRS,

My attention has been fortuitously called to your advertisement enquiring for a copy of the 1st edition of Mortimer Scrivens' *Country Tilth*. I am the fortunate possessor of a 1st edition of this much sought-after item, which I shall be willing to sell if we can come to a suitable financial arrangement. I need hardly remind you that 1st editions of Mortimer Scrivens are a considerable rarity in the market, and I shall await your offer with some interest.

Yours faithfully,

HENRY WINTERS

Mr Henry Winters to Miss Honoria Winters

DEAR HONORIA,

I trust that your health is profiting by what I still consider to be your unnecessary visit to Harrogate. Do you remember a book of essays by Mortimer Scrivens called *Country Tilth*, which used to be, and had been for upwards of twenty-five years, in the middle shelf on the right-hand side of the fireplace? I have looked for it, not only there but in all the other shelves, without result, and I can only conclude that you have taken it up to your bedroom recently and that it has since been put away in some hiding place of your own. It is of the *utmost importance* that I should have this book at once, and I shall be obliged by your immediate assistance in the matter.

The weather remains fine, but I am gravely inconvenienced by your absence, and shall be relieved by your return.

Your affec. brother,

HENRY WINTERS

Miss Honoria Winters to Mr Henry Winters

DEAR HENRY

Thank you for your letter. I am much enjoying my stay here, and Frances and I have been making a number of pleasant little 'sorties' to places of interest in the neighbourhood, including one or two charming old churches. Our hotel is very quiet, thanks to the fact that it has no licence to provide intoxicating drink, with the result that an extremely nice class of person comes here. Already we are feeling the beneficial effects of the change, and I hope that when I return—on Monday the 24th—I shall be completely restored to health.

Frances sends her kindest remembrances to you, for although you have never met her, she has so often learnt of you in my letters that she feels that she knows you quite well!

Your affectionate sister,

HONORIA

P.S. Don't forget to tell Mrs Harding in advance if you are not going to London next Thursday, as this was the day when we had arranged for the window-cleaner to come. She can then arrange for any other day suitable to you. You lent that book to the Haverhills when they came to tea about two years ago, together with your viola book, I remember because you told me to fetch it for you. I haven't seen it since, so perhaps you lent it afterwards to somebody else.

Messrs Warbecks Ltd. to Mr Brian Haverhill
DEAR SIR,

re *Country Tilth*

We have received notice of a copy of the 1st edition of this book in private possession, but before entering into negotiations with the owner it would be necessary to have some idea of the outside price which you would be prepared to pay. We may say that we have had no replies from the trade, and if this copy is not secured, it may be difficult to obtain another. First editions of this author are notoriously scarce, and we should like to feel that, if necessary, we could go as high as £5, while endeavouring, of course, to obtain it for less. Trusting to have your instructions in the matter at your early convenience,

Yours faithfully,

H. & E. Warbecks Ltd.

Mr Brian Haverhill to Messrs Warbecks Ltd.
DEAR SIRS,

Country Tilth

I had assumed when I wrote to you that a first edition of this book, being of no literary value, would not have cost more than a few shillings, and in any case £1 would have been my limit, including your own commission. In the circumstances I will ask you to let the matter drop, and to send me your account for any expense to which I have put you.

Yours faithfully,

BRIAN HAVERHILL

Mr Henry Winters to Mr Brian Haverhill
DEAR SIR,

I now find, as must always have been known to yourself, that at the time of my lending Mrs Haverhill *The Care of the Viola* by Reynolds Chapman, I also lent her, or you, a 1st edition of *Country Tilth* by Mortimer Scrivens. In returning the first named book to me two years later, you ignored the fact that you had this extremely rare book in your possession, presumably in the hope that I should not notice its absence from my shelves. I must ask you therefore to return it *immediately*, before I take other steps in the matter.

Yours faithfully,

HENRY WINTERS

Mr Brian Haverhill to Messrs Warbecks Ltd.

DEAR SIRS,

This is to confirm my telephone message this morning that I am prepared to pay up to £5 for a 1st edition of *Country Tilth*, provided that it is in reasonably good condition. The matter, I must say again, is of the most urgent importance.

Yours faithfully,

BRIAN HAVERHILL

Brian Haverhill to Sally Haverhill

O hell, darling, all is discovered. I had a snorter from that devil this morning, demanding the instant return of *Country Tilth*, and this just after I had told Warbecks not to bother any more! They had written to say that they only knew of one copy in existence (I told you nobody would keep the damn thing) and that the man might want £5 for it. So naturally I said '£5 my foot'. I have now rung them up to withdraw my foot, which I had so rashly put in it, and say '£5'. But £5 for a blasted book which nobody wants to read—and just because of a beer-ring which is its only real contact with life—seems a bit hard. Let this be a lesson to all of us never to borrow books, at least never from T.T's. Alternatively, of course, to return them in less than two years—there is that …

Messrs Warbecks Ltd. to Mr Henry Winters
DEAR SIR,

Country Tilth

If you will forward us your copy of the 1st edn. of this book for our inspection, we shall then be in a position to make what we hope you will consider a very satisfactory offer for it in accordance with its condition. Awaiting a reply at your earliest convenience, as the matter is of some urgency,

Yours faithfully,

H. & E. Warbecks Ltd.

Mr Henry Winters to Mr Brian Haverhill
SIR,

Country Tilth

Unless I receive my copy of this book within 24 hours I shall be compelled to consult my solicitors.

Yours faithfully,

HENRY WINTERS

Mr Brian Haverhill to Messrs Warbecks Ltd.
DEAR SIRS,

Country Tilth

In confirmation of my telephone message this morning I authorize you to make a firm offer of £10 for the 1st edn. of this book for which you are negotiating, provided that it is delivered within the next 24 hours.

Yours faithfully,

BRIAN HAVERHILL

Messrs Warbecks Ltd. to Mr Henry Winters
SIR,

Country Tilth

We are still awaiting a reply to our letter of the 18th asking you to forward your copy of the 1st edn. of this book for our inspection. We are now authorized by our client to say that he is prepared to pay £10 for your copy, provided that its condition is satisfactory to him, and that we receive delivery of it by the 22nd inst. After that date he will not be interested in the matter.

Yours faithfully,

H. & E. Warbecks Ltd.

Mr Henry Winters to Mr Brian Haverhill

SIR,

The enclosed copy of a letter from Messrs Warbecks speaks for itself. You have the alternative of returning my book *immediately* or sending me your cheque for £10. Otherwise I shall take legal action.

H. WINTERS

Sally Haverhill to Brian Haverhill

Darling one, *what* do you think has happened!!! This morning we drove into Taunton just after you rang up, Mother having suddenly remembered it was Jacqueline's birthday to-morrow, and in a little bookshop down by the river I found a copy of *Country Tilth* in the 6d. box! Quite clean too and no name inside it, so I sent it off at once to Mr Winters, with a little letter just saying how sorry I was to have kept it so long, and not telling a single 'other sort' except for being a little sarcastic which I'm sure is quite a gentlemanly thing to be. So, darling, you needn't bother any more, and after I come back on Monday (HOORAY!) we'll go up to London for a night and spend the £10 I've saved you. What fun! Only of course you must ring up Warbecks *at once* …

Mrs Brian Haverhill to Mr Henry Winters

DEAR MR WINTERS,

I am sending back the other book you so kindly lent me. I am so sorry I kept it so long, but it had *completely* disappeared, and poor Brian has been looking everywhere for it, and worrying *terribly*, thinking you would think I was trying to steal it or something! Wasn't it crazy of him? As if you would!—and as if the book was worth stealing when I saw a copy of it in the 6d. box at Taunton this very morning! I expect you'll be wondering where I found your copy. Well, it was most odd. I happened to be looking in my dressing-case just now, and there is a flap in the lid which I hardly ever use, and I noticed it was rather bulging—and there was the book! I've been trying to remember when I last used this particular dressing-case, because it looks as though I must have taken the book away with me directly after you so kindly lent it to me, and of course I remembered that it *was* just before I came to see my people, which I do every year at this time, that we came to see you!

I must now write and tell Brian the good news, because after turning the house upside down looking for it, he was actually *advertising* for a copy to replace it, and offering £10—ten *pounds*, think of it, when its actual value is sixpence! Wouldn't it have been awful if some horrible mercenary person who happened to have a copy had taken advantage of his ignorance of book prices and swindled him? But, whatever its value, it doesn't make it any the less kind of you to have lent it to me, or careless of me to have forgotten about it so quickly.

Yours most sincerely,

Sarah Haverhill

P.S. Isn't this hot weather delightful? Just perfect for sun-bathing. I can see you and Miss Winters simply *revelling* in it.

Portrait of Lydia

(1950)

Arthur Carstairs was born in London in 1917, to the sound of one of those air-raids which have seemed so small an affair since, but which were so terrifying then. His mother was continuously frightened any-how, for her husband was a subaltern in Flanders, soon to be killed. Mrs Carstairs and her baby retired to a cottage on the outskirts of the country-town of Kingsfield, and lived as best they could on what little money there was. When he was old enough, Arthur went as a day-boy to Kingsfield Grammar School. Not surprisingly he grew up a quiet, rather shy, industrious boy, with none of the vices and few of the picturesque virtues, clinging to his mother, more from a sense of duty than because he desired no other companionship. When she died on his twentieth birthday, he had never kissed a girl, nor climbed a mountain, nor swum in the sea, nor spent a night in the open, and all the adventures he had had were adventures of the mind, romantic, exciting, but, as he well knew, not for him. Mr Margate, one of Kingsfield's three solicitors, and a good friend of his mother's, had given him his articles, and had promised him a post in the office when he had passed his finals. It seemed to him now at twenty-one that he would remain in Kingsfield for ever, a commonplace lawyer whom the world passed by. Perhaps, he thought sometimes, it would be better if he tried for a job in London when he was qualified. In London adventure waited on the doorstep, as his reading of Stevenson assured him. In London jewelled hands beckoned to you from broughams ...

On his mother's death her cottage had been sold, and he lived now in lodgings close to Mr Margate's office. Occasionally after dinner he would go round to the Cap and Bells and have a glass of beer; not because he liked beer, nor the atmosphere of public houses, but because he felt that in this way he was seeing life. He was a nice-looking boy, with an earnest, innocent face which appealed to ageing barmaids; who called him 'Ducks', as if they really meant it, and made him feel a man. And a rather highly coloured sporting gentleman called Platt, who frequented the Cap and Bells, had made friends with him one night over a double cherry-brandy, and had received, as one man of the world from another, all Arthur's confidences. This encouraged him to think more hopefully of the future. He told himself that, when he had passed his finals, he would open out a little more, spending at least three evenings a week at the Cap and Bells. He might even learn to play billiards, which Platt had offered to teach him. His own game was chess; but an offer to teach Platt chess had been unacknowledged at the time, and not repeated. Presumably, in the noisy environment of the Public Bar Platt had not heard.

On this January evening in 1939 Arthur had just finished dinner and was sitting over his books, when his landlady put her head in at the door and said suspiciously, 'There's a lady to see you.'

He looked up with a start, trying to make sense of it, and then asked nervously, 'Who is it?' He had the absurd idea that Doris the barmaid had come to fetch him, and that Mrs Heavitree didn't approve of her.

'Didn't give a name. Said she wanted to see you professionally.'

'Oh! Oh well, you see, the office is closed, and she may have gone round to Mr Margate's house, and he may be out, and she may have been sent—' He broke off, thinking ashamedly, 'Why am I such a coward, why am I apologising for what is none of her business?' and said firmly, looking as much like a solicitor as he could, 'Show her up, please, Mrs Heavitree.' As she closed the door, he hurried into his bedroom and brushed his hair. A pity that the remains of a rice pudding were on the table, but if she were a nice old lady they could laugh it off together.

There was a knock at the door. He called 'Come in!' and she came in.

Arthur stood up to receive her. He had been preparing to say 'Good evening, Mrs—er—won't you sit down and tell me what I can do for you?' What he did say was, 'Good lord!'

She was young, she was lovely, she was, everything which he had hoped that a girl might be, she was the girl of his dreams. He stood gaping at her.

She had a low, deep voice, wonderfully sweet. She said, 'Do forgive me, Mr Carstairs, for coming at this time,' and he pulled himself together and said, 'Not at all, sit down, won't you?' Apologies for the springs of the arm-chair and the death-throes of the rice pudding rose to his lips, but her pretty, 'Thank you,' and the smile she gave him left him speechless. He told himself that, as once or twice before, he had fallen asleep over his books, and presently would wake.

'Mr Carstairs,' she said, 'you are a solicitor, are you not?'

'Well—er,' he said, 'yes, and—er—no, I mean I shall be—I hope—in a short time, as soon as I have passed my final examination, but actually I'm not yet qualified. Does it matter?' he added anxiously.

'Oh dear!' she said. 'I thought you were a solicitor.'

'Well, I am in a way. What it comes to is that I could give you my advice, my help, unprofessionally, I mean without payment—but then,' he hurried on, 'of course I shouldn't want that anyhow, I mean—'

She smiled and said, 'You mean I could thank you without offending your legal etiquette?'

'Yes, of course, I mean—er—well, perhaps you had better tell me what it is. I expect it will be all right.'

'It's a question of a will. Must you have a qualified solicitor to write a will for you?'

This was easy.

'Anybody can write a will. People generally employ a solicitor so as to be sure of covering all the ground, and the solicitor employs a special legal language so as to be sure of doing this. But anybody can write in plain English on a piece of paper "I leave my gold cigarette-case to John Smith," and if it's properly signed and witnessed, John Smith gets it.'

She smiled at him delightedly and said, 'Then there you are! You read this will which my father has made, you assure him as a friend that it is legally correct, it is signed and witnessed, and then we thank you, we show our gratitude'—she held him for an endless moment with her wonderful eyes—'in any way you wish. So long, of course, as it does not include six-and-eightpence.'

She laughed as she ended, and her laughter was divine music to him. Nobody had ever laughed like that.

'That's right,' he said, laughing too.

'Then you will come with me?'

'Of course, if you really—'

'To Norton St. Giles?'

He nearly said, 'To the ends of the earth!' but stopped himself just in time.

'Norton St. Giles? I don't think I—'

'It's a village about twenty-five miles from here. We're a little way out of it. The Old Barn.'

'Twenty-five miles! I say! But I don't understand.' He frowned at her, trying to remember that he was nearly a solicitor. 'It doesn't make sense.'

She rose from the broken chair as if it were a throne, and held out her hand to him.

'Nevertheless, because I ask you, you will come—Arthur?'

He was on his feet, taking her hand in his, saying huskily that he would come, seeing the squalid room as it would be if she left him alone in it, romance and beauty gone from his life for ever. All the same, it didn't make sense. Perhaps that was what was so attractive about it.

She pressed his hand, thanking him with her eyes, and, surprisingly, sat down again. She smiled at him, and said, 'I knew I could be sure of you. So now let's make sense of it.'

He pushed his books further out of the way, and leant forward, chin on hands, watching her eagerly.

'My name is Lydia Clyde. My father and I live alone together. I am all that he has left in the world, and I am devoted to him. He is, I am afraid, a sick man.' She put her hand to her left breast. 'He may die at any moment, the doctors tell us; but he and I'—she gave a confident little laugh—'we don't believe the doctors. And yet sometimes—do you understand?—we do believe. For weeks now he has been insisting that he must make a will, so as to leave me provided for. You know how it is; one puts off doing a thing for years, telling oneself that there is no hurry, and then, when one suddenly decides to do it, every wasted minute seems of importance. So I arranged with a London friend of ours, a lawyer, to come down for a night. I would meet him at the junction, for we are many miles from a station. But he is not there! So I ring up my father, and I learn that our friend has telegraphed to say that he is prevented from coming. My father implores me to find some other lawyer and bring him back with me. He dare not put it off any longer. Foolish, unreasonable, I know, he may live for twenty years yet, but'—she shrugged her shoulders—'sick men *are* unreasonable. And I cannot have him worrying. So'—she broke off, and looked at him gratefully—'you!'

'Yes, but how'—

'You have met a man, Roger Platt, at—the Cap and Bells, is it?'

'Is he a friend of yours?' he asked, surprised.

'We have known him a long time, but that is not to say that he is a man I approve of altogether. Poor Roger! He is not'—she smiled at him confidingly—'our sort. But he has spoken to me of you. He has a great admiration for you, did you know? So, when I was so badly in need of a friend, a friend who was also a lawyer, but a friend who was young enough not to mind doing an unusual thing, I remembered suddenly what he had said of you. You will come? I have my car outside.'

'Of course,' said Arthur, flattered to think that he had made such an impression. But he looked at her in a puzzled way, for there was still something which didn't make sense.

'What is it?' she asked, suddenly alarmed.

'Your father—'

'Yes?'

'You are his only child. Then why the urgent need for a will? Everything will be yours anyhow.'

She gave him the most pathetic look which he had ever received from a human being. She turned away from him, and her lovely head drooped upon her shoulder. 'Don't you understand?' she whispered.

To show that he was a man of the world and practically a qualified solicitor he said quickly that he did, of course he did, but—and stopped, hoping that she would explain.

'I didn't want to tell you,' she murmured, 'I wanted to keep my poor little secret. But I cannot have secrets from my friend. You see, Arthur, I am his daughter, but—oh, must I say it?' She looked forlornly at him.

'Oh!' Now he understood. 'You mean—he never married your mother?'

She bowed her head.

He got up, saying, 'I'm a fool, forgive me. I'll just get my coat.' As he went into his bedroom she looked at her watch. It was 7.47.

They said little on the way. As they wound out of the half-lit streets into the deep blackness of the country lanes she asked him if he were ever frightened in a car, and he said, 'Not with you.' She gave him her hand for a moment, saying simply, 'I am a good driver and the roads will be empty.' He was too happy to be frightened. Once or twice his heart turned over, but her reassuring smile, her little apology, brought forgetfulness. They flashed through a village and she said, 'Barton Langley, half-way,' and he looked at his watch to find that it was only just after eight. Twelve-and-a-half miles, that was fifty miles an hour! Fifty miles an hour on a pitch-black night with a lovely girl, this, he told himself, was life. He closed his eyes happily, and went into a dream …

'There! Thirty-three minutes. That's as good as I've ever done at night. Come along!'

She switched off the engine, took his hand, and drew him after her. She opened the front door into darkness, saying, 'The lights went this evening, you must keep hold of me,' and he was glad to be still holding her hand. They went into a room on the left.

It was a man's room, lit now by many candles; plainly furnished with a couple of comfortable chairs and a sofa, all in green linen covers on which were brightly coloured patchwork cushions. At a gate-legged table with a check tablecloth, an elderly man was playing Patience. He rose, sweeping the cards together, as Lydia said, 'Darling, this is Mr Carstairs, who has very kindly come to help us.'

Mr Clyde bowed low from behind the table, saying, 'Mr Carstairs, I am your most obliged, humble servant.' He was an oddly old-fashioned figure, thought Arthur, in his black velvet jacket and black stock, with an eyeglass, dependent from a black ribbon, now in his eye. He had a long, pale rather melancholy face in a setting of crinkly, silver hair, but his eyes shone alertly, and his hand, as he held it out, did not tremble. After all, thought Arthur, why should Lydia's father be more than fifty? It's only the hair which makes him seem old.

'I'll get the drinks,' said Lydia. 'Have you got the will there, Father? We mustn't keep Mr Carstairs.' She took a candle and went out. Arthur turned to watch her go, saw the picture on the wall, and gave a gasp of astonishment. Mr Clyde, fumbling among some papers on his table, presumably for the will, said, 'Ah, you have seen my Corot.'

Arthur was surprised, for he did not associate Corot with nudes, and it was certainly difficult to associate him with this particular one. She sat on a rock, her crossed feet just in the water, and she was leaning back on her hands, looking up into the sunlight, her eyes bright with the joy of living. She was so real, he felt, that if he called to her she would look down and smile at him, and say, 'Ah! there you are!' happy to have found him; as Lydia was happy to have found him such a little while ago. For the face was the face of Lydia; alive; unmistakable.

He looked quickly away, and saw what he supposed was the Corot on the other wall. Pale, delicate fantasy, a dream world, an eggshell world which broke at a touch, insubstantial faeryland which somehow made the other picture doubly alive, filling the room with Lydia.

'It's lovely,' stammered Arthur, and the old man chuckled to himself.

And now Arthur was to be startled into admiration again, for on a small table in the window a chess-board was laid out, with the most elaborately carved red and white ivory men which he had ever seen. The knights were real knights, the bishops real bishops; to sit down behind them would be to fight a battle, not to play a game. He wondered how long it would take to get used to them; whether it would upset one's game not to have the familiar pieces under one's hand. He longed to try.

Lydia came back with a tray. Arthur felt shy of her suddenly. He wanted to look at the picture again, and then at her. He was afraid to look at either, to look at the picture under her eyes, or to look at her with the secret of the picture showing in his own eyes.

'I must have left it in the other room,' said Mr Clyde, coming from behind his table. 'No, no, Lydia,' he cried testily, 'I am *not* dying. I *can* walk into the other room. I am *not* going upstairs.' He took a candle and went out.

She felt his uncomfortableness. She took his hand and deliberately turned him round to the picture. They looked at it together.

'Are you shocked?' she asked gently.

He blushed and said, 'It's too beautiful for that—I've never—it's just beauty. Oh, Lydia!'

'I was a model before my father found me again. It was either that or—the other thing. You don't despise me?'

'No, no, no!'

'I think it is only a few special people who recognize me. To most it is just'—she shrugged—'Aurora or June Morning or Sea Maiden. But you are different. I knew—didn't I say so?—that I could have no secrets from you.' She pressed his hand and left it as the old man came back.

'Now, Mr Carstairs, here you are. It's quite short, as you see, and I don't want any nonsense about messuages and hereditaments, because I haven't got any. These ridiculous doctors order me from one place to another, and my life is lived, you might say, in short leases.'

Arthur read the will and said: 'It seems all right. I see you just say "my daughter Lydia". I think—'

'Exactly. As you notice, I've left a space there.'

'Well, legally—er—it's a question of—I mean—'

'I've told him, Father,' said Lydia.

'Then what are you stammering about, young man? Go ahead.'

'Well, is her name Clyde?'

'Yes. She took it by deed poll as soon as—well, some years ago.'

'That's good. Any other Christian name?'

'Lydia Rosaline,' said Lydia.

'Then I should say "my daughter Lydia Rosaline Clyde, who is now living with me", and I don't see how there could be any doubt.'

'That's what I want. Thank you.' He sat down and began to write.

'We shall need another witness, of course,' said Arthur.

'We only want two, don't we?' said Lydia. 'You and me. Why, what's the matter?'

It was absurd that anybody shouldn't know what he knew so well. He smiled at her as he would have smiled at a child, and said, 'A witness can't benefit from a will, you know. We need some other independent person. A servant will do.'

'Father, did *you* know that?'

'I take no interest in the artificialities of the Law,' said Mr Clyde grandly. 'I leave them to this young man.'

'But we have no servant here!' cried Lydia. 'A woman comes in, but she is ill and hasn't been coming this week—what are we to do?'

'One of your neighbours?'

'We hardly know them. Father's health—Oh, if I'd only known, we could have brought Roger with us!'

'Then as you didn't,' said Mr Clyde, 'may I suggest that the simplest thing would be to go and fetch him now?'

'But Father!' She looked at her watch. 'Half-past eight, I couldn't be back before nine-forty, say, and to keep Mr Carstairs waiting about all that time—'

'You'll keep him waiting about much longer, if you're going round from one strange house to another trying to persuade somebody to come out on a damned cold night, and probably getting nobody in the end. Don't you worry about Mr Carstairs, I'll look after him. You play chess, Mr Carstairs?'

'Yes, rather, I—er—'

'Well, if you'd like a game—'

'Oh, I say, I'd love it!'

'There you are, my dear, you aren't the only attraction in this house. Now then, don't waste any more time, off you go.'

'Well, if you really don't mind—Arthur?'

'It's quite all right—Lydia!'

'You're very sweet.' She gave him a warm loving smile, glanced up at her picture, and said in a low voice, 'I shall be watching over you. Look at me sometimes.' She pressed his hands. Mr Clyde busied himself with the chessmen.

It was a curious game which they played. The strangeness of the pieces; the insistent presence of Lydia; the urge to look at her which made it so difficult to concentrate on the board; a sort of nightmare feeling that he could not escape from his opponent, that every move was a foolish move to which the counter was inevitable and should have been foreseen—and then, unable to be resisted any longer, Lydia, beautiful, desirable, filling the room. The game came to an end with the noise of wheels on the gravel, so completely was it in the other man's control.

'Nine thirty-five!' cried Lydia gaily. 'I beat our record, Arthur.'

'I should say she did,' said Platt. 'Evening, Carstairs. I'm all of a tremble still.'

Arthur nodded to him; as the family solicitor might nod to some rather undesirable member of the family with whom he had a business appointment.

'It's good of you to come, my boy,' said Mr Clyde. 'Now then, Mr Carstairs, tell us what we have to do.'

'Lead me to the dotted line,' said Platt, taking out his pen, 'and watch me spell my name. You'll be surprised.'

The will was signed 'Philip Clyde', and witnessed.

'Exhausting,' said Platt, putting his pen away. 'I must have a drink, Lyd.'

'Only a small one, darling, you're going to drive us back.'

'That's nice.'

'And you'll take forty-five minutes exactly.'

'When they tell you, Carstairs, don't argue, just do it.'

'Arthur?' She looked at him, decanter poised over glass.

'Just a very little,' he said nervously. He had never drunk whisky before.

'There! And a very small one for me. I like driving fast, but I don't like being driven fast. We'll sit comfortably together at the back without hitting the roof. Through Barton Langley, Roger, it's the better way.'

'Oh, right.'

The moon had risen, relieving the blackness a little. Arthur and Lydia sat in silence together, a rug wrapped round them, clasping hands beneath. He saw nothing but her face beside him, her picture on the wall, and a magic future in which, somewhere, somehow, they were together for always ...

'The Cap and Bells,' said Platt, as the car came to rest, 'and that's that, as far as I'm concerned. Lyd, you can take Carstairs home. And a very good night to you both.'

'Thank you for everything, darling, ever so much.'

He got out of the car, waved to them, and went inside. She moved into the driver's seat, and Arthur sat next to her. It was only a few hundred yards to his lodging. The street was empty. She turned to him, holding out her arms. He clung to her, kissing her cheeks clumsily, whispering, 'Oh, darling! Oh, Lydia!' She guided his mouth to her own. He had never known such ecstasy. Oh, to die like this in her arms, his soul drawn slowly through his lips to rest in hers!

He was almost suffocating when she released him. She said smilingly, 'Better than six and eightpence?' and then, 'Darling, you must go.' She reached across him and opened the door on his side. 'Quick.'

'I shall see you again—soon?'

'I expect so,' she smiled. 'In a day or two. Good-bye, darling, and thank you a thousand times. You can't think what a help you have been.'

He was out on the pavement; she had pulled the door shut, kissed her hand and was gone. He stumbled up the stairs to his sordid little room. It was ten-thirty. Just three short hours, and he had experienced a new world. He undressed. He lay in bed in the dark, seeing her picture on the wall.

That was Tuesday. On the Thursday morning he was summoned to Mr Margate's room. Vaguely apprehensive, feeling, as he had felt ever since, that he had done something unprofessional on that evening and was to be reprimanded, he went in. There was another man there. Mr Margate said, 'Oh, good morning, Arthur. This is Inspector Wells. I'll leave you to him. Answer his questions and help him in any way you can.' Completely bewildered, a little alarmed at contact with the police, yet relieved that his conduct as a solicitor was not to be impeached, Arthur waited. The Inspector sat negligently on the corner of Mr Margate's desk, one leg swinging. He was a stocky, pleasant-looking man with a gentle, rather tired voice.

'Just a few questions,' he murmured. 'Nothing much.' He smiled in a friendly way and added, 'I can hardly ask you to sit down in your own office, but you'd be more comfortable.'

Arthur sat down.

'Never mind for the moment why I'm asking these questions. If you do happen to guess, well, you're a lawyer and can keep a confidence. That right?'

'Of course.'

'Know a man called Platt? Roger Platt?'

'I've met him once or twice.'

'When did you last see him?'

'Tuesday night.'

'Where? At what time?'

'At about ten-thirty, going into the Cap and Bells.'

The Inspector was silent for a little, swinging his leg, and then said, 'I'm trying to confirm his account of himself on Tuesday evening. It involves, among other people, some friends of his called Clyde, who live at Norton St. Giles, and yourself. Now give me *your* account.'

Arthur gave it. The Inspector smiled and said, 'I gather that the lady is not ill-looking.' Arthur blushed and said, 'Yes, I mean no.'

'All the same, if you can drive fifty miles on a dark winter's night for a lady, you can drive fifty miles for a mere policeman on a nice sunny morning. Can't you?'

Arthur couldn't keep the excitement out of his eyes and voice as he asked, 'Do you mean you want me to come with you to Norton St. Giles—now?'

416

'That's the idea. I gather that it finds favour with you.'

Arthur blushed again and said defensively, 'Well, it's better than stuffing in an office.'

'No doubt. Now just a word before we start. You would, of course, vouch for the honesty and integrity of your friends the Clydes?'

'Of course!'

'Although you only met them on Tuesday. Well, I'm not saying you're wrong. But would you also vouch for Mr Roger Platt?'

'N-no,' said Arthur. 'I suppose I wouldn't.'

'You wouldn't—and I'm not saying you're right. You see, the police can't come to these quick decisions. To the police every man might be a liar, and every woman is one. I don't feel bound to accept the Clydes' word, nor Platt's, nor yours. But if you all agree on something, then it's probably the truth. You've told me that Platt was in a certain place at nine thirty-five on Tuesday night in the company of yourself and Mr and Miss Clyde. If he was there, then he can't have been thirty-five miles away at nine-fifteen—in which case I've no more interest in him. So, with your permission, we'll just make sure that you're speaking the truth, and that that's where you were yourself at nine thirty-five. No offence?'

'Of course not.'

'Right. Then let's go. I've warned them that we're coming.'

They went out to the police-car. A constable-driver was studying a map.

'Found the way, Lewis?'

'There seems to be two ways, sir. I don't know that there's much choice.'

'Perhaps Mr Carstairs can tell us.'

Arthur was about to explain that it was much too dark to see anything, when he remembered. 'We go through Barton Langley,' he said, with the assurance of one who always did.

'That's right,' said Lewis. 'I thought that looked the better way.'

'All right, then. Step on it.'

It was like coming home to be in that room again; to see the picture, the two pictures, and the great chessmen under the window, and old Mr Clyde with his Patience spread out on the chequered tablecloth, and now, making her even dearer, Lydia in a chair before the fire busy with her needle. 'I've brought a friend of yours with me,' the Inspector had said, and her eyes had lit up, and she had cried, 'Oh, how nice!' and held out a hand to him, and the old man had chuckled and said, 'Hallo, boy, come for your revenge?' The Inspector had managed it all very tactfully, leaving Lydia a little bewildered, a little anxious for Roger, and the old man cynically amused.

'Yes, you want to keep your eye on that gentleman, Inspector. Reckless young devil. You never know what he'll be up to next. What's he done now? Didn't run over anybody, did he, when he drove Mr Carstairs back?'

'Of course he didn't, darling. I don't know what it's all about.'

'Just a matter of confirmation, Miss Clyde,' said the Inspector vaguely. 'You know how it is, one friend recommends a book, and you say "Really?" Another friend recommends it, and you say "Oh, I must get it." Then a third friend recommends it, and you really do get it. Same with evidence.'

Now he was saying good-bye to Lydia. Now he was saying good-bye to the other Lydia, the Lydia of the picture—oh, Lydia, my lovely!—and then he was in the car, and perhaps would never see her again.

'And that's where you were at nine thirty-five on Tuesday night, Mr Carstairs?'

'Yes.'

'Playing chess with Mr Clyde when Miss Clyde came back with Platt?'

'Yes.'

'Certain?'

'Yes.'

'Good enough,' said Inspector Wells regretfully, and began to talk about football.

Six years later Arthur was in Cairo. He had been half round the world; he had kissed girls of many nationalities; he had climbed mountains, swum in strange seas and spent more nights under the stars than he could count. He had seen life and he had seen death. Now he was in Cairo, having what he called a spot of leave.

A hand came on his shoulder and turned him round. He saw a pleasant-looking middle-aged man in captain's uniform.

'Carstairs, surely?' said the other. 'Though it's a long time since we met.'

'I'm afraid,' began Arthur, looking at the man again, and went on, 'Yes, but I do know your face, only—I'm sorry—I can't for the moment—'

'I used to be Inspector Wells. Field Security now. Same job really.'

'Of course! Nice to meet you again. Are you dug in here? I'm just on leave.'

'Then you must let me give you a drink. Groppi's suit you?'

'Anything you say. It's your home town.'

They sat out at a little table with their drinks, each of them, because he was in the company of someone who knew his own particular corner of England, stirred by a vague feeling of happiness.

'Did you ever see your friends the Clydes again?' asked Wells, after they had exchanged immediate news about themselves.

'No,' said Arthur shortly. He could still feel ashamed of his utter surrender to that revelation of Lydia; still remember with contempt the feverish anxiety in which he had waited for some message from her, had written to her imploringly and reckoned the hours by the deliveries of a postman who never came, had hired a bicycle at last and ridden out one Sunday to find the house in possession of new tenants who could give him no forwarding address. And although five years in the Army had put her now in her right place, some-where well below the W.A.A.F.s and the A.T.S. and the pretty Italian girls with whom he had fallen in love since, he could still imagine himself meeting her again and discovering that nothing had changed between them.

'I could give you news of them if you were interested.'

'Oh? Yes, I should like to hear.' He tried to sound indifferent, but already his heart was beating out an absurd message that she was here in Cairo—now! Was that the news?

Wells puffed at his pipe for a little, as if wondering where to begin.

'I could have told you this five years ago or more. In fact, I went round to see you, but you'd already joined up. Funny our meeting like this. I often wondered—when I asked you all those questions, did you know what I was after?'

'Not at first. I hardly ever bothered with the papers in those days. Afterwards, when I heard about the jewel robbery at Glendower House, I wondered if it was that.'

'It was.'

'And you thought Platt might have done it? I shouldn't have put it past him.'

'Well, yes and no. It wanted somebody quicker and neater and more active to do the actual robbery, but there was evidence to show that he had been interesting himself in the lay-out of the house— hanging around, taking her ladyship's maid to the pictures, that sort of thing. My idea was that he prepared the ground, and somebody else nipped in and did it. Possibly there was a third person in the background who organized it all.'

'But you never got them?'

'Oh yes, we did. Not then, but later on when they worked it again in another part of the country, and we found some of the Glendower stuff on them. And then we got the whole story out of them, from Platt chiefly. A nasty bit of work, Platt.'

'Platt?' said Arthur, astonished. 'You mean he *was* in the Glendower show?'

'Oh, yes. The girl actually did it, of course, and it was Clyde who had worked it all out. A great organizer that man, and a great artist. Pity he had to go to prison, he'd have done well in the Army.'

'The girl?' cried Arthur. 'What are you talking about, Wells? What girl?'

'Lydia.'

Arthur gave a loud mocking laugh. Wells raised his eyebrows, shrugged, and said nothing. A little disconcerted, Arthur said, 'Perhaps I'm getting it all wrong. When did the robbery take place?'

'Everybody was at dinner, all the bedrooms empty. It was the night of the Hunt Ball, but the women didn't really plaster themselves with the stuff until they were ready to start. So she made a pretty good haul. Accidentally, as we thought at first, she knocked over the ladder as she came down. It crashed on to the terrace, and brought everybody out. The moon had just risen, and they saw a figure running, sex unknown. Time, definite and fixed, nine-fifteen.'

'And twenty minutes later she was thirty-five miles away! Ha-ha!'

Wells didn't say anything, and Arthur asked a little anxiously, 'Glendower *is* thirty-five miles from Norton St. Giles, isn't it?'

'Ten miles due south of Kingsfield, and another twenty-five north. That's right.'

'Well, then!'

'This is the ingenious part.' He put a hand for a moment on Arthur's knee, and said, 'Don't think that you have anything to reproach yourself with. I was taken in just as badly, and I was a policeman.'

'What on earth do you mean?'

'Well, you see, Carstairs, you never were at Norton St. Giles. You were never more than a mile from Kingsfield—and ten miles from Glendower House.'

'But—but, my good man, I went there with *you*!'

'Oh, next morning, yes.'

'To the same house.'

'No.'

'But I could swear—'

'You couldn't swear it was the same house, because you never saw the house that night. You saw one room.'

'All right, then, the same room.'

'No.'

'Really, Wells, I know I was an innocent young fool in those days, but I wasn't blind.'

'Everyone is blind to the things at which he isn't looking. What did you see in that room? That picture. What else? Go on, describe the room to me.'

'The other picture, the Corot. The chessmen on the table by the window. The big table with a check table-cloth—er—dammit, it was six years ago—oh yes, there were some patchwork cushions, and—er—' He tried to think, but all he could see was Lydia.

'You see? Everything you remember was movable. It could all have been put in a car, and taken from one house to another; from Clyde's house in Norton St. Giles to Platt's house outside Kingsfield. Oh, he knew his stuff, that man Clyde. He knew that a young bachelor living in lodgings doesn't take in a room as a woman does, or even as a married man might. Give him something to fix his eyes on, and the rest goes by. So he gave you the portrait of Lydia and the chessmen—your two loves, so to speak—and they furnished the room for you.'

'But she drove me there—'

'In the dark, to Barton Langley and back, same as when Platt drove you home. When Lydia left you and Clyde playing chess, she drove straight to Glendower House, ten miles, did the job, and drove back to Platt's house where you were just finishing your game. Platt, who was in the pub until nine, walked over and met her outside. Then they burst in together, straight from their supposed twenty-five-mile drive, and full of it. Easy.'

Arthur sat there, trying to take it in, trying in the light of this revelation to remember all that she had said to him, all the lies which she had told him.

'Was he really her father?' he asked.

'Oh, yes, undoubtedly.'

Well, at least she had told the truth about that.

'Oh, sorry,' said Wells, 'I see what you mean. No, no, Clyde was her husband.'

'Her *husband*?'

'Yes, he's quite a young man. It was Platt who was her father.'

Lies, lies, nothing but lies! All lies!

'I daresay it didn't give the girl much chance, having a father like that. Just a common crook. Clyde was the genius, an artist in every sense of the word. He painted that picture, you know.'

'Oh?' He didn't want to think of the picture now.

'Typical of him.' Wells laughed gently. 'It wasn't the girl at all. Just a professional model for Dawn or Summer, or whatever he called it. He painted in his wife's face specially for the occasion. Thought that it would occupy your attention more. He thought of everything.'

All of it lies, and this the crowning lie of all! He could forgive her everything but this, this outrage on his modesty. Damn her! And who the hell cared? Edna was having dinner with him to-night. A really good sort. And quite pretty.

'Oh well,' he said indifferently, 'that was a long time ago. I was a bit younger then. What about another drink? It's my turn this time.'

The Balcony

(1950)

Albert Edward Wilberforce Pyrke C.B.E. (Albert Edward after the Prince of Wales, and Wilberforce after the Bishop, both parents having taken a hand) was sixty-two when he fell out of a balcony on the eighth floor of Cavendish Mansions. Although his death was accidental, this did not immediately explain to his widow why he arrived on the pavement without coat, waistcoat and shoes, nor relieve the shareholders of Pyrkes Ltd., of the fear that their Chairman was thus avoiding prosecution. In fact, he had often told Sheila that her little balcony was dangerous, but she had only laughed at him. Now he had proved it. The shares went down and up again, nothing was wrong there; and Mrs Pyrke, assured by Sheila that the shoes had been hurting him, and that it was a particularly hot afternoon, soon forgot the unpleasantness of those first few days. So relieved, indeed, were the shareholders, and so pleasantly surprised the widow when the will was proved, that Justice demanded a revised verdict upon him; in whose white light the text on his tombstone began to seem not so ironical as was at first feared. Meanwhile Albert Edward Wilberforce Pyrke was awaiting a more impartial judgment in another place.

This was, or seemed to be, a large, empty reception room on an upper floor. He remembered dying, all but that last, awful moment, but he was not sure whether he had immediately woken up to find himself here, or whether centuries of oblivion had passed while he waited with all the others for Judgment Day. Seeing himself, as he had seen himself through life, as a special case, he doubted if he were the sort of person one would keep waiting so long; nor could he believe that his memory of that last hour with Sheila would be so clear if it had happened so long ago. In a moment, then, the door would open, and a voice would say 'Mr Wilberforce Pyrke, please', and he would be passed along to St. Peter; alone, not with a million jostling dead. It was St. Peter, wasn't it, who received you, asked you a few polite questions, and gave you the freedom of the place? One ought to know for certain; nobody liked being called by the wrong name. He could ask the attendant casually, emphasizing at the same time that he had dropped the Albert Edward in his own name years ago. He didn't want that dragged up against him.

He was not frightened. He had made his fortune as honestly as anybody in the City; no shareholder had lost money in his companies save by his own stupidity; he had given a helping hand to most of his poor relations. Not to all of them, of course, not Muriel the suffragette, nor Howard who hadn't joined up in 1914, nor that damned parson cousin who preached at him; but all the deserving ones. Yes, and helped them again, if they had shown their gratitude properly. He had subscribed to charities regularly; and though he did not go to church himself (because he played golf, and you can't do both), he had given the Vicar £100 a year for the good of the parish, and an extra £100 for repairing the tower. Presumably St. Peter had all that down. The only serious fault which might be found with him was in the matter of Sheila, and her two—two, that was all—her two predecessors. Well, one couldn't help one's nature; and if Agnes ceased of her own wish to be a wife (though a dear, good woman, all the same), what was one to do? St. Peter was a man of the world, he would make allowances. Of course, if they passed you on afterwards to St. Ursula or St. Teresa or one of those, he would have to look out. They just wouldn't understand.

So he waited; not frightened, yet not complacent; just pleasantly assured, pleasantly interested. At any moment now his name would be called, 'Mr Wilberforce Pyrke, please' …

He was standing, and had now been standing for some little time, in the middle of a room which seemed to be about 60 feet long and 30 feet wide. Behind him was the door from which presently he would be summoned. In front of him were long windows opening on to a balcony, whose parapet hid from him all but a violet-blue sky: the sort of sky which he had noticed sometimes abroad (when he had leisure to look at the sky), but which was rarely to be seen in England. Evidently the weather here was good. He thought of walking to the balcony and seeing what the country was like, but feared that this might take him out of hearing when his name was called. 'Plenty of time for looking about later,' he told himself. All the same, he had been here now for—how long was it? Automatically his hand went to his watch; automatically the thought flashed through his mind that he had left his watch on Sheila's dressing-table, silly of him; and, with the thought, he looked down, and found, to his shocked surprise, that he was naked.

For the first time a trickle of fear crept round his heart. Until now he had had as support the assurance of a hundred contacts with other men, teaching him that he could hold his own with any. He had discussed production with Cabinet Ministers, he had talked without embarrassment to the King when receiving his decoration, had made speeches, opened bazaars, given away prizes. An interview with St. Peter was just another occasion. But now—naked! It was damnably unfair. There was St. Peter covered from neck to ankle in the sort of bath-towelling which Saints seemed to go in for, and there was he, Wilberforce Pyrke, feeling a perfect fool, catching the devil of a cold, and not even a handkerchief to blow his nose on. How could he stand up for himself under cross-examination, however mild, knowing all the time that at sixty-two one's figure didn't look at its best? Better than most men's of his age, he thought, looking down at himself with a slight renewal of complacency, but not what it was once. Now if he had died at thirty, he could have shown St. Peter something.

Yes, it was unfair. Not cricket. Leaving behind a nasty feeling that they were going to take every advantage which they could. Tricky, that's what they were. And then to keep him hanging about for all this time—bad staff work? Or trickiness again? Trying to work on his nerves. All right then, if that's how they treated you up here, they couldn't expect courtesy in return. He would sit out on the balcony and enjoy the view, and they could damned well come and fetch him when they wanted him.

He walked to the window, looking about him as he went. The walls of the room were queerly opalescent, seeming to have no positive substance, no final resting place for the eye. All the colours of the spectrum were there, until one tried to give one's impression of any particular colour an abiding form; then it was there no longer. A phrase which he remembered from some book came into his mind: 'Its walls were of jasper.' Was this jasper? He went closer, in order to feel it; half a dozen strides, and ... and he was still in the middle of the room. He laughed uneasily, hoping to reassure himself, and went quickly on, as had been his first purpose, towards the balcony ... But he was still in the middle of the room.

Then he was really frightened. He called out, 'St. Peter! St. Peter!' and then, 'Here, for God's sake, somebody!' He bent down to touch the floor, wondering if it was so slippery that he could not walk, or if it was just that the room moved as he moved. He touched nothing. He realized suddenly, surprised that he had not noticed it before, that his feet felt nothing, neither heat nor cold. Very cautiously he tried to sit down, and found that though he still felt nothing, he was in a sitting position, and somehow sustained. It was the same when he lay down, and when he stood up again. He put a hand on his leg and up his side, and felt nothing. Yet he could see himself as clearly as he had seen himself in Sheila's room—was it a few hours ago? But now he was a ghost, a disembodied spirit. It came home to him then, as it had not yet come, that death made a difference; that all the pleasures of the flesh had been put away for ever. Well, he must get used to the idea, difficult as it might be at first. After all, ghosts had their advantages. They could not be imprisoned. They were free to walk through walls, so he had always understood. Yes, but if the walls were ghosts too? If all were unreal, but the invisible self within himself? What then?

Suddenly he began to cry in a weak, helpless sort of way ... and put the back of his hand to his eyes, but could not wipe away the tears which he knew were there.

Days, or weeks, or years passed—how could he tell when there was neither day nor night, sunrise nor sunset, to mark the passing of time? He was still there in the middle of the room. It was clear to him now that Judgment Day and St. Peter and all that was just a tale for children. Nobody was coming for him. Nobody would ever say 'Mr Wilberforce Pyrke, please'. Nobody bothered about you when you were dead. When you were dead, they took everybody and everything away from you, and left you alone in empty, infinite space. Yes, but you weren't dead; that was the horror of it.

He remembered a text from one of the many funerals and memorial services which he had attended (not that he liked them, but it was bad form not to show up): 'We brought nothing into the world, and it is certain that we can carry nothing out.' St. Paul, wasn't it? In one of those letters he was always writing. But he was alive when he wrote it, he didn't really know. Of course one left one's property behind, one's friends, one's credit, in a way one's name. One would expect that. But this absolute nothingness was different. If they had let him keep a pencil, a pack of cards, a dictionary: dammit, even a piece of string to tie and untie, a wall to touch, to examine, to make marks on with a finger-nail—if they had left him anything! What Heaven, it seemed to him now, prison would have been: surrounded by solid walls; in front of work, however lowly, waiting to be done; spoken to however roughly by real people, however much unloved. But nothing was left to him—*nothing*! An eternity of doing nothing, and nothing to do it with.

But wait! Something *was* left to him. His mind. They had had to leave him that.

His mind. Well, they could have that too, if they liked. If he went out of his mind—and it wouldn't take much more of this to make him—then he would be all right. He would be imagining himself Julius Caesar or a poached egg or something, and be perfectly happy. But even as the idea came into his mind, he resisted it. They had left him this one thing, and now let them take it away from him if they could. He would fight for it; he had always been a fighter; my God, how I shall fight for it!

If only he had been a poet, a novelist, a musician, he could have sat here happily, writing, composing, as happily alone with himself as he would have been in the real world. If only he had read as he should have done, he could have comforted himself now with poetry—*Paradise Lost*, Shakespeare and *The Lays of Ancient Rome*—for hours at a time. Of course, some of those poets would look pretty silly now, lacking his expert knowledge; he would be able to criticize them, and tell them where their imagination had failed them. Paradise! He knew a bit more about Paradise than Milton did.

Yes, but what else did he know? How else employ his mind? The arts, all the worlds of the imagination, were closed to him; a pity, he saw now, that he had neglected them; but what about the world of affairs? What about—figures?

He laughed aloud (or so it seemed to him) as he thought of figures. He put his tongue out, and made a face at St. Peter. (For some reason, St. Peter was to be regarded as his chief enemy.) He almost said, 'Sucks to you, old man.' For here was occupation for the mind, occupation without end. He would begin in a small way, multiplying 123456789 by itself. Keeping all the figures in his head. Remembering nine lines of figures, keeping them all in their proper places, and then adding them up. Talk about Mental Arithmetic; there was an example for you! It would take him—how long? Hours, of course; perhaps days. And so he could go on, making up other problems for himself, for as long as he liked. Sucks to St. Peter.

He multiplied by nine, and found to his bewilderment that the answer was 1111111101. Extraordinary! He multiplied again to make sure, and it still was. Apparently it always had been, and always would be. And he had never known! 'Well, well,' he thought, 'we live and learn,' and then laughed at himself, and said ruefully, 'We die and learn.' Eight ones, a nought and a one, easy to remember. He started on the next line, wondering if something equally remarkable was coming out. It began promisingly 21345—could it possibly be 6? It was. And 7?—7. Well well, well! To think of it! 987654312! Another easy one to remember. It simply couldn't go on like this. Absurdly excited, he began to multiply by seven. His excitement died; the great thrill was over. It took him several attempts, and a good deal of mental crossing out, before he had committed the answer to memory—864197523. Nothing there ... Except that every figure came once and once only. That was odd. Would it always be like that? And why? He had never thought of figures in this way before, and now it was all becoming rather interesting. In a sudden burst of enthusiasm he cried, 'Damn it all, I'll *cube* it!'

Days passed, weeks passed, years passed—who could tell when there was neither dawn nor dusk, sleeping nor waking, when the deep violet-blue of the sky beyond the balcony never wavered, never changed its intensity. He had done the task which he had set himself; something which nobody had ever done before. All of it meaningless, he saw now. It told you nothing, it led you nowhere. Surely there was something better to do with his time than this?

Something he had heard somebody say once: 'Every man has at least one book inside him.' Something like that. What did it mean?

That every man could write a book? No, that was nonsense. He certainly couldn't, for one. Or did it mean—yes, surely that was it—that every man's life was material for a book? Well, it was the one thing which a man would know, his own life. No need to invent anything, no need to wonder what happened next. One just put down all that one remembered. Exactly as it happened …

Why not? …

Why ever not? …

Of course, it wouldn't do just to go on thinking aimlessly, picking out a scene from this or that year—nursery, school, office, army—as it happened to come into his head. It must be consecutive; it must be 'written'; it must be committed to memory, so that at the end he had the whole book complete in his mind. Could that be done? If it were written in short paragraphs, each paragraph learnt by heart as it was finished, and then repeated to himself, and then repeated with all the preceding paragraphs: one; two, one-two; three, one-two-three; four, one-two-three-four; yes, it could be done like that. It would mean that he would be saying the first paragraph over to himself thousands and thousands of times. Well, he had eternity in front of him. But it would be something to do, something tremendous to do, something (he felt with complete conviction) good to do.

It would be a book whose like had never been seen. Every autobiography ever written was less than the truth. The author was making himself out greater or smaller than he really was. He was boastful or deprecating. However he had lived, there were things in his life, if only thoughts, which he dared not reveal to others. But this time there were no others. There was not even a posterity to discover and decipher the manuscript after he was dead. He was dead now, and there would be no manuscript. He could 'write' uninhibited, perhaps the first man who ever did. He would have nothing to hide, because there was nobody from whom to hide it.

How long would it take him? Ten years, fifty years, a hundred years, what did it matter? What were years to him? A phrase came into his head, which he had used himself when addressing shareholders: 'The immediate future is amply provided for.' Immediate—ten years! He laughed happily. He felt very happy suddenly.

Now then, to begin. He would begin with a short paragraph, because of saying it so many times.

'I was born on May 15th, 1886. My father was Joseph Preston Pyrke, M.A., the Vicar of Withamsted in Somerset. My mother was Grace Brackenbury before she married my father. I was their only child.'

He said it over and over again until it was part of himself. Then he went on to the second paragraph.

'Withamsted is a small village in the north-east corner of Somerset. We lived in the Vicarage. I was christened Albert Edward Wilberforce ...'

How many years? But he was nearly at the end.

'... I told her that it was the last time. I was paying her well, and I don't think she minded, because of course I was getting a bit old. I told her that that was why. The real reason was that I had just heard that I was in the running for a knighthood, and of course I shouldn't get it if Agnes divorced me. So I was taking no more risks.

'It made me feel very noble that I was going to be faithful to Agnes again. I wandered to the window and stood for a moment on the little balcony. You could look right over London. It was the last time, so that was why I was looking. I didn't throw myself down—at least, not meaning to—but something made me fall. I am not very clear about this. I don't mean Sheila, of course; I mean giddiness, or perhaps some sort of devilish compulsion. But the balcony was dangerous. I had told Sheila so.

'Well, that was my life. At least, all that I can remember of it.'

It was finished. How many years? Well, it wasn't quite finished yet. Now he had to go right through it from the beginning:

'I was born on May 15th, 1886 ...'

And as he reached the last words, the summons came. Not from the door, as he had once expected, but from the blue immensity outside.

'Albert Edward Wilberforce Pyrke!'

Eagerly he jumped up, and walked with firm, quick steps to the balcony.

Christmas Party

(1950)

I

'Oh, there's a letter from Ruth, how nice.'

'What does she say?'

'Wait a moment, dear, I must find my glasses.'

'Telling you the train, I expect. Might I have the marmalade? Some day it will be explained to me why it's always on your side of the table when you don't eat it. Jessie must have a reason, but it escapes me. Thank you. You told Ruth that Raymond and Coral were coming by the 4.50?'

'Yes, but I don't know if Stephen can get off so early. They keep him so late sometimes.'

'In a Government office? That will be news to a lot of people.'

'Now then ... Oh dear, Penelope has a slight cold.'

'Babies always look as though they had slight colds, I don't see how anyone can tell the difference. You don't mean that they're not coming?'

'Oh no, no. By the 4.50, that's a comfort. So now they can all come together.'

'Better tell Hoskings.'

'I told him yesterday that he'd have to meet Raymond—well yes, perhaps I'd better just give him a ring, or he'll be wondering about the others. I'm so glad Mark is coming by train. I don't like him dashing about the country on that motor-bicycle, particularly at night.'

434

'Mark? You didn't tell me about that. Has he written? When?'

'This morning, dear. It's here. Just a postcard to say "Coming by 4.50".'

'May I look?'

'It was only a postcard, dear. I thought you would have read it.'

'Never saw it. I was wondering why he hadn't written to me. May I—Thank you. "Coming by 4.50. Mark". Good. You'd better tell Hoskings he'll want both cars—or shall I go and meet them for one?'

'Better leave it to Hoskings, dear. You'll be wanting to make the cocktails.'

'That's true ... And I must make sure the television set is working. I'm glad I got that in time for Christmas. I don't suppose they've any of them seen one. I know Mark hasn't.'

'Yes, dear, but don't let us sit in the dark *all* the time.'

'No, no, of course not. But there it is, if they want it.'

'Yes, and that reminds me, the bedside light in Coral's room has gone. Put in a new bulb for me, Gerald, they always look as if they were waiting to explode when I do it.'

'Right ... I say, Helen, you do think that Coral will like that what do you call the thing?'

'*Boutonnière.* Oh, I'm sure she will, dear. It was very expensive. And Ruth will love the bedroom slippers.'

'She'd better. I'd put her over my knee and give her a damned good spanking with them if she didn't. Can't do that to Coral unfortunately, not being one's own daughter. She's not exactly—'

'What, dear?'

'Easy. Except on the eye, of course.'

'Well, we know who we wanted Ray to marry, but when you look round at all the extraordinary girls he might have married, I don't think that we must complain.'

'There's still Mark, of course. Not that he'll be thinking of it for some time yet. And who said that I was complaining of Coral? It's a pleasure to look at her. All I say is that she's not exactly one of us. So damned aloof. D'you think they're happy? Why haven't they got any children? Been married two years.'

'Gerald dear, are you suggesting that young married people can't live happily together in a small flat unless they have children; or that they can't have children unless they are happy?'

'Leave it, Helen, leave it. And I'll have half a cup, and I mean half. A little more milk this time, you never give me enough milk.'

'All the same, I think I know what you meant. There, is that better? And peel me an apple, will you, darling? Or, better still, share one with me, I don't really want more than half. You mean that husband and wife don't always agree about children, and if they are quarrelling about it, then they aren't happy.'

'Practically what I said, wasn't it? What does Ruth think?'

'If she thinks about it at all, she thinks that now she has given you a grandchild, any other baby in the family would be a—what's the word?'

'Mistake.'

'No, dear. I could have thought of that for myself. Anti-climax, that's it.'

'Ruth seems to forget that her baby is a Rawson, not a Merridew.'

'I don't suppose she forgets, she just doesn't think it matters.'

'One doesn't want the family to die out.'

'Well, dear, it won't be doing it this morning, so we'll just have to wait and see. You reminded Philbeach to bring in some holly?'

'Of course. Not too much of it about this year, I'm afraid.'

'Oh, I expect he'll find some, he always does. I wish I had a few flowers for Coral's room. Such a bad month.'

'Nothing in the greenhouse?'

'Not for picking. Oh well, she'll understand. And there's the new *Vogue*, she'll like that. The girls had better have breakfast in bed, then there won't be so much pressure on the bathrooms.'

'What will Jessie say to that?'

'I daresay I can make it all right with Jessie. Coral's so decorative in bed, that always appeals to them, and of course she'd do anything for Ruth.'

II

'By the way, Coral, did you write and tell Mother the train?'

'Just as you like, darling.'

'What did you think I said?'

'Yes, darling.'

'Coral, I'm asking you. Did you write and tell Mother the train?'

'Did I write and tell Mother the train? Did—I—write—no, it's no good, sweetie, I'm not with you. The author and I are in a little shack in the Adirondacks, and at any moment the postman will knock twice. It's very difficult being suddenly asked about mothers. What were you saying, darling?'

'Oh, never mind. I was just wondering, I didn't notice you were reading. Sorry.'

'What did you wonder, darling?'

'I just asked if you had written to tell Mother about the train.'

'No, precious, I thought *you* were going to.'

'As a matter of fact, I did.'

'You did?'

'Yes.'

'Ray darling, one of us is definitely going downhill. Taking a long distance view of the situation from my little eyrie in the Adirondacks, it seems to me that if a letter has been written to your mother telling her about the train, our united purpose is achieved. She now knows about the train. Obviously there is a flaw somewhere, but for the moment I don't see it.'

'You told me *you* were going to write. It was just by chance that I happened to mention it.'

'You have mentioned it every day for the last week, darling. It couldn't have been a coincidence every time.'

'I mean just by chance I happened to mention it in my letter to Mother.'

'Ah well, it's the same train whether you mentioned it by chance or by grim purpose, so that's all right. What a very, very ugly word "mention" is. Let's not mention it again.'

'It would have been rather more polite, don't you think, if *you* had written to her, and said how much you were looking forward to coming down for Christmas?'

'More polite, perhaps, but not so truthful, darling. And it still wouldn't have told her what train we were coming by. What train are we, by the way? Something tells me I ought to know.'

'Obviously the 4.50. It's the only good one.'

'Would it be obvious to your mother too? Because if so—'

'Oh God, why do we have to madden each other like this? At least, I suppose I madden you, I know you're maddening me.'

'Am I, sweetie? I'm so very sorry. Let me return to my little shack.'

'Coral darling, what *is* the matter? Would you rather we *didn't* go down to Wheatleys for Christmas?'

'Much.'

'Coral!'

'You didn't really want to know, did you, darling? It was just a rhetorical question. I was supposed to say "Don't be so absurd," and you would have said "Well, then?"'

'I had no idea.'

'That shows what a good wife or a good actress or a good something I am.'

'What's the matter with Wheatleys?'

'As an hotel, darling, nothing. Comfortable beds, central beating, log fires, first class cuisine, fully licensed, constant h. and c., the usual offices conveniently placed—which is always, I think, *so* important—willing service and every possible home comfort. Oh, I nearly left it out—delightful rural surroundings.'

'But you just can't stand the family. Is that it?'

'You want me to continue the inventory? Very well, sweetie. If I had met your father out anywhere, we should have got on madly together, and everybody would have said "Who's Coral's new boyfriend?" As the father of a family in the bosom of his family, and being a bit frightened of me anyway, he doesn't seem to sort of co-operate. I forget now whether I did kiss him or didn't kiss him when we first met, but whichever it was, it must have been wrong. Or done in the wrong way. Your mother naturally doesn't like me. She probably had a girl in her mind for you—you must tell me about her one day—and is always comparing me with her, and thinking how much nicer it would have been if only little Margot had been coming down to them for Christmas. Mark is a thoroughly nice person, but I should like him more if he weren't always telling me about the girl he is in love with. This is always slightly annoying for anybody moderately good-looking, but it is more annoying when you have just worked yourself up into taking an interest in Betty and telling yourself that she can't be as frightful as she sounds, and then find that it isn't Betty any longer, it's Sally. All this is rather silly and personal, I know, because Mark is an extremely attractive boy—or would be, if he weren't always moaning for somebody else when I see him. Stephen is all right; naturally I have a strong feeling for him as a fellow-alien. But I've seen so many Stephens with watch-chains and striped trousers and a dispatch-case in the cloaks that I don't really get much of a kick out of them. He explained the Gap to me last time we dined there, and I felt it yawning between us more and more widely as the evening wore on. Still, I think I like him more than any of you do. No man bores me all the time: there's always something. As for Penelope, she's just like any other baby of that age. One says "*Isn't* she sweet?" or "*Hasn't* she grown?" whichever sounds the less unlikely, and looks around for somebody else. Oh, I was forgetting Jessie. Jessie and I get on very well together. I'm taking her down an old dress of mine. She'll look ghastly in it, but she won't know. There!'

'You haven't mentioned Ruth.'

'No, darling, I thought I'd better not.'

'You mean you hate her?'

'No, sweetie, it's just that Ruth and I took one look at each other three years ago, and rushed off to Reno and got a divorce for incompatibility.'

'I always felt that she was rather unenthusiastic about *you*, but I thought you liked *her* well enough.'

'That, darling, is one of the incompatibles. Our idea of good manners.'

'I admit she is a little outspoken—'

'She admits it too in the most charmingly outspoken way. I suppose all those years in the Sergeants' Mess saying "Eyes right"—'

'She was a Section Officer.'

'Was she, darling? Somehow I always see her in the Sergeants' Mess.'

'Well, thank you for being so frank about us all.'

'*Vous l'avez voulu, Georges Dandin.*'

'So now we know where we are.'

'Well, darling, I'm not sure about that, but at least we know where we shall be for Christmas.'

'What I don't know is where you'd *like* to be.'

'The reason why you don't know, sweetie, is that you have never asked me.'

'All right, I'm asking you now—at least, it's too late now, of course, but suppose I'd said a month ago "Darling, where would you like to go for Christmas?" what would you have said?'

'Oh, Raymond, my idiot child, don't you see that if you *had* said that, then it wouldn't have mattered *where* we went? I'd probably have said "Wouldn't you like to go to Wheatleys, darling, because if you'd like it very much—" and perhaps I should have found that you didn't really like it as much as all that, and would rather have been going off alone with me to a little inn in the Cotswolds or an hotel in Paris, or—oh, I don't know, but it would have been fun talking it over. And if I had felt that you couldn't bear Christmas anywhere but at Wheatleys, and were just being sweetly unselfish about it, why of course I would have said "Oh, darling, let's go to Wheatleys." But—oh, well.'

'Yes … I see … I'm sorry, darling.'

'Sweetie!'

'Next year—'

'Yes, next year. Ray … *Darling? This isn't the Adirondacks!* Help, help!'

III

'Stephen!'

'Yes?'

'Come here a moment, old thing.'

'What is it?'

'Steve—*ern*!'

'Damn. Oh, all right … What is it?'

'You haven't upset anything?'

'Not that I know of. Did you want me to?'

'Silly old boy, I just wondered what the damn was about. Oh, I don't mind, one gets used to swearing in the Army. Did a bit of it myself if it comes to that. I wondered if you had spilt the ink.'

'I haven't.'

'Well, are you busy at the moment?'

'I am trying, in the face of constant interruption, to finish that report.'

'Oh well, you've missed the post now. Look, old man, the point is, which of your dressing-cases are you taking? Because, if you take the big one, then we can fill up with the presents and one or two things of mine and Baby's. *You* won't want much.'

'No, not much. Only my dressing-case to myself.'

'Play the game, old thing. We're all in this together. Naturally if I had any room left over in mine for anything of yours—all I want to know is which dressing-case you're taking, and then I shall be able to make my own plans. Don't forget that I've got Baby to think of.'

'I wish you would think of her as a unit and not as a species. The name is Penelope.'

'Time enough for that, old man, when she knows we're talking about her.'

'I frequently refer to you as "Ruth" rather than "Woman" when you don't know that I am talking about you. The cases seem to be parallel.'

'Yes, well, I can't discuss parallelograms now, I've got to do the packing. You're taking the big dressing-case, is that all right?'

'No, I'm taking the small one.'

'Aren't you being just a little bit obstructive, old man? Why is it so necessary for you to take the smaller one, when the whole side benefits if you take the larger one?'

'I might say, my dear Ruth, that the smaller one was your wedding-present to me, and that I cannot bear to spend a single night away from it. What I do say is that the other one isn't really a dressing-case at all. It has none of those invaluable partitions for brushes, combs, nail-scissors, tweezers and the now unfashionable razor-strop. Only when fortified by the companionship of your dressing-case do I feel sufficiently sure of myself to face a week-end at Wheatleys.'

'It's a damned good one, though I say it myself. It put me back eighty-five guineas.'

'Indeed? Not a sum to be lightly left behind in the box-room. I shall take it with me.'

'Oh well, if you're going to play for yourself and not for the side— What did you mean by "facing" a week-end at Wheatleys? It sounds as if you didn't *like* going there.'

'I hope so. I couldn't dislike it more.'

'My dear old thing, what *do* you mean?'

'When, as a very young member, I was first privileged to enter the Athenaeum, I felt like a new boy at school. Nobody talked to me.

Everybody seemed to know everybody except myself. The only place where I didn't feel an outcast was in the lavatory. By repairing thither every few minutes and washing my hands vigorously and in obvious haste, I managed to give myself, and I hope others, a continuous impression that I was on my way to be the life and soul of the party in some more social corner of the club. Making the necessary allowances for the difference in the intellectual atmosphere and the size of the lavatory, I have felt much the same at Wheatleys.'

'Oh, nonsense, Stephen. You get on well enough with Coral, anyhow. Don't think I haven't noticed it.'

'Coral and I are as friendly as any two castaways would be who accidentally found themselves in the same caravan in an Esperanto Holiday Camp. If we didn't talk to each other, we should have to learn Esperanto. It is a pity that we bore each other so profoundly. On the intellectual plane, I mean.'

'The only plane that interests Coral is the slap-and-tickle plane.'

'Naturally I shall leave Penelope's education in your hands, but you must see that she doesn't pick up any coarse expressions from her mother.'

'Sorry, old man, but five years in the Army—Don't think that I don't like Coral. I like her very much.'

'Oh, I realized that you liked her very much. The signs are unmistakable.'

'It's only that I don't think that she is the right wife for Raymond. I'm sure she's ruining him.'

'Ah, I hadn't realized that. Financially or morally?'

'Both, I should say … What did you mean by Esperanto? Or didn't you?'

'My dear Ruth, I am in the habit of choosing my words. I meant that your family, like every other family, has a language of its own, consisting of unintelligible catch-phrases, favourite but not generally known quotations, obscure allusions, and well-tried but not intrinsically humorous, family jokes. For instance, there was a constant reference last Christmas to somebody or something called Bufty.'

'Pufty.'

'I accept the correction, without admitting that it is in itself elucidatory.'

'It was terribly funny. It was when Raymond was four years old. Let me see, I was six, because it was the day before my birthday, so he would be just short of four. We had taken a house by the sea—'

'Yes, dear, and you all shrieked with laughter, and you have been saying "Pufty" to each other ever since. One needs to have lived in the atmosphere of a family joke to appreciate it properly. Bald narration rarely does it justice. That is the point which I was endeavouring to make.'

'The point being that you are bored stiff at Wheatleys?'

'Let us say rendered uncomfortable by the realization that I am not there on my own merits, but merely as witness to Penelope's legitimacy; so that when the Vicar's wife says archly to her "Where's Daddy?", you can answer truthfully for her "In the lavatory".'

'Well! Why didn't you tell me all this before I fixed it up? We could have gone to *your* people if you had said so.'

'Nothing would have induced me to say so. You would have found it extremely unpleasant. My mother would have taken you up into her room and shown you countless photographs of myself as a baby, and told you how much, much more beautiful I was than Penelope. Father, unlike yourself, strongly objects to women in slacks, calling constant attention to the place where he particularly disapproves of them. My brother, whom I dislike profoundly, would make love to you and then try to borrow a fiver. My sister and you would loathe each other even more enthusiastically than you and Coral do. It would be an interesting but not a happy Christmas.'

'I don't loathe Coral, and I'm quite sure she doesn't loathe me. I've always tried to help her. If I had had her in my section, I could have done a lot for her.'

'Leaving the question of Coral's higher education for the moment, you now see that I am not a family man, my dear, and that I think family parties are a mistake.'

'In other words, you would rather we spent Christmas here—just the three of us?'

'Yes, Ruth. Or, if you and Penelope liked to go to Wheatleys—just the one of us.'

IV

'Then you won't come, Mark?'

'Darling, I've told you, I can't possibly. You know how I'd love to. Oh, Sally, do try to understand.'

'I understand perfectly. I'm going to St. Moritz with the Campbells, they've asked me to bring a man with me, I've invited you, and you've turned me down. It's all quite simple, and rather humiliating.'

'Darling, don't be such an idiot. I might have been stuck in an office instead of on my own, and then how could I possibly have come? There's nothing humiliating about asking a man to go out with you, and then finding that he's booked up.'

'Obviously if you had been stuck in an office, I should never have thought of you. But you're perfectly free; and, if you're going to be a writer, I should have thought that the more experience of every kind you got, the better. And there's a good deal of difference between asking a man to go to a dance with you—or having two tickets for Wimbledon or something—and choosing him out of everybody else to spend a fortnight in Switzerland with you, practically alone.'

'Oh God, don't I know? It's wonderful of you. Don't I wish like hell that I could come? You talk as if I were doing it on purpose. I'm just as sick about it as you are, only—'

'I'm not in the least sick about it, don't flatter yourself. There are plenty of other people in the world—Rex would jump at it—'

'Oh lord, not that little twerp?'

'At any rate he isn't tied to his mother's apron-strings, as some people are.'

'I've told you that this has nothing to do with Mother. It's Father.'

'Daddy's little boy.'

'All right, if you care to put it like that. I don't know that it helps.'

'Sorry, forget it. It's just that I simply can't understand you, Mark. You've always pretended to be rather keen about me.'

'Yes, I think you can start with that assumption fairly safely. If this weren't the Ritz Bar, I'd illustrate it for you. What publishers call profusely.'

'All right, you're keen about me … Well, naturally, of course, you're fond of your people—'

'Not naturally, but I am.'

'Yes, and no doubt you'd have quite a good Christmas with them—'

'Well, we'll have a family four-ball one morning, I expect, and I like seeing my niece, she's rather fun, and Father has a new T.V. set—oh, it won't be so bad.'

'Exactly. You're not wildly excited at the prospect?'

'I'm certainly not.'

'Would you enjoy coming to Switzerland with me?'

'Ten thousand times more.'

'One might almost say that you *would* be wildly excited at the prospect?'

'One might. Only wildly is a very tame word.'

'Then why on *earth*—'

'You'd better have another drink, hadn't you, darling? This is where we came in.'

'No, go on, I want to understand. You are of age and your own master. You have the choice of two things, neither of them in any way wrong. And you deliberately choose the "not so bad" one instead of the "wildly exciting" one. I can't make sense of it.'

'Well, try, darling. I'll put it in words, more or less, of one syllable. My people like having all the family round them at Christmas in the old family home. Silly, sentimental, old-fashioned, mid-Victorian, Christmas-number, anything you care to call it. But they *like* it. Raymond was away a couple of years in the war, of course, but Ruth was always stationed in England, and I was at school through most of it, so the war didn't make very much difference. We've always been together at Christmas ever since I can remember. I'd far sooner be in Switzerland with you; I'd far sooner be anywhere with you. When you began about Switzerland this evening, I was just wondering if I dare ask you to spend Christmas with us at Wheatleys. Rather apologetically, because we haven't much to offer you. Well, that's off. You're going to Switzerland. But I can't come with you, because I've told them that I'm coming home. They are expecting me, and it will disappoint them terribly, particularly Father, if I don't come. I'm very fond of them both, and very grateful, because I do think, so far as I'm concerned, that they have been model parents. Well, that's all. *Somebody's* got to be terribly disappointed—me or them. Or as we writers say, I or they. And since I'm doing the choosing, I don't see how I can possibly avoid choosing myself. That's all.'

'I see.'

'You don't. Not in that voice.'

'You didn't think of *my* disappointment, I suppose?'

'You told me not to flatter myself.'

'You needn't. Give her my love, won't you?'

'Who?'

'This other girl, in the country.'

'Sure you won't have another drink?'

'No, thanks. I must ring up Rex. I think Rex, don't you?'

'I think so, from what I've seen of him. Nice curly hair, definitely not Daddy's little boy, and probably in the black market for nylons. Shall we go?'

V

'Good-bye … good-bye.'

'Good-bye.'

'Good-bye, Father.'

'Good-bye, my boy. Come again soon.'

'Good-bye, Penelope, bye-bye, darling.'

'Grannie's saying good-bye to you, darling, say "Bye-bye, Grannie." Oh, she said "Gannie"! Did you hear her, Stephen? Yes, darling, that's who she is—Gannie. Good-bye, Mother, I'll send you the pattern.'

'Any time, dear. Good-bye. Good-bye.'

'Good-bye …'

'Well—that's over. I think they enjoyed themselves, Helen.'

'Oh, I'm sure they did, darling.'

'Mark looked a bit run down, I thought.'

'He hadn't quite such a good appetite as usual, but I expect it's just that he's in love again.'

'Mark? Nonsense. Working too hard, probably, and not getting enough exercise … I think they all liked their presents.'

'Oh, I'm sure they did. Is that the pen Mark gave you?'

'Yes, one of those patent things. Writes five miles or something. Just what I wanted. Wonder how he knew.'

'Oh, well, I expect he knew somehow. Did you like your pipe?'

'Haven't tried it yet, but it looks all right. I expect Ray helped her choose it. She was looking very pretty, I thought. Particularly in that blue thing.'

'Coral? Yes, she's almost too attractive. I hope dear Ray is happy. I wish I could get to know her better. I'm sure she's a nice girl really.'

'Much more friendly this time, I thought, what I saw of her. Next time you go up to London, why not take her out to lunch, and—'

'Yes, I think I will, Gerald, that's a good idea. But don't expect me to go up in a balloon with Stephen, because I just couldn't manage it.'

'Oh, there's more to Stephen than you think. For one thing he's a damned good putter.'

'I daresay, dear. I wouldn't get to know about it in a balloon.'

'I told you, or didn't I, that Mark and I beat them 2 and 1. We were playing pretty well—well, we generally do when we play together—but Ray was right off his drive, and if it hadn't been for Stephen's short game, particularly his putting—though of course that doesn't say that he's easy to live with ... Ruth was looking as well as ever, I thought. Wonderful health that girl's got. Mark tells me that they think a lot of Stephen in the Treasury. Ruth will be Lady Rawson one day, you'll find. How will you like *that*, Helen?'

'Well, as long as she doesn't expect Jessie to call her Your Ladyship, I shan't mind. I'm just going down to the pillar-box, dear. Can I post anything for you?'

'I'll go, I'll go. Give me your letters.'

'It's quite all right, dear, I shall like the little walk.'

'I'll come with you ... You know, Helen, much as I like having them all here for Christmas, I must say it's a great relief when they've gone, and we are alone together again.'

Murder at Eleven

(1950)

Yes, sir, I do read detective-stories. Most policemen will tell you that they don't. They laugh at 'em, and say that they aren't like real life, and that tracking down a murderer isn't a matter of deduction and induction and all the rest of it, which you do by putting your finger-tips together or polishing your horn-rim spectacles, but of solid hard work, over a matter of months maybe. Well, so it is for the most part, I'm not denying it. But why should I want to read books which tell me what I know already? The more detective-stories are unlike the sort of story I'm living, the better I'm pleased. I read 'em for the same reason that you read 'em—to get away from my own life for a bit.

Ever reasoned out why murderers in detective stories are always shooting themselves, or getting killed in a car crash, or falling over a cliff? Ever noticed that? I mean why a story-book murderer hardly ever gets brought to trial? Of course, sometimes it's because he's the heroine's Uncle Joseph, and it spoils the honeymoon if you suddenly wake up and remember that your Uncle Joseph is being hanged that morning. But there's another reason. Proof. All this amateur deducting and inducting is very clever, and I don't say it doesn't find the murderer sometimes; but it doesn't *prove* he's the murderer. Any Police Inspector knows half a dozen murderers he'd like to see with a rope round their necks, but he can't do anything about it. Proof—that's the trouble. I don't mean the sort of proof which convinces a reader who knows anyhow that his favourite detective is always right; I mean the sort of proof which convinces a Jury when the Judge has taken out all the bits which aren't legal evidence, and the prisoner's Counsel has messed up the rest of it. And that's saying nothing about the witnesses who have let you down. No, it's an easy job being an amateur detective, and knowing that you've only got to point out to the murderer that logically he must have done it, to be sure that he'll confess or commit suicide in the last chapter. It isn't so easy for a country Inspector like me, with a Super and a Chief Constable and a Judge and a Jury to satisfy. Murderers? There're hundreds of 'em walking about alive now, all because they didn't come into detective stories.

All the same, I did know an amateur detective once. Clever he was, he worked it all out, just the way they do in detective-stories. Helped me a lot. But there you are. We were both quite certain who the murderer was, and what could we do? Nothing. I put in everything I knew, all the old solid routine stuff, but I couldn't take the case any further. No proof. Only certainty. I'll tell you about it if you like.

Pelham Place it was called, and a fine place too. Mr Carter who lived there was a great one for birds. He had what they call a Bird Sanctuary in the middle of the park. It was in a wood, and there was a lake in the middle of the wood, fed by a little river, and all sorts of water-birds came there, ousels and kingfishers and so on, and he used to study them and photograph them for a book he was writing about them. I don't know whether it would have been a good book, because he never wrote it. He was killed one day in June, hit on the head with what we call a blunt instrument, and left there. Of course he had a lot of notes and photographs for the book, but it never got finished.

He hadn't made a will, and everything was divided equally between the four nephews, Ambrose and Michael Carter, and John and Peter Whyman. Ambrose, that was the eldest, the one who lived there, wanted to hand the place over to the National Trust, which he said was what his uncle always meant to do, but the others wouldn't agree, so it was sold and they divided up the money. When war came, the Army took it over, and of course that was the end of any sort of bird sanctuary.

Ambrose—that's my amateur detective—looked after the place and helped his uncle with the birds and the book. He said that watching birds wasn't so much different from watching people, and it was the best way of training your powers of observation which he knew, and there was a lot of detective work in it too, and I daresay he was right. It was natural that he should feel more keenly about the place, and want to carry out his uncle's wishes, and equally natural that the other three shouldn't. John and Peter were brothers. John was an actor, mostly out of work, and Peter had just got engaged, he was a barrister but hadn't had any briefs yet, so they both wanted all the money they could get. Michael Carter was Ambrose's cousin, he was in business and doing pretty well, but he had an expensive wife, and money was money. So there it was.

The first I heard of it was from Ambrose, who rang up and said that Mr Henry Carter of Pelham Place had been murdered, and could I send somebody up at once. I couldn't get hold of our doctor, he was on a case somewhere, so I left a message for him, took a sergeant with me and drove off. I don't know why, but I had expected to find the body in the house, sort of taken it for granted, and I was a bit surprised when Mr Ambrose Carter—I'd come across him once or twice, of course—who was waiting for me at the front door, said, 'Round to the left here and take the first fork on the right,' to the driver, and got into the car. And then he said, 'Sorry, Inspector, hope you don't mind my giving orders, it's in Sanctuary Wood. We can get a bit nearer to it this way.' Seemed to have his wits about him, which is what I like.

Well, this is what had happened. Mr Carter had gone out to his sanctuary at about ten in the morning the day before. He generally spent the whole day there and came back in time for dinner, but every now and then he'd stay the night, so as to be ready for them at the first light, so when he didn't turn up the night before nobody missed him.

'Where did he sleep?' I asked.

'There's a hut there. You'll see.'

'Food?'

'Yes, and a spirit lamp and all that. It's quite comfortable. I've spent a night there more than once.'

'So nobody thought anything of it when he wasn't there at dinner?'

'Well, there was comment, naturally, but we were just a family party, and most of us knew what Uncle Henry was like.'

'Then when did you get anxious—or didn't you?'

'He would have been back in the morning for a bath and what little breakfast he had, he always was. John, my cousin, and I went to look for him. We thought perhaps he'd been taken ill. John's there now, not that there was the slightest chance of anybody interfering with—with the body. Nobody ever goes there. It's complete sanctuary.'

If that was right, then it was a family job. So I'd better give you an idea of the family as I meet them. Ambrose and John both had what I call actors' faces though they weren't a bit alike. John Whyman was tall and dark and handsome with the sort of Irving face, you know what I mean? About thirty and a bit cynical-looking. Ambrose Carter, a little older, had one of those round blank comedian's faces which can take on any expression, d'you know the sort? Medium height. Might be fat one day.

He stopped the car and we walked a short way across the park to a wood. The lake in the middle of the wood—well, it was a large pond, really, I suppose—was as lovely a thing as I've seen, and the trees—but we'll skip all that or I shall be all night talking. John Whyman was sitting on a log, smoking a cigarette, and he looked at his watch as we came up and said, 'A whole bloody hour,' and Ambrose said, 'Sorry, John, couldn't have been quicker, this is Inspector Wills.' He hadn't seen anybody or anything, of course, and I sent him off in the car with Sergeant Hussey, and told Hussey to wait at the house for the doctor and bring him back. And I wrote out a message for him to send, because I could see that we would want more help. And then Ambrose and I looked at the body.

'Fond of him?' I said.

'Enough not to kill him, do you mean?' he said, looking at me rather comical.

'I didn't mean that, sir, at all,' I said, and it's true, I didn't.

'Sorry, Inspector. And the answer is that we got on very well together. I liked my job, but I can't say that I either liked or disliked him. He was a little—inhuman. More interested in birds than men, and had never had any great affection for anybody, I should say.'

'I know the sort,' I said.

Mr Carter lay on his back. His head and his right wrist were broken, as if he'd put his arm up to defend himself from the first blow, and been killed by the next. It looked as if he'd been dead for some time.

'When was he last seen alive?' I asked.

'About half-past nine yesterday morning,' said Ambrose.

'Well, he wasn't alive more than two or three hours after that, I should say, but we'll know more when the doctor comes.'

'Meanwhile, what about his watch, that ought to tell us something.'

I bent down to look at his wrist. The watch had been badly smashed but I could see the time. Eleven o'clock. Murder at eleven, I said to myself. Good title for a detective story.

'Hallo, that's funny,' said Ambrose. 'I could have sworn—' He stopped suddenly.

'What?' I asked.

'He wore his watch on his left wrist,' he said, a little lamely. It sounded as if it wasn't what he'd been going to say.

'Where was it when you and Mr Whyman first saw him?'

'Where it is now, I suppose,' he said, staring.

'You didn't notice particularly?'

'I noticed that his wrist and his watch were smashed, without paying much attention to it. Subconsciously I assumed it was his left wrist, as that's where you keep a watch. That's why I was surprised.'

'You're certain that Mr Carter did?'

'Absolutely. Look, you can see the strap-mark on his left wrist.'

It's true, you could. I should have come to it in time, but he was quicker. Bird-watching.

He walked round the body, and looked down from behind it. Then he laughed softly to himself.

'What's the joke, sir?'

'Well, well, well,' he was saying. I went over to him and looked too. The watch was the wrong way round.

'You see what happened, Inspector? The murderer broke Uncle Henry's wrist before he managed to kill him. Then he changed the watch to the broken wrist, and broke it too. So now you know that the murder took place at precisely eleven o'clock. Which you wouldn't have known otherwise.'

'Looks like it,' I said.

'Like tying another man's tie for him. More difficult than you think. You're looking at the watch the other way round. What's right for you is wrong for him.'

'What it comes to,' I said slowly, 'is that he wanted us to put the murder at his own chosen time.' I wasn't going to be hurried.

'Right.'

'Which means that it *didn't* take place at eleven.'

'Right. Which means—what, Inspector?'

'Which means,' I said, rather proud at seeing it, 'that the murderer probably has an alibi for eleven.'

'Probably?' he said, surprised like. 'Certainly; or why alter the watch? Well, we know *something* about him.'

'But that's all we do know. We don't know what time he hasn't got an alibi for. The time of the murder.'

'Oh, I wouldn't say that,' he said rather airily. You know what I mean—rather sure of himself.

The ground was dry and hard. No footprints or anything like that. I had a couple of men coming, and they could look for the weapon, but they wouldn't find it, because it was probably in the middle of the lake. As soon as the doctor came I wanted to get back to the house, and ask a few questions. Meanwhile I might as well listen to Mr Ambrose, if he fancied himself as Sherlock Holmes, because he seemed to have ideas, and good ones too. We sat down on a log together and smoked.

'Let's have it, sir,' I said.

'Have what?'

'What you've got up your sleeve, about the time of the murder.'

'Nothing up my sleeve, Inspector, I assure you. Your guess is as good as mine.'

'I haven't started guessing yet,' I said. 'You go first.'

'D'you mean it? Good!' He beamed at me. 'First of all, what would you say the limits are, I mean from the condition of the body?'

'We shall have to wait for Dr Hicks to tell us that. And he'll make 'em pretty wide. Maybe six hours or so.'

'As much as that? Oh well, let's see what we can do. Now the first thing—Oh!' He stopped suddenly, and looked uncomfortable.

'Yes, sir?' I said.

'I was forgetting. Of course, that's the first thing to be settled.' He was talking to himself rather than to me, and I waited a little, and then said, 'What is?'

'Where are you looking for your murderer, Inspector?'

'Haven't begun to look yet, sir.'

'Inside the house or outside?'

'I shall want to see everybody inside, of course. And I daresay a lot of people outside too. Any reason yourself, sir, for thinking it was one or the other?'

'The best of all reasons for thinking it was outside.'

'You mean the best of all reasons for hoping it was outside?'

He laughed and said, 'I suppose I do,' and then to himself, 'I suppose that's all I mean, dammit.'

'I should like you to be frank with me,' I said. 'A murderer's a murderer, even if he's a relation.'

'That's true.' He threw his cigarette-end away, and lit another. 'I'll give you both sides,' he said. 'A tramp or a trespasser, an outsider of some kind, comes whistling through the wood, knocking at the undergrowth with the stick he carries, making the hell of a row, and disturbing all the birds. My uncle rushes out at him furiously—as he certainly would—and asks him what the devil he thinks he's doing. There's a fight, the tramp hits him in self-defence, loses his head, and hits him again. Easy.'

'Except for the watch,' I said.

'Exactly, Inspector, you've got it. Except for the watch. In the first place, a tramp wouldn't think of it; in the second place, he'd have a long way to go for an alibi, and a tramp's alibi isn't much good anyway; and in the third place, he wouldn't dare to put the watch on, in case the body was found before the false time was reached, or put it back in case Uncle Henry had been seen alive afterwards.'

'Doesn't that apply to any murderer who fakes the time?' I asked.

'Yes. Except in special circumstances.'

'And those are—?'

'That you know that the murdered man is going to remain in a certain place for a certain time, and, dead or alive, will be visited by nobody.'

'Which was true in this case, and which everybody in the house knew?'

'Yes,' he said, rather reluctantly.

'And, I suppose, the outside men, gardeners and gamekeepers and so on—they would know too?'

'That's true,' he said, brightening up. 'Oh, well, then, just as a bit of theorizing, here you are. If you murdered a man at three, and were altering his watch to two or four, which would you choose.'

'Which would you, sir?' I asked.

'Two o'clock, obviously.'

'I don't see the obviously.'

'Well, if I make it two o'clock, it's because I've already got an alibi for two. But if I make it four, it's because I hope to get an alibi for four; and I can't be absolutely certain that I shall. Something might go wrong. I might be with somebody then, but his memory might be bad, or he mightn't have a watch, or he might be a notorious liar. The other way I have made certain of a perfect alibi first, and I put *back* the watch to a time when I can prove I was elsewhere. Even if it is an unplanned murder, there's such a time somewhere.'

Well, that was true enough. Perhaps I should have thought of it, perhaps I shouldn't, I don't know.

'All right then,' he went on. 'The murder took place *after* eleven. How long after? If it were very soon after he couldn't have an alibi for eleven which was watertight. He's got to allow a margin for watches being wrong, and another for his distance from the place of the alibi—in this case, the house, presumably; a good twenty minutes away, if he walked, for he would hardly dare to leave a car about. I think that one's feeling would be for a good safe margin of an hour. You've got your alibi for eleven and a bit after, you kill at twelve, and you put the watch back to eleven.'

'Then why not kill at one or two or three? Still safer by your reckoning.'

'Lunch,' he said. Just like that.

'Does a murderer let his lunch interfere with his plans?' I laughed, sort of sarcastically.

'Not *his* lunch, the dead man's. You can tell, can't you, when a dead man had his last meal?'

'That's right, sir, stupid of me.'

'Uncle Henry would have his at any time between twelve-thirty and one-thirty, and what's the good of pretending he died at eleven, if he'd just finished his lunch? No, Inspector, the absolute limits for the time of death are eleven-thirty to twelve-thirty, and the nearer to twelve the better.'

Well, that was clever, it really was, and I couldn't see anything against it.

'All right, sir,' I said. 'He was killed at twelve. That means that the murderer has no alibi at all for twelve and a watertight one for eleven.'

'As you say, Inspector.'

'In that case, sir, I will ask you where *you* were at eleven and twelve.'

He gave a great shout of laughter.

'I knew you would,' he said, twinkling at me. 'I felt it coming.'

'Nothing meant, sir, of course, but we have to know these things. Same with everybody at the house.'

'Of course. Well, let's think. Times a bit vague; general plan—I walked over to Weston to lunch with some friends. Name given on demand. I left the house a bit after ten, and went over to the garage; talked to a chauffeur and a gardener or two till ten-thirty, and got there, I suppose, at twelve-thirty. It's four miles, isn't it, through the fields, but it was a hot day, and why hurry?'

'Why not take the car, sir? I suppose there was a car available?'

'Mrs Michael wanted to go into town to do some shopping. Besides,' he patted his stomach and looked at mine, 'walking's good for the figure.'

'Meet anybody?'

'Not to remember or identify.'

'Did the others know you were going?' I asked.

'We discussed plans a bit at breakfast. Michael was—oh, but you'll prefer to ask them yourself. Sorry.'

I thought that I might as well know what they had planned to do, even if they didn't do it, or pretended they hadn't. So I told him to go on.

'Michael always brings down masses of papers with him, he's the sort of man who works in the train. I told him he could have my room, and I'd send him in a drink later, and he told his wife that he'd be busy all morning. Peter and his girl—well, you know what the plans of a newly engaged couple are, Inspector. As long as they are together, they don't mind where they are. I wanted to fix John up for golf, he's always very keen, but an agent or a manager or somebody was ringing him up at eleven, and that would have made it rather late. So he said that, as soon as his call had come through, and he'd done his business, he'd take an iron out in the park and knock round a bit. I don't know if he did, or what he did, or, in fact, what any of them did, but that's what was said at breakfast.'

He got up suddenly, as if he had an idea, and I asked him what it was, because I'd had a sudden idea too.

'His notes,' he said. 'What idiots we are!'

'I was just going to ask you,' I said, and I was, because I thought if he was watching a couple of birds nesting or something he'd make a note of the times when things happened, or anyhow make a note of the time of any photograph he'd taken. That hidey-hole! You wouldn't have known it wasn't a great beech trunk with bushes all round, and inside a regular home from home. And there was his diary, and the last entry was 10.27! 'What d'you know about that?' I said to Mr Ambrose.

'It's funny,' he said, picking up the diary and turning the pages backwards and forwards. 'After all our clever theorizing, too. He would hardly go an hour and a half without an entry or a photograph. Hallo!'

'What?'

'Last entry comes at the bottom of the page. Coincidence?'

'You mean a page might have been torn out? A page going on to twelve o'clock?'

'Yes.'

'If so, the corresponding page would be loose.'

We looked. There was no loose page, but the corresponding page way back in March was missing. We knew, because an entry broke off in the middle and never went on. Well, it all fitted in, and Mr Ambrose looked rather pleased with himself again.

Well, that was my amateur detective, and very good too, I thought; and now I'll tell you what the professionals got. Mr Carter's last meal was breakfast, and, putting his lunchtime at twelve-thirty, he was killed between nine forty-five and twelve-thirty. So our guess at twelve was probably right. But when I came to alibis—and remember, the murderer had to have one for eleven, but not for twelve—things began to go a bit wrong. There was a woodman called Rogers who had no alibi at all, and the other employed men gave each other alibis for the whole morning. Mr Michael Carter was shut up in Mr Ambrose's study all the time, or so he said. He was a solid, bossy sort of man, looked older than Ambrose, though he wasn't.

'Nobody came in that you can remember?'

'A maid brought me a whisky and soda some time in the course of the morning. I hadn't ordered it, but I drank it.'

'When would that be, sir?'

'She might know; I don't.' Much too busy a man to notice such trifles, he seemed to be saying.

Doris, the maid, confirmed this, but was uncertain of the time. 'It was his elevenses as you might say, sir, only Hilda sitting down on a queen wasp and naturally having to go upstairs to put something on and me helping her and then taking it in myself, well it all made it late like.'

Mr Peter and Miss Mayfield, that was his girl, gave each other complete alibis, as did the chauffeur and Mrs Michael. Of course you'll say that Mr Peter's real alibi, for twelve o'clock, being only confirmed by a girl in love with him, wasn't very satisfactory. But how I looked at it, if the girl was going to give him an alibi anyhow, all that business of changing the hands of the watch to eleven, and then smashing it, was pointless. Any time was alibi-time for him.

Mr John Whyman was the one I was most disappointed in. His call had come through at ten-thirty—not eleven, as he had expected and I had hoped; it was over by ten thirty-five; and he took an iron and half a dozen golf balls, and went off into the park. All of which was confirmed by the Post Office and Mrs Michael.

So there we were, and, after all our checking up, the possibilities came down to these:

1. Michael Carter, assuming his drink had come in at 11.10, as he would have known; which gave him an alibi for eleven o'clock in the wood; and no alibi for twelve.

2. Rogers; but only if John Whyman had altered the watch when left alone with the body, and had torn out the page of the diary. Why should he do this? Because he was afraid he might be suspected of the murder, being the hardest-up of the nephews, and having discussed with Ambrose the possibility of getting help from his uncle.

3. Any tramp, with John Whyman assisting again. But this was very unlikely, as the wood was in the middle of a private park, a long way from the road.

In the last two cases why didn't John make the time ten-thirty, when he had an alibi, instead of eleven when he hadn't?

No reason. So you can take out 2 and 3, and that leaves Michael Carter.

And then I'm blessed if that wretched little Doris didn't come and say that what with one thing and another, and talking it over with Hilda like, and not noticing the time Hilda making such a fuss and all, it was twelve o'clock before she took in the whisky. So Mr Michael Carter was out too—and nobody did it.

I had a good think about it that night. I lay in my big chair, and put a pipe on and a drink handy, and another chair for my feet. Because the Super was wanting to take a hand, and I thought I should like to tell him who'd done it before he got all the credit for himself, or called in Scotland Yard.

The first thing I thought about was the watch.

Now it couldn't be clearer than it was that the murderer had done some funny business with that watch so as to fool us about the time.

Look at what we had. The mark on the left wrist showing where it was usually worn; the fact that it was upside down, showing that it was put on the other wrist by somebody else; and the page torn from the diary, showing that the real time of death was being hidden from us. What could be clearer than that?

'Nothing,' I said to myself … and then found myself saying 'Nothing' again in a wondering sort of voice, and going on, 'Nothing. Absolutely nothing. The murderer *couldn't* have made it clearer!'

Silly of me, wasn't it, not to have seen it before? Why should the murderer want to make it so clear to us that eleven o'clock was the wrong time, unless it was because eleven o'clock was the right time? You see, if he had broken the watch in the ordinary way on the left wrist, then, whatever time he'd put the hands at, he couldn't be sure we'd accept it. Because everybody knows that the hands of a watch or clock can be altered to suit a murderer's plan. So he did a double bluff. He made us think that he had to get the watch on the right wrist because the wrist was already broken, and he let us think that he hadn't noticed the clues he was leaving behind. In fact, the murder took place at eleven, and this was the murderer's clever way of making us think that it didn't.

Mr Michael Whyman, then, could have done it. He had no alibi for eleven. Everybody was out of the house by ten thirty-five, and he was alone until twelve when Doris brought in the drink. I took my feet down, and told myself that I had solved the case … and then I put my feet up again and told myself that I hadn't. Because Ambrose and John could have done it equally well. Neither of them had an alibi for eleven. So I had a drink and lit a fresh pipe, and went on thinking.

Motive and opportunity made it pretty certain that one of the four nephews did it. If the one who did it was trying to make us think that the murderer had an alibi for eleven, wouldn't he make sure that one at least of the other three had such an alibi? Only so could he feel safe. Well, what about it? Did Michael know where Ambrose was at eleven? No. Ambrose might have been anywhere. So might John.

Did John know where the others were? No. He didn't know where Ambrose was, and even if he knew that Michael was in Ambrose's office, he wouldn't know if Michael could prove it. Did Ambrose—and at that I shot out of my chair, banged my fist into my palm, and shouted 'Ambrose!'

He had ordered a drink to be sent in to Michael at eleven. That was to be Michael's alibi. John, he knew, had a telephone call coming in at eleven; that would be John's. It wasn't his fault that both alibis failed him. Ambrose! The amateur detective who had led me on, who had pointed out the mark on the left wrist, and the upside-down watch, and the missing page of the diary; who was taking no risks with a stupid country policeman, but handing it all to him on a plate. Ambrose, who had asked all of them their plans at breakfast and known where everybody would be. Ambrose, who had so casually let me know that two of his cousins had an alibi for eleven. Ambrose, who had proved so convincingly that the murder took place at twelve, when neither cousin would have an alibi! Ambrose!

Well, there you are, sir. If he hadn't been so clever, if he hadn't done so much amateur detecting in the wood, I shouldn't have tumbled to it. Helped me a lot, he did. There didn't seem any way of getting legal proof, and we never did prove it. But, as I said at the beginning, we both knew who'd done it.

A Rattling Good Yarn

(1950)

I

Most people have heard of Michael Hartigan. It is a well-known name behind the counter, where faces light up when he gives it, and voices say shyly, 'I read your last book, Mr Hartigan,' before adding for the record, 'Then I'll see that that goes off at once, Mr Hartigan.' Mr Hartigan likes this. He likes it all: the recognition, the letters, the invitations, the speeches, the press paragraphs, and, of course, the money. Who wouldn't?

Michael Hartigan writes the Lord Harry books. His publishers print a first edition of 50,000 copies, if they have the paper, and sell it before publication; and there are, of course, serial rights, film rights, radio rights and all the rest of it. Even so, there may be superior persons in Bloomsbury and the backwaters of our older universities who have never heard of Lord Harry; it is also possible that, as the result of insomnia, shipwreck or other Act of God, one or two of them may be temporarily among my own readers. For their benefit some introduction to Mr Michael Hartigan's hero seems necessary.

Lord Henry Wayne (only called Lord Wayne alternatively in the first book, which has now been withdrawn) was the son of the Duke of Scarborough. He was amateur heavyweight champion in the year when he won the Grand National, besides scoring a century against

Oxford. I fancy he won the mile too. I think I remember some mention of it in the first Lord Harry book, at a time when the Wambesi head-hunters seemed to be gaining on him; but, as I say, this one is now out of print. One way and another it had given Hartigan a good deal of trouble. Not foreseeing the future, Lord Harry had pledged himself to Estelle da Suiza, the lovely girl whom he had rescued from the Wambesis when she was on the point of being sacrificed to the Sacred Crocodile. They were married a little later in the Brompton Road. At this time Hartigan was employed in a bank, and there was no immediate thought of a second book. But the acceptance of the first, and its subsequent sales, were sufficiently encouraging for him to try again. It seemed a pity to waste such a well-equipped hero, and almost inevitable that his visit to the Bagoura Hinterland should lead to the rescue of the beautiful Maddalena Ramona as she was being pegged down to an ants' nest. Estelle, meanwhile, was on a visit to her mother at Harrogate; for naturally one wouldn't want one's wife around when rescuing. Unfortunately a similar situation arose in the next six books, in the course of which Estelle went four more times to her mother at Harrogate, and twice to a nursing-home in Portland Place. This proved very helpful, but Lord Harry's style was still a little cramped. So it was that in the ninth book Michael Hartigan took a fateful decision. The poisoned chocolates ('from an admirer') which had been sent to Lord Harry by his old enemy the Ace of Spades, were eaten by the lovely Estelle. The inevitable end came as a relief to the public (who thought that she was seeing too much of her mother), and gave Lord Harry a freedom of expression which he had not hitherto enjoyed. Now he could clasp one lovely heroine after another to his breast, so long as nothing was said about marriage.

Michael Hartigan was a good business man. His early training had given him an insight into the economic laws which govern industry, and he understood why he grew richer and richer as his books became more and more popular. What he didn't see was why his publishers should. John Smith wrote a bad book, and they made £10 out of it. Michael

Hartigan wrote a good one, and they made £10,000. Why? What had *they* done? Nothing. There was no justice in it. A stickler for justice at this time, he acquired a controlling interest in a publishing firm, and became, in effect, his own publisher. This made things much fairer. Now the man who was earning the money was the one who was receiving it.

He received so much that with the publication of his twelfth book he was living in a large flat in Park Lane and employing two secretaries. But he had no illusions about himself. This was what his friends liked in him.

On a certain afternoon in December, Miss Fairlawn, the one he didn't take out to lunch, buzzed through to what she called his inner sanctum to say that a—

'Just a moment,' said Michael. 'With one bound Lord Harry reached the stake to which the half-fainting Natalie was bound, damn, tied. A quick slash of his knife—no—As the oncoming savages—no—The astonishment of the High Priest at this sudden apparition gave him a moment's quarter—grace—dammit, what's the word—breathing-space. Taking full advantage of it he—no— with a quick flick—flash—hasty flick—with a—hell, who cares?' He switched off the dictaphone. 'Well, Miss Fairlawn, what is it? And remember that savages are oncoming all the time, and we mustn't keep Natalie waiting.'

'Oh, I'm sorry, Mr Hartigan. There's a gentleman here who wants to see you.'

'Did you tell him that I didn't want to see *him*?'

'Yes, but—it's all very peculiar.'

'Who is he, anyhow? Press or public?'

'That's what's so peculiar. He says—really, Mr Hartigan, I don't know what to make of it—he says he's Michael Hartigan.'

'You mean he said *I* was? He's right. I am.'

'No, no, that's what *I* said, and *he* said *he* was.'

'Crackers,' said Mr Michael Hartigan after a little thought. 'Does he look crackers?'

'Well, no. He's very young.'

'That means nothing. You can start at any age. You can be born crackers, if it comes to that. Is he listening to all this?'

'Oh no, he's in the lobby. I really think you should see him, Mr Hartigan.'

'Oh, well, if you think so.'

Mr Hartigan brushed his hair, filled and lit the pipe with which he received visitors, puffed out a cloud of smoke, and called, 'Come in!' To his surprise a small, unattractive boy in spectacles, clutching a dirty bowler hat, edged through the door.

'Well, young man,' said Michael genially, 'what's all this in aid of? Sit down, make yourself comfortable. My time is your time.'

The visitor sat nervously down.

'I understand,' he said gruffly—'that is, I have been informed, that you write books under the—'

'Just a moment,' said Michael. 'Quite apart from everything else, hasn't your *voice* cracked rather early?'

'What do you mean? I'm eighteen and a quarter.'

'Mr dear sir, I do beg your pardon. In that case you must have a cigarette. There's a box at your elbow.'

'Er, I—thank—I think—er, no. *No!*'

'Just as you like. Or don't like. Well, now tell me all.'

'What I want to know is are you the man who writes these ghastly books under the name of Michael Hartigan?'

'Or should it be "over" the name? I never know. It doesn't matter, of course. Yes, Mr—er—I am. I gather, sadly, that you are not one of my admirers. By the way, I'm afraid I didn't get *your* name.'

'Michael Hartigan.'

'No, no, that's *my* name. You had all this out with my secretary. We don't want to get wound up about it again. What do they call you at school? Are you still at school, by the way?'

'Er, I—no—I mean, yes.'

'Surely there can't be any doubt in your mind? It's the sort of thing one usually knows so well. Well, what do your friends there call you?'

'Er—Scruffy.' It came out unwillingly.

'An excellent name,' said Michael kindly. 'With your permission, and so that we shall know which one of us is talking, I shall call you Scruffy. Now then, Scruffy, what's the trouble?'

'I want to know if your name is really Michael Hartigan.'

'It is.'

'I don't believe it.'

Michael shook his head sadly. 'When you are an old man, Scruffy, sitting in your bath-chair at Eastbourne, you will regret this.'

'*I'm* Michael Hartigan!'

'Are you sure?'

'Of course I am. Look at that!' He held out his bowler hat. 'Look inside!'

A little reluctantly Michael looked inside, and read on the dirty lining, 'M. R. Hartigan, 256.'

'My dear Hartigan,' he said, 'this is indeed a moment in our lives.' He got up, shook hands solemnly with his visitor and sat down again. 'I shall dedicate my next book to you. "To Michael Hartigan, in admiration and friendship". That'll make the critics think a bit—if,' he added, 'they ever do think.'

'The chaps all believe that you're my father.'

'I hope not,' said Michael, considerably alarmed by this. 'Can't you tell them that I am much too young, much too careful, and much too—well, tell them. Or couldn't your father come down one day and watch you rally the School forward in the second half, and then you could introduce him?'

'Good lord, I don't play rugger now I'm in the Sixth. Allow me a little self-respect.'

'The things I would allow you, Mr Hartigan, you wouldn't believe. Well, you now have my permission to return to your school friends and tell them that you are *not* my son. Was that what you wanted?'

'What I want is that you should stop using my name. I'm going up to Oxford with a scholar next autumn, and I'm going to be a writer, and how can I write when you've bagged my name?'

'You must do what I seem to have done, Scruffy. Bag somebody else's.'

'There you are!' said Scruffy triumphantly. 'I knew it wasn't your real name. You've got no right to it at all.'

'I assure you I have every right. Deed poll, and all that.'

'If you had to write all this frightful tripe, why couldn't you have stuck to your own name, instead of ruining mine?'

'Oh, believe me, I did want to. For months I had been imagining well-groomed men saying to delicately nurtured women across the dinner-table, "*Have* you read *The Priestess of the Crocodiles*?" For months I had imagined bearded members of the Athenaeum Club saying to each other across the billiard table, "Who *is* this Thomas Hardy everybody's talking about?" For months—'

'Is *your* name Thomas Hardy?'

'Was, Scruffy, was. But I bore no grudge against the other Mr Hardy for that. *I* didn't burst into his flat and ask him what the devil he meant by it. *I* didn't whine that he had ruined my literary career by making my name a household word. No, I just sat down at the instigation of my publisher, and thought of Michael Hartigan. So my advice to you, Scruffy, is to pull up your socks—or, of course, pull down what seem to be your pants, I don't mind which—and do the same.'

'It's pretty good cheek, you know,' said Scruffy, with dignity, 'to assume that the cases are parallel. Thomas Hardy, despite his old-fashioned attitude to the novel and his lack of style, was at least a conscientious writer with some knowledge of agricultural matters; whereas—'

'Keep the rest of your fascinating essay for the school Literary Society,' said Michael, getting up. 'Here is your hat. What does "R" stand for?'

'Russell,' muttered Scruffy unwillingly. He didn't know why he said it, when he wanted to say, 'What the hell's it got to do with you?'

'Then you can write your interesting masterpieces under the name of Russell Hartigan. I shan't object. And now,' said Michael, 'rustle off.'

He opened the door.

II

This was the only meeting between the two Michael Hartigans, and Scruffy never forgot it, nor forgave the other his share in it.

Scruffy went through life neither forgetting nor forgiving. He hated almost everybody because almost everybody exposed him in some way. He hated tall people because he was short, good-looking people because he knew himself to be ugly. He despised games because he had never been able to play them; he was contemptuous of good manners because his own manners were so graceless; he scorned pretty girls because he felt that he was an object of scorn to them. Even though he was clever, and was at times assured of it, he hated the more clever for his moments of doubt, and the equally clever for his inability to look down on them. The whole world was in a conspiracy against him. Whatever anybody else did, it was done with the idea of showing up M. R. Hartigan.

So now he hated Michael for his good humour, his ease of manner, his obvious attraction for women (women, ha!); for the absence of all the pomposity, stupidity and conceit which had been imagined for him. Even if the other had exhibited these undesirable qualities, Scruffy would still have hated him for his success, and for his lack of shame in it. And this was Michael Hartigan, the only Michael Hartigan whom the world would now know! Scruffy's righteous indignation accompanied him to Oxford in the autumn.

At Oxford he wrote for the undergraduate papers, contemptuous little articles such as undergraduates love. Whether by pulling up his socks or (as suggested) pulling down his pants, he managed to think of a new name for himself: Gryce. As Russell Gryce he had a small circle of admirers, who looked forward to his triumphant descent on London. His father, a hardware manufacturer, who thought little of writers but never ceased to wonder how they did it, said that he would stake his son for two years in London, and if he wasn't earning a living by then he would have to come into the hardware business. Scruffy left Oxford, settled in London and changed his name by deed poll to Gryce. This annoyed his father considerably, but his word was his bond, and what he had said he wouldn't go back on.

'But if you think I'm going to address my letters to him "Russell Gryce, Esquire"—'

'I'll address them, dear,' said his wife. 'Besides, you know you never do write.'

Scruffy began with a novel of Oxford life. It was to be the first real novel of Oxford life, but publishers didn't think so. He wrote an entirely original play, released from the old-fashioned strait-jacket of plot and counterplot. It was thought by managers to owe something to Tchekov. This annoyed Scruffy almost as much as it would have annoyed Tchekov. He wrote many other things, but was seldom rewarded. His contempt for the theatre and the publishing world was now extreme. He saw no future for himself save as a critic.

It was when the two years were nearly over, and he was still far from earning a living, that he came across Archibald Butters again. Archie was a round-faced, beaming, hospitable youth, a contemporary at Oxford, who had sat at Scruffy's feet imbibing culture. He had admitted apologetically that he knew nothing about literature and all that, but knew what he liked; in which respect he differed from Scruffy, who knew a great deal about it, but was never sure of liking anything until it had been rejected by the public. At first he was Scruffy's only friend and admirer; but as Russell Gryce got better known, Archibald Butters was a little overlooked, although it was always a pleasure to have a free meal in his hospitable rooms. Meeting him now, Scruffy found himself hoping that another free meal would be offered him; perhaps even a succession, such as might postpone the hardware business for a few days longer.

'Scruffy, old man!'

'Hallo, Archie.'

'I say, you're just the man I wanted! I've been trying to find you in the telephone book.'

'You wouldn't find me in the book. I've changed my name, you know.'

'I didn't. What? Why? Been left money?'

'Russell Gryce.'

'Oh, of course. Well, that's lucky, because it's really Russell Gryce I wanted to see. Because, old man, it's the most wonderful thing. The old governor died last June—well, of course, that wasn't so good, but it *was* last June—and it turned out he was practically a million-aire. Well, not quite that, but anyway I've got a nice whack of it, and I'm going to start a paper—literary monthly, like we always said we would, remember?—and I simply must have *you*. Look, let's go and have a drink, and I'll tell you all about it, and then we could go and have dinner somewhere, and you can tell *me*. Old boy, we'll wake them up. Gosh, I *am* glad to have run into you like this!'

III

That was how the 'advanced literary monthly' *Asymptote* was born. Scruffy had naturally supposed that he was to be Editor, with a satellite Butters making seasonal appearances, cheque-book in hand, admiration on lips. In this he was to be disappointed. Archie had grown up since Oxford days. He now knew everything about liter-ature and all that; and, with a cheerful certainty which he had only exhibited at Oxford when talking about food, he gave Scruffy the benefit of it.

He spoke of Gertrude Stein ('and I'm sure you agree with me, old man') as pathetically old-world, 'though, mind you, I'm not saying not all right for prep schools still.' He dismissed E. E. Cummings, 'the modern Longfellow' as a poet who left nothing to the imagination, 'drawing-room ballad stuff, old boy, we must do better than that.'

'I've got Brant as Editor, bit of luck there, and Speranza—you know him, of course, the man who invented Indifferentialism—as assistant. Brant wants a monthly review of novels, we must keep in touch with the lower orders, he says, and I said I knew just the man. That's you, old boy. Fifteen pounds a month, I thought, for an article of about 2,000 words, and of course you'll have the pick of the books, and sell as many as you like. Ought to be a good thing. We thought you might call it 'The Sheep and the Goats'. See the idea? Give the goats hell, same as you did at Oxford and do what you can for the real writers. They'll most of them be writing for us, of course, but one can't let personal considerations stand in the way.'

Scruffy's mind was in confusion. He was bewildered by the extra-ordinary change in Archibald Butters; a change the more remarkable because it seemed to have had no effect on his personality. He was the same cheerful, friendly soul as before, but with a new set of values and a new assurance, which he wore like a new and well-fitting suit of clothes; something which, with money in his pocket, he had decided to buy.

Scruffy was also confused by the strange mixture of powder and jam which he was being asked to swallow. Somebody was wanted to 'keep in touch with the lower orders', and they had immedi-ately thought of *him*! As against this, his Oxford articles were still remembered, and the hardware business could now be forgotten. He wanted to hate Archie for his money, his mental growth, his new self-confidence and, most of all, his patronage; but the presence of a bottle of Burgundy inside him, and the promise of security ahead of him, left his hatred unstabilized. He told himself that once on the review, in whatever capacity, he would put Archie in his proper place.

Asymptote was undoubtedly advanced, but with a month's rest between numbers its readers were able to keep up with it. A long poem consisting almost entirely of punctuation marks raised '!'s' and '?'s' from one or two foolish correspondents ... until the Editor reminded them that Browning was thought unintelligible when he first began to write. Puzzled (S.W.7), who had forgotten about this, was reassured. Art (and it made all the difference to Anxious at Ponders End) could not stand still. Under the guidance of *Asymptote* it advanced at the double.

Whatever of humiliation Scruffy had considered himself entitled to feel at that inaugural meeting, he soon lost when he began to write his monthly article. He had objected to the title 'The Sheep and the Goats' on the ground that the distinction between them was not sufficiently marked for what would mainly be a non-agricultural public, some of whom might prefer goats. Moreover, as an attribute of advanced fiction, would not 'sheeplike' raise less interesting anticipations than 'goatish'? If all one's goats were sheep, following the old trail, and one's sheep exhibited goat-like tendencies, what then? This being agreed, the final decision was for 'Gold and Tinsel'.

In his new position Scruffy justified the good opinion of himself which he had struggled so hard to hold. If a magazine which scarcely anybody saw can be said to have a feature, 'Gold and Tinsel' became the feature of *Asymptote*. The few subscribers enjoyed it because the writer was so obviously enjoying it. At last he had a platform from which he could get back at the world. Everything and everybody that he hated could be dragged in somewhere, and held up to contempt. Most of all, and in almost every number, the man who had robbed him of his birthright: Michael Hartigan.

'This month we propose to review one novel only: *Lord Harry to the Rescue*. It will be asked, "Have we then, nothing on the other side to show our readers, no gold to match the tinsel?" The answer is that when a Hartigan book appears on the bookstall, all else seems shining gold; so that we dare not estimate, we cannot estimate rightly, the true worth of any other.'

This was the beginning of the only full-length review which Michael ever had. One would have supposed that Scruffy could have worked off his hatred in 2,000 words, or at least kept what was over for the next Lord Harry book. But Michael had become his King Charles' head, a head for which a place could always be found.

'Severely as we have castigated him, let not Mr Sprott suppose that we place him among the Hartigans of the bookshops. We would not so insult him; we would not so betray our sense of literary values. All we ask of Mr Sprott is that he should abandon creative writing in favour of some other activity.' That did for Mr Sprott *and* Mr Hartigan. 'Although we have considered *Chased Bodies* to be worthy of inclusion in our Gold section, Mr Firkin must not be complacent. One can be illiterate, and yet above a Hartigan; one can be a writer of near-genius, and yet below a Proust. Mr Firkin has still something to learn.'

All this was good reading for Anxious and Puzzled, if not for Michael Hartigan. It was good reading for those non-subscribers who picked up *Asymptote* in their clubs and found in 'Gold and Tinsel' the only matters which they could understand. And it was a great day for Scruffy himself when a publisher's advertisement attributed to Russell Gryce the opinion that *Dead Grass* was a novel which nobody interested in modern fiction could afford to leave unread. It was a greater day still when another publisher boasted of one of his more unsaleable books that it 'bore the hall-mark of *Asymptote*'s gold standard'.

As the result of this public recognition Scruffy saw himself suddenly as not only the blaster but the maker of reputations. It would be for 'Gold and Tinsel' to herald a still newer and more sideways approach to creative fiction than had yet been seen; it would be for Russell Gryce to place the laurel wreath firmly on the brow of whomever he chose as the new Master.

He chose J. Frisby Withers, author of *Metronomic Beat*. Mr Withers had written three other novels, each of them more disordered than the one before. To the old-fashioned reader they suggested an almost illegible, much corrected, first pencil draft, which had been pulled together with a '*stet* everything', and handed over to a typist whose six easy lessons had not taken her up to capital letters and punctuation marks. The result was chaotic, but very impressive. In fact, it was Russell Gryce's considered opinion that *Metronomic Beat* was the most profoundly impressive contribution to creative fiction in our time.

IV

One would not have expected Michael Hartigan to be an original subscriber to *Asymptote*, and in fact he was not. But he subscribed to a press-cutting agency. Miss Fairlawn read all the cuttings which came in, destroyed the unflattering ones, and passed on the others. She came into the inner sanctum one morning, put a bunch of them on Michael's desk, and stood hesitating.

'And then there's this one, Mr Hartigan,' she said, holding it up.

'Good?'

'By no means, Mr Hartigan.'

'Then I don't want to see it. Why should I?'

'Well, I think it's libellous, Mr Hartigan. I thought you might want to do something about it. It's—it's disgraceful! People oughtn't to be allowed to write such things!'

'As bad as that? Let's have a look.' He took it, said 'Oh, one of *those* papers,' and began to read. Miss Fairlawn watched him anxiously, tears in her eyes, muttering 'Abominable' to herself.

'We must face it bravely,' said Michael, putting down the cutting. 'Russell Gryce doesn't care for us. Who is he? Ever heard of him?'

'Never!' cried Miss Fairlawn indignantly.

'Probably I missed a catch off his bowling at school, or did him out of the Divinity prize. These things rankle.'

'Do you want me to do anything about it, Mr Hartigan?'

'Such as?'

'Making an appointment with your solicitors, so that you could bring an action against him.'

'I'd sooner kick him and be fined forty bob. Much cheaper and much more pleasurable. Well, we'll see. Meanwhile, let me have every cutting by this fellow. In fact, I think it would be a good idea to take in his damned rag, what's it called, *Asymptote*. Will you do that?'

'Very well, Mr Hartigan.'

So for six months Michael read *Asymptote*, and comforted himself with the thought that nobody else read it. And more and more he wondered about Russell Gryce, and damned his soul. Then one day, at what was called a Literary Lunch, he saw the hated name on the table plan; located the seat; and knew that somewhere he had seen that face before. All through the meal and the first speech he was searching his memory, but in vain. Suddenly he banged the table, and cried '*Scruffy!*' Luckily the speaker was just sitting down, and it passed as an Italian expression of enthusiasm.

Scruffy!

Michael went back to his flat, still murmuring 'Scruffy' to himself. The new number of *Asymptote* was in, and J. Frisby Withers was making his bow to posterity. What Russell Gryce had not realized was that Alstons Ltd., who had recently assimilated the Daffodil Press and so become the publishers of *Metronomic Beat*, were also the publishers of the Lord Harry books. Michael, being in effect Alstons Ltd., realized it at once. He began to smile gently. He went on smiling to himself for quite a long time.

The meaning of the smile was not immediately clear to Scruffy. A chaste little advertisement of *Metronomic Beat* quoted *Asymptote*. 'Russell Gryce, the well-known critic writes ...' and Scruffy read it, and looked modestly down his nose. This was fame.

But next week there was another advertisement.

Messrs Alstons Ltd. have the honour to announce
TWO NEW BOOKS.

LORD HARRY AT BAY by Michael Hartigan, METRONOMIC
BEAT by J. Frisby Withers.

RUSSELL GRYCE, the famous critic of *Asymptote*, calls this 'the most
profoundly impressive contribution to creative fiction in our time'.

A protective circle round the advertisement made it clear that this
was Messrs Alstons' only contribution to creative fiction that week,
and one gathered that Mr Gryce thought it impressive.

Scruffy didn't like it. The Editor of *Asymptote* didn't like it. Even
Archie Butters didn't like it. In a dignified letter to the publishers the
Editor pointed out that the advertisement was misleading. Alstons
Ltd. expressed surprise. They could not believe that any intelligent
reader of *Asymptote* had been misled; but rather than mislead even
one person they would withdraw the advertisement in its present
form. They withdrew it a fortnight later.

Michael had an uncle, who was the Bishop of St. Bees. The Bishop
was a kindly man, and when his nephew sent him a book to read ('which
my firm has just published, I wonder what you will think of it') he did
his best. In the following weeks the advertisement took a new form.

METRONOMIC BEAT
By
J. Frisby Withers

RUSSELL GRYCE, the famous critic, writes: 'Profoundly impressive.'
THE BISHOP OF ST. BEES writes: 'Undoubtedly clever.'

The Bishop had written a good deal more, beginning with 'but';
space, however, was limited.

At this period the money which Michael earned, whether as author or publisher, meant very much less to him than it did to the Chancellor of the Exchequer. Anything on the debit side of the account was so much off income-tax; and if 'annoying Scruffy' could be counted as legitimate expenses, it was a much cheaper amusement than buying a new car. But, as it happened, the money was beginning to come back. Continuous advertisement was so swelling the sales of *Metronomic Beat* that it justified (or nearly) the next announcement.

It is reassuring to find that the literary taste of a critic like Russell Gryce is at one with that of the general public; it is good to know that a popular best-seller can win the approval of such an eclectic review as *Asymptote*. Such has been the fortunate destiny of *Metronomic Beat*, whose fifth large edition is announced to-day. It was this book that Mr Russell Gryce, the famous critic of *Asymptote*, speaking for the average man, proclaimed 'the most impressive contribution to creative fiction of our time.

Michael was enjoying himself, almost as much as Scruffy had once enjoyed himself. If there were times when he felt sorry for Scruffy, he read again the review of *Lord Harry to the Rescue*, and hardened his heart. Nobody should be allowed to get away with that sort of thing.

Scruffy was not enjoying himself. When he went in now to the office of *Asymptote*, the Editor gave him a cold nod, Speranza said 'Oh—you?' and turned away, and even Archie made an excuse for leaving him—'Just a moment, old man'—and never came back. They all seemed to be telling him that it was not *Asymptote*'s business to boom best-sellers, not their business to ally themselves with Bishops. He dreaded to look at the Sunday papers now. What new indignity was waiting for him?

Next Sunday he knew.

THE POPULAR TASTE

METRONOMIC BEAT (8th Edn)

MR RUSSELL GRYCE, the popular critic, writes: 'The most impressive contribution to creative fiction of our time'.

MR MICHAEL HARTIGAN, the popular author, writes: 'A rattling good yarn'.

'And if that doesn't do it,' said Michael to the admiring Miss Fairlawn a week later, 'nothing will.'

But it did. Russell Gryce, the popular critic, was already in the train, on his way to the hardware business.

The River

(1950)

I

'The marriage arranged between Mr Nicholas Deans and Miss Rosemary Paton will not now take place.'

I knew them both. I am remembering them now, and that astonishing August morning when I read the announcement in *The Times*, and then read it aloud to Mary, and we stared at each other across the breakfast table.

'Nicky and Roma?' cried Mary. 'Darling, it's crazy! Why, they were here only a month ago, jibbering with love! What on earth does it mean?'

I didn't know. This was in 1937. Perhaps if I had known then, one of us might have done something. We didn't know until two years later, when the Second World War was beginning, and Rosemary had married young Wayne. I am remembering it all now, because at breakfast this morning two paragraphs in the paper caught my eye. The first recorded a posthumous and extremely belated award to an airman who had died very bravely. I had just read this, and had it still in my mind as I turned to the 'Forthcoming Marriages'. At the bottom of the column it said that the marriage arranged between Squadron Leader A and Miss B would not now take place. Nicky fought in the Battle of Britain, rose to be a Squadron Leader with a chest full of medals, and died as

482

bravely as any of them. Somehow it brought it all back. There was Mary across the table, looking not a day older: the same table, the same china. I almost expected to hear her cry, 'Nicky and Roma? Darling, it's crazy!'

II

Mary's people had lived at Castle Craddock for hundreds of years. Her father was one of those survivors of the really old families whose founders had somehow been overlooked when baronies were being given out, and who were much too proud to accept titles from upstart Plantagenets and their successors. George Craddock, D.L., J.P. could look any so-called peer in the face, and down his nose at most of them. He became my father-in-law, and I got to know him fairly well. I admired him, liked him, and was rather afraid of him. In the way of wives, Mary used to tell me that he was very fond of me. Well, I wouldn't say that, but he was surprisingly kind to me; particularly when it was broken to him that Mary and I loved each other. Nobody, of course, was good enough for Mary, but he may have thought that at least an unpretentious middle-class professional man was better than an upstart Earl. In any case, Mary could always get round him, even on such an important matter as her marriage.

I was a very young architect in those days, and, leaving out the 'very young', still am. By 1914 George Craddock had reluctantly reached the conclusion that horseless transport had come to stay. Nobody, of course, would want to rush about the country for pleasure in one of those contraptions, but for anybody who lived ten miles from a station they might be useful for shifting luggage, or even guests, from one point to another. So my firm was commissioned to turn an old barn adjoining the stables into a garage, with rooms for a chauffeur above it. My chief went down for the night, made his reconnaissance, and came back to draw up his plans. Then, luckily for me, he fell ill, and it was left to me to see his plans carried out. So, for the first time, I spent a night at Castle Craddock, and met Mary.

We have been married thirty-four years now, and I suppose I am a little more worthy of her than I was; by which I mean that I have done well in my profession, and that nobody could live with Mary for thirty-four years and not be a better man. But I still look across the table at her, and wonder how I dared to ask her to marry me. She was so young, and so old; so innocent, and so wise; so gay, and so serious; so simple, and so precious. I can still remember the agonies I went through when I knew that I was in love with her. I imagined myself telling her; saw her kind, pitying smile; heard old Craddock's ringing laugh; read in *The Morning Post* next week of her engagement to the Duke of This or the Earl of That, and laughed bitterly myself at my own folly. Madness! Still, I suppose I should have had to propose to her anyhow, even without the assistance of Master Nicholas Deans. But I do not know whether, without him, she would have accepted me.

It was the last time I had come down professionally, the last day on which I could pretend that it was necessary for me to be there. There was, as always, company in the house, but on that last morning I had somehow managed to get her alone. We went for a walk. It had rained heavily for a week, but now it was fine and warm again, and if I hadn't been so hopeless I should have been happy. We went down through the pines to the river. Normally it ran gaily and peacefully enough, and in very dry weather an active person could cross it jumping from rock to rock, but now it was a swirling yellow torrent, and only here and there was the top of a boulder momentarily visible in the foam. I told myself that, if only Mary would fall in, I could jump in after her, and we should both be drowned; and perhaps, if she wasn't already in love with somebody else, we should still be together in Heaven, and—well, anyhow, we should still be together. It seemed bad luck on Mary to drown her like this, so I told myself that, if only we had brought one of the puppies with us, and it fell in, then I would jump in and be drowned, and that that was better than the misery which was all I could look forward to for the next fifty years. And

I told myself that, if by a miracle the puppy and I came safely to shore, some of Mary's love for the restored puppy would carry over to me, and she might even—well, you see the sort of state I was in. And it was while all this absurd, romantic, heroic, but not really at all heroic nonsense was going through my mind that Master Nicholas Deans obligingly fell in; and, as near as might be unconsciously, I went in after him. Who wouldn't have done, with the mother shrieking fifty yards upstream, and his girl standing by his side?—particularly if she were already unhooking her skirt, the silly little idiot. I pushed her out of the way and jumped.

It was pure luck that Master Deans and I met, because I couldn't have done anything about it if we hadn't. I grabbed him, and found more than ever that I couldn't do anything about it. I tried to take some small part in events with my left arm, but it hit one of those submerged rocks with a wallop, and that seemed to be that. If it is possible to be extremely happy and extremely angry and extremely frightened at the same time, then that's what I was; or perhaps first one and then the other. Happy because now Mary would never forget me; angry with the river for being so damnably discourteous; and frightened because I was about to die and I didn't know what it was going to be like. I'm afraid that I never thought of Master Deans.

Well, the river took a sudden turn, and we were washed up in a sort of little backwater, and we struggled out. By that time Mary, who could run like Atalanta, was ready for me, while Mrs Deans was still wringing her hands and crying a hundred yards behind. Mary didn't say 'My hero!' or 'Are you hurt?' or 'Is he dead?' she took Master Nicholas Deans from me, turned him upside down, and said:

'You'll find the Craddock Arms down stream by the bridge. Tell them what happened, and ask them to ring up the house. They'll know what to do. Then come back and help. You'd better bring a blanket with you.'

I didn't feel much like running, and I had an idea that I was going to be sick in a moment, but I ran. And then I ran back with the blanket, and a double brandy inside me, feeling like somebody else, and wondering why his left arm looked so silly. Mary, who had been brought up to know everything that a young girl on a desert island, surrounded by wreck-survivors and wild animals, ought to know, was kneeling over Master Deans and pumping air into him in the most professional way. His mother had been sent up the hill where she could see the house, and told to wave to it when help began to come. She would have been a nuisance anywhere else.

'Anything I can do?' I asked.

'Watch me,' panted Mary, 'because you'll have to take over soon.'

'I doubt it,' I said, and passed out.

I had had a fortnight's holiday coming to me; and I spent it at Castle Craddock; the first few days in bed, rather unnecessarily, but I didn't mind because Mary looked after me. It is not quite clear how we became engaged. She said afterwards that it was she who proposed, and that it was when I knocked her down so brutally that she realized that she loved me. I suggested that the moment of revelation came not when I courteously motioned her to one side, but when Mrs Deans, who was a young and pretty widow, flung her arms round my neck and kissed me; and that that husky noise next morning, which she may have thought was a water-pipe, was me proposing to her. She said, 'Well, anyhow, darling, I'm jolly well going to marry you.' I suppose that in the ordinary way we should have seen too much of this Mrs Deans, who had been a complete stranger and now looked like being a friend for life; but the First World War was at hand, and life very soon left the ordinary. Mrs Deans was whirled back to London in a torrent of gratitude; Master Deans, being only two, said nothing of moment; and I married Mary, spent a short but ecstatic honeymoon with her, returned her to her father, and went into the Army.

III

My office was in Bedford Square. We had a flat above it, which I used when I had to, and which Mary and the children used as little as possible, preferring our cottage in Kent. She came up for a night in July 1935, so that we could celebrate the coming-of-age of our engagement—anything for a celebration was our motto. The always difficult question of whether to dine before the play or sup afterwards, or both, was solved by an invitation to a cocktail party at the Savoy, which fitted in very nicely. It was given by a Mrs Paton, who was a distant cousin of Mary's. I didn't know many of the people there, and was beginning to get a bit bored, when our hostess brought a middle-aged woman up to me, and introduced us. For once I caught the name: Mrs Fellowes.

After we had talked a little, she smiled at me and said, 'You don't recognize me?'

I didn't and said so. I might have added that if I saw her again to-morrow, I shouldn't. She had one of those faces which seem to be about a good deal.

'Well, it was a long time ago that we met, and I've changed my name since then.'

'Your dress too, probably,' I smiled. 'That makes a difference, you know.'

'All the same, I recognized *you*, and you were in pyjamas when I last saw you.'

'Coming out of the bathroom? With sponge?'

'In bed,' she said with an arch smile.

She was obviously enjoying the conversation. I wasn't. Not with her, and on this particular day. I wanted to say, 'Were you bringing my morning tea?' but it would have been rather rude.

I said, 'Sorry, I give it up.'

'I used to be Mrs Deans.'

'That seems to strike a note,' I lied, 'but I'm blessed if I can remember. Mrs Deans,' I murmured to myself, hoping it would come back to me.

'I suppose you're always diving into rivers and saving people's lives?' she said, rather huffed.

'Good Lord! Of course!'

I remembered her. I remembered suddenly that she had kissed me, had come into my bedroom to say good-bye, and that but for her, or the boy—was it a boy? Yes, I was sure it was.

'How is he?' I asked, as if he might still have a bit of a cold. With another flash of memory I got the name. 'Nicholas, I mean.'

She beamed at me for remembering the name.

'That's Nicky over there,' she said, nodding towards a young man and a girl standing by the serving-table. 'Would you like to meet him?'

'Very much.' And then I hesitated. 'I say, you haven't told him?'

'He doesn't even know that he fell in. I thought it best not to say anything about it.'

'I'm sure you were right. Let's go on saying nothing about it.'

That was how I met Master Deans again. The girl to whom he was talking was Rosemary Paton. He had just been introduced to her.

IV

Mrs Fellowes, fortunately, lived with her new husband somewhere in the North. Nicky was in London, reading for the Bar. He and Roma got engaged one week-end in our cottage. But for Nicky, Mary and I might not have been there, so it was only right that we should have helped him (if we did) to his happiness. We loved Nicky, and I think he loved us; the children adored him. Roma was a very nice girl, but—

It is a funny thing that whenever, at this time, I thought or said or wrote that Roma was a very nice girl, I always went on '*but*—' and then stopped. Because I never discovered what the 'but' was. She was extremely pretty; she was intelligent and could see a joke; she was nice to everybody, and as considerate as a pretty girl is expected to be; she could ride and swim and play golf and lawn-tennis better than most; and I had never heard her say an unkind word about anybody. But—But what? I couldn't explain, except by saying that something seemed not to be ticking over properly, and I wanted to shake her until it came into play. 'I wanted to shake her.' Was that it? That there didn't seem to be anybody there? Well, that was as near as I could get.

Nicky was tall and dark and eager, with a thin sensitive face, and black hair which kept falling over his left eye and had to be tossed back, and he always seemed to have just discovered, or to be on the point of discovering, whatever exciting thing it was for which he was looking. When two people have been married for over twenty years, their life together, however happy, has a certain regular pitch which can strictly be called monotony. Nicky made a week-end an adventure; not only for himself, but for us. Even the servants—and Mary was always on happy family terms with her staff—used to light up when she told them that Mr Deans was coming.

In the holidays, when the children were at home, we could only manage one guest at a time. It was not until the Easter term of 1937 that Roma and Nicky came down together. They had met again in London a few weeks earlier, and it was obvious at once that they were madly in love with each other. When they came back from a walk on the Sunday afternoon and announced that they had just got engaged, we were a little surprised. In our old-fashioned way we had assumed that they were already engaged; indeed, we shouldn't have been astonished to hear that this was their honeymoon. They had been embarrassingly devoted to each other all the week-end, and embarrassingly unembarrassed in front of us.

Well, we realized that we had lost Nicky for the time being. They came down again at the end of June, and, as far as they were concerned, we might not have been there. In fact, we began to feel a little like an engaged couple ourselves. They were being married in October, and were having a golfing holiday together in August.

They said good-bye to us on the Monday. They wrote their usual charming bread-and-butter letters. And we heard no more of them until that morning when I opened *The Times* and read that the marriage arranged between them would not take place.

'Darling, it's crazy!' cried Mary. 'What on earth does it mean?'

'Some silly quarrel, I suppose.'

'But you don't make a quarrel public in *The Times* one day, and then announce next day that you've made it up.'

That was true. It was obviously more than a temporary quarrel. It was final.

'What does one do?' I asked. 'Write and sympathize? But with which? Presumably one of them wanted it, and one didn't. One is glad and one is sorry.'

'Well, we can't just leave it. I could write to Marjory'—that was Mrs Paton—'but she may not know any more than we do.'

We thought it over.

'I'll write to Nicky,' I said at last, 'and you write to Roma. And we'll just say how sorry we are, and make it clear that if it helps them to confide in somebody, here we are, and, if not, we shall quite understand. That sort of thing.'

So that was what we did. And Roma said politely, 'Thank you very much, but I don't want to talk about it'; and Nicky said, 'It's very decent of you and just like you both, but there's nothing to be said except that I deserve to have lost her, and that it was I who broke it off.'

And what that meant neither of us knew.

V

We didn't see Roma again until April, 1939, when Mary went to her wedding. I made some excuse of business. Whatever had happened, I was on Nicky's side. So was Mary, of course, but Roma was some sort of cousin, and the Craddocks take their relations seriously.

'How did she look?' I asked.

'Radiantly happy, and as pretty as ever.'

'Glad to see you again?'

'I don't think she thought of it as "again". It might have been two years ago, and she was marrying Nicky.'

'H'm!' I said; which meant—well, I don't know what it meant, except that I never understood the girl.

We hadn't seen Nicky. He had gone in madly for flying, had given up the Bar, and had got a job as a test pilot with an aeroplane company in the Midlands. We heard from him from time to time, but he didn't come down to Kent any more. Not for lack of invitations.

And then, a week before war broke out, he invited himself. I drove in to meet him.

'I had to see you all again before the show started,' he said. 'I shall be looking so beautiful in my uniform that you won't recognize me.'

'R.A.F., of course?'

'Yes. How's everybody?'

'Grand. Longing to see you.'

'Martin left school?'

'You mean for good? No, another year, thank God. Elizabeth will want to be a nurse or something, I suppose. What a hell of a business.'

'Oh well, it had to come.'

We had a delightful week-end, almost like old times. We sat up late on Sunday night, after the children had gone to bed. And then quite suddenly he said:

'Let's go down to the garden-house.'

'Won't it be too cold to sit?' said Mary.

'Then get a coat, darling.'

'I think I will too,' I said, 'just in case.'

'As a matter of fact, it's damned hot,' he shouted after us.

We sat out in the still night, one of us on each side of him, my cigarette-end glowing as I drew on it, his face clear cut suddenly in the darkness as he relighted his pipe. We were all silent for a little. Then he gave a long sigh.

'I want to get this off my chest,' he began, 'before—' He left it at that, and went on, 'You two darlings are the only people I could tell it to, and I should like you to know the worst of me.'

'Carry on,' I said. 'It won't be as bad as you think.'

'Pretty bad,' he said.

I felt rather than saw Mary's hand go out and touch his for a moment.

'Well, here it is. I think we told you that we were going to stay with some people in Devonshire—your part of the world, isn't it, Mary?—we were supposed to be playing golf, they were all mad about it. I drove Roma down. For the first three days and nights it rained without stopping. There we all were, and Roma and I couldn't get alone, and it was general hell. On the fourth morning it suddenly cleared up. Everybody rushed to play golf, but we wanted to get away from them all, so we got into the car and drove off. We fetched up for lunch at a pub called the Craddock Arms. I don't suppose you know it, but—'

'I had a drink there once,' I said.

'Oh, did you? Oh well, then, you'll have seen the river.'

'I have.'

'But not as it was then. It hadn't been like that for more than twenty years, they said at the pub. It was just a raging torrent with waves spouting up on the rocks in mid-stream. We had Duncan with us—you remember Roma's Scottie? He had been sitting at the back, as good as anything, all the way, and we took him along the river to stretch his legs, while they got the lunch ready.'

He stopped. The night was very still. We waited.

'Have you ever frightened yourself with your own imagination? I mean by seeing something which isn't there, so clearly that it is there and you're terrified of it? Off and on all my life I have lain in bed, awake, and seen a river like that, and shuddered with fear, and thought, "My God, fancy falling in!" And there it was. Just as I had imagined it.'

He stopped again to relight his pipe. By the flame of the match Mary and I looked at each other.

'We were walking up stream. Roma had let go of my hand, and was running in front with Duncan, pretending to chase him, and Duncan dodged and fell in. Roma shrieked, "Oh, darling!" All right, now tell me that a sensible person doesn't risk almost certain death for a little dog. Go on. Tell me.'

'He doesn't,' said Mary. 'It's sentimental and idiotic.'

'All right. He doesn't. It's sentimental and idiotic. Human beings are more precious than little dogs, aren't they? Their lives are more valuable. Aren't they? More worth saving?'

'One hopes so,' I said.

'One hopes so. So I did nothing. I just stood there. Damn it, I said calmly to myself, one doesn't risk almost certain death for a little dog. Sensible, that's what I was. Realistic. Not sentimental. Not idiotic. Not—' he paused and added very gently, 'not like Roma.'

Mary gave a gasp. I said, 'Good lord, you mean Roma went in?'

'Whipped off her skirt, and in like a flash. Roma! The girl I loved. Into that raging torrent. Now ask me what I did. Go on!' he shouted. 'Ask me!'

'All right,' I said. 'What did you do?'

'Nothing.' He said it so sadly, so gently, that we hardly heard it. 'Nothing,' he said wonderingly to himself.

Once more there was silence. Once more he put a match to his pipe. Once more Mary and I looked at each other in the flame of it; and she shook her head, meaning 'Not yet'.

'I told myself—I pretended to tell myself that there was nothing I could do. Roma was at least as good a swimmer as I, and I couldn't have helped her. But of course it wasn't that. I was terrified. You've read of people being rooted to the ground in fear. It was like that. I couldn't have jumped for a million pounds. Oh well, that's silly, Roma was worth much more than a million pounds to me. But if I were to have been shot for cowardice the next morning,

I couldn't have jumped. There wasn't a muscle in my body over which I had any control. I can't expect you to believe this, but—' He broke off suddenly, shaking his head, as if it were beyond even his own understanding.

'Don't be silly, darling,' said Mary, 'of course we believe you. Tell us what happened to Roma.'

'She caught Duncan up—you know what she's like in the water—and collared him. They were close in shore luckily, where there weren't any rocks and the current wasn't so fast. The river swung round suddenly and they got washed into a little backwater. All danger being over, I became active. I was full of resource. I trotted up stream and fetched her skirt. I trotted down stream with it. And, at the grave risk of wetting the ends of my trousers, I helped them out.'

'*Did* you wet the ends of your trousers?' asked Mary anxiously.

Nicky gave a great laugh, and said, 'Good old Mary, how I do love you two,' and went on with his story, more quickly, more naturally.

'Well, there we all were; Duncan frisking about and shaking himself, Roma wringing the water out of her hair, and I not knowing what on earth to say or do. And then, as soon as she had got into her skirt, she took my hand and said, "Come on, darling, let's run for the inn. I shall have to go to bed while they're drying my clothes, but we can have lunch upstairs if you don't mind my not looking my best in the landlady's nightgown. What fun! Or perhaps it would be nicer if I didn't wear one at all. Don't you think so, darling?" And she gave me a loving look, and squeezed my hand. It was uncanny. It was just as if I had been somewhere else when it happened, and had strolled up and found them on the bank.'

'Poor Nicky. Horrible for you.'

'Yes. Well, it was all like that. Tact. Perfect tact. Not once did she give a hint that anything out of the way had happened, that she had noticed anything, that there was anything for either of us to worry about. With one half of my mind I felt that it was wonderful of her to spare my feelings like this, and with the other half I wished to God she would jeer at me and call me a coward.'

'It was difficult for her,' I said, doing my best for a girl I had never really liked.

'It must have been. But then the whole situation was impossible. There were times in the next few days when I could almost persuade myself that this was my old daydream come back, and that I was imagining it all. And then one morning I heard her talking rubbish to Duncan, and saying, "Did he fall in the river and ask his missis to pull him out?" or something like that. It had happened all right.'

'So you broke it off?'

'Yes. It would always have been between us. Perhaps if we had really had it out—I don't know—but hushed up like that—and anyway a girl can't be expected to marry a coward. Not when she's as brave as Roma. That river—if you could have seen it! No, I couldn't live up to her, she couldn't live down to me. As soon as we got back to London, I wrote.'

Then Mary said an odd thing. Or so I thought at the time.

'Did Roma know what you were talking about in your letter?' she asked.

'Well, you see, I'd been finding it difficult to be as loving as I had been. I always had that moment in my mind. You can't make love when you're thinking of something else all the time. Roma actually thought that I was falling for another girl there. We did have a silly quarrel about that, a girl I'd hardly spoken to. In my letter I just said that, after what had happened, it was obvious that we couldn't be happy together. She may have thought that I meant the quarrel.'

'I'm sure she did,' said Mary. 'How do you feel about Roma now?'

'Do you mean am I still in love with her? Not a bit. I expect it was mostly physical, you know. One gets over that more easily.'

'That's good. Now, Nicky, John has something to tell you. But I think that before he begins I should like to say something about Roma. It's only lately that I have got her clear in my mind, and in any case it wouldn't have done any good talking about it before. You thought that Roma was being tactful—sweetly, unbearably tactful. She wasn't. Tact means considering people's feelings, and Roma has never found it necessary to do that. Rosemary Paton is the supreme egotist. She is the centre of her own stage all the time, and everybody and everything else is just a cue or an audience or a property for her. You didn't exist for her at all when Duncan fell in, except as an audience in the wings. It never went through her head for a moment that you were a coward. You weren't on in the great dog-rescuing scene, so how could you be brave or not brave? And what did it matter to her if you felt this or that off-stage, so long as you were there on your cue, and played your part properly, when the love-scene came on? Roma's whole world is Rosemary Paton—and you are well out of it.'

So that explained Roma; explained that 'but' which used to worry me. I saw it now. She was a dead woman in a dead world of her own.

'I daresay you're right,' said Nicky indifferently. 'That's Roma. But I'm where I was.'

'Well, now John is going to tell you where you were twenty-five years ago. Go on, darling.'

I had known that this was coming, and had been wondering how to deal with it. No friendship between men can survive the knowledge that one has saved the other's life.

'All right,' I said. 'Now listen, Nicky, because this is important, and really quite simple. You say that all your life you have had terrifying visions of a river, that you recognized this as the river you'd always imagined, and that physically and literally you couldn't have gone in whatever the moral compulsion?'

'Yes.'

'Well, it's natural enough. When you were two years old, you did go into that river, at, I should say, that very spot, and the river was pretty much as you saw it more than twenty years later. Terrifying.'

'You're mad!'

'No, it's a fact. And if you like to observe that the world is a very small place, or the arm of coincidence a very long one, you may.'

'How do you know?'

'Your mother talked about it that day we met you.'

He turned to Mary.

'Is this true?'

'Of course, Nicky.'

'Why should my mother talk about it to you?'

Before she could answer, I said:

'Because Mary was there. Your body came to shore in that same backwater. You were dead, Nicky. I don't suppose you knew, but Mary lived at Castle Craddock when she was a girl. She found you there dead, and she restored you to life.'

Mary gave a short hysterical laugh and said, 'Don't be such an idiot, Johnny. Of course he wasn't dead.'

'Who knows?' I said. 'Who knows what happens when the drowned are restored to life?'

Nicky gave a great sigh, squaring his shoulders as if he were easing them of the burden which he had been carrying for two bitter years.

'So you see,' I went on, 'when your mother met Mary again after all that time—well, naturally, when I was introduced to her, she was full of it. We talked of nothing else. And she told me that she had thought it better not to say anything to you; and, like a fool, I said that I was sure she was right. But of course we were desperately wrong. You've had the thing gnawing away inside you all these years, and known nothing about it. So, my dear Nicky, wash out the idea that you are, or were, a coward; or, if you insist, you must give us much better evidence than you have given us to-night.'

There was a long silence this time, a very long silence. It was lighter now, or perhaps I was getting more used to the darkness. I could see Nicky's face. He was looking up into the sky, with that eager look which he always used to have, as if he were on the verge of discovery.

He turned to Mary.

'Did I say thank you nicely at the time,' he said, 'or was I too young?'

'A bit too young, Nicky.'

'Then I'll say it now. Thank you, darling.' He picked up her hand, kissed it, and let it go. 'You'll see. I won't let you down.'

He didn't. He didn't.

The Wibberley Touch

(1950)

I

It may be within the memory of my friends that recently I recorded the facts which led to my expulsion from The Towers (whither I had gone in all good faith on a Christmas visit) by the direction of the third Mrs Aldwinckle (Bella). It was a melancholy business, which reflected, as I showed, the greatest discredit, both on that lady herself and her step-daughter (Gabrielle). My indecision as to which of them I should marry being thus set at rest (as it would have been in one sense anyhow by the discovery at The Towers that Mr Aldwinckle, though senile, was still officially alive), I was now maturing my matrimonial plans in another direction; as it happened, the second and divorced Mrs Aldwinckle, Claudine. My feelings, therefore, can be imagined when I received a letter from her solicitor a few days ago, threatening me, on her behalf, with a writ for malicious slander! The idea of marrying a woman who goes about pursuing innocent and spotless men with writs for slander is so repugnant to me that I decided at once that I should have to look elsewhere for a mate; but further reflection showed me that first and foremost I owed my friends a plain statement of the facts. For once again I have been abominably treated by one of Mr Aldwinckle's many wives; once again I have been the victim of cruel circumstance. In an unfortunate situation in which anybody might have found himself I acted throughout, not only with discretion, but with a high degree of ingenuity—and this is my reward! Let my friends judge. Let the facts speak for themselves.

II

The second Mrs Aldwinckle, Claudine, had married again, and was the widow of a rich manufacturer called Pagham. It is an unlovely name, and the opportunity, which I proposed to give her, of changing it to Wibberley would no doubt have been welcome to her. At the time of which I write I was already calling her by her Christian name, and making a few careless enquiries as to how the late Mr Pagham had left his money. These were most satisfactory; indeed, by a flight of fancy one might say that the air was already charged with the distant music of wedding-bells.

On this fatal Wednesday evening (as it proved to be) I was taking her out to dinner. This was the first time that I had had this pleasure, so naturally it was to be something of an occasion. We were dining at a newly opened restaurant unknown to either of us, of which I had heard a good account: the Hirondelle. I had already decided on champagne.

In good heart, then, I drove up to her house in Green Street, telling the cabman to wait. This meant a little extra on the clock, but at the time I did not grudge it; now, of course, I know that it was wasted money. We were both of us in evening dress, and made, if I may say so, a handsome and well-matched couple. Claudine, being what I may call the *ex*-mother of Gabrielle, was naturally some years older than myself, but remarkably well preserved; I, for my part, had been from childhood intellectually ahead of my contemporaries, and have continued to give an impression of maturity somewhat beyond my years.

I think it was Shakespeare who observed that the course of true love never did run smooth, and almost immediately I had an example of this.

I had been hoping that after dinner I should not only see Claudine home, and thus have an opportunity of indicating the warmth of my feelings in the taxicab, but that I might even be invited upstairs for a moment, when I could make a more pronounced revelation of my passion. Indeed, I saw myself coming away from Green Street an accepted suitor and the happiest of men. How different the dream from the reality!

'Is that you, Cecil?' she called out from her bedroom. 'Where are you taking me?'

'The Hirondelle,' I replied. And I added, 'If that is all right with you?'

'Nice. Do you know the telephone number?'

'Yes. Why? Anything particular you want ordered?' I admit that I felt a little hurt at the suggestion that I could not be trusted in the matter.

'Heavens, no. I leave that to you. With confidence, my dear man. But Paul will probably be ringing up, and I said I'd leave the number. Give it to Annette, will you? And mix us both a drink.'

Her maid came in. I make a habit of jotting down the details of engagements in my book, and was thus able to give Annette the number she required. I may say that I objected strongly to the intrusion of this Paul, whoever he might be, and felt that some explanation was necessary.

Claudine joined me just as I had got the drinks ready, and I am bound to say, in the teeth, so to speak, of what has since transpired, that she looked extremely well. A propensity for issuing writs cannot disguise the fact that she had a good figure, a flair for dress, and a very clever maid.

'Here's to everybody,' she said as she drank.

'And to you above all,' I replied, my eyes meaningly on hers. 'Cigarette?'

I put down my glass and whipped out my cigarette-case; with a flick of the finger my lighter was ready for her. Women appreciate this sort of well-bred dexterity in their men.

'Thank you.' She blew out a cloud of smoke. 'About Paul. I was hoping we might have danced somewhere afterwards, or something, but I suddenly remembered this party I'd promised to go to, and Paul said he might be able to call for me. He's going to ring up and let me know.'

'My dear Claudine,' I said, 'I should have driven you home in any case, and I could have driven you equally easily to your party.'

'Not quite as easily, darling, it's right in the wilds of the country. Richmond or somewhere.'

'Would that be Richmond in Yorkshire?' I asked, not without irony.

'I shouldn't be surprised. It's an anniversary of something, and I'm hoping Paul will tell me before we get there whether it's a birth, a marriage or a death.'

I must confess that the 'darling' mollified me, though I still felt that Paul was not essential to the success of the evening.

We drove off. I took her hand in mine, but some sudden need to touch up her hair arose, and I was unable to retain it. In any case we had a very short way to go. As soon as we arrived, I mentioned that there would be a telephone call later for Mrs Pagham. A careless motion of the hand indicated the lady of whom I was speaking; and if I a little over-emphasized the ugly 'Pagham', there was an underlying suggestion both in my voice and in the glance which I gave her that the name was not irremediable.

I had ordered a table up against the wall, so that we should sit together. I was glad to find that ours was the last on that side of the restaurant, and that for the moment the table on Claudine's right was vacant. Though the place was otherwise crowded, and there was a pleasant hum of conversation, we were, so to put it, in a little island of our own. I think I may say that I am a good host; the food was excellent, and the wine, a vintage Lanson, above reproach. We talked gaily. I had been keeping a witty anecdote from *The Reader's Digest* for this very occasion, and it went well. We also had some amusing passages again about the Aldwinckle family. Once more she confirmed the severe judgment I had been compelled to pass upon the present

Mrs Aldwinckle (Bella), and we laughed together over it. It was a merry evening.

However, all good things must come to an end. As we sipped our coffee the waiter arrived with the bill. Although it was discreetly folded, I caught sight of the final figure. It was, as I had feared, in the neighbourhood of £4 10s. 0d. I continued, however, to talk gaily, and she was smiling at my whispered comment on the hat of the woman now sitting next to her—(for I should explain that the Hirondelle does not insist on evening dress, and the two women who had taken the empty table were both in hats)—she was smiling, I say, at some pleasantry of mine on this rather ridiculous red hat, when the telephone summons came.

'That's Paul at last,' said Claudine, getting up—rather too eagerly, I thought. 'Forgive me, Cecil.'

I rose and bowed as she moved away. It seemed to be the tactful moment for paying the bill. Women must always feel slightly embarrassed when their menfolk fumble in their note-cases, and a man of the world seeks to spare them this embarrassment. I put my hand in my pocket for my note-case—

My note-case was not there!

III

My cousin Bernard, the naturalist and big-game hunter, tells of an occasion when, faced by a charging rhinoceros, he whipped his trusty rifle to his shoulder, and then realized that he was armed with nothing more lethal than a butterfly net. I suppose that his feelings on that occasion were much as mine were now. Instinct told him what to do. He sprang behind a tree and climbed rapidly up it, remaining there until the rhinoceros wearied of looking for him, and returned to its former avocations. Instinct alas! was of no help to his cousin Cecil. To dive under the table and remain there until the restaurant closed would be of little ultimate value. To borrow the money from Claudine was equally impossible. One does not take a lady out to dinner and cut short her prettily expressed thanks at the close of the meal by saying 'I wonder if you could lend me five pounds.' I might have asked the *maître d' hôtel* to take a cheque, but we were both strangers to him, and I should have become involved in a considerable argument ending in the return of Claudine and an offer from her to lend me the money. This, and I am sure every man of spirit will agree with me, was not to be endured.

So, what? (as I believe the Americans say).

The Wibberleys observe quickly and think quickly. They are rarely at a loss. A little to my right, by Claudine's vacant place, was her bag, which she had left behind when called to the telephone. She had told me once that she always carried 'Five or ten pounds' with her, 'in case', to which I had retorted quickly, 'Where else would you carry it?' This *jeu d'esprit* came into my mind now. Here was a heaven-sent opportunity to borrow the money without embarrassment to her. For the moment I did not quite see how to return it with an equal regard to her feelings, but doubtless I should think of something. The immediate need was to pay the bill. I sidled cautiously towards the bag, therefore, while maintaining an airy nonchalance towards my surroundings; pulled the bag behind my back with the right hand, felt for it with my left, and sidled carelessly back to my original place. I now had the bag out of sight between myself and the wall. This manoeuvre was necessary; for the idea of prying into a lady's bag in her absence, and in the full sight of others, is abhorrent to a man of any feeling.

I opened the bag. In an inside flap there was an embroidered silk note-case. In the case (and you can imagine the sigh of relief which escaped me) were five £1 notes. I tucked them into the bill, and was about to return the empty case to the bag, when, as if from Heaven itself, inspiration descended upon me.

The late Duke of Wellington—or, more accurately, the early Duke of Wellington—said that it was necessary to know what was happening on the other side of the hill; by which he meant that we must deduce what goes on in the other person's mind. So it was now. My whole plan was visible to me in a flash. I foresaw exactly each move which would follow, and had my answer to it. Let me make it clear to less agile minds.

It is quite impossible to lose five separate pound-notes out of a note-case. It is not wholly impossible to lose a note-case out of a bag. I slipped the empty case into my pocket. At some time or other Claudine would discover her loss. When? Not to-night, for she was going on to a party. Presumably Paul (preoccupied as I was, I recognized gladly that such men may have their uses) presumably this interloper would drive her home. She would sleep until a late hour in the morning, thus making it unlikely that she would have need of the note-case until the afternoon. So far, I trust, my friends have followed me. So far, indeed, they might have reasoned for themselves. But now comes what I might call the Wibberley Touch.

Immediately on my return I should take five pounds from the note-case which I had left behind, and transfer them to hers. At twelve-thirty next morning I should ring her up from my flat. I should speak as from the Hirondelle, saying that I had dropped in there in order to engage a table for lunch in the following week. I had been told that a note-case had been found under our table last night, and I had been asked if it belonged to the lady who was with me. Would Claudine see if hers was missing, and, if so, describe it to me so that I could satisfy the management?

I could foresee what would happen. She would give a scream of dismay, rush for her bag, confirm the loss, give me a confused description of the note-case, and beg me to get it back for her. I would calm her down, and promise to call with it that afternoon. So active is my mind that even now I was shaping a few phrases appropriate to the restoration of her property, such as would lead gracefully to an expression of the hope that in future we should hold all our possessions in common.

The waiter came back. I pushed the plate towards him, magnanimously telling him to keep the change. I restored the bag to its original place. I lit another cigarette and puffed it luxuriously. No one, I think, will deny that I was extricating myself from an extremely unpleasant position with consummate address. It is true, of course, that my story to Claudine would deviate (or seem to the self-righteous so to do) from the strictest accuracy. Doubtless the Duke of Wellington was condemned by such people for misleading the enemy by a feint on this or that wing. I venture to think that our reputations will not suffer. Indeed, I do not mind confessing that for my part I experienced no twinges of conscience. I was, on the contrary, extremely pleased with myself.

It was at this moment that I saw Claudine weaving her way through the tables towards me. *She was carrying her bag in her hand!* ...

I cannot pretend that I was immediately master of myself. Momentarily my appearance was such that Claudine associated it with an entirely irrelevant crab salad with which I had begun the dinner. I corrected her, pulled myself together, and lit a cigarette for her.

'Well,' I said gaily, 'what news from the Rialto?'

'Paul is coming round now. We'll give him five minutes.'

'Don't you want—' I began, and left it there tactfully.

'I tidied up when I went to the telephone. That's why I was so long.'

Of course! And that is why she took her bag with her. I should have realized this.

She thanked me for a delightful dinner. Little did she know how nearly she had paid for it! (Little did the red-hatted woman next to her know that she *had* paid for it.) For the few minutes remaining to us I tried to be my usual light-hearted self; I think I may say not unsuccessfully.

I accompanied her to the door, not stopping on the way for my hat and coat. There was a Rolls-Royce waiting for her. I am not a Socialist, but I dislike ostentation. I said nothing on this subject, however, and Paul (as I suppose it was) got out. I bowed and left them. I returned to the lounge, lit a cigarette, and gave myself up to thought.

IV

There was an unpleasant character on the air during the war who used to pose some trifling problem to his listeners, and then ask them 'What would *you* do, chum?' In less revolting language I will now ask my friends what they would have done in my place. I think they will agree that so far my conduct has been irreproachable, and it was an ill reward for my ingenuity that the lack of restraint with which this red-hatted woman scattered her belongings about the restaurant should have brought me to such an *impasse*. Some of my friends may think that she would have been rightly punished if I had gone home and said no more of the matter. But I felt otherwise. It was my duty, I conceived, to return the note-case and the money to her, and to do this in the way which would cause us both the least embarrassment.

But how?

It was clear to me that I could not approach her with the case until I had replaced the money in it. This entailed either a visit to my Club or a return to my flat; and by the time I was back in the restaurant, the two women might have left. I was assuming of course that the other woman would have enough to pay for both of them. Charitably I hoped that she would; for the plan which I was now maturing would postpone the restoration of the note-case until the morrow. My friends will wonder how this could be accomplished without the ignominious confession that I, Cecil Wibberley, was to all appearances a penitent 'thief'. Well, they will see.

I took one of my cards from my pocket-book, and wrote on the back:

'It is of urgent importance that you should get in touch with me. This will be explained if you will ring up between 11 and 12 to-night, or 9 and 10 in the morning.'

I added my telephone number, and gave the card, together with a shilling from the loose change in my pocket, to a page-boy.

'Take this to the lady in the red hat,' I said, pointing her out to him through the glass doors. 'You need not wait for an answer.'

He seemed an intelligent lad, but I watched him until he had handed over the card. Then I collected my hat and coat and left the restaurant.

I had no doubt that she would accept the challenge. What woman could have resisted it? Probably she would have discovered by then that she had mislaid her note-case; for I have observed that, when two women eat together, the discussion as to which of them has been entertaining the other usually ends in each paying her own share. Even so, she would be unlikely to connect my message with her loss, but assume it to be an affair of gallantry. Was it likely that she would hesitate? Let us admit that there *are* unpleasant men about who pursue and prey upon women, and that, for all she knew at this point, I might be one of them. But what had she to fear? There was no need even to give me her name until she had heard what I had to say.

It was as I had foreseen. At 11.45 that night she rang up. I took off the receiver and said, 'Cecil Wibberley speaking.'

'Mr Wibberley? I got your card,' a voice said, and gave a slightly self-conscious laugh. 'I'm wondering what it is all about.'

To put her at her ease I said: 'It is rather a long story, but no doubt you would prefer that I should give it to you over the telephone. I am entirely in your hands in the matter.'

With the same little laugh she said: 'Well, I think perhaps you had better begin on the telephone, and we'll see how we get on.'

'Then I will come to the point at once. Did you miss your note-case at the Hirondelle this evening?'

I am extremely responsive to impressions. I could sense the disappointment which underlay her surprise at this unromantic opening.

'Good gracious!' she said.

'Well?'

'I certainly did, and I've been looking for it ever since I got home. Why?' and her voice became a little sharper. 'What do *you* know about it?'

'A good deal,' I said calmly. 'In fact, I have it here by my side at this moment.'

'It had a lot of money in it,' she said quickly, for all the world as if I could be suspected of stealing it!

'It still has,' I said; and if there was a note of reproof in my voice, who shall blame me?

'Well, I'm glad of that, but I should very much like to know how you come to have it. You aren't a pickpocket?' she added with a forced laugh.

I laughed too, and said lightly, 'A pickpocket, dear lady, might return an embroidered silk note-case to its fair owner for senti-mental reasons, but he would hardly return five unsentimental £1 notes.'

'Oh, I *am* getting them back, am I?'

'But of course.'

'That's good. And when may I expect it?'

'Whenever you say.'

'Well, there's nothing to prevent you posting it to-night, is there?'

'Addressed to The Charming Lady in the Red Hat, London?' I said. 'Certainly. I'll put it in an envelope and slip down to the pillar-box. Good-bye.'

'Mr Wibberley!' she called quickly.

'Yes?'

'Good Heavens, I thought you'd gone.'

'You could have rung me up again.'

'So I could. Listen, let's go back to where we started, shall we? You said you had rather a long story to tell me. How long?'

'Ten minutes.'

'Yes, well, it looks as though you'll have to have my name and address anyhow, doesn't it?'

'Not at all,' I said coolly. 'You invent a name for yourself like Florence Nightingale, you give me the address of your old nurse in Yorkshire, you write to her to-night asking her to send on all letters addressed to Florence Nightingale, and I delay posting your property until to-morrow night. It will be quite easy.'

'You seem to be a very ingenious person,' she said, with a laugh in which a faint note of resentment was to be discerned.

'I have to be in my profession,' I replied.

'Oh, what's that?'

'That is part of the long story, Miss Nightingale.'

She laughed in appreciation of my sally, and said, 'Then I think you had better bring the note-case and the story round to-morrow at, say, twelve-thirty. I'm going out to lunch, but we could have a quick one first.' And she gave me her name, and the address of her flat in Chelsea.

'That's charming of you,' I said. 'We shall all be there at twelve-thirty. Good night.'

I will confess that I was not displeased with my share of the conversation, nor with the subtle way in which I had forced an invitation from her. For I felt that my story would need all the personal charm which I could exert, if I were to get, as they say, away with it.

I presented myself punctually at twelve-thirty next morning, and she opened the door to me. She was a Mrs Trant, living, I gathered, apart from her husband; much the same age as Claudine, but plumper and more provocative. She gave me a glass of indifferent sherry, and said, 'Well, now for the story.' She was evidently determined to be business-like. So was I.

'First let me give you this,' I began, and I handed over the note-case. 'I ventured to look inside,' I added, 'hoping to find some means of identification, and in this way ascertained that there were five £1 notes within. Is that as it should be?'

'Five, that's right. The story, please, I can't wait.'

'It is quite simple. Did you happen to notice the woman at the table on your left?'

'Naturally I saw what she was wearing and what she looked like. I didn't notice her particularly.'

'I did. I was sitting some way away from you, but looking in your direction. You had put your bag down by your side; and while you were talking to your companion, I saw her surreptitiously extract the note-case from it. Almost immediately afterwards she left the room and went to the telephone-box, presumably to contact a confederate outside. The man at her table, I don't know if you remember him'—to my relief she shook her head—'I should say that he was innocent of his companion's character. I was not. So I followed her. We had a little talk together, and I persuaded her to give up the note-case.'

That was all. A perfectly simple, straightforward story. But obviously she would not allow me to leave it there.

'Persuaded her!' she said indignantly. 'Why didn't you have her arrested?'

'There are official reasons,' I said with a note of authority in my voice, 'why it is not considered advisable to arrest her just yet.'

'Oh!' Mrs Trant thought this over, and then said, 'Does that mean you're a policeman?'

'Temporarily,' I smiled. 'I am in M.I.5, but lent to Scotland Yard for special duties.'

'M.I.5—that's the Secret Service, isn't it?'

'That is so,' I bowed.

'Well, fancy! All the same,' she went on, 'it was very inconvenient being without the money last night. What I'm wondering is why you didn't give it back to me at once.'

I was wondering, too, but I couldn't very well say so.

'Isn't it perfectly obvious, dear lady?' I said, playing for time.

'Not exactly.'

Luckily it became so to me almost as I said it. The Wibberleys, as may have been remarked, are very quick thinkers.

'She returned to her seat by your side,' I explained patiently. 'If I had given it to you then, you would have demanded her instant arrest. As I have said, this was contrary to public policy. We are hoping that, if we leave her at liberty, she will lead us eventually to—well, to a certain organization. She left altogether a little later, giving me just time to write you a note and follow her. Which, you understand,' and I finished my glass of sherry with an air, 'was why I had come to the restaurant in the first place.'

This last statement, of course, was strictly true. The fact that I was so ingeniously weaving truth and what in a sense might be called untruth into the fabric of my story may have gone to my head. For, without really thinking, I found myself adding:

'She is known to us at Scotland Yard as Flash Annie.'

V

If there were any justice in the world: if true character were rewarded according to its worth; if man's honourable love met with an equally honourable response; indeed, if any of Mr Aldwinckle's multitudinous wives had had a sense of humour, this story would either not have been begun or would have ended differently.

Last week I received the following letter:

'Mrs Arthur Pagham begs to inform Mr Wibberley that she met your friend Mrs Trant at a dinner party last night. She behaved in such a peculiar way to Mrs Pagham that I had to ask our host for an explanation. He took her on one side, and came back to Mrs Pagham later to say that the woman had had the impertinence to mistake me for a notorious crook called Flash Annie. Naturally she insisted on a full explanation from her.

'Mrs Pagham has only two things to say to you. One—that she has instructed her solicitor to issue a writ for slander; and the other, that for the first time in my life I have come to recognize the sound judgment and good sense of the present Mrs Aldwinckle.'

Illiterate, too, you see. I am well rid of her.

A Savage Game

(1950)

'Forget the detective story. I'm not saying that because I have written one detective story I am a good detective. What I do say is that any writer who makes his living by creative fiction is well fortified to do what your policeman have to do.'

'And what's that?'

'Invent a story which accounts for all the facts and suspicions and discrepancies which the case presents. That's our daily job, inventing stories; making a definite pattern of a number of incidents. Dammit, I could contrive some sort of story out of any assortment of facts: a spot of candlegrease, a badly sharpened pencil, a canary which wouldn't sing any more and a man who went to bed one night in his wooden leg.' Even as he said this, Coleby began to wonder what the story would be. Better start with the canary ...

Colonel Saxe went to his desk and unlocked a drawer. He took out a loose-leaf file of papers and said, 'Like to try?' Coleby came back to his surroundings suddenly, and said, 'Oh—what's that?'

'Our latest murder.' The Chief Constable sat down again and began to turn the pages. 'You'd better look at this. It shows you the house in relation to the rest of the town. That's important.'

Coleby looked at it, and said plaintively, 'Can't I have a plan of the room, with X marks the spot?'

'That particular room doesn't matter so much. Still, here you are: bedroom where the body was found, living-room where the girl and the man were drugged.'

Coleby took them, and said, 'Drugs too. I *am* going to enjoy this.'

'I'll just give you the set-up. Wavetree—silly name—is a bungalow about three hundred yards outside Easton, which is a small country town in my district. It's got a bit of garden, front and back, and there are half a dozen houses, mostly pretty good ones with a fair amount of land, between it and the town. There were four people at the bungalow that Sunday afternoon. Norris Gaye, the owner, now deceased: elderly, miserly, an invalid, or anyway preferred to live like one, and generally, I should say, a crotchety unpleasant person and a great trial to his niece Phyllida. She is thirty minus, very capable, very good-looking in a big, healthy way, if you know what I mean—Captain of Hockey type— and ran the house and her uncle single-handed. Phyllida's brother, Douglas—hot-tempered, who-the-devil-are-*you* sort of cove, lives in London, test driver for racing cars, generally dashed down to lunch on a Sunday, and dashed off again, but whether from love for his sister or to keep in with his rich uncle, I can't say.'

'Did they know he was rich?'

'I think so. Even living as he did, he must have had something to leave. In fact, the girl gets an annuity of £500 and the boy the residue, about £20,000. The fourth person was Mark Royle. You may have come across him: thirty plus, French and German scholar, translates books. Very reliable, I've known his people for ages; very intelligent, Field Security in the war, and did a good job. I say all this, because he is our chief witness.'

'You wouldn't let me make him the murderer?'

'That's up to you: you'll see. Personally I have no doubts about him. Well now, there's a confectioner's in the town where people go for coffee in the mornings. A few weeks ago Royle and Phyllida had run into each other, literally, just outside it, and when he had picked her parcels up, and apologized—well, there they were having coffee together, and telling each other their names. And it wasn't surprising, seeing what a good-looking couple they are, that they were doing it again next morning. And so on.'

'Both fancy-free at the time?'

'More or less. The girl wears an engagement ring, rather a good one, but the fellow was missing-believed-killed in the war, as Royle was not sorry to hear. I suppose she saw him looking at it and wondering. He seems to have fallen for her rather. And then one Sunday he came to lunch.'

'To ask Uncle?'

'Oh no. She wanted him to meet her brother, that's all, or her brother to meet him. Just friendly on her part; probably still thinking of the other man. The three of them lunched together in the dining-room; Uncle was being an invalid in his bed-sitting-room, looking out on to the front garden; and after lunch they went into the living-room. Phyllida told her brother to light the fire while she got the coffee. It was a log fire, already laid, and Douglas, when he had got it going, wandered about rather impatiently, looking at his watch. Royle sat down in the arm-chair on the right of the fireplace as you face it. Phyllida came back with the coffee. She put the tray on the table behind Royle's chair and said, "Pour it out, Douglas. I must just make sure that Uncle's all right. The cream's for Mr Royle, special." Apparently they had had some joke about that at the coffee-shop. Of course, it wasn't real cream, just the top of the milk, and only enough for one. You'll see the point of all this directly.'

'I'm seeing it now. Who put the sleeping tablets in what?'

'Exactly. Douglas poured out the three cups, put sugar in his own and Phyllida's, pulled up a stool next to Royle, and put on it the third cup, the cream jug and the sugar bowl. Royle put in the sugar, poured in the cream very gently so that it rested on the top, and left it for the sugar to melt. Apparently this was a little way of his. Douglas drank his straight off, put his cup back on the tray, and, as Phyllida came back, said, "Sorry, old girl, but I must dash." She suggested that he should say good-bye to his uncle, and he went out and was back again, Royle says, in a couple of minutes; the door was open and they watched him into his uncle's room and back. Phyllida looked at him a little anxiously when he came back, or so Royle thought, and said, "All right?" and Douglas said, "Most genial, but then I wasn't making a touch, and that's all he's afraid of." They went out to his car, and saw him drive off at a hell of a bat towards the town.'

'Exit First Murderer,' said Coleby. 'Or not?'

'You'll see. The other two went back to the living-room. Now then, I'll read Royle's actual statement, starting from there.' He drew out the pages and read. Coleby lay back, listening to the words of Royle, imagining the scene.

'I sat down in the chair, and she sat on the sofa, which was on the other side of the fireplace and at right angles to it. She drank her coffee and put the cup down on a little table behind the sofa, and then we talked about her brother. After a bit she said, "Oh dear, I do feel so tired, it's very rude of me," and I said, "Nonsense! Put your feet up and be comfortable." So she did. I finished my coffee, and was trying to listen to some story she was telling me, but for some reason I couldn't keep my eyes open. I put my hand up, as if to shield them from the fire, so that she wouldn't notice. Then I suddenly realized that she wasn't talking any more, and I opened my eyes with an effort, and saw her lying there, utterly still. Her hand drooped to the ground, and the firelight flickered in her ring. She might have been dead. I knew that I ought to do something. I think I knew then that we had both been drugged, but I couldn't take my eyes off that enormous ruby; it got bigger and bigger until it filled the whole room and swallowed me up … and by that time I suppose I had passed out. I woke up to a smell of burning, and thought vaguely of breakfast, and it took me a little time to realize that I wasn't in bed at home. One of her shoes had fallen off, and I suppose a bit of burning wood had shot on to it, and the leather was smouldering gently. Then I knew where I was. I tried to revive her, but she was still completely out. I went into Mr Gaye's room to find out his doctor's telephone number. He was dead. So I rang up the police. It was just five o'clock.'

Saxe returned the statement to the file, and Coleby opened his eyes.

'Very good picture. Or is there too much detail? Oh well, you can take that either way. Now for the body.'

'Gaye had been stabbed through the heart by a double-edged knife of some sort, but there was no trace of the weapon. It was an hour before the girl was brought round, and able to make a statement. Wherever it overlapped Royle's, it confirmed him exactly. Of course we analysed all the coffee things. Result: traces of an opiate in the two cups, nothing in the third or in the coffee-pot, cream jug or sugar basin.'

'And the only person who could possibly have dropped anything in the cups was the brother—at least, according to Royle.'

'Yes, and the cups were the only possible medium.'

'So you sent out an all-station call for Douglas.'

'No.'

'You surprise me. I should have thought your Inspector would have jumped at it.'

'He didn't, for the simple reason that Douglas was already arrested. He was stopped in the town for dangerous driving, lost his temper, laid out a couple of constables, and was now safely locked up. Damned young fool.'

'But very convenient for you.'

'So we thought. But, you see, we searched him, we searched the car, and there was no weapon!'

'It could have been thrown away anywhere.'

'Where? When? The others saw him off, remember, streaking towards the town. Within a minute he was in trouble with the police. We've searched the room and the garden outside the window of the room, we've searched the front gardens on each side of the road, and the dagger is simply not there. But in any case, Coleby, if it was hidden under his coat when he drove off, why should he throw it away at once? By doping the coffee he had given himself at least a couple of hours' start, and could have dropped it in a pond or river a hundred miles away, where it would never be found. Also with a murder behind him, wouldn't he take damned good care *not* to get into the hands of the police?'

'You'd think so. Yes.'

'So there we are. I'll bet my last shilling that Douglas drugged that coffee, but I'm damned if I can see how he can have killed his uncle. And I'll put my shirt on Royle as an utterly honest and reliable witness, but that means that the girl couldn't have done it either. So there it is. Now make up a story to account for everything, and I shall believe that you really are an author.'

'Dear Saxe, I can give you one straight off. The girl stabbed him when she went to see him after lunch; hid the knife temporarily in the back garden where you never looked, and disposed of it afterwards. To give her a perfect alibi Douglas drugged the two of them, and witnessed that his uncle was alive after Phyllida had left him. To give himself a certain amount of cover, he deliberately got himself arrested. If you'd picked him up two hours later, the absence of the knife wouldn't have been in his favour. Joint murder by the two legatees.'

'Good God, Coleby,' said Saxe, staring at him. 'I believe you've got it.'

'Yes, but I don't like it. It doesn't do justice to my creative powers. Any policeman could have thought of it. Also it leaves no alternative suspect, which is bad art, and, from the murderer's point of view, bad management. No, it won't do; there's something damnably wrong somewhere. I was picturing the scene in my delightfully imaginative way—see press cuttings—and something went wrong suddenly. Let me take that plan of the room and Royle's statement to bed with me, and I'll tell you the true story to-morrow.'

* * *

'Well, got the story?'

'Yes. Your Hockey Captain did it on her own, hoping that her little brother would be hanged, thus scooping the pool. Nice girl.'

'Impossible!'

'That's what she hoped you'd think.'

'I suppose you mean that, being in love with the girl, Royle made up his story to save her?'

'Who said anything about Royle? Royle is the perfect witness. That's why the girl bumped into him outside the coffee-shop.'

'You're suggesting that she deliberately picked him up?'

'Well, you see, he was just what she wanted: good character, observant and a slow starter with his coffee.'

'My dear Coleby, how could she possibly have known beforehand that he drank his coffee slowly—for whatever that's worth?'

'She'd watched him on other mornings. Why not? Now I'll tell you what happened.'

'In your story,' smiled Saxe, leaving himself free to laugh at it or profit by it.

'In a story,' said Coleby firmly, 'which may or may not—I haven't decided yet—include a very stupid Chief Constable. Here we go. The morphia was in the cream. Don't interrupt. All went as Royle told you; and there are the two of them sitting by the fire; and in the car, bumping into policemen, which was the last thing she wanted, a witness that the uncle was alive. The plan demands that she shall be the first to drink her coffee, and so now she drinks it. She pretends to feel sleepy, and puts her feet up. Just as he is beginning to fade away, she goes out with a bump, or so it seems; and of course the fact that oblivion, as we novelists say, is descending on him, too, makes it all very convincing. As soon as he is right out, she gets up, and in her quick athletic way stabs that very tiresome uncle. She has a nice little untraceable grave in the back garden waiting for the dagger, and in it goes. She washes out the cream-jug, pours a little undoped cream into it which she has carefully put aside, gives herself a little more coffee, drops in the morphia, stirs and swallows. Then she lies down again on the sofa and—genuinely this time—passes out. And there she is, and there she has been all the time when Royle wakes up, and there is the dope in the coffee-cups and nowhere else. End of story.'

'Good lord, you know,' said Saxe in astonishment, 'it *could* have happened like that!'

'If there is one thing that Author Coleby prides himself on, it is his realism. It could.'

'But that doesn't say that it did. It's just a story.' Coleby was silent. 'Or have you got any proof? Yes, you said there was something wrong in Royle's statement. Is that it?'

'Not in Royle's statement. Couldn't be more accurate. No; something wrong in my visualization of the scene. Or so I thought. But on consulting Plan C again in my bedroom I found that there was nothing wrong in my visualization of the scene. So then I knew that the hockey eleven was going to lose its popular young captain.'

'You'll have to explain.'

'I insist on explaining. I've been looking forward to explaining ever since 1.30 a.m. When your Inspector arrived on the scene, Phyllida was lying on the sofa with her feet towards the fireplace. Or so I saw her; and I could almost smell the burning shoe—what size does she take, sevens?—which Royle thought was his breakfast. But Royle's last view of her before he passed out included the ruby on her engagement finger, hanging over the side of the sofa. You can only get it there, feet by the fire, if the sofa is on the right of the fireplace. And I'd been picturing it on the left; after, I suppose, a casual glance at the plan.'

'But it *is* on the left.'

'Exactly. Which means that she was lying in a drugged stupor with her head to the fire at two-thirty, and in the same drugged stupor with her feet to the fire at five. Silly girl.'

'My God!'

'Yes.'

'I think I'll telephone,' said Saxe, getting up.

'It may not take you far,' said Coleby, 'but at least you can dig up the back garden. And you might give Royle a hint, or a French novel to translate, or something, to take his mind off the girl. Quite apart from losing your star witness if he marries her, you don't want to spoil his young life. He wouldn't be happy with Phyllida. Too violent for him. Not hockey; lacrosse, I think, don't you? A savage game.'

Bread Upon the Waters

(1950)

'Kindness doesn't always pay,' said Coleby, 'and I can tell you a very sad story which proves it.'

'Kindness is its own reward,' I said. I knew that somebody else would say it if I didn't.

'The reward in this case was the hangman's rope. Which is what I was saying.'

'Is it a murder story?'

'Very much so.'

'Good.'

'What was the name of the kind gentleman?' asked Sylvia.

'Julian Crayne.'

'And he was hanged?'

'Very unfairly, or so he thought. And if you will listen to the story instead of asking silly questions, you can say whether you agree with him.'

'How old was he?'

'About thirty.'

'Good-looking?'

'Not after he was hanged. Do you want to hear this story, or don't you?'

'Yes!' said everybody.

So Coleby told us the story.

* * *

Julian Crayne (he said) was an unpleasantly smooth young man who lived with his Uncle Marius in the country. He should have been working, but he disliked work. He disliked the country too; but a suggestion that he should help the export drive in London with a handsome allowance from Marius met with an unenthusiastic response; even when he threw in an offer to come down regularly for week-ends and bring some of his friends with him. Marius didn't particularly like his nephew, but he liked having him about. Rich, elderly bachelors often become bores, and bores prefer to have somebody at hand who cannot escape. Marius did not intend to let Julian escape. To have nobody to talk to through the week, and then to have a houseful of rowdy young people at the week-end, none of whom wanted to listen to him, was not his idea of pleasure. He had the power over his nephew which money gives, and he preferred to use it.

'It will all come to you when I die, my boy,' he said, 'and until then you won't grudge a sick old man the pleasure of your company.'

'Of course not,' said Julian. 'It was only that I was afraid you were getting tired of me.'

If Marius had really been a sick old man, any loving nephew such as Julian might have been content to wait. But Marius was a sound sixty-five, and in that very morning's newspaper there had been talk of somebody who had just celebrated his hundred-and-fifth birthday at Runcorn. Julian didn't know where Runcorn was, but he could add forty years to his own age, and ask himself what the devil would be the use of this money at seventy; whereas now, with £150,000 in the bank, and all life to come—well, you can see for yourself how the thing would look to him.

I don't know if any of you have ever wondered how to murder an uncle; I mean an uncle whose heir and only relation you are. As we all know, the motives for murder are many. Revenge, passion, gain, fear, or simply the fact that you have seen the fellow's horrible face in the paper so often that you feel it to be almost a duty to eliminate it. The only person I have ever wanted to murder is—well, I won't mention names, because I may do it yet. But the point is that the police, in their stolid unimaginative way, always look first for the money motive; and if the money motive is there, you are practically in the bag.

So you see the very difficult position in which Julian was placed. He lived alone with his uncle, he was his uncle's heir, and his uncle was a very rich man. However subtly he planned, the dead weight of that £150,000 was against him. Any other man might push Marius into the river and confidently wait for a verdict of Accidental Death; but not Julian. Any other man might place a tablet of some untraceable poison in the soda-mint bottle and look for a certificate of Death from Natural Causes; but not Julian. Any other man might tie a string across the top step of the attic stairs—but I need not go on. You see, as Julian saw, how terribly unfair it was. The thing really got on his mind. He used to lie awake night after night thinking how unfair it was; and how delightfully easy it would be if it weren't for this £150,000.

The trouble was that he had nobody in whom to confide. He wished now, and for the first time, that he was married. With a loving wife to help him, how blithely they could have pursued, hand in hand, the search for the fool-proof plan. What a stimulant to his brain would have been some gentle, fair-haired creature of the intelligence of the average policeman; pointing out the flaws, voicing the suspicions which the plan might raise. In such a delicate matter as this two heads were better than one, even if the other head did nothing but listen with its mouth slightly ajar. At least he would then have the plan out in the open, and be able to take a more objective view of it. Unfortunately the only person available was his uncle. This also seemed to him extremely unfair.

What he had to find—alone, if so it must be—was an alternative suspect to himself; somebody, in the eyes of the police, with an equally good motive. But what other motive could there be for getting rid of such an estimable man as Marius Crayne? A bore, yes; but would the average Inspector recognize boredom as a reasonable motive? Even if he did, it would merely be an additional motive for Julian. There was, of course, the possibility of 'framing' somebody, a thing they were always doing in detective stories. But the only person in a position to be framed was old John Coppard, the gardener; and the number of footprints, fingerprints, blunt instruments and bloodstained handkerchiefs with the initials J.C. on them necessary to offset the absence of motive, was more than Julian cared to contemplate.

I have said that Uncle Marius was a bore. Bores can be divided into two classes: those who have their own particular subject, and those who don't need a subject. Marius was in the former, and less offensive, class. Shortly before his retirement (he was in the tea business) he had brought off a remarkable double. He had filled in his first football Pool form 'just to see how it went', distributing the numbers and the crosses in an impartial spirit, and had posted it 'just for fun'; following this up by taking over a lottery ticket from a temporarily embarrassed but rather intimidating gentleman whom he met in the train. The result being what it was, Marius was convinced that he had a flair, or, as he put it, 'a nose for things'. So when he found that through the long winter evenings—and, indeed, during most of the day—there was nothing to do in the country but read detective stories, it soon became obvious to him that he had a nose for crime.

Well, it was this nose which poor Julian had had to face. It was bad enough, whenever a real crime was being exploited in the papers, to listen to his uncle's assurance that once again Scotland Yard was at fault, since it was obviously the mother-in-law who had put the arsenic in the gooseberry tart; it was much more boring when the murder had taken place in the current detective story, and Marius was following up a confused synopsis of the first half with his own analysis of the clues.

'Oh, I forgot to tell you, this fellow—I forget his name for a moment—Carmichael, something like that—had met the girl, Doris—I mean Phyllis—had met Phyllis accidentally in Paris some years before—well, a year or two, the exact time doesn't matter; it was just that she and this fellow—what did I call him?—Arbuthnot ...'

And it was at just such a moment as this that Julian was suddenly inspired.

'You know, Uncle Marius,' he smiled, '*you* ought to write a detective story.'

Marius laughed self-consciously, and said that he didn't know about that.

'Of course you could! You're just the man. You've got a flair for that sort of thing, and you wouldn't make any of the silly mistakes all these other fellows make.'

'Oh, I daresay I should be all right with the deduction and induction and so on, that's what I'm really interested in, but I've never thought of myself as a writer. There's a bit of a knack to it, you know. More in your line than mine, I should have thought.'

'Uncle, you've said it!' cried Julian. 'We'll write it together. Two heads are better than one. We can talk it over every evening and criticize each other's suggestions. What do you say?'

Marius was delighted with the idea … So, of course, was Julian. He had found his collaborator.

Give me a drink, somebody.

Yes (went on Coleby, wiping his mouth), I know what you are expecting. Half of you are telling yourselves that, ironically enough, it was Uncle who thought of the fool-proof plan for murder which Nephew put into execution; and the rest of you are thinking what much more fun it would be if Nephew thought of the plan, and, somewhat to his surprise, Uncle put it into execution. Actually it didn't happen quite like that.

Marius, when it came to the point, had nothing much to contribute. But he knew what he liked. For him one murder in a book was no longer enough. There must be two; the first one preferably at a country-house-party, with plenty of suspects. Then, at a moment when he is temporarily baffled, the Inspector receives a letter inviting him to a secret rendezvous at midnight, where the writer will be waiting to give him important information. He arrives to find a dying man, who is just able to gasp out 'Horace' (or was it Hoxton?) before expiring in his arms. The murderer has struck again!

'You see the idea, my boy? It removes any doubt in the reader's mind that the first death was accidental, and provides the detective with a second set of clues. By collating the two sets—'

'You mean,' said Julian, 'that it would be taken for granted that the murderer was the same in the two cases?'

'Well, of course, my dear boy, of course,' said Marius, surprised at the question. 'What else? The poacher, or whoever it was, had witnessed the first murder, but had foolishly given some hint of his knowledge to others—possibly in the bar of the local public-house. Naturally the murderer has to eliminate him before the information can be passed on to the police.'

'Naturally,' said Julian thoughtfully. 'Yes ... Exactly ... You know,' and he smiled at his uncle, 'I think something might be done on those lines.'

For there, he told himself happily, was the fool-proof plan. First, commit a completely motiveless murder, of which he could not possibly be suspected. Then, which would be easy, encourage Uncle Marius to poke his 'nose for things' into the case; convince him that he, and he alone, had found the solution; and persuade him to make an appointment with the local Inspector. And then, just before the Inspector arrives, 'strike again'. It was, as he was accustomed to say when passing as a Battle of Britain pilot in Piccadilly bars, a piece of cake.

It may seem to some of you that in taking on this second murder Julian was adding both to his difficulties and his moral responsibility. But you must remember that through all these months of doubt he had been obsessed by one thing only, the intolerable burden of motive; so that suddenly to be rid of it, and to be faced with a completely motiveless killing, gave him an exhilarating sense of freedom in which nothing could go wrong. He had long been feeling that such a murder would be easy. He was now persuaded that it would be blameless.

The victim practically selected himself; and artistically, Julian liked to think, was one of whom Uncle Marius would have approved. A mile or two away at Birch Hall lived an elderly gentleman of the name of Corphew. Not only was he surrounded by greedy relations of both sexes, but in his younger days he had lived a somewhat mysterious life in the East. It did not outrage credibility to suppose that, as an innocent young man, he might have been mixed up in some secret society, or, as a more experienced one, have robbed some temple of its most precious jewel; and though no dark men had been seen loitering in the neighbourhood lately, at least it was common knowledge that Sir George had a great deal of money to leave, and was continually altering, or threatening to alter, his will. In short, his situation fulfilled all the conditions which Uncle Marius demanded of a good detective story.

At the moment Julian had no personal acquaintance with Sir George; and though, of course, they would have to be in some sort of touch with each other at the end, his first idea was to remain discreetly outside the family circle. Later reflection, however, told him that in this case he would qualify as one of those mysterious strangers who were occasionally an alternative object of suspicion for the police, the more particularly, since he was himself of a dark, even swarthy, complexion. It would be better, he felt, to be recognized as just a friendly acquaintance; obviously harmless, obviously with nothing to gain, even something to lose, by Sir George's death.

In making this acquaintance with his victim, Julian was favoured by fortune. Rejecting his usual method of approach to a stranger (an offer to sell him some shares in an oil-well in British Columbia), he was presenting himself at the Hall as the special representative of a paper interested in Eastern affairs, when he heard a cry for help from a little coppice which bordered the drive. Sir George, it seemed, had tripped over a root and sprained his ankle. With the utmost good will

Julian carried him up to the house. When he left an hour later, it was with a promise to drop in on a bedridden Sir George the next day and play a game of chess with him.

Julian was no great chess-player, but he was sufficiently intimate with the pieces to give Sir George the constant pleasure of beating him. Between games he learnt all he could of his host's habits and the family's dispositions. There seemed to him to be several admirable candidates for chief suspect, particularly a younger brother of sinister aspect called Eustace, who had convinced himself that he was to be the principal legatee. Indeed, the possibility of framing Eustace did occur to him, but he remembered in time that a second framing for the murder of Marius would then be necessary, and might easily be impracticable. Let them sort it out among themselves. The more suspects the better.

Any morbid expectations you may now have of a detailed account of the murder of Sir George Corphew will not be satisfied. It is enough to say that it involved the conventional blunt instrument, and took place at a time when some at least of the family would not be likely to have an alibi. Julian was not at this time an experienced murderer, and he would have been the first to admit that he had been a little careless about footprints, fingerprints and cigarette ash. But as he would never be associated with the murder, this did not matter.

All went as he had anticipated. A London solicitor had produced a will in which all the family was heavily involved, and the Inspector had busied himself with their alibis, making it clear that he regarded each one with the liveliest suspicion. Moreover, Uncle Marius was delighted to pursue his own line of investigation, which, after hovering for a moment round the Vicar, was now rapidly leading to a denunciation of an under-gardener called Spratt.

'Don't put anything on paper,' said Julian kindly. 'It might be dangerous. Ring up the Inspector, and ask him to come in and see you tonight. Then you can tell him all about it.'

'That's a good idea, my boy,' said Marius. 'That's what I'll do.'

But, as it happened, the Inspector was already on his way. A local solicitor had turned up with a new will, made only a few days before. 'In return for his kindness in playing chess with an old man,' as he put it, Sir George had made Julian Crayne his sole legatee.

Very unfair.

Call me Sally

(1953)

The sixth Earl of Halstead left Oxford in 1922, a serious young man, politically minded. Being as yet a commoner, he stood unsuccessfully for a division in Essex at the 1923 election. He tried again both in 1924 and 1929, still without success. He was also unsuccessful in a bye-election in 1930. However, success came to him at last. In 1933 he succeeded his uncle the fifth Earl, and entered the House of Lords. In the previous years he had married Sarah Anne Ashley, and had become the father of two children, both girls. His hobbies are old manuscripts and first editions.

I take no interest in peers as such, and even less in politics; I merely transcribe these facts from my *Who's Who?*, to which I hurried as soon as I came back from the Brett-Lorimers' party. I was up in London next day, lunching at the club. This gave me an opportunity to consult *Burke's Peerage* which goes into these matters more wholeheartedly. Sarah Ann was the only daughter of the late Robert Hearn and, more importantly, widow of James Ashley. James Ashley had died in February, 1932; which, as I happened to know, was three months after he had divorced his wife but three months before the divorce could have been made absolute. Technically, then, she had been a widow when she married again in August, and no doubt Lord Halstead, who had remained serious and politically minded, was

531

glad that she could be thus catalogued; even though no longer, so to speak, a first edition.

Mrs Brett-Lorimer's party had been a bigger one than was usual in our corner of the world, and less intimate. As a stranger she may have wished to assert herself by exhibiting an old circle of acquaintance fully up to the standard which she had been meeting in her new neighbourhood. We have our Countess too, and when I have to introduce one of my other guests to her I just say, 'You know Lady Hazelwood,' and more often than not he or she does. This must be wrong, for Mrs Brett-Lorimer, taking me up to a charming figure which seemed to be the focal point of the party, said impressively, 'Let me present you to the Countess of Halstead—Mr Evan Hill,' and as Lady Halstead turned from the last person so honoured and held out her hand, I saw this unmistakable light of recognition in her lovely eyes, and, without thinking, I said 'Sally!' The look was smoothed out, a faint surprise lifted what was left of her eyebrows, and I apologized suitably. For a moment I had mistaken her for an old friend. 'Oh, I don't think we've met, have we?' she said and added charmingly, 'I'm sure I shouldn't have forgotten!' We talked for a moment of nothing in particular, and then I was moved on, still a little embarrassed. Naturally as soon as I got home I looked up Halstead in *Who's Who?* She was Sally, all right.

It began, you may say, on the 21st of April, 1931, when I opened a letter from Hugh Carris, The Croft, Castle Colne, Essex, a gentleman unknown to me. I was just down from Cambridge, reading for the Bar, but in between times I did a little writing, nothing creative, just a few articles to bring in a few guineas on subjects of which I had acquired a superficial knowledge, mostly from encyclopaedias. One such subject, in which I had shown perhaps a trifle more interest than usual, was about the Montgolfier brothers, inventors of the balloon. Mr Carris, it seemed, was really excited by balloons. He had six autograph letters from Joseph to Etienne, dated 1782, which were obviously the high-water mark in his ballooning world; so valuable that he didn't dare to trust them to the post but would like to show them to me if I cared to come down some Saturday night. One caught the 2.22 from Liverpool Street and changed at Marks Tey to the branch line. I would be met at the station.

Well, I was very young, didn't often get invited to the country at week-ends, and spring was here. So, having arranged for the next Saturday but one, I spent the intervening nights with the Montgolfiers, hoping not to give myself away for the fraud that I was. And on the Saturday I caught the 2.22 from Liverpool Street.

As I was waiting at Marks Tey for the local train, a breathless voice behind me said, 'Is it Mr Hill?' I turned round and looked into two large childlike eyes, which were now a little apprehensive.

'Yes,' I said.

'That's good!' She smiled happily all over her face. 'Good both ways,' she explained. 'I mean it might have been the Prince of Wales which would have been awkward, and then,' she hesitated and with what I can only describe as a slightly pink look went on, 'you might have been—well, for all my husband and I knew, you might have had a long white beard. I am so glad you haven't.'

I went a little pink too and said I had shaved it off this morning. It wasn't terribly funny, but we both laughed. It was that sort of warm golden afternoon.

'I've been shopping in Colchester all day,' she explained, 'so I thought I'd pick you up here. You don't want to go in that stuffy slow train and it takes twice as long.'

'That's very kind of you, Mrs Carris.'

'Oh, call me Sally!' she said quickly. 'Everybody does and it's so much easier.'

Christian names were not in such immediate use then as they are now, and I was young enough to blush and say awkwardly 'Sally!'

'You are Evan, aren't you? Do you mind?'

'Of course not.' And after that we got on grandly together.

She looked about sixteen, a child not a married woman; the daughter, I should have supposed, of this old-sounding gentleman who had written to me, not the wife. I was as sentimentally romantic as one was at my age, and I was already regretting Hugh Carris and wondering if there was any chance of his falling out of a balloon at about the time when briefs were pouring in on me. Say next November. These coincidences can be pleasant to think about but rarely come off.

The car was an old Morris two-seater, with a dicky at the back into which we put my bag.

'Was what you expected a Rolls?' she asked.

'The whole setup is different,' I said. 'Particularly this chauffeur. I'm not complaining.'

She laughed. 'Neither am I. Are you prepared for a shock?'

'Another?'

'Well, same sort of, really. I'm also the cook. At least for tonight.'

'Are you a good cook?'

'Not bad, in the fried potato omelette and hotting up class. Our cook's local and there's a baby coming somewhere in the family, so I've had to give her the night off. We don't live in any sort of style, you know. Just the cook.'

'No butler, no footmen? Stop the car, I want to get out.'

'I can see I shan't have any trouble with you,' she said.

The country was lovely, all fruit blossom and pale greens. We came to this house—well, it was only a cottage with a thatched roof and yellow plaster walls up which clematis, I think it was, struggled carelessly. The front door opened onto what house agents would call a large hall with a sitting room on its left, and a passage at the back which led to a kitchen at one end, a dining room at the other, and a staircase with twisted oak rails in between. Sally picked up a letter from a table in the hall, glanced at it, murmured, 'Whatever?' and led the way upstairs.

'You're in here,' she said, opening the door to a little bedroom. 'Bath here,' she went through the bathroom to another door displaying a large room with two beds in it, 'and us. Now you know it all. And I'll just remind you that the bathroom has three doors. Bolt them all when you are using it, of course, but please, Evan, don't forget to unbolt them all when you leave.'

'I swear I won't,' I said, holding up my right hand.

'Good. Then you can have first go at the bathroom now, and I'll expect you downstairs. We'll have tea in the garden, shall we?'

I was in the little hall when she came down, an open letter in her hand. She said:

'I say, another shock! My husband has had to—well I don't know if he had to, but he has gone up to London. Something to do with some letters which somebody rang up and wants to buy, written to somebody called Montgollifer.'

'Montgolfier, the first men to go up in a balloon.'

'Oh Lord!' Her dark blue eyes opened wide. I had never seen such eyes. 'You're his balloon man. I mean that's why you're here, to see the letters.'

'That's why I was here, Sally, but now ...' I tried to look gallant and I dare say I looked a fool. Quite properly she ignored my silliness and said. 'You mean if my husband comes back this evening without the letters, you won't just burst into tears?'

I shook my head and damned the letters.

'Oh well then that's all right, then. Let's have tea. Coming to help?'

We made the tea and drank it in the garden under the apple trees, chattering happily. And then we washed up. She was so pretty and innocent, it was like a children's picnic.

'It's only for tonight,' said Sally. 'Mrs Clayton will be back tomorrow morning and we can leave the dinner things for her.'

We explored the garden after tea, and a little wood at the back of it. Then we came back to our deck-chairs and did a crossword together. At seven o'clock she was meeting Carris. But at six-thirty the telephone bell rang. It was in the dining room and we could hear it through the open window.

'Do you mind?' she said, jumping up. 'It may be Hugh.'

She went in. I heard her say 'Hallo! Is it Hugh? … Whatever … wait a moment while I shut this window. All these cuckoos and bees …'

She shut the window and I heard no more. About five minutes later she came out looking rather bewildered.

'He is selling the letters,' she said.

'Really, Sally? I don't care a damn about the letters. In fact—'

'No, but I mean it was only an agent he saw and he's got to see the principal tonight, which means he is to stay staying in London.' She broke off awkwardly wrinkling her forehead, and said, 'Do you know anything about these things? I ought to but …'

'About what? Autograph letters? Balloons? Business? Nothing.'

'No, us. I don't mean that. I mean etiquette and propriety and what all the neighbours say, if we had any.'

'Oh!'

'I asked Hugh, and he said "Don't be so damn silly. I suppose he is a gentleman." I said I thought you were. Are you a gentleman, darling.'

I must have gone very red. Possibly because I was wishing I wasn't one, possibly because of this unexpected 'darling'. She didn't look the sort who flings it about. At my stammers she said, 'Oh I'm sorry.' And then, 'You aren't married or engaged or anything?' I shook my head. 'Oh well then who's to mind?'

'Nobody,' I said firmly, 'and I think it's all very silly and Victorian, don't you?'

'Idiotic! I never think about things like that anyway.'

She didn't look as if she did. I felt more and more certain that her husband was a dried-up stick of a man, middle-aged before his time, and she a child, and their marriage like something in an old-fashioned novel, a mockery. All the same I couldn't help being a little uncomfortable. She might be an innocent child, but I wasn't and she was enchanting and it was springtime. Though she was safe from everything but my thoughts, I feared lest even these should harm her.

Carris was spending the night with a brother in London (dismissed by Sally with a wrinkled nose as 'Stuffy') and would be back in time for lunch. I had not been asked for the night and was wondering whether I ought to set off for the first possible train or wait for his arrival and, as it were, official recognition. When it came out that my best train left the junction just before his arrival so that one journey with the car would do for both, 'though it does seem sort of inhospitable,' and when she followed this up with, 'As a matter of fact he sounded a bit frightened of meeting you after not having the letters to show,' then the decision seemed to be taken out of my control. And for some odd reason, not that I knew just what I was doing, the situation lost all its embarrassment. We were in the kitchen getting the dinner ready, and once more it was a nursery picnic, intimate but innocent. We had a carefree evening together, a carefree breakfast the next morning.

Just before I went off, I saw from my bedroom window Mrs Clayton arriving, an extraordinary pyramidal figure, and heard Sally greeting her and asking after the new baby. Then there was a shout of 'Evan are you nearly ready, darling? We ought to be starting,' and I hurried down, bag in hand. We drove to the station.

'Thank you so much,' I said again, this time through the carriage window. 'I have enjoyed it.'

'So have I, Evan. I can't tell you. Good-bye.'

'Shall we both meet again, Sally? I do hope so.'

'Sure to,' said Sally gaily. 'Some place, some time.'

We did. But it was twenty years later.

It is more important to the young to be in love than to love a particular person. Sally lasted me for a month's fantasy, but by October when I was called to the Bar, though she was never out of my memory, my daydreams were getting along happily with some unmarried lovely more lately seen. So Carris might have fallen out of a dozen balloons, and I should not have minded, nor indeed, unless the descent had been so spectacular as to have claimed the headlines, would not have known about it.

While waiting for briefs I spent a good many hours in the Courts, absorbing their etiquette and studying the mannerisms of famous counsel so as to decide on my model. I had dropped into the divorce court on one dull November morning and found myself listening to Ashley v. Ashley and Another. Mr James Ashley of Apple Orchard, Littlethorp, Essex was petitioning for divorce from Sarah Ann Ashley, the co-respondent being unnamed and unknown. Counsel for the petitioner was in the middle of his opening speech when I slipped in. At first I found myself listening to him professionally and I decided that, had I been he, I should not have wasted so much good theatrical oration on what was, after all, an undefended case. It was not until James Ashley went into the witness-box that I began to be interested in the story.

I didn't like him. He was a man of about forty, cold, correct and utterly unforgiving. An exhalation of hate diffused from the witness box through the court, hate too implacable, one felt, to have flourished only on his wife's unfaithfulness. Yes, he remembered the week-end of May the 2nd, he had gone to Birmingham to attend the wedding of his cousin. His wife had not accompanied him? 'No,' he said fiercely, and I seemed to hear in that one word the whole story of her unconformity with his background, and his bitter resentment of it. There had been no arrangement for anyone to stay with her? 'I arranged,' he said, clearly irate, 'that Mrs Clayton was staying with her.'

'Who is Mrs Clayton?'

'The cook. She was deliberately sent away.'

'Yes, well, we shall be hearing from her directly. I was referring to visitors from outside.'

'She had a visitor from outside.'

'I think Mrs Clayton must tell us about that too, as you did not see him yourself. What His Lordship and I wish to know is whether any previous arrangement had been made between yourself and Mrs Ashley for a visitor in your absence.

'No.'

And so it went on. A plan of the cottage was put up. Apart from the cook's room there were only two bedrooms, a large and a small, with a bathroom connecting them.

'That small room being your dressing room?'

'Yes.'

I began thinking professionally again, noting how counsel kept the witness from giving anything but first hand evidence.

'And when you returned on Monday morning, was Mrs Ashley there?'

'No.'

'You then questioned Mrs Clayton and, as the result of what she told you, you instituted these proceedings?'

'Yes.'

'And you have not seen Mrs Ashley since?'

'My solicitors saw her.'

'Yes, well, they can tell us anything relevant. Thank you, Mr Ashley.'

He left the witness box and was followed by Mrs Florence Clayton.

And even when I saw that pyramidal figure again, I still didn't understand. I assumed that this was before, or after, her service with Sally. I told myself that the neighbourhood was obviously full of Mrs Claytons, all pyramidal, all intermarried and looking alike, that in any case my one glimpse of her was no sort of identification. Yes even when I heard her telling the court how Mrs Ashley had suggested that she could go home that Saturday afternoon, 'May 2nd, that's right,' because her brother's wife was having a baby. 'But Lord bless you your Lordship it wasn't to be ready for another week by the doctor's reckoning as I told Mrs Ashley at the time, and then Annie being late as you could count on, two weeks over, like the last and to my own knowledge and ten days with Georgie the time before, well I couldn't help wondering.'—Yes, even then it was somebody else's stay …

Until suddenly I heard my own name.

'And she calls up the stairs, "Evan darling," she calls and down he comes with his bag in his hand, bold as brass. No I never seen him before, just an ordinary young fellow …'

One talks about one's heart stopping still, but I think mine did then. And when it started working again, it seemed to be pumping all the blood to my face and then draining it out again, and I felt that the whole court must know that I was the ordinary young fellow, that I was 'Another'. I turned my head down partly to hide myself, partly to look, as I had to look, in the little diary which I carried with me. You know, as I knew, this had to be May the 2nd when I slept in Sally's house, I in the little room, she in the big one, with the bathroom in between …

But I had been staying with Mrs Carris at The Crofts, not with Mrs Ashley at Apple Orchard.

The odd thing was that it took me some little time to realize this. My first reaction was simply the indignation of perfect innocence, the exasperation of the man who has got himself entangled in somebody else's trouble through no fault of his own. Then, when I had finished being sorry for myself, I began to be sorry for Sally, equally blameless, equally entangled. Why ever, I thought bewildered, why ever didn't she let me know what was happening so that I could have rushed back to defend her? Between us, surely, we could have convinced her husband.

But suppose she didn't want to convince him. Suppose—

He had come home to find her gone. Already, then, she had decided to leave him. Wouldn't it be natural for her to seize the great chance which his suspicion offered, the chance of a final separation? The chance, some day, to marry again? She was not involving me for I was unknown to all but herself. At the same time she did not dare to tell me what she was doing, in case I had conscientious scruples about divorce. So she had just let the case go by default, glad to be free of him. And I, who knew her and had now seen and heard him, understood why she had to be free. Yes, all my sympathies were with Sally. She was the sweet innocent child I had thought her, but how injured I had not known. As for the detestable Hugh Carris—

No, James Ashley—

Well, which?

And why … and how …? I took a firm hold on my still wandering mind and began again.

I am not one of those people who tear up letters as soon as they have been answered, but every so often, when my pockets are bulging and my desk littered, I make a slight clearance, keeping any which seem still to be of interest. There was a chance, then, that I had saved my first, my only fan letter. So when I got back to my rooms, I looked for and found the original invitation from Hugh Carris, written below the embossed heading The Croft, Castle Colne, Essex. It expressed great interest in my ridiculous article; it invited me to choose a Saturday and come down for the night; it informed me of the trains and that I changed at Marks Tey for the local line; it assured me that I should be met at Castle Colne. And I had chosen May 2nd, caught the train, and got out at Marks Tey.

So far, then, I am staying with Mr Hugh Carris at The Croft. But now Mrs Sarah Anne Call-Me-Sally Ashley of Apple Orchard intervenes. She will save me the slow train journey and drive me the rest of the way. I am ignorant of the country, of the man I am staying with, of the house I am going to. She drives me to Apple Orchard. She explains the absence of her 'husband' Hugh, Hugh Carris, with whose reasons for inviting me she is fully acquainted, as she is with the train and the day on which I am coming.

So what is the answer?

First, that she must know Hugh Carris well; second that the kidnapping of his guest is part of a well considered plan for getting a divorce from her husband, a divorce in which the guest is to play an anonymous but important part.

Was Carris a party to that plan, and, if so, was the intention that he should marry her when she was free? Well, I had written to him accepting his invitation, and I had not come. Nevertheless, I had sent a letter to Mrs Carris at The Croft, addressing her as Sally and thanking her for a delightful visit. He may not have been an accessory before the fact but he must have been an accessary after it.

Sally! So young, so innocent! And all the time balancing precariously and confidently between the danger of involving me too deeply and the fear of leaving too little evidence behind her. It was beautiful, for instance, how she had timed Mrs Clayton's return, so that I was seen, but no more than seen, just 'Evan darling', an easy-going fellow, coming downstairs from the marriage suite with a week-end bag. How cleverly she had prepared the supposed letter, the supposed telephone call from her husband, from 'Hugh'. How could I help feeling hurt and indignant, remembering my own attraction to her, and my fond assumption that she was a little attracted by me, when now I realized that I was just a walker-on in her life, in her well contrived plan, an anonymous Mr X, who would have served equally well if he had been Mr Y or Mr Z, and she had called 'Harry darling' up the stairs to him! To have received so much enchantment from her, and to have been allowed to offer nothing of my own in exchange was something which the sensitive vanity of youth could not easily forgive.

But in a little while I was forgiving her. She had fooled me, but in what I believed to be a good cause. Even as an irresponsible joke it would have been well and gaily done; as a way of escape from James Ashley it was magnificent. I applauded her. Indeed if I had known where she was now living, I should have written to congratulate her.

But then—I'm afraid I was a bit slow in those days, and perhaps I am still—I remembered that I was a barrister, a servant of the law, whose duty it was to uphold the law. The decree had been improperly obtained, for there were no grounds for divorce. The court had been, as it was fond of saying, grossly deceived.

I am a layman now, and my respect for the law takes second place to my respect for my own beliefs. These beliefs have broadened since those days, but even then my sympathies were with Sally, and I felt that she had a right to be freed from her husband. But barristers cannot indulge unorthodox feelings. It was my serious duty to disclose the facts to the proper authorities, taking the chance that I might be disbelieved. Believed or disbelieved, it wouldn't do my career much good, but I can honestly say that I wasn't thinking of that. I was thinking of Sally. She was a liar and a good actress, but what woman isn't? As against this, she had courage, she had gaiety and (don't let us pretend that it doesn't matter) she had an enchanting way with her. I was damned if I would be the interfering prig who tied her up again to that cold implacable man. No, I would say nothing, and to hell with the Bar. I began to think that I had chosen the wrong profession.

So it was fortunate for me that an uncle who had ignored me until now should suddenly decide that he wanted me in his firm, his only son having unexpectedly received a call to the Church. I accepted gladly. He offered very generous conditions, and by the time May came round again, I was running my own little car. On Sunday May the 2nd I drove into Essex and reached Apple Orchard. It was, of course, the cottage at which I had stayed. Then I looked for The Croft. It was only a couple of miles away and quite a big place.

It was wonderful to have seen Sally again at the Brett-Lorimers'. She was forty now (*Burke's* has no scruples about mentioning a lady's age) and as enchanting as ever, looking as little like forty as she had looked like twenty when first I had met her. Why had she denied that meeting? To have involved me in her divorce case was bad; but then she couldn't have guessed that I had been in court on that day. Had it not been for the chance visit, I should have known nothing about her divorce. Indeed I should not even have discovered that she had played a trick on me. For I had thought her to be Mrs Carris, and now she was Lady Halstead. Well, what was wrong with that? Carris, as she could have explained and as *Burke's* had now told me, was the family name of the Earls of Halstead. The present Earl had been Hugh Carris when he wrote to me, had still been Hugh Carris when he married her.

I shall confess now, if indeed confession is necessary of anything so obvious, that I never really got Sally out of my head. Perhaps that is why I am still a bachelor. Seeing her again, I found myself again her champion, ready to seek excuse for anything she did.

So when I say that it was a guilty conscience which made her dis-own me, I mean that it was a conscience guilty on her husband's behalf rather than on her own. It was his part which had been the ignoble one. He wanted Sally, but he wanted safety more. It was her sudden plan, when she learnt that my visit to him coincided with her husband's absence, to use me to win her freedom, the freedom to which Carris, with his political career to consider would not help her. And in effect he said, 'Do what you like to get free, and then I will marry you, but don't draw me into your plans.' The only help she wanted from him was a letter to leave in the hall in case I remem-bered his handwriting and a telephone call at six-thirty. The letter was written, the call made, but oh so innocently; a little note giving her particulars of a book he recommended, an enquiry for an address she had promised to give him, nothing to do with the plan. Of course he knew nothing about that. She must have loved him madly, seeing him so clearly yet always excusing him to himself, always protecting him.

Am I being fanciful about her, about him? Probably. For I am afraid that if after all these years he did fall out of a balloon, I should not be sorry. That is why I continue to make myself agreeable to the Brett-Lorimers, so that, if the widowed Countess of Halstead should ever be among us again, I shall once again be presented to her with all due formality, and once again with this freedom granted to me twenty years earlier call her 'Sally'.

Happy Ever After

(Undated)

I

Of all the dailies, weeklies and monthlies, from the *Morning Mercury* to *Right Thinking*, which thundered so incessantly out of the Swart press, Thursday's *Happy Homes* was closest to the heart of Thomas Henry Swart, first Lord Wheatfield.

Tom Swart was a romantic little button-nosed man who could believe anything which he wished to believe, except, at times, that he was Lord Wheatfield. When people addressed Lord Wheatfield in his presence, he looked around for the fellow, recovered himself, and said, 'Oh—ah—yes, quite so.' He catered in his various periodicals for clergymen, nudists, dog-followers, psychic researchers, schoolboys, jumper-knitters and riders of bicycles, with equal conviction of their importance to their community, with equal assurance of the value of his services. At the banquet which was given to him when he accepted the peerage for his wife's sake (he had been a widower for twenty years, but 'she would have wished it') he had put it on record that his one contribution from boyhood had been 'to make the world a jollier place', and he had hardly needed to add that it takes all sorts to make a world. He was quite genuine. One had only to look at his round, red face with its little button nose and protruding blue eyes, to be convinced of his sincerity.

Important to the community in their different ways as jumper-knitting and nudism might be, Lord Wheatfield had no doubt where true jolliness lay. It was in the happy marriage, which made the happy home where jollity reigned and love laughed at everything, including locksmiths. *Happy Homes* told husband and wife, mother and expectant mother, everything which they needed to know for happiness; and if some of the more technical information pulled in subscribers from without the marriage ring, this was merely a risk which had to be taken.

A feature of the paper was a well-illustrated article with the title 'Happy Home number 159', or whatever the figure might be. Every week an address would be chosen at random from among the registered subscribers, and, after due warning and the assurance of welcome, a visit made by reporter and photographer. The interview started off on the assumption that the home was a happy one; and if there did happen to be a lack of jollity in the atmosphere of the house or the artificial faces of its occupants, this was covered up by the pleasantly facetious approach to his subject of the interviewer.

But Lord Wheatfield was not satisfied. He was expressing his dissatisfaction one morning to his nephew Hartley Wilkes, the editor of *Happy Homes*. The Swart millions had been made just in time for Hartley to enjoy an education which had been denied his cousins and brothers. He was, as his uncle often remarked, a Public School and Oxford man.

'The trouble is, my boy,' said His Lordship, 'that you're getting into a groove. Now here's this happy home number 160.' He tapped it with a pencil. 'What is its secret? Well, Mrs Percy Doolittle tells us. Mrs Percy Doolittle says, "My husband and I realized from the commencement of our marriage that true happiness depends not only on a community of interests but on a good appreciation of the doctrine of give-and-take." Very sound. Very true. Mrs Alfred Stackhouse had put it a little differently the previous week.' He opened another copy of the paper. 'Here it is. "For a truly happy marriage an appreciation of the doctrine of give-and-take is not sufficient. Some real community of interests must also be present." You see these are not their own words, my boy. They are words put into their mouths by the young man you sent to interview them.'

'They haven't got any words of their own,' said Hartley. 'They're dumb.' And he added, 'Of course that may be the secret of a happy marriage.'

'Now my boy, none of your Oxford cynicism. Do you always send down the same young man?'

'The one who can spell, Jefferson.'

'Is he married?'

'Not to notice.'

'Then how come he knows what makes a happy home?'

'He says his little piece, and they say OK or that's right. I don't see what more you want.'

'I want a good deal more. I want the genuine views of genuine people. Their own ideas, not yours or Jefferson's. Now what I propose is that we offer a prize for the best list of rules drawn up by a happy married couple from their own experience of a happy married life. Something that makes it worthwhile for all classes to go in for. Say a thousand pounds.'

'Good Lord!' said Hartley. He thought for a moment and asked, 'Can I resign and go in for it?'

'I was not aware that you were married.'

'No, but I could get married.'

Lord Wheatfield quite rightly ignored this. He went on, developing his idea.

'Yes, I see now, we must have a time qualification. Competitors must have been married for—what shall we say, fifteen years?'

'I shan't resign,' murmured Hartley.

'What's that? Don't mutter, my boy.'

'What I said was, do you want to run a competition entirely for the middle-aged? Think of the photographs!'

'You're quite right, Hartley. We must have two divisions. Between five and fifteen years, and over fifteen. Five hundred pounds and a silver loving cup for each. Yes, I see it all.' He leant back, closing his eyes. 'A personally conducted tour through England, calling in at all five centres.' He waved a pencil to and fro, personally conducting it. 'Arrival at our offices for presentation of suitable gifts to losers. Grand luncheon on return to London, Mansion House if we can get it, for presentation of loving cups and cheques by the Home Secretary, or can I persuade H.R.H.? Yes, this is big, my boy. Put all our papers on to it. We'll make the final announcement to-morrow in the *Mercury*. Silver car with Cupid on the radiator. Make the country car conscious before the start … Cupid's chariot … Photographs. Yes I seem to see …'

Observing that his Proprietor was in a trance, the editor of *Happy Homes* left him and returned to his cubby-hole.

II

Miranda's married life, she often told herself, was one of uninterrupted happiness. She had been married for sixteen years, and in all that time she could not remember a single real quarrel which she had had with Philip. It was true that he grumbled sometimes, but she had only to sit on his knee and call him her Growly Old Bear and tickle his ear and threaten to eat him up before he could eat his little Miranda, and he stopped grumbling at once—darling Philip; but she had always known that he had never meant it. And when they differed, as of course husband and wife couldn't help doing sometimes, he was always so sweet about it. He never shouted at her, as some husbands did, or insisted on having his own way; he was always perfectly reasonable and saw almost at once that her way was really the best, though of course, as she was the first to admit, there was a good deal to be said for his way, if things had been just a little bit different.

She had been married at nineteen, so she was still under forty, still pretty in her plump little way. The plumpness was a trial to her, in fact the only trial in her married life. Nature had so clearly meant her to be a fairy-like creature; a dryad (or an oread, she was never quite sure of the difference) dancing in diaphanous draperies to the little people of the forest, communing with the birds who would alight gently on her outstretched hands. So she had always seen herself. At nineteen, though her legs were never quite long enough for an oread, she was gracefully slim, and a pretty enough picture for any man, dancing in her nightgown at the end of their father's Hampstead lawn on Midsummer Night. This was how Philip, who lived next door, had first seen her, just before her mother saw her and called out from her bedroom window, 'Miranda! What on earth do you think you are doing? Come in at once!' She hadn't known then that Philip was watching her; but when he told her on their honeymoon, she promised to dance for him in her nightgown on every Midsummer Night in future. By that time of course it meant less to her, and after fifteen years it wasn't meaning very much to anybody, so she gave it up, and became a writer instead.

Philip was a writer too, but he wrote history books, full of dull facts, very different from her own whimsical fancies. They lived in the country, and she had had a little hut made in the wood which bordered the garden, her Wendy House she called it. Here she could be quite alone with Nature. Here, in this enchanted spot, elves of various kinds visited her and whispered secrets of the forest and laughed their tinkling laughs and scuttled away. It is not easy to write while constantly interrupted by elves, but every now and then she would get a story or a poem done and then, as a treat for her darling Philip, she would read it to him after dinner, indicating by changes in the voice which character was speaking. She had a cooing voice for doves and a twittering voice for the smaller birds, and a brownie voice and a hob-goblin voice, and a very special royal voice for the Queen of the Fairies, and of course her own voice for the narration. She could feel Philip's enjoyment of it all as he leant back in his chair, the newly opened *Times* on his knee, and she sitting cross-legged at his feet;

such a relaxation after his full day's history; and she spared herself no pains. It was quite a performance. Indeed, she had thought at one time of going onto the stage, but had remembered, after writing to one or two people, that it could take her away too much from her darling Philip.

It would have been nice if some of these charming fancies had been published. A few years ago she had made a collection of them and Philip, after a little coaxing and nibbling of his ear, had sent them to an editor he knew. The editor wrote a most encouraging letter back, saying how much he liked them personally, but fearing that they were a little above the heads of his rather earth-bound readers. So, after that, she wrote them only for Philip. Only Philip was worthy to hear the secret of the elves. This brought them even more closely together.

The elves, she saw now, were their children, for they had no other. Philip had not really wanted children; her instinct, which never failed her, told her this. Babies, Philip knew, would have taken something away from her spirituality. Their homely needs would have brought her too close to earth. Then, too, as they grew up they would have come between her and darling Philip, as children so often did, marring their perfect unity. Ah, if only all marriages were as happy, as united, as theirs, what a beautiful, beautiful place this world would be!

And now here was a chance of leading others along the right road. At first, just the notion of teaching them was enough, but then she thought how wonderful to win the prize! It would be her secret from Philip, the first she had ever had. Think of his excitement when he opened the morning paper one day, and saw that they, Mr and Mrs Welby, were acclaimed the happiest couple in England! Well, no, not quite that, but the ones who knew best how to achieve true happiness. And five hundred pounds earned by her own pen! She could hardly wait to get to the Wendy House and begin.

She would write her rules in verse. Since she had this rare gift, it would be a sin to waste it. But remembering what the editor had said, she saw that she must be practical.

Make work a song
The whole day long.
Then happiness
Your lives will bless!

Live and let live,
If wrong, forgive;
If wrong, withdraw—
Such is the law!

It was difficult to keep this up. She tried a variation of metre.

Begin each day anew,
Your quarrels put behind you.
The morning skies are blue,
Their laughter seeks to find you!

'Tis little things which make up life,
Small change of harmony or strife.
Take care of these symbolic pence
And here reward will be immense!

The next one came in that flash which we call inspiration. It was as if somebody else was holding the pen.

There's more in the world than we know!
There's more in our hearts than we show!

And charged with significance as it was, yes it had all that elusive quality which she associated with herself. As did the last one.

Remember one and one make two,
But each is one, and one is you,
And me the other. So begun,
We prove that one and one make one!!

It is impossible for the more earth-bound clod not to feel that this means something.

III

The life of Mr and Mrs Joseph Bloxham was just as idyllic.

They had been married for twelve years, and, as far as he had noticed, had never had a day's disagreement. 'You wouldn't find a happier couple in the whole length and breadth of England,' Joe Bloxham would boast to his friends at the Golf Club bar; and there is no doubt that he was very happy. He had a reason to be. The little woman, as he spoke of her affectionately, was a first class cook, so that even in the most difficult days he was accustomed to enjoy his dinner. It was just as well, since it was at dinner that they met.

'And a damn good dinner too. Course I don't say I don't manage to bring back a bit of pork sometimes, never knew its mother, but even if I haven't been lucky, she never lets me down.' He drank and dried his moustache on the back of his hand. 'I'll tell you two funny things about women from my experience of them. They don't like pork, and they love standing in queues. Gives them a chance of gossip with the neighbours.'

Happy though they were together, Joe Bloxham was wise enough to realize that happiness must not be strained too far. It was for this reason that he spent Saturday afternoons and Sundays at the Golf Club, leaving the little woman at home to amuse herself as she pleased. 'I've known husbands,' he would say, 'who drag their wretched wives around the course, make 'em carry their clubs as likely as not, and then curse 'em for moving when they're playing a shot. Well, that's not my way. If Rosie's happier at home, it's damn selfish to drag her out. No, let's each go our own way, and then over the dinner table we can tell each other what we've been doing.' And on Saturday and Sunday evenings Mr Bloxham was meticulously careful to tell her.

They had no children living. Rosalind's only baby had died at birth. She was willing enough, bless her brave, generous little soul, to have another, but Mr Bloxham, who had gone through hell when the first was coming, was too tender-hearted to let his wife suffer again.

'I could see how it was,' he said at the bar. 'She knew I wanted a son to carry on the name and was ready to sacrifice herself. But what a selfish brute I should have been if I had allowed it! How those parson fellows can let their wives go on and on! Well, it may be all right for them. They're not sensitive, got no imagination as well. I suppose I'm different somehow. I shall never forget what I went through that first time. No, not again! Just as well, perhaps,' he added after a drink, 'seeing what's happening to the country. Prices and taxes as they are, we'd never have managed a decent school for the little chap. As I pointed out to Rosie.'

Mr Bloxham didn't see the *Morning Mercury* in the ordinary way, and it was from his friends at the bar that he first heard of the competition. They suggested jokingly that he should go in for it. 'Well, I dare say I could tell 'em a thing or two,' he said complacently, 'but what's the good? You know how it goes. First prize to the Proprietor's bedridden aunt, second prize to the sister's mother-in-law. But you're right, though. Rosie and I could tell 'em.' On the Monday he bought a copy of the *Mercury* on his way to the office. For the rest of that morning he seemed busier than usual. The day's work went like this:

Six steel-shafted rules for a happy married life

4. In a foursome the partners consult each other, but the more experienced one has the final word. So it must be in married life.
5. 'Head down.' Watch what you are doing. A hasty word, a hasty action, and you will find yourself in the rough.
6. 'Slow back.' Slow to anger, slow to take offence.
7. 'Don't press.' Don't press an argument too far or too strongly. Be reasonable, and the other will see reason.
8. 'Follow through.' Don't leave a quarrel or misunderstanding unfinished. Follow it out and clear it up.
9. 'Steady on your feet.' Reliable, true to your connections, so that each knows what the other stands for.

No golfer can fail to be helped by this.

IV

A cheque for fifty pounds and a guarantee of good billing brought together a suitable panel of announcers, actresses and admirals to serve as judges. Contrary to his usual practice, Lord Wheatfield awarded himself a casting vote. The competition had become the darling child of his creative genius. Since all the other competitors had said much what Mrs Doolittle and Mrs Stackhouse had said, if in slightly more fancy words, the judges had no difficulty in awarding the Over Fifteen Prize to Mr and Mrs Welby, whose verse contribution was so outstanding. 'Don't know how they do it,' said Admiral Seaworthy, shaking a puzzled head at Miss Julia Herrick. 'Never could myself.' Miss Herrick, however, knew a boy who did, and suggested that it was just a knack. 'Ah!' said the Admiral, comforted. For the Under Fifteens the field was more open. Indeed, but for the Chairman, the names might have been put into a hat and well shaken. The Chairman, luckily, could make up his own mind.

For it happened that the Wheatfield Park which had recently become Tom Swart's ancestral estate, and from which he derived his title, included a private golf course. It became necessary, then, for the new owner to learn not only the history of the resident ghost, but the theory of golf from the resident professional. His handicap, starting from the late hundreds, had now worked down to an approximate putt-conceding thirty-four, and his enthusiasm had matched inversely it's descent. When he was not thinking about his putting, he was thinking about his stance. Hearing that the panel showed signs of cracking, he stepped in; and no sooner had he read Mr and Mrs Joseph Bloxham's entry than the whole business was settled. The Bloxhams and the Welbys were announced as the happy occupants of Cupid's Chariot.

It was on a fair morning in May that the chariot set forth. Lord Wheatfield's first rule was that it should be preceded by outriders on silver-plated motorcycles; indeed, with a vague memory in his mind of some picture or other, he had toyed with the pretty thought that they should ride backwards, scattering rose petals in front of the happy couples as they went. 'Went into what?' asked his nephew, and His Lordship agreed that they would have to be careful.

'You really want the Household Cavalry for this,' said Hartley. 'More dignified.'

'All right, all right, my boy, it was just a passing fancy. I suppose,' he went on coldly, 'you have no objection to outriders in the ordinary way?'

'You mean facing the ordinary way?' He shook his head. 'Better not. Outriders eat so much.'

For this or some other reason outriders were dropped.

Cupid's Chariot was one of those wide American cars which take three people comfortably in the front. Next to Hartley, who was both driver and conductor, sat the two happy wives; at ease in the back sprawled the two happy husbands.

'Brought a flask along,' said Joe, tapping his hip pocket. 'Thought it was a good idea in case we had to make speeches.'

'Speeches!' said Philip with a start. 'Yes, I suppose so.'

'Do much speaking?'

'No.'

'You write books, don't you? History books.'

'Yes.'

'That reminds me, we shan't have to pay income tax on this five hundred, shall we? I mean with all this hullabaloo—well, I mean, the whole of England knows we've had it.'

'It can hardly be described as one's regular source of income. Fortunately.'

'Not mine, anyway,' laughed Joe. 'Bit different for you, perhaps, being a professional scribbler. I liked those verses of yours. Very neat, I thought. Go in for poetry much?'

'Not much.'

'Never tried your hand at historical plays? Like Shakespeare?'

'Never.'

'Yes, I liked those verses of yours,' said Joe, and waited for Philip to pick up his cue. Lacking this assistance, he went on:

'You know, I thought mine was rather a good idea. Looking at marriage from the golfing point of view. Original.'

'Evidently the judges agreed with you.'

'D'you play golf at all?'

'Not at all.'

'Old man Wheatfield is crazy about it. Asked what my handicap was, and when I told him that I—er—' He gave a modest laugh. 'Well I happen to be scratch, you see, and when I told him, what do you think he said?'

'I've no idea.'

'He said, "Mr Bloxham, I'd give half my fortune to have your handicap." So I said, "Well, if it comes to that, Lord Wheatfield, I'd give half my handicap to have your fortune." Made him laugh no end.' He joined in the laugh, and as Philip didn't, said, 'You don't play golf?'

'Still not, no.'

'Pity.'

They drifted into silence. 'It's just a week of hell anyhow,' thought Philip. 'This fellow can't make it worse.' He wondered for the hundredth time if he could have refused to take part in it, and decided for the hundredth time that he had had no choice once their names were in the papers. And knowing Miranda.

Miranda, meanwhile, was finding it equally difficult to interest Rosalind in her charming fancies. Her assertion of a belief that this was really Cinderella's coach and that at any moment it would be turned back into a pumpkin, and that they would find themselves being drawn by the little wild wee things of the forest, brought out a short sharp laugh from the happy wife beside her. Hartley gallantly came to the rescue.

'Talking of being drawn by wild wee things,' he said, 'there's a hairy little man in my Bristol office who will probably want you to give him a sitting. He does cartoons.'

'Oh!' said Miranda. 'I didn't mean—'

'And talking of pumpkins—you know, Mrs Welby, you've got something there. In a kind of way this car did start as a pumpkin. Lord Wheatfield began his career by selling marrows. On barrows.' He thought of adding that the first barrow was at Harrow but decided against it. 'Of course, he worked up to pomegranates afterwards, and so, gradually, turned to literature. But the pumpkin was, so to speak, the inspiration of the whole thing.'

'Oh, how romantic!' cried Miranda.

'Yes, isn't it? But it's a family secret, so don't let it go any further, please.'

'Oh, I won't.'

'I'm his nephew, you see, so that's how I know.'

'I had no idea!' said Miranda. 'Are you really? Actually his nephew?'

'Really and actually.' He was silent for a little, and then said, 'At least, I've always been told so. This opens up an entirely new field of thought. I wonder—I suppose—I couldn't—of course he did go to Paris for a week-end about then—but I couldn't be his—what is it Mrs Bloxham?'

'N-n-nothing,' said Rosalind, handkerchief to mouth.

'I thought,' said Hartley, 'we'd stop at Newbury for a drink. If everybody wants one as badly as I do.'

At Newbury—('Here, you sit at the back, Rosie')—Joe changed places with his wife. He was getting tired of Philip's silence. There was still silence at the back of the car, but, with Bristol in sight, Rosalind spoke.

'I suppose,' she said, looking at Philip and away again, 'we are both too loyal and well brought up to say anything.'

Philip turned to her. She was tall and fair and not in the least like Miranda.

'I suppose,' he sighed, 'we are. But,' he added, 'I am of the opinion that a sympathetic and understanding silence would be quite in order.'

'I am of the same opinion,' smiled Rosalind.

'Indeed,' said Philip, warming to it, 'I would go much further. I would suggest that in moments of extreme embarrassment or absurdity, a certain amount of—how shall I put it?'

'Eye-catching?'

'Exactly. A certain amount of discreet eye-catching would bring relief to the feelings.'

'Might, in fact, make the whole ghastly week just bearable,' said Rosalind. 'Shall we shake hands on it?'

They shook hands on it.

V

Cupid's Chariot had returned to London on the Saturday. At ten o'clock on the Monday morning Lord Wheatfield prepared to run through the final arrangements for the luncheon. He had invited all the famous people who were known to accept such invitations, and most of them had accepted. He had prepared his speech; photographers had been mobilized; and Hartley had sampled and approved of the champagne. Lord Wheatfield rang the bell and sent for his nephew.

'Well, my boy,' he said rubbing his hands, 'so you brought them back safely. No accidents, eh?'

'If there had been, I shouldn't be here,' said Hartley with dignity. 'I should have been the first to leave the car.'

'I hope you—yes, I suppose you would. Ha-ha! Well, from all accounts, you did a very good job. It seems—Hartley!'

'What's the matter?'

'All right, all right, silly of me. I thought for a moment that you might have so little appreciation of the occasion as to suppose that you could attend it in baggy flannel trousers with a hole in them. Obviously you mean to go home and change.' He looked down affectionately at his own morning coat and striped trousers.

'Oh, I get you. Well, the fact is, Uncle Tom, I wasn't quite sure what sort of an occasion it was going to be. It begins to look as if you and I aren't going to be wearing very much, and everybody else will be in black.'

'Are you going crazy? I don't know what you're talking about.'

'You see, if there isn't going to be any luncheon, we shouldn't be too popular.'

'Not going to be—the sooner you explain what you mean, the better I shall be pleased. And stop fiddling with that paper knife! Sit down over there and speak up.'

Hartley sat down, taking the paper knife with him.

'I'm trying to break it to you gently,' he said. 'I'm nervous.' He coughed and began 'Mrs Welby—'

'Good heavens! Dead?'

'Not as good as—I mean as bad as that. Her husband has left her.'

'Left her? Left what?'

'Flat.'

'Whose flat? I don't know what you're talking about. Put that paper knife down! Now then!'

'All right. In basic English here you are. At long last Philip has left his Miranda. As Miranda so well said: "There's more in our hearts than we show." Philip, after bottling up his very natural feelings for sixteen years, has run away. And I don't blame him.'

If Tom Swart had not been a man of lightning decisions, he would not have been Lord Wheatfield.

'Well,' he said aggressively, 'what's that got to do with the luncheon? Mr Welby has been taken suddenly ill. Naturally Mrs Welby would have preferred to be at the bedside of her husband, but she bravely recognizes that she must keep faith with her public.'

'And collect the cheque. Quite. But I doubt if the luncheon will be a good advertisement for *Happy Homes*. Because, you see, Uncle Tom, and quoting Miranda again, "Remember One and One make Two." Realizing this, Mr Welby has run away with Mrs Bloxham. And now may I play with your paper knife?'

All this happened more than a year ago. In case anybody is interested, I may just add that they all lived happy ever after. Mr Joseph Bloxham is happy as personal secretary and golf instructor to Lord Wheatfield, who is delighted to have got his handicap down to twenty-four. Hartley is as glad to have seen the last of *Happy Homes* as Miranda Torgood is thrilled to have succeeded him. It is unlikely that the Proprietor will allow her to organize another competition on the secrets of a happy marriage; but even if he does, it is doubtful if that infatuated couple, Philip and Rosalind Welby, will go in for it.

The Southey Manuscript

(Undated)

This naturally leads me to a consideration of what my friend Mr Harold Appleby-Dodds (of Ambleside) calls 'the Southey MS'.

When Mr Appleby-Dodds heard that I was writing this book, and that all sorts of odd things were getting into it, he generously offered to let me include the extraordinary story which follows. The story falls into four sections to which, for clarity, I have given headlines. The rest of it is as Mr Appleby-Dodds sent it to me. He has been a little imprecise as to the date on which his great discovery was made, but he assures me that there is a good reason for this.

Here, then, is the first publication of the Southey MS.

I

Statement by Harold Appleby-Dodds, Esq., B.A., F.S.A., author of *With Wordsworth in the Lake District*, *Wordsworthiana*, *In the Lake District with Wordsworth*, etc.

It was in August 19—, while roaming in the hills which look down upon the placid Vale of Grasmere, that I discovered the remarkable document which I now make public. The document, consisting of two pages of manuscript, one in prose, the other in verse, lay in a crevice in a little outcrop of rock halfway up the slope of Loughrigg

Fell, and it was on my descent that I first noticed it. Assuming it to be something which had slipped out of my pocket on the way up, I replaced it and thought no more of the matter, being concerned only with the business of getting safely down. Indeed, it was not until some years later (19—, to be exact) when clearing out an old cupboard for the vicar's jumble sale that I came across the coat again, and so found myself emptying out the pockets. It was then that for the first time I gave the manuscript my close attention. It was obviously one of considerable importance.

The first page of the manuscript spoke for itself in terms as convincing to me as to any fair-minded person who now reads it. Here it is, one of those graceful introductions so beloved of the poet, explaining the circumstances in which the latest creation of his inspired pen came to be written. Which poet? you ask. Read on, and you will have as little doubt as I had. Read but the title of the poem and you will have your clue.

'Jones! When I walked with you and Wilkinson'

That trumpet voice cannot be mistaken. It is Wordsworth himself who speaks to us.

II

Wordsworth speaking:

'Jones! When I walked with you and Wilkinson'

I distinctly recollect the occasion when these lines were suggested to me. It was in the autumn of 1819 that a gentleman, who announced himself as the Reverend Robert Herrick, came to me with a letter of introduction from Mr Keats, my friend and fellow poet. Mr Herrick was suffering from an unhappy love affair, being in alternate moods of ecstasy and despair over a lady of the name of Julia; and it was the hope of Mr Keats that our Lakeland air and the grandeur of our mountains would combine to restore him to a more independent outlook. With this end in view, I suggested an excursion to the

Langdale Fells, Mr Southey being our companion on this journey. Unfortunately, Nature was hindered in her restorative work by one of those seasonal mists which shrouded her beauties; and though I kept our guest in touch with the different features and interests which he would have seen had they been visible, he continued in a state of dejection. In the endeavour to rouse him from this mood I declaimed some of the nobler and more elevating lines from such poems as I had then written or was contemplating. Barely had I uttered the first line before he burst out with some wild references to Julia, the young woman of whom he was enamoured. Again and again I attempted with some new passage to calm him, and again and again, with some rhapsody or complaint about Julia, he would interrupt me. Finally, I desisted. At this point there came into my mind a walk with my friend Mr Jones, when he was similarly emotionally disturbed. But how differently he had responded to the comfort which I had essayed to give him! Immediately the first line of the sonnet which follows slipped into my consciousness, and before our excursion was over the whole composition had assumed its present shape. I might add that my friend Mr McBean of Glasgow, to whom I sent a copy, considered it to be one of the finest of my sonnets, and frequently said so to my sister.

III

Further remarks by Harold Appleby-Dodds, Esq., author of *Wordsworthiana*, *Southeyana*, *Coleridgeana*, etc.

The reader can imagine with what eagerness I turned to the second page of the manuscript, hoping to share the felicity of Mr McBean. He can imagine also with what astonishment my eyes encountered, not a noble sonnet of fourteen lines beginning 'Jones! When I walked with you and Wilkinson', but a poem of three eight-line verses which had no connection whatever either with Mr Jones or Mr Wilkinson! Moreover, it was clear that

Wordsworth could not possibly be held responsible for more than half the lines.

What was the explanation?

My first thought was that Southey, obscured by the mist from the observation of his companions, had jotted down as much of their conversation, if such it can be called, as came to him; and that in some way this record had taken the place of the sonnet. But in that case where was the sonnet, and why was it not included in the poet's published works? A hasty visit to Glasgow, in the hope that some surviving member of the McBean family might have the precious copy in his possession, proved abortive; partly owing to the abnormal number of McBeans available, and partly owing to the difficulty in many cases of reconciling their mode of speech with the language in which I had supposed that we were conversing.

But on giving the manuscripts a renewed consideration, I came to a different conclusion. There was no lost masterpiece of Wordsworth, because Wordsworth had not only not written the sonnet implied but had not even written the introduction! The whole MS, it was now clear to me, was a *jeu d'esprit* of Southey's in mischievous mood. He had heard Wordsworth and Herrick declaiming against each other and had amused himself later by making an imaginary poetic version of the encounter, prefacing it with an introduction which Wordsworth might have written to an imaginary sonnet. As will be seen, the two poets speak in alternate lines. It is not, of course, suggested that the antiphonic poet (if I may call him so) was the Reverend Robert Herrick who wrote *Hesperides*. The author of those sprightly poems was born in 1591, and even if the announcement of his death in 1674 had been premature, he would have been 228 years old at this time, and in no condition either for climbing fells or (one hopes) indulging in amorous speculations. But the visitor to Rydal was almost certainly a descendant of the older poet; and by a pleasant, if uncritical, exercise of the imagination we may titillate ourselves with the whimsical fancy that the Julia here referred to was herself descended from the Julia who figures so largely in the *Hesperides*.

Here, then, is the second page of the manuscript.

IV

The second page:

> The world is too much with us; late and soon
> I think of Julia and am like to swoon.
> How sweet it is, when Mother Fancy mocks,
> To picture Julia tying up her locks.
> Earth has not anything to show more fair
> Than is the ribbon in my Julia's hair.
> Dull would he be of soul who could pass by
> The light that beckons from my Julia's eye.
>
> It is a beauteous evening, calm and free.
> I wait for Julia neath my almond tree.
> Breathless with adoration; the broad sun
> Will find my waiting barely yet begun.
> Getting and spending we lay waste our powers—
> Sometimes I wait for hours and hours and hours:
> Thoughts that do often lie too deep for tears
> Have made it seem like years and years and years.
>
> Once did she hold the gorgeous East in fee,
> Submissive to her will, and now holds me.
> (A noticeable man with large grey eyes
> Was Henry East, and famous for his ties.)
> We have given our hearts away, a sordid boon,
> To one as fickle as the inconstant moon.
> Milton! Thou should'st be living at this hour,
> Thy Paradise Regained in Julia's bower!

V

Final statement by Harold Appleby-Dodds, Esq., author of *Whither Wordsworth?*, *Wordsworth: whither?*, etc.

It only remains to add that Southey's sense of mischief has prompted him to a further irreverence, mercifully not carried beyond the opening couplet. It will be remembered that Mr Herrick came to Rydal with an introduction from Keats. Southey, we must suppose, had wickedly imagined an encounter in the neighbourhood of Hampstead similar to the one overheard by him in the Langdale Fells. On the back of the poem given above he had written:

'I stood tiptoe upon a little hill

'And got my chin on Julia's windowsill.'

Fortunately, he realized in time that this was hardly a posture for a beneficed clergyman and pressed the matter no further.

I may perhaps be forgiven for intruding my private affairs upon the notice of the reader as far as to say that I have just added a codicil to my will, bequeathing the MS of Southey's *jeu d'esprit* to the British Museum.

Such is Mr Appleby-Dodds's story. It only remains to add that, in sending it to me for publication, he was good enough to let me study the original documents here described. It was evident that two words in the fourth line of the poem had been corrected, the original version of them being still just decipherable. As first conceived, then, the third and fourth lines would have run:

'How sweet it is when Mother Fancy mocks

'To picture Julia pulling up her socks.'

Whether the poet pictured the lady as engaged literally or figuratively in the exercise mentioned is not clear, but in either case it would seem that a more modern voice than Southey's was speaking to us. I say no more. It is for the British Museum to judge.

In It Together [fragment]

(Undated)

The big man in the red waistcoat detached a piece of tobacco leaf from his lower lip, flicked it off the end of his finger, and spoke.

'If you want to know what's happened, I can tell you what's happened. This is what's happened.'

'Don't keep saying "what's happened",' said Derrick testily.

'Why not?'

'Because it irritates me.'

The big man, his uncomprehending eyes on Derrick, removed his cigar, blew a cloud of smoke across the table, patted both sides of his moustache, and replaced the cigar. He was in no hurry.

'Well,' said Derrick weakly, 'what's happened?'

'Somebody's got wind of it, that's what's happened.'

'Oh my God!' said Derrick in a whisper to himself; and then aloud, and coldly, 'Obviously.'

'That's what's happened, you can take my word for it. Somebody's got wind of it.' He threw another cloud of smoke across the table and added, 'Somebody's got wind of it.'

Derrick screwed his face up in agony.

'Don't keep saying—oh never mind.' Opening his eyes again, he saw that the big man was still looking at him, unmoved, uncomprehending. A new anxiety added itself to the others. 'Your cigar band will catch light directly,' he said plaintively.

Henshaw, nodding his thanks, pushed the band a little lower down.

'Somebody's got wind of the business,' he said. 'Take my word for it.'

The red waistcoat settled down in little hillocks to the edge of the table; each button rested in a little valley of its own. Red was the colour which Derrick most disliked in waistcoats. It seemed to him that this had always been so. His mind went back to—what other red waistcoats had he seen? He could remember none; and yet, if he had always hated them so, they should have left some mark on his memory. Perhaps he was being unfair to Henshaw; perhaps Henshaw's waistcoat was the only one. But then, did not that make it worse? By what right did Henshaw destroy a man's faith in red waist-coats by one private exhibition of them? 'Them' or 'it'? Had Henshaw several? Whenever he saw Henshaw, morning, afternoon or evening, there also was the red waistcoat. Perhaps he had one for each day of the week, as of old one had razors. For what an invention the safety razor was! And yet there were people who still used the old-fashioned sort. Henshaw probably. And prided themselves on it for some reason. Automatically Derrick's hand went up to his chin.

'That's what's happened,' said Henshaw confidently.

Derrick flinched again. God, how slowly their minds moved! Other people's minds. At a cinema half a dozen sentences were put on the screen, and one had to wait for minutes before the crowd had assimilated them. Minutes! It seemed like hours sometimes. What were their brains doing all that time? They had to say things over and over again to themselves before any sort of meaning emerged. How hellish to be born with a brain like that! No—how heavenly! Never to have to wait for other people! Wasn't there some proverb—an army takes its time from the slowest man? Did the slowest man realize that the army was taking its time from him? Probably, and chuckled to himself. The slow man sets the pace for the army; the stupid man sets the pace for the country. How heavenly to be born slow and stupid! Never to be looking back! Never to be waiting—waiting—waiting— for fools to catch up.

'Somebody,' said Henshaw, clinching the matter, 'somebody—I don't say who, mind—has got wind of the business.'

And then, taste (thought Derrick). Taste in dress, taste in decoration, taste in the employment of words. Wasn't it time that the world was made for the unfastidious? 'Somebody has got wind of the business.' Got wind of! Bad enough to say it once; but to keep saying it! There was something horrible about these sporting metaphors, or military metaphors interlaced with business or politics; something that made one shudder. The stupid, the insensitive, the unfastidious, they were the lucky ones. Nothing touched them. Nothing touched a man like Henshaw. The world waited for him; the world adapted itself to him.

'Well?' said the big man.

The band of his cigar was in danger again; in danger on two fronts, as he would have put it. Derrick watched it, fascinated. Would he let it burn, or would he cut it?

'Well,' said Henshaw, 'we must face the position. Somebody knows something, that's how I see it.'

He took out a pen knife, and, holding his cigar between finger and thumb, slit the band with care. It disengaged itself gently and fluttered to the table. Even there, it had a fascination for Derrick. When at last he raised his eyes, Henshaw was puffing at the stump of his cigar, the stump supported jauntily now on the blade of his knife.

'Well, what do you suggest?' said Derrick irritably. He pushed his pince-nez more firmly onto his nose.

Henshaw considered him over the top of the knife. (Mistake to waste an inch of a cigar like this.) Why didn't the damn fool gum his glasses to his nose, if they wouldn't stick on naturally? Funny how that sort of fool always had something the matter with his eyes. The governing classes. By God, what a crowd! Fatuous fools with monocles; finicking fools with pince-nez; pompous fools with horn-rimmed spectacles. The governing classes! Lord, but the world could get a move on if it wasn't for these glass-eyed fools.

'I wonder,' said Henshaw thoughtfully.

No good expecting Derrick to help him. He would have to think this out for himself. How could a man think with a head like Derrick's? Even if you had a brain, where could you keep it with a head like that? Narrow heads! Glass eyes! And always fidgeting. Like a nervous horse. Almost made me want to pat him and say, 'Whoa there! Steady!' Narrow head like a horse. No room there for a brain; only room for prejudices. Jostling each other inside that narrow box. Poor stunted sort of fellow, Derrick … Now his glasses are slipping off again. Gum them on, you damn fool. Well, they were in it together now. One could only make the best of it.

My Dear Vincent [fragment]

(Undated)

'The case, my dear Vincent,' said the famous detective, putting the tips of his fingers together, and gazing at the aspidistra, 'presented one or two points of interest. The first thing which struck me was the peculiarity of the dying man's last words. "Hentall is all right." Now as far as the defalcations were concerned, Hentall was obviously all right; just as obviously as the others were all wrong. Once the police were called in, the apprehension of the guilty parties was in safe hands. It was plain, then, that the dying man was absolving Hentall of complicity in the murder, since there was no need to absolve him of complicity in the misappropriation. This gave us two facts:

'One, McDonald knew that he had been poisoned.

'Two, he also knew that Hentall was innocent.

'As regards the first point, it seems strange that a man who has been given only a year to live should guess at once, when feeling suddenly ill, that he has been poisoned; and as regards the second, it seems still more strange that he should know at once which of five men who had had access to his medicine should be innocent—rather than which of the five might be guilty.

'Having got thus far in my consideration of the problem, I then turned my attention to the dead man's other message to the police: the cryptic words which were found on his desk. Again, we are forced to the same conclusion: namely that the message did not refer to the misappropriation, as to which Hentall could give the police all the information they needed, but to the murder; and again, we are met with the extraordinary fact that the dead man knew that he was being poisoned. But now we have a new and still more extraordinary fact: that the dead man, having something relative to his murder to communicate to the police, put his communication into the difficult form of a cryptogram. Moreover, since he was actually telephoning to the police when death overtook him, he must have written the message first, when apparently in his usual health. How, then, could he know that death was coming?

'At this moment the obvious, the only possible conclusion began to confront me. In some way he must have connived at his own murder, for it is only thus that he could have known that death was coming to him. Immediately I realized this I saw that everything else fitted into its place. Previously I had wondered why the medicine was taken at the unusual hour of 10.15 a.m.; why the office boy had been asked to take it out of its cupboard; why he had hesitated at the last dose (by which time he should have been used to the taste) rather than at the second. No, my dear Vincent, it is not true to say that these other facts fitted into their place immediately. One further adjustment was necessary. I had to tell myself that Mr McDonald had not merely connived at his own murder, he had instigated it. He had, in fact, brought it about.'

'Suicide?' gasped his heavy-witted companion.

'Suicide,' said the Superintendent.

'But—'

'Remember the facts, my dear Vincent. One: he had in any case no more than a year to live. Two, he had been swindled out of a good deal of money.'

'But surely ...' began the other.

'You are overlooking the third fact,' said the famous detective, removing his fingertips in order to scratch his ear, and then putting them together again. 'He was a Scotsman.'

'Hell,' said the Superintendent, quoting from one of the Restoration dramatists, 'knows no fury like a woman scorned—and he might have added "or a Scotsman who has been swindled".'

'You mean,' gasped Vincent again, 'he committed suicide in order to involve his office in the suspicion of murder?'

'Exactly. That was to be their punishment. Imprisonment was not enough for a man who has swindled a Scotsman; he must also know the terror of being suspected of murder.'

'Then the cryptogram,' said his companion, exerting his subnormal intellect to the utmost, 'was ... was ...'

'Exactly,' agreed the great detective again.

Vincent waited hopefully for further light.

'There are limits,' said the Superintendent, 'even to a Scotsman's fury. The four suspects were to go through the furnace of ... of ...'

'Suspicion?' said his companion obligingly.

'Exactly. But only for so long as it took the police to solve the cryptogram. And then at the very last moment he remembered that the innocent Hentall would also be going through the ... the ...'

'Furnace?' suggested Vincent.

'Exactly. And tried to save him from it.'

'But the cryptogram?' said Vincent, after a long silence in which we could almost hear his brain not working.

'Elementary, my dear Vincent. The five letters in the last line are the clue. SCRLS. To a lover of Stevenson such as myself those magic initials would always stand out. SC — RLS. Scott, Stevenson. I went to that place in the library where the complete works of Stevenson followed those of Sir Walter Scott. Separating them was a single volume. On a sheet of notepaper inside that volume I found a complete confession.'

The Superintendent unstuck the tips of his fingers and poured himself out another drink.

'Just for interest,' said Vincent, 'what was the volume?'

'It was a book,' said the Superintendent, 'by perhaps the most brilliant writer alive to-day. *The Red House Mystery*.'

Also Available

In his classic autobiography A. A. Milne, with his characteristic self-deprecating humour, recalls a blissfully happy childhood in the company of his brothers, and writes with touching affection about the father he adored.

From Westminster School he won a scholarship to Cambridge University, where he edited the university magazine, before going out into the world, determined to be a writer. He was assistant editor at *Punch* and went on to enjoy great success with his novels, plays and stories. And of course he is best remembered for his children's novels and verses featuring Winnie-the-Pooh and Christopher Robin.

This is both an account of how a writer was formed and a charming period piece on literary life – Milne met countless famous authors including H. G. Wells, J. M. Barrie and Rudyard Kipling.

OUT NOW

Also available

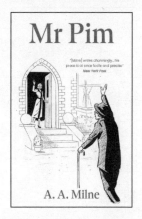

Gentle chaos sets in when the absent-minded Mr Pim calls in to see George Marden, bearing some innocent news…

George is a fine upstanding citizen and a stickler for doing the right thing. He has a devoted wife, Olivia, and is guardian to his somewhat flighty niece, Dinah. But his careful peace is broken when Mr Pim casually announces that he's recently seen an ex-convict from Australia, Telworthy.

The only thing is that the character sounds awfully like Olivia's first, and supposedly deceased, husband… and if he's really still alive, then Olivia is a bigamist.

OUT NOW

Also available

Two
People

"[Milne] writes charmingly... his
prose is at once facile and precise"
New York Post

A. A. Milne

How well can you ever know another person?

Happily married, Reginald and Sylvia seem to lead a perfect, and perfectly quiet, life. They have more than enough money and their own country house. But when success overtakes them, and allure of London life pulls Reginald in, they find parts of themselves they never knew. Where does their happiness really lie?

Reminiscent of Evelyn Waugh, this wry, intimate examination of a relationship is a gem of 1930s literature.

OUT NOW

Also available

Jenny Windell is obsessed with murder mysteries, so when she discovers her estranged aunt dead at her country home, the stage is set for her own investigation.

Worried that being the first at the scene of the crime will make her a suspect and ruin her inquiry, she flees. On the run, she befriends Derek Fenton, the dashing younger brother of acclaimed crime writer Archibald Fenton, and persuades him to join her in her attempts to solve the crime and outsmart dim-witted Inspector Marigold.

An affectionate send-up of the classic Golden Age murder mystery, this charming comedy is A. A. Milne at his most delightful.

OUT NOW

Also Available

Chloe Marr is young, beautiful and so irresistible that countless people fall in love with her, and friends are hypnotized by her charm and warmth. Her origins are a mystery and, in London society, such mystique carries both allure and suspicion.

But when an untimely exodus pulls Chloe from the people around her, they soon realize nobody really knows the truth about anybody else...

A. A. Milne's ability to portray interwar society is second to none, and this classic novel of an elusive Mayfair delivers his signature humour and lightness of touch.

OUT NOW

Also Available

The Rabbits, as they call themselves, are Archie Mannering, his sister Myra, Samuel Simpson, Thomas of the Admiralty, Dahlia Blair and the narrator, with occasional guests. Their conversation is almost entirely frivolous, their activity vacillates between immensely energetic and happily lazy, and their social mores are surprisingly progressive.

Originally published as sketches in *Punch*, the Rabbits' escapades are a charming portrait of middle-class antics on the brink of being shattered by World War I, and fail entirely to take themselves seriously.

So here they all are. Whatever their crimes, they assure you that they won't do it again – A. A. Milne

OUT NOW

About the Marvellous Milne series

The Marvellous Milne series brings back to vivid life several of
A. A. Milne's classic works for grownups.

Two collections – *The Complete Short Stories*, gathered
together in full for the first time; and *The Rabbits*
comic sketches, originally published in *Punch* and
considered by many to be his most distinctive work
– showcase Milne's talent as a short story writer.

Four carefully selected novels – *Four Days' Wonder*,
Mr Pim, *Chloe Marr* and *Two People* – demonstrate
his skill across comic genres, from the detective
spoof to a timeless and gentle comedy of manners,
considering everything from society's relationship
with individuals, to intimate spousal relationships.

Alongside this showcase of Milne's talent is his classic
memoir *It's Too Late Now*, providing a detailed account of
how his writing career was formed, as well as proving a
charming period piece of the literary scene at the time.

The full series –
It's Too Late Now
Mr Pim
Two People
Four Days' Wonder
Chloe Marr
The Complete Short Stories
The Rabbits

About the author

A. A. Milne (Alan Alexander) was born in London in 1882 and educated at Westminster School and Trinity College, Cambridge. In 1902 he was editor of *Granta*, the University magazine, and he moved back to London the following year to enter journalism. By 1906 he was assistant editor of *Punch*, where he published a series of short stories which now form the collection 'The Rabbits'.

At the beginning of the First World War he joined the Royal Warwickshire Regiment. While in the army in 1917 he started on a career writing plays and novels including *Mr Pim Passes By*, *Two People*, *Four Days' Wonder* and an adaptation of Kenneth Grahame's *The Wind in the Willows* – *Toad of Toad Hall*. He married Dorothy de Selincourt in 1913 and in 1920 had a son, Christopher Robin.

By 1924 Milne was a highly successful playwright, and published the first of his four books for children, a set of poems called *When We Were Very Young*, which he wrote for his son. This was followed by the storybook *Winnie-the-Pooh* in 1926, more poems in *Now We Are Six* (1927) and further stories in *The House at Pooh Corner* (1928).

In addition to his now famous works, Milne wrote many novels, volumes of essays and light verse, works which attracted great success at the time. He continued to be a prolific writer until his death in 1956.

Gyles Brandreth is a former *Punch* contributor and lifelong admirer of the work of A. A. Milne. A friend of Christopher Robin Milne, Gyles wrote *Now We Are Sixty* with the composer Julian Slade in the 1980s, a play celebrating A. A. Milne, in which the young Aled Jones starred as Christopher Robin.

Note from the Publisher

To receive updates on further releases in the Marvellous Milne series – plus special offers and news of other humorous fiction series to make you smile – sign up now to the Farrago mailing list at farragobooks.com/sign-up